I0821269

David Bowie

THE GOLDEN YEARS

ROGER GRIFFIN

This edition published by Omnibus Press and distributed in the United States and Canada by The Overlook Press, Peter Mayer Publishers Inc, 141 Wooster Street, New York, NY 10012. For bulk and special sales requests, please contact sales@overlookny.com or write to us at the above address.

(A Division of Music Sales Limited)
14/15 Berners Street,
London, W1T 3LJ, UK.

Cover & book designed by Paul Tippett and Adrian Andrews for Vitamin P.
Picture research by Dave Brolan, Roger Griffin, Ian Whent and Paul Tippett.

ISBN 978-1-4683-1069-6

Printed in China.

A catalogue record for this book is available from the British Library.

Cataloguing-in-Publication data is available from the Library of Congress.

Visit Omnibus Press on the web at www.omnibuspress.com

David Bowie

THE GOLDEN YEARS

ROGER GRIFFIN

OVERLOOK OMNIBUS

FOR EDIE AND GENE

FOREWORD

Australia was a strange place to be a Bowie fan in the early Seventies. He wasn't exactly a cult, but he was rarely on the radio or mentioned in the papers.

The UK music weeklies that reported Bowie's evolution from the mid-Sixties onwards were not available in Australia, so we relied on local equivalents like *Go-Set* and *RAM*, whose editor Anthony O'Grady saw *The Man Who Sold The World* (the 'dress cover') languishing in a record store bargain bin on its initial 1971 release. Bowie didn't trouble the charts here until much later.

Bowie's first appearance on Australian television was the 1975 BBC documentary *Cracked Actor*, in which a fan observed that Bowie "intentionally keeps himself a mystery." Whatever Bowie's intention, he was certainly a mystery to me, as were all those people listed on the back of his records. How did Bowie find these brilliant musicians, producers, designers and photographers?

This book is an attempt to piece it all together – the story of 1970 to 1980, recalled by Bowie and his collaborators, friends and witnesses, of what and how it all happened. Bowie made his money after 1980, but in the Seventies he made his art.

Roger Griffin
July 2016

PROLOGUE

In 1964 David Jones was one of the many hopefuls coming into London scrounging for gigs, haunting the Marquee Club by night and Denmark Street by day, looking for breaks. He had the right hair and the right clothes – scavenged from Carnaby Street discard bins with Marc Feld (later Bolan) – and fronted a few bands. As he recollected later, he thought he could 'fake it' in rock'n'roll.

By 1967 he was David Bowie and his manager Ken Pitt had secured him a recording contract. His debut album, *David Bowie* (released the same day as *Sgt. Pepper*), sank without trace and he spent 1968 immersed in Buddhism, studying mime with Lindsay Kemp and pondering his next move.

Knowingly or not, Pitt had already provided Bowie with the necessary catalyst in December 1966, when he returned from a New York meeting with Warhol with an acetate advance copy of *The Velvet Underground & Nico*. Bowie fixated on this band that personified the New York *demimonde*, subverted rock song orthodoxy and rejected hippie rhetoric. He too regarded tribalism with suspicion ('Join Our Gang', 'The London Boys' and 'Cygnet Committee') and consciously avoided association with styles, fads and movements.

Like Lou Reed, Bowie had been experimenting with characters and narratives to write from several points of view. Warhol and Kemp showed Bowie how the artist could disappear from their work behind a wall of noise, lights, imagery and make-up.

Mary Angela 'Angie' Barnett, a fast-talking, intelligent, sophisticated, connected and ambitious ex-pat American, was a student at Kingston Polytechnic when she met Bowie in April 1969 at The Speakeasy. A mutual friend – Calvin Mark Lee, who worked for Mercury Records – had asked Bowie to join him and Angie at an invitation-only King Crimson showcase gig.

It transpired Lee had been sleeping with both of them and rightly figured that they should meet. Angie was no stranger to controversy and, as their relationship began, she schooled Bowie in the art of the dramatic gesture. There were always 'incidents occurring'. The morning after their second night together, Bowie went to leave so Angie threw herself down the stairs. Bowie calmly stepped over her, saying "see you later."

With a new record deal, Bowie's fortunes finally turned around in July with 'Space Oddity', released with perfect timing nine days before the Apollo XI moon landing, followed by his eclectic second album (also called *David Bowie)* in November. It received lukewarm reviews, but by then 'Space Oddity' had reached number five in the UK charts and Angie had found them a flat in Haddon Hall, a huge rambling place in Beckenham. In the next few years, Haddon Hall would become their salon – a Warhol Factory-like creative hub that attracted the people who were crucial in the creation of 'David Bowie'.

Contents

July 21 1969, the day after the moon landing, in the flat Bowie shared with Mary Finnigan at 24 Foxgrove Road, Beckenham.

JANUARY

SUNDAY 4

★ LIVE

Beckenham Arts Lab
The Three Tuns
Beckenham, Kent, England

Bowie had started the Beckenham Arts Lab at The Three Tuns pub in May 1969 with a friend Mary Finnigan.

They organised it – like the others springing up at the time – as a collective of local artists working with various media. By 1970, input from other artists was dwindling and it had become more like a residency for Bowie. He later expressed his frustration to John Peel.

ABOVE: Bowie holds court at the Beckenham Arts Lab.
BELOW LEFT: Arts Lab co-founder Mary Finnigan.
OPPOSITE: Bowie at Finnigan's Beckenham flat where he lived in 1969.

Bowie (1970)

It's impossible to call it an Arts Lab because of the simple fact that most people won't participate. They prefer to have things fashioned for them. [340]

Tony Visconti (1976)

It never happened because everyone was in awe of David. It turned out as David's appreciation society. All the local Beckenham kids would come to the Arts Lab every week just to see David's set and talk to him and be close to him after the set was over, because he'd just had that hit record. But as soon as he saw that, it took him about four months to realise that it was a complete bust and he gave it all up. [332]

THURSDAY 8 JANUARY

▲ RECORDING

Trident Studios
17 St Anne's Court, Soho
London, England

'The Prettiest Star'

Tony Visconti: Producer
David Bowie: Vocals/Guitar
Marc Bolan: Lead Guitar
Delisle Harper: Bass
Godfrey McLean: Drums

Bowie had written 'The Prettiest Star' the previous month for Angie, who was with her parents in Cyprus for Christmas. He played her a demo over the phone. "As I heard David's voice sing those tender, loving words I just cried," she later recalled.

In 1967 Bowie was recording for Decca subsidiary Deram with little success. His publisher David Platz introduced him to producer Tony Visconti. They clicked immediately and since then Visconti had produced several Bowie recordings including the 1969 *David Bowie* album, though not the single 'Space Oddity'.

For this session, held in the early hours of Bowie's birthday, Visconti brought in Delisle Harper and Godfrey McLean, both from the soul band Gass. He also invited Marc Bolan (whom he had been producing) to play lead guitar. Bolan was keen to show off his newly acquired guitar skills, inspired by his visit to Eric Clapton's house where he'd watched the master at work.

Tony Visconti (2010)
All I wanted to do was promote Marc as an electric guitarist; I thought it would have been a great coup to have him play on David's record. David was extremely happy to have Marc play on the record and he was always happy for Marc's success. [195]

Bowie's manager Ken Pitt dropped in to watch the session and met Bolan's wife June in the control room. "You're David's Mr Ten Percent, aren't you?" sheasked him. Pitt replied, "I don't work that cheaply." [044]

Bowie (1976)
Marc was just going through the stumbling with learning to play lead guitar and I liked some of the mistakes he was making and asked him if he'd like to come along and play lead guitar on it… and he produced a beautiful solo. [332]

Tony Visconti (2010)
But after Marc had played this brilliant solo – and he also played on another track too called 'London Bye Ta-Ta' – June just sniped at David, "He's too good for you! He shouldn't play on your music!" and she dragged Marc out. It was one of the few times that I saw him at a loss for words. [195]

▲ RECORDING

'London Bye Ta-Ta'

Tony Visconti: Producer/Bass
David Bowie: Vocals/Guitar
Marc Bolan: Lead Guitar
Godfrey McLean: Drums/Congas
Rick Wakeman: Piano
Lesley Duncan/Sue/Sunny: Backing Vocals

Visconti brought in session pianist Rick Wakeman, who had played on 'Space Oddity', which Gus Dudgeon had produced after Visconti passed on it.

Rick Wakeman (1976)
I'd done a few sessions for Tony Visconti, for Strawbs – that's before I joined them – and for one or two other people, the band called Junior's Eyes. Gus didn't know anybody that played Mellotron. [332]

Gus Dudgeon (1974)
Someone said, "I know a great one who plays at the Top Rank Ballroom"… so we brought him in… and he looked kind of nervous. For some reason we didn't have the chords we wanted written out so I just told him I wanted a melancholy Mellotron sound, not the quality sound, but the sad sound. He got halfway through, made one mistake, started again and did it straight through. Amazing. That was Rick Wakeman. [263]

Bowie had first recorded 'London Bye Ta-Ta' (also with Tony Visconti) in March 1968 for Decca. Frustrated after Decca had rejected several proposed singles, Bowie had decided to write some 'pop rubbish'. It was submitted as a B-side with 'In The Heat Of The Morning' as a proposed single. After Decca rejected both songs Bowie left the label and signed to Philips.

Following the success of 'Space Oddity', Decca and Ken Pitt met to discuss a compilation of Bowie's recordings for the label, which would include some unreleased songs. However, as the 'London Bye Ta-Ta' master tape had since been lost, Pitt and Philips A&R executive Ralph Mace decided it should be re-recorded as the A-side of a proposed single with 'The Prettiest Star'.

By March, Angie's affection for her tribute, 'The Prettiest Star', would prevail over Pitt's preference as the new single. 'London Bye Ta-Ta' was again shelved, remaining unreleased until 1989.

❚ Released: *Sound+Vision* (Ryko 1989)/ *David Bowie* (EMI 2009).

ABOVE: American expat producer, arranger and bass player Tony Visconti in the studio, 1969. He and Bowie began their 50-year working relationship in 1967 on the proposed single 'Let Me Sleep Beside You'.
LEFT: Marc Bolan in December 1969. Visconti produced several hit singles and albums for T.Rex.
OPPOSITE: Bowie in 1969.

★ **LIVE**

The Speakeasy
48 Margaret Street
Covent Garden
London, England

David Bowie: Guitar/Vocals
Tony Visconti: Bass
Tim Renwick: Guitar
John Cambridge: Drums

Bowie's birthday night appearance at the club was somewhat thrown together as it had been booked initially as a solo performance, but Bowie asked Visconti to accompany him on bass. He then called Tim Renwick, a guitarist from Junior's Eyes, most of whom had played on the 1969 *David Bowie* album.

Their drummer John Cambridge was in the club having a drink with Roger Fry, an Australian roadie who used to work for Cambridge's old band in Hull, The Rats. Bowie spotted him and asked if he happened to have his drums with him. They were in his car outside, so he set up and joined in the gig. Afterwards Bowie asked Cambridge to join the permanent band he was putting together.

Tim Hughes was at the club, reporting on Bowie for *Jeremy* magazine:

This is the Speakeasy, the club for Top Pop People. David is doing the late night spot. Perched precariously on two boxes – a luminous elfin face surrounded by an aureole of blonde curls – he looks very vulnerable. He works hard. Numbers from the LP… Jacques Brel, some bawdy poems by Mason Williams, 'Buzz The Fuzz'.

Throughout the act there is a smattering of blasé applause. The reaction is disturbingly muted. It's all over and David joins us at the bar. The elfin face looks puzzled. "I can't believe it. The manager says I got a good reception. If that's what happens when they like you – what happens when they hate you?" [156]

ABOVE: The Speakeasy served as a late-night meeting place for the music industry from 1966 to the late 1970s. Other musicians who played at the club include Elton John, Cockney Rebel, The Rolling Stones, The Crazy World Of Arthur Brown, Pink Floyd, Yes, Jimi Hendrix and The Beatles.

FRIDAY 9 JANUARY

PRESS

Tim Hughes visited Haddon Hall with Johnnie Clamp, who photographed Bowie for the *Jeremy* article:

The house is a monstrous folly of a place in deepest Beckenham. Light on. Door open. No sign of David. He's just popped down to the shops for paraffin and meat for the night's stew. David takes us on a conducted tour of his mansion – ramshackle, yet strangely beautiful in its decay. Sweeping staircases, stained-glass windows, moulded ceilings, carved and tiled fireplaces. Liberty print blocks, art deco lamps, William Morris screens. There is an almost childlike excitement about the way he pounces on each new treasure. It's infectious. "We have only been here for a month, and we've hardly started yet. There is so much to do and it's the wrong time of the year." We wonder if he doesn't get professional help. "No, it's my first real place and I want to do it by myself." [156]

Published: *Jeremy*, March.

ABOVE: The Three Tuns pub in Beckenham, Kent.
BELOW: Aberdeen University, Scotland.

SUNDAY 11 JANUARY

★ LIVE

Beckenham Arts Lab
The Three Tuns
Beckenham, Kent, England

TUESDAY 13 JANUARY

▲ RECORDING

Trident Studios
17 St Anne's Court, Soho
London, England

'The Prettiest Star'
'London Bye Ta-Ta'

WEDNESDAY 14 JANUARY

★ LIVE

Old Tiger's Head
Lewisham
London, England

THURSDAY 15 JANUARY

▲ RECORDING

Trident Studios
17 St Anne's Court, Soho
London, England

'The Prettiest Star'
'London Bye Ta-Ta'

SUNDAY 18 JANUARY

★ LIVE

Beckenham Arts Lab
The Three Tuns
Beckenham, Kent, England

THURSDAY 22 JANUARY

★ LIVE

Beckenham Arts Lab
The Three Tuns
Beckenham, Kent, England

SATURDAY 24 JANUARY

◆ AWARDS

1969 'NEW MUSICAL EXPRESS' READERS' POP POLL

British Male Singer #11
World Male Singer #12
New Disc Singer #4
Best British Disc #10

WEDNESDAY 28 JANUARY

► TRAVELLING

Bowie travelled up to Scotland with Angie, Tony Visconti and percussionist Tex Johnson for his appearance on Grampian Television, stopping overnight in Glasgow. Johnson had played with Delaney & Bonnie and Friends and had met Visconti through their mutual dealings with Denny Cordell. He went on to play for Eric Clapton and Joe Cocker.

THURSDAY 29 JANUARY

✪ TELEVISION

Grampian Television
Queens Cross
Aberdeen, Scotland

'CAIRNGORM SKI NIGHT'
'London Bye Ta-Ta'

Jimmy Spankie: Presenter

Bowie performed 'London Bye Ta-Ta' – still planned to be the next single – accompanied by the in-house Alex Sutherland Band, which comprised vibes, Cordovox, acoustic guitar, drums and a string section.

Broadcast: February 27 (Grampian Television).

FRIDAY 30 JANUARY

★ LIVE

Johnston Halls
Aberdeen University
Aberdeen, Scotland

With Junior's Eyes unavailable, Bowie played the annual formal ball accompanied by Tony Visconti on bass and Tex Johnson on congas.

SATURDAY 31 JANUARY

✪ THEATRE

Gateway Theatre
Leith Walk
Edinburgh, Scotland

'THE LOOKING GLASS MURDERS'

Bowie arrived in Edinburgh with Angie to join rehearsals with Bowie's old mime teacher Lindsay Kemp. In 1968 Bowie had worked with Kemp on a production of *Pierrot In Turquoise*. Kemp was working on a new adaptation in Edinburgh and, hearing that Bowie was headed his way, had contacted Ken Pitt to ask if Bowie would be available.

For the production Bowie reprised the role of Cloud and wrote two new tracks, 'Harlequin' and 'Columbine', as well as a new lyric for 'London Bye Ta-Ta', which became 'Threepenny Pierrot'. These were recorded as a backing track along with Bowie's 'When I Live My Dream'. Kemp's pianist Michael Garrett played organ.

Still on a shoestring budget, Bowie and Angie accepted Kemp's invitation to sleep on his floor for the night.

FEBRUARY

SUNDAY 1

THEATRE

Gateway Theatre
Leith Walk
Edinburgh, Scotland

'THE LOOKING GLASS MURDERS'

Brian Mahoney filmed the production for the Scottish Television avant-garde arts series *Another World*, renamed *Gateway* after the theatre.

Broadcast: July 8 on *Gateway* (Scottish TV).

Released: *Love You Till Tuesday* DVD (Universal 2004).

TUESDAY 3 FEBRUARY

LIVE

The Marquee Club
90 Wardour Street, Soho
London, England

David Bowie: Vocals/Guitar
Tim Renwick: Guitar
Tony Visconti: Bass
John Cambridge: Drums
Junior's Eyes: Support Act

Supporting Bowie at The Marquee was Junior's Eyes, playing their final gig, due to singer Mick Wayne's drug problems. With Cambridge already on board, Bowie asked Tim Renwick to join his new band, but he declined.

Tim Renwick (1987)

It was a very hard decision to make, but while I enjoyed working with David, there were certain things I couldn't relate to. I never doubted he would make it, though; I knew it was just a matter of time before he found his feet. [177]

For some time, Cambridge had been raving to Bowie and Visconti about a guitarist he'd played with in The Rats back in Hull – Mick Ronson. Now in need of a strong guitarist, Bowie told Cambridge, "All right, bring him down."

Back in Hull, Cambridge heard that Ronson was working for the council and found him on a rugby pitch, marking out the lines in creosote. Ronson was initially reluctant to throw in a steady job but was swayed by the prospect of advancing his musical career. Ronson was still playing locally with The Rats at the time.

ABOVE: John Peel, early champion of Bowie and Bolan. For decades his radio show gave important exposure to alternative artists via his Peel Sessions, recorded live in the BBC studios. OPPOSITE: Guitarist Mick Ronson, whose unique style and string arrangements defined Bowie's sound between 1970 and 1973.

Mick Ronson (1987)

It was a pretty frustrating sort of period, trying to become popular outside the local scene. It was really enjoyable playing gigs, but there was always that frustration – we want to be a big band. [043]

Cambridge persuaded Ronson to come down to London to check out Bowie's act at The Marquee. After the show, he introduced Bowie to Ronson. The party adjourned to La Chasse, a private members club in Wardour Street for music industry folk, and ended up at Haddon Hall.

Mick Ronson (1984)

We just sat around in David's flat. I picked up a guitar and jammed with him. Bowie said, "Hey, do you wanna come down to this radio show and play with me?" [077]

Bowie (1995)

When I first heard him play, I thought "Ooh, that's my Jeff Beck. He is fantastic, this kid is great", and so I sort of hoodwinked him into working with me. [354]

WEDNESDAY 4 FEBRUARY

PRESS

There was no time to rehearse for the radio show as Bowie had a meeting with film executive Rex Sheldon about the possibility of writing the theme music for *Silver Lady*, a film about Rolls and Royce, the founders of the famous company. Although the film was never made, Sheldon asked Bowie to perform at an upcoming concert for the Mencap charity.

That was followed in the afternoon by an interview at Pitt's flat with Penny Valentine for a feature on the *Disc* awards. Editor Ray Coleman had informed Ken Pitt in January that Bowie would receive the award for Brightest Hope at the ceremony on February 13 and the article would run in *Disc* the following day. Penny Valentine asked Bowie if he felt established after his recent success and the upcoming award.

"I suppose I want success, but not for the reason that people would think. I want to establish myself so that I can fulfil other desires by using success as a springboard and then swiftly dis-establish myself. I suppose people think I am an escapist, but I getdrunk with the things I want to do – and my own ambitions come before any career as such. Of course I'm pleased about the award. It's probably based more on 'Space Oddity' than anything, because that single stuck in people's minds… The next album will be more solid. As the first side will be completely augmented it means specially writing a whole set of new material. The second side will be just me with guitar." [299]

Published: *Disc*, February 14.

THURSDAY 5 FEBRUARY

PRESS

Prior to the performance, Bowie was interviewed by George Tremlett, a journalist friend who later wrote *The David Bowie Story* in 1974. Afterwards Ronson returned to Hull to finish up at his council job.

RADIO

BBC Paris Studio
Lower Regent Street
London, England

BBC RADIO 1
'THE SUNDAY SHOW'
Introduced by John Peel.

SOLO ACOUSTIC
'Amsterdam' (Brel/Shuman)/
'God Knows I'm Good'/
'Buzz The Fuzz' (Rose)/
'Karma Man'

WITH VISCONTI/CAMBRIDGE
'London Bye Ta-Ta'/
'An Occasional Dream'

FULL BAND
'The Width Of A Circle'/**'Janine'**/
'Wild Eyed Boy From Freecloud'/
'Unwashed And Somewhat Slightly Dazed'/
'Fill Your Heart' (Rose/Williams)/
'I'm Waiting For The Man' (Reed)/
'The Prettiest Star'/
'Cygnet Committee'/
'Memory Of A Free Festival'

Jeff Griffin: Producer
David Bowie: Vocals/Guitar/Keyboards
The Tony Visconti Trio:
Mick Ronson: Guitar
Tony Visconti: Bass
John Cambridge: Drums

Producer Jeff Griffin had been commissioned to produce a new series of one-hour concert programmes. Impressed with Bowie's performance at the Purcell Room the previous November, Griffin was confident Bowie had the talent to carry a whole show in the longer format. Following a morning rehearsal at Haddon Hall, the group left for an afternoon soundcheck at the BBC studio – another opportunity to rehearse – to prepare for Ronson's debut appearance with Bowie.

Mick Ronson (1984)
So, we went down to this radio show and I played along with him. I didn't know anything, none of the material. I just sat and watched his fingers. I didn't really know what I was doing, but everybody seemed to like it. I don't know if it was treated as an audition or not, I never really thought of it like that, I was just playing, it was a normal thing for me. After that he said, "Well, how about coming along and playing with me all the time?" So I agreed. That was pretty much straight after the show. [077]

Tony Visconti (2006)
David suggested he play the radio show with us – we were very under-rehearsed which was plain for all to hear. [047]

Bowie (2000)
We rehearsed in the morning and did the show very badly. [170]

Peel asked Bowie, "Are you going to be doing gigs with this band?", to which he joked, "Well, looking at them… no." Bowie went on to explain he'd met Ronson only two days before through Cambridge and they would indeed be doing gigs together.

Broadcast: February 8 without 'I'm Waiting For The Man' as the radio session ran over time.
Released: *Bowie At The Beeb* (Virgin/BBC 2000)

The BBC was originally unable to include this performance on the *Bowie At The Beeb* compilation as the master tape was missing. Due to the BBC's tight budget, tapes were often wiped and reused after their broadcast. However, Bowie was able to lend the BBC a copy from his personal collection.

SUNDAY 8 FEBRUARY

★ **LIVE**

Beckenham Arts Lab
The Three Tuns
Beckenham, Kent, England

✪ **RADIO**

The Sunday Show broadcast (BBC Radio 1).

THURSDAY 12 FEBRUARY

★ **LIVE**

Beckenham Arts Lab
The Three Tuns
Beckenham, Kent, England

ABOVE: The Café Royal.
RIGHT: Manager Ken Pitt signing copies of his 1983 memoir *David Bowie: The Pitt Report*.
OPPOSITE: At the Café Royal in his 'awards suit', February 13.

FRIDAY 13 FEBRUARY

◆ **AWARDS**

Café Royal
Regent Street
London, England

'DISC & MUSIC ECHO' AWARDS

Bowie was voted Brightest Hope and accepted the award from presenter (and fellow recipient) DJ Tony Blackburn. He then went over to Ken Pitt and gave him the trophy – a gold disc in a leather case – saying, "This is for you."

SATURDAY 14 FEBRUARY

► **TRAVELLING**

Bowie, Angie, Visconti and Liz Hartley took a quick trip to Hull to visit Ronson, who had left his job and was preparing to move into Haddon Hall with them.

During the week Ronson had told *Hull Daily Mail*: "I've been offered jobs in London before, but nothing as secure as this. I didn't want to go back there and find myself in debt with my equipment again, and the money from this job means I shall be able to live properly. The Hype has a record, 'Prettiest Star', for release shortly and after that we shall be off on bookings up and down the country. The main thing for me now, what I'm really after, is just to get myself known." [157]

Bowie had told Ken Pitt that he wanted to introduce a strong element of hype into the launch of the band, to which Pitt replied, "Then why not call it The Hype?"

In Hull, Ronson introduced Bowie to Stuart George, who had been working with The Rats. Stuey George – as he was known – later became Bowie's bodyguard.

Penny Valentine's article 'A New Star Shoots Upwards' was published in *Disc*, sparking a new wave of interest from the media.

SUNDAY 15 FEBRUARY

★ **LIVE**

Beckenham Arts Lab
The Three Tuns
Beckenham, Kent, England

MONDAY 16 FEBRUARY

✪ **PRESS**

Anne Nightingale's *Daily Sketch* column reported that Bowie could be "the giant heartthrob that Scott Walker was" and that Bowie's next single release would be 'The Prettiest Star'. This was news to Ken Pitt.

Ken Pitt (1976)
I discovered there had been a lot of pressure put on behind my back to get 'The Prettiest Star' put out. I had a vested interest in 'The Prettiest Star' in that David, by way of a present, had given me the publishing rights to it, so I would have been delighted to see it released but I was not concerned with the publishing but getting a hit record and I thought that 'London Bye Ta-Ta' was by far and away the best. [332]

Ken Pitt (1983)
Ralph Mace explained that the tape of 'The Prettiest Star' was the one that had been delivered to him by Tony Visconti and the choice had been David and Angela's. The labels had been printed and the records were being pressed with 'Conversation Piece' as the B-side. [034]

THURSDAY 19 FEBRUARY

★ **LIVE**

Beckenham Arts Lab
The Three Tuns
Beckenham, Kent, England

ABOVE: The Roundhouse.
OPPOSITE: Visconti and Bowie onstage at the Roundhouse.

SUNDAY 22 FEBRUARY

★ LIVE

Implosion
The Roundhouse
Chalk Farm
London, England

DAVID BOWIE & HYPE

David Bowie and Hype (billed as David Bowie) supported Caravan, The Groundhogs and Bachdenkel at the regular Sunday night event, Implosion.

Prior to this, Bowie and Angie had suggested to the others at Haddon Hall (where most of the band were now living) that some sort of stage wear was needed to spice up the act. As the band rehearsed, Angie browsed the Charing Cross Road shops with neighbour and friend Mark Pritchett, buying costumes for the band based on different characters they had dreamt up.

Visconti's girlfriend Liz Hartley, a creative seamstress, added the finishing touches. Visconti became Hypeman, John Cambridge was Cowboy Man, Ronson was Gangster Man, while Bowie was, according to him, "no one in particular" but he got out the silver catsuit he used to promote 'Space Oddity'.

Bowie (1989)

Bolan was there, and he was open-mouthed that we had the balls to camp it up so much. I think that was the first glam-rock performance. It was all jeans and long hair at that time, and we got booed all the way through the show. People hated it. They absolutely loathed what we were doing. It was great! [323]

Tony Visconti (2006)

Musically it was a great gig, although we were heckled initially, and called a variety of homosexual epithets. [047]

FRIDAY 27 FEBRUARY

✪ TELEVISION

Cairngorm Ski Night broadcast on Grampian Television, including Bowie's performance of 'London Bye Ta-Ta'. Advertising read: "Join the party of skiers as they relax to the best of Scottish après-ski entertainment provided by the resident team."

SATURDAY 28 FEBRUARY

★ LIVE

Basildon Arts Lab
Basildon
Essex, England

Hype, described as "David Bowie's New Electric Band", shared top billing with High Tide and was supported by Iron Maiden (not the later, more successful heavy metal band).

High Tide included two of Bowie's collaborators from the past and the future – Tony Hill from Turquoise (1968) and Simon House, who later joined Hawkwind and played violin on Bowie's 1978 tour.

"He was **open-mouthed** that we had the **balls** to camp it up."

Bowie on Marc Bolan's reaction to the gig at the Roundhouse

MARCH

SUNDAY 1

★ LIVE

Beckenham Arts Lab
The Three Tuns
Beckenham, Kent, England

TUESDAY 3 MARCH

★ LIVE

White Bear
Hounslow
London, England

THURSDAY 5 MARCH

★ LIVE

Beckenham Arts Lab
The Three Tuns
Beckenham, Kent, England

Bowie's last appearance as part of the Beckenham Arts Lab.

FRIDAY 6 MARCH

★ LIVE

University of Hull
West Refectory
Hull, Yorkshire, England

A homecoming concert for Ronson and Cambridge. Another ex-Rat, Benny Marshall, joined them on 'Unwashed And Somewhat Slightly Dazed', reprising his harmonica part from the *David Bowie* album.

RIGHT: Dutch (top) and Italian (bottom) releases of 'The Prettiest Star'.

■ **SINGLE RELEASED**

'The Prettiest Star' (3:11)/
'Conversation Piece' (3:05)
UK (Mercury 1135)

'The Prettiest Star'

▮Reissued: *Sound+Vision* (Ryko 1989) (mono single version).

▮Reissued: *Best Of David Bowie 1969/1974* (EMI 1997) (stereo version).

▮Reissued: *David Bowie* (EMI 2009) (stereo version)

'Conversation Piece'

Tony Visconti: Producer
David Bowie: Vocals/Guitar
Mick Wayne: Guitar
John Lodge: Bass
John Cambridge: Drums

Recorded during the *David Bowie* (1969) album sessions.

▮Reissued: *Space Oddity* (Ryko 1990) (mono single version).

▮Reissued: *David Bowie* (EMI 2009) (stereo version).

True to Ken Pitt's predictions, the single sold poorly and received a lukewarm response from radio although the music press was supportive:

Derek Johnson (*NME*)
A rather unexpected follow-up in that this is a complete contrast to 'Space Oddity'... a thoroughly charming and wholly fascinating little song.

Peter Jones (*Record Mirror*)
David comes near to croaking in his emotionless voice but it's still very effective. Chart cert.

Penny Valentine (*Disc*)
David Bowie has been very clever by not trying to repeat 'Space Oddity' – an impossible task anyway – and yet managing to steer clear of his album material, which would have been far too heavy for a single... This has the most compact, catchy melody I've ever heard. A hit indeed.

■ ALBUM RELEASED

'THE WORLD OF DAVID BOWIE' COMPILATION

UK (Decca SPA 58)

SIDE ONE

1. **'Uncle Arthur'** (2:05)
2. **'Love You Till Tuesday'** (3:08)
3. **'There Is A Happy Land'** (3:05)
4. **'Little Bombardier'** (3:22)
5. **'Sell Me A Coat'** (2:57)
6. **'Silly Boy Blue'** (3:47)
7. **'The London Boys'** (3:19)

SIDE TWO

1. **'Karma Man'** (3:02)
2. **'Rubber Band'** (2:16)
3. **'Let Me Sleep Beside You'** (3:23)
4. **'Come And Buy My Toys'** (2:07)
5. **'She's Got Medals'** (2:23)
6. **'In The Heat Of The Morning'** (2:57)
7. **'When I Live My Dream'** (3:22)

Ken Pitt and Bowie drew up a track list for this collection of Bowie's earlier recordings for Decca. The compilation drew largely from the 1967 debut album *David Bowie* (produced by Mike Vernon), with four tracks dropped to make way for 'The London Boys', a 1966 B-side, and three previously unreleased tracks that reflected his development and current direction – 'Let Me Sleep Beside You', 'Karma Man' and 'In The Heat Of The Morning'.

Recorded in 1967 and 1968, they were Tony Visconti's first productions for Bowie.

Bowie had dismissed the songs at the time as 'pop rubbish', but in October 1969 Bowie played 'Let Me Sleep Beside You' on the *Dave Lee Travis Show* radio session with a new heavier backing from Junior's Eyes.

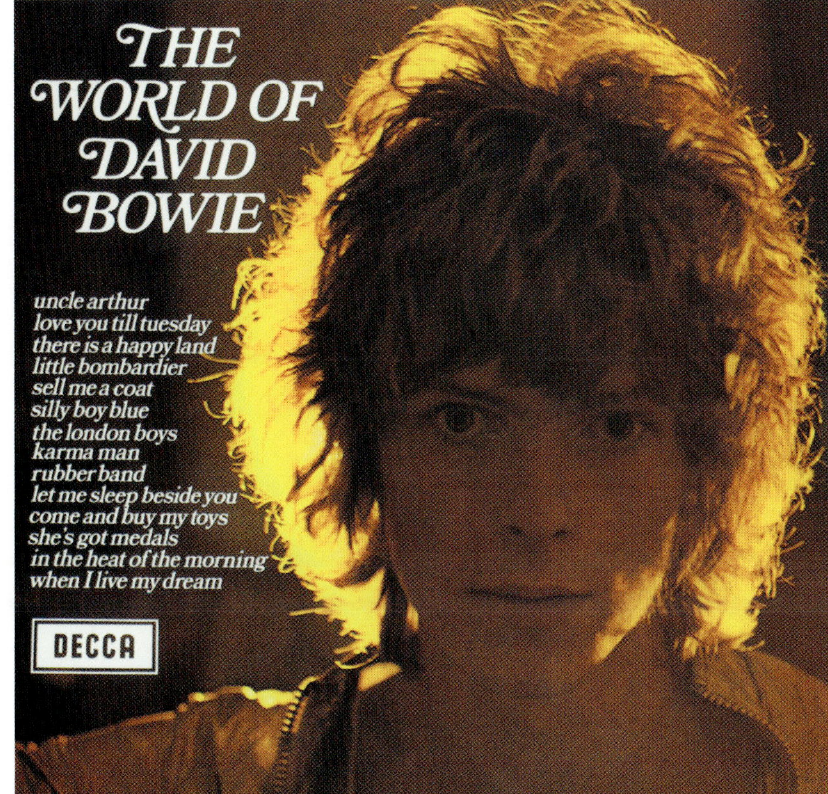

ABOVE RIGHT: Arts Lab friend Ted Bebbington supplied the cover photo for the first compilation of Bowie's work for Decca/Deram.
RIGHT: Regent Street Polytechnic.

Introducing the song on air, Bowie explained to Brian Matthew, "We've got a number that we've dug up today which was written about four years ago and hasn't been out of the house. It's the first airing it's had anywhere."

Asked why it hadn't been recorded, Bowie replied, "My mother thought the lyrics were dirty."

By 1970 Bowie was less dismissive of the songs, as was Decca, which went on to reissue any Bowie product in the vaults to recoup their investment in him. This was the first of several compilations and was reissued in 1973 with a new Ziggy era cover photo.

SATURDAY 7 MARCH

★ LIVE

Regent Street Polytechnic
London, England

DAVID BOWIE & HYPE

Gavin Petrie (*Disc*)

David Bowie, in ten-league boots and groovy gear, presented his new backing group line-up Hype, at London's Regent Street Polytechnic on Saturday. He needs an expert on sound balance who should effectively solve the teething problems of the new line-up. David had much more confidence and stage presence with this backing group, and as his songs are suitable for grooving to as well as just listening to, the brightest hope could well change categories.

This show was a disaster. The volume on Mick Ronson's lead guitar was so high that not only did he block out David's singing but also completely overpowered John Cambridge's drums. The volume also cleared the seats in a direct line with his speaker. That magic that makes for greatness is there but suppressed, sometimes even hidden. If my ears ever recover I expect to see David plus Hype in a few months time… shining through.
[241]

■ Published: 'Bowie's Bow', *Disc and Music Echo*, March 12

"My mother thought the lyrics were dirty."

Bowie on 'Let Me Sleep Beside You'

WEDNESDAY 11 MARCH

★ **LIVE**

Atomic Sunrise
The Roundhouse
Chalk Farm
London, England

Sharing the bill with Genesis, this performance was part of the week-long Atomic Sunrise festival. For the event, Angie and Bowie further developed his stage attire, on this occasion with a metal choker necklace, a satin cape and buccaneer- style thigh-length leather boots.

The set included 'Memory Of A Free Festival', 'The Supermen', 'I'm Waiting For The Man' and Lennon's 'Instant Karma'.

Atomic Sunrise, the concert film, was screened at The Roundhouse on March 11 and 12, 2013.

✪ **PRESS**

Raymond Telford interviewed Bowie during the day for *Melody Maker*:

I think a lot of people are expecting another 'Space Oddity', and 'Prettiest Star' is nothing like it. I'm sure this is why the BBC isn't plugging it. Everyone wanted another song with the same feel as 'Space Oddity' but as I'd done it, I didn't see the point of doing it again.

I'm very happy with the band. Although we're all happy with the set-up, I can't see it becoming a really permanent thing. I want to retain Hype and myself as two separate working units whereby we can retain our own identities.

The gigs we've done so far have gone better than I expected. We played the Roundhouse recently and it was great. The Roundhouse audiences seem to be something apart from the usual blasé London audiences. The best audiences I know are up north where they really appreciate you. In London the audiences are very aware that they are living in the place where it's all supposed to be happening, so inevitably they have this cool attitude. [290]

▮ Published: 'Hype and David Bowie's Future', *Melody Maker*, March 28.

THURSDAY 12 MARCH

★ LIVE

Royal Albert Hall
London, England

SOLO SHOW

Bowie had promised film producer Rex Sheldon to appear on the show organised by Irish philanthropist Michael Sugrue for Mencap charity. Bowie played a 20-minute set, which was well received, despite most of the crowd being there to see the main act, Irish tenor Josef Locke. Also on the bill were The Faces.

After the show Pitt, Bowie and Angie strolled from the Royal Albert Hall to Piccadilly, where Bowie told Pitt of their plans to get married.

FRIDAY 13 MARCH

★ LIVE

Locarno Ballroom
Sunderland
Northumberland
England

HYPE

Hype performed a one-hour set, again dressed in character costumes.

SATURDAY 14 MARCH

★ LIVE

University of Surrey
Guildford
Surrey, England

SOLO SHOW

THURSDAY 19 MARCH

★ LIVE

Beckenham Arts Lab
The Three Tuns
Beckenham, Kent, England

SOLO SHOW

Bowie and Angie spent the afternoon at Kensington Antique Market, choosing Angie's wedding dress for the following day. Bowie opted for black satin trousers.

After Bowie's set at The Three Tuns, where artist/actress friend Clare Shenstone also played a solo acoustic set, they all spent the evening at Haddon Hall.

LEFT: Bowie and Hype return to The Roundhouse for the Atomic Sunrise festival.

FRIDAY 20 MARCH

▼ SOCIALISING

Bromley Registry Office
Beckenham Lane
Bromley, Kent, England

BOWIES' MARRIAGE CEREMONY

They arrived half an hour late after oversleeping and found Bowie's mother Peggy Jones already there. Bowie hadn't told her about the ceremony but she'd heard a rumour and followed it up with Ken Pitt, who told her, "If he wants me to go to his wedding, he'll invite me."

Bowie had invited only the Haddon Hall crowd. Tony Visconti would have been best man but had a Strawbs recording session that day. Those who attended included Liz Hartley, John Cambridge, Roger Fry and Clare Shenstone. Bowie had asked Cambridge to be a witness but Mrs Jones pushed forward to sign the register herself. Clare Shenstone was the second witness and signatory.

To their surprise, the local press greeted them outside – Bowie's mother had alerted both the Bromley papers.

In lieu of a reception the party went to the Swan & Mitre pub across the street, where Bowie told *The Bromley Times* that there would be no honeymoon. "Unfortunately, I'm far too busy working."

SATURDAY 21 MARCH

▲ RECORDING

Trident Studios
17 St Anne's Court, Soho
London, England

'Memory Of A Free Festival'

Following the commercial failure of 'The Prettiest Star', Mercury's Robin McBride had requested a new version of 'Memory Of A Free Festival', which he felt had more chart potential as the next single. The song would be split over two sides with the A-side fading early on the 'sun machine' chorus. He suggested to Visconti that this could be achieved by picking up the tempo to reach the chorus earlier.

Bowie and Angie also visited Ralph Mace, who had left Philips and was working for Soho-based music publisher Famous Music.

OPPOSITE: Bowie and Angie pose with his mother, Peggy Jones. ABOVE: Bowie and Angie outside Bromley Registry Office, where they were married. This enabled Angie, then aged 20, to obtain a work permit in Britain.

SUNDAY 22 MARCH

▲ RECORDING

Trident Studios
17 St Anne's Court, Soho
London, England

'Memory Of A Free Festival'

MONDAY 23 MARCH

▲ RECORDING

Trident Studios
17 St Anne's Court, Soho
London, England

'Memory Of A Free Festival'
'The Supermen'

The band also began work on a new song, 'The Supermen', but Bowie and Ronson became increasingly frustrated with John Cambridge's difficulty with the rhythm.

John Cambridge (1986)
I just couldn't get it right and even Mick was saying, "Come on, it's easy," which makes you feel worse. [013]

The song traced back to 1965 when Bowie was in The Manish Boys. Working on their single 'I Pity The Fool' was a young session guitarist, Jimmy Page.

Bowie (1997)
He just got a fuzz box and he used that for the solo. He was wildly excited about it and he was quite generous that day and he said, "Look, I've got this riff but I'm not using it for anything so why don't you learn it and see if you can do anything with it." [331]

WEDNESDAY 25 MARCH

✪ RADIO

Playhouse Theatre Studios
Northumberland Avenue
London, England

BBC RADIO 1
'SOUNDS OF THE 70s'
ANDY FERRIS
'I'm Waiting For The Man'/
'The Width Of A Circle'/
'The Wild Eyed Boy From Freecloud'/
'The Supermen'

Bernie Andrews: Producer

▌Broadcast: April 6 (BBC Radio 1) except 'The Supermen'.

▌Released: 'I'm Waiting For The Man' on *BBC Sessions 1969–1972 (Sampler)* (NMC 1996).

▌Released: 'The Wild Eyed Boy From Freecloud' on *Bowie At The Beeb* (Virgin/BBC 2000).

MONDAY 30 MARCH

★ LIVE

Croydon Star Hotel
Croydon
Surrey, England

TUESDAY 31 MARCH

⊙ BUSINESS

Frustrated with his lack of success after several years under Pitt's management, Bowie told him he was "thinking of going it alone". Although Bowie was surviving on live work, he was keen to devote more time to recording. Pitt reassured him by scaling back live engagements and advanced Bowie £200.

APRIL

WEDNESDAY 1

⊙ BUSINESS

Pitt and Visconti met to discuss the schedule for recording the new album, with Tony Visconti producing. *Memory Of A Free Festival* was floated as a title to tie in with the new single. As the budget was tight, recording time would be booked in downtime at the Trident and Advision studios.

THURSDAY 2 APRIL

▲ RECORDING

Trident Studios
17 St Anne's Court, Soho
London, England

'Memory Of A Free Festival'

FRIDAY 3 APRIL

▲ RECORDING

Advision Sound Studios
23 Gosfield Street
West London, England

'Memory Of A Free Festival'

Visconti hired a Moog synthesiser from George Martin's Air Studios. It was installed by Martin's engineer Chris Thomas, who had worked on The Beatles' *White Album*.

Ralph Mace dropped in at the session and saw Ronson was having difficulty with the instrument. An accomplished keyboard player himself, Mace told Ronson, "I can save you a lot of time if you let me do that."

SATURDAY 4 APRIL

▲ MIXING

Trident Studios
17 St Anne's Court, Soho
London, England

'Memory Of A Free Festival'

Bowie and Visconti began mixing the new single.

MONDAY 6 APRIL

⊙ BUSINESS

After the friction during 'The Supermen' sessions, Bowie (with Ronson and Angie's encouragement) reluctantly told John Cambridge that they were looking for a new drummer. He explained it was not dissatisfaction with his drumming, but a need for a drummer with arrangement skills.

TUESDAY 7 APRIL

⊙ BUSINESS

Following Cambridge's early morning departure for Hull, Ronson suggested another ex-Rat, Mick 'Woody' Woodmansey. Bowie phoned to invite him down to Haddon Hall for an audition, which he passed. Like Ronson, Woodmansey threw in his Hull job and moved in.

Together with Ronson and Visconti, Woodmansey signed a new separate record contract for Hype with Philips. Hype was paid an advance of £4000, which they put towards a new PA system and new tyres for the van.

Photographer Pete Sanders took some publicity pictures of Ronson, Woodmansey and Visconti, who had begun soundproofing the basement at Haddon Hall to create an in-house rehearsal space.

Tony Visconti (1982)

We'd just go into the basement and make a lot of noise, and David would drift down every now and then for 15 minutes and say, "Hey! What's going on?" when we could get him away from Angie, so we had a lot of sketchy songs that we'd written in the basement. [015]

SUNDAY 12 APRIL

★ LIVE

Harrogate Theatre
Harrogate
North Yorkshire, England

2 SOLO SHOWS

On Ronson's recommendation, bassist Trevor Bolder came down from Hull to see Bowie's show.

TUESDAY 14
WEDNESDAY 15 APRIL

▲ MIXING

Advision Sound Studios
23 Gosfield Street
West London, England

'Memory Of A Free Festival'

Mixing of the single completed.

FRIDAY 17 APRIL

▲ RECORDING

Trident Studios
17 St Anne's Court, Soho
London, England

'THE MAN WHO SOLD THE WORLD' ALBUM
'All The Madmen'

Tony Visconti: Producer

Recording of the new album began with a four-hour session starting at 1am. With little in the way of prepared material, it fell to the band to work up Bowie's song ideas in the studio.

Bowie (1971)

I used to have periods, weeks on end, when I just couldn't cope any more. I'd slump into myself... I felt so depressed, and I really felt so aimless, and this torrential feeling of 'what's it all for anyway?' A lot of it [the album] went through that period, 'Width Of A Circle' was definitely that – I went to the depths of myself in that. I tried to analogise the period of my life from when I left school to that time – to the making of that LP. Just for my own benefit, not really for any listener's benefit. [096]

Tony Visconti (1982)

David had 'Space Oddity' under his belt, and he was living off those royalties and had become very complacent – this man would not get out of bed and write a song, and he had a commitment to make an album! [015]

Tony Visconti (1974)

I have a pretty positive approach to work so I was very unhappy about the situation. With a lot of persuasion I managed to get David to give us some chord changes to work on and we ended up with the ridiculous situation where the entire production for the whole album was set – except for the melody and words. [126]

Tony Visconti (1985)

Mick Ronson, Woody Woodmansey and myself would be making up backing tracks, having got a brief from David – it was E chord for 16 bars, then an A chord for four bars and a B chord for two bars – and we were just banging out these backing tracks, and David would come into the studio and say whether he liked it or not. [019]

Tony Visconti (1982)

It's hard to say how much you do when you write a song with someone else, and even though we weren't credited as writers, Mick and I were getting the chord changes together. 'Width Of A Circle' was the only track that was written, and that was only the first part of the song that was written. The second part, where it goes into a boogie, was written in the studio, and Mick and I definitely wrote all that, and David just threw all his words and melody on top.

'All The Madmen', for instance, originally had a working title of 'The Man Who Sold The World'. Later, we just laid down the chords, the arrangements, the guitar solos, the synthesisers, the recorders, and David would be out in the lobby of Advision, holding hands with Angie. [015]

Ralph Mace (1986)

It was creation in the studio. They began with a basic idea from one instrument or one vocal line. They would start adding and then they would change according to their whims. They got a core of the sound and then they started overdubbing and if it worked they kept it and if it didn't they would do it again, and it was a creative build-up, a synthesis. David would bounce ideas off people. There was a lot of creative interplay with all the people there. [13]

⊙ BUSINESS

Still concerned about Ken Pitt's management, Bowie met with Olav Wyper, who suggested three lawyers. He chose the first on the list – Tony Defries, who had worked with producer Mickie Most. Defries told Bowie he would get him out of Pitt's management contract.

Bowie (1976)

He said, "I'm Tony Defries and I'm going to make you a star!" [laughs] I said "Oh yeah?" And he did... so they say – I've read about it. Yeah, that's when Tony Defries entered my life – and me wallet! [332]

FRIDAY 24 APRIL

BUSINESS

Bowie and Angie wrote to Ken Pitt advising him that he would no longer be considered Bowie's personal manager.

SATURDAY 25 SUNDAY 26 APRIL

▲ RECORDING

Trident Studios
17 St Anne's Court, Soho
London, England

'THE MAN WHO SOLD THE WORLD' ALBUM

MONDAY 27 APRIL

★ LIVE

Poco-a-Poco Club
Stockport
Cheshire, England

SOLO SHOW

Bowie took the stage alone as Woodmansey had injured his finger the week before. He invited The Purple Gang (another band on the evening's bill) to back him but they lost their nerve and declined.

WEDNESDAY 29 APRIL

BUSINESS

Pitt's response to Bowie's letter rejected claims of mismanagement and suggested they discuss ways of ending their professional relationship.

THURSDAY 30 APRIL

▲ RECORDING

Trident Studios
17 St Anne's Court, Soho
London, England

'THE MAN WHO SOLD THE WORLD' ALBUM

LEFT: Tony Visconti and Bowie recording *The Man Who Sold The World* at Trident Studios on May 4.

MAY

▲ RECORDING

Haddon Hall
42 Southend Road
Beckenham, Kent, England

'Tired Of My Life' (acoustic demo)

The song, originally written when Bowie was 16, was considered for the album but was dropped without being recorded. Bowie used the melody as the basis of 'It's No Game' in 1980 and also kept some lyrics in the middle eight. The demo was bootlegged widely and remains unreleased.

FRIDAY 1

▲ RECORDING

Trident Studios
17 St Anne's Court, Soho
London, England

'THE MAN WHO SOLD THE WORLD' ALBUM
'She Shook Me Cold'
(working title 'Suck')

MONDAY 4 MAY

▲ RECORDING

Trident Studios
17 St Anne's Court, Soho
London, England

'THE MAN WHO SOLD THE WORLD' ALBUM
'Running Gun Blues'
'Saviour Machine'

Ralph Mace, who had worked on 'Memory Of A Free Festival', again played Moog on 'Saviour Machine'.

✪ PRESS

A visiting Swedish journalist, Bosse Hansson, interviewed Bowie upstairs at Trident. Hansson told Bowie, "You are going to be the Bob Dylan of the Seventies." Bowie dismissed the comparison, saying, "His songs are boring and he has a bad voice." [007] Bowie expressed his disappointment (shared by many) with Dylan's semi-retirement more eloquently the following year on 'Song For Bob Dylan'.

TUESDAY 5 WEDNESDAY 6 MAY

▲ RECORDING

Trident Studios
17 St Anne's Court, Soho
London, England

'THE MAN WHO SOLD THE WORLD' ALBUM

ABOVE AND OPPOSITE: Bowie being interviewed upstairs at Trident Studios during *The Man Who Sold The World* sessions on May 4.

THURSDAY 7 MAY

⊙ BUSINESS

Bowie and Defries met Ken Pitt at his flat to discuss a settlement of his management contract. Having invested significant amounts of money and time in Bowie, Pitt asked to be compensated for loss of future earnings. Defries stalled for time to consider the situation and the matter was settled later.

SUNDAY 10 MAY

◆ AWARDS
★ LIVE
✪ TELEVISION

Talk Of The Town
Charing Cross Road
Westminster
London, England

'IVOR NOVELLO' AWARDS
'Space Oddity'

Joint winner with Peter Sarstedt, Bowie picked up the award for Most Original Song for 'Space Oddity', which he performed solo with guitar, accompanied by an orchestra conducted by Les Reed. Bowie and Angie attended the celebration dinner following the event.

▮Telecast live to Australia, USA and Europe and broadcast on BBC Radio 1.

TUESDAY 12 WEDNESDAY 13 SUNDAY 17 MAY

▲ RECORDING

Advision Sound Studios
23 Gosfield Street
West London, England

'THE MAN WHO SOLD THE WORLD' ALBUM

Recording moved to Advision, with three sessions from 2pm to midnight.

THURSDAY 21 MAY

★ LIVE

The Penthouse
Scarborough
Yorkshire, England

Mark Pritchett made a guest appearance on guitar for Woodmansey's first live appearance with Bowie.

FRIDAY 22 MAY

▲ RECORDING

Advision Sound Studios
23 Gosfield Street
West London, England

'THE MAN WHO SOLD THE WORLD' ALBUM
'The Man Who Sold The World'

'The Man Who Sold The World' was the last song recorded for the album, with Bowie writing the lyrics on the spot at the last minute, which had been the pattern throughout the recording period. On later albums Visconti became accustomed to Bowie's approach, but at the time found it frustrating.

Tony Visconti (1985)

By the last week, I didn't have a vocal on two of the tracks and this is where it actually began – David writing on microphone. He'd start singing spontaneously. It was really wonderful. When he was hot, he was hot, but for me the whole thing was not so good. I had two big conflicts – getting this done technically, which I was struggling with, and also managing to get a good performance out of David. I had a record company screaming for final mixes, not even sure that they wanted this album. As far as they were concerned, this was the last they had to do with David Bowie and I wasn't delivering the goods. [019]

With the vocals recorded and the mixes done, the album was complete. Later, outside Defries' office on Regent Street, Visconti told Bowie he'd had enough. On top of his frustration with Bowie, Visconti was distrustful of Defries, and wary of the blind faith Bowie had in his new manager.

Tony Visconti (1986)

David was also assigning his personal power to other people… when he meets someone, and he falls in love – forget it. The person's the one until he's severely hurt. I said to David, "If you go with Tony Defries, I'm not going to go with you." [013]

Tony Visconti (2006)

As I turned to walk away from David, the look on his face just seemed to say "Why oh why?" I felt terrible but Marc [Bolan] was about to become almost a full-time job for the next two years of my life. [047]

SATURDAY 23 MAY

▶ TRAVELLING

With the album complete, Bowie and Angie headed off to Scotland for a belated honeymoon.

JUNE

TUESDAY 16

★ LIVE

Cambridge University May Ball
Jesus College
Cambridge, England

Coming on after Deep Purple at 4am, Bowie and Hype played an acoustic set with Woodmansey on bongos and Mark Pritchett, who later recalled their performance as being haphazard.

FRIDAY 26 JUNE

■ SINGLE RELEASED

'Memory Of A Free Festival Pt 1' (3:59)/
'Memory Of A Free Festival Pt 2' (3:31)
UK (Mercury 6052 026)

▮ Reissued: *Space Oddity* (Ryko 1990) and *David Bowie* (EMI 2009).

JULY

SATURDAY 4

★ LIVE

Queens Mead
Recreation Ground
Bromley
Kent, England

The all-day outdoor concert was organised by Fleetwood Mac's Peter Green and included Mark Pritchett's band Rungk, who would form the basis of Arnold Corns the following year. The name Hype was dropped from the billing and Bowie would be advertised as 'David Bowie' from this point, whether solo or with backing group.

SUNDAY 5 JULY

★ LIVE

Implosion
The Roundhouse
Chalk Farm Road
London, England

MID JULY

✪ TELEVISION

'EDDY READY GO!'
'Memory Of A Free Festival'

Eddy Becker: Presenter

Bowie appeared on the Netherlands show, performing solo on the keyboard. According to Ruud Altenburg, *Eddy Ready Go!* was recorded to Ampex tapes, which have all been wiped.

▮ Broadcast: July 18 (NCRV)

SATURDAY 18 JULY

★ LIVE

Fickle Pickle Club
Cricketers Inn
Southend-on-Sea
Essex, England

AUGUST

SATURDAY 1

★ LIVE

Rock With Shelter
Southend-on-Sea
Essex, England

Bowie, accompanied by Ronson on bass, appeared at this festival staged to raise funds for Shelter, a housing charity.

TUESDAY 4 AUGUST

▲ RECORDING

With Tony Visconti producing, Hype recorded four songs without Bowie for a proposed album. The project was abandoned at that point – the tracks were left unmixed with no vocals.

With live work drying up and no wage being offered, Ronson and Woodmansey moved out of Haddon Hall and returned disillusioned to Hull. They reformed The Rats with Benny Marshall and Trevor Bolder under a new name, Ronno.

Visconti and Liz Hartley had already moved out to set up home in Penge, as communal living was "wearing a bit thin" with "arguments about mundane things like grocery shopping". [047]

Tony Visconti (2006)

Haddon Hall had also become overcrowded with not just us, Angela and David, Mick Ronson, Woody Woodmansey, and Roger the Lodger, but also a constant stream of visitors staying late into the night. [047]

SEPTEMBER

With his band gone and no work on the horizon, Bowie became despondent and frustrated with Defries, who had promised much but delivered little. Angie stepped into the breach, chasing up work and suggesting new approaches.

Four months after its completion, *The Man Who Sold The World* was in limbo. Philips had internal problems since the departure of ousted general manager Olav Wyper. He told Ken Pitt in 1982, "I left Philips and went to RCA and it seemed to me that it all went quiet for David."

With him went Bowie's support at the label, and post-production of the album stalled.

Tony Visconti (1986)

There were only four people in the world who liked that album at the time – me, Mick Ronson, Woody Woodmansey and David. The record company didn't. [013]

Fortunately Robin McBride came over from Chicago to push album production forward and Bowie began formulating a cover concept. Back in June, Pitt had mused, "I wonder if Andy Warhol would design the album cover, or do a portrait we could use. Or Hockney?"

With Pitt gone and Philips in disarray, this ambitious idea never materialised. Bowie turned instead to another Pop artist, Mike Weller – a friend who had designed posters for the Beckenham Arts Lab and visited Haddon Hall occasionally. Weller was part of the politicised Penge Artists Union and related to the album's themes of oppression and malevolence.

He produced an illustration of John Wayne carrying a gun in front of Cane Hill, a mental hospital where Weller had recently visited a friend. Unbeknownst to Weller, this referenced 'All The Madmen', which Bowie wrote about his schizophrenic half-brother Terry, who was a patient there.

Bowie (1972)

'All The Madmen' was written for my brother and it's about my brother. He's the man inside, and he doesn't want to leave. He's perfectly happy there – perfectly happy. Doesn't have to work, just lies there on the lawn all day, looking at the sky. He's very happy. [096]

Weller's painting *Metrobolist*, which Bowie adopted as the album title, would be the front cover.

Bowie told Philips art director Mike Stanford that he wanted a gatefold sleeve to reveal a series of photographs showing him in a 'domestic environment', i.e. Haddon Hall, with its art deco screens and antique finery.

Stanford brought in designer/photographer Keith MacMillan. 'Keef' was well known from his work for labels like Vertigo, which Olav Wyper had launched in 1969. Keef's iconic cover for Black Sabbath's debut, released in February, was typical of his work.

ABOVE AND OVERLEAF: Photo session for *The Man Who Sold The World* at Haddon Hall with Keith 'Keef' MacMillan - in the kitchen and a casual dress variant of the front cover. OPPOSITE: On the set of Netherlands pop show *Eddy Ready Go!* in July.

Eye magazine describes Keef's "imagined rural past" as "located in some magical time before the First World War but after *Sgt Pepper*. He combines references from the Pre-Raphaelites, pagan ritual, PH Emerson's photographs, Edwardian fashion and the legend of King Arthur, to create a future-past that is both carnivalesque and downbeat, shaped by small pleasures and overshadowed by a sense of doom." [055]

The Man Who Sold The World, basically.

Keef arrived at Haddon Hall to photograph Bowie in his domestic environment – including the garden – and in his 'man's dress'. Bowie had recently purchased two medieval-style velvet gowns from the Mr Fish boutique where his old friend Geoff MacCormack worked. Bowie chose one of these gowns and reclined on a couch in the style of Pre-Raphaelite painter Dante Gabriel Rossetti.

Robin McBride then returned to Chicago with the master tapes and the artwork, along with Bowie's specific instructions.

Bowie's publishing contract with Essex Music's David Platz had expired and Defries was looking for a new deal. Laurence Myers suggested Bob Grace of Chrysalis Music, and arranged for Bowie to meet him.Chrysalis was a new label set up by Terry Ellis and Chris Wright. A year before, following their success with Ten Years After and Jethro Tull, they had brought in Bob Grace to set up their publishing company.

Bob Grace (1987)

David came up to interview me with his wife, and he really did have some idea of where he was going. Played me what was then his latest single, 'Holy Holy', which I thought was great; of course I'd loved 'Space Oddity', and I took him on simply because I thought he was great and his songs were great. Everyone was telling me not to, that he was a has-been. [043]

OCTOBER

TUESDAY 6

Arrangements were made to record the next single, 'Holy Holy', with producer/bass player Herbie Flowers, who had played on 'Space Oddity'. More recently he had produced Top 10 hits for Blue Mink, with whom he played bass.

FRIDAY 23 OCTOBER

BUSINESS

Bowie and Defries met with Bob Grace and Chris Wright to sign Bowie's publishing deal with Chrysalis Music. Bowie had been impressed by Bob Grace and was looking to him to provide career support, having found Defries so far lacklustre in this respect, though he was conscientious where money was involved.

To Chrysalis, Bowie was still a relatively untried artist, with one hit and otherwise modest sales, but he had already recorded a new album and was writing new material. As such he represented a good proposition for a publishing company.

Nevertheless, Chris Wright baulked at Defries' asking price of £5000, an unprecedented amount for Chrysalis, but he deferred to Grace's unwavering faith in Bowie's talent.

Under the contract, David Bowie was obliged to supply a minimum of 100 songs, 70 of which were to be "commercially recorded". As the agreement was retroactive this included six of the nine songs on *David Bowie* not owned by Essex as well as the songs from *The Man Who Sold The World*.

With the contract signed, Bob Grace booked time at Radio Luxembourg Studio to record demos. Bowie had no difficulty fulfilling Grace's expectations.

Bob Grace (1987)

All of a sudden, all these great songs suddenly started appearing. We used to do all the demos at the Radio Luxembourg Studios. We could never have more than a couple of inches of lead on the guitars, otherwise it acted as an aerial and picked up the mini-cab rank down the road. That was why the place was so cheap. But it suited us, simply because David was writing so much stuff. [177]

ABOVE AND TOP: The cover of the first (US) issue of *The Man Who Sold The World*, with Beckenham Arts Lab artist Mike Weller's illustration *Metrobolist* (the original album title) on the front, featuring Cane Hill mental hospital. Unbeknownst to Weller, Bowie's half-brother Terry Burns was a patient there.

SATURDAY 24 OCTOBER

The following day, Visconti's latest production for Marc Bolan, T. Rex's 'Ride A White Swan', reached No.2 in the UK singles chart.

NOVEMBER

WEDNESDAY 4

ALBUM RELEASED

'THE MAN WHO SOLD THE WORLD'

US (Mercury 61325)

Released April 10, 1971 in UK

SIDE ONE

1. **'The Width Of A Circle'** (8:07)
2. **'All The Madmen'** (5:38)
3. **'Black Country Rock'** (3:33)
4. **'After All'** (3:52)

SIDE TWO

1. **'Running Gun Blues'** (3:12)
2. **'Saviour Machine'** (4:27)
3. **'She Shook Me Cold'** (4:13)
4. **'The Man Who Sold The World'** (3:58)
5. **'The Supermen'** (3:39)

All songs by David Bowie

Tony Visconti: Producer/Remixer

Ken Scott: Engineer

David Bowie: Vocals/Guitar/Stylophone

Mick Ronson: Guitar/Vocals

Tony Visconti: Bass/Piano/Guitar

Mick Woodmansey: Drums/Percussion

Ralph Mace: Moog Synthesiser

Mike Weller: Illustrations

Bowie was horrified to find that Mercury had ignored most of his artwork instructions. The gatefold and photography were gone and they had removed the text from the speech bubble ("roll up your sleeves and show us your arms") leaving it blank. Mike Weller's cover illustration was not credited.

SELECTED REISSUES

- LP (RCA 1972).
- CD (RCA 1984).
- CD (remastered) (Ryko 1990).

BONUS TRACKS

1. 'Lightning Frightening' (3:38)
2. 'Holy Holy' (1971 Spiders version) (2:20)
3. 'Moonage Daydream' (Arnold Corns version) (3:52)
4. 'Hang On To Yourself' (Arnold Corns version) (2:51)

- CD (remastered) (EMI 1999).
- CD (mini LP replica) (Toshiba EMI 2007).

MONDAY 9
FRIDAY 13
MONDAY 16 NOVEMBER

▲ RECORDING

Island Studios
Basing Street, Notting Hill
London, England

'Holy Holy'

Herbie Flowers: Producer
David Bowie: Vocals/Guitar
Herbie Flowers: Bass
Alan Parker: Guitar
Barry Morgan: Drums

Like Visconti, producer Herbie Flowers also played bass on the session, along with most of his band Blue Mink.

A dispute arose with Mercury after Bowie had promised each musician £35 rather than the standard session rate of £12. After intervention from Defries, McBride paid the musicians the promised fees. A similar dispute, also involving Herbie Flowers, would occur in 1974.

ABOVE: Island Studios. BELOW: Herbie Flowers, who would return to Island with Bowie and Alan Parker for the *Diamond Dogs* sessions in late 1973.

DECEMBER

Bowie and Brian Eno were both present at a performance by Philip Glass and his ensemble at the Royal College of Art. Glass' minimalism would significantly influence their later work.

Brian Eno (2008)
This was one of the most extraordinary musical experiences of my life – sound made completely physical and as dense as concrete by sheer volume and repetition. For me it was like a viscous bath of pure, thick energy. Though he was at that time described as a minimalist, this was actually one of the most detailed musics I'd ever heard. It was all intricacy and exotic harmonics.
[038]

TUESDAY 1

■ SINGLE RELEASED

PROMO
'All The Madmen' (3:14)/
'All The Madmen' (3:14)
US (Mercury DJ-311)

This single, intended to promote *The Man Who Sold The World*, played the same on both sides – a 3:14 edited down mono mix with the first chorus and middle eight taken out. Stock copies with the red Mercury label backed with 'Janine' (Mercury 73173) were produced but not released.

ABOVE: Chrysalis Music publisher and Bowie's de facto manager Bob Grace.
OPPOSITE: Bowie at home, the songs "pouring out of him".

JANUARY

With a new publishing contract from Chrysalis, Bowie continued to write prolifically. At home in Haddon Hall he had moved a grand piano into Tony Visconti's old room overlooking the garden. The switch from guitar to piano produced a new way of writing, with the added quirk of having to play around a stuck piano key.

Angie Bowie (2011)
He loved that piano. David is a fantastic musician, because his approach is not studied, it's by ear. He has an ability to pluck a song from those first moments when he plays with an instrument. Writing on the piano opened up his possibilities, because of its association with so many kinds of music – classical, cabaret, every style. [113]

Determined to be a good songwriter, Bowie developed a work ethic that astonished his friends. Bob Grace, now Bowie's de facto manager since Defries was largely absent at the time, became used to Bowie's constant calls about his latest songs, which they would record at Radio Luxembourg Studio.

Bob Grace (2009)
He was incredibly prolific. Songs were just pouring out of him and it was getting intimidating. [281]

MONDAY 4

⊙ BUSINESS

Laurence Myers sent Bowie's song 'How Lucky You Are' to manager Gordon Mills for his consideration as a potential recording for Tom Jones.

WEDNESDAY 6 JANUARY

⊙ BUSINESS

Mercury Records publicist Ron Oberman contacted Defries to request arrangements for Bowie to undertake a promotional visit to America and talk up the new album to selected media. Oberman knew it was unlikely that Bowie could break *The Man Who Sold The World* in America, but he was confident that Bowie would charm some good publicity from the media.

Bowie's work permit would not allow for live performance but he packed his guitar, knowing he would find opportunities to play.

FRIDAY 15 JANUARY

■ SINGLE RELEASED

'Holy Holy' (3:13)/
'Black Country Rock' (3:32)
UK (Mercury 6052 049)
Reissued: *Five Years 1969-1973* (EMI 2015)

▮ In 1990 Ryko reissued *The Man Who Sold The World* with bonus tracks. Although 'Holy Holy' was listed as a 'single A-side from 1970', Bowie completists were disappointed to find it was the version rerecorded later with the Spiders.

MONDAY 18 JANUARY

✪ TELEVISION

Granada Studios
Quay Street
Manchester
Lancashire, England

'SIX-OH-ONE NEWSDAY'
'Holy Holy'

Bowie performed the new single on acoustic guitar wearing a dress from Mr Fish. On the set at Granada, Bowie met Roger Damon Price, who told him about an idea he was working on called *The Tomorrow People* – a television show featuring a master race called The Homo Superior.

TUESDAY 19 JANUARY

▲ RECORDING

Radio Luxembourg Studio
Hertford Street
London, England

'Oh! You Pretty Things' (demo)

At four in the morning Bowie woke up with a song going round in his head – an infectious melody and a phrase, 'Gotta make way for the Homo Superior'. After quickly getting it down on the battered piano, Bowie called Bob Grace. Grace was due to attend MIDEM, a music trade fair in Cannes, the next day, so he told Bowie, "Come up, I can record an interview with you and we can do the demo."

WEDNESDAY 20 JANUARY

⊙ BUSINESS

At the MIDEM festival Bob Grace approached legendary hit-making producer Mickie Most with an acetate of 'Oh! You Pretty Things'.

Bob Grace (1986)
I played him the demo and he said, "Smash!" You knew if Mickie listened to the whole demo and didn't stop you, you were probably going to get a record. [013]

SATURDAY 23 JANUARY

► TRAVELLING

LONDON – WASHINGTON

Bowie arrived in Washington alone (Defries chose not to accompany him and Angie was heavily pregnant) to begin the promotional tour arranged by Ron Oberman. Dressed in a blue maxi-coat and white chiffon scarf, Bowie was whisked off to the Dulles Airport Customs Hall for questioning by bemused officials for 45 minutes. A guard muttered "fag" as Bowie walked off to be greeted by Ron Oberman, who was there with his parents.

Michael Oberman (2005)
I was a music columnist for the Washington Star. ***I had written about David in 1968 based on his success in the UK. So his first stop was DC/Maryland and my parents picked up Bowie and my brother at the airport. Ron had flown in from Chicago (where Mercury was headquartered at the time).*** [402]

Bowie met Michael Oberman at the family home in Silver Spring and they took him for dinner in Washington.

Ron Oberman (2009)
Hofberg's delicatessen had the best corned beef that I'd ever had in my life, so we went to the restaurant and had a great dinner there. He got a lot of stares. [040]

Michael Oberman (2011)
Actually, we ate at Emerson's... a few doors down from Hofberg's. Our booth had a curtain which a waitress promptly closed after we ordered. [400]

MONDAY 25 JANUARY

✪ MEDIA

Washington DC, USA

Following interviews with a local underground paper and radio station, Bowie and Ron Oberman left by train for Philadelphia and the first round of interviews.

TUESDAY 26 JANUARY

✪ RADIO

Philadelphia
Pennsylvania, USA

Interviewed on 94 WYSP Radio.

WEDNESDAY 27 JANUARY

▼SOCIALISING

New York City
New York, USA

After checking in to a midtown Holiday Inn, Bowie spent the day sightseeing in Manhattan, visiting Nat Sherman ('Tobacconist to the World'), record shops in Times Square, the Metropolitan Museum of Modern Art and East Side antique stores.

In the evening Bowie and Mercury Records' Paul Nelson braved the icy January weather to hear Tim Hardin play in a Greenwich Village coffee house.

FRIDAY 29 JANUARY

▼SOCIALISING

New York City
New York, USA

The Velvet Underground were playing Fridays and Saturdays at the Electric Circus at 23 St Marks Place. Bowie had been a fan ever since Ken Pitt gave him their first album in 1967, and having just heard the the 1970 LP, *Loaded*, he was eager to catch their set, but was unaware the band's line-up had changed dramatically since then.

Bowie (2004)

When I first came to America, around 1971, my New York guide told me one day that The Velvet Underground were to play later that night at the Electric Circus, which was about to close. I was the biggest fan in the UK, I believe. I got to the gig early and positioned myself at the front by the lip of the stage. The performance was great, and I made sure that Lou Reed could see that I was a true fan by singing along to all the songs.

After the show, I moved to the side of the stage to where the door of the dressing room was located. I knocked, and one of the band members answered. After a few gushing compliments, I asked if I could have a few words with Lou. He looked bemused but told me to wait a second. After only moments, Lou came out, and we sat and talked about song writing for ten minutes or so.

I left the club floating on cloud nine – a teenage ambition achieved. The next day, I told my guide what a blast it had been to see the Velvets live and meet Lou Reed. He looked at me quizzically for a second, and then burst into laughter. "Lou left the band some time ago," he said. "You were talking to his replacement, Doug Yule." [066]

ABOVE AND OPPOSITE: Bowie at the Holiday Inn in New York.

■ SINGLE RELEASED

RONNO

'4th Hour Of My Sleep' (Zimmerman) (3:08)/
'Powers Of Darkness' (Marshall) (3:32)
UK (Vertigo 6059 029)
Picture sleeve released Germany/Sweden

Mick Ronson: Guitar
Tony Visconti: Bass
Woody Woodmansey: Drums
Benny Marshall: Vocals

Bowie (1972)

I didn't believe it till I came here, till I got off the plane. From England, America merely symbolises something – it doesn't actually exist. And when you get off the plane and find that there actually is a country called America, it becomes very important then. [096]

FEBRUARY

MONDAY 1 – TUESDAY 9

► TRAVELLING

✪ PRESS

Bowie and Oberman flew to Detroit, checking in at another Holiday Inn, on Grand Boulevard, where Bowie was interviewed by Dave Marsh (*Creem* magazine) and photographed by Charlie Auringer.

Their next stop was Minneapolis for more interviews, then on to Chicago for a meeting with Mercury's A&R boss Robin McBride at their head office. From there they flew to Detroit, then Milwaukee for more interviews, and onto Atlanta and Houston.

WEDNESDAY 10 FEBRUARY

✪ MEDIA

► TRAVELLING

HOUSTON – SAN FRANCISCO – SAN JOSE

During a round of radio station appearances, Bowie's provocative choice of dress was too much for one local, who called Bowie a 'fag' and pulled a gun on him.

Bowie flew to San Francisco and was met by Mercury Records' Lewis Seigel, who had arranged for him to be accompanied on his West Coast visit by *Rolling Stone* writer John Mendelsohn who reported, "In the studios of San Francisco's KSAN-FM [Bowie] assures the incredulous DJ that his last album was, very simply, a collection of reminiscences about his experiences as a shaven-haired transvestite." [205]

In San Jose, Mendelsohn and Bowie visited a radio station for an interview and Bowie was invited to play some records. Mendelsohn went through the racks and came up with The Stooges' 'I Wanna Be Your Dog'. Bowie was transfixed by Iggy Pop and tracked down a copy of *Fun House*. For the rest of their trip Bowie pumped Mendelsohn for stories of the 'world's forgotten boy'.

SATURDAY 13 FEBRUARY

► TRAVELLING

LOS ANGELES

Bowie and Mendelsohn flew to Los Angeles and were met by DJ Rodney Bingenheimer. His time as Bowie's guide in Los Angeles led to a lasting friendship, with Bowie encouraging him to open his English Disco.

Bowie was in America primarily to talk up the album but his own motivation was to absorb the aspects of American culture at that time. He would listen to stories of the exploits of punk cult figures Iggy Pop and Lou Reed, and imagined a combination of the two – nihilistic, literate, self-destructive and charismatic. Also thrown into the mix was the delusional UK rocker Vince Taylor and the manic Legendary Stardust Cowboy. Out of all this, Bowie came up with a composite – an archetype of a doomed rock star.

While in Hollywood, Bowie stayed with RCA executive and producer Tony Ayres and, using the recording equipment there, made a demo of 'Moonage Daydream'.

As he scrawled the lyrics to another song on Holiday Inn stationery, Bowie told Bingenheimer and Ayres he was writing about an imaginary character called Ziggy Stardust. At Ayres' studio Bowie recorded a multitrack demo of 'Hang On To Yourself' and gave the tape to Ayres to pass on to Gene Vincent, who was also there recording demos. Ayres indulged his guest's requests to record new ideas whenever inspiration struck. Noting Bowie's abundant songwriting talent and his disappointment with Mercury's handling of the album artwork, Ayres suggested he think about signing to RCA and arranged for Bowie to meet with RCA's West Coast publicity head. RCA was then relying mainly on Elvis Presley, who, as Ayres explained, "can't last forever".

SUNDAY 14 FEBRUARY

▼SOCIALISING

Bowie was invited to jam with Mendelsohn's band Christopher Milk. Bowie decided to walk the several blocks of Sunset Boulevard in his dress to A&M studios on La Brea in Hollywood. Arriving with his acoustic guitar, Bowie sat out most of the jam but joined in for the Velvets' 'I'm Waiting For The Man'.

Later Bowie, Bingenheimer and Mendelsohn attended a number of Valentine's Day parties, the first of which was at the home of attorney Paul Feigen. Still armed with his guitar, Bowie took centre stage, cross-legged on a waterbed playing 'All The Madmen', 'Space Oddity', 'Amsterdam' and 'Hang On To Yourself' to the guests. (Bingenheimer recorded the performance and later played part of it on his radio show in the Nineties.) After losing their attention, Bowie eventually

Mendelsohn wrote: "In Hollywood, at a party staged in his honour, he blows the minds of arriving hot-panted honeys with Edy Williams hair, welcoming them lispily in his gorgeous gown before excusing himself so he can watch [Warhol superstar] Ultra Violet give interviews from a milk bath at a party held a few blocks away in her honour. 'I refuse to be thought of as mediocre,' Bowie asserts blithely. 'If I am mediocre I'll get out of the business. There's enough fog around. That's why the idea of performance-as-spectacle is so important to me.'

"He plans to appear on stage decked out rather like Cleopatra in the appropriate heavy make-up and in costumes that will hopefully recall those designed in the Thirties by Erté." [193]

ABOVE AND BELOW: Unplugged – entertaining the Valentine's Day party from a waterbed.
OPPOSITE: Doing the rounds with 'The Mayor of Sunset Strip', Rodney Bingenheimer, who championed Bowie on the West Coast.

Bowie spent the rest of his time in Los Angeles being driven around by Bingenheimer in Tom Ayres' Cadillac to radio station interviews – KMAC, CMIS and KYMS.

Bowie also watched a performance by Biff Rose, an eccentric songwriter known as 'the hippy Randy Newman'. Bowie had been playing Rose's songs 'Buzz The Fuzz' and 'Fill Your Heart' in his set and would record the latter for *Hunky Dory*.

THURSDAY 18 FEBRUARY

►TRAVELLING

LOS ANGELES – LONDON

Back in England after a direct flight from Los Angeles, Bowie was fired up from his first US trip and told everyone about his new character "who looks like he's landed from Mars".

Bowie (1972)

America was an incredible adrenalin trip. I got very sharp and very quick. Somehow or other I became very prolific. I wanted to write things that were more… immediate. [205]

The 'Holy Holy' single had sunk without trace while he was away. Undeterred, Bowie focused all his attention on his new songs.

THURSDAY 25 FEBRUARY

▲RECORDING

Radio Luxembourg Studio
Hertford Street
London, England

THE ARNOLD CORNS SINGLE
'Moonage Daydream'
'Hang On To Yourself'

David Bowie: Vocals/Guitar
Mark Pritchett: Guitar
Pete De Somogyl: Bass
Tim Broadbent: Drums

Bob Grace arranged more sessions for Bowie to test out the new songs with Rungk.

Still contracted to Mercury, Bowie decided to test the new material in a pseudonym concept, The Arnold Corns, a prototype for the Ziggy Stardust project. Fred Burrett, a young designer friend now renamed Freddie Burretti, was the lead singer in name only. His real functions would be to design Bowie's clothes and facilitate his assimilation of the Kensington gay

MARCH

TUESDAY 9
WEDNESDAY 10

▲ **RECORDING**

Radio Luxembourg Studio
Hertford Street
London, England

'Lady Stardust' (demo)
'Right On Mother' (demo)

▮ 'Lady Stardust' demo released on *Ziggy Stardust* (Ryko 1990).

FRIDAY 26 MARCH

▲ **RECORDING**

Kingsway Studios
Kingsway
London, England

PETER NOONE SINGLE
'Oh! You Pretty Thing'
'Right On Mother'

Mickie Most: Producer
Peter Noone: Vocals
David Bowie: Piano/Backing Vocals
Herbie Flowers: Bass
Clem Cattini: Drums

While Bowie was in America, Mickie Most had taken 'Oh! You Pretty Things' to Herman's Hermits singer Peter Noone, telling him, "I think I found your first solo record." On hearing the intro Noone said, "That's it, it's perfect!"

Noone told *Melody Maker*, "We wanted the same feel as the demo [Bowie] sent us, so he played piano on the record." Later he told Paul Trynka, "He could only play the song in F#, which became the new key. Suddenly with him playing the piano, the song came alive. We cut it sort of half-live, I kept the original scratch vocal and then just doubled the high notes. It was mixed in 30 minutes." [295]

The song was renamed 'Oh You Pretty Thing' and in keeping with his wholesome pop image, Noone also changed the line "the earth is a bitch" to the more radio-friendly "the earth is a beast".

Johnny Arthey wrote a new arrangement, opening with the chorus instead of the familiar piano intro and first verse.

Bowie later told Chris Welch, "Although I really wanted Leon Russell to sing it, I suppose Herman has done it quite well."

'Right On Mother' was to be the flipside but it was held over until October as the B-side of Peter Noone's second single, 'Walnut Whirl'.

LEFT: Ex-Herman's Hermit Peter Noone.
ABOVE: The UK cover of *The Man Who Sold The World* became known as the 'drag' or 'dress' cover to distinguish it from the US 'cartoon' cover, the German circular foldout cover and the RCA reissue 'kick' cover.
OPPOSITE: Angie, Bowie and Freddie Burretti photographed at home on July 20 by Peter Stone for Don Short's *Daily Mirror* story 'Dressed For The Bowie Life'.

APRIL

THURSDAY 1

✪ **PRESS**

John Mendelsohn's feature on Bowie in America, 'David Bowie: Pantomime Rock', was published in *Rolling Stone*. The profile was everything Ron Oberman had hoped for, giving American readers their first impression of Bowie – charming, clever and outrageous. It didn't boost album sales, but Mendelsohn had put Bowie on the map.

SATURDAY 10 APRIL

■ **ALBUM RELEASED**

'THE MAN WHO SOLD THE WORLD'
UK (Mercury 6338 041)

Almost a year after its completion, the album was finally released in the UK with the 'drag cover' (as it later became known), photographed by Keef. Designed as a Dante Gabriel Rossetti parody, the cover was printed on textured stock to simulate a canvas.

Promotional copies of *The Man Who Sold The World* were sent out to the press with 500 press kit folders made up with new photos, biography and cuttings.

Bob Grace had also called in Bill Harry – one of London's top publicists – to generate momentum for Bowie's stalled career. He saw the key aspect to promote was Bowie's sophisticated visual sense. Bowie showed him an array of imagery and themes, including the Egyptian ideas he had described to John Mendelsohn in February. Bowie requested Chrysalis photographer Brian Ward – on the strength of his work with Jethro Tull – for a session to photograph Bowie's new look.

With Bill Harry, Bowie did the rounds of Fleet Street, talking up the album and surreptitiously raiding their filing cabinets, replacing their old file photos with the new Brian Ward shots. The curly-haired Bowie of 'Space Oddity' fame was consigned to history.

SATURDAY 17 APRIL

✪ **PRESS**

In his feature for *Melody Maker*, 'Why Does David Bowie Like Dressing Up In Ladies Clothes?', Chris Welch was bemused by Bowie's new dress sense and focused more on what went wrong after 'Space Oddity'. Fired up by his US visit, Bowie dismissed his setback as temporary and enthused about the resurgence in his writing.

FRIDAY 23 APRIL

▲ **RECORDING**

Trident Studios
17 St Anne's Court, Soho
London, England

'Rupert The Riley'
'The Man'
(later titled 'Lightning Frightening')
'How Lucky You Are' ('Miss Peculiar')

Ken Scott: Engineer
Mickey King: Vocals
David Bowie: Backing Vocals/Saxophone
Mark Pritchett: Guitar
Herbie Flowers: Bass
Barry Morgan: Drums

Bowie produced another pseudonym project – Mickey King's All Stars – to test some new songs, this time with Mickey King (another friend from the Kensington club scene) as lead vocalist.

The previous month Bowie had told *Disc & Music Echo*, "It's funny how I suddenly seem to have taken off as a songwriter. But that is what living down here has done for me. I'm wrapped up in my friends and include them in my songs. One of my songs, 'Rupert The Riley', is about the car." [114]

Bowie had hoped 'Rupert The Riley' might become a hit for King with its classic pop arrangement – a key change making up for the absence of a middle eight.

The finishing touch was a sound effect of roadie Roger Fry starting up the Riley, which Bowie had recorded on his Revox outside Haddon Hall.

Since writing the song, Bowie had been seriously injured after his 1932 Riley Gamecock stalled on the way to London. He got out and cranked the starting handle, forgetting he had left the car in gear. It lurched forward and plunged the handle into his thigh. Fortunately this happened outside Lewisham Hospital, where he spent some days recuperating.

The most significant outcome of the session was a conversation with engineer Ken Scott during a break in recording.

Ken Scott (2005)

He came into Trident one day to produce a single for a friend and because I'd worked with him before, I was put on the session. Around that time, I was getting fed up with just engineering, and in a tea break I happened to say to him, "You know what? I'm a bit frustrated. I want to start moving into the production side." He said, "Well, I've just got a new manager, and I'm about to start a new album. I was going to do it myself but I don't know if I can, how about working with me?" [088]

▮ 'Rupert The Riley' was never officially released, but two different stereo mixes with and without sound effects later appeared on bootlegs.

▮ 'The Man' was first released as 'Lightning Frightening' on the 1990 Ryko reissue of *The Man Who Sold The World* as it was thought to be recorded in 1970 with Visconti, Renwick and Cambridge. Ryko used a mono mix that fades in, since the start of the master tape was accidentally chopped off and lost during the Ryko mastering. However, a complete stereo version (sourced from copies made prior to this) circulates on bootlegs.

▮ 'How Lucky You Are' was knocked back by Tom Jones' manager and this version fared no better. It was deemed unfit for release, as was a later recording with Bowie on lead. Both versions remain in the Bowie vaults, available only on bootlegs.

SATURDAY 24 APRIL

✪ **PRESS**

The *Daily Mirror* ran a half-page feature, 'Dressed For The Bowie Life' by Don Short. The article, illustrated with a photo taken in the back garden at Haddon Hall, focussed on Bowie's 'dress', which Bowie downplayed.

FRIDAY 30 APRIL

■ **SINGLE RELEASED**

PETER NOONE
'Oh You Pretty Thing' (2:55)/
'Together Forever'
(Vangarde/Fishman) (2:30)
UK (RAK 121)
Chart Peak No.12

Chrysalis Music published the sheet music for Noone's hit 'Oh You Pretty Thing' and highlighted Bowie as not only the author of that song, but also his own album and the Arnold Corns single.

MAY

SATURDAY 1

✪ **PRESS**

David introduced Freddie Burretti to the press as Rudi Valentino, 'the new Mick Jagger', adding that Arnold Corns would be the next Rolling Stones.

Curious magazine featured Bowie and Burretti on their May/June cover.

The image was one of a series that Brian Ward shot of Bowie, Burretti (in various outfits) and Bob Grace in biker leather. Burretti also posed holding a boa constrictor, which Bowie later claimed was the origin of Alice Cooper's snake act.

THURSDAY 6 MAY

⊙ **BUSINESS**

Bob Grace wrote to BBC producer Jeff Griffin to confirm Bowie's booking for a John Peel radio session on June 3. Bowie had enlisted guitarists Tim Renwick from Quiver and Tony Hill from High Tide, with Herbie Flowers on bass and Terry Cox on drums. All but Tony Hill had played on the 1969 *David Bowie* album.

FRIDAY 7 MAY

■ **SINGLE RELEASED**

THE ARNOLD CORNS
'Moonage Daydream' (3:52)/
'Hang On To Yourself' (2:51)
UK (B&C Records CB 149)

▮ Reissued on *The Man Who Sold The World* (Ryko 1990) and *Ziggy Stardust* (EMI 2002).

Bob Grace (1987)

We decided to lease three of the demos to B&C Records [an offshoot of Charisma Records], simply to try and get some money back. I think we got £300 for the three masters. Because David was still contracted to Mercury we couldn't use his name, so David came up with Arnold Corns. He never told anyone what it meant. [043]

▼ **SOCIALISING**

RONNO
London Temple Club
London, England

Bowie took Bob Grace to Ronno's showcase set at London Temple Club. The support act on the night was Beggars Opera, a prog-rock group (also on Vertigo) founded by guitarist Ricky Gardiner, who later worked on Bowie's *Low* and Iggy Pop's *Lust For Life*.

ABOVE: Bowie and his clothes designer/protégé/experiment Freddie Burretti on the cover of *Curious* magazine.
OPPOSITE: Producer Ken Scott, whom Bowie described as "my George Martin". By 1971 Ken Scott's CV included engineering The Beatles' *White Album*, *Magical Mystery Tour* and several of their solo projects, including George Harrison's *All Things Must Pass*. After engineering Bowie's *The Man Who Sold The World* he moved into production. *Hunky Dory* was the first album he co-produced with Bowie, followed by *The Rise And Fall Of Ziggy Stardust And The Spiders From Mars*, *Aladdin Sane* and *Pin Ups*.
OVERLEAF: Major label publicity for Peter Noone's new single, which was the first fruits of Bowie's prolific songwriting in 1971.

INSTANT PHASER
POWER SUPPLY

OH! YOU
PRETTY
PETER NOON
MORE O'FERRALL LTD.

WEDNESDAY 12 MAY

▼SOCIALISING

Bowie and Angie attended the marriage of George Underwood and Birgit Graversen at Bromley Register Office. George Underwood was an old friend of Bowie's from his schooldays. In 1962 they had a fight after Bowie tried to steal his girlfriend.

Bowie (1973)

He threw a punch at me! It caught me in the eye, and I stumbled against a wall and on to my knees. At first he thought I was kidding – it wasn't a very hard punch. But it had obviously caught me at rather an odd angle. [226]

He was rushed to hospital and after four months of operations, Bowie was left with faulty depth perception and a permanently dilated left pupil. As a result, Bowie appeared to have different coloured eyes, giving him an otherworldly appearance.

George Underwood (1973)

I'm sure David doesn't think about it nowadays – but every time I see him again after a long break, I'm reminded of what I did to him, all those years ago! [226]

Despite this setback, the two remained firm friends, playing in the King Bees. Their single, 'Liza Jane', released in June 1964 on Vocalion Pop, was Bowie's first commercially released recording.

Underwood had trained as an illustrator but Bowie was encouraging him to resume his musical career, inviting him to guest on the upcoming radio session. Bowie also agreed to produce some sessions at Advision Studios for Underwood to record three Bowie songs, which Defries would shop around the labels for a deal.

George Underwood (2006)

'Hole In The Ground' was written by David, Herbie Flowers on bass, Tim Renwick on guitar and Terry Cox on drums. Also David was playing guitar on it. The B-side was just a continuation of the record without any vocals, which we were going to call 'Lump On The Hill'. 'Time' was an early version (originally titled 'We Should Be On By Now') with some different lyrics from the one that appeared on Aladdin Sane ***a few years later. I think 'Song For Bob Dylan' was the same session.*** [392]

ABOVE: Bowie and Angie (far left) attend the wedding of his childhood friend George Underwood, who was responsible for Bowie's eyes appearing to be different colours. They remained lifelong friends and Underwood worked as a designer/illustrator on several Bowie-related projects, including the back cover of *David Bowie*, the MainMan logo and the cover of the unreleased 1972 Ziggy live album.

THURSDAY 13 MAY

BUSINESS

Stevie Wonder turned 21, meaning he was no longer contracted to Motown Records and could now take control of his own business affairs. Tony Defries had been in negotiations with him through Don Hunter, an associate who worked at Motown. He had planned to take over Wonder's management, but Wonder decided to negotiate a new contract with Motown. The proposed deal had occupied most of Defries' time, meaning he'd had little involvement in Bowie's career.

FRIDAY 14 MAY

BUSINESS

Following his failed bid to manage Stevie Wonder, Tony Defries finally refocused on getting Bowie away from Mercury Records.

Defries met with Mercury's Robin McBride, Irwin Steinberg and Charlie Fasch, who came to the Londonderry Hotel buoyant and optimistic. They were expecting Bowie to re-sign with them for another three years, but were in for a rude shock.

Defries stated unequivocally that the contract was to be terminated forthwith and that Bowie would not record another note for Mercury. To their counter-demand for a third album they were owed under contract, Defries responded with the same 'piece of crap' strategy employed by The Rolling Stones to get off Decca. Knowing that forcing this point and paying for the production of unreleasable material was pointless, Mercury unwittingly demanded what Defries wanted all along – full reimbursement for all costs associated with *The Man Who Sold The World* and the other recordings made under the contract.

Defries now had two albums to sell later on to the highest bidder.

Bowie's disappointment with Mercury over the handling of the last album was still fresh in his memory. As before with Pitt, Bowie sat mutely throughout proceedings with Angie, watching the axe fall, apparently in his favour.

ABOVE: Peter Noone performs 'Oh You Pretty Thing' (without Bowie on piano) on *Whittaker's World Of Music* (LWT) on May 29.

With Mercury out of the picture, Defries continued with his plans, registering a new company, Minnie Bell Music Limited, which he later renamed MainMan.

Defries had been studying the managerial strong-arm techniques of the likes of Klein (Beatles, Stones), Peter Grant (Led Zeppelin) and Albert Grossman (Janis Joplin, Bob Dylan). By the early Seventies every aspect of the music business was bigger, and these men had pioneered deals that reflected their artists' potential or established popularity, ensuring financial security for both manager and artist at the label's expense – rather than the old business model where the inverse applied.

More significantly, Defries also modelled himself on Colonel Tom Parker. Like Elvis' ex-carny manager, Defries made it clear who was working for whom.

▮ 'David Bowie – Man for McLuhan' article, featuring an interview by Patrick Salvo, published in *Circus* magazine.

Tim Renwick was unavailable for an upcoming radio session and Tony Hill had dropped out so Bowie called up Ronson, who was at his lowest ebb and living with his parents in Hull. Live work had dried up and the Ronno single had been unsuccessful.

Mick Ronson (1987)

It did nothing at all. Vertigo offered us a simple deal – here's a studio, go and make a record. That was it. And when the single flopped, things simply fell apart. Then David called and asked us if we wanted to come back and do some more stuff with him. [177]

Ronson jumped at the offer and took the next train to London. At Haddon Hall Bowie proposed that Ronson assemble a new version of Ronno, retaining drummer Woody Woodmansey. Ronson returned to Hull to try out bass players. In the end the job went to Trevor Bolder, another of Ronson's Hull friends who had auditioned. Bolder had already seen Bowie play and had visited Ronson at Haddon Hall the previous year. His extensive musical experience – including playing trumpet and piano tuning – would prove to be a significant factor in The Spiders From Mars.

THURSDAY 27 MAY

TELEVISION

'TOP OF THE POPS'

Peter Noone performed 'Oh You Pretty Thing' accompanied by Hot Chocolate's Tony Wilson (in place of Herbie Flowers) on bass and Bowie, who played piano in a dress.

▮ The video of the performance was wiped by the BBC, whose budget necessitated the recycling of their tapes.

SUNDAY 30 MAY

Angie gave birth to their son at Bromley Hospital, following a long labour and suffering a cracked pelvis in the process. Bowie was at home, listening to *After The Goldrush* when he got the call, as he explained on John Peel's radio show a week later: "I'd been listening to a Neil Young album and they phoned through and said that my wife had had a baby on Sunday morning and I wrote this about the baby. It's called 'Kooks'."

Bowie and Bob Grace visited Angie and the baby, whom they named Duncan Zowie Haywood Jones. Later Zowie called himself Joe before settling on Duncan Jones.

JUNE

THURSDAY 3

RADIO

BBC Paris Studio
Lower Regent Street
London, England

BBC RADIO 1
'IN CONCERT'
JOHN PEEL
'Rupert The Riley'
'The Man'
(later titled 'Lightning Frightening')
'How Lucky You Are' ('Miss Peculiar')

Jeff Griffin: Producer
David Bowie: Vocals/Guitar/Piano
Mick Ronson: Guitar/Vocals
Trevor Bolder: Bass
Woody Woodmansey: Drums
Mark Pritchett: Rhythm Guitar
George Underwood/Dana Gillespie/Geoff MacCormack: Vocals

Bowie planned the show to be a preview of the forthcoming album, but it became something of a "community thing", which Peel noted, with approval, as "an astonishing number of friends" from Bowie's neighbourhood took turns on vocals. Despite the session's casual atmosphere, Bowie and his band were nervous before the show. The new material was unfamiliar and Bowie had not performed live for some time.

Trevor Bolder (2009)

I wasn't supposed to be playing bass – it was supposed to be Herbie Flowers, but he couldn't do it so I played. I had to learn 12 songs in about two hours. [281]

Bolder had problems during rehearsal, earning a rebuke from Bowie, so retreated to the dressing room to relearn his parts and played the whole show without mistakes.

George Underwood remembered, "It was a bit nerve-racking. David was nervous. You can hear it in his voice when he is talking." Bowie's voice occasionally faltered and gave out entirely during 'Oh! You Pretty Things'. The recording of the song was duly dropped from the broadcast and deleted from the BBC archives.

Peel introduced Mark Pritchett as a member of Arnold Corns, saying it was a great pity that no one at the BBC had played their single. He announced 'Looking For A Friend' as their next single to be recorded, adding they were "shortly to be recording an LP as well".

Ronson, Woodmansey and Bolder were introduced as members of Ronno, who were planning an album with Bowie "involved in some way or another".

Benny Marshall had also attended rehearsals and was mentioned in Peel's introduction as a member of Ronno, but he had returned to Hull before the recording.

George Underwood took the lead on 'Song For Bob Dylan' (also referred to here as 'Here She Comes') in anticipation of a planned single, which Bowie produced during this period. Dana Gillespie sang 'Andy Warhol' and backing vocal on 'It Ain't Easy', as she would on the version Bowie would soon record.

The show was judged a success despite Bowie's misgivings and, for a while, he considered making it a travelling road show, along the lines of *Mad Dogs And Englishmen*.

Broadcast: June 20 (BBC Radio 1).

'Bombers'/'Looking For A Friend'/'Almost Grown'/'Kooks' released on *Bowie At The Beeb* (Virgin/BBC 2000).

ABOVE: Portrait by Marcellus Hudalla, taken in the Gem offices, Regent Street. OPPOSITE: Brian Ward photo session for *Hunky Dory* cover.

DANA GILLESPIE

Defries began planning his own management empire, modelled on The Beatles' Apple Corps. He would have a stable of artists working on each other's projects as well as their own. Apple had collapsed, but Defries was certain his would succeed. And he had David Bowie. Defries had recently begun a relationship with Gillespie and signed her to Gem, convinced that she too would be a star. She was an old flame of Bowie's, having met him one night at The Marquee Club in 1965 when he was in the Manish Boys and she was a folk singer, recording singles for Pye and Decca, before moving into theatre. Defries would now revive her musical career, after freeing her from her theatrical contracts.

In between *Hunky Dory* sessions, Bowie and Ronson would produce recordings of her songs at Trident Studios, starting with her version of Bowie's 'Andy Warhol', previewed on the BBC session.

FRIDAY 4 JUNE

The members of Ronno returned to Hull to prepare for their move down to London. Bolder and Woodmansey initially joined Ronson at Haddon Hall, sleeping on mattresses on the gallery level before they moved to a flat nearby in Beckenham (although, according to Bolder, they moved out the following year).

The band rehearsed in the basement until it became too cramped, after which they moved up to the hall, near the living room where Bowie had his piano by the window.

TUESDAY 8 JUNE

RECORDING

Trident Studios
17 St Anne's Court, Soho
London, England

'HUNKY DORY' ALBUM
'Song For Bob Dylan'

Hunky Dory sessions began with Ken Scott co-producing with Bowie. Scott was a natural choice, having engineered Bowie's previous two albums and, more recently, the tracks with Mickey King.

They started working on one of the songs from the Peel session earlier in the week, 'Song For Bob Dylan'.

Bowie (1976)

That laid out what I wanted to do in rock. It was at that period that I said, "Okay, Dylan, if you don't want to do it, I will." I saw that leadership void. Even though the song isn't one of the most important on the album, it represented for me what the album was all about. If there wasn't someone who was going to use rock'n'roll, then I'd do it. [332]

The *Hunky Dory* sessions were characterised by immediacy and spontaneity and, unlike the previous album, Bowie was present throughout and focused on the moment.

Ken Scott (2005)
It was very much him knowing what he wanted right from the get-go. I think he knew all along what was going to happen, but he didn't always tell you. You had to be ready. And with David almost all of the lead vocals are one take. And no need to put them in tune afterward. Even if you could. [088]

Trevor Bolder (2011)
Our approach was very off the top of our heads. We'd go in, David would play us a song – often one we hadn't heard – we'd run through it once, and then take it. No time to think about what you're going to play. You'd have to do it there and then. In some respects, it's nerve-racking, but it gives a certain feel. [113]

Woody Woodmansey (2011)
There was incredible pressure in getting a track recorded right. Many times we'd go in with a track to record and at the last minute David would change his mind and we'd do one we hadn't rehearsed! We would be panicking, as he didn't like doing more than three takes to get it. Nearly every track I recorded with David was first, second or third take – usually second. He knew when a take was 'right'. [113]

Bowie also began recording demos of other songs for what would become *Ziggy Stardust*.

SATURDAY 12 JUNE

■ **CHART**

Boosted by the *Top Of The Pops* appearance and a concerted publicity campaign, including a billboard, Noone's single 'Oh You Pretty Thing' peaked in the UK chart at No.12.

Peter Noone (2009)

David was sitting around waiting to get out of his record deal, and when it became a hit he felt we'd done him a favour because he could pay his rent that month. At the time I remember thinking David Bowie was the next Paul McCartney. [281]

As the song's publisher, Bob Grace was naturally delighted with the success and income it would bring. However, his partners at Chrysalis – an avowedly alternative label – were appalled to be associated with a mainstream pop single.

THURSDAY 17 JUNE

▲ **RECORDING**

Trident Studios
17 St Anne's Court, Soho
London, England

THE ARNOLD CORNS
'Looking For A Friend'
'Man In The Middle'

Roy Thomas Baker: Engineer
Rudi Valentino: Vocals
David Bowie: Vocals/Guitar
Mick Ronson: Vocals/Guitar/
Lead Guitar on 'Man In The Middle'
Trevor Bolder: Bass
Woody Woodmansey: Drums
Mark Pritchett: Vocals/Lead Guitar on 'Looking For A Friend'

A second Arnold Corns recording session for the supposed album *Looking For Rudi* produced only two songs, neither of which were released. 'Looking For A Friend' was Freddie Burretti's only vocal appearance. Other mixes and takes of the song have Bowie singing the lead.

'Man In The Middle' was composed and sung by Mark Pritchett, with Bowie on backing vocal.

▮ Both tracks released on the semi-official 12-inch EP *Man In The Middle* (Krazy Kat 1985).

ABOVE: Glastonbury Fair. As dawn breaks, Bowie makes his way from the Eavis farmhouse to the Pyramid Stage. Angie made him a blue 'magician cloak' to wear, as she was tired of seeing him in T-shirts.
OPPOSITE TOP: The 1971 Glastonbury festival featured the first incarnation of the Pyramid Stage. Built from scaffolding and metal sheeting, the structure was a one-tenth replica of the Great Pyramid of Giza. The festival was filmed by Nicolas Roeg and Peter Neal and released in May 1972 as *Glastonbury Fayre*. There is no footage of Bowie's performance in the film.
OPPOSITE BOTTOM: Two priests walk among the festival crowd.

MONDAY 21 JUNE

GLASTONBURY FAIR

Bowie was booked to perform at the inaugural Glastonbury Fair by DJ/promoter Jeff Dexter. Accompanied by Bob Grace, Tony Defries, Dana Gillespie and Roger ('The Lodger') Fry, Bowie took the train from Paddington, then booked into a small hotel in Shepton Mallet.

Bowie was originally due to perform on Tuesday 22nd at 7.30pm but was rescheduled to perform at midnight, before being moved again to the following morning.

Jeff Dexter (2016)

David had wandered 'off piste', hanging out with 'Toad', aka Toni Attell, actress and mime artist with the theatre troupe that were holing up in the farm cottage, joined by a couple of other musicians too, Linda Lewis and Terry Reid.

WEDNESDAY 23 JUNE

★ **LIVE**

'The Supermen'/'Quicksand' (announced but not played)/'Changes'/'I'd Like A Big Girl With A Couple Of Melons'/'Oh! You Pretty Things'/'Kooks'/'It's Gonna Rain Again'/'Memory Of A Free Festival'/'Amsterdam'/'Song For Bob Dylan'/'Bombers'

GLASTONBURY FAIR

Around five in the morning – assisted by Roger the roadie – Bowie appeared on the main stage to play to the waking crowd. The set – mainly *Hunky Dory* songs – included 'I'd Like A Big Girl With A Couple Of Melons', a ribald take on 'Oh! You Pretty Things' which he followed it with.

Bowie returned to London invigorated by the experience and more determined than ever. Dana Gillespie later reflected, "It all got more serious after that weekend."

▮ His live set at Glastonbury was recorded but remains unreleased. Some of the live recordings made during the festival (though not Bowie's) were released in *July 1972 on the triple LP Revelations – A Musical Anthology For Glastonbury Fayre.*

LATE JUNE

⊙ BUSINESS

The success of 'Oh You Pretty Thing' and the Glastonbury performance confirmed Bob Grace's instincts and Tony Defries realised the extent of Bowie's potential. Grace was more involved with Bowie than Defries and had become his de facto manager. At a meeting with Grace and Terry Ellis at Chrysalis, Defries accused Grace of trying to steal his client. Grace apologised, explaining, "I'm just trying to do my job as a publisher." [007]

Defries also dispensed with PR Bill Harry, feeling that he too was taking over his job. Just prior to this, Bill Harry had secured Bowie a feature article in the *Daily Mirror* titled 'Right Then, Which One Is Dad?' with photos by Ray Burton of Bowie and Angie at home with Zowie at Haddon Hall. Bowie was pictured wearing the same high-waisted Oxford bags and floppy hat he'd worn to Glastonbury.

Defries replaced Bill Harry with Dai Davies, who arranged the cover story on Arnold Corns for *Curious* magazine.

Defries also formalised the severance of Bowie's Mercury contract and cleared Ronson of his contractual commitments to Philips in readiness for a new contract. With Dana Gillespie also cleared of her obligations, Defries and Myers planned a Gem promotional album, one side showcasing Bowie's new songs, the other Gillespie's.

Dana Gillespie (2011)

His attitude was "I'll take care of this." He made sure nobody had any hassles to deal with, and was free to create. [295]

THIS SPREAD: The Bowies show off (almost) one-month-old Zowie for the *Daily Mirror*, June 29.

JULY

FRIDAY 9

▲ RECORDING

Trident Studios
17 St Anne's Court, Soho
London, England

'HUNKY DORY' ALBUM
BOWIE/GILLESPIE PROMO
'It Ain't Easy'
'Bombers' (2 takes)

Recording sessions for the first songs earmarked for Bowie's side of the promotional LP and *Hunky Dory*. Bowie's cover of Ron Davies' 'It Ain't Easy' would be held over for *Ziggy Stardust*.

As on the John Peel radio session, Dana Gillespie sang backing vocals on 'It Ain't Easy'. Rick Wakeman, brought in by Bowie to play piano on the album, played harpsichord.

Rick Wakeman (2009)
David called me up to his house in Beckenham, Kent, as he wanted to play me some songs. I sat at his beautiful grand piano while he played all the songs that were to appear on the* Hunky Dory *album on his battered 12-string guitar. [281]

Rick Wakeman (2011)
I enquired about the state of the instrument he was playing. David replied, "Rick, very soon you too will be recording music, and you will realise if it sounds good on rubbish like this, then it will sound amazing when it is completed in the studio." [169]

Ken Scott (2009)
The piano we used was an 1898 Bechstein, and there wasn't another one quite like it. It's the same piano used by The Beatles on 'Hey Jude'. [281]

Rick Wakeman (2009)
David very much let me have free rein. I had worked a lot with Ken Scott as well, so they both knew my style of playing. David simply said to play the music as piano pieces in my style. [281]

▮ 'Bombers' released on *Hunky Dory* (Ryko 1990).

WEDNESDAY 14 JULY

▲ RECORDING

Trident Studios
17 St Anne's Court, Soho
London, England

'HUNKY DORY' ALBUM
BOWIE/GILLESPIE PROMO
'Quicksand' (4 takes/take 4 used)

SUNDAY 18 JULY

▲ REHEARSING

Near Victoria Station
London, England

Rodney Bingenheimer was in town and took some photographs of the rehearsals. Bob Grace introduced Bowie to Chameleon, a new group he was signing to Chrysalis' Butterfly Productions. Bowie gave them a demo of 'Star', which he wanted to produce for them, but Chrysalis insisted on using a 'proper' producer. Chameleon recorded it with John Schroder, but it was never released.

WEDNESDAY 21 JULY

▲ MIXING

Trident Studios
17 St Anne's Court, Soho
London, England

BOWIE/GILLESPIE PROMO

★ LIVE

The Country Club
Haverstock Hill
London, England

Bowie, Ronson, Woodmansey and Rick Wakeman played a set based around the tracks earmarked for *Hunky Dory*, plus 'The Supermen', 'Memory Of A Free Festival', 'Buzz The Fuzz', 'It Ain't Easy', 'Amsterdam' (Brel) and 'It's Gonna Rain Again'.

With the prospect of a new album deal and tour for his Ziggy Stardust stage concept, Bowie invited Wakeman to join as keyboardist and musical arranger.

The promise of a good fee appealed to Wakeman as the two had considerable respect for one another. Bowie urged him to take time to consider, but that night Wakeman got a call from Chris Squire with an invitation to join Yes, which he accepted.

THURSDAY 22
SATURDAY 24 JULY

▲ MIXING

Trident Studios
17 St Anne's Court, Soho
London, England

BOWIE/GILLESPIE PROMO

MONDAY 26 JULY

Following a final seven-hour mixing session, the promotional LP was pressed privately with green Gem labels, ready for Defries to present to record companies.

■ ALBUM RELEASED

'DAVID BOWIE & DANA GILLESPIE ROUGH MIX'
UK (BOWPROMO1)

SIDE ONE
DAVID BOWIE
1. **'Oh! You Pretty Things'** (3:12)
2. **'Eight Line Poem'** (2:55)
3. **'Kooks'** (2:58)
4. **'It Ain't Easy'** (Davies) (3:01)
5. **'Queen Bitch'** (3:17)
6. **'Quicksand'** (5:07)
7. **'Bombers'/'Andy Warhol' intro** (3:30)

SIDE TWO
DANA GILLESPIE
1. **'Mother Don't Be Frightened'** (Gillespie) (4:15)
2. **'Andy Warhol'** (2:44)
3. **'Never Knew'** (Gillespie) (3:32)
4. **'All Cut Up On You'** (Gillespie) (3:23)
5. **'Lavender Hill'** (Gillespie) (3:22)

After doing the rounds of the industry, the album circulated among collectors and became one of the most sought-after Bowie rarities. The mixes differ to varying degrees from the later album versions.

FRIDAY 30 JULY

▲ RECORDING

Trident Studios
17 St Anne's Court, Soho
London, England

'HUNKY DORY' ALBUM
'The Bewlay Brothers'

Ken Scott (2011)
That was almost a last-minute song. Just down the street from Trident, there was a tobacconist, which apparently gave him the inspiration for the name. He came in and said, "We've got to do this song for the American market." I said, "OK, how do you mean?" He said, "Well, the lyrics make absolutely no sense, but the Americans always like to read into things, so let them read into it what they will." [113]

Bowie (2000)
It's another vaguely anecdotal piece about my feelings about myself and my brother, or my other doppelganger. I was never quite sure what real position Terry had in my life, whether Terry was a real person or whether I was actually referring to another part of me. [113]

Bowie (2008)
I used Bewlay as a cognomen – in place of my own. This wasn't just a song about brotherhood so I didn't want to misrepresent it by using my true name.

The circumstances of the recording barely exist in my memory. It was late, I know that. I was on my own with my producer Ken Scott, the other musicians having gone for the night.

Unlike the rest of the Hunky Dory album, which I had written before the studio had been booked, this song was an unwritten piece that I felt had to be recorded instantaneously.

I had a whole wad of words that I had been writing all day. I had felt distanced and unsteady all evening, something settling in my mind. I distinctly remember a sense of emotional invasion.

I do believe that we finished the whole thing on that one night. [067]

OPPOSITE: Michael Stroud's studio portrait of Bowie with Dana Gillespie, May 17.

AUGUST

SUNDAY 1

★ LIVE

The Marquee Club
90 Wardour Street, Soho
London, England

DAVID BOWIE & MICK RONSON

Bowie and Ronson played as a duo to a small crowd.

Bowie signed a six-year recording agreement with Gem management, thus giving Defries the power to license Bowie's recordings to record companies rather than Bowie signing directly with them.

MONDAY 2 AUGUST

The Roundhouse
Chalk Farm Road
London, England

ANDY WARHOL'S 'PORK'

The cast of *Andy Warhol's Pork* arrived in London for a 26-night run at The Roundhouse in Camden. For the past three years, Warhol had habitually recorded all his conversations on a portable tape recorder. Tony Ingrassia had constructed a play from these, primarily his phone conversations with Factory 'star' Brigid Polk. These deadpan exchanges, re-enacted by a Warhol-like character (played by Tony Zanetta) and 'Amanda Pork' (played by Kathy Dorritie aka Cherry Vanilla), were accompanied by unsavoury and outrageous behaviour from the cast of eight, stage-managed and photographed by Leee Black Childers.

Leee Black Childers (1986)

There was a lot of sex going on, a lot of really sick stuff. Geri Miller would douche on stage; Pork would shoot speed through her blue jeans. All Vulva (Wayne County) would talk about was shit. [043]

The ensuing media uproar, including a *Daily Mirror* exposé, provided enough free publicity to fill The Roundhouse for most of the season.

FRIDAY 6 AUGUST

▲ RECORDING

Trident Studios
17 St Anne's Court, Soho
London, England

'HUNKY DORY' ALBUM
'Life On Mars?'
'Song For Bob Dylan' (version 2)

ABOVE: Director Tony Ingrassia (front, left) and Andy Warhol with the cast of their play *Pork* at La Mama Experimental Theater Club in New York, May 10.
RIGHT: Wayne County in character as Vulva.
OVERLEAF: Tony Zanetta as the Warhol character B. Marlowe and Kathy Dorritie (aka Cherry Vanilla) as Pork. Both would soon become an integral part of MainMan and Bowie's success.

Bowie (2008)

I took a walk to Beckenham High Street to catch a bus to Lewisham to buy shoes and shirts but couldn't get the riff out of my head. Jumped off two stops into the ride and more or less loped back to the house up on Southend Road.

Rick Wakeman came over a couple of weeks later and embellished the piano part and guitarist Mick Ronson created one of his first and best string parts. [067]

Suzi Fussey/Ronson (2009)

He used to write the strings sitting in the toilet. Without even a keyboard. Only by ear. It was quiet in there. [040]

With the album sessions complete, Bowie and Grace went to Ken Scott's home to select the tracks for *Hunky Dory*.

WEDNESDAY 11 AUGUST

★ LIVE

The Country Club
Haverstock Hill
London, England

DAVID BOWIE & MICK RONSON

Bowie and Ronson again played as a duo, on guitar and piano respectively, with Angie working the lights.

The performance was plagued by sound problems. The support band, Tucky Buzzard, had no such problems so Angie and Defries approached their engineer Robin Mayhew for help. He had been using a new type of PA that allowed a singer to move about through an auditorium. Seeing the potential freedom this would offer Bowie, Defries put him and Rats' old roadie Pete Hunsley on retainers to develop and run a new PA system, regardless of the cost.

In the audience was a contingent from the *Pork* production. Leee Black Childers and Cherry Vanilla had been doing the rounds of live shows in London since their arrival, gaining free entry by posing as journalists from *Circus* magazine. Both were avid readers of the rock press, and Leee Black Childers remembered Mendelsohn's profile of Bowie in *Rolling Stone* back in April.

Leee Black Childers (2010)

One day I saw this little ad for David Bowie playing at the Country Club, on Haverstock Hill and I said "Let's go see him." And they said "Who's he?" and I said "All I know is I read somewhere that he wears dresses" and Wayne County said "Dresses? Okay let's go!" [369]

To their disappointment, Bowie was wearing his usual baggy pants and floppy hat, not a dress in sight. Bowie noted their arrival and introduced them to the audience before launching appropriately into 'Andy Warhol'. Cherry Vanilla registered her approval by exposing a breast. The Warhol crowd had Bowie rapt.

Leee Black Childers (1986)

I think he was a lot more impressed with us than we were with him. It was hard to say anything about David. Angela was smarter, Dana was sexier and Ronson was cuter. [043]

Nevertheless, Cherry Vanilla admitted he had something – poetry, charisma, sex appeal – but above all musicianship. He just needed a little help to get these things to coalesce.

Wayne County (2009)

We kind of took him under our wing and we all decided to help him out. You know, glam him up and make him more outrageous. [040]

Afterwards, as both parties mingled at a club – Yours And Mine – Bowie sat back, watching. As Childers observed, "He was rarely a participant in anything." What Bowie absorbed from the *Pork* cast was, he explained, "that idea of creating a personality and surrounding himself with similar people". [040]

Bowie was both jealous and dazzled by this outrageousness, but it was left to the equally brash Angie to turn it into something that Bowie had in mind but was yet to articulate. That night, County overheard Angie telling him "that he needed to change his image and start getting some attention too". [040]

THURSDAY 12 AUGUST

▼SOCIALISING

Invited by Childers and Vanilla the night before, Bowie, Angie, Gillespie, Defries and Burretti were at The Roundhouse to see *Pork* and be introduced to the cast. Bowie and Angie were transfixed by the spectacle and returned night after night.

Angie Bowie (2010)

It had a big impact on me. It made me know the kind of stage show that I thought would make David a star. That's all I was looking at, from that point of view. I was there to borrow. I thought OK, we've done Lindsay Kemp, we've done the ballet thing, done the folk stuff. Now how are we going to make this rock band different from anything else? And I thought the only way we can do it is if we go beautiful. If we go great tailoring, gorgeous fabrics, handsome men, all just looking amazing, young and handsome and fabulous! [369]

⊙BUSINESS

Earlier in the day, Defries' role as manager became official as Bowie signed a contract with Gem, backdated to April 1970 and 'limitless'.

FRIDAY 13 AUGUST

⊙BUSINESS

Defries flew to New York for ten days of negotiations with record companies, some of whom had shown interest in signing Bowie. Confident he would be returning with deals for his two artists, Defries played the Bowie/Gillespie LP to A&R executives at CBS, Bell, RCA and United Artists.

John Cale had left The Velvet Underground and was dividing his time between solo work, sessions and production. In 1971 he was at Warner Brothers in A&R (Artists & Repertoire). Since the recent revolution in the music industry, major labels were employing young hip A&R executives – 'house hippies' – to act as a conduit between the 'suits' and the artists. As such they were the first port of call for a manager looking for a deal.

Defries had sent an acetate of *Hunky Dory* to Warners which Cale loved, describing it as "unique and strange and very unorthodox". He had fought hard for the label to accept the deal on the table.

ABOVE: Velvet Underground co-founder John Cale, in his A&R role at Warner Bros, encouraged the company to sign Bowie in 1971, to no avail.

John Cale (2009)

It's a very difficult thing to fight for in a large corporation like that if nobody understands where they're going with it. [040]

Bell was receptive but Defries had the first real expression of interest from United Artists.

Bill Roberts (UA) (1972)

Mike Stewart [UA President] and Tony Defries agreed upon an equitable deal and we proceeded to draw up contracts. Before they could be signed Bowie apparently received an alternative deal from RCA with greater revenues. Marty [Cerf] and I were both crushed. [270]

Defries opted for RCA when their newly appointed A&R head Dennis Katz made a last-minute bid to top the United Artists offer.

Although Katz was unfamiliar with Bowie's earlier albums, he was so impressed by the *Hunky Dory* tracks on the sampler that he needed little persuasion to agree to the terms Laurence Myers and Defries proposed.

RCA had always been Bowie and Defries' favoured option, appealing to Defries' Colonel Parker aspirations and to Bowie for its Elvis association. RCA had relied (comfortably) on Elvis Presley, The Archies, The Monkees, Perry Como and the immensely successful *The Sound Of Music* soundtrack. Their sole concession to the turbulent Sixties was signing Jefferson Airplane.

However, by 1971, Elvis' sales were in decline and there was a feeling at the company that the label lacked credibility. To salvage RCA's image, Dennis Katz was brought in to sign new artists. He was assisted by in-house producer Richard Robinson and his wife, Lisa Robinson, an influential music journalist who edited the magazine *Rock Scene* and contributed columns to *New Musical Express*.

Richard Robinson (2009)

RCA was in a situation where it was a major corporation of the old school trying to survive, and not being quite sure what was going on. [281]

On the advice of these arbiters of cool, Katz signed The Kinks and Lou Reed, who had left The Velvet Underground. They urged Katz to sign Bowie.

Under the contract Bowie would deliver RCA three albums over a two-year period. The advance of $37,500 per album RCA had agreed to pay was, by industry standards, a modest asking price and reasonable, given that Bowie's previous albums for Mercury had sold poorly. But Defries knew he could always improve a deal. Once he had the master tapes of those albums back from Mercury, he would be able to lease them to RCA for $20,000, to which RCA agreed.

Myers had also included a crucial proviso in the contract. As a precaution designed to give Gem control over the back catalogue, the clause called for the reversion of all the masters of Bowie's RCA recordings and the Mercury albums after 15 years. It was a demand, admitted Myers later, which he borrowed from Allen Klein.

Laurence Myers (1987)

All the deals I did had that clause, and there were certain companies who I simply couldn't deal with because they refused to accept it. One of them is CBS. [043]

Bob Grace had played acetates to CBS A&R Dan Loggins, who had in turn recommended Bowie to CEO Clive Davis. Whatever it was that Davis objected to – Myers' clause or Bowie's effeminacy – he passed on signing 'the next Bob Dylan' and stayed with the Dylan he had.

RCA, however, agreed to the reversion clause. At that point few envisaged Bowie's career lasting until 1986.

SATURDAY 14 AUGUST

✪PRESS

'The Space Oddity Comes Down To Earth' by James Johnson published in *NME*.

SUNDAY 15 AUGUST

▼SOCIALISING

Tony Zanetta was invited for lunch at Haddon Hall, where Bowie grilled him about New York, Warhol and The Factory.

FRIDAY 27 AUGUST

⊙BUSINESS

Gem's negotiating lawyer in the US, Normand Kurtz, informed Myers and Defries by telegram that Bowie was effectively free of Mercury and now with RCA, pending signing of contracts.

Irwin Steinberg confirmed that Mercury would return Bowie's recordings and artwork on payment of $17,844 – representing Mercury's total investment in Bowie's career.

SATURDAY 28 AUGUST

▼SOCIALISING

Following the last show of *Pork*'s run at The Roundhouse, the Bowies joined the celebrations backstage and at the new Hard Rock Café in Mayfair.

SEPTEMBER

WEDNESDAY 8

▶ **TRAVELLING**

Bowie flew to New York with Angie, Ronson and Defries to sign the RCA contract. Myers had opened the negotiations with RCA but Defries stage-managed the trip in a manner that reflected the importance of the signing. He began by booking them into the prestigious Warwick Hotel in the same suite The Beatles had occupied on their 1965 US East Coast tour.

As soon as they arrived, Angie called Tony Zanetta, who came up to the hotel. Bowie reintroduced him to Defries (they had met when Zanetta came to London with *Pork*) as the actor who played Andy Warhol. Defries seized on the Warhol connection, telling Zanetta (now called Z as Defries was 'Tony') that Warhol's films were not being handled properly – he should be making Hollywood films and getting rich.

Defries appointed Zanetta as New York liaison, instructing him to set up a meeting with Warhol. The unemployed actor was given a crucial role: creating a buzz around Bowie and ushering him through the New York *demimonde*.

THURSDAY 9 SEPTEMBER

⊙ **BUSINESS**

At RCA Records' New York head office on Sixth Avenue, Bowie signed his recording contract and met the RCA executives, including Dennis Katz's assistant Richard Robinson and his wife, Lisa.

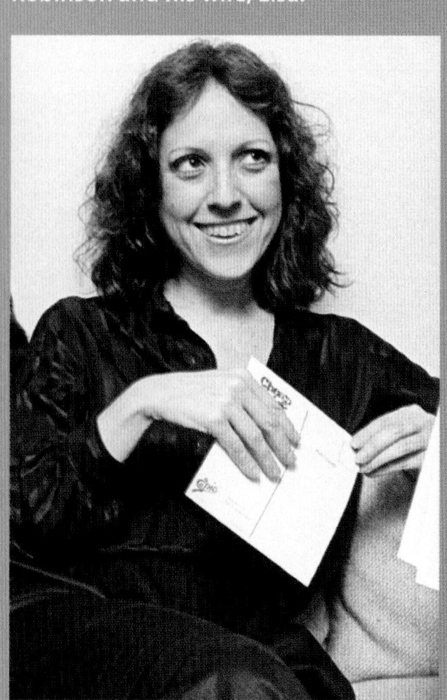

Lisa Robinson (1990)

I was there at the behest of my husband, Richard Robinson, who was one of RCA's 'house hippies' and partially responsible for signing Bowie, Lou Reed and the Kinks to that label. I also wrote a column for the English music weekly New Musical Express, *so Bowie wanted to meet me. He also wanted to meet Lou Reed and Iggy Pop, both of whom were friendly with my friend Danny Fields.* [256]

▼ **SOCIALISING**

Robinson and fellow journalist Fields occupied a pivotal position inside the back room at Max's Kansas City, the centre of the New York underground music scene. Fields helped her to arrange dinner at the Ginger Man restaurant on East 36th Street where Bowie met Lou Reed. Robinson recalled, "Lou wasn't the most gregarious social animal." However, he warmed to Bowie and later said, "I knew there was somebody else living in the same areas I was."

Victor Bockris (2010)

Lou was very pleased to be there and David treated him very sensitively by making him the centre of attention and letting him talk rather than David talking a lot. Lou loves to talk; he needs, like all great talkers, a receiver. Lou's very bright, he would've seen it that way. [369]

Back at the Warwick, Reed played demos of his planned album to Bowie and Ronson. When Bowie in turn played him an acetate of *Hunky Dory*, Reed was impressed with Bowie's new songs, particularly (and unsurprisingly) his Velvets tribute 'Queen Bitch'. Responding to Bowie's Warhol tribute, Reed joked that The Velvet Underground once had an idea to produce an Andy Warhol doll which, when you wound it up, did nothing at all.

Later that night the party moved on to Max's Kansas City where Lisa Robinson introduced Bowie to Danny Fields, the Elektra A&R executive who had signed The Stooges. Elektra had since dropped them after two albums and Iggy was at a loose end – without a band, in the grip of a heroin habit and staying with Fields.

Iggy Pop (1974)

I was sitting around Danny Fields' one night watching Mr Smith Goes To Washington, *and I was deep into it when Danny calls from Max's. Says, "You remember this guy David Bowie?" A year ago in* Melody Maker *he'd listed me as his favourite singer or something. So Danny says, "Grab a cab down to Max's, he wants to meet you." So I said okay, but I couldn't tear myself away from the movie, because Jimmy Stewart was so sincere. Fields kept calling me, saying, "Listen, man, do yourself a favour." 'Cause Fields was kinda like my second mind. So finally after about a hundred calls, I made it down there just as they were about to close. It was ridiculous.*

They said "Are you hungry?" and I said "Uh-huh!" I hadn't eaten in about four days, so they took me out and I ordered two dinners. This was the exact time that I wanted to approach Tony [Defries] about managing me, so we talked about it, and I signed my soul. [052]

Danny Fields (2010)

I was sort of semi-managing Iggy then and his career was nowhere and there had been a drug problem and it was severe. I didn't have any money, I didn't have any power, I didn't have anything except I loved them – "I love you, I love your songs and I love your music." He shouldn't have been, at that point in his life, falling asleep in my house with a black and white Western on television 'cause there was nothing better for him to do or nothing more promising. I sort of, "David… here, you take him". [369]

BELOW LEFT: Lisa Robinson, an influential and supportive journalist who was one of Bowie's trusted contacts in the US underground music scene.
LEFT: Lou Reed, London 1972.
BELOW: A&R Danny Fields, who signed The Stooges to Elektra, and graphic designer Arturo Vega, who created the Ramones logo.
OPPOSITE: Iggy Pop in freefall, April 1971.

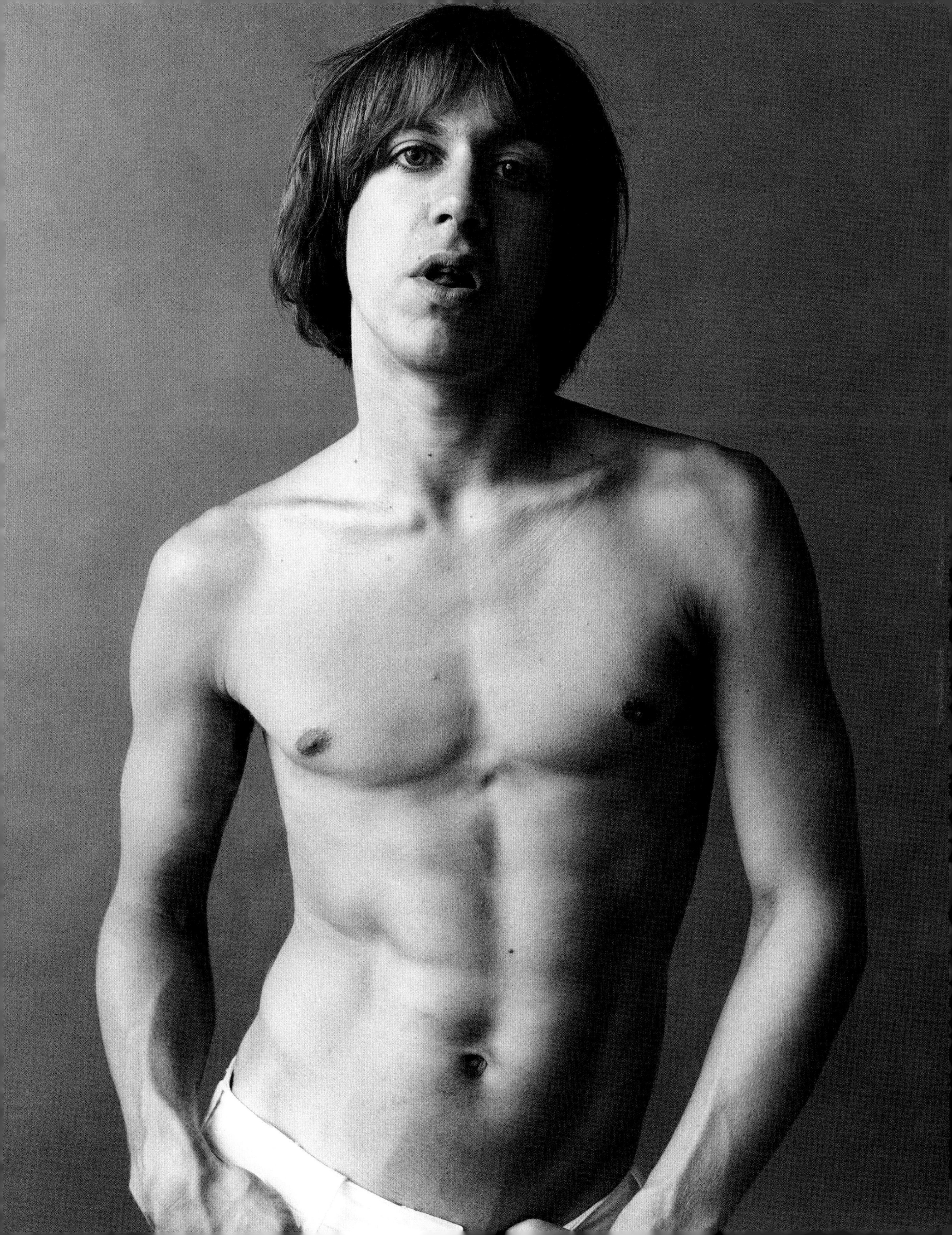

ABOVE: Andy Warhol at The Factory in May with film producer Paul Morrissey and Warhol superstar Joe Dallesandro.

FRIDAY 10 SEPTEMBER

BUSINESS

Over breakfast at the Warwick Hotel, Defries and Bowie discussed Iggy Pop's situation amid a flurry of phone calls. Nothing could be done until Iggy rid himself of the ruinous heroin addiction that had contributed to The Stooges' implosion. Iggy was put up at the hotel to begin a methadone programme.

TUESDAY 14 SEPTEMBER

SOCIALISING

Tony Zanetta took Bowie, Angie, Ronson and Defries to meet Andy Warhol at The Factory at 33 Union Square in New York.

Bowie (1974)

We got in the lift and went up and when it opened there was a brick wall in front of us. We rapped on the wall and they didn't believe who we were. So we went back down and back up again till finally they opened the wall and everybody was peering around at each other. That was shortly after the gun incident. I met this man who was the living dead. Yellow in complexion, a wig on that was the wrong colour, little glasses. I extended my hand and the guy retired, so I thought, "The guy doesn't like flesh, obviously he's reptilian." He produced a camera and took a picture of me. And I tried to make small talk with him, and it wasn't getting anywhere.

But then he saw my shoes. I was wearing a pair of gold-and-yellow shoes, and he says, "I adore those shoes, tell me where you got those shoes." He then started a whole rap about shoe design and that broke the ice. [093]

Bowie (1997)

I was wearing a pair that Marc Bolan had given me – brilliant canary yellow, semi-wedge heel, semi-point rounded toe. [Warhol] used to design shoes in his advertising so we had something to talk about. [331]

Bowie had brought along an acetate of 'Andy Warhol' which he played to him.

Bowie (2011)

He hated it, loathed it. He went "Oh, uh-huh…" then just walked away. I was kind of left there. Somebody came over and said, "Gee, Andy hated it." I said, "Sorry, it was meant to be a compliment." "Yeah, but you said things about him looking weird. Don't you know that Andy has a thing about how he looks? He's got a skin disease and he really thinks that people see that." [113]

Meanwhile Defries told director Paul Morrissey how to market his Warhol films and offered to distribute them in the UK. Bowie was introduced to Glenn O'Brien and occasional Warhol impersonator Allen Midgette.

Allen Midgette (2009)

He said, "I'm going to be the greatest drag rock'n'roll star in the world." I said, "Great, how long are you going to be in New York?" He said, 'I'm leaving tomorrow, I'm going to Rome… I'm going to have my clothes fitted by Valentino." [429]

At some point Bowie took part in a 15-minute 'screen test' filmed by Michael Netter. Bowie, used to 'acting' when put in front of a camera, performed a mime routine (involving pulling out his intestines) from his Lindsay Kemp days.

The Warhol screen test subverted the Hollywood casting process by requiring nothing from its subject. Visitors to Warhol's studio were filmed as potential 'stars', not by acting a role but by simply being themselves.

Warhol wrote in 1975, "That screen magnetism is something secret – if you could only figure out what it is and how to make it, you'd have a really good product to sell. But you can't even tell if someone has it until you actually see them up there on the screen. You have to give screen tests to find out." [048] Factory photographer Billy Name explained, "Andy wanted to capture the essence of the person only, no interference." [428]

TUESDAY 21 SEPTEMBER

✪ RADIO
Studio T1
BBC Kensington House
Shepherd's Bush
London, England

BBC RADIO 1
'SOUNDS OF THE 70s'
BOB HARRIS

'The Supermen'/
'Oh! You Pretty Things'/
'Eight Line Poem'/'Kooks'/
'Fill Your Heart'/'Amsterdam'/
'Andy Warhol'

John Muir: Producer
John White/Bill Aitken: Engineers
David Bowie: Vocals/Guitar/Piano
Mick Ronson: Bass/Lead Guitar/Vocals

Bowie and Ronson performed as a duo for Bowie's only BBC radio session to be recorded in stereo.

▮Broadcast: October 4 (without 'The Supermen').

▮'The Supermen' and 'Eight Line Poem' released on *Bowie At The Beeb* (Virgin/BBC 2000).

ABOVE: 'Whispering' Bob Harris, host of *The Old Grey Whistle Test* and co-founder of *Time Out* magazine.
RIGHT: Journalist and editor of *ZigZag* magazine Kris Needs in 1977.

'HUNKY DORY'

An acetate was produced of *Hunky Dory* with a track listing much the same as the final version, but without 'Eight Line Poem' and differing track times on half of the songs. 'Bombers' was originally intended to segue to the studio chat intro of 'Andy Warhol' ("It's War*hol*, actually") but was replaced by Biff Rose's 'Fill Your Heart', which Bowie had recorded at Bob Grace's suggestion.

'Fill Your Heart' had already been covered by Tiny Tim and appeared on the flipside of 'Tiptoe Through The Tulips'. The song was often in Bowie's set during this period and, prior to that, Bowie had also been performing Rose's 'Buzz The Fuzz' (recorded on a February 1970 BBC radio session – still unreleased).

SATURDAY 25 SEPTEMBER

★ LIVE
The Friars Club
Borough Assembly Hall
Aylesbury
Buckinghamshire, England

'Fill Your Heart'/
'Buzz The Fuzz'/'Space Oddity'/
'Amsterdam'/'The Supermen'/
'Oh! You Pretty Things'/
'Eight Line Poem'/'Changes'/
'Song For Bob Dylan'/'Andy Warhol'/
'Queen Bitch'/'Looking For A Friend'/
'Round And Round'/
'I'm Waiting For The Man'

This live date at the small club was the first to feature the line-up later billed as The Spiders From Mars as Trevor Bolder made his live debut proper (he had played on the Peel session in June). As Rick Wakeman had recently joined Yes, Bowie called up an old friend from Kent, ex-Animal Tom Parker, to accompany them on piano.

Kris Needs, a Bowie fan who had designed the flyers for the night, was also there to report on the gig for the local Buckinghamshire paper.

Kris Needs (1987)

I met him backstage before the show and he was nervous as hell. He had just got back from New York, and was full of talk about the people he'd met there, Lou and Warhol. [043]

Bowie dressed up for the occasion, having spent the morning with Angie at Kensington Market, and took to the stage in baggy black culottes and a feminine beige jacket open to his naked chest. Inspired by his brush with the Warhol superstars and underground glamour, he experimented with stage make-up and encouraged the band to do the same.

The format was similar to his recent shows, beginning with semi-acoustic numbers with Ronson, building to more up-tempo songs with the full band.

After the acoustic numbers, Bowie moved to piano for 'Oh! You Pretty Things' and 'Eight Line Poem' before introducing Tom Parker, "to take over piano and play it properly for the rest of the evening".

Introducing 'Queen Bitch' as a song about Lou Reed, Bowie was surprised at the cheers of recognition at the mention of The Velvet Underground.

SUNDAY 26 SEPTEMBER

★ LIVE
Implosion
The Roundhouse
Chalk Farm Road
London, England

DAVID BOWIE & MICK RONSON

OCTOBER

MONDAY 4

★ LIVE
Seymour Hall
Seymour Street
Marylebone
London, England

DAVID BOWIE & MICK RONSON

The Gay Liberation Front benefit concert was the last documented appearance of Bowie and Ronson playing as a duo.

FRIDAY 15 OCTOBER

▲ REHEARSING
Underhill Studios
1 Blackheath Hill
Greenwich
South East London, England

Work began on *Ziggy Stardust* with ten days of rehearsals at Underhill, an inexpensive two-roomed studio opened by Will Palin in September.

■ SINGLE RELEASED
PETER NOONE
'Walnut Whirl'
(Flowers/Tatham/Banks) (2:45)/
'Right On Mother' (2:32)
(RAK 121)

The B-side was written by Bowie, who also played piano on the session. One of the many demos Bowie had recorded for Bob Grace in late 1970, 'Right On Mother' was another jaunty piano-led number celebrating his mother's acceptance of his living with his girlfriend.

NOVEMBER

SUNDAY 7

▼SOCIALISING

Rainbow Theatre
Finsbury Park
North London, England

ALICE COOPER

Bowie attended the last night of Alice Cooper's *Love It To Death* European tour at the Rainbow Theatre.

His interest piqued by reports of the show's extravagant theatricality, Bowie brought along the rest of his band to show them the effect of the costumes and make-up.

Trevor Bolder (1995)
It was very theatrical and we all thought it was great, but David said, "Wait till you see what we can do." They were wearing make-up and were a really heavy band, and it looked good, so we went along with it too. [007]

▲RECORDING

'THE RISE AND FALL OF ZIGGY STARDUST AND THE SPIDERS FROM MARS'

Ken Scott: Producer

Mike Stone: Engineer

Soon after he'd returned from New York, Bowie had contacted Ken Scott to book recording time at Trident for a new album. "You're not going to like it," Bowie told him. "It's much more like Iggy Pop – more rock'n'roll." [013]

Ken Scott (1987)
I don't know how he got the impression I didn't like rock'n'roll. What he'd come up with was incredible. [013]

MONDAY 8 NOVEMBER

▲RECORDING

Trident Studios
17 St Anne's Court, Soho
London, England

'Star' (original title 'Rock'n'Roll Star')
'Hang On To Yourself'

THURSDAY 11 NOVEMBER

▲RECORDING

Trident Studios
17 St Anne's Court, Soho
London, England

'Star'
'Hang On To Yourself'
'Ziggy Stardust'
'Looking For A Friend'
'Velvet Goldmine'
'Sweet Head'

Having scrapped the first takes from the first session, two tracks were re-recorded. Other songs recorded on the day (like many others during the *Ziggy* sessions) would be deemed unsuitable for the album and remained unreleased for several years:

'Looking For A Friend'
▮Never officially released, but surfaced in high quality on the bootleg *1971 Outtakes From EMI Masters*, leading to the rumour it was being considered for release.

'Velvet Goldmine'
▮'Space Oddity' (reissue B-side) (RCA 1975).

▮*Rare* (RCA 1982).

▮*Ziggy Stardust* (Ryko 1990).

▮*Ziggy Stardust* (EMI 2002).

'Sweet Head'
▮*Ziggy Stardust* (Ryko 1990).

▮*Ziggy Stardust* (EMI 2002).

FRIDAY 12 NOVEMBER

▲RECORDING

Trident Studios
17 St Anne's Court, Soho
London, England

'Moonage Daydream'
'Soul Love'
'The Supermen'
'Lady Stardust'

'The Supermen'

▮*Revelations – A Musical Anthology For Glastonbury Fayre* (Revelation 1972).

▮*Hunky Dory* (Ryko 1990).

▮*Ziggy Stardust* (EMI 2002).

SATURDAY 13 NOVEMBER

✪ MEDIA

RCA ran a full-page ad for *Hunky Dory* in *Billboard*, featuring excerpts of glowing reviews from US critics and Bowie's notes explaining each song, handwritten on Warwick Hotel stationery during the September New York trip.

'Changes'...
This album is full of my changes and those of some of my friends.

'Oh! You Pretty Things'...
The reaction of me to my wife being pregnant was archetypal daddy – Oh he's gonna be another Elvis. This song is all that plus a dash of sci-fi.

'Eight Line Poem'...
The city is a kind of high-life wart on the backside of the prairie.

'Life On Mars'...
This is a sensitive young girl's reaction to the media.

'Kooks'...
The baby was born and it looked like me and it looked like Angie and the song came out like – if you're gonna stay with us you're gonna grow up Bananas.

'Quicksand'...
The chain reaction of moving around throughout the bliss and then the calamity of America produced this epic of confusion – Anyway, with my esoteric problems I could have written it in Plainview – or Dulwich. There is a time and space level just before you go to sleep when all about you are losing theirs and whoosh void gets you with its cacophony of thought – that's when I like to write my songs.

'Fill Your Heart'...
Biff Rose song.

'Andy Warhol'...
A man of media and anti-message, with a kind of cute style.

'Bob Dylan'...
This is how some see B.D.

'Queen Bitch'...
A song on a Velvet Underground – Lou Reed framework s'about London sometimes.

'The Bewlay Brothers'...
Another in the series of David Bowie confessions – *Star Trek* in a leather

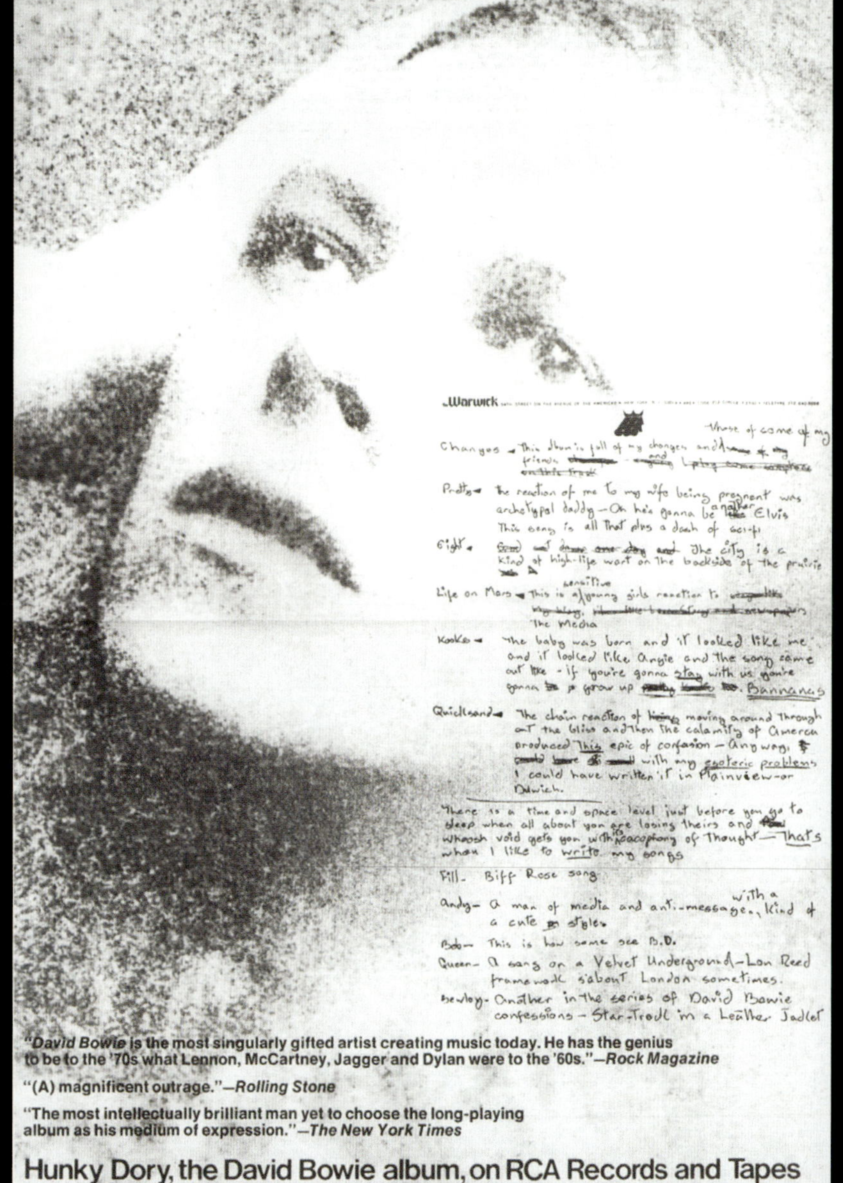

ABOVE: Full page ad for *Hunky Dory*, featuring Bowie's handwritten notes on each song. OPPOSITE: Alice Cooper's onstage electric chair. The commotion Cooper and his band (originally named The Spiders) were causing in Britain was not lost on Bowie, who took his own band (soon to be named The Spiders) to see what all the fuss was about.

MONDAY 15 NOVEMBER

▲ RECORDING

Trident Studios
17 St Anne's Court, Soho
London, England

'Five Years'
'It's Gonna Rain Again'
'Shadow Man'

'Shadow Man'

▮ Never commercially released, a fairly rough but complete take (no overdubs) circulated among collectors. A high-quality version surfaced on the bootleg *1971 Outtakes From EMI Masters*, prompting speculation that EMI had prepared unreleased material as potential bonus tracks for the 1999 reissues.

Also recorded by this stage were 'Round And Round', 'Amsterdam' and a new Spiders makeover of 'Holy Holy'.

'Round And Round'
(Berry)

▮ 'Drive-In Saturday' (single B-side) (RCA 1973).

'Amsterdam'
(Brel/Schuman)

▮ 'Sorrow' (single B-side) (RCA 1973).

'Holy Holy'
The Mercury single had flopped but Bowie was never one to waste a good song and put it up for a Spiders makeover. With Ronson, Bolder and Woodmansey on board, the song took on a new life with a solid meaty sound and a dynamism lacking in the flat acoustic treatment of the single.

▮ 'Diamond Dogs' (single B-side) (RCA 1974).On the eve of *Hunky Dory*'s release, Bowie had already recorded enough songs for the follow-up album and an early track list for *Ziggy Stardust* was drawn up:

SIDE ONE
1. **'Five Years'**
2. **'Soul Love'**
3. **'Moonage Daydream'**
4. **'Round And Round'**
5. **'Port Of Amsterdam'**

SIDE TWO
1. **'Hang On To Yourself'**
2. **'Ziggy Stardust'**
3. **'Velvet Goldmine'**
4. **'Holy Holy'**
5. **'Star'**
6. **'Lady Stardust'**

Ron Davies' 'It Ain't Easy' was again to be held over as there were already two covers.

Even as Brian Ward was preparing US press kits with the recent *Hunky Dory* photos, Bowie was moving on from his Lauren Bacall/Greta Garbo image, starting with a haircut from Trevor Bolder, who used to be a hairdresser. Bolder feathered the back and sides and emphasised the length by cropping the top – the first stage of the creation of the Ziggy Stardust hairstyle.

Ken Scott: Producer, assisted by The Actor (David Bowie)
David Bowie/Mick Ronson: Arrangers
David Bowie: Vocals/Guitar/Piano/Saxophones
Mick Ronson: Guitar/Mellotron/Vocal
Trevor Bolder: Bass/Trumpet
Mick Woodmansey: Drums
Rick Wakeman: Piano
Brian Ward: Photographer
Terry Pastor (Main Artery): Hand-colourist
Recorded at Trident Studios, London, England

SELECTED REISSUES
- CD (RCA 1984).
- CD (remastered) (Ryko 1990).

BONUS TRACKS
1. 'Bombers' (2:38)
2. 'The Supermen' (alternative version) (2:41)
3. 'Quicksand' (demo) (4:43)
4. 'The Bewlay Brothers' (alternative mix) (5:19)

- CD (remastered) (EMI 1999).
- CD (mini LP replica) (Toshiba EMI 2007).

DECEMBER

■ SINGLE RELEASED
'Changes' (2:32)/
'Andy Warhol' (3:03)
US (RCA 74-0605)
Chart Peak No.66

FRIDAY 17 DECEMBER

■ ALBUM RELEASED
'HUNKY DORY'
UK (RCA SF 8244)
Chart Peak No.3
(September 1972 reissue)
US (RCA LSP-4623)
Chart Peak No.176

SIDE ONE
1. **'Changes'** (3:33)
2. **'Oh! You Pretty Things'** (3:12)
3. **'Eight Line Poem'** (2:53)
4. **'Life On Mars?'** (3:48)
5. **'Kooks'** (2:49)
6. **'Quicksand'** (5:03)

SIDE TWO
1. **'Fill Your Heart'** (Williams/Rose) (3:07)
2. **'Andy Warhol'** (3:58)
3. **'Song For Bob Dylan'** (4:12)
4. **'Queen Bitch'** (3:13)
5. **'The Bewlay Brothers'** (5:21)

ABOVE: Bowie showed pictures of Lauren Bacall and Greta Garbo to photographer Brian Ward and told him, "I want to look like this". The cover photo was cropped and printed on 12" x 12" matte stock, which was hand-coloured by Terry Pastor, George Underwood's partner at Main Artery. The US release had the title on a sticker on the shrink wrap. In other countries the title was embedded in the artwork.
OPPOSITE: RCA promotional photo which featured on the back cover.

Bowie's concept for *Hunky Dory*'s cover was fitting for an album of songs rooted in American imagery. The Garbo-like cover portrait, one of a series Brian Ward had shot at his Heddon Street studio, was both Hollywood nostalgia and Warhol modernism, and alluded to the silver screen in 'Life On Mars?' and 'Andy Warhol'.

In contrast, the back cover testified to the personal nature of the songs, with Bowie's left-handed scrawl annotating the tracks, paying tribute to their origins.

SATURDAY 25

▼ SOCIALISING
Bowie, Angie and Zowie spent Christmas in Cyprus with Angie's parents.

DAVID BOWIE
Exclusively on RCA
RCA Records and Tapes

JANUARY

Richard Cromelin's feature 'David Bowie: The Darling of the Avant Garde', published in *Phonograph Record*.

Hunky Dory had been in the shops for six weeks and, despite positive reviews, sales were sluggish. Unconcerned, Bowie was looking ahead to the new album and the imminent cover shoot.

Before Christmas he had his hair cropped short, but Angie felt it needed something else. She asked local hair stylist Sue Fussey over to Haddon Hall. Fussey, who worked in the Evelyn Paget salon on Beckenham High Street opposite The Three Tuns, was well aware of the Bowies and thought Angie was "the most exciting thing to hit Beckenham before or since". [013] Fussey decided Bowie's hair was too "Rod Stewart-ish" and reshaped it into the familiar Ziggy cut, though the colour came later.

TUESDAY 4 – THURSDAY 6

▲ **REHEARSING**

Underhill Studios
1 Blackheath Hill
Greenwich
South East London, England

Three days rehearsing of new material for the *Ziggy Stardust* album, preparing for the upcoming UK tour.

FRIDAY 7 JANUARY

■ **SINGLE RELEASED**

'Changes' (2:02)/
'Andy Warhol' (3:03)
UK (RCA 2160)

Derek Johnson (*NME*)
Not a disturbing or fantasy disc like some of Bowie's previous singles, but a shrewd insight into the contemporary scene.

SATURDAY 8 JANUARY

▼ **SOCIALISING**

Bowie celebrated his 25th birthday with a party at Haddon Hall. Among the invited were Lou Reed, in town to record his solo debut album *Lou Reed*, his producer Richard Robinson and Richard's wife Lisa.

Lisa Robinson (1990)
***Bowie greeted us at the door of his London house wearing the patterned Ziggy jumpsuit, red vinyl boots and his hair was chopped off in that short spiky orange style – all of it a far cry from the Greta Garbo of the year before – and I remember saying to him, "Ahh, so you've seen* Clockwork Orange.*"** [256]

Bowie hadn't seen it as it would be another five days before its UK premiere. The film opened December 19 in the States.

▮ *Melody Maker* ran a full-page ad for *Hunky Dory*.

TUESDAY 11 JANUARY

✪ **RADIO**

Studio T1
BBC Kensington House
Shepherd's Bush
London, England

BBC RADIO 1
'SOUNDS OF THE 70s'
JOHN PEEL
'Ziggy Stardust'/'Queen Bitch'
'Waiting For The Man'/'Lady Stardust'

John F Muir: Producer

The radio session was initially booked in order to promote *Hunky Dory*, but Bowie chose only 'Queen Bitch' – the most Ziggy-ish of the tracks. He performed 'Ziggy Stardust' in nearly identical fashion to the album cut.

▮ Broadcast: January 28.

RIGHT: Upstairs in Brian Ward's Heddon Street photographic studio, Bowie poses as Ziggy Stardust for the first time, transformed by stage garb inspired by *Clockwork Orange* and newly cropped hair by Sue Fussey.

"Bowie greeted us at the door of his London house wearing the patterned Ziggy jumpsuit."

Lisa Robinson

THURSDAY 13 JANUARY

Clockwork Orange opened at The Warner West End in London. Shortly afterwards Bowie took the band to see it and came away with another key element for the Ziggy image.

Bowie (1993)
I was determined that the music we were doing was the music for the Clockwork Orange *generation and I wanted to take the hardness and violence of those* Clockwork Orange *outfits – the trousers tucked into big boots and the codpiece things – and soften them up by using the most ridiculous fabrics. It was a Dada thing. This extreme ultraviolence in Liberty fabrics.* [111]

Angie Bowie (2009)
Freddie Burretti worked for this Greek tailor called Andreas, so I'd brought Freddie and his girlfriend, Daniella [Parmar], down to Haddon Hall. David and Freddie then got together and designed these outfits for the Ziggy Stardust thing. David designed the bomber jackets and the tight-fitting pants with the lace-up boots. [155]

Trevor Bolder (1976)
He started dragging us downstairs to this girl – who used to look after Zowie [Sue Frost] – and trying costumes on! And it slowly worked into a band with costumes. I think he slowly brought us into it, rather than pushing it at us, because I think that if he'd pushed it at us, I think we might have pulled away, thinking like "What's he trying to do to me, I'm not wearing that!" And it was good. [332]

Woody Woodmansey (2009)
At first we were very reticent about the outfits and the make-up. Mick Ronson hated the outfits. In fact he packed his bags and left. David asked me to go after him and handle it. I spent a good hour or so on Beckenham train station with him! [155]

Mick Ronson (1972)
When we were first talking about it, I had a few different ideas, but I was caught on an off-time. I had a lot on my mind. I can get very stubborn. [274]

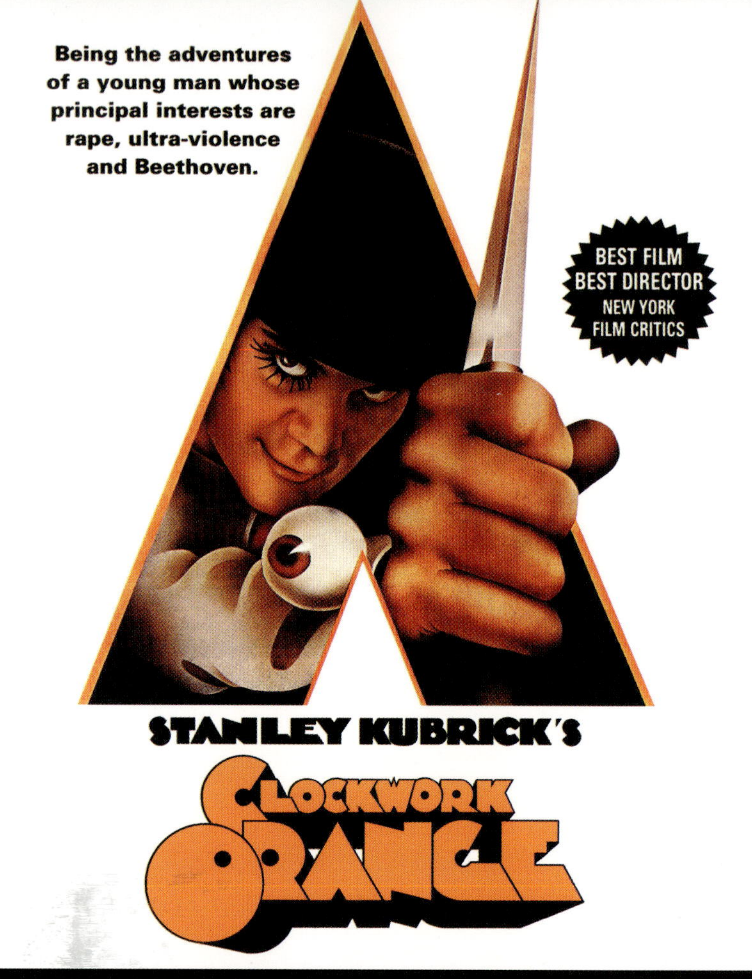

ABOVE: The *Clockwork Orange* film poster illustrated by airbrush artist Philip Castle who also worked on the *Aladdin Sane* sleeve.
OPPOSITE: Brian Ward's 'kick' shot was used later in the year for the cover of RCA's *The Man Who Sold The World* reissue.

Bowie (1995)
Mick came from Hull. Very down-to-earth, as were the rest of the Spiders: "What do you mean, make-up?" I reverted to things like, "You looked very green tonight onstage… I think if you wore make-up you'd look a little more natural-looking," and sort of lies like this, and gradually got them into areas of costume and theatre. Actually, when they realised how many girls they could pull when they looked so sort of outlandish, they took to it like a fish to water. [354]

Mick Ronson (1972)
Actually it makes me want to be more outrageous, if anything. I like shocking people. We want to excite kids, make them feel good, so they can't take their

MID-JANUARY

✪ PHOTO SESSION
Heddon Street, Soho
London, England

'ZIGGY STARDUST' ALBUM COVER

Brian Ward: Photographer

The cover photo session for the *Ziggy Stardust* album began on a cold wet afternoon in Ward's studio at 29 Heddon Street, just off Regent Street.

Bowie (1993)
Upstairs in the studio we did the Clockwork Orange *look-alikes that became the inner sleeve. The idea was to hit a look somewhere between the Malcolm McDowell thing with the one mascara'd eyelash and insects. It was the era of* The Wild Boys *by William S Burroughs. That was a really heavy book that had come out in about 1970, and it was a cross between that and* Clockwork Orange *that really started to put together the shape and the look of what Ziggy and the Spiders were going to become.*

They were both powerful pieces of work, especially the marauding boy gangs of Burroughs' Wild Boys *with their Bowie knives. I got straight on to that. I read everything into everything. Everything had to be infinitely symbolic.* [285]

Ward suggested they do more photographs in the street but with poor weather and the fading light the band declined.

Despite suffering from flu, Bowie ventured out to the street in the drizzling rain. A few doors down, Bowie posed in the doorway of No. 23 where Ward shot black and white photos from various angles. Next door, No. 21, was the home of furriers K West. As Bowie posed beneath their sign, Ward lined up the shot and took four frames, one of which became the final front cover. (The sign was removed some 20 years later by a fan, who later described his act as preservation, arguing it was deteriorating from age and other attempts to take it.)

Bowie (1993)
It's such a shame that sign went. People read so much into it. They thought K West must be some sort of code for 'quest'. It took on all sorts of mystical overtones. [285]

More photos were taken from different angles around the corner in the alley that leads to Regent Street. Here Bowie posed under a streetlight and in the phone booth where Ward shot the back cover image.

Terry Pastor, George Underwood's partner in Main Artery, later hand-coloured the prints for the artwork. He airbrushed a yellow tint – as he had done for *Hunky Dory* – to Bowie's hair, which at that stage was still a natural light brown. The guitar, a red Gibson Les Paul that Bowie had borrowed from Mark Pritchett, had the same yellow tint applied.

Terry Pastor (2007)
*I was given a black and white photograph printed on matte paper – David Bowie's management wanted some colour put into it. I applied the colour using photo dyes with an airbrush (a DeVilbiss Super 93). The lettering for the front cover (which isn't included on this print) was Letraset'd (rub-down transfer lettering) – a very hands-on way of doing things, but in 1972 that was the

TUESDAY 18 JANUARY

✪ RADIO

Maida Vale Studio 5
Delaware Road
London, England

BBC RADIO 1
'SOUNDS OF THE 70s'
BOB HARRIS
'Hang On To Yourself'/
'Ziggy Stardust'/
'Waiting For The Man'/
'Queen Bitch'/'Five Years'

Jeff Griffin: Producer

▮Broadcast: February 7.

▮Released: *Bowie At The Beeb* (Virgin/BBC 2000). Initial pressings duplicated 'Ziggy Stardust' from the May 16 session instead of this version.

WEDNESDAY 19 – SUNDAY 23 JANUARY

▲ REHEARSING

Theatre Royal
Stratford
East London, England

SATURDAY 22 JANUARY

✪ PRESS

Michael Watts interview:

David's present image is to come on like a swishy queen, a gorgeously effeminate boy. He's as camp as a row of tents, with his limp hand and trolling vocabulary. "I'm gay," he says, "and always have been, even when I was David Jones." But there's a sly jollity about how he says it, a secret smile at the corners of his mouth. He knows that in these times it's permissible to act like a male tart, and that to shock and outrage, which pop has always striven to do throughout its history, is a ball-breaking process. And if he's not an outrage, he is, at the least, an amusement. "Why aren't you wearing your girl's dress today?" I said to him (he has no monopoly on tongue-in-cheek humour). "Oh dear," he replied, "You must understand that it's not a woman's. It's a man's dress." [303]

▮Published: 'Oh! You Pretty Thing', *Melody Maker*.

Defries expected it to run as the paper's front-page story but was infuriated to learn that King Crimson's split was the lead. Nevertheless, it was Bowie's photo and headline that dominated the cover.

Chris Charlesworth (2009)
As Melody Maker's news editor at the time, I was a party to the decision to stick him on the front page. We were all pretty broad-minded on** Melody Maker **so the gayness didn't put us off him. I don't recall any adverse reaction from anyone. [040]

Michael Watts (2003)
I think he said it very deliberately. I brought the subject up. I think he planned at some point to say it to someone. He definitely felt it would be good copy. He was certainly aware of the impact it would make. [086]

Bowie (2002)
The irony of that was that it virtually went unnoticed other than by the** NME. ***It certainly wasn't a newspaper thing. It was still kind of underground. I found that I'd been able to get a lot of tension off my shoulders by being able to almost out myself in the press in that way, in very early circumstances, so I wasn't going to get people crawling out the woodwork. I knew that at some point I was going to have to say something about my life.

It's taken on far more in retrospect than actually it was at the time. I'm quite proud that I did that. On the other hand I didn't want to carry a banner for any group of people, I didn't like that aspect of it: this is going to start overshadowing my writing and everything else that I do. [116]

SUNDAY 23 JANUARY

✪ PRESS

Robert Hilburn's review published in the *LA Times*: "*Hunky Dory* contains all the humour, intelligence, irony and personal vision that one expects from our best musical minds… from the splendour of the instrumentation to the range/intensity of Bowie's voice to the quality of the lyrics. A major talent." [142]

WEDNESDAY 26 – FRIDAY 28 JANUARY

▲ REHEARSING

Theatre Royal
Stratford
East London, England

OPPOSITE: *Melody Maker* photographer Barrie Wentzell recalls: "It was a rather overcast day in London and Mick Watts and I went over to interview David at his manager Tony Defries's rather small and grubby office. As we entered, David was sitting very pretty in this amazingly bright outfit, lazily smoking a cigarette and reading a book. "Hello, come in," he said smiling and after we got over the shock of the new Bowie look, Mick did a funny interview and I took pictures. One was used on the front page of the *Melody Maker* for the next week's issue."

"David's present image is to come on like a swishy queen, a gorgeously effeminate boy."

Michael Watts

SATURDAY 29 JANUARY

★ LIVE

The Friars Club
Borough Assembly Hall
Aylesbury
Buckinghamshire, England

The Spiders, though not yet billed as such, returned to The Friars Club in their new glammed-up catsuits: Ronson in gold, Bolder in blue and Woody in pink.

The atmosphere was very different to the previous engagement there – the audience had doubled, bolstered by London kids taking the train up, and the backstage area was now off limits.

Heralded by Walter Carlos' *Clockwork Orange* theme, Bowie appeared in the new green jumpsuit amidst dazzling strobe lights.

Queen members Roger Taylor and Freddie Mercury were in the audience to witness the rebirth of Bowie, tonight billed as the Most Beautiful Person in the World. Every effort was made to make good on this claim, with Bowie changing (during an extended version of Cream's 'I Feel Free') into a patterned cream satin blouse and white sequined pants.

Also in the audience again was Kris Needs, who was bowled over by the transformation from last September. This time the Spiders were match fit, the PA was delivering and the sonic assault never let up. By the time they got to the climax of 'Rock'n'Roll Suicide', Needs told Paul Trynka, "The place was in total uproar."

The Friars Club had paid a mere £110 to host what Needs described as "the night that invented the Seventies".

ABOVE AND OPPOSITE: A star is born: Ziggy's debut leaves Aylesbury's The Friars Club "in total uproar".

✪ PRESS

The local newspaper proclaimed the next day, 'A Star Is Born'.

'David Bowie' by Danny Holloway was published in *NME*. Holloway had interviewed Bowie at Haddon Hall in Beckenham. He noted the newly cropped hairstyle. "Oh yes," said Bowie, "I had it cut a couple of weeks ago. I'm still getting used to it… I'm just an image person. I'm terribly conscious of images and I live in them."

Bowie continued to play down the dress controversy, saying, "I'm certainly not embarrassed by it… But unfortunately, it all detracted from the fact that I was also a songwriter."

The interview also revealed the pace at which Bowie was shifting from one idea to the next, preferring to look ahead. "The melodies I do write please me temporarily and have a very singular effect on me. I quickly put them down. I write songs very quickly because I get bored very quickly with

Rather than talk about *Hunky Dory*, Bowie played him tapes of the *Ziggy* album: "We're gonna rock on stage. We'd like to consider ourselves to be in the same sphere as The Who. We want to be visually exciting. When Alice [Cooper] came out and I saw what he was doing, I decided to veer away from that angle because I didn't want people to compare me with Alice. I would have loved to put on a theatrical show like that, but I wouldn't have wanted to fall into that category. But I do have plans for a theatrical experience if and when the money comes in." [151]

Holloway's review, 'Bowie At His Brilliant Best', said of *Hunky Dory*: "It's very possible that this will be the most important album from an emerging artist in 1972, because he's not following trends – he's setting them. *Hunky Dory* is a masterpiece from a mastermind." [152]

FEBRUARY

WEDNESDAY 2

A master tape was prepared with 'Port Of Amsterdam', 'He's A Goldmine' and 'Holy Holy' replaced by 'It Ain't Easy', 'Suffragette City' and 'Rock'n'Roll Suicide.'

RCA's Dennis Katz had listened to the November 15 acetate of the album and told Defries that all it needed was a single. Bowie responded by writing 'Starman', which would replace 'Round And Round' in the album's final running order.

Shortly afterwards, Bowie was interviewed for radio to discuss *Hunky Dory*, but the conversation turned to the upcoming album. To Bowie's surprise, the interviewer already knew of the changes to the track listing and asked him about 'Round And Round', 'Holy Holy', 'Amsterdam' and other tracks that had been dropped.

Bowie (1972)

'Round And Round' would have been the perfect kind of number that Ziggy would have done on stage. I think probably what happened is that it was a jam. We jammed 'Round And Round' for old times' sake in the studio. The enthusiasm of the jam probably waned after we heard the track three times and we replaced it with a thing called 'Starman'.

I certainly haven't destroyed any of those tracks – I kept them all. I think that maybe we could put them out as a budget album or something at a later date… the stuff that never really got used. Because there are quite a few… there's a thing called 'Bombers' which is kind of a skit on Neil Young… also it's quite funny.

Do you want to know some titles – things in the can we have never released? There's a thing called 'He's a Goldmine' ['Velvet Goldmine']. 'He's a Goldmine' is lovely. But probablythe lyrics are a little bit too provocative. I think they'll keep that out for a bit. [376]

FRIDAY 4 FEBRUARY

▲ RECORDING

Trident Studios
17 St Anne's Court, Soho
London, England

'Starman'
'Suffragette City'
'Rock'n'Roll Suicide'

With the last three master takes in the can, the *Ziggy Stardust* recording sessions were complete.

Bowie (2003)
There was a sense of French chanson in ['Rock'n'Roll Suicide']. It wasn't obviously a Fifties pastiche, even though it had that rhythm that said total Fifties. But it actually ends up as being a French chanson. That was purposeful. I wanted that blend, to see if that would be interesting. [112]

For 'Suffragette City', Ken Scott programmed an ARP synthesiser that Ronson played to emulate a driving horn section.

Ken Scott (2009)
[On 'Starman'] Mick Ronson did the arrangements for strings and guitar. That Morse code sound is actually a piano and two guitars, an octave apart, then we bounced them all down to make one track. It seemed to make sense in that there was this idea of something coming from another planet.

So we then put it all through a phaser. There are two versions of 'Starman' – one a loud Morse code version and one a quiet version. And I only remember doing one mix of it, and I can't tell you which one I did. I've no idea where the second came from. [155]

▮ The 'Morse code' version appeared on the initial UK album release and the single in some countries. The US issues and all subsequent releases (except the 1980 compilation *The Best Of Bowie*) used the version where the 'Morse code' sound was lower in the mix.

MONDAY 7 FEBRUARY

✪ TELEVISION

BBC Television Centre
London, England

'THE OLD GREY WHISTLE TEST'
'Queen Bitch'/
'Oh! You Pretty Things'/
'Five Years'

After Bowie wore a dress for his *Top Of The Pops* appearance with Peter Noone, the BBC had ruled out further television appearances. However, one of the booked acts dropped out at the last minute and Bowie was finally offered the spot.

In a small studio, they filmed three songs with Bowie singing live vocals over backing tracks, specially mixed for the performance. Just as they had done on the recent radio session, they added a *Ziggy Stardust* track to the *Hunky Dory* songs.

Mindful of BBC censorship, Bowie recorded two takes of 'Oh! You Pretty Things'. On the first take he took out the line 'the earth is a bitch', repeating the 'written in pain' lyric instead. The second take retained it.

▮ Broadcast: February 8 on BBC 2 (without 'Oh! You Pretty Things'). Neither take of 'Oh! You Pretty Things' was broadcast until an *Old Grey Whistle Test* special in 1982, when presenter David Hepworth noted the clip had "evaded the hands of the efficient BBC tape wiper".

▮ All three songs plus take 1 of 'Oh! You Pretty Things', as a hidden track, released on *Best Of Bowie* DVD (EMI 2002).

THURSDAY 10 FEBRUARY

✪ RADIO

BBC RADIO 1
'SCENE AND HEARD'

Interviewed by Johnny Moran.

★ LIVE

Toby Jug
Tolworth
South London, England

ZIGGY STARDUST UK TOUR

David Bowie: Vocals/Guitar
Mick Ronson: Lead Guitar
Trevor Bolder: Bass Guitar
Woody Woodmansey: Drums
Nicky Graham: Piano

FRIDAY 11 FEBRUARY

★ LIVE

Town Hall
High Wycombe
Buckinghamshire, England

SATURDAY 12 FEBRUARY

★ LIVE

Great Hall
Imperial College
London, England

Bowie had recently seen footage of Iggy Pop walking across the audience's shoulders at the 1970 Cincinnati Pop Festival and tried it out on the Imperial College audience. Unaccustomed to this, they let him tumble ignominiously to the floor – Ray Stevenson's photograph captured the moment (opposite). Bowie quickly recovered and carried on with the show as if it hadn't happened.

Melody Maker
Don't expect Danny La Rue or any Alice Cooper rubbish with boa constrictors and electric chairs. The costumes – and there were several changes – are the gilt on the lily, but they're not the substance.

The music is muscular, witty and assured performances. What other group would dare to do 'I Feel Free' before a London audience, complete with Cream rip-off solo – so calculated as to be a thing of glorious absurdity? Because Bowie and his band are nothing if not superb parodists, right down to the way in which Ronson walked to the front of the stage and invited the front row to caress the body of his guitar.

Dedicated to bringing theatrics back to rock music, David Bowie swirled and captivated at London's Imperial College on Saturday, queening his way through old and new songs, before a house packed to the door. And they hung on every word that dropped from his lips. [197]

▮ Clips from the concert, including 'Suffragette City', broadcast on *Pop 2* (French TV).

RIGHT: Bowie and the Spiders play to a packed Great Hall at Imperial College.

"And they hung on every word that dropped from his lips."

Melody Maker

MONDAY 14 FEBRUARY
★ LIVE
Brighton Dome
Brighton
East Sussex, England

FRIDAY 18 FEBRUARY
★ LIVE
University of Sheffield Rag Ball
University Park
Sheffield
South Yorkshire, England

WEDNESDAY 23 FEBRUARY
★ LIVE
Chichester College
Chichester
West Sussex, England

In response to requests to turn Ronson's volume down, the roadies readjusted the controls on his amp so when Ronson turned it to 10, it was the equivalent of 8.

THURSDAY 24 FEBRUARY
★ LIVE
Wallington Public Hall
Wallington
Surrey, England

FRIDAY 25 FEBRUARY
★ LIVE
Avery Hill College
Eltham
London, England

SATURDAY 26 FEBRUARY
★ LIVE
Happenings
Mayfair Suite
Belfry Hotel
Sutton Coldfield
West Midlands, England

MONDAY 28 FEBRUARY
★ LIVE
Glasgow City Hall
Candleriggs
Glasgow
Scotland

SHOW CANCELLED

Bowie's first appearance with the band in Scotland got as far as unloading the gear at the venue. At that point, the venue's manager explained that the band's PA was too large for the stage. Faced with playing using a stripped-down system, Bowie and the band refused to go on and the concert was cancelled.

TUESDAY 29 FEBRUARY
★ LIVE
Locarno Ballroom
Sunderland
Tyne and Wear, England

SHOW CANCELLED

Gem cancelled this date as well on the grounds that it would have been a civic function and therefore inappropriate for Bowie.

MARCH

WEDNESDAY 1
★ LIVE
Bristol University
Bristol, England

Bowie and the Spiders played to another sparsely attended hall but nevertheless delivered a strong show.

Meanwhile Defries took the completed *Ziggy Stardust* master tapes and artwork to RCA in New York for approval.

SATURDAY 4 MARCH
★ LIVE
Gaiety Lounge Show Bar
South Parade Pier
Southsea
Hampshire, England

Another engagement at another unsuitable venue, supported by Bridget St John, an old friend from the Beckenham Arts Lab days.

Bridget St John (1999)
There was a huge storm, a hovercraft overturned, that was such a weird night. And there he was in his platform heels and I remember thinking, oh, that's not the same guy that I remember. [386]

The roadies had their own problems moving the gear to the venue at the end of the pier. The equipment cases couldn't be rolled along the open decking, so they had to carry them there and back again after the gig.

TUESDAY 7 MARCH
★ LIVE
Yeovil College
Yeovil
Somerset, England

SATURDAY 11 MARCH

★ LIVE
Southampton Guildhall
Southampton
Hampshire, England

TUESDAY 14 MARCH

★ LIVE
Chelsea Village
Glen Fern Road
Bournemouth
Dorset, England

FRIDAY 17 MARCH

★ LIVE
Town Hall
Birmingham
Warwickshire, England

The Birmingham gig was another half-filled hall but it marked two important milestones in the evolution of Ziggy Stardust. Backstage Sue Fussey took the Ziggy hairstyle to its next stage, feathering it and dyeing it red, and Bowie met photographer Mick Rock, whose work with Bowie immortalised the Ziggy image. Rock was there to cover the show for *Rolling Stone,* having pitched the idea to the magazine's London editor. Before the performance, he poked his head around Bowie's dressing-room door and introduced himself. Bowie responded, "I like your name. It can't be real..."

According to Rock, they hit it off straight away and Bowie invited him to come back to Beckenham after the show to do an interview. Rock then shot his first frames in the dressing room before Bowie took the stage.

Mick Rock (2002)
I didn't know how to shoot a live concert then, so there is a certain looseness of framing. It was actually through David that I learnt how to shoot live. [037]

Mick Rock's report:

The venue is half-empty, and those in attendance are more spellbound than boisterous, but Bowie performs with the energy and fervour of a man with a goal. He seems totally out of context in such dull surroundings. [258]

On the train back to London, Bowie and Mick Rock found they shared a fascination with outsiders like Iggy Pop, Lou Reed (whose 'White Light White Heat' featured in the set that night) and Syd Barrett, whom Rock had befriended at Cambridge and photographed on several occasions, including for the cover of his album *The Madcap Laughs*.

Mick Rock (1999)
So we kind of swapped stories. I swapped him Syd Barrett stories and he swapped tales of Iggy and Lou. So that was probably the first bonding with David when we found a certain taste in common. It tended to be the more esoteric and extreme variety, these two of course among the manifestation of exactly that attitude and philosophy. [374]

Mick Rock returned to Haddon Hall a few days later for his first proper photo session with Bowie. By that time Sue Fussey had intensified the red of Bowie's hair, and the Ziggy hairstyle was complete.

Bowie (2002)
Sue did a straightforward copy. The cut and colour were both Kansai's – Schwarzkopf red was the colour. [037]

Bowie (1993)
The Ziggy hairstyle was taken lock, stock and barrel from a Kansai display in Harper's in February '71. He was using a kabuki lion's wig on his models, which was brilliant red. And I thought it was the most dynamic colour, so we tried to get mine as near as possible. [111]

LEFT: With Ronson at Wallington Public Hall on February 24.

FRIDAY 24 MARCH
★ LIVE
Mayfair Ballroom
Newcastle upon Tyne
Northumberland, England

MONDAY 27 MARCH
⊙ BUSINESS
Mott The Hoople bass player Pete 'Overend' Watts called Bowie to tell him the band would be splitting at the end of their *Rock & Roll Circus* UK tour.

Dale Griffin (1976)
Overend, who had always been a big fan of Bowie, phoned him up.He'd got his phone number from a tape David sent us of 'Suffragette City', which he thought we might like to do for a single. He said, "The band's split, y'know, what's happening with you?" – hoping for some job as a bass player, maybe. David was quite shocked that the band had broken and said, "Listen, don't do anything, I'll work something out, you mustn't break up." [332]

Bowie (1972)
It was the first song I've written for somebody else. They were at the point of breaking up as a band and I told them not to, because I thought they were a very good band. I told them I'd write them a hit single. And I did. It was easy. [229]

Bowie arranged to meet with Mott at Gem's offices to play them the song, 'All The Young Dudes'.

Ian Hunter (2009)
He just sat on the floor of Defries' office in Regent Street and played it on an acoustic guitar. I knew straight away it was a hit. There were chills going down my spine. It's only happened to me a few times in my life. We grabbed hold of it. I'm a peculiar singer but I knew I could handle that. [229]

Dale Griffin (1976)
By that time, we were completely baffled and bewildered. We didn't know what we were doing. We were in no state to do anything for ourselves. We couldn't believe that anybody would give 'All The Young Dudes' away. [332]

Bowie offered to produce their single and Defries offered to manage them, but Ian Hunter was suspicious of Defries and deferred their signing. He discreetly collected all the management contracts from the band and filed them away at home in his piano stool, where they remained unsigned. Defries proceeded regardless to pay off the band's contract with Island and negotiate a new record deal with CBS.

TUESDAY 28 MARCH
▲ MIXING
Bowie and Ken Scott remixed 'Starman' for release as the next single.

FRIDAY 31 MARCH
Bowie's management contract with Gem was renewed for a ten-year term with Bowie receiving £300 a week salary for providing services of "writing lyrics and/or music, composer, arranger, etc". Bowie signed the document, oblivious to the fact that it made him an employee of Defries who would be controlling all of Bowie's revenue. It would be two years before he realised the arrangement with Defries was far from a partnership with equal shares of the profits.

OPPOSITE: Mott The Hoople on tour in Los Angeles, with Mick Ralphs and Ian Hunter by the rooftop pool of The Continental Hyatt House on November 24.

"I told them I'd write them a hit single. And I did. It was easy."

David Bowie

APRIL

SUNDAY 9

▼ **SOCIALISING**

Civic Centre
Guildford
Surrey, England

MOTT THE HOOPLE

Having sent flowers to Mott's dressing room for every show, Bowie turned up at the Guildford gig with Defries and Angie.

"She told me David had taken four hours to get ready," Hunter later recalled. "He was shaking, real nervous. He thought we were a lot heavier than we were… heavy duty punks. He was slightly disappointed to encounter 'ordinary blokes'. He just liked what we represented." [229]

MONDAY 17 APRIL

★ **LIVE**

Lord's Club, Civic Hall
Gravesend
Kent, England

THURSDAY 20 APRIL

★ **LIVE**

The Playhouse
Harlow
Essex, England

FRIDAY 21 APRIL

★ **LIVE**

Free Trade Hall
Manchester
Lancashire, England

Future Joy Division members Ian Curtis and Stephen Morris were in the audience.

Stephen Morris (2008)
Bowie apparently asked Ian if there was a club he could go to, where he could hear some Northern soul. [298]

ABOVE: French release of 'Starman'.
OPPOSITE: Bowie takes time out from redecorating Haddon Hall – unbeknownst to the landlord – to chat with Rosalind Russell from *Disc* and photographer Michael Putland and play them some of his favourite records.

FRIDAY 28 APRIL

■ **SINGLE RELEASED**

'Starman' (4:16)/
'Suffragette City' (3:25)
UK (RCA 2199)
Chart Peak No.10

Bowie's first Top 10 hit since 'Space Oddity' in 1969. Meanwhile, *Hunky Dory* became Bowie's first album to make the charts, reaching No.176 in America.

NME
Bowie proves he's not just a pretty face on this cosmic 45… 'Starman' is obviously single of the week.

SATURDAY 29 APRIL

★ **LIVE**

Town Hall
High Wycombe
Buckinghamshire, England

SHOW CANCELLED

SUNDAY 30 APRIL

★ **LIVE**

Guildhall
Plymouth
Devon, England

MAY

WEDNESDAY 3

★ **LIVE**

Aberystwyth University
Aberystwyth, Wales

SATURDAY 6 MAY

★ **LIVE**

Kingston Polytechnic
Main Hall
London, England

▮ 'I Feel Free' released on *Rarest One Bowie* (Golden Years 1995).

Interview feature by Rosalind Russell published in *Disc & Music Echo*.

Photographer for the article, Michael Putland, had arrived at Haddon Hall to find Bowie up a stepladder in his quilted Ziggy jumpsuit. With George Underwood's help, Bowie was painting the ceiling silver and decorating the walls with large blue circles.

In May 1976, long after Bowie had moved out, he was sued over the flat, which his former landlord claimed was painted in a "garish and unsightly fashion", as *NME* reported. "Mr Ralph Hoy says he was unable to re-let the flat in Beckenham, Kent, for nine months and then only at less than its true market value."

SUNDAY 7 MAY

★ **LIVE**

Hemel Hempstead Pavilion
Hertfordshire, England

THURSDAY 11 MAY

★ **LIVE**

Assembly Hall
Worthing
West Sussex, England

FRIDAY 12 MAY

★ **LIVE**

Central London Polytechnic
London, England

Among the audience were members of T. Rex (though not Bolan) and Steve Harley, who later said that the show inspired him to form Cockney Rebel. The show was photographed by Mick Rock.

SATURDAY 13 MAY

★ **LIVE**

Summer Ball
Slough Technical College
Slough
Berkshire, England

SUNDAY 14 MAY

▲ **RECORDING**

Studio 2
Olympic Studios
117 Church Road
Barnes
South West London, England

MOTT THE HOOPLE SINGLE
'All The Young Dudes'

David Bowie/Mick Ronson: Producers
Keith Harwood: Engineer

Bowie played rhythm guitar, sang distinctive backing vocals and came up with the idea of cramming them all (including Stuart George and Nicky Graham) into the studio lavatory to record handclaps for the choruses.

TUESDAY 16 MAY

✪ RADIO

Maida Vale Studio 4
Delaware Road
London, England

BBC RADIO 1
'SOUNDS OF THE 70s'
JOHN PEEL
'White Light White Heat'/
'Moonage Daydream'/
'Hang On To Yourself'/
'Suffragette City'/'Ziggy Stardust'

Pete Ritzema: Producer

Nick Gomm: Engineer

▮Broadcast: May 23 (BBC Radio 1).

▮Released: *Bowie At The Beeb* (Virgin/BBC 2000).

FRIDAY 19 MAY

★ LIVE

Oxford Polytechnic
Headington
Oxford, England

MONDAY 22 MAY

✪ RADIO

Studio 2
Aeolian Hall
New Bond Street
London, England

BBC RADIO 1
'JOHNNIE WALKER LUNCHTIME SHOW'
'Starman'/'Space Oddity'/
'Changes'/
'Oh! You Pretty Things'

Roger Pusey: Producer

▮Broadcast: June 6.

▮Released: *Bowie At The Beeb* (Virgin/BBC 2000).

TUESDAY 23 MAY

✪ RADIO

Maida Vale Studio 5
Delaware Road
London, England

BBC RADIO 1
'SOUNDS OF THE 70s'
BOB HARRIS
'Andy Warhol'/'Lady Stardust'/
'White Light White Heat'/
'Rock'n'Roll Suicide'

Jeff Griffin: Producer

▼ SOCIALISING

Bowie and Mott The Hoople celebrated the completion of the 'All The Young Dudes' single at a party that night in London.

▮Broadcast: June 19 (BBC Radio 1).

▮Released: *Bowie At The Beeb* (Virgin/BBC 2000) except 'White Light White Heat'.

THURSDAY 25 MAY

★ LIVE

Chelsea Village
Glen Fern Road
Bournemouth
Dorset, England

SATURDAY 27 MAY

★ LIVE

Ebbisham Hall
Epsom
Surrey, England

MONDAY 29 MAY

⊙ BUSINESS

On the eve of Bowie's career breakthrough, Laurence Myers was concerned that the revenue Bowie had generated hadn't justified the mounting debts and split with Defries, who agreed to pay out Gem £29,000 for investment thus far and pledged to pay $500,000 from Bowie's future earnings. In doing so, Defries assumed sole responsibility for Bowie's financial future.

JUNE

FRIDAY 2

★ LIVE

Newcastle City Hall
Newcastle upon Tyne
Northumberland, England

In the audience at Newcastle was future *Smash Hits* journalist and Pet Shop Boy Neil Tennant, who later called it his "favourite gig ever".

Neil Tennant (2011)

At the climactic moment of the concert when Bowie sang "Wham! Bam! Thank you ma'am!" in the song 'Suffragette City', the audience was showered with these promotional posters of Bowie as Ziggy and I grabbed one. Later my friends and I waited in a crush of fans outside the stage door. Bowie emerged and signed my poster in pencil. The late Mick Ronson, his legendary guitarist and musical arranger, signed it also. I was very happy. [391]

Mick Nixon

Armed with his own fine vocals and stage presence, an immaculate sound system, a light show and above all the best rock band I have seen or heard for years, he took the audience by storm. It really was a shame that the 2,500 capacity hall was only one-third full. But it was not surprising. The music loving fans of Tyneside could have had no idea of the goodies that were in store. David Bowie has hardly hit the heights – until now that is.

He showed himself to be the supreme showman. Straight from the first note the sound quality was amazing. The volume was full blast but the details were in no way muffled – as is so often the case. The end of the 60-minute set was met by a genuine spontaneous standing ovation. The band took a little time to return for the encore – so that David could change outfits again. [375]

SATURDAY 3 JUNE

★ LIVE

Liverpool Stadium
Liverpool
Merseyside, England

The PA system overloaded the electrical system so Bowie played his acoustic set while the problem was rectified. Once power was restored, Bowie and the band ended the show with a storming 'Suffragette City'.

SUNDAY 4 JUNE

★ LIVE

Preston Public Hall
Preston
Lancashire, England

The Public Hall was a smallish venue, an old ballroom with sprung floors, but the 2,000 to 3,000-strong crowd had the floor bouncing up and down.

TUESDAY 6 JUNE

★ LIVE

St George's Hall
Bradford
West Yorkshire, England

OPPOSITE: Bowie delivers the goods for Neil Tennant (above) and others at Newcastle City Hall.

> **"It was my favourite gig ever."**
>
> **Neil Tennant**

■ **ALBUM RELEASED**
'THE RISE AND FALL OF ZIGGY STARDUST AND THE SPIDERS FROM MARS'
UK (RCA SF 8287)
US (LSP-4702)
UK Chart Peak No.5
US Chart Peak No.75

SIDE ONE
1. **'Five Years'** (4:42)
2. **'Soul Love'** (3:34)
3. **'Moonage Daydream'** (4:40)
4. **'Starman'** (4:10)
5. **'It Ain't Easy'** (Davies) (2:58)

SIDE TWO
1. **'Lady Stardust'** (3:22)
2. **'Star'** (2:47)
3. **'Hang On To Yourself'** (2:40)
4. **'Ziggy Stardust'** (3:13)
5. **'Suffragette City'** (3:25)
6. **'Rock'n'Roll Suicide'** (2:58)

David Bowie/Ken Scott: Producers
David Bowie/Mick Ronson: Arrangers
David Bowie: Vocals/Guitar/Saxophone
Mick Ronson: Guitar/Piano/Mellotron/ARP Synth/Vocals
Trevor Bolder: Bass
Mick Woodmansey: Drums
Rick Wakeman: Harpsichord on 'It Ain't Easy'
Dana Gillespie: Backing Vocals on 'It Ain't Easy'
Brian Ward: Photographer
Terry Pastor (Main Artery): Hand-colourist
Recorded at Trident Studios London, England

ABOVE: Bowie posing for the *Ziggy Stardust* cover in Heddon Street on a cold, wet January night. The Spiders declined to leave the comfort of Brian Ward's studio upstairs, where the band shots were taken. The back cover (below) was shot in a phone box at the end of the alley around the corner.

SELECTED REISSUES
▮CD (RCA 1984).

▮CD (remastered) (Ryko 1990).

BONUS TRACKS
1. 'John, I'm Only Dancing' (2:43)
2. 'Velvet Goldmine' (3:09)
3. 'Sweet Head' (4:14)
4. 'Ziggy Stardust' (demo) (2:35)
5. 'Lady Stardust' (demo) (3:35)

▮CD (remastered) (EMI 1999).

▮CD 30th Anniversary 2 CD Edition (remastered) (EMI 2002).

BONUS DISC
1. 'Moonage Daydream' (Arnold Corns version) (3:53)
2. 'Hang On To Yourself (Arnold Corns version) (2:54)
3. 'Lady Stardust' (demo) (3:33)
4. 'Ziggy Stardust' (demo) (3:38)
5. 'John, I'm Only Dancing' (2:49)
6. 'Velvet Goldmine' (3:13)
7. 'Holy Holy' (2:25)
8. 'Amsterdam' (Brel/Shuman) (3:24)

▮CD (mini LP replica) (Toshiba EMI 2007).

▮CD/DVD/LP 40th Anniversary Edition (EMI 2012). Remastered by original Trident Studios engineer Ray Staff on limited edition vinyl plus DVD featuring a 5.1 mix in high resolution audio, and 2003 Ken Scott mixes of 'Moonage Daydream' (instrumental), 'The Supermen', 'Velvet Goldmine' and 'Sweet Head'.

James Johnson (*NME*)
By now everybody ought to know he's tremendous and this latest chunk of fantasy can only enhance his reputation further.

Richard Cromelin (*Rolling Stone*)
Although Lady Stardust himself has probably had more to do with androgyny's current fashionableness in rock than any other individual, he has never made his sexuality anything more than a completely natural and integral part of his public self, refusing to lower it to the level of gimmick but never excluding it from his image and craft. To do either would involve an artistically fatal degree of compromise.

David Bowie has pulled off his complex task with consummate style, with some great rock & roll… with all the wit and passion required to give it sufficient dimension and with a deep sense of humanity that regularly emerges from behind the Star facade. The important thing is that despite the formidable nature of the undertaking, he hasn't sacrificed a bit of entertainment value for the sake of message. I'd give it at least a 99,

IGGY & THE STOOGES

Ziggy Stardust arrived the same day as Stooges Ron and Scott Asheton. They had been summoned to London, where Iggy Pop and James Williamson were holed up in St John's Wood. Having no musical (or social) simpatico with any of Bowie's London crowd, they had decided to call on the Asheton brothers to reunite The Stooges and begin work on The Stooges' third album.

Ron, however, was relegated to bass as Williamson had displaced him as Iggy's guitarist and collaborator at the end of 1971. Supervised by Tony Zanetta, Iggy had successfully kicked his heroin habit and had signed with Columbia after serenading the company president Clive Davis with 'Shadow Of Your Smile'.

When the Ashetons joined them they began a rigorous rehearsal routine, but with no recording schedule the group became frustrated. They told Defries, "We're a band, let us play!" but he was loath to set them loose on the live circuit when Bowie was in his ascendancy.

WEDNESDAY 7 JUNE

★ LIVE

City Hall
Sheffield
South Yorkshire, England

THURSDAY 8 JUNE

★ LIVE

Town Hall
Middlesbrough
Yorkshire, England

✪ PRESS

Mick Rock's feature article 'David Is Just Not Serious' published in *Rolling Stone*.

FRIDAY 9 JUNE

► TRAVELLING
▼ SOCIALISING

Bowie flew to New York with Defries and Mick Ronson for a three-day promotional trip. Their first stop: Elvis Presley's New York live debut at at Madison Square Garden.

Bowie (1997)

[Elvis] was a major hero of mine. And I was probably stupid enough to believe that having the same birthday as him actually meant something. I came over for a long weekend. I remember coming straight from the airport and walking into Madison Square Garden very late. I was wearing all my clobber from the Ziggy period and had great seats near the front. The whole place just turned to look at me and I felt like a right idiot. I had brilliant red hair, some huge padded space suit and those red boots with big black soles. I wished I'd gone for something quiet, because I must have registered with him. He was well into his set. [079]

Mick Ronson (1986)

An orchestra, the works, sitting in the eighth row, these forty-year-old women throwing their handkerchiefs about. I couldn't believe it. [013]

✪ PRESS

Bowie was interviewed at the Helmsley Park Lane Hotel by Lillian Roxon, an Australian music writer who had moved to New York.

ABOVE: Iggy Pop onstage in 1971 with the Stooges, Ann Arbor. LEFT: Elvis plays Madison Square Garden for the first time, with Bowie and Ronson in the audience.

ABOVE AND OPPOSITE: Bowie and the Spiders performing 'Starman' on *Lift Off With Ayshea*.

SATURDAY 10 JUNE

★ **LIVE**

Leicester Polytechnic
Leicester, England

SHOW CANCELLED

A gig scheduled for Leicester Polytechnic was cancelled as Bowie was still in New York, talking up the album and catching up with Wayne County and Leee Black Childers. They were given a pile of *Ziggy Stardust* LPs to circulate among the right circles. Bowie also looked in on Lou Reed, inviting him to play at an upcoming benefit concert for Friends of the Earth at the Royal Festival Hall, which Bowie would be headlining.

NME reported that Mott The Hoople would also be playing as special guests, but they later declined the invitation. Ian Hunter suspected they would be given 20 minutes "with a lousy sound system" to make Bowie sound better by comparison. "I knew what the bugger was up to," Hunter later said.

MONDAY 12 JUNE

"Now I know how he does it," Bowie told Angie on his return to Haddon Hall, recalling Elvis' sexual charisma on stage. "I think Ziggy changed probably on the Monday night. It was probably Elvis Stardust for about a week," Bowie recalled in 2000. [170]

TUESDAY 13 JUNE

★ **LIVE**

Colston Hall
Bristol, England

THURSDAY 15 JUNE

✪ **TELEVISION**

Granada Studios
Quay Street
Manchester
Lancashire, England

'LIFT OFF WITH AYSHEA'
'Starman'

Bowie and the Spiders flew to Manchester to appear on episode 60 of the Granada TV children's show *Lift Off*. Incongruously, Bowie and the Spiders came on after a glove puppet owl called Ollie Beak.

▌Broadcast: June 21 (Granada).

FRIDAY 16 JUNE

★ **LIVE**

Town Hall
Torquay
Devon, England

SATURDAY 17 JUNE

★ **LIVE**

Town Hall
Oxford
Oxfordshire, England

During the soundcheck Bowie hatched a plan for a new stage move involving Mick Ronson, based on Hendrix's 'play it with your teeth' gimmick. It occurred to Bowie that "one person gnawing the guitar was one thing, but two people, well, that was two things… probably. I got all excited about this brave new idea and told Mick that, whatever happened tonight, he should just keep going." [037]

Bowie also warned Mick Rock before they went on that night to get ready for something he planned to do on stage. During the climax of 'Suffragette City', the capacity crowd witnessed the famous moment when Bowie simulated fellatio on Ronson's guitar and Mick Rock was ready in the wings to capture it.

SUNDAY 18 JUNE

⊙ **BUSINESS**

Mick Rock met up with Bowie at Defries' office to show him the previous night's photos, having developed and printed them overnight. With some Tippex borrowed from Defries' secretary, Bowie wrote on the photo, "Thanx to all our people for making Ziggy. I love you. Bowie x."

Bowie and Rock then persuaded Defries to run it as a full-page ad in the July 15 *Melody Maker*.

MONDAY 19 JUNE

★ **LIVE**

Southampton Guildhall
Southampton
Hampshire, England

WEDNESDAY 21 JUNE

✪ TELEVISION

Granada broadcast Bowie's performance of 'Starman' on *Lift Off With Ayshea*, then wiped the tape of the episode.

★ LIVE

Civic Hall
Dunstable
Bedfordshire, England

Billed as 'David Bowie and The Spiders From Mars', to associate with the album title.

Bowie (1976)

It was 'Ziggy Stardust And The Spiders From Mars', and somewhere along the line the Spiders got attached to David Bowie. So then the confusion set in about who was Ziggy and who was David Bowie, and even I didn't quite understand how that happened. Suddenly I had a band called the Spiders and I was willing to go with it because it worked on stage and I liked the ambiguity of not being able to separate the personas. [332]

The supporting band that night was The Flamin' Groovies, whose records had been produced by Richard Robinson. The high energy San Francisco band raised the stakes, and with Mick Rock filming and photographing the performance, Bowie pulled out all the stops, ripping off his shirt and chasing Mick Ronson around the stage.

Michael Watts (*Melody Maker*)

To those who had seen his act before this year the format was not new. That's to say he started the set rockin' like a bitch before cooling down somewhat with 'Changes', a song of mixed tempos, and then the darkling, apocalyptic message of 'Five Years', which owes something lyrically to Lou Reed ("I think I saw you in an ice-cream parlour drinking milk shakes cold and long"). And then the acoustic passages with Ronson ('Space Oddity' and 'Andy Warhol'), culminating in a solo version of 'Amsterdam', a febrile account of rough trade, as delightfully coarse as navy blue serge.

"Now some golden oldies for you." He announced the number as written by Jack Bruce and Pete Brown. All his fans, of course, needed no telling. 'I Feel Free', ripping out of the stereo PA system, choreographed by the flickering strobe lighting, it's not what you do, it's the way you do it. My, how they clapped and whistled.

The band returned for an encore. It was 'Waiting For The Man'. But something rather strange was happening up there on stage. During the instrumental break Bowie began chasing Ronson around the stage, hustling him, trying to press his body close. The attendants at the exits looked twice to see if they could believe their eyes. The teenage chickies stared in bewilderment. The men knew but the little girls didn't understand. Jees-us! It had happened.

It should be recorded that the first act of fellatio on a musical instrument in the British Isles took place at Dunstable Civic Hall. How do you top that? You don't. You get off stage. [304]

▮ Mick Rock's silent colour footage from the concert was synced with the audio from the Santa Monica concert on October 20, 1972. It was released as a one-track VHS video of 'Ziggy Stardust' to promote the album *Santa Monica '72* (Golden Years 1994).

SATURDAY 24 JUNE

▲ RECORDING

Trident Studios
17 St Anne's Court, Soho
London, England

'John, I'm Only Dancing' (2 takes)
'I Can't Explain' (2 takes)

David Bowie/Ken Scott: Producers

▮ This earlier and tougher recording of 'I Can't Explain' remains unreleased, as Bowie decided not to include it on the Ryko reissue of *Pin Ups*.

SUNDAY 25 JUNE

★ LIVE

The Greyhound
Park Lane
Croydon
Surrey, England

The queue stretched around the block and 1,000 people were turned away due to overcrowding. Bowie's PR, Dai Davies, later issued a press release stating: "Bowie wishes to apologise… He intends to play another gig as soon as possible."

The support act that night, Roxy Music (Mark Pritchett's suggestion), had released their debut album on June 16 and were gaining popularity since their appearance on *The Old Grey Whistle Test* (performing 'Ladytron') four days after that. Backstage Bowie met their keyboard player Brian Eno for the first time.

Bowie (2002)
Eno, looking quite the glam rocker at the time, was so bright and mercurial and we quickly found we shared a number of similar musical passions. We had both been lucky enough to have been present at Philip Glass' first London show in 1970 and we wittered on about maybe working together at some point in the future. I was not to meet Ferry, to whom I was introduced by Amanda Lear, until a year or two later at a party in New York. [037]

NME announced that the special guest at the Festival Hall show was likely to be Lou Reed. Gem's press release explained that, although he had live commitments in America, "the feeling is that he will come and that he will appear with David. It's certainly on the cards."

ABOVE: Brian Eno prepares for Roxy Music's show at the Royal College of Art in London on July 5. On the same day, Bowie and the Spiders were at the BBC performing 'Starman' on *Top Of The Pops* (opposite).

MONDAY 26 JUNE

▲ RECORDING

Studio 2
Olympic Studios
117 Church Road
Barnes
South West London, England

'John, I'm Only Dancing'

David Bowie: Producer
Keith Harwood: Engineer

Nine takes were recorded of the new song, one of which was selected for the next single. The Spiders were joined by violinist Lindsay Scott who could be heard at the end of each chorus, doubling Ronson's ascending guitar. The echo on the handclaps was achieved by recording them in the entrance hall.

THURSDAY 29 JUNE

▲ RECORDING

As 'Starman' climbed the UK singles chart, Bowie was invited to perform it on *Top Of The Pops*, which required a backing tape to accompany his live vocal. Four instrumental takes were recorded.

FRIDAY 30 JUNE

★ LIVE

Queens Hall Royal Grammar School
High Wycombe
Buckinghamshire, England

SHOW CANCELLED

The engagement had been cancelled in mid-June because they were, according to Gem, "saturated with gigs around that weekend". Nevertheless, the promoter had continued to advertise in the hope of holding Bowie to his original promise to perform at the charity engagement.

▼ SOCIALISING

Instead, Bowie, Iggy Pop and Mick Rock went to the Wembley Empire Pool to see Alice Cooper's last UK show, supported by Roxy Music.

After meeting Alice Cooper backstage, Bowie renewed his determination to make his stage show more theatrical.

⊙ BUSINESS

Tony Defries changed the name of his company Minnie Bell Limited to MainMan Limited and commissioned George Underwood to design the logo.

JULY

▲ RECORDING

Studio 2
Olympic Studios
117 Church Road
Barnes
South West London, England

MOTT THE HOOPLE SINGLE
'All The Young Dudes'

David Bowie: Producer
Keith Harwood/Dave Hentschel/Ted Sharp: Engineers

SATURDAY 1

★ LIVE

Winter Gardens Pavilion
Weston-super-Mare
Somerset, England

SUNDAY 2 JULY

★ LIVE

Rainbow Pavilion
Torquay
Devon, England

WEDNESDAY 5 JULY

✪ TELEVISION

BBC Television Centre
London, England

'TOP OF THE POPS'
'Starman'

Bowie and the Spiders recorded their appearance with Nicky Graham on piano.

Woody Woodmansey (2009)
I recall waiting to go on, standing in a corridor, and Status Quo were opposite us… and they had on their trademark denim. Francis Rossi looked at me and said, "Shit, you make us feel old." [155]

This television appearance, broadcast the following evening, was a watershed moment, transfixing the kids and bewildering parents nationwide. Musicians of the coming punk and new wave generation have since cited this as their equivalent of The Beatles on Ed Sullivan in 1964.

Ian McCulloch (1999)
As soon as I heard 'Starman' and saw him on* Top Of The Pops*, I was hooked. All my other mates at school would say, "Did you see that bloke on* Top Of The Pops*? He's a right faggot, him!" And I remember thinking, "You pillocks", as they'd all be buying their Elton John albums, and* Yessongs *and all that crap. It made me feel cooler. [044]

Dave Gahan (2008)
Bowie gave me a hope that there was something else. This world that he seemed to be a part of – where was it? I wanted to find it. I just thought he wasn't of this earth. [040]

▮ Broadcast: July 6 (BBC 1).

▮ Released: *Best Of Bowie* DVD (EMI 2002).

FRIDAY 7 JULY

▲ REHEARSING

Underhill Studios
1 Blackheath Hill
Greenwich
South East London, England

Lou Reed arrived in London and immediately joined Bowie and the Spiders in rehearsals for the following night's set at the Royal Festival Hall.

SATURDAY 8 JULY

★ **LIVE**

Royal Festival Hall
South Bank
London, England

'Hang On To Yourself'/ 'Ziggy Stardust'/'Life On Mars?'/ 'The Supermen'/'Starman'/'Changes'/ 'Five Years'/'Space Oddity'/ 'Andy Warhol'/'Amsterdam'/ 'I Feel Free'/'Moonage Daydream'/ 'White Light White Heat'/ 'Waiting For The Man'/'Sweet Jane'/ 'Suffragette City'

The show was in aid of Friends of the Earth, with the proceeds going to the Save the Whale Fund. Compere Kenny Everett introduced Bowie as the "next biggest thing to God".

NME's article 'Reed to Join Bowie?' heightened expectations of Lou Reed appearing at the show as Bowie's special guest in his first UK appearance.

ABOVE: Bowie and Reed share the stage at the Royal Festival Hall to help save the whales.

Bowie (2002)
It was part of my crusade to present these fantastic underground artists to the world and get them an audience. You'd occasionally see things in the **NME** ***about the Velvets, but I would almost put money that there was never an article about Iggy in the British music press until I introduced him to England. And if there had been more than half a dozen articles in the five or six years before I got Lou into view again… They were totally abandoned, there was nothing about them. I had a real joy in "you ain't seen nothing yet", these are two great influences who will influence rock from this point on.*** [116]

Reed had been drinking heavily as he waited in the wings. Bowie's short introduction brought rapturous applause from the 3,000-strong crowd; then Reed tottered, discreetly shepherded by roadie Will Palin, to his spot. Together they launched into 'White Light White Heat'.

Bowie (2002)
Lou had gone shopping for an extraordinary and what looked to me to be a glam-ish Mexican number, in black and silver. As another gesture to this glam thing he had also put on lots of eye make-up over a white skin base. Very fetching and a little ominous. Just right, of course. We had a ball, playing and singing together, racing full tilt through 'White Light White Heat', 'Sweet Jane' and the essential 'Waiting For The Man'. [037]

Ray Coleman *(Melody Maker)*
When a shooting star is heading for the peak, there is usually one concert at which it's possible to declare, "That's it – he's made it." For David Bowie, opportunity knocked loud and clear last Saturday at London's Royal Festival Hall – and he left the stage a true 1972-style pop giant, clutching flowers from a girl who ran up and hugged and kissed him while a throng of fans milled around the stage. It was an exhilarating sight. [091]

Charles Webster *(Record Mirror)*
A triumph for the showmanship as well as music. His talent seems unlimited and he looks certain to become the most important person in pop music on both sides of the Atlantic." [312]

Japanese photographer Masayoshi Sukita, in London doing photo sessions for T. Rex, heard about Bowie and went to the concert, but without his camera.

Masayoshi Sukita (2011)
In 1972 there was very little information about David Bowie in Japan and when I had arrived in London I had never even heard his name. I was immediately interested and intrigued. [042]

After witnessing the dramatic effect Bowie had on his audience, Sukita's stylist Yasuko 'Yacco' Takahashi arranged a meeting with Defries and Mick Rock to present his portfolio. The timing was perfect, as Bowie had expressed a desire to tour Japan. Defries and Rock, impressed with Sukita's work, immediately arranged a series of portrait sessions.

THURSDAY 13 JULY

✪ PHOTO SESSION

MASAYOSHI SUKITA

In the evening Sukita shot his first session with Bowie at a London studio borrowed from his friend Hiroshi Yoda. One of the close-ups was later blown up to giant proportions and displayed in the foyer of the Rainbow Theatre.

FRIDAY 14 JULY

✪ PRESS

Dennis Katz arrived in London with 19 American music journalists in tow – including Lillian Roxon, Henry Edwards, Ron Ross, Lisa Robinson and Dave Marsh – whom RCA and MainMan had flown in for the finale of the first UK Ziggy Stardust tour.

Their first-hand reports of the Bowie phenomenon would prepare American audiences for the coming tour. They were installed at the Inn On The Park, given cocktails at RCA, then wined and dined at an Italian restaurant.

▼SOCIALISING

LOU REED

KING'S CROSS CINEMA

London, England

Bowie, Angie and Ronson watched Lou Reed play his first UK show (apart from his guest spot with Bowie). Reed took the stage after midnight with a set of 13 (mostly) Velvets songs, some of which he had re-recorded for his *Lou Reed* album. Mick Rock was there to photograph the show and captured the iconic image that became the cover of *Transformer*.

SATURDAY 15 JULY

★LIVE

Friars Borough Assembly Hall

Aylesbury

Buckinghamshire, England

The UK Ziggy Stardust tour wound up at the same venue where it began in January.

Defries set the hype machine in motion with a full-page ad featuring Mick Rock's guitar fellatio shot which appeared that day in *Melody Maker*.

ABOVE AND RIGHT: Lou Reed and Iggy Pop on consecutive nights at King's Cross Cinema, where Mick Rock shoots two iconic record covers: *Transformer* and *Raw Power*.

Henry Edwards (*After Dark*)

It looks like hype. Periodically roadies appear on stage and toss Bowie posters to the audience. It's a bit of a business borrowed from Alice Cooper's recent London appearances and already a rock theatre cliché. The audience seems not to mind. They eagerly grab the souvenirs. Balloons float through the air and are helped along by the jolly crowd. The friendly mob, however, refuses to be worked up to the fever pitch that the poster throwers seem to demand.

The King of Camp Rock has put on quite a show. Here is an authentic songwriting and singing talent. Here is an act that has been carefully staged and then polished to perfection. It is filled with ideas and moments borrowed freely from other rock acts like Alice Cooper, MC5, The Stooges,The Velvet Underground, T. Rex, even The Beatles. As with all glossy novelties, it seems to have almost no substance. Bowie has always seemed to be manufacturing an act for the public. [118]

After the show Bowie got a bloodied nose in the crush of fans as he beat a hasty retreat to his pink Rolls-Royce. They returned to London, followed by a coach load of journalists, in time to see Iggy & The Stooges make their UK debut at the King's Cross Cinema. Defries had organised the concert to show off his latest signing to the press.

▼SOCIALISING

IGGY & THE STOOGES

KING'S CROSS CINEMA

London, England

At 2am Iggy Pop took to the stage, glammed up in silver jeans and silver hair.

Nick Kent (*NME*)

The total effect was more frightening than all the Alice Coopers and Clockwork Oranges put together, simply because these guys weren't joking. [173]

Mick Rock had already shot The Stooges in their "trashed out basement rehearsal studio off the Fulham Road" as none of the music papers had any photos of the band. At the King's Cross Cinema, Rock took another iconic photograph – his second in as many days – that became the cover of *Raw Power*.

SUNDAY 16 JULY

✪ PRESS

Dorchester Hotel
Park Lane
Mayfair
London, England

The Defries publicity blitz reached its climax with an extended press conference for all of the American journalists, press agents and record company executives.

Mick Rock (2002)
David was planning this tour for the fall of 1972 and the idea was to generate some press. David was starting to be a big deal in England and Lou and Iggy had both recently arrived and obviously they were invited for part of the flavouring of things. [037]

In his room at the Dorchester, Bowie kept them waiting, postponing the marathon of interviews for three hours before making his entrance.

After two weeks of recording with Mott The Hoople, Bowie played Charles Shaar Murray a tape of the album, which included a cover of The Velvets' 'Sweet Jane'.

"I've got Lou singing it at the moment," Bowie explained. "I've got to put Ian on, but he doesn't know the lyrics yet. Lou phrased it so Ian can pick up how it was. The album is fabulous. They've never written better stuff." [212]

Charles Shaar Murray (*NME*)
Lou Reed and his band are there, all the Spiders, and curled up in a corner, in a Bolan T-shirt, eye shadow and silvered hair, is Iggy Pop. [212]

Mick Rock (1999)
I knew I was going to get this picture no matter what happened. I was not letting anybody out until I got a shot of the three of them together. At the time it wasn't really a big deal. Because David was just breaking and just starting to garner a lot of attention and Iggy and Lou were still underground figures. That's the only time the three of them were in a photograph together. And of course Iggy was wearing a T. Rex T-shirt. And he's got a pack of Lucky Strike in his mouth. It just happened. That was just one of those great fortuitous things. [374]

However, not all the Spiders were there. Mick Ronson, uncomfortable with the hoopla surrounding the 'guitar fellatio' ad published the day before, had gone to Toronto, to play on Pure Prairie League's RCA album *Bustin' Out*.

MONDAY 17 JULY

▼ SOCIALISING

Bowie, Angie, Woodmansey and Bolder left for a two-week holiday in Cyprus. Bowie was involved in a head-on collision at a level crossing outside Kyrenia, where they were staying at a coastal resort. Bowie escaped injury but was charged in court with dangerous driving. The charges were dropped after he paid damages for the other car.

SATURDAY 22 JULY

✪ PRESS

Record Mirror reported on Bowie's plans for the near future. These included an appearance on the *Flip Wilson Show* in the US before the August Rainbow gig, and a tour of Japan, New Zealand and Australia later in the year, although none of these happened.

FRIDAY 28 JULY

■ SINGLE RELEASED

MOTT THE HOOPLE
'All The Young Dudes' (3:33)/
'One Of The Boys'
(Hunter/Ralphs) (5:35)
(CBS S 8271)

David Bowie/Mick Ronson: A-side Producers

ABOVE: Cover of *Revelations*, a live album from Glastonbury 1971, which included Bowie's new studio version of 'The Supermen'.
OPPOSITE: Lou Reed in 1973.

SATURDAY 29 JULY

■ ALBUM RELEASED

'REVELATIONS –
A MUSICAL ANTHOLOGY FOR GLASTONBURY FAYRE'

The triple album, featuring highlights from the 1971 festival, would have included songs from Bowie's set but the organisers were denied permission and asked to surrender the master tapes, which Angie collected and lost soon afterwards.

Instead, Bowie contributed the Spiders' update of 'The Supermen', recorded during the *Ziggy Stardust* sessions on November 12.

SUNDAY 30 JULY

► TRAVELLING

Bowie, Angie, Woodmansey and Bolder flew back to the UK, and were thrown about in the turbulence of an electrical storm. Bowie had already begun to ponder his mortality, presciently telling Mick Rock back in March, "I get worried about dying. At the moment it's this terrible travel thing. I keep thinking we're going to crash." [258]

Bowie took his latest close call as an omen and vowed never to fly again – and didn't until 1977. For the next few years Defries incorporated this phobia into Bowie's publicity, making it a romantic affectation.

While Led Zeppelin and The Rolling Stones toured in customised chartered jets, Bowie would traverse continents by train and sail to America, arriving like a latter-day Oscar Wilde.

AUGUST

THURSDAY 10 – MONDAY 14

▲ REHEARSING

Rainbow Theatre
Finsbury Park
North London, England

In preparation for two shows booked (and sold out) at the Rainbow Theatre on August 18–19, the band began rehearsals. Lindsay Kemp was brought down to design and choreograph the elaborate Ziggy Stardust show Bowie had been wanting to stage since seeing Alice Cooper's outrageous stage presentation. Flushed with recent success and an impressive fee of £1,000 for the first night, Bowie seized the chance to realise his vision for this second stage of the UK tour.

FRIDAY 11 AUGUST

▲ RECORDING

Trident Studios
17 St Anne's Court, Soho
London, England

LOU REED
'TRANSFORMER' ALBUM

David Bowie/Mick Ronson: Producers
Ken Scott: Engineer

While Bolder and Woodmansey continued rehearsals using backing tapes, Bowie and Ronson began production work on Lou Reed's new album at Trident.

Reed had readily agreed to Bowie's offer to produce his album, feeling that they had the chemistry that was missing from the recording of his first album. Reed recalled the response he had from RCA: "They said, 'The first record was a flop so go make another one.' You know in those days they gave you a chance, you could go make another one."[349]

Bowie (1997)
I was petrified that Lou said yes he would like to work with me in a producer capacity, because I had so many ideas and I felt so intimidated by my knowledge of the work that he had already done. [363]

Lou Reed (2001)
With Ronno and David there was a real simpatico, which is certainly part of the situation I had in the Velvets and it was miles above where I'd been on the first* Lou Reed *record, where there was nothing simpatico. [349]

Ken Scott (2001)
The whole set-up for this was to try and make it a lot more basic than a lot of the Bowie things that we'd done in the past. [325]

Lou Reed (2001)
I just ran over the songs with them. By that I mean the chord structure and the melody. [349]

The result was a modern hybrid of Bowie and Reed with an overall theme – Reed's New York, specifically Warhol.

Along with 'New York Telephone Conversation' and 'Make Up', 'Vicious' was a song Reed wrote in 1968 for a proposed Broadway musical to be produced by Andy Warhol and Yves St Laurent, and inspired by a conversation with Warhol.

Lou Reed (2001)
Andy said, "Why don't you write a song called 'Vicious'?" I said, "Vicious? What kind of vicious?" He said, "Vicious, I hit you with a flower." I thought, "Oh, what a great idea." [349]

Reed had written 'Andy's Chest' about the attempted assassination of Warhol by Valerie Solanas. At Trident the Velvets song was stripped back and slowed down to accommodate Reed's dense lyrics, then built up with layers of Bowie's backing vocals. Another Velvets holdover, 'Satellite Of Love', was given a similar treatment.

Lou Reed (2001)
David's amazing at background vocal parts – 'bom bom bom' – that's okay, that's really great, but the really great thing is the high note at the end. Very few people could do that. I just loved when he did that, I mean – what a move. I think everything is really about details and that was the exclamation mark. When he goes up like that… really pure and beautiful. [349]

'Walk On The Wild Side' began as a song Reed had written in 1971 for a planned theatrical adaptation of Nelson Algren's 1956 novel. The play never happened but Reed adapted it as an ode to the Warhol 'superstars'.

Lou Reed (1973)
I have always thought it would be kinda fun to introduce people to characters they maybe hadn't met before, or hadn't wanted to meet, y'know. The kind of people you sometimes see at parties but don't dare approach. That's one of the motivations for me writing all those songs in the first place. [175]

Herbie Flowers, whom Bowie had called in for three days' work, came up with the twin interlocking bass lines, which gave the song much of its character. Double tracking carried the added benefit of doubling his session fee of £12 for three hours.

Herbie Flowers (2001)
I put the double bass down first with the guitar and the drums. So then I asked Ken if I could go straight back down and overdub the electric bass in tenths, just to give it a little bit more atmosphere or character. [349]

Over the next ten days, Bowie and Ronson shuttled between the Rainbow Theatre and Trident, where Mick Rock shot a series of close-ups of Bowie to be projected during the concerts.

SATURDAY 12 AUGUST

▲ REHEARSING

Rainbow Theatre
Finsbury Park
North London, England

Lindsay Kemp arrived with a troupe of dancers to begin three days of choreography rehearsals.

SUNDAY 13 AUGUST

★ LIVE
★ GUEST APPEARANCE

Civic Hall
Guildford
Surrey, England

MOTT THE HOOPLE

Bowie and Reed, having finished work on *Transformer*, attended the show with Defries. To thunderous applause Ian Hunter brought Bowie on for 'All The Young Dudes'.

Earlier that day Mott The Hoople had performed the song on BBC's *Top Of The Pops*.

WEDNESDAY 16 – FRIDAY 18 AUGUST

▲ REHEARSING

Rainbow Theatre
Finsbury Park
North London, England

Prior to the first Rainbow show, keyboard player Nicky Graham fell foul of Angie and was shown the door by Defries. Ken Scott recommended Procol Harum's Matthew Fisher.

OPPOSITE: Bowie gives one of his critically acclaimed performances at London's Rainbow Theatre.

SATURDAY 19 SUNDAY 20 AUGUST

★ LIVE

Rainbow Theatre
Finsbury Park
North London, England

Lloyd Watson/Roxy Music: Support Acts

George Underwood: Programme/ Poster Designer

Natasha Korniloff: Astronettes' Spider Web Costume

The second UK tour kicked off with two sold-out shows at the Rainbow Theatre, heralded by *Record Mirror*'s front page 'Bowie Sell-Out'.

The Rainbow concerts opened with a screening of *Un Chien Andalou*, the 1929 silent surrealist short film by Luis Buñuel and Salvador Dalí, followed by 'Ode To Joy' as Bowie "emerged from shadows" through a cloud of dry ice. With a photo of Bolan projected on the screen, they launched into 'Lady Stardust'.

The set now included the forthcoming single 'John, I'm Only Dancing' and 'Starman', where Bowie acknowledged both the venue and the song's melodic origin by inserting a snatch of 'Somewhere Over The Rainbow'.

As the show progressed, the screen showed a series of images of Bowie, landscapes and art compiled by Mick Rock, who also filmed the show for his (still unreleased) documentary *Ziggy Across The Rainbow*, which included interviews with fans and guests such as Elton John.

FRIDAY 25 AUGUST

■ SINGLE RELEASED

THE ARNOLD CORNS

'Hang On To Yourself' (2:55)/
'Man In The Middle' (4:10)
(B&C CB 189)

With Bowie's stock at an all-time high, B&C cashed in on his abandoned project without his permission.

✪ PROMO VIDEO FILMING

Rainbow Theatre
Finsbury Park
North London, England

'John, I'm Only Dancing'

Mick Rock: Director

With Bowie and the band still based at the Rainbow, Mick Rock hired a cameraman to shoot Bowie and the Spiders on stage, miming to a record player hooked up to the house sound system. Bowie's close-ups revealed a tiny anchor drawn on his cheek, inspired by Samantha (from the US television show *Bewitched*), who occasionally wore tiny tattoos on her face.

Footage from the shows of The Astronettes dancing was later incorporated into the film by an editor whom Rock engaged for a marathon session, which he says lasted "eight or nine hours, all in one night, and in the morning the editor rolled over and had an epileptic fit on the floor." [037]

Mick Rock's natural flair for composition created a stylish film whose stark spotlit minimalism provided a stylistic template for the music video. The spectral images of the spidery Astronettes anticipated the Goth aesthetic adopted by Siouxsie Sioux and Bauhaus.

▮ Released: *The Video Collection* VHS/Video CD/Laserdisc (PMI 1993)/ *Best Of Bowie* DVD (EMI 2002).

SATURDAY 26 AUGUST

The Rainbow shows received glowing reviews. Charles Shaar Murray was greatly impressed with the theatricality, which "made Alice [Cooper] look like a third-form dramatic society". As well as the "finest body of work of any contemporary songwriter", he concluded, "there really isn't anything going that tops the current Ziggy show." [213]

Gavin Petrie in *Disc*, however, was critical of the choreography in the Rainbow shows, saying it had detracted from the music. Bowie, earlier stung by Defries' opinion that Kemp's involvement hadn't worked, had already decided to restyle the rest of the tour with simpler stage wear and white lights.

Matthew Fisher was unable to continue with the tour as his wife was expecting a baby. Bowie remembered Bob Sargeant from Chrysalis act Mick Abrahams Band. Their drummer Ritchie Dharma, who had recently worked on *Transformer*, told Bowie that Sargeant was away and suggested Robin Lumley (with whom he was collaborating), who jumped at the offer.

SUNDAY 27 AUGUST

★ LIVE

Locarno Centre
Electric Village
Bristol, England

MONDAY 28 AUGUST

▲ REHEARSING

Rainbow Theatre
Finsbury Park
North London, England

Bowie and band prepared for the third and last show, added by popular demand.

WEDNESDAY 30 AUGUST

★ LIVE

Rainbow Theatre
Finsbury Park
North London, England

THURSDAY 31 AUGUST

★ LIVE

Starkers
Royal Ballrooms
Boscombe
Bournemouth
Dorset, England

In New York City, Tony Zanetta, president of the newly incorporated MainMan Limited, set up their headquarters at 240 East 58th Street.

SEPTEMBER

FRIDAY 1

★ **LIVE**
St Leger Festival
Top Rank Suite
Doncaster
South Yorkshire, England

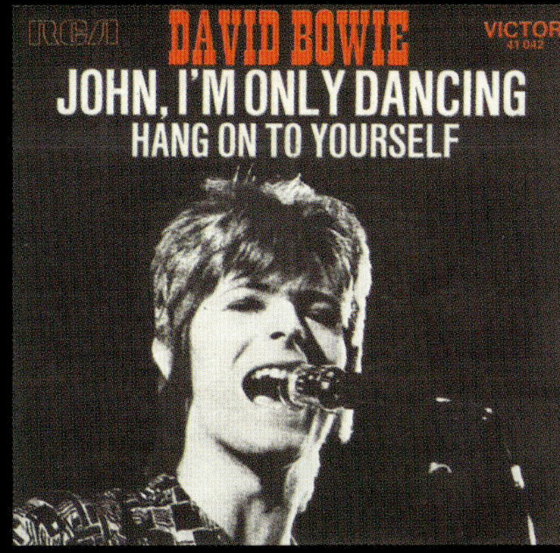

■ **SINGLE RELEASED**
'John, I'm Only Dancing' (2:43)/
'Hang On To Yourself' (2:38)
UK (RCA 2263)
Chart Peak No.12

Bowie (1993)

It was my attempt to do a bisexual anthem, and it was incredibly successful. I was amazed that the Beeb played it. [007]

NME's Danny Holloway, usually supportive of Bowie, was disappointed with the single, finding Bowie's "screeching vocal" and Mick Ronson's "agitating guitar" an "irritating combination".

SATURDAY 2 SEPTEMBER

★ **LIVE**
Hardrock Concert Theatre
Stretford
Manchester
Lancashire, England

"Interest in Bowie at Hardrock has been phenomenal – the phones haven't stopped ringing all week," Hardrock owner Mike O'Shea told *Record Mirror*. "We've managed to arrange a second show, and both concerts are certain to be sell-outs." [248]

Pianist Roy Young sat in with the band and "had the audience eating out of his hand", according to *Record Mirror*. Bowie kept Young in mind and in 1975 asked him to play on *Station To Station*. He couldn't, but the next year Young was flown in for the *Low* session.

Over a thousand fans were turned away from the sold-out show, which opened the newest of the UK purpose-built rock 'supervenues'. *NME* reported the new venue "outdoes both London's Rainbow and its Sundown chains in technical apparatus and specification" and boasted 24-track mixing, quadraphonic sound and a revolving stage." [232] After the acclaimed Rainbow concerts and with two albums in the charts, Bowie and the Spiders were now moving into star mode. Defries encouraged them to live the part, putting them up at Manchester's upmarket Excelsior.

SUNDAY 3 SEPTEMBER

★ **LIVE**
Hardrock Concert Theatre
Stretford
Manchester
Lancashire, England

In the morning Defries announced to the band and crew that RCA had high expectations of their imminent US tour, on par with The Beatles' success. "You will all have to learn to look and act like a million dollars!" he told them.

Defries then asked roadie Will Palin what was needed for the tour. Palin explained they would need their own backline set-up – they had been hiring it up until now. He guessed £20,000 worth. Within days all the gear was purchased and ready to ship for the tour.

MONDAY 4 SEPTEMBER

★ **LIVE**
Top Rank Suite
Liverpool
Lancashire, England

TUESDAY 5 SEPTEMBER

★ **LIVE**
Top Rank Suite
Sunderland
County Durham, England

Mott's 'All The Young Dudes' single peaked at No.3 in the UK. Ian Hunter said in 1974, "We got our morale back and decided to keep going." [074]

WEDNESDAY 6 SEPTEMBER

★ **LIVE**
Top Rank Suite
Sheffield
South Yorkshire, England

THURSDAY 7 SEPTEMBER

★ **LIVE**
Top Rank Suite
Hanley
Stoke-on-Trent
Staffordshire, England

✪ **PRESS**
Interviewed by Paul Raven for *Mirabelle* magazine:

RAVEN: *Why do you wear such way-out costumes?*

BOWIE: *Why not? I enjoy wearing them and so does the group. When I go out onto a stage I try to make the performance as good and interesting as possible, and I don't just mean by singing my songs and moving off. I think if you're really going to entertain an audience then you have to look the part, too. I feel very comfortable in the clothes I wear and they're part of me, and part of my act.*

RAVEN: *Do you enjoy working for other groups?*

BOWIE: *You mean Mott The Hoople, do you? Well, it's good working with them because in the studio they've got a feel for what's right. I was pleased with their version of my song, 'All The Young Dudes'.* [247]

As Robin Lumley was not available for the US tour, auditions were held for a new pianist, but with no success.

ABOVE: French release of 'John, I'm Only Dancing'.
OPPOSITE: Following the July photo session with Masayoshi Sukita, Tony Defries decided to invite two other key photographers – ex-AFAP clients David Bailey and Brian Duffy – to create some high-quality studio shots for Bowie's upcoming US and Japan tour promotion. At this stage, neither Bailey nor Duffy were familiar with Bowie's work. Although this Duffy session was not used, Bowie was sufficiently impressed with Duffy to ask him back the following January to shoot the cover of *Aladdin Sane*.

FRIDAY 8 SEPTEMBER

■ ALBUM RELEASED

MOTT THE HOOPLE
'ALL THE YOUNG DUDES'
UK (CBS 965184)
Chart Peak No.12

SIDE ONE
1. **'Sweet Jane'** (Reed) (4:20)
2. **'Momma's Little Jewel'** (Hunter/Watts) (4:26)
3. **'All The Young Dudes'** (3:31)
4. **'Sucker'** (Hunter/Ralphs/Watts) (4:58)
5. **'Jerkin' Crocus'** (Hunter) (4:00)

SIDE TWO
1. **'One Of The Boys'** (Hunter/Ralphs) (6:46)
2. **'Soft Ground'** (Allen) (3:16)
3. **'Ready For Love/After Lights'** (Ralphs) (6:46)
4. **'Sea Diver'** (Hunter) (2:54)

Mott The Hoople/David Bowie: Arrangers
David Bowie: Producer/Saxophone
Mick Ronson: Strings Arranger/Brass on 'Sea Diver'
Mick Rock: Sleeve Concept/Art Direction
George Underwood: Colour Retoucher
Recorded in May at Trident Studios
July at Olympic Studios

Ian Hunter (1974)
We'd always got a murky, dirty sound without much clarity. We didn't know how to do it properly. We had wanted to be a classy band. When David took over, the sound got clear. We learned a lot of things about arranging and production; it was a technical change. [074]

ABOVE: All in the family – sleeve by Mick Rock and George Underwood, produced by Bowie.
RIGHT: Pianist Mike Garson in 1974. After joining Bowie in 1972, Garson played a prominent role on the *Aladdin Sane* album.

Ian Hunter (2009)
Everything got finished real quick because Bowie had to go somewhere. We were halfway where we were going and halfway where we'd been but we knew the standard now. We weren't sure about how the Dudes album sounded. He took some of the power away. [229]

■ The 1998 *All The Young Dudes: The Anthology* box set and the 2006 reissue of the album include a mix of 'All The Young Dudes' which combines Bowie's original guide vocal with the finished backing track.

SUNDAY 10 SEPTEMBER

► TRAVELLING

Iggy & The Stooges began recording the *Raw Power* album at CBS Studios in London, with sessions continuing for four weeks.

Bowie and Angie boarded the *QE2* for America, accompanied by George and Birgit Underwood. After Defries' objections to Lindsay Kemp's choreography of the Rainbow shows, Underwood was asked to stage design the US tour.

FRIDAY 15 SEPTEMBER

Defries met with RCA in New York. As they were underwriting the tour, RCA had appointed Gustl Breuer to liaise with MainMan on expenditure. RCA told Breuer, then the vice-president of their classical section, he would now have "the great chance of working with David Bowie", to which Breuer replied, "What is a David Bowie?" Defries saw this as an advantage, stepped forward and embraced Breuer, saying, "You're our man." [013]

SUNDAY 17 SEPTEMBER

Arriving in New York, the Bowies and the Underwoods were met on the Manhattan waterfront by Breuer, who later recalled that Angie "looked like a gentile Barbra Streisand who was very much in command of the whole situation". [013]

He settled them into a suite at The Plaza with an invitation to call him at home if there was a problem. As soon as he got home the phone was ringing. Angie was shrieking that "everything was fucked up". He returned to the hotel to rectify the matter and Angie apologised.

MONDAY 18 SEPTEMBER

⊙ BUSINESS

The rest of the tour party arrived in New York. On Annette Peacock's recommendation Bowie invited Mike Garson to audition to play piano on the tour. Garson's background was more jazz than rock, having played with Mel Tormé, Nancy Wilson and Martha Reeves, among others.

Mike Garson (2011)
I had played with all those people, so I was looking for something different and they seemed plenty different!

I went into shock when I went into RCA Recording Studios to audition because I see this one guy with red hair, one guy with this blonde hair, one guy with the silver-black hair with this kind of weird beard. You know, each member of The Spiders From Mars had a look, and they were in full apparel that day and I come in wearing dungarees and a T-shirt from giving a piano lesson in Brooklyn.

I actually left the piano student to babysit my one-year-old daughter because my wife wasn't home, and I had to go right then and there to audition. I went in there and I thought, "What the hell is this?" But I liked them. Mick Ronson conducted the audition and David was listening in the studio.

I said, "Mr David Bowie, I'm sorry that I don't know who you are, but I certainly will play my best." I only played about eight seconds on the song called 'Changes' and Mick said, "You got it." I hadn't even started. He obviously was a good enough musician to figure out that I could play from whatever I played in those first eight bars or eight seconds. A week later I'm in Cleveland, Ohio for the first show of The Spiders From Mars.
[406]

TUESDAY 19 SEPTEMBER

▼SOCIALISING

Oscar Wilde Room
Mercer Arts Centre
Broadway Hotel
New York City
New York, USA

NEW YORK DOLLS

After the show Bowie and the Spiders (minus Bolder), Angie, Mick and Sheila Rock met the Dolls – the start of Bowie's friendship with their singer David Johansen and his fixation with Johansen's girlfriend Cyrinda Foxe.

ABOVE: New York Dolls: David Johansen (front) with Jerry Nolan, Johnny Thunders, Arthur Kane and Sylvain Sylvain.
BELOW: David Johansen and Cyrinda Foxe, 1974.

WEDNESDAY 20 SEPTEMBER

►TRAVELLING

The touring party left New York for Cleveland on a chartered Greyhound bus, staying overnight in Pennsylvania. Throughout the American tour, Bowie and a small entourage travelled by Greyhound bus, train and car. The rest of the tour crew, including Leee Black Childers and Cherry Vanilla, would fly ahead to do advance publicity and prepare venues.

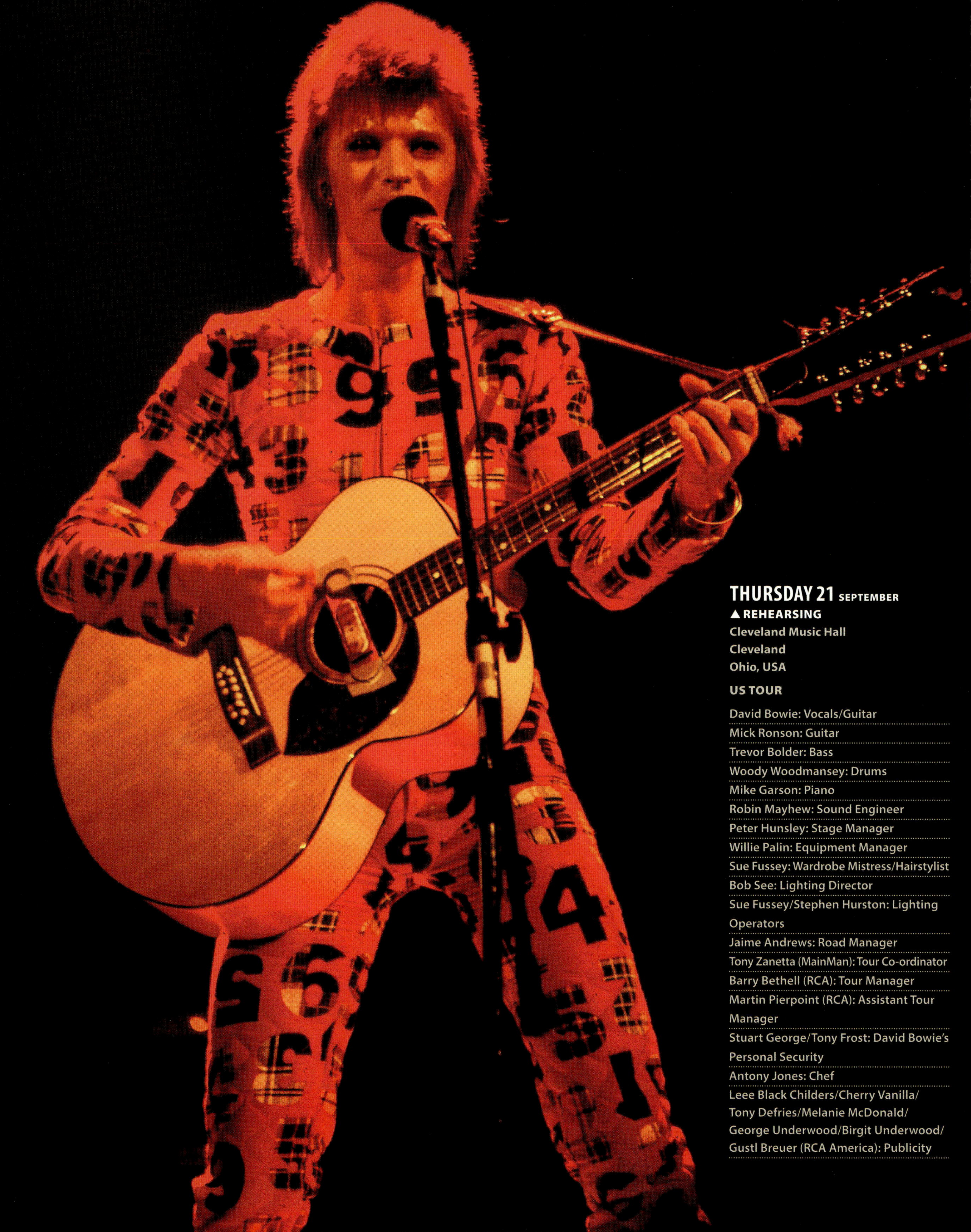

THURSDAY 21 SEPTEMBER

▲ REHEARSING

Cleveland Music Hall
Cleveland
Ohio, USA

US TOUR

David Bowie: Vocals/Guitar
Mick Ronson: Guitar
Trevor Bolder: Bass
Woody Woodmansey: Drums
Mike Garson: Piano
Robin Mayhew: Sound Engineer
Peter Hunsley: Stage Manager
Willie Palin: Equipment Manager
Sue Fussey: Wardrobe Mistress/Hairstylist
Bob See: Lighting Director
Sue Fussey/Stephen Hurston: Lighting Operators
Jaime Andrews: Road Manager
Tony Zanetta (MainMan): Tour Co-ordinator
Barry Bethell (RCA): Tour Manager
Martin Pierpoint (RCA): Assistant Tour Manager
Stuart George/Tony Frost: David Bowie's Personal Security
Antony Jones: Chef
Leee Black Childers/Cherry Vanilla/Tony Defries/Melanie McDonald/George Underwood/Birgit Underwood/Gustl Breuer (RCA America): Publicity

FRIDAY 22 SEPTEMBER

★ **LIVE**

Cleveland Music Hall
Ohio, USA

Bowie's first US public performance was heralded by a publicity campaign staged by Cherry Vanilla and Leee Black Childers, who did the rounds of the local media, ensured the records were available in the shops and checked the venues were adequate.

Bowie was rapturously received by the ecstatic 3,200-strong crowd who rushed the stage at the end of the show.

He was interviewed earlier in his hotel room by the local newspaper and a reporter from *Cream*. Timothy Ferris reported on the interview as part of his coverage of the tour. His feature, 'David Bowie in America', published in November, was Bowie's first *Rolling Stone* cover story.

SATURDAY 23 SEPTEMBER

► **TRAVELLING**

CLEVELAND – MEMPHIS
Greyhound bus

SUNDAY 24 SEPTEMBER

★ **LIVE**

Ellis Auditorium (North Music Hall)
Memphis
Tennessee, USA

▼ **SOCIALISING**

The sold-out show was followed by a party at The Memphis Downtowner Inn.

LEFT: Bowie and Ronson at the Cleveland Music Hall.

WEDNESDAY 27 SEPTEMBER

✪ PRESS

Bowie and the Spiders returned to stay at The Plaza Hotel. Bowie later recalled he had his "first big-time star interviewer" that night.

Al Aronowitz was renowned mainly for hooking up Dylan with The Beatles when they visited New York. At that meeting of legends, Dylan "turned them on" and Lennon changed his attitude to songwriting. Aronowitz had been dining off the story ever since and now regaled Bowie with stories of how he influenced rock history.

Then Aronowitz left, saying, "Oh, by the way, I won't be going to your show tomorrow night. The Carnegie Hall people were very rude to me once." [037]

THURSDAY 28 SEPTEMBER

★ LIVE

Carnegie Hall
New York City
New York, USA

RCA announced that the show was a complete sell-out. In reality, MainMan had papered the house, distributing most of the tickets to journalists and New York scene makers such as Cyrinda Foxe and Geri Miller. The resulting shortage of tickets ensured Bowie's New York debut was the hottest ticket in town, attracting stars such as Tony Perkins, Todd Rundgren and Alan Bates.

Andy Warhol was there to witness Bowie's transformation from the shy creature he had met the previous September.

Lisa Robinson, who described the concert as a triumph, wrote: "I wonder what went through Andy's head as he sat in Carnegie Hall listening to David's tribute to him."

Warhol had virtually ignored the song when Bowie had presented it to him a year earlier and now the kids were clamouring for it. Lee Radziwill

Bowie had contracted a 48-hour flu and struggled with some high notes, but the huge response from the audience kept him going. "It was very rewarding because the audience were wonderful, and I wanted to sing so much better," he told Lisa Robinson in 1983. Watching Angie and Cyrinda Foxe at the after-show party inspired Bowie to write 'Watch That Man' the following morning.

⊙ BUSINESS

Bowie signed a new contract of employment with MainMan (erroneously dated September 31), mistakenly thinking it was giving him partnership in the company.

ABOVE: Bowie's suite at the Plaza Hotel, New York. OPPOSITE: Live at Carnegie Hall.

OCTOBER

'David Bowie: Fleeting Moments In A Glamorous Career' published in *Phonograph Record* magazine. The extensive cover story by Ron Ross detailed Bowie and Defries' combined efforts to break America, including Bowie's 1971 US promotional trip, the RCA signing and the press junket Ron Ross had joined in July to report the Bowie phenomenon.

SUNDAY 1

★ LIVE

Music Hall
Boston
Massachusetts, USA

The concert (like others in New York and Los Angeles) was recorded for a planned live album, which got as far as mixing and George Underwood's cover artwork before it was shelved.

▮ 'John, I'm Only Dancing'/'Changes'/'The Supermen' on *Sound + Vision* (Ryko 1989).

▮ All three plus 'Life On Mars?' on *Aladdin Sane* 30th Anniversary 2 CD Edition (EMI 2003).

MONDAY 2 OCTOBER

► TRAVELLING

Bowie and the tour party travelled to New York to record new material and begin mixing Lou Reed's *Transformer* album.

WEDNESDAY 4 OCTOBER

▲ RECORDING

RCA Studio D
155 East 24th Street
New York City
New York, USA

'Untitled Track'

David Bowie: Producer
Mike Moran: Engineer

THURSDAY 5 OCTOBER

▲ RECORDING

RCA Studio D
155 East 24th Street
New York City
New York, USA

'Untitled Track'

David Bowie: Producer
Joe Lopes: Engineer

FRIDAY 6 OCTOBER

▲ RECORDING

RCA Studio D
155 East 24th Street
New York City
New York, USA

'The Jean Genie'

David Bowie: Producer
Mike Moran: Engineer

'The Jean Genie' began life as a jam based on The Yardbirds' 'I'm A Man' one night on the Greyhound bus between dates.

The recording happened just as spontaneously, when the Spiders kicked off the session jamming on the riff "as a laugh", as Bolder recalled in 1995. Bowie told them, "I like it, let's keep it."

With a hastily written lyric, the song quickly took shape – a thumbnail sketch of an Iggy-type character moving through New York's underground, delivered in a stream of consciousness street rap. Having recently met French novelist Jean Genet, Bowie subconsciously adapted the alliterative name for the character.

They recorded the backing track in one take, deciding to ignore the mistake before the chorus, and added some overdubs, including Bowie's harmonica part. He said in 1973 that the "wanted to get the same sound The Stones had on their very first album. I didn't get that near to it, but it had a feel that I wanted – that Sixties thing."

An hour and a half after they started the session, 'The Jean Genie' was not only complete but catchy enough to release as the next single.

► TRAVELLING

In the afternoon, Bowie, Zanetta, the Underwoods, Breuer and Antony Jones boarded *The Broadway Limited* at Penn Station New York for the overnight trip to Chicago.

SATURDAY 7 OCTOBER

▲ **RECORDING**
RCA Studios
Chicago
Illinois, USA

'John, I'm Only Dancing'

David Bowie: Producer

Bowie and the Spiders recorded a new version for possible inclusion on the next album, but this version was never issued.

★ **LIVE**
Auditorium Theatre
Chicago
Illinois, USA

'Hang On To Yourself'
'Ziggy Stardust'/'The Supermen'
'Queen Bitch'/'Changes'
'Life On Mars?'/'Five Years'
'Space Oddity'/'Andy Warhol'
'My Death'/'The Width Of A Circle'
'John, I'm Only Dancing'
'Moonage Daydream'
'Starman'/'Waiting For The Man'
'White Light White Heat'
'Suffragette City'/'The Jean Genie'

SUNDAY 8 OCTOBER

► **TRAVELLING**
Gustl Breuer joined the touring party, which boarded *The Wolverine* in the morning, arriving in Detroit in the afternoon.

★ **LIVE**
The New Fisher Theatre
Detroit
Michigan, USA

Iggy flew over with the master tapes of *Raw Power* and caught up with Bowie after the sold-out show. Iggy regaled him with stories of riots in the city, inspiring Bowie to write 'Panic In Detroit'. Also backstage was feted backing singer Claudia Lennear, who had worked with Ike & Tina Turner on the Rolling Stones 1969 US tour and appeared in the concert films *The Concert For Bangladesh* and *Mad Dogs And Englishmen*. Bowie asked her "for some input" and they agreed to work together in the near future.

MONDAY 9 OCTOBER

► **TRAVELLING**
At 8.15am, the entourage reboarded *The Wolverine*, changing trains to *The Abraham Lincoln* in Chicago, and arrived in St Louis late that night, checking in at The Cheshire Inn.

WEDNESDAY 11 OCTOBER

★ **LIVE**
Kiel Auditorium
St Louis
Missouri, USA

Despite the efforts of Leee Black Childers and Cherry Vanilla to drum up publicity, the audience was well below the 10,000 capacity and scattered about in numbered seats.

Bowie (2002)
Only a few hundred stalwart fans showed. I got them to come down to the front, to the orchestra pit, and gave them a real intimate show, talk going back and forth between us all night. [037]

THURSDAY 12 OCTOBER

Bowie, Ronson, Jones and Breuer travelled by limo to Nashville, staying at the Ramada Inn while Zanetta and the Underwoods stayed in St Louis for two days.

▲ **MIXING**
RCA Studio B
Nashville
Tennessee, USA

'John, I'm Only Dancing'
'Changes'
'The Supermen'
'Life On Mars?'
(recorded live in Boston, October 1)
'The Jean Genie'
(mono/stereo versions)

Ken Scott later remixed the track 'The Jean Genie' for the album with wider separation of the instruments across the channels.

FRIDAY 13 OCTOBER

► **TRAVELLING**
Bowie, Ronson, Jones and Breuer rejoined the group in St Louis.

SATURDAY 14 OCTOBER

► **TRAVELLING**
In the morning the Bowie party boarded *The National Limited* for the trip from St Louis to Kansas City.

SUNDAY 15 OCTOBER

★ **LIVE**
Memorial Hall
Kansas City
Kansas, USA

Originally scheduled for the 12th before being moved at the last minute, resulting in another near empty venue. To make matters worse, Bowie fell off the stage.

MONDAY 16 OCTOBER

► **TRAVELLING**
Bowie left Kansas City at 2am and traversed the expanse between Kansas and Los Angeles on *The Super Chief* luxury train. Like *The Zephyr*, it boasted the Vista Dome observation car, which gave them a panoramic view of the passing scenery.

Bowie (2002)
A couple of the band or friends, gladly one and the same most of the time, would often come and sit with me on these stretches. Ronson would love it, so too would my old chum George Underwood and his wife Birgit. At about 10 at night we'd creep up there, the air rich with the smell of grass, and laze around with guitars and a bottle of wine, watching the western moon get bigger and shinier into the early hours of the morning. [037]

The rest of the entourage left at noon and flew to Los Angeles. At The Beverly Hills Hotel they proceeded to take Defries' conspicuous consumption policy to the extreme, charging everything to room service. In the end it was Bowie who was footing the bill as his arrangement with MainMan meant that every cent of his record sales went straight to paying back RCA advances and MainMan expense accounts.

TUESDAY 17 OCTOBER

✪ **PHOTO SESSION**
Bowie arrived in Los Angeles at 9am, and met up with the rest of the touring party at The Beverly Hills Hotel.

With some time off before the next date, they spent their days by the hotel pool and their nights at Rodney Bingenheimer's new E Club on Sunset Strip. Subsequently renamed Rodney's English Disco, the club acquired legendary status as the epicentre of Seventies decadence and glamour and a crucible for the next generation of rock stars.

Mick Rock photographed Bowie in the grounds of the hotel, trying out some ideas for the planned 'The Jean Genie' promo film he would shoot in San Francisco. Bowie wanted the film to "locate Ziggy as a kind of Hollywood street-rat" with a "consort of the Marilyn brand" [037] and called Cyrinda Foxe – Warhol's own Marilyn figure – to ask her to fly in from New York. For the shoot Bowie had two bomber jackets sent over from London – black for him, bright yellow for her.

Following the hour-long photo session, Bowie, Rock and the Underwoods went to Sunset Boulevard for the LA premiere of Andy Warhol's *Heat*, while other members of the tour party opted for *Deep Throat*.

OPPOSITE: At the Beverly Hills Hotel Bowie tries out ideas for the 'Jean Genie' video shoot with Mick Rock.

WEDNESDAY 18 OCTOBER

▲ MIXING

Western Sound Studios
Los Angeles
California, USA

IGGY & THE STOOGES
'RAW POWER' ALBUM

Bowie spent three days remixing *Raw Power* with Iggy. Defries had rejected Iggy's initial mix and told him CBS would refuse to release it. Iggy had been left to his own devices, producing the album himself despite having little studio expertise, so when it came to mixing, he found his options were limited.

James Williamson (2001)

He found out that the guy who had recorded it originally had not gotten a lot of level on certain things, like the bass and drums, especially the bass, so he didn't have a lot to work with. Then Iggy, on his mix, he left a bunch of guitar stuff on there that probably shouldn't have been left in, and just odds and ends. [404]

Iggy turned to Bowie in the hope that he could produce something fit for release.

Bowie (1991)

He wanted me to mix **Raw Power*****, so he brought the 24-track tape in, and he put it up. He had the band on one track, lead guitar on another and him on a third. Out of 24 tracks there were just three tracks that were used. He said, "See what you can do with this." I said, "Jim, there's nothing to mix." So we just pushed the vocal up and down a lot. On at least four or five songs that was the situation, including 'Search And Destroy'. That's got such a peculiar sound because all we did was occasionally bring the lead guitar up and take it out.*** [147]

Bowie's mix caused much debate in the ensuing years, with complaints that he'd knocked the edges off the sound. In 1997 Iggy attempted to "give this thing its due sonically, and I didn't have that before", but the result attracted equal criticism. Bowie's, which was generally agreed to be better overall, was remastered for a deluxe reissue in 2010.

FRIDAY 20 OCTOBER

Meanwhile, MainMan was running out of money. Several of the previous shows had suffered from low attendance and in New York they had papered the house, earning nothing. The rising costs of keeping up appearances threatened the whole tour. Defries arrived in Los Angeles to survey the mayhem – observers likened it to Fellini's *Satyricon* – and his solution to the immediate problem was to convince RCA to advance MainMan more money, but other measures would have to be taken.

⊙ BUSINESS

Defries handed over the MainMan reins to Tony Zanetta, who would make key decisions concerning the tour and keeping down the spiralling costs. By this time the entourage had grown to 46 and Defries was rightly concerned about the hangers-on they were attracting. He suspected some of being undercover reporters or doing something "potentially harmful to us". Groupies were to be "sent home without breakfast".

★ LIVE

Santa Monica Civic Auditorium
Los Angeles
California, USA

Warhol was in the crowd to witness another landmark Ziggy show – as well as Bowie's imitation of him, which was captured for posterity and broadcast live by KMET-FM, giving Bowie invaluable exposure. As a result it was quickly bootlegged and remains the essential 1972 tour document.

▮ Released: *Santa Monica '72* (Golden Years 1994).

▮ Released: *Live Santa Monica '72* (remastered) (EMI 2008).

SATURDAY 21 OCTOBER

★ LIVE

Santa Monica Civic Auditorium
Los Angeles
California, USA

The second show was promptly booked and sold out, thanks to radio exposure and Bingenheimer's tireless promotion. Angie meanwhile returned to Britain with Zowie, prompting gossip that either she had been banished, was jealous of Cyrinda Foxe or tired of no longer being the centre of attention.

FRIDAY 27 OCTOBER

✪ PROMO VIDEO FILMING

'The Jean Genie'

Mick Rock: Director
Mick Rock/Jerry Slick: Cameramen

Bowie's idea for the video was played out on the street in San Francisco.

Mick Rock had gone out to scout locations for the 'Hollywood street-rat' film idea and suggested the aptly named Mars Hotel on 4th Street near the corner of Howard Street (before its 1974 demolition). Rock filmed Bowie leaning against the wall like a hustler while Cyrinda Foxe cavorted in the background.

Later, in a studio, cameraman Jerry Slick (Grace Slick's ex-husband) shot more footage of Foxe dancing and pouting to camera while Bowie and the Spiders mimed to the song, resplendent in newly tailored stage outfits.

Mick Rock (1999)

We shot Bowie and Cyrinda on the streets outside the Mars Hotel fairly early in the day. He played the Winterland that night. I remember Sylvester and his band were one of the support acts. [004]

★ LIVE

Winterland Auditorium
San Francisco
California, USA

Also supporting were The Phlorescent Leech & Eddie (ex-Turtles and Frank Zappa), whose drummer Aynsley Dunbar later played on *Pin Ups* and *Diamond Dogs*.

LEFT AND OVERLEAF: Mick Rock shoots the clip for 'The Jean Genie' in San Francisco.

SONGS
50¢ 50¢
TUBORG
slim jim

SATURDAY 28 OCTOBER

★ LIVE

Winterland Auditorium
San Francisco
California, USA

Both Winterland shows were only half full, adding to MainMan's economic woes, so they decided to cut their losses and cancel the Dallas and Houston dates, which were selling slowly.

✪ PROMO VIDEO FILMING
'The Jean Genie'

In the morning Mick Rock looked at the previous day's footage and decided they needed more for the clip, but they had used the entire modest budget of $350.

Mick Rock (1999)
Somehow I got some more dollars off Defries to rent an Arriflex camera, a silent one, and I went and shot all the live stuff myself the next night, because David did two nights at the Winterland. So I filmed him singing 'The Jean Genie' that night, processed overnight and, because there was no time, edited in one ten-hour rush. I had to chop it up a lot to keep everything in synch with his live performance, which was fairly close to the recorded version, as he'd only just recorded it. [004]

▮ Released: *The Video Collection* (PMI 1993)/*Best Of Bowie* DVD (EMI 2002).

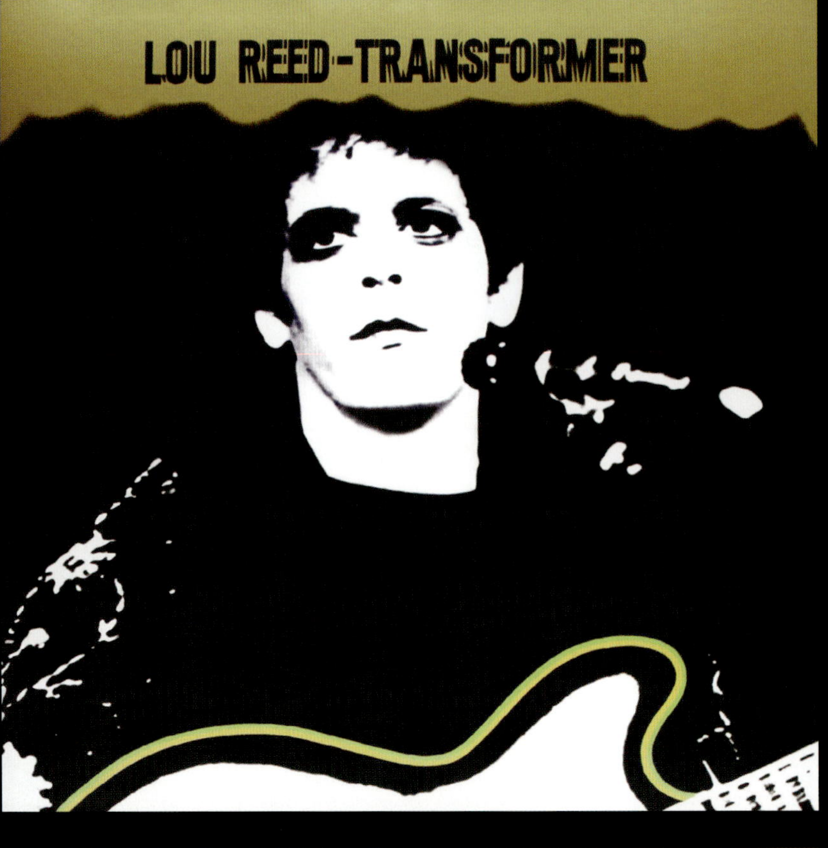

ABOVE AND RIGHT: Mick Rock had shot the cover photo of Lou Reed on stage at the King's Cross Cinema. Later, Reed went through the contact sheet with him and selected a frame. Rock inadvertently printed it slightly out of focus, but he and Reed were happy with the result – so much so that Karl Stoecker's photos of the model Gala Mitchell and Reed's friend Ernie Thormahlen, originally intended for the front, became the back cover.

NOVEMBER

▮ *The Rise And Fall Of Ziggy Stardust And The Spiders From Mars* released in Japan.

WEDNESDAY 1

★ LIVE

Paramount Theatre
Seattle
Washington, USA

The touring party arrived in Seattle and checked in at The Edgewater Inn, famous for hosting The Beatles in 1964. The poorly attended show proved to be another let-down after the success in Los Angeles. The journey from Seattle to Phoenix inspired Bowie to write 'Drive-In Saturday'.

■ SINGLE RELEASED
'The Jean Genie' (3:59)/
'Hang On To Yourself' (3:35)
US (RCA 74-0838)

SATURDAY 4 NOVEMBER

★ LIVE

Phoenix Celebrity Theatre
Arizona, USA

With no bookings until New Orleans the band stayed put after the poorly attended show, sweltering in the Phoenix heat. During the layover, Bowie shaved off his eyebrows, emulating Kansai Yamamoto's models in his 1971 London fashion show. Bowie later said it was done either in a drunken stupor, or because Mott The Hoople turned down his offer of 'Drive-In Saturday' as their next single.

WEDNESDAY 8 NOVEMBER

■ ALBUM RELEASED

LOU REED
'TRANSFORMER'
(RCA 2303)
UK Chart Peak No.13
US Chart Peak No.29

SIDE ONE
1. **'Vicious'** (2:55)
2. **'Andy's Chest'** (3:17)
3. **'Perfect Day'** (3:43)
4. **'Hangin' Round'** (3:39)

SIDE TWO
1. **'Make Up'** (2:58)
2. **'Satellite Of Love'** (3:40)
3. **'Wagon Wheel'** (3:19)
4. **'New York Telephone Conversation'** (1:31)
5. **'I'm So Free'** (3:07)
6. **'Goodnight Ladies'** (4:19)

All songs written by Lou Reed
David Bowie/Mick Ronson: Producers
Lou Reed/David Bowie/Mick Ronson: Arrangers
Mick Ronson: String/Bass Arranger
Ken Scott: Engineer
Ken Scott/Mike Stone/Lou Reed/ David Bowie/Mick Ronson: Mixers
Lou Reed: Guitar/Keyboards/Vocals
Herbie Flowers: Bass Guitar/Double Bass/ Tuba on 'Goodnight Ladies'/'Make Up'
Mick Ronson: Lead Guitar/Piano/ Recorder/ Backing Vocals/String Arrangements
John Halsey: Drums
Ronnie Ross: Baritone Saxophone on 'Goodnight Ladies'/'Walk On The Wild Side'
David Bowie/The Thunderthighs – Karen Friedman/Dari Lalou/Casey Synge: Backing Vocals
Barry DeSouza/Ritchie Dharma: Drums
Klaus Voormann: Bass
Recorded at Trident Studios London, England

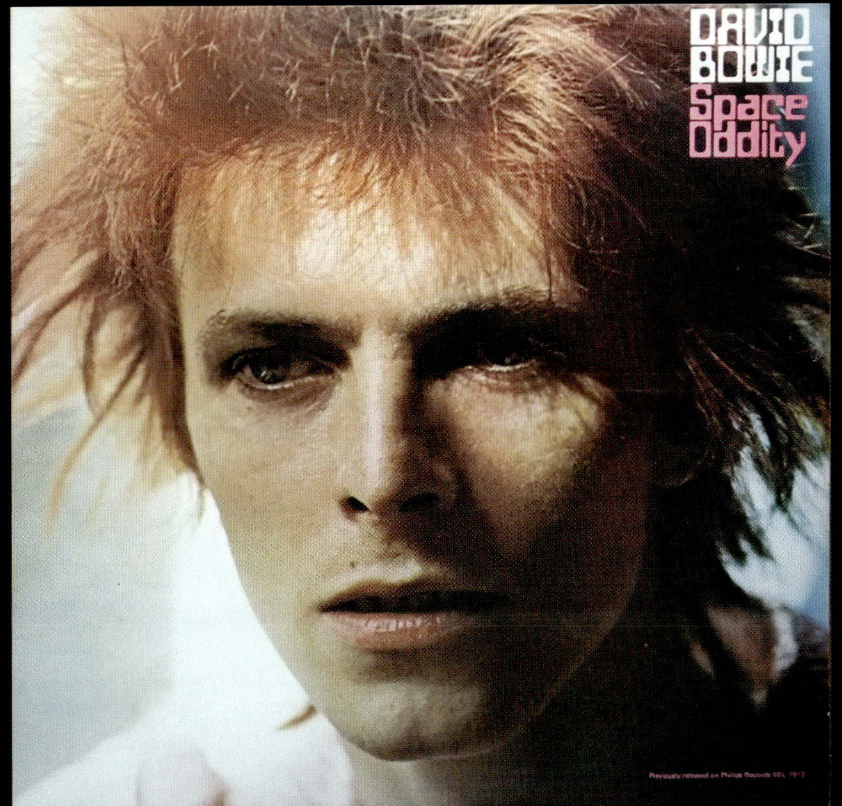

ABOVE: Mick Rock's photos from Haddon Hall earlier in the year provided the front and back covers of *Space Oddity*.
RIGHT: *The Man Who Sold The World* featured a Brian Ward photo on the front and a Mick Rock photo on the back.

FRIDAY 10 NOVEMBER

■ **ALBUM RELEASED**
'SPACE ODDITY' (reissued)
(RCA LSP 4813)
UK Chart Peak No.17
US Chart Peak No.16

■ **ALBUM RELEASED**
'THE MAN WHO SOLD THE WORLD'
(reissued) (RCA LSP 4816)
UK Chart Peak No. 26
US Chart Peak No.105

RCA reissued Bowie's Philips/Mercury albums with new artwork, updated promotional photographs, liner notes and fine print on the back reading 'recorded in 1969' and '1970' respectively. Initial pressings included a poster of the cover photo and an inner sleeve with lyrics.

For the reissue of the 1969 album *David Bowie*, RCA used the masters of *Man Of Words/Man Of Music* (the US version of the album), which omitted the out-take 'Don't Sit Down' from the track-listing.

■ **EP RELEASED**
'DAVID BOWIE' PROMO
'Space Oddity' (3:24)/
'Moonage Daydream' (4:30)/
'Life On Mars?' (3:45)/
'It Ain't Easy' (Davies) (2:52)
US (RCA EP-45-103)

Given away at some shows on the tour.

SATURDAY 11 NOVEMBER
★ **LIVE**
Majestic Theatre
Dallas
Texas, USA

SHOW CANCELLED

SUNDAY 12 NOVEMBER
★ **LIVE**
Majestic Theatre
Dallas
Texas, USA

SHOW CANCELLED

TUESDAY 14 NOVEMBER
★ **LIVE**
Layola University
New Orleans
Louisiana, USA

Bowie began reworking the song 'Time', previously recorded by George Underwood for a planned single and including a reference to Billy Murcia ('Billy Dolls'), the New York Dolls drummer who had died on November 6 from asphyxiation following a drug overdose at a London party.

FRIDAY 17 NOVEMBER
★ **LIVE**
Pirate's World
Amusement Park
Dania
Miami
Florida, USA

The new song 'Drive-In Saturday' made its live debut. Charles Shaar Murray, reporting on the gig for *NME*, described the transfixed state of the audience, too incredulous to move, coming over more like "religious worshippers at some demonic ceremony than a bunch of people who've come together to hear some rock and roll". To help the reissue, 'The Width Of A Circle' was reintroduced to the set, which allowed the Spiders to come to the fore in the long instrumental passages.

An RCA representative told Murray that the *Ziggy* album, at 150 in the charts before the tour and now at 94, would soon rise to the fifties as a result of the show. After all, he explained, "Americans don't buy records unless they've seen a show." [214]

George and Birgit Underwood arrived in Miami from Los Angeles with artwork for the planned *Ziggy Stardust – US Tour* live album.

George Underwood (2006)
I like the 1972 album, because I painted that completely on my own without anyone telling me what to do. It was my invention. I only had about 10 days to do that artwork. [392]

MONDAY 20 NOVEMBER
★ **LIVE**
Municipal Auditorium
Nashville
Tennessee, USA

WEDNESDAY 22 NOVEMBER
★ **LIVE**
The Warehouse
New Orleans
Louisiana, USA

FRIDAY 24 NOVEMBER
■ **SINGLE RELEASED**
'The Jean Genie' (3:59)/
'Ziggy Stardust' (3:13)
UK (RCA 2302)
Chart Peak No.2

■ **SINGLE RELEASED**
LOU REED
'Walk On The Wild Side' (Reed) (3:37)/
'Perfect Day' (Reed) (3:42)
UK (RCA 2303)
Chart Peak No.10

ABOVE: Italian release of 'The Jean Genie'.
OPPOSITE: Bowie performing in a shirt borrowed from Cyrinda Foxe.

Reed's ode to the 'superstars' of Warhol's Factory was an unusual choice for a single, but it gave Reed his first hit in the UK (where the BBC censors missed the line "even when she was giving head").

SATURDAY 25 NOVEMBER
★ **LIVE**
Public Auditorium
Cleveland
Ohio, USA

Chrissie Hynde was a student at Kent State University – where she witnessed the 1970 campus shootings – and already a dyed-in-the-wool rock fan, particularly of Lou Reed and Iggy Pop. She joined the capacity crowd to witness Bowie's triumphant return to Cleveland and blagged her way backstage, but she was too overawed by Bowie and chatted with Ronson instead.

▮ 'Drive-In Saturday' released on the *Aladdin Sane* 30th Anniversary 2 CD Edition (EMI 2003) and possibly sourced from the recording of the two shows by radio station WMMS (not broadcast).

SUNDAY 26 NOVEMBER
★ **LIVE**
Public Auditorium
Cleveland
Ohio, USA

TUESDAY 28 NOVEMBER
★ **LIVE**
Stanley Theatre
Pittsburgh
Pennsylvania, USA

WEDNESDAY 29 NOVEMBER
The entourage reached Philadelphia and checked in to the Warwick, a historic hotel in Rittenhouse Square.

★ **LIVE**
★ **GUEST APPEARANCE**
Tower Theatre
Philadelphia
Pennsylvania, USA

MOTT THE HOOPLE

Bowie introduced the band and joined them for 'All The Young Dudes' and played sax on 'Honky Tonk Woman'.

▮ Released: *All The Way From Stockholm To Philadelphia* (Angel Air 1998).

THURSDAY 30 NOVEMBER
★ **LIVE**
Tower Theatre
Philadelphia
Pennsylvania, USA

The concert's promoter Rick Green introduced David Bowie to his aide Pat Gibbons, who became Bowie's acting manager in 1976.

DECEMBER

FRIDAY 1

★ LIVE

Tower Theatre
Philadelphia
Pennsylvania, USA

SATURDAY 2 DECEMBER

★ LIVE

Tower Theatre
Philadelphia
Pennsylvania, USA

Bowie narrowly averted disaster during the encore, when he fell off the lip of the stage. He saved himself by hooking his legs onto the rail of the orchestra pit and carried on singing while upside down.

SUNDAY 3 DECEMBER

➤ TRAVELLING

Bowie and the Spiders returned to New York to continue work on the *Aladdin Sane* album.

MONDAY 4 – MONDAY 11 DECEMBER

▲ RECORDING

RCA Studios
155 East 24th Street
New York City
New York, USA

'ALADDIN SANE' ALBUM

David Bowie/Ken Scott: Producers

Mike Moran: Engineer

The sessions included 'Aladdin Sane', 'The Prettiest Star', 'Drive-In Saturday' and 'All The Young Dudes', with Bowie playing saxophone.

Mike Garson (2006)

On the first run through of 'Aladdin Sane' I played a blues solo and David said he wasn't looking for that sound, so he asked me to play a Latin solo, then he told me, "That's good, but I'm looking for that wild avant-garde music you were playing on the New York jazz scene in the Sixties," so I played that style and we recorded that in just one take! [191]

Bowie (1991)

You wouldn't think of bringing a fringe avant-garde pianist into the context of a straight-ahead rock'n'roll band, but it worked out well. It brought some really interesting textural qualities to the album that wouldn't have had quite the same feel on it if Mike hadn't been there. [153]

▮ 'All The Young Dudes' released on *Rarest One Bowie* (Golden Years 1995)/ *Best Of 1969/1974* (EMI 1997)/ *Aladdin Sane* 30th Anniversary 2 CD Edition (EMI 2003).

SUNDAY 10 DECEMBER

▼ SOCIALISING

After a day at the studio, Bowie met up with Ian Hunter for dinner at the Stage Deli. Bowie played him some of the new recordings, including 'All The Young Dudes', which Hunter felt was inferior to Mott's version.

As they compared notes, Bowie gave Hunter some telling advice – a band could not be run as a democracy. The statement reflected Bowie's growing feeling that the Spiders had run their course. The undervaluing of Bolder and Woodmansey was further encouraged by Defries, even as Bowie and the Spiders stood on the cusp of success.

MONDAY 11 DECEMBER

✪ PRESS CONFERENCE

RCA Studio 3
155 East 24th Street
New York City
New York, USA

WEDNESDAY 13 DECEMBER

✪ PROMO VIDEO FILMING

RCA Studio 3
155 East 24th Street
New York City
New York, USA

'Space Oddity'

Mick Rock: Director

RCA commissioned Mick Rock to make a film clip for the single. Rock and Bowie came up with the economical idea of using the studio control room as a metaphor for the space capsule – Major Tom still alone, wearily strumming an acoustic guitar.

ABOVE: Bowie and Ronson at the press conference: "America is the loneliest place in the world. I found a general insecurity and need for warmth. There are very few people who actually consider themselves Americans. It's very sad."

Bowie (2002)
I really hadn't much clue why we were doing this, as I had moved on in my mind from the song… I know I was disinterested in the proceedings and it shows in my performance. [037]

► **TRAVELLING**
After five hours of filming, Bowie prepared for the journey home to England. After Mick Rock saw him off at the dockside, Bowie boarded RHMS *Ellinis* for the week-long Atlantic crossing, during which he was inspired to write the lyrics for the song 'Aladdin Sane'.

Mick Rock (2002)
The next day I went back to film the oscilloscope and other studio equipment. I viewed the studio as Major Tom's 'tin can'. [037]

▮Released: *The Video Collection* (PMI 1993)/*Best Of Bowie* DVD (EMI 2002).

THURSDAY 21 DECEMBER
Bowie was welcomed home as a conquering hero, thanks in part to Charles Shaar Murray's reviews filed from America earlier in the month. Full-page ads in the music weeklies announcing "Bowie's Back!" had listed UK tour dates, several of which were already sold out.

SATURDAY 23 DECEMBER
★ LIVE
Rainbow Theatre
Finsbury Park
North London, England

Charles Shaar Murray's *NME* article 'Rainbowie' announced Bowie's first homecoming show, which was added after the Christmas Eve concert had sold out. Bowie, wrote Murray, "is virtually unassailable". Supporting on the British dates was Stealers Wheel.

SUNDAY 24 DECEMBER
★ LIVE
Rainbow Theatre
Finsbury Park
North London, England

Charles Shaar Murray's review of the concert noted the beginnings of Ziggymania, with "young girls reaching out for our hero's supple limbs and squealing in the customary manner". The show was slightly truncated, dropping the acoustic set and Lou Reed songs. Of the new songs, only 'The Jean Genie' made the cut. "That American tour has really honed the Spiders to perfection – the show is tougher, flashier and more manic than it's ever been before." Presciently Murray added, "Maybe it's time for Ziggy to retire and for David to usher in the next phase."

THURSDAY 28 DECEMBER
★ LIVE
Hardrock Concert Theatre
Stretford
Manchester
Lancashire, England

Also supporting in Manchester was Fumble, a Fifties revivalist band who had caught Bowie's attention with their album cover and included Sean Mayes, who later played on Bowie's 1978 tour and *Lodger*.

In the audience at the Hardrock was another with whom Bowie would share a stage – Steven Morrissey, 13 at the time and obsessed with Marc Bolan and The New York Dolls.

ABOVE: Morrissey, whose live cover of 'Drive-In Saturday' was released as a B-side in 2008.

Steven Morrissey (2012)
I would be there at noon, and I would be pressed against the door 12 hours before anybody was ever going to think about opening. And I would race to the stage, and an industrial crane couldn't move me from that spot. You would have to blowtorch me off the front of the set if you wanted to move me. I was there, wanting some form of evidence, commitment. Wanting the world to change. Someone to do it for me. That's what I saw. And so that's what I wanted to provide. [230]

As Bowie was leaving the venue, Morrissey wrapped up a two-pence coin in a piece of paper with his phone number written on it and pushed it through the window of Bowie's Daimler.

In 1995 post-Smiths Morrissey was opening for the European leg of Bowie's *Outside* tour. After two weeks Morrissey left the tour following a dispute, but in 2006 he told David Fricke that the Manchester show was "full of wonderment for me… Bowie was going where nobody else had gone before with the music and the visuals. He was extraordinary." [426]

FRIDAY 29 DECEMBER
★ LIVE
Hardrock Concert Theatre
Stretford
Manchester
Lancashire, England

A second night was added due to huge public demand, capping a year of almost relentless touring and recording.

"Bowie was going where nobody else had gone before with the music and the visuals. He was extraordinary."

Morrissey

1973

JANUARY

■ **SINGLE RELEASED**
'Space Oddity' (5:05)/
'The Man Who Sold The World' (3:53)
US (RCA 74-0876)
Chart Peak No.15

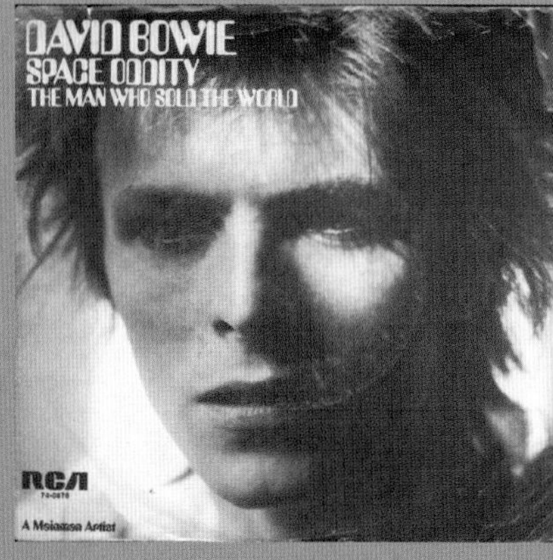

TOP RIGHT: Bowie's first gold record from RCA, for 100,000 sales of *Ziggy Stardust* in the UK, presented to him at BBC Television Centre.
ABOVE: US 'Space Oddity' single.
OPPOSITE AND OVERLEAF: Live at Newcastle City Hall. Ian Dickson got around the Defries ban on unauthorised photography by posing as an usher and concealing his camera and 105mm lens under his jacket.

WEDNESDAY 3

✪ **TELEVISION**
'TOP OF THE POPS'
BBC Television Centre
Studio TC8
London, England

'The Jean Genie'

In the middle of their sell-out UK mini tour, Bowie and the Spiders iced the cake with a live performance of 'The Jean Genie' on *Top Of The Pops*. Bowie played maracas and harmonica while Ronson cranked up the volume, deafening the television engineers.

They recorded three takes, the last of which was chosen for broadcast the following evening, despite the band missing their cue on the final section. Among the dancers visible by the stage were Daniella Parmar and her flatmate Wendy Kirby. Bowie had asked them and Freddie Burretti to come along as he was feeling nervous about the show.

Wendy Kirby (2011)
He comes across as very confident, but he was always very shy and didn't really want to go on* Top Of The Pops. *Angie was the one with all the energy. [416]

Kirby, Parmar and Burretti had frequented the Sombrero club where Bowie met them in 1971 and he acknowledged their influence in 'All The Young Dudes': "Wendy's stealing clothes from Marks & Sparks, and Freddie's got spots from ripping off the stars from his face."

Wendy Kirby (2011)
We were the 'young dudes' who shaved off our eyebrows just for camp, because you could paint them on higher up – that gave us a strange unearthly look which David adopted. He was always open to suggestions and went through our wardrobes like a magpie! [416]

Bowie (2002)
Daniella Parmar was the first girl I had seen with peroxide white hair with cartoon images cut and dyed into the back. [037]

Downstairs in the BBC canteen the futuristically dressed Spiders were asked what parts they were playing in *Doctor Who*, which was being filmed in another studio.

Backstage RCA presented Bowie with his first gold record for *Ziggy Stardust*, which had sold over 100,000 copies in the UK.

▮Broadcast: January 4 (BBC 1).

After the broadcast the BBC taped over the performance. It was assumed to be lost forever until John Henshall, a cameraman on the show, revealed in 2011 that he had a broadcast quality 2-inch tape copy.

Shortly after the taping Henshall had asked *TOTP* producer Johnnie Stewart for a personal copy to include in his company's show reel. At the time Henshall ran a company called Telefex, which specialised in visual effects including the fisheye effect he used on the 'The Jean Genie'. The tape was digitised in December 2011 and premiered at Missing Believed Wiped at BFI Southbank, before being included in BBC 2's *Top Of The Pops* December special.

✪ **RADIO**
BBC RADIO 1
'SCENE AND HEARD'
Interviewed backstage by Nicky Horne.

▮Broadcast: January 6.

FRIDAY 5 JANUARY

★ **LIVE**
Green's Playhouse
Glasgow, Scotland

2 SHOWS

SATURDAY 6 JANUARY

★ **LIVE**
Empire Theatre
Edinburgh, Scotland

SUNDAY 7 JANUARY

★ **LIVE**
Newcastle City Hall
Newcastle upon Tyne
Northumberland, England

MONDAY 8 JANUARY

▼ **SOCIALISING**
Bowie spent his birthday with the Spiders and Stuart George at RCA's Washington pressing plant in County Durham. The publicity stunt included a tour of the production line and a birthday cake.

TUESDAY 9 JANUARY

★ **LIVE**
Preston Guild Hall
Preston
Lancashire, England

ABOVE AND OPPOSITE: Duffy's (opposite top) contact sheets reveal the variations that were considered for the *Aladdin Sane* cover – such as including the rest of the Spiders (opposite bottom) – before the sleeve design was finalised.

✪ PHOTO SESSION
Kitchen Tool Shop
Swiss Cottage
Camden
London, England

'ALADDIN SANE' ALBUM COVER

Brian Duffy: Photographer
Brian Duffy/Celia Philo: Designers

With *Aladdin Sane* sessions nearing completion, Bowie worked on concepts for the cover. Defries approached Brian Duffy, whom he knew in the Sixties when he represented The Association of Fashion & Advertising Photographers.

Along with David Bailey and Terence Donovan, Duffy invented a new documentary style of fashion photography, producing a body of work that challenged conventions of portraits, reportage and advertising – he was one of the few photographers to have shot two Pirelli calendars, including the one in 1973.

At his north London studio, Duffy introduced Bowie to Celia Philo, his design partner in the Kitchen Tool Shop, and Elizabeth Arden make-up artist Pierre Laroche.

Bowie later described his concept for the Aladdin Sane character as "a lightning bolt. An electric kind of thing. Instead of, like, the flame of a lamp, I thought he would probably be cracked by lightning. Sort of an obvious-type thing, as he was sort of an electric boy." [184]

In 2009 Duffy recalled, "Bowie was interested in the Elvis ring which had the letters TCB [Taking Care of Business] as well as a lightning flash." [262]

Duffy noticed that the National logo on the rice cooker in the studio bore a similar but shorter device, which he drew onto Bowie's face. Laroche then filled in the blue and red with lipstick and applied a purple 'death mask' wash to Bowie's face.

Illustrator Philip Castle, known for his *Clockwork Orange* poster and soundtrack cover, later airbrushed the teardrop to Bowie's collarbone, adding to the aura of stillness. Duffy wanted to make him look like "a statue that's wet".

Castle had also worked with Duffy and Allen Jones on the Pirelli calendar, which they revisited for the inside gatefold. Castle applied a silver airbrush to Duffy's photo, completing the statuesque androgynous image.

Following the success of *Ziggy Stardust* and 'The Jean Genie', Defries was in a position to commission a lavish sleeve for the new album, reasoning that RCA would give it more promotional support, which would justify the expense.

Brian Duffy (2010)

Tony realised that in order to get the record company really going, you had to get them up to their neck in debt, which was of course a masterstroke. He wanted to make the most expensive cover he possibly could get a record company to pay for, because he realised that if it cost five thousand pounds, "so what, one way or the other." If it cost five thousand pounds, the record company were now having to pay attention.

Tony said, "Can you make it expensive?" No problem. One: dye transfer, a genius method of being able to spend the most amount of money to get a reproduction from a colour transparency onto a piece of paper. Two: get the plate made in Switzerland – the most expensive place in the world to get plates made. Then to employ me to design it and create it – even better, more wasteful. Then we went to Conway's who were the most expensive typographical house – more money. [358]

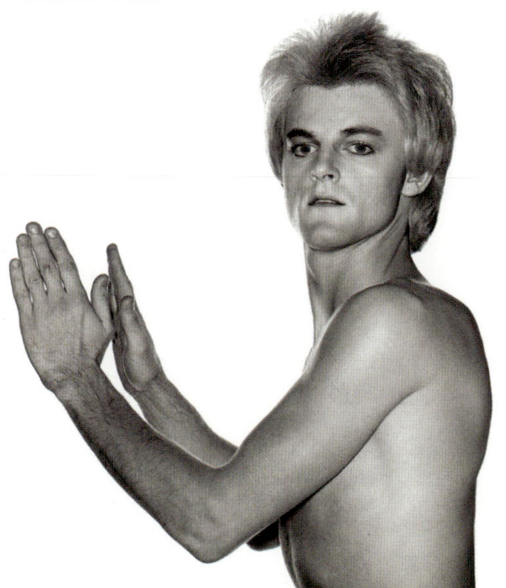

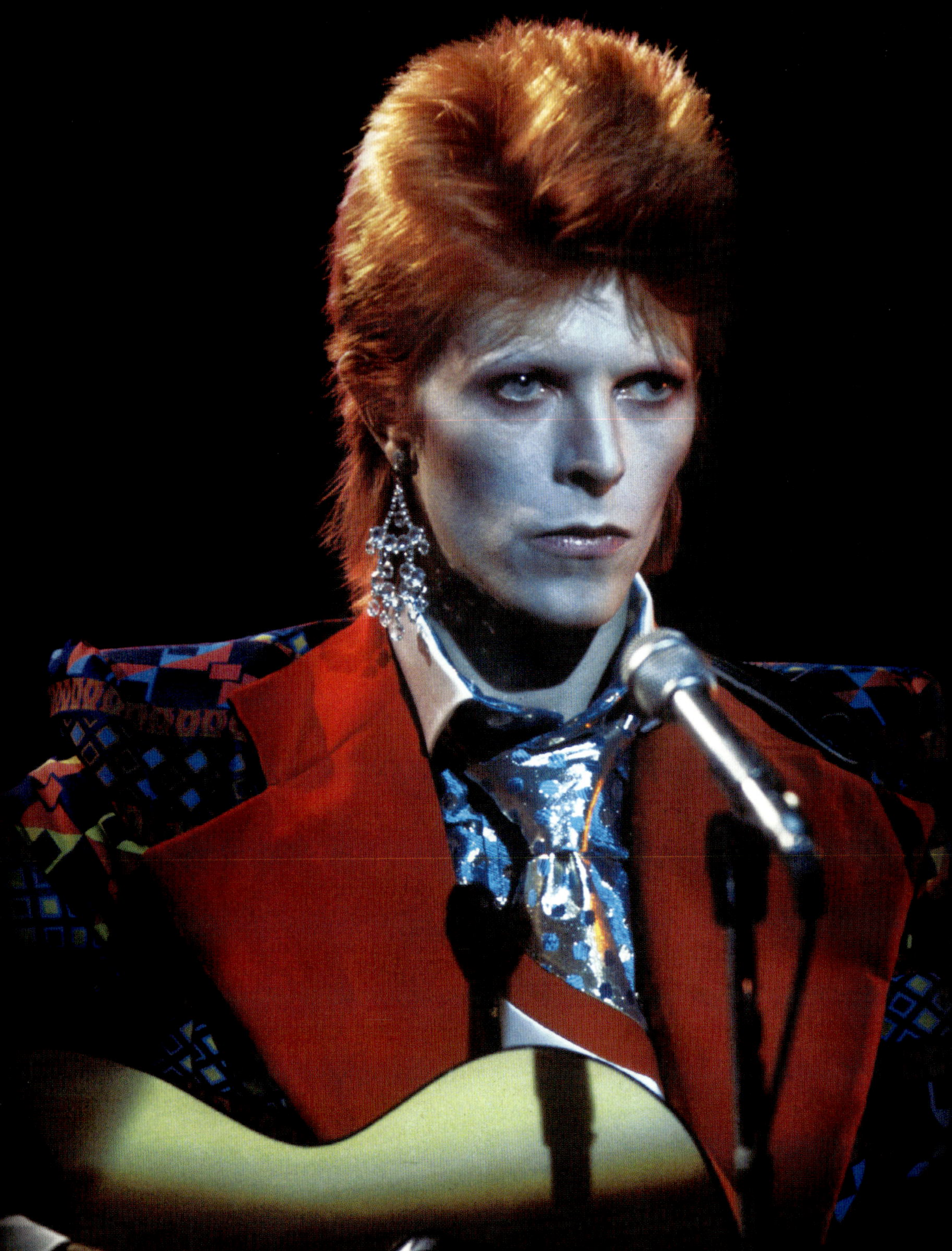

WEDNESDAY 17 JANUARY

✪ TELEVISION

'RUSSELL HARTY PLUS POP'
LWT (London Weekend Television)
Studio 3
South Bank Television Centre
London, England

'Drive-In Saturday'/ interview/ 'My Death'

Nick Barrett: Producer
Mike Mansfield: Director

Bowie appeared on Russell Harty's chat show to perform his new single, promote the new album and satisfy the curiosity of mainstream Britain, answering Harty's direct questions about his sexuality and religious beliefs with candour.

Charles Shaar Murray reported from the studio for the tech run-through prior to the taping: "There's a stir over at the corner of the studio as Bowie and his entourage enter at the side. David is looking more than somewhat bizarre in a green quilted tuxedo and yellow trousers, waistcoat and boots. His eyebrows have vanished, replaced by finely sketched red lines. He's wearing red eye shadow, which makes him look faintly insect-like. He's thinner than ever. With him Trevor Bolder, with sideboards yet un-silvered, looking faintly bemused; Mick Ronson with his second best Les Paul and striped satin jacket; and Woody Woodmansey in a city gent outfit that contrasts oddly with his extravagantly deranged blond coiffure." [216]

The Spiders rehearsed 'Drive-In Saturday', miming to a backing tape, and Bowie practised his move to where he would sit with Harty in matching armchairs. The crew put away the amps and drums and set up the dual mic and a stool, on which Bowie rehearsed his solo number 'My Death', which Murray described as 'riveting': "Even the technicians have stopped fussing around with the lights, carrying ladders and muttering into their headsets. As Bowie approaches the last section, one of his guitar strings gives way under the strain and hangs away from the neck, one razor thin silver streak under the lights. He cracks up the entire studio by announcing the calamity in the song, and then finishing perfectly." [216]

Backstage Sue Fussey, Pierre Laroche and Fred of East End (Freddie Burretti's trading name) then prepared Bowie's hair, make-up and clothes for the taping.

"He vanishes to reappear moments later in full splendour in a more than somewhat mind-snapping outfit which he is to describe as 'a parody of a suit and tie'. A solitary ornate earring dangles from one ear." [216]

▮ Broadcast: January 20
LWT (London Weekend Television).

'Drive-In Saturday' released on *The Video Collection* (PMI 1993).

'Drive-In Saturday' and interview released on *Best Of Bowie* (EMI 2002).

ABOVE: Technical rehearsal before the taping.
OPPOSITE: Bowie plays Brel's harrowing 'My Death' on *Russell Harty Plus Pop* following a candid interview with Harty.

FRIDAY 19 – WEDNESDAY 24 JANUARY

▲ **RECORDING**
Trident Studios
17 St Anne's Court, Soho
London, England

'ALADDIN SANE' ALBUM
'Cracked Actor'
'1984' (early version)
'John, I'm Only Dancing'
(saxophone version)
'Lady Grinning Soul'
'Let's Spend The Night Together'
'Time'
'Panic In Detroit'

David Bowie/Ken Scott: Producers

On the Saturday of the final sessions at Trident, Charles Shaar Murray watched the progress of the new tracks:

"The door swings open and the entrant is nearly knocked off his teenage feet by a blast furnace rendition of 'John, I'm Only Dancing' clawing its way out of the jumbo-sized speakers. The new cut of 'John' has a murderously high energy level, which by comparison makes the single version sound like one man with a three-stringed acoustic. It virtually blisters the ears to make it even more obvious that the Spiders are one of our best bands. All but two cuts from the new album were finished by Saturday – and that particular brace of tunes lacked only vocals. The excellent reason was that Bowie had not yet written the lyrics." [216]

Pianist Matthew Fisher observed Bowie directing the brass players 'Bux' Wilshaw and Ken Fordham.

Matthew Fisher (2009)

He issues very strange instructions to people – not in the prosaic way I would do it. He was talking to the brass players using terms like "renaissance" and "impressionist" – it was very esoteric, but people seemed to understand. [045]

Mike Garson (1986)

'Time' was an almost swing or Dixieland style, and he liked my concept on that because it had to do with time, and I was playing in another time zone and he was talking about time. [013]

Ken Scott (1986)

We wanted to make it that much rougher. Ziggy was rock'n'roll but polished rock'n'roll. David wanted certain tracks to go like The Rolling Stones – unpolished rock'n'roll. [013]

Bowie (1991)

The idea was to fuck the sound up. On 'Let's Spend The Night Together' the wobbly noise in the break was an ARP 2600, and it had patch wires, but by the time I went onstage they'd already brought out the Minimoog, and that's what we adopted for live work; it was much more convenient to cart around the country. [153]

Mike Garson (2003)

'Lady Grinning Soul' brought out the romantic playing in me that comes from composers like Franz Liszt and Chopin. I mixed this with elements of Liberace and Rodger Williams, which were styles of music that were always put down because they were so mainstream. I played in a very un-dissonant way here, where 'Aladdin Sane' is about as dissonant as you can get. [325]

Bowie has said that 'Lady Grinning Soul' was about "someone I met, that I found enchanting. It was a London song." In 2014 Claudia Lennear revealed that she was the inspiration for the song, confirming what was long rumoured. Bowie told her after the Academy Awards, "You are my Lady Grinning Soul."

They had first met in Detroit in 1972 and reconnected when she was passing through London. Bowie had asked her to join the US tour in New York to sing the Juanita Franklin and Linda Lewis vocal parts. This was announced in the music press, but the idea was dropped in favour of having musicians doubling up on backing vocals.

For this Bowie turned to his childhood friend Geoff MacCormack, who had worked sporadically in music, at one stage singing jingles for radio DJ Emperor Rosko's show, and was now selling advertising space for *Construction News*.

LEFT AND OPPOSITE: A Richard Imre photo session showcases new stage outfits for the 1973 *Aladdin Sane* tour.

Geoff MacCormack (2008)

David lived in the same hometown as my mother did, so we kept in touch. My girlfriend at the time worked in a fashion store in London. The little jackets that David and his band wore, the little tight-fitting nylon zip-up jackets, they actually came from the shop. So one day, at my office, a phone call came in from David. He simply said, "You're coming to America." [280]

MacCormack also contributed back-up vocals on 'Panic In Detroit' – one of the last tracks completed – and played congas after Woodmansey refused to play a Bo Diddley rhythm, saying it was "too obvious".

John 'Hutch' Hutchinson, who in 1969 had played with Bowie in Feathers and had since moved back to Scarborough, read an article in *Melody Maker* where Bowie mentioned he was looking for a guitarist for the US tour. Hutchinson asked John Cambridge for Bowie's address and wrote to Haddon Hall.

John Hutchinson (2004)

Mick Ronson and David phoned me at work and said, "We're going to New York next week. Can you come?" My role was to play 12-string because David had previously played 12-string with The Spiders From Mars but he wanted more freedom to move around the stage. And the idea was that he'd get someone to play guitar who could also do backing vocals. I think there was a bit of a budget cut so we didn't get backing vocalists.

So Geoff MacCormack and I practised our falsettos and we did the girly vocals instead. [368]

After the losses incurred on the previous US tour, RCA and Defries agreed to restructure the next tour, playing more shows in fewer, larger cities. RCA would pay the hotel bills but MainMan would cover the rest of the expenses. Defries trimmed the entourage down to the essentials: the band, road crew and Bowie's retinue – Sue Fussey (wardrobe/hairdresser/PA), travelling companion Geoff MacCormack, Pierre Laroche (make-up) and bodyguards.

THURSDAY 25 JANUARY

▶ TRAVELLING
SOUTHAMPTON – NEW YORK
SS *Canberra*

Defries took advantage of a cheap berth for Bowie and MacCormack on the *SS Canberra*. The crew had changed their schedule and needed to get the liner back to New York in a hurry. To defray expenses, P&O offered a discount for passengers with carry-on luggage.

Mick Rock went to see Bowie and MacCormack off from Southampton and photographed them in their cabin.

Geoff MacCormack (2009)
Since we were such old pals, he decided I should keep him company when he sailed to America, instead of taking a plane with the band. Most passengers were well-to-do, semi-retired or retired old folks, so we stood out like a sore thumb. As the brass band played while we were leaving the quay, I remember being mildly concerned that the ship's officers might not take to us too kindly. [054]

SATURDAY 27 JANUARY

◆ AWARDS
'NEW MUSICAL EXPRESS' READERS' POP POLL

Male Rock Singer #3
Album *Ziggy Stardust* #3

■ CHART
'Space Oddity'
US Billboard Hot 100
Chart Entry No.71

TUESDAY 30 JANUARY

▶ TRAVELLING
Bowie and MacCormack arrived in New York and were taken to The Gramercy Park Hotel in Lexington Avenue, instead of the more expensive Plaza used on the previous visit. Defries had written to Gustl Breuer concerning the 1973 tour: "We would like to stay in good hotels but do not require the most luxurious."

RIGHT: RCA Studio A in New York was Bowie's base for rehearsals, promotion and photo sessions with Masayoshi Sukita.

WEDNESDAY 31 JANUARY

At Trident Studios, Ken Scott put together an *Aladdin Sane* master tape comprising 11 tracks, ending with the new 'sax' version of 'John, I'm Only Dancing'.

FEBRUARY

■ SINGLE RELEASED
LOU REED
'Walk On The Wild Side' (Reed) (3:37)/
'Perfect Day' (Reed) (3:42)
US (RCA 74-0887)
Chart Peak No.16

Like the BBC, US censors missed the reference to "giving head", but they replaced "the coloured girls" with "all the girls" and Lou Reed had his first US hit.

Holly Woodlawn (2008)
One day a friend called me and said, "Turn on the radio!" They were playing 'Walk On The Wild Side'. The funny thing is that, while I knew The Velvet Underground's music, I'd never met Lou Reed. I called him up and said, "How do you know this stuff about me?" He said, "Holly, you have the biggest mouth in town." [284]

SATURDAY 3

A full-page colour ad in *Billboard* advertised the 'Space Oddity' single rising in the US charts.

SUNDAY 4 – TUESDAY 13 FEBRUARY

▲ REHEARSING
RCA Studio A
155 East 24th Street
New York City
New York, USA

Rehearsals for the tour were held in the large cinema-like studio RCA used for recording soundtracks.

✪ PRESS
Cherry Vanilla interviewed Bowie at the studio as part of the tour publicity.

John Hutchinson (2012)
The rehearsals were very easy going. The sax players were good readers and Mike Garson is brilliant. Mick Ronson had written chord sheets and we were to use old-fashioned big-band-style music stands throughout the world tour. The result of that was that I couldn't have played without the sheets – that way you never learn the songs, never commit them to memory.

John Hutchinson (1985)
We were supposed to be in New York in secret for the first week while we were rehearsing for the tour, but the word soon got around so there was plenty of attendance at the hotel after a few days. [009]

Masayoshi Sukita (2011)
A few days before the show at Radio City Music Hall, Bowie did a photo session, a rehearsal and an interview at RCA Studios. Yasuko Takahashi was working as the stylist, running here and there with costumes by Kansai Yamamoto that she'd brought over from Japan. They looked marvellous. [042]

Yasuko 'Yacco' Takahashi contacted Kansai in Japan, advising him to come to New York to meet Bowie.

SUNDAY 4 FEBRUARY

▼ SOCIALISING
Bowie and Hutchinson headed downtown with MacCormack and Stuart George to see their old favourite Charles Mingus perform at The Village Gate.

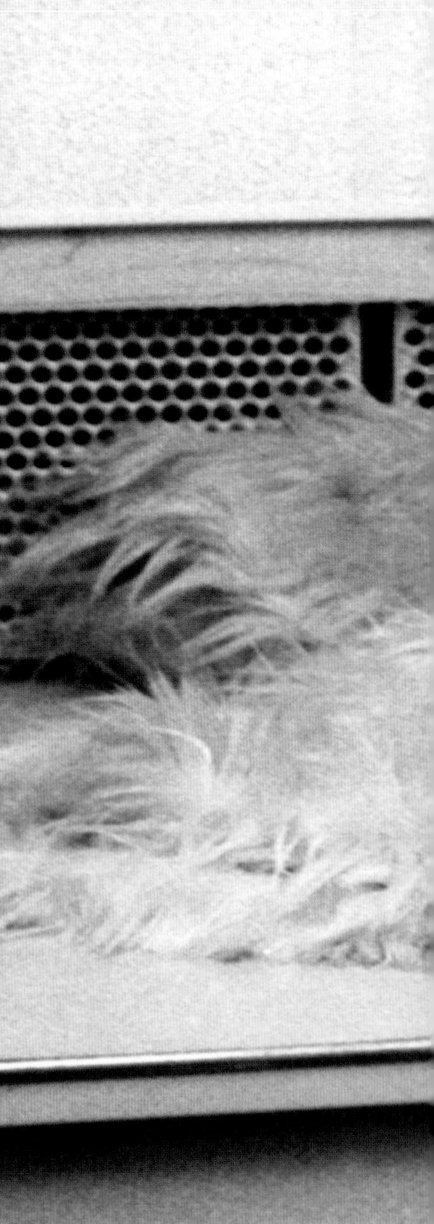

MONDAY 5 FEBRUARY

▼SOCIALISING

The group spent several evenings that week at Max's Kansas City.

Geoff MacCormack (2009)

It was the coolest place in New York. On any given night you'd usually find a Jagger, Lennon or Lou Reed, as well as a couple of film stars. David dragged me down there to see Biff Rose. But, to be honest, his set wasn't my cup of tea and I think David was a bit underwhelmed.

Then another guy came on and sat down at the same piano and began playing something equally gloomy. We'd have left there and then if we hadn't had beers to finish. Just at the point where it was all getting too much, he strapped on a Fender Telecaster and the band struck up an anthem called 'Does This Bus Stop At 82nd Street?' That was the first time David and I saw Bruce Springsteen. [054]

Bowie (1998)

The moment they kicked in he was another performer. All the Dylanesque stuff dropped off him and he rocked. I became a major fan that night and picked up* Asbury Park *immediately. [231]

Bowie was so impressed by *Greetings From Asbury Park NJ*, he recorded three of the songs – 'Growin' Up', 'Spirit In The Night' and 'It's Hard To Be A Saint In The City' – later that year.

WEDNESDAY 7 FEBRUARY

▼SOCIALISING

Stevie Wonder performed at Carnegie Hall supported by The Main Ingredient, which featured future Bowie collaborators Carlos Alomar and Emir Ksasan. Following his concert, Motown threw him a party at Genesis discotheque. Bowie and MacCormack went along to meet Wonder and watched R&B legends Aretha Franklin and Gladys Knight put on an impromptu show, but it was the striking young Afro-American girl on back-up who had Bowie's attention.

Ava Cherry had arrived in New York from Chicago, hoping to make it as a model and worked as a cocktail waitress in between modelling jobs, but her passion was soul music. Her manager brought her to the party hoping to advance either career.

ABOVE: Stevie Wonder's party at Genesis nightclub, where Bowie met Ava Cherry. OPPOSITE: Bowie at Radio City Music Hall, New York.

Introductions were made and Bowie asked her if she was a singer. She told him that she was and that she loved his records. The attraction was mutual and over the next few days they became lovers. Cherry was shocked to find he was married, and more so by Angie's apparent acceptance of the situation.

Ava Cherry (1986)

I was freaked out. I didn't want to give anyone the impression that I was in the habit of going out with married men, but David said, "She does what she wants to do and I do what I want to do." [013]

Bowie asked her to join the US tour later in the year. Following an informal audition for Defries she packed up her New York life and returned to Chicago to wait for the call.

THURSDAY 8 FEBRUARY

⊙BUSINESS

A second show at Radio City Music Hall was added, announced by a full-page ad in *The Village Voice*: "SOLD OUT so he will do it there again."

MONDAY 12 FEBRUARY

▼SOCIALISING

Bowie and Angie spent the evening at Max's Kansas City, where they spotted Todd Rundgren and his girlfriend Bebe Buell and introduced themselves.

Bebe Buell (1997)

I told him, "I'm Bebe Buell and this is my boyfriend Todd Rundgren." He looked at Todd and said, "I've heard of you, you're supposed to be pretty fucking smart." Todd said, "Yes I am, and I hear you're supposed to be ripping me off." David looked at him like he was out of his mind. [023]

Bowie told Buell that Angie was returning to London the following day and asked her to show him around New York.

TUESDAY 13 FEBRUARY

▼SOCIALISING

Bowie called Bebe Buell in the morning and they spent the day together shopping for clothes, finishing up at Nirvana, a penthouse Indian restaurant near Central Park. Then they met up with Hutchinson and Defries at Radio City Music Hall to watch a show by New York dance troupe The Rockettes. Inspired by the sight of one of the dancers descending to the stage on a silver gyroscope, Bowie requested that it be incorporated into his concert there the next night.

▲REHEARSING

Following the show the tour band reconvened for a final rehearsal ahead of the first concert of the US tour. Sue Fussey had to pull apart and re-stitch the Spiders' stage costumes, which had arrived from England, as none of them fitted.

While Bowie was enjoying the high life in New York, trouble was brewing in the ranks concerning salaries. In a casual conversation, Mike Garson had revealed he was on £500 a week and was shocked to find the Spiders were still being paid the same meagre pay of £50 they had started on.

Trevor Bolder (2007)

We thought, hang on, what's going on here? So we saw Defries before the Valentine's Day gig at Radio City Music Hall and demanded a rise or we were going home on the next plane. Bowie took offence, said that we were disloyal and that we owed him everything, although we could barely live on our wages. [057]

Mick Ronson sought advice from Dennis Katz, who had left RCA to practise entertainment law. Katz told the Spiders that they were contractually obliged to complete the tour, but he agreed to help them set up a separate deal with CBS.

Trevor Bolder (2012)

Defries found out about it and he told us not to go with CBS, that RCA would put the money up for us to do an album with them and give us the same deal. And we agreed. But in the meantime he got Ronson to the side and said, "You don't need those two. You can do a solo album instead." So he could keep control of Ronson, as well as the whole situation. So he broke it all up to keep control of it. Which is stupid, really. But that's what money does. [411]

WEDNESDAY 14 FEBRUARY

US TOUR II

David Bowie: Vocals/Guitar/Minimoog/Percussion
Mick Ronson: Musical Director/Lead Guitar/Vocals
Trevor Bolder: Bass Guitar/Vocals
Mick Woodmansey: Drums
Mike Garson: Piano/Mellotron
John Hutchinson: Rhythm Guitar/12-String Acoustic Guitar
Geoff MacCormack: Percussion/Vocals
Ken Fordham: Tenor/Baritone/Alto Saxophone
Brian Wilshaw: Tenor Saxophone/Flute
Robin Mayhew: Sound Engineer
Peter Hunsley: Stage Manager
Mick Hince/Willie Palin: Equipment Managers
Stuart George: David Bowie's Personal Security
Sue Fussey: Wardrobe Mistress/ Hairstylist
Bob See: Lighting Director
Ron Meadows/Stephen Hurston: Lighting Operators
Jaime Andrews: Road Manager
Tony Zanetta (MainMan): Tour Co-ordinator
Barry Bethell (RCA): Tour Manager
Martin Pierpoint (RCA): Assistant Tour Manager

★ LIVE

Radio City Music Hall
New York City
New York, USA

An A-list audience, including Salvador Dali and Bette Midler, turned out to see the elaborately staged first show of the second US tour. The packed house watched Bowie's dramatic 'descent from the gods' on the gyroscope as Walter Carlos' 'Beethoven's Ninth' boomed through the speakers. From the opening song the pace never let up throughout the first set. After a break they reappeared with another theatrical flourish.

John Hutchinson (2004)
Our entrance was up from the floor, on a stage riser. It was steam curtains behind us… and that was just a taste for the next few months. [368]

Mike Garson (2002)
It was the ultimate in drama because the encore number was 'Rock'n'Roll Suicide' and after the song ended he fell on the floor. He definitely went unconscious for a while and then the doctors, nurses came in and he was fine but… it was scary. [370]

Bowie (1973)
I just fainted; but I'm always fainting. I always manage to faint at the right time, though. [125]

After the show Bowie was introduced to the designer Kansai Yamamoto, who on Yacco's advice had dropped everything to fly to New York to be at the concert. Backstage he presented Bowie with five new outfits as a gift, which became the basis of the Aladdin Sane wardrobe.

Bowie (2000)
He presented me with virtually an entire wardrobe because he knew I was wearing copies of his stuff and he realised Ziggy was becoming very popular. It was the first real connection between a designer and a rock star. [030]

▮ Recorded by RCA.

ABOVE: Angie Bowie, Cyrinda Foxe and Kansai Yamamoto in the front row at Radio City Music Hall. OPPOSITE: Bowie wows New York glitterati at Radio City Music Hall.

THURSDAY 15 FEBRUARY

✪ PRESS CONFERENCE

Gramercy Park Hotel
New York City
New York, USA

Defries explained Bowie's faint to Michael Watts as "just a lack of eating and sleeping".

Bowie slept for 12 hours recuperating at the hotel, where Watts visited him in the afternoon. When Bowie played him a tape of *Aladdin Sane*, Watts remarked that it sounded more remote than previous albums and lacked the warmth of *Hunky Dory*. Bowie agreed: "God, I listen to that album and think how happy I must have been." [305]

★ LIVE

Radio City Music Hall
New York City
New York, USA

▌Recorded by RCA.

FRIDAY 16 FEBRUARY

★ LIVE

Tower Theatre
Philadelphia
Pennsylvania, USA

SATURDAY 17 FEBRUARY

★ LIVE

Tower Theatre
Philadelphia
Pennsylvania, USA

2 SHOWS

SUNDAY 18 FEBRUARY

✪ TELEVISION

'THE MIKE DOUGLAS SHOW'
Studio A
KYW-TV Studios
Philadelphia
Pennsylvania, USA

▌Broadcast: February 19 (CBS).

★ LIVE

Tower Theatre
Philadelphia
Pennsylvania, USA

2 SHOWS

MONDAY 19 FEBRUARY

★ LIVE

Tower Theatre
Philadelphia
Pennsylvania, USA

2 SHOWS

FRIDAY 23 FEBRUARY

★ LIVE

War Memorial Auditorium
Nashville
Tennessee, USA

SATURDAY 24 FEBRUARY

✪ PRESS

'Gay Guerrillas & Private Movies' by Charles Shaar Murray published in *NME* and 'Stranger In A Strange Land' by Michael Watts published in *Melody Maker*. Bowie used both interviews to announce that he would be making, starring in and writing the music for a film of Robert Heinlein's *Stranger In A Strange Land*. The nonexistent project was part of Defries' plan to legitimise Bowie as an entertainer in America. He reasoned that if Bowie was seen to be moving into films, real film offers would follow.

SUNDAY 25 FEBRUARY

★ LIVE

Ellis Auditorium (North Hall)
Memphis
Tennessee, USA

2 SHOWS

MONDAY 26 FEBRUARY

▼ SOCIALISING

Dolph Smith, a teacher at the Memphis Academy of Art, was exhibiting a series of watercolours he had made based on the lyrics of 'Space Oddity'. He had heard an interview with Cherry Vanilla on FM100 and contacted her through the station. She visited the school and told Bowie that he should see the exhibition.

Bowie arrived at 9.45pm with Ronson, Woodmansey and Cherry Vanilla, who photographed the event. Smith and his son Tim presented Bowie with a watercolour entitled 'A Paper Airplane Having Just Spotted A Fallen Comrade'.

Dolph Smith (2008)

Bowie walked throughout the school. He quietly looked into the small metal department and a student was working on a piece. She apparently had not known about him being there and kind of freaked when she looked up. David must have looked at the piece and held it because she entitled it 'David Bowie Touched This Piece'. [403]

MARCH

THURSDAY 1

★ **LIVE**

Masonic Temple Auditorium
Detroit
Michigan, USA

✪ **PRESS**

Nick Kent was in Detroit when he found out Bowie was at the Hilton. An audience with Bowie was usually impossible but with Defries out of town on business, Kent managed to get a request through and reported on the night's gig: "His exhaustive touring is starting to point to a real performer somewhere under the uncertain, often awkward posing he's been forced to use in order to justify his presence on the stage… [the show] has changed drastically into a far more respectable professional effort."

Back at the Hilton, Stuart George led him to a private suite where Bowie was holding court. "Oh, so you're Nick Kent," said Bowie. "My, aren't you pretty. And I thought all English music writers looked like Richard Williams." [174]

FRIDAY 2 MARCH

■ **SINGLE RELEASED**

LOU REED
'Vicious' (Reed) (2:55)/
'Satellite Of Love' (Reed) (3:40)
UK (RCA 2318)

★ **LIVE**

Masonic Temple Auditorium
Detroit
Michigan, USA

SATURDAY 3 MARCH

✪ **PRESS**

NME confirmed reports that Bowie would be starring in a film adaptation of Robert Heinlein's *Stranger In A Strange Land* and writing the incidental music, but work would not begin for at least 18 months.

A spokesman said, "Suggestions that David is to give up touring to concentrate on an acting career are completely wrong. Obviously the film will interrupt his live work, but he will be on tour both before and after his movie commitment."

The Chicago Tribune listed a concert at Aragon Ballroom in Chicago on March 4, and RCA's tour ad listed March 5, but there is no evidence either took place.

ABOVE: Bowie and Stuart George (left). The train with Bowie and his entourage arrived at Union Station, Los Angeles and was greeted by a large contingent of fans, including Patty Clark (seen opposite page, left) from teen magazine *Star*. The June issue breathlessly reported: "The shiny doors of the metal beast swung open and Patty rushed up to a dazzling, zoot-suited Bowie, planting a Star smacker right on his smiling lips and handing him a bouquet of pink baby roses and a copy of *Star*. Winking at Patty, Bowie whispered something into her ear and I could see her blush." OPPOSITE BOTTOM: Bowie at the Hollywood Palladium.

FRIDAY 9 MARCH

▼ **SOCIALISING**

The queens of the Los Angeles groupie scene, Sable Starr and Lori Maddox, headed over to the Hilton to meet Bowie when they heard he was in town. Later Bowie picked them up from the Hyatt in his limo to take them to The Rainbow, the epicentre of rock music on Sunset Strip.

Bowie was dancing when a drunken patron yelled, "Fucking faggot!" Bowie ignored him so he lunged forward to throw a punch, but Stuart George was suddenly on him and bustled him outside.

SATURDAY 10 MARCH

★ **LIVE**

Long Beach Auditorium
Long Beach
California, USA

Mick Jagger came to see the Long Beach concert and dropped in backstage to meet Bowie for the first time.

MONDAY 12 MARCH

★ **LIVE**

Hollywood Palladium
Hollywood
California, USA

▼ **SOCIALISING**

After the concert Bowie hosted an end of tour party at Lost on Larrabee (an organic restaurant) attended by Ringo Starr and Klaus Voorman, among others.

TUESDAY 13 MARCH

▼ **SOCIALISING**

On a rare night off, Bowie took Claudia Lennear to see Bette Midler's show at the Music Centre in Long Beach, where Bowie got a standing ovation as they walked in.

The audience gave Midler the same at the end of her show, though Bowie declined to stand up until Midler glared at him. "The son of a bitch!" she joked to Nick Kent later. "Oh, he's a very sweet boy… I think he's very… um… talented. You know what I mean? In the nicest sense of the word… He's certainly very smart." [174]

MONDAY 19 MARCH

► **TRAVELLING**

Bowie and MacCormack boarded the SS *Oronsay* for the journey to Japan to continue the tour. Again the one-class liner was a far cry from the luxury he'd enjoyed on the *QE2*.

TUESDAY 20 MARCH

► **TRAVELLING**

Bowie and MacCormack arrived in San Francisco and, unhappy with the accommodation on the 'Old Rancid', decided to spend the night ashore at a club with Bette Midler.

WEDNESDAY 21 MARCH

► **TRAVELLING**

SAN FRANCISCO – VANCOUVER

FRIDAY 23 MARCH

✪ **PRESS**

In Vancouver, Bowie gave interviews on board and was given a guided tour of the city by local RCA reps.

WEDNESDAY 28 MARCH

▼ **SOCIALISING**

Bowie and MacCormack spent the day sightseeing in Honolulu before returning to the ship in the evening.

APRIL

■ **SINGLE RELEASED**
'John, I'm Only Dancing' (2:41)/
'Hang On To Yourself' (2:38)
UK (RCA 2263)

This version, later referred to as the 'saxophone version', replaced stocks of the original single version but retained the original catalogue number.

▮ Reissued on initial pressings of *Changes One Bowie* (RCA 1976)/ *Sound + Vision* (Ryko 1989)/ *Best Of 1969/1974* (EMI 1997)/ *Aladdin Sane* 30th Anniversary 2 CD Edition (EMI 2003).

■ **ALBUM RELEASED**
'ROCK'N'ROLL NOW'
PROMO COMPILATION
Japan (RCA SPLD-1052)

■ **ALBUM RELEASED**
'ALADDIN SANE'
ADVANCE PROMO
Japan (RCA 6100)

THURSDAY 5
► **TRAVELLING**
Masayoshi Sukita photographed Bowie and MacCormack as they sailed into Yokohama to a rapturous reception from fans and Japanese RCA reps bearing a huge welcome banner.

At the Imperial Hotel in Tokyo they were greeted by Kansai, who had designed nine new costumes to add to the five he had given Bowie in New York.

Bowie (1973)
They're based on the traditional Noh drama costumes. Some of the great Noh actors wear as many as 15, one on top of the other, so that they can peel them off layer by layer. [160]

Bowie quickly embraced Kansai as an important collaborator, who represented both the exoticism of the East as well as the cutting edge of haute couture. Defries too recognised his importance and proclaimed he would represent Kansai through MainMan Tokyo.

FRIDAY 6 APRIL
The rest of the band and entourage arrived in Tokyo and joined Bowie and MacCormack at the hotel.

✪ **PRESS CONFERENCE**
Imperial Hotel
Tokyo, Japan

■ **SINGLE RELEASED**
'Drive-In Saturday' (4:30)/
'Round And Round' (Berry) (2:39)
UK (RCA 2352)
Chart Peak No.3

The first release of 'Round And Round' recorded during the November 1971 *Ziggy Stardust* sessions.

SATURDAY 7 APRIL
▲ **REHEARSING**
RCA Nippon Victor Studios
Tokyo, Japan

SUNDAY 8 APRIL
★ **LIVE**
Shinjuku Koseinenkin Kaikan
Tokyo, Japan

Hysteria greeted Bowie's first Japanese show. The media reported him as a sensation and "possibly the most interesting performer ever in the pop music genre".

Bowie (1973)
We were faced with an audience that we presumed didn't understand a word of what I was saying. There I was more physical than on any other tour that I've ever done. Literally, I activated the whole thing with my hands and my body. I needn't have sung half the time. The Japanese are theatrical and far more aware than either England or America. [219]

TOP LEFT: Bowie and MacCormack aboard *SS Oronsay*, on arrival at Yokohama.
ABOVE LEFT: Press conference, Imperial Hotel.
LEFT: Shinjuku Koseinenkin Kaikan, Tokyo.
OPPOSITE: Bowie in Japan photographed by Leee Black Childers.

MONDAY 9 APRIL

▼SOCIALISING

Bowie and Angie spent the day attending a tea ceremony in the Imperial Gardens at the Emperor's Palace with Ronson. In the evening they saw a performance by kabuki star Tomasa Boru. After the show Boru showed Bowie the techniques of applying kabuki make-up, which Bowie would incorporate into the Aladdin Sane image.

TUESDAY 10 APRIL

★LIVE

Shinjuku Koseinenkin Kaikan
Tokyo, Japan

⊙BUSINESS

As Bowie revelled in the rapturous reception, Bolder and Woodmansey again confronted Defries as the pay rises he'd promised them had still not materialised. Defries dismissed them with the curt observation that the roadies were worth more to him. They stormed out in disgust and it was left to Ronson to talk them out of quitting the tour.

By this time Defries had reached a stand-off with RCA concerning the US arena tour planned for later in the year. RCA refused to underwrite another tour while Bowie's record sales in America remained unremarkable. Since Bowie was tiring of the Ziggy concept anyway, Defries and Bowie made the decision to 'retire' Ziggy – and, by extension, the act – at the end of the UK tour.

They would dispense with Bolder and Woodmansey, avoid the ignominy of a cancelled tour, buy some time to write new material and create demand. MainMan would then focus on Ronson's solo career, but in the meantime Ronson would have to keep this to himself, toe the line and keep the band on the rails long enough to finish the tour.

Sue Fussey/Ronson (2012)

It was decided in Japan. Mick was sworn to secrecy. "And if you do this for us, you're going to be the next star, you're going to be doing this next thing, but you can't tell the boys." [355]

Mick Ronson (1975)

The fucking Master Plan. I never believed in all that. It might have seemed great as an idea but those plans never work. [162]

WEDNESDAY 11 APRIL

★LIVE

Shinjuku Koseinenkin Kaikan
Tokyo, Japan

The last of the three sell-out shows in Tokyo.

When Bowie's travel itinerary for his return to England via the Trans-Siberian Railway was devised in March, Leee Black Childers had persuaded Defries to let him accompany Bowie and MacCormack, arguing there should be a photographic record of the trip. After problems obtaining the necessary travel visas, Childers caught up with the tour in Tokyo.

THURSDAY 12 APRIL

►TRAVELLING

TOKYO – NAGOYA
Shinkansen Bullet Train

★LIVE

Kokaido
Nagoya, Japan

ABOVE: Duffy's statuesque – and expensive – sleeve.
OPPOSITE: Aladdin Sane's take on the Pirelli calendar, seen in the gatefold.

FRIDAY 13 APRIL

ALBUM RELEASED

'ALADDIN SANE'

UK (RCA RS 1001)

Chart Entry No.1

SIDE ONE

1. **'Watch That Man'** (4:30)
2. **'Aladdin Sane (1913-1938-197?)'** (5:15)
3. **'Drive-In Saturday'** (4:38)
4. **'Panic In Detroit'** (4:30)
5. **'Cracked Actor'** (3:01)

SIDE TWO

1. **'Time'** (5:10)
2. **'The Prettiest Star'** (3:28)
3. **'Let's Spend The Night Together'** (3:10)
4. **'The Jean Genie'** (4:06)
5. **'Lady Grinning Soul'** (3:53)

All songs by David Bowie except 'Let's Spend The Night Together' (Jagger/Richards)

David Bowie/Ken Scott: Producers

David Bowie/Mick Ronson: Arrangers

Ken Scott/Mick Ronson: Mixers

Ken Scott/Mick Moran: Engineers

David Bowie: Vocals/Guitar/Harmonica/Keyboards/Saxophone

Mick Ronson: Guitar/Piano/Vocals

Trevor Bolder: Bass

Mick Woodmansey: Drums

Mike Garson: Piano

Ken Fordham: Tenor/Baritone/Alto Saxophone

Brian 'Bux' Wilshaw: Tenor Saxophone/Flute

Linda Lewis/Juanita 'Honey' Franklin: Backing Vocals

Geoff MacCormack: Backing Vocals/Congas

Brian Duffy/Celia Philo: Cover Designers

Brian Duffy: Photographer

Phillip Castle: Cover Art

Pierre Laroche: Make-up

Recorded at Trident Studios London, England

The album qualified for gold on release having received advance orders of 100,000 in the UK.

Bowie (1976)

Aladdin Sane is Ziggy Stardust meets fame. Ziggy Stardust the album was an objective point of view and Aladdin Sane is himself talking about being a star, I think, and hitting America, because I'd had that first experience of America so I had plenty of material for it. Subjective talking, really. Showing the break-up. [332]

Bowie (1973)

The album was written in America. The numbers were not supposed to form a concept album, but looking back on them, there seems to be definite linkage from number to number. There's no order; they were written in different cities, and there's a general feeling on the album which at the moment I can't put my finger on. It's a feeling I've never yet produced on an album; I think it's the most interesting album that I've written, musically as interesting as any of the things I've written. [216]

Charles Shaar Murray (*NME*)

The album's changed slightly since I first heard the tapes in that the recut 'John, I'm Only Dancing' has been replaced by 'Let's Spend The Night Together', originally intended as the B-side of 'Drive-In Saturday', and a then incomplete track called 'Zion' has been replaced by 'Lady Grinning Soul'. [217]

Murray's review led to years of speculation about 'Zion', generally assumed to be a seven-minute piece Bowie played to Martin Hayman during the July *Pin Ups* sessions.

SELECTED REISSUES

- CD (RCA 1984).
- CD (remastered) (Ryko) 1990).
- CD (remastered) (EMI 1999).
- CD 30th Anniversary 2 CD Edition (remastered) (EMI 2003).

BONUS TRACKS

1. 'John, I'm Only Dancing' (saxophone version) (2:45)
2. 'The Jean Genie' (single mix) (4:07)
3. 'Time' (single edit) (3:43)
4. 'All The Young Dudes' (mono mix) (4:12)
5. 'Changes' (live) (3:20)
6. 'The Supermen' (live) (2:42)
7. 'Life On Mars?' (live) (3:25)
8. 'John, I'm Only Dancing' (live) (2:40)
9. 'The Jean Genie' (live) (4:10)
10. 'Drive-In Saturday' (live) (4:53)

The six live tracks were recorded during the 1972 US tour for a planned live album.

- CD (mini LP replica) (Toshiba EMI 2007).
- CD 40th Anniversary Edition (EMI 2013).

Yubin Chokin Kaikan
Hiroshima, Japan

Promoter Daniel Nenishkis told *Billboard* magazine that Bowie was the first rock singer to receive a standing ovation from a Hiroshima audience.

■ CHART
'Drive-In Saturday'
UK Top 30 Chart Entry No.16
Charting 10 weeks

MONDAY 16 APRIL

★ LIVE
Kokusai Kaikan
Kobe, Japan

TUESDAY 17 APRIL

★ LIVE
Koseinenkin Kaikan
Osaka, Japan

WEDNESDAY 18 APRIL

★ LIVE
Shibuya Kokaido
Tokyo, Japan

Shibuya Kokaido
Tokyo, Japan

The Japanese audiences were accustomed to the heavy police presence, but usually became hysterical as Bowie came on. At the last show of the Japan tour, Angie and Tony Zanetta felt the audience was even more excited and resorted to screaming and swinging chairs around. In the resulting chaos, the venue suffered structural damage and police demanded that RCA hand over those responsible.

▼ SOCIALISING
Oblivious, Bowie and MacCormack spent the rest of the evening with two girlfriends in a quiet restaurant.

Geoff MacCormack (2010)
I knew he was trying to think of some angle that would allow us to stay in Japan, but there was no way. [045]

SATURDAY 21 – TUESDAY 24 APRIL

►TRAVELLING

YOKAHAMA – NAKHODKA

Felix Dzerjinsky

A crowd of fans gathered at the dockside in a rainstorm to see off Bowie and MacCormack as they boarded the *Felix Dzerjinsky* bound for Nakhodka, the eastern terminus for the Trans-Siberian Railway and the only port in the Russian Far East that was open to foreigners.

Leee Black Childers planned to catch up with them once he received his Russian visa. In the meantime he had to get Angie and Tony Zanetta out of Japan following the fracas the night before At Tokyo airport, police were watching flights bound for London and San Francisco, so Childers got them onto a flight to Honolulu.

During the passage Bowie and MacCormack realised they were being followed by two men who introduced themselves as KGB and questioned them about their politics. Later that night the crew put on a show in traditional Russian costume. Bowie decided to reciprocate with an acoustic set, playing a couple of songs with MacCormack on his bongos before continuing alone with 'Amsterdam' and 'Space Oddity'. Afterwards a Russian radio official invited them to play in Vladivostok.

Geoff MacCormack (2008)

There must have been no more than 200 people there. Most people didn't know who he was, though there were a few Japanese tourists who did. By and large the people watching him play thought he was just this kind of redheaded freak. [280]

Geoff MacCormack photographed Bowie in their 'soft class' compartment on the Trans-Siberian Railway.

СССР

TUESDAY 24 – MONDAY 30 APRIL

► TRAVELLING

NAKHODKA – VLADIVOSTOK – KHABAROVSK – IRKUTSK – KRASNOYARSK – NOVOSIBIRSK – SVERDLOVSK (YEKATERINBURG) – MOSCOW

Trans-Siberian Railway

From Nakhodka they took the boat train to Khabarovsk, where they were joined by UPI news correspondent Bob Musel. Musel had met with Angie in London after the plan for Bowie's train journey was announced at the end of March. Musel decided to cover it as part of his ongoing *Great Train Journeys* series. Musel also had a musical past as a songwriter in the Fifties and had seen Bowie perform in July 1972. As it turned out, he was an invaluable travelling companion, having spent years as UPI's Moscow correspondent.

Bowie and MacCormack boarded the Trans-Siberian Railway for the 6,650-mile trip to Moscow. Two Canadian girls went into shock as Bowie appeared on the train wearing platform-soled boots and a blue raincoat, carrying a guitar. "David Bowie! On our train!" they shrieked as he made his way to his compartment next to Musel's. They were travelling 'soft class' – the Russian equivalent of first class.

Bowie (1973)

There are three ways you can travel. Deluxe – two bunks in a simple compartment, sharing a toilet and bathroom with the rest of the carriage – that's what I had. Then there's first class, which is four bunks per compartment, and hard class – bunks right up both sides with people sleeping on the floor. [125]

TOP: Sightseeing in Moscow. ABOVE: Bowie filming the May Day activity from his room at the Intourist Hotel in Moscow OPPOSITE: Leee Black Childers' photo of Bowie that almost got them arrested.

"I won't fly," he told Musel, "because I've had a premonition I'll be killed in a plane crash if I do. If nothing happens by 1976 I'll start to fly again.

But I love trains and I'd probably take this ride anyway, it's supposed to be the greatest of them all." [225]

Bowie had become fascinated with film and throughout the trip he shot footage on a 16mm camera that he picked up in Japan. Years later he edited it together using his ambient pieces recorded in Berlin as soundtracks.

Leee Black Childers finally obtained his Russian visa and flew from Japan to Russia, joining Bowie on the train at Irkutsk.

The journey continued without incident until Sverdlovsk, where Childers persuaded Bowie, who rarely ventured from the compartment, to come out with him to stretch his legs on the platform.

Leee Black Childers (1986)

I was taking pictures of David and sneaking pictures of the soldiers who were on the platform with us but unfortunately they caught me at it. The soldiers came and tried to get my camera but I was fighting back. David began to film it all. Then they got really crazy, trying to get David's movie camera and to arrest us. [043]

Fortunately two burly female train attendants, who had been looking after Bowie's compartment, intervened and literally carried them back onto the train while fending off the guards.

MONDAY 30 APRIL

► TRAVELLING

On their arrival in Moscow, guides escorted Bowie and MacCormack to the Intourist Hotel (a high-rise hotel on Tverskaya Ulitsa built in 1970, since demolished) where they checked in.

They spent the rest of the day sightseeing with Bob Musel, who knew the city well. When Musel suggested they go out for a meal, Bowie insisted they eat 'like the Russians' so he took them to the GUM department store cafeteria and was unsurprised when Bowie found the food inedible.

They abandoned the meatballs and moved on to the National Hotel, next door to their own, where they dined on smoked salmon, caviar and fresh sturgeon.

"I won't fly, because I've had a premonition I'll be killed in a plane crash..."

David Bowie

MAY

■ **ALBUM RELEASED**
IGGY POP & THE STOOGES
'RAW POWER'
US (CBS KC 32111)
Chart Peak No.182

Mixed by David Bowie.

TUESDAY 1

▶ **TRAVELLING**

Bowie, MacCormack and Musel attended the May Day parade in Moscow.

WEDNESDAY 2 THURSDAY 3 MAY

▶ **TRAVELLING**
MOSCOW – POLAND – EAST BERLIN – WEST BERLIN – PARIS

While Bowie and MacCormack continued on the train, Leee Black Childers flew ahead to Berlin. During the journey through Poland an over-zealous train guard attempted to break down their compartment door, demanding they produce travel documents before soldiers intervened.

Childers met them in Berlin to change trains for Paris, but they mistakenly boarded a train to Belgium. After a frantic changeover, the three arrived in Paris where they met up with Angie, Cherry Vanilla and RCA press officer Andrew Hoy at the George V hotel.

✪ **PRESS CONFERENCE**

A press conference for the French media was held in the Rouge Room.

Asked who his next collaborator would be, Bowie replied, "I really have no idea. There's nobody that I have in mind whom I want to work with. I have no idea if anybody wants to work with me. At the time, I had time. Now, time's another commodity I have less and less of."

Another writer asked him if he'd ripped off Iggy Pop and Lou Reed. Bowie replied, "You should ask Iggy Pop and Lou Reed." [218]

▼ **SOCIALISING**

Bowie, Angie and MacCormack went out for dinner with Charles Shaar Murray and *NME* photographer Joe Stevens.

FRIDAY 4 MAY

▶ **TRAVELLING**
PARIS – BOULOGNE – DOVER – LONDON

After delays checking out of the George V Hotel, Bowie and entourage (Angie, MacCormack, Childers, Vanilla and Hoy) arrived at the Gard du Nord to find the 12.30 boat train to Calais had already left.

"Seven thousand miles, and we miss the bleedin' train on the last leg," Bowie groaned. They would have to take the hovercraft from Boulogne to Dover, which to Bowie was as bad as a plane. "It flies – it's death," he pronounced.

They whiled away the wait for the train to Boulogne at the Cafe du Nord Brasserie with *Melody Maker* writer Roy Hollingworth and photographer Barrie Wentzell. Bowie picked up the tab for the sandwiches and beers as the *Melody Maker* team was broke.

Bowie told them, "I'm sick of being Gulliver. You know, after America, Moscow, Siberia, Japan. I just want to bloody well go home to Beckenham, and watch the telly. I've got to work harder this year than I've ever worked in my life. You know that? We're going to do a 79-date tour of America this year in about as many days. I might die. But I have to do it.

"I've gone through a lot of changes. It's all happened on my way back from Japan. You see, Roy, I've seen life, and I think I know who's controlling this damned world. And after what I've seen of the state of this world, I've never been so damned scared in my life." [150]

Following the hovercraft ordeal, he regained his composure at Dover with a cup of tea and a British Rail sausage roll. Meanwhile fans were gathering to welcome him home at Charing Cross station. The train finally rolled in to the sound of a high-pitched howl from the mass of teenage girls who mobbed Bowie as he stepped from the train.

ABOVE LEFT: Bowie changing trains at Berlin Bahnhof, West Berlin for the next leg to Paris. LEFT: Bowie and Angie at the Café du Nord Brasserie in Paris. OPPOSITE: On the train from Dover to Charing Cross.

Levi's.

Bowie runs the gauntlet at Charing Cross station. Barry Wentzell recalls "The way girls materialised out of nowhere was amazing. They seemed to have some sort of telepathy and knew far more about his movements than we ever did. You can tell he's glad to be back."

SATURDAY 5 MAY

▼ SOCIALISING

Bowie was welcomed home with a party at Haddon Hall. Among the friends were Tony Visconti with Mary Hopkin, Lindsay Kemp, Mick Ronson, Chelita Secunda, Ken Scott, Freddie Burretti, George and Birgit Underwood and Charles Shaar Murray, who had become the 'Bowie correspondent' for *NME*.

Sue Fussey made a cake with red and blue streaks and 'Welcome Home Aladdin Sane' written across the top. Also there from MainMan were Andrea (Bowie fan club assistant) and Corinne Schwab.

Corinne Schwab (2001)

I first met David at a welcome home party at Haddon Hall in 1973. He and Geoffrey [MacCormack] had just arrived back from Japan on the Trans-Siberian Express. My first impression was how tired and skinny he seemed! The famous red hair was a bit crumpled but his essence, the warmth and kind gentleness was there (through that worldly weariness) and he hugged Andrea and me and made us feel welcome. Andrea and I had been working at MainMan for several months and had not actually met him yet. [389]

Life at Haddon Hall by this time had become impossible, with fans camping outside day and night. Angie arranged to rent Diana Rigg's apartment in Vale Court on Hall Road, Maida Vale.

During the week Bowie and the band rehearsed for the last leg of the tour at Manticore, a converted Odeon cinema in Fulham owned by Emerson, Lake & Palmer. Paul and Linda McCartney dropped in and stood at the back for a while before approaching the stage.

John Hutchinson (2012)

Linda went and talked to David briefly. Paul came over to me and we talked about the Harptone 12-string I was playing. "George has one of those," he said. I said, "Bob Dylan has one, too." They didn't stay long. Paul said, "Okay, show-off" to me, and went. It was a dream sequence but it really did happen that way.

MONDAY 7 MAY

■ ALBUM RELEASED

'ALADDIN SANE'

US (RCA LSP-4852)

Chart Peak No.12

▼ SOCIALISING

Bowie and Angie attended the premiere of *Hitler: The Last 10 Days* at the Empire Cinema, Leicester Square. Princess Margaret was guest of honour.

TUESDAY 8 MAY

▼ SOCIALISING

Having renewed his friendship with Tony Visconti, Bowie suggested they go out to see Peter Cook and Dudley Moore's show *Behind The Fridge* at the Cambridge Theatre in the West End. Bowie and Angie picked up Visconti and his wife, Mary Hopkin, from their flat in Courtfield Gardens, Kensington.

Tony Visconti (2006)

David took the lift up to our flat to collect us. I was giving the babysitter instructions when David walked into our kitchen dressed in full Ziggy Stardust regalia. The babysitter, unbeknownst to me, was a Bowie fan. She dropped the pan filled with warm water that contained the baby's bottle on the kitchen floor and shrieked. David was amused. [047]

The Bowies and Viscontis proceeded to the theatre in Bowie's limo, which was so large it became wedged between the cars parked on either side of the street.

Tony Visconti (1982)

Angie heckled Peter Cook and Dudley Moore all night, and it was quite a bizarre evening, but exactly the evening I expected, strained and full of tension and real culture shock. As you may know, Mary, my wife, is a very subdued, laid-back and, in her own description, 'twee' person, and here we were going out with these two extroverts in the personas of David and Angie Bowie. However, we bridged the gap very quickly and got friendly again. [015]

LEFT: Arriving at the Empire Cinema in Leicester Square.
BELOW: Backstage at the Cambridge Theatre with Peter Cook and Dudley Moore. Bowie was a fan, as was Eno, who described his friendship with Bowie as "tinged by echoes of Pete and Dud".
OPPOSITE: The first night of the *Aladdin Sane* UK tour at Earls Court (top) was marred by bad sightlines and Bowie's inadequate PA system.
FOLLOWING SPREAD: Ziggy's last tour kicks off in London. Crowds gather outside Earls Court, including a teenage Sid Vicious and Angie.

SATURDAY 12 MAY

★ LIVE

Earls Court
London, England

UK TOUR II

The opening concert of the tour was a disaster after Defries judged Bowie to be big enough to warrant booking the 18,000-seat Earls Court – more than twice the size of anywhere Bowie had played before. Defries got his sums right – tickets sold out in the first three hours – but he overlooked the fact that the arena was not yet designed for rock concerts. Bowie's PA system was woefully inadequate; the acoustics were terrible, made worse by the band performing at floor level. The inevitable result was a crush at the front as fans attempted to get a better view, and the band had to leave the stage while security tried to quell the riot.

The music papers had a field day the following Saturday, with front-page stories featuring headlines like 'Bowie Fiasco – What Went Wrong?' and 'Aladdin Distress'. Bowie had Defries change the venue for the end of the tour from Earls Court to the Hammersmith Odeon.

Bowie (1973)
Personally, I'm not worried by what is said about it… we were the first band to experiment with the place, and if I remember rightly the Rainbow had exactly the same kind of reception when it first opened as a venue. We had a similar problem with Earls Court apparently. After about three-quarters of the way back, everything was totally lost and it became just an aerodrome. Somebody had been put in charge of getting the acoustics together, and it hadn't been done sufficiently well. [219]

■ CHART

LOU REED
'Walk On The Wild Side'
UK Top 30 Chart Entry
Charting 9 weeks

SHOW SOUVENIR
The David Bowie Tour 1973

THE SPIDERS

TUESDAY 15 MAY

▶ TRAVELLING

✪ PRESS

David and the Spiders took the train from Kings Cross to Aberdeen for the shows in Scotland. In the evening they checked into the Imperial Hotel, where Martin Hayman (*Sounds*) and Ray Fox-Cumming (*Disc*) interviewed Bowie. Fox-Cumming asked him about film projects, namely *Stranger In A Strange Land*.

"I don't think I'm going to do that one," said Bowie. "John Schlesinger has asked me to do a film for him and has left me to choose the story. I've chosen the story, but I can't say more than that. We're still waiting for the copyright, but if all goes well I might do it in spring 1974." [125]

WEDNESDAY 16 MAY

★ LIVE

Aberdeen Music Hall
Aberdeen, Scotland

2 SHOWS

Despite Bowie and the crew spending the day in preparation, the two sold-out shows suffered from sound problems.

THURSDAY 17 MAY

★ LIVE

Caird Hall
Dundee, Scotland

The tour coach stopped by the side of the A92 for a band photo opportunity before travelling on to Dundee, where they checked in to the Angus Hotel.

FRIDAY 18 MAY

★ LIVE

Green's Playhouse
Glasgow, Scotland

2 SHOWS

Bowie (1973)

We had, I think, four couples making it in the back row, which was fabulous. It's the first time I've heard of that happening. There was also a whole row of seats physically torn out of the floor, which sounds like the Fifties to me. That's what my brother used to do in Brixton. Can you imagine how much energy has to be used to tear out a theatre seat? [219]

SATURDAY 19 MAY

★ LIVE

Empire Theatre
Edinburgh, Scotland

Geoff MacCormack snapped Bowie perusing the local paper in the dressing room as the Spiders prepared for the show.

The Monty Python troupe was also in Edinburgh for their first Farewell Tour. In the coming years Bowie and the Pythons would often cross paths. Bowie became a fan and friend, as did Led Zeppelin, Pink Floyd and George Harrison, all of whom helped Python with film financing.

Bowie's first encounter with the Pythons was inauspicious. After Bowie's concert (where the audience rose to cheer Angie as she took her box seat) they headed off to a gay club where they found Graham Chapman and his partner David Sherlock sitting at the table that Angie had reserved. "Do you know who we are?" she demanded but to no avail.

ABOVE: Bowie at Kings Cross station before boarding the train to Aberdeen.

Back at the Post House Hotel, Bowie's entourage put other Python noses out of joint, partying late into the night.

Michael Palin (1973 diary entry)

Went to bed. Could not get to sleep, owing to presence of David Bowie and his acolytes in the hotel. Bowie is currently the hottest touring property in Britain, having recently played to 18,000 in Earls Court. Tonight Bowie was in Edinburgh – and staying about a couple of doors down on the same floor as myself. They weren't exactly noisy, there was just so many of them. From 2am to 3am and beyond it was like trying to sleep through the invasion of Poland. [028]

ABOVE: Bowie rocks Brighton at the Dome, May 23.

SUNDAY 20 MAY

In the morning Michael Palin and fellow Pythons watched Bowie and entourage check out of the hotel.

Michael Palin (1973 diary entry)

At 12pm sauntered down to the lobby, which was filled with the Bowie party's gear, and Bowie attendants. What a relief from roomfuls of grey suits – this morning it was almost as though squatters had moved in. Tall, gangling men dressed in denim moved through the throng like a dozen Jesuses, sharply dressed chicks sat around smoking – everyone wore a relaxed air of confidence – they were, after all, part of the hottest road show in Britain. With our Sunday papers and our conspicuous lack of hangers-on we looked very dull and anonymous.

Outside the hotel was Bowie's splendid personal conveyance, a chunky black and white Dodge Van, which looked like nothing I had ever seen – it was an armoured car, in effect – with thick steel sides and black windows. A stylish version of a Black Maria. [028]

MONDAY 21 MAY

■ SINGLE RELEASED

LOU REED

'Satellite Of Love' (Reed) (2:53)/
'Walk And Talk It' (Reed) (3:24)
US (RCA 74-0964)

David Bowie/Mick Ronson:
A-side Producers
B-side from *Lou Reed*

★ LIVE

Theatre Royal
Norwich
Norfolk, England

2 SHOWS

TUESDAY 22 MAY

★ LIVE

Odeon Theatre
Romford
Essex, England

WEDNESDAY 23 MAY

★ LIVE

Brighton Dome
Brighton
East Sussex, England

✪ TELEVISION

'NATIONWIDE' (BBC TV)

Bernard Falk and a BBC film crew arrived to shoot a short segment on the Bowie phenomenon.

Bowie (2002)

One of their 'Good Heavens, whatever next?' – type reports. Lots of confused questioning and following me swanning around backstage, putting silly clothes on. It was all too funny. [037]

At Brighton Bowie was filmed on stage and off, arriving at the Bedford Hotel, where fans were interviewed outside the door to his room, returning to the hotel in full stage costume after the show and leaving for Lewisham the next morning.

THURSDAY 24 MAY

★ LIVE

Lewisham Odeon
Lewisham
South London, England

"It's good to be home," Bowie told the audience which included 'Boy George' O'Dowd.

Boy George (1995)

I spent the day hanging around Lewisham, watching the crowd well up. Hundreds of Ziggy and Angie clones. Girls in fox-fur stoles and pillbox hats, boys in glitter jackets. Bowie was an alien. [025]

FRIDAY 25 MAY

★ LIVE

Bournemouth Winter Gardens
Bournemouth
Dorset, England

✪ TELEVISION

'NATIONWIDE' (BBC TV)

The BBC crew followed the tour to Bournemouth where they shot more live footage of 'Watch That Man', 'Hang On To Yourself' and 'Time'.

SUNDAY 27 MAY

★ LIVE

Civic Hall
Guildford
Surrey, England

2 SHOWS

MONDAY 28 MAY

★ LIVE

Civic Hall
Wolverhampton
Staffordshire, England

TUESDAY 29 MAY

★ LIVE

Victoria Hall
Hanley
Staffordshire, England

■ CHART

LOU REED
'Walk On The Wild Side'
UK Chart Peak No.10

WEDNESDAY 30 MAY

★ LIVE

New Theatre
Oxford
Oxfordshire, England

THURSDAY 31 MAY

★ LIVE

King George's Hall
Northgate
Blackburn
Lancashire, England

Lancashire Evening Telegraph
Bowie sent a packed St George's Hall [sic], Blackburn absolutely wild last night. By the end of the concert, everybody in the hall was standing up, many on their chairs for a better view. Two girls even got on to the stage and had to be bodily carried away by stewards.

JUNE

FRIDAY 1

★ LIVE

St George's Hall
Bradford
West Yorkshire, England

SATURDAY 2 JUNE

★ LIVE

University of Leeds
Woodhouse Lane
Leeds
West Yorkshire, England

2 SHOWS CANCELLED

Earlier in the day the matinee and evening shows at Leeds were cancelled. MainMan later told the press of the venue's "inadequate technical facilities" – the stage was too small and backstage was unsuitable for a dressing room. "It would have meant David walking through the audience to get to the stage which is out of the question." The shows were rescheduled for later in the month.

SUNDAY 3 JUNE

★ LIVE

New Theatre
Coventry
West Midlands, England

MONDAY 4 JUNE

★ LIVE

Gaumont
Worcester
Worcestershire, England

TUESDAY 5 JUNE

✪ TELEVISION

'NATIONWIDE' (BBC TV)

The show included the 12-minute feature on Bowie's UK tour, filmed in Brighton and Bournemouth.

WEDNESDAY 6 JUNE

★ LIVE

City Hall
Sheffield
South Yorkshire, England

2 SHOWS

Among the audience were Glenn Gregory and Martyn Ware, future members of Human League spin-off, Heaven 17, who took their name from a fictitious band mentioned in *Clockwork Orange*.

▼ SOCIALISING

After the show Bowie and the entourage partied in the bar at the Hallam Tower hotel. Lulu and Labi Siffre were also in town and put on an impromptu show.

Lulu (1973)
We knew each other vaguely. One night we were all together and started to sing, and Mike Garson was playing piano, and David said: "I'd love to write a song for you." I said, great, never thinking it would come through. But he came through, and said, "I'd like to record you." And it happened. [313]

Bowie (1974)
We started talking about the possibility of working together, although nothing concrete was arranged. However, I was keen to get something fixed up, because I really have always thought that Lulu has incredible potential as a rock singer. I didn't think this potential had been fully realised and the nearest record she'd got to performing as a rock star was way back when she recorded 'Shout'. [227]

After Bowie and Lulu disappeared together, Angie went looking for him, knocking on all the doors of the hotel as the band and crew looked on with amusement.

THURSDAY 7 JUNE

★ LIVE

Free Trade Hall
Manchester
Lancashire, England

2 SHOWS

Cherry Vanilla (1973)
Hysterical little girls were of course dragged off the stage but uniquely enough, little boys got on stage. They were calm and after they straightened out their clothes went over to David, shook his hand and patted him on his back – gave the power salute and calmly walked off. David loved it. Stu couldn't deal with it. [400]

FRIDAY 8 JUNE

★ LIVE

Newcastle City Hall
Newcastle upon Tyne
Northumberland, England

2 SHOWS

Cherry Vanilla (1973)
Newcastle was the peak of aggro on this tour. Bowie arrived at 7.00 for a 6.00 show – traffic, so he said – I had police all over the north and Midlands looking for him. I asked BBC Newcastle three times to leave backstage and they tried sneaking back, trying to get at Dave. [400]

SATURDAY 9 JUNE

★ LIVE

Preston Guild Hall
Preston
Lancashire, England

Live at the Free Trade Hall, Manchester.

SUNDAY 10 JUNE

★ LIVE

Empire Theatre
Liverpool
Lancashire, England

2 SHOWS

Two more future Bowie-influenced musicians attended the Liverpool show, Ian McCulloch (Echo & The Bunnymen) and Marc Almond (Soft Cell), who had been 'bottled' by thugs on the way to the show. All was forgotten when Bowie reached out and took Almond's hand during the finale of 'Rock'n'Roll Suicide'.

Marc Almond (2008)
I was a mess of blood, glitter and cheap, badly applied make-up, but in a state of near religious ecstasy. [298]

The shows were typical of most of the *Aladdin Sane* UK tour – plagued by the mayhem of hysterical fans constantly invading the stage to be repelled by over-zealous security. On some nights the show had to be stopped to prevent further injuries.

At Liverpool Bowie took the step of calling off security, which backfired terribly when the crowd surged forward, trashing the orchestra pit in front of the stage. At one point, Bowie stopped the show to tell a heckler, "When you entered the theatre, you must have seen the sign 'Artist at work'. Well you came to see us. When you go to work, we will come and see you. Until then, fucking shut up."

Melody Maker
Liverpool won't forget David Bowie in a hurry. There's a couple of dozen smashed seats, two broken crash barriers, and one young kid in hospital after Sunday night at the Empire Theatre. If you wanted to see Bowie the musician you had to forget it, and get swept along in the mass reaction to Bowie the blatant sex machine.

MONDAY 11 JUNE

★ LIVE

De Montfort Hall
Leicester
Leicestershire, England

TUESDAY 12 JUNE

★ LIVE

Central Hall Theatre
Chatham
Kent, England

2 SHOWS

WEDNESDAY 13 JUNE

✪ PROMO VIDEO FILMING

'Life On Mars?'

Director: Mick Rock

In a Ladbroke Grove studio Mick Rock shot the clip for the 'new' single. Bowie wore a new Freddie Burretti suit with make-up by Pierre Laroche.

Bowie (2002)
I always knew when Pierre Laroche was having a bad day, as he would give me green eye shadow, which he knew I hated. [037]

Mick Rock (2007)
We had two cameras and we also used stills, so it was relatively sophisticated for its era. It stands up. I didn't make a single penny out of those films at the time. However, once David split from MainMan and made his final settlement he gave me the visual rights. He has always been a gentleman. [057]

Released on
The Video Collection (PMI 1993)/
Best Of Bowie (EMI 2002).

★ LIVE

The Gaumont State
London, England

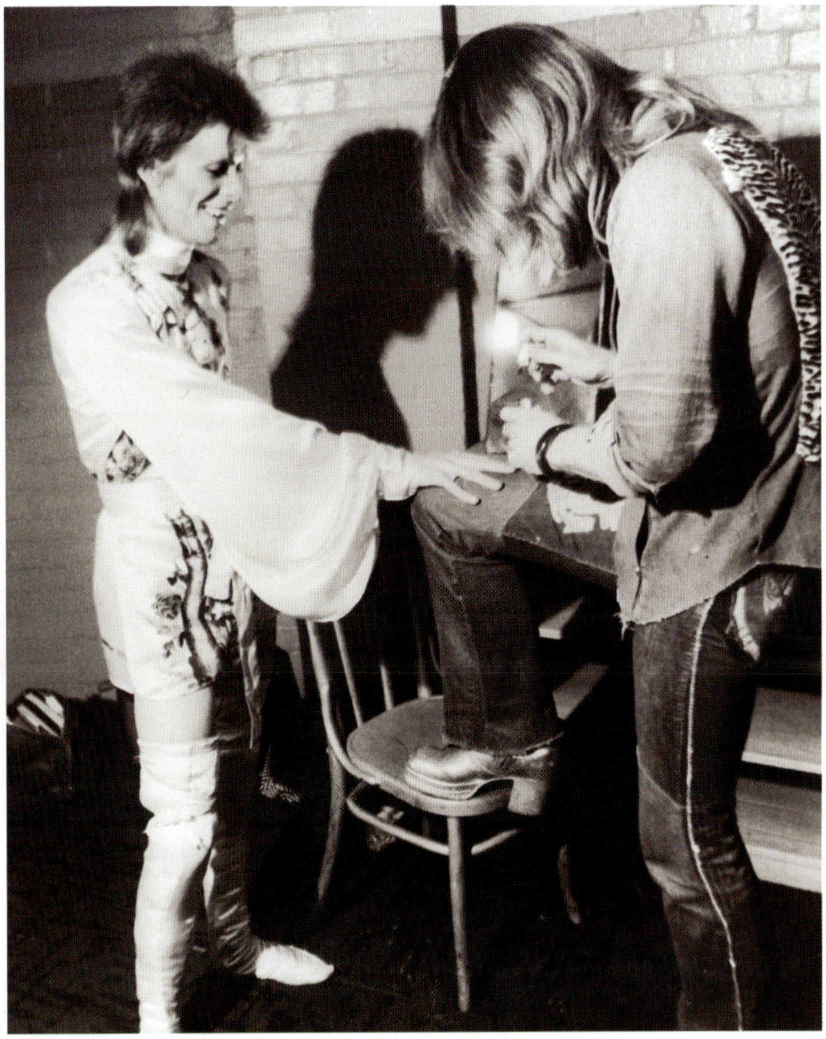

THURSDAY 14 JUNE

★ LIVE

Salisbury City Hall
Salisbury
Wiltshire, England

Bowie successfully stagedived – he had failed to pull off a similar Iggy-inspired stunt a year before – but injured his ankle in a jump from the PA stack.

Mike Garson (1985)

I thought, "This guy thinks he can fly." There may be some acrobats could have handled that. He's a pretty rubbery guy, but I knew it was too high. He went flying past me at the piano and just wiped out. [016]

He performed the encore in a chair, telling the audience, "I've a few things to say. Firstly, I think I've broken my ankle. Not really, but it hurts a bit."

ABOVE LEFT AND RIGHT: Make-up and nails by Pierre Laroche. OPPOSITE: Mick Rock's elegant film of 'Life On Mars?' – an early prototype of music video as an art form.

FRIDAY 15 JUNE

★ LIVE

Taunton Odeon
Taunton
Somerset, England

2 SHOWS

Bowie ignored doctors' advice and soldiered on with the shows, sitting through the performance, falling into the audience and eventually being carried off.

SATURDAY 16 JUNE

★ LIVE

Town Hall
Torquay
Devon, England

MONDAY 18 JUNE

■ SINGLE RELEASED

'Time' (3:38)/
'The Prettiest Star' (3:25)
US (RCA APBO-0001)

▮Single edit reissued on *Aladdin Sane* 30th Anniversary 2 CD Edition (EMI 2003).

★ LIVE

Colston Hall
Bristol, England

2 SHOWS

TUESDAY 19 JUNE

★ LIVE

Southampton Guildhall
Southampton
Hampshire, England

Replaced scheduled Portsmouth Guildhall show.

THURSDAY 21 JUNE

★ LIVE

Birmingham Town Hall
Birmingham
Warwickshire, England

2 SHOWS

FRIDAY 22 JUNE

★ LIVE

Birmingham Town Hall
Birmingham
Warwickshire, England

2 SHOWS

■ SINGLE RELEASED

'Life On Mars?' (3:48)/
'The Man Who Sold The World' (3:55)
UK (RCA 2316)
Chart Peak No.3

■ SINGLE RELEASED

SIMON TURNER
'The Prettiest Star' (2:42)/
'Love Around' (King) (2:21)
UK (UK Records UK 44)

Turner, a child actor turned singer, was dating Daniella Parmar and so became friends with Angie Bowie, for whom the song was originally written. Johnny Arthey was credited with the arrangement, despite it being identical to Tony Visconti's on Bowie's original 1970 single. Later in the year, Defries signed Turner to MainMan but nothing came of it.

▮Reissued on *Oh! You Pretty Things: The Songs Of David Bowie* (Castle Music 2006).

SATURDAY 23 JUNE

★ LIVE
Gliderdrome
Boston
Lincolnshire, England

SUNDAY 24 JUNE

★ LIVE
Fairfield Halls
Croydon
Surrey, England

2 SHOWS

MONDAY 25 JUNE

★ LIVE
New Theatre
Oxford
Oxfordshire, England

2 SHOWS

TUESDAY 26 JUNE

★ LIVE
New Theatre
Oxford
Oxfordshire, England

WEDNESDAY 27 JUNE

★ LIVE
Top Rank Suite
Doncaster
South Yorkshire, England

THURSDAY 28 JUNE

★ LIVE
Bridlington Spa Ballroom
Bridlington
East Yorkshire, England

FRIDAY 29 JUNE

★ LIVE
Leeds Rolarena
Leeds
West Yorkshire, England

2 SHOWS

Audiences were down at both shows, which replaced the cancelled dates at Leeds University.

Trevor Bolder (1995)
That was really surprising. We were completely sold out everywhere else but because we had cancelled the original Leeds gig, most people decided to stay away. It was odd suddenly playing to a small audience again, but it was fair enough. You should never cancel a gig. [007]

SATURDAY 30 JUNE

★ LIVE
Newcastle City Hall
Newcastle upon Tyne
Northumberland, England

2 SHOWS

ABOVE: Live on stage in Croydon.
OPPOSITE: Live at Hammersmith.
OVERLEAF: Bowie arrives at the Hammersmith Odeon stage door.

■ CHART
'Life On Mars?'
UK Top 30 Chart Entry
Charting 13 weeks

JULY

■ SINGLE RELEASED
LOU REED
'Vicious' (Reed) (2:55)/
'Goodnight Ladies' (Reed) (4:18)
US (RCA APB0-0054)

David Bowie/Mick Ronson: Producers

MONDAY 2

★ LIVE
Hammersmith Odeon
London, England

Celebrated filmmaker DA Pennebaker and his crew arrived in London at RCA's behest to film the concert the following night.

DA Pennebaker (2002)
We hurried to the Hammersmith Odeon, where the next-to-the-last concert was about to take place. I had never seen an audience like that... made up of one gigantic group of back-up singers... they were wonderful. We were only supposed to do a half-hour show for RCA. It was supposed to be a thing on this new record they'd invented that could do visual and audio at the same time called SelectaVision and they only wanted half an hour. Five minutes into that night's concert, I realised that there was a feature film here, crying to be made.

That night we filmed bits of the concert, as well as the audience to check the lighting. It was an incredibly exciting concert experience, a long way from the Dylan concerts I had filmed for Don't Look Back. *And Bowie himself was stunning. I have never seen anyone turn on an audience, men as well as women, the way he did that night. The minute he strode out on stage I could see that he was a character looking for a film.* [373]

After the show, Peter Harvey (*Record Mirror*) interviewed Ronson, Bolder and Woodmansey at the Hertford Hotel. The Spiders talked about the coming American tour, but they didn't have any plans after that. Presciently, Woodmansey mused, "You don't know what is going to come up next or what you might fancy doing next; whether it's to do with music or what." [138]

"I had never seen an audience like that... made up of one gigantic group of back-up singers."

DA Pennebaker

ROCK & ROLL
HERE TO

THE

TUESDAY 3 JULY

★ LIVE

Hammersmith Odeon
London, England

Mike Garson medley/ 'Hang On To Yourself'/ 'Ziggy Stardust'/'Watch That Man'/ 'Wild Eyed Boy From Freecloud'– 'All The Young Dudes'– 'Oh! You Pretty Things'/ 'Moonage Daydream'/'Changes'/ 'Space Oddity'/'My Death'/ 'Cracked Actor'/'Time'/ 'The Width Of A Circle'/ Band Introduction/ 'Let's Spend The Night Together'/ 'Suffragette City'/ 'White Light White Heat'/ 'The Jean Genie'–'Love Me Do'/ 'Round And Round'/Farewell Speech/ 'Rock'n'Roll Suicide'

"Ladies and Gentlemen, straight from his fantastically successful world tour, including the United States of America… Japan… now his home country… for the last time… David Bowie!"

Barry Bethel's stage introduction said it all without anyone realising. The last concert of the 1973 UK tour was also the swan song of the act known as Ziggy Stardust and The Spiders From Mars.

Throughout the concert camera flash bulbs popped, creating a strobe effect. Pennebaker felt the audience was an integral part of his film, and had arranged signs to be put up, asking everyone to bring flash bulb cameras and take as many pictures as possible.

Peter Harvey ***(Record Mirror)***
It was immediately obvious that David, the band and all their crew, had wound up to a terrific pitch. There was never quite this level of tightness and certainty before. Maybe having Ken Scott (David's engineer) to record the show on 16-track put an edge on the sound. Whatever it was, the performance was inspired. [139]

After introducing the band ("No, it's not Suzi Quatro on lead guitar…") they raced headlong into 'Let's Spend The Night Together' ("This is for Mick"), 'Suffragette City' and yet another costume change. "I'd like to do a number by a guy who tonight is in London somewhere making an album and I think he's a friend of mine… anyway he's one of the best songwriters around today. His name's Lou Reed!" Bowie announced as they launched into 'White Light White Heat'.

As a favour to Mick Ronson, Bowie brought on Jeff Beck – who was mid-tour with Beck Bogert & Appice – for a guest spot.

Mick Ronson (1973)
Jeff Beck was my idol. I used to copy everything he did. That's why I was so knocked out when he agreed to come and play on the last couple of numbers. [259]

The Yardbirds-derived 'The Jean Genie' segued to 'Love Me Do', followed by 'Round And Round' and then Bowie stepped up to the mic to announce, "Of all of the shows on this tour, this particular show will remain with us the longest because not only is it the last show of the tour, but it's the last show that we'll ever do. Thank you."

None were more surprised than the band, though some had prior knowledge of his intention.

Geoff MacCormack (2008)
David told me ahead of time that it would be his last show. I felt quite guilty knowing that, especially as I was one of the lowly cats in that particular performance. [280]

Tony Visconti (2002)
Mick Ronson was told about it and David said, "Do you want to tell the guys or shall I tell the guys?" and Mick said, "Well, we'll wait until after the show, and… you tell them." [373]

John Hutchinson (2004)
To us it was just another gig. We were actually planning on going back to the States. The first clue that I had that something was a little bit different about that gig was that David said to me, "Don't start 'Rock'n'Roll Suicide'. Don't play the intro until I give you the nod." I thought, "Well, he must be going to say something." Well, he did. He said, "Thanks very much, we're all retiring." You know – 'we'. The band kind of looked at each other and I started playing. [368]

Trevor Bolder (2012)
I kept looking at Woody, and Woody was playing away, going "I don't know what's going on." [411]

Woody Woodmansey (2012)
It didn't equate with what we'd been talking about three days earlier so we didn't know whether that was true or not. [411]

John Hutchinson (2004)
When we came off, people were looking at each other. Woody and Trevor were taken aback – we were all saying, "What did he say?" We got fired on stage. And as it turned out, that was the last gig that we did, but we didn't know about it at the time. [368]

Mike Garson (2012)
It was not a big deal to me. It could have gone on another five or ten years but David was done with it. Any artist at any time is entitled to be done with something. [411]

DA Pennebaker (2002)
We were sworn to secrecy by Tony Defries, who assured us that only Bowie himself knew this and would reveal it to the audience sometime during the final performance. [373]

Charles Shaar Murray (1993)
I was the one who got the tip-off, thereby enabling NME to have its 'Bowie: That's It, I Quit' cover story rolling off the presses before Bowie had made the onstage announcement. [223]

Melody Maker's Michael Benton had also been told and during the day he interviewed Mick Ronson at the Hertford Hotel, where the band and crew were staying, and asked if it was really the end. "No, we haven't even started yet," Ronson told him. "We can do anything we want. Bowie can't be the same all the time, he has to change. Instead of doing tours, we'll concentrate on films and records. I'll be working with David on his films. The other Spiders will be getting things together on their own merits. They'll be glad of the rest." [058]

OPPOSITE: Hammersmith Odeon, July 3. Bowie plays the part of Ziggy for the last time. OVERLEAF: "Gimme your hands, cos you're wonderful" – Hammersmith Odeon, London.

"David told me ahead of time that it would be his last show. I felt quite guilty knowing that…"

Geoff MacCormack

✪ **FILM**

'ZIGGY STARDUST AND THE SPIDERS FROM MARS'

A MainMan Production in association with Pennebaker-Hegedus Films.

DA Pennebaker: Director
Tony Defries: Executive Producer
Jim Desmond/Mike Davis/Nick Doob/Randy Franken/DA Pennebaker: Cameramen
Robin Mayhew: Concert Sound/Ground Control
Ken Scott: Concert Recording/Trident Studios 16-track
Steve Lysohir/Phillip Mesure: Assistants
Stacy Pennebaker: Unit Manager
Edith Van Slyck: Associate Producer
Lorry Whitehead: Editor
Alan Brewer: Post-production Supervisor

DA Pennebaker (2002)
The three of us [Pennebaker, Jim Desmond and Nick Doob] were the main cameras. Then we had a neighbour who had shot a camera (allegedly) so we brought him along and then we got somebody there who had a tripod and a camera and we put them up in the balcony and they shot the long shots. [373]

- Film broadcast as *Bowie '73 With The Spiders From Mars* in US (ABC 1974).
- Screened as *A London Show* in Italy.
- Screened as *Bowie* at Edinburgh Film Festival (1979).
- General release as *Ziggy Stardust And The Spiders From Mars: The Motion Picture* (20th Century Fox 1983).
- Reissued on VHS (various 1984), Videodisc (RCA 1984), DVD (Image 1998) and remastered DVD (EMI 2003).
- Soundtrack released as *Ziggy Stardust: The Motion Picture* (RCA 1983).
- Reissued on CD (Ryko 1992) and remixed CD (EMI 2003).

▼**SOCIALISING**
Café Royal
Regent Street
London, England

THE LAST SUPPER

Directly after the concert the who's who of London society joined Bowie for a lavish end of tour party, which lasted till dawn.

Celebrity guests included Ringo and Maureen Starr, Mick and Bianca Jagger, Lou Reed, Lulu, Keith Moon, Edgar Broughton, Spike Milligan, Elliot Gould, Tony Curtis, Britt Ekland and Barbra Streisand, who was in London to film a TV special and had asked Bowie to dinner that night. Some invitees, such as the McCartneys, did not attend.

John Hutchinson (2012)
I don't think Woody went to the Café Royal party. I probably took his place in the Spiders limo as I went with Mick and Trevor to the 'do'. Ringo passed me outside the gents and we exchanged some northern banter about the 'big time'. I found Colin Scott (an old friend, a great folk singer) at a table with Princess Nina of Nina and Frederik fame and so I spent the evening with them mostly.

As the guests were treated to large amounts of champagne, smoked salmon, turkey and strawberries and cream, Bowie and Angie had gone back to their suite at the Hyde Park Hotel to change before making their entrance to a round of applause and flash bulbs. DA Pennebaker shot some silent footage of the occasion.

Settling into a velvet-covered throne-like chair, Bowie held court before moving round to Jeff Beck. Also at the table were Dana Gillespie, Mick Ronson, Penelope Tree, Barry Bethel and drummer Aynsley Dunbar, who was playing on Lou Reed's *Berlin* album. Lulu had also been at the concert. "I want to make a motherfucker of a record with you. You're a great singer," Bowie told her and promised to hook up in the next few days, before going into a huddle with Reed and Jagger. [298]

Bowie (2002)
I remember that I spent most of my time chatting and laughing with Jagger and Lou Reed (who, by the way, can be wickedly funny). The Lou 'kiss' picture, of course, is merely a lean-in to yell something above the volume produced by the DJ. [037]

Dr John provided live entertainment while a disc jockey kept the music going with rock and soul records and the Bowies and Jaggers took to the dance floor.

John Hutchinson (2012)
David and I were on the dance floor at the same time – I usually won't dance but I had to dance with the Princess Nina – and we nodded 'alright?' and that was the last time I saw David.

Trevor Bolder (2005)
At the party I heard people talking about how the tour wasn't going to happen. Bowie didn't say anything and there were no last words… we could have sat down and discussed it. [188]

Bowie told Peter Harvey, "It's been a great run, but this scene is all finished for me now. It's time I moved on. I've had lots of film offers and will probably take one of them up." [140]

He told Ray Fox-Cumming he didn't want to do any concerts again "for a long, long time – not for two or three years at least".

Radio Luxembourg's Kid Jensen was the first to break the news at 10pm that David Bowie had retired on stage that night.

ABOVE: Angie with Bianca Jagger at Bowie's end of tour party at the Café Royal. OPPOSITE: Arriving with Angie and (over her shoulder) Pierre Laroche. OVERLEAF: The star-studded Last Supper. Back: Edgar Broughton, Bianca Jagger, Bowie, Angie Bowie, unknown; Front: Ringo Starr, Celia Hammond, Jeff Beck, Lulu, Mick Ronson and Maureen Starkey.

WEDNESDAY 4 JULY

⊙ BUSINESS

MainMan newsletter #1 announced, "The world's largest rock and roll tour, David Bowie USA Tour III, has been cancelled. The massive arenas of 80 US and Canadian cities will not now, or perhaps ever again, hold within their walls the magic essence of a live Aladdin Sane. Bowie will spend the summer in France and Italy recording, relaxing and writing the script of his future."

Bowie (1981)
About 48 hours later, I'm sitting there thinking, "What have I said? I don't think I really meant that at all. I'm feeling better already." But too late. I know I really pissed off Woody and Trevor. They were so angry. I hadn't really told them that I was splitting the band up. But that's what Ziggy did, so I had to do it too. [329]

Bowie (1989)
They wanted to remain doing what we were doing and I didn't. I was going somewhere else and they didn't want to go. They were quite happy to play Jeff Beck covers. But I knew what I wanted the band to do. [110]

Woody Woodmansey (2007)
We had discussed new directions musically and we were not really into the soul thing David was looking at doing next. On reflection I think it was a good decision. [393]

Bowie (2002)
It was a big decision for me and it actually took me time to make it. Also, I was incredibly drained. We toured, the schedules that MainMan were putting us on were insane. [116]

Tony Zanetta (2009)
It was to be this mega-mega-tour. But the truth of it was, the business didn't warrant a tour like that. David's stardom was illusory, it was more in the press. It didn't translate into real numbers. So the promoters were very hesitant to do the kind of deal and the really major arena tour that Defries wanted to do. 'Retiring' was a business decision. [040]

In Chicago, Ava Cherry received a telegram from MainMan saying that the tour was off.

Ava Cherry (1987)
That was my first lesson – that you shouldn't count on things unless you're absolutely sure they are going to happen. I took all the money I had and decided to go to Europe anyway and find him and tell him what he did was low and tacky. [121]

THURSDAY 5 JULY

⊙ BUSINESS

Confirmation of Woodmansey's sacking came on the morning of his wedding to girlfriend June. MainMan called Mike Garson, who was presiding over the ceremony as an official of the British Church of Scientology. Garson waited until after the wedding to break the news to him.

Mike Garson (1986)
Woody was devastated. This was his life and he thought he was going to the top with David. [013]

Trevor Bolder (2012)
I was really upset, and with Mick doing a solo album, I was wondering what was gonna happen to me. I think the reason he broke the band up was that Woody was being very odd with him. Woody had gotten into Scientology through Mike Garson. And, in a way, Woody thought he was God because he found religion. And he just disagreed with everything that David was doing. [411]

Mick Ronson (1975)
When we talked about a Spiders album, which was before I did Slaughter On 10th Avenue, *Woody wanted as much say about what was written and recorded as I was gonna have. I didn't think that was fair because Woody didn't know the technical or production side of music and so I just told them "It's not on." So I told them they should do their own things and I went and did* Slaughter. *I used Trevor on the albums and on my solo gigs, but I had another drummer.* [132]

At the Hyde Park Hotel, Bowie began planning the *Pin Ups* album, working through a pile of records with Scott Richardson, an aficionado of the era. Richardson met Angie through The Stooges when they returned to Ann Arbor after finishing *Raw Power* and Angie had followed them. After an affair with Ron Asheton, she took up with Richardson and returned with him to London, where he became friends with Bowie and Ronson, with whom he also collaborated.

They picked 12 songs to record, including two apiece from favourites The Who, The Pretty Things and The Yardbirds.

Lulu visited and listened to a few Bowie tracks to record as a single, settling on 'The Man Who Sold The World' and 'Watch That Man'.

Lulu (2008)
I didn't think it would happen but he followed up two days later. He was übercool at the time and I just wanted to be led by him. I loved everything he did. I didn't think 'The Man Who Sold The World' was the greatest song for my voice, but it was such a strong song in itself. I had no idea what it was about. [298]

Bowie (1976)
To give her a song about finding angels and devils inside yourself was a naughty thing to do but it seemed right at the time. [332]

Bowie visited Reed at Morgan Studios, where he was recording his *Berlin* album with producer Bob Ezrin, to ask Aynsley Dunbar (Ronson's recommendation) and Jack Bruce to join the sessions in France.

Dunbar accepted the offer but Jack Bruce declined, being committed to West, Bruce & Laing. Trevor Bolder was called to a meeting at the hotel, where Bolder confronted Bowie about Woody's sacking.

Trevor Bolder (1995)
Mick told me to keep my mouth shut or I wouldn't be working, because David would get rid of me as well. David had actually said to me, "If you don't like it, you can clear off and we'll get another bass player as well." When everything calmed down, David said to me, "Come over here, I've got some songs to play you." And he played me all the songs he was going to do on Pin Ups. [010]

The songs were all familiar to Ronson and Bolder, who'd played most of them in covers bands over the years. Dunbar had been in The Mojos, whose 1964 hit 'Everything's Alright' was shortlisted for *Pin Ups*.

Ken Scott (2006)
The initial move of bringing in Aynsley worked. I don't think it would have been better with Woody and I'm all for new participants to stir things up a little. [394]

▼ SOCIALISING

Bowie and Angie attended the premiere of *Live And Let Die* at the Odeon Leicester Square.

FRIDAY 6 JULY

Paul McCartney said of Bowie's retirement, "I don't know why he is giving it up. I should have asked him. I met him last night at the premiere of *Live And Let Die*… I think it's a pity, because I haven't seen his show yet! I'd like to see it. So come on, David. Just do a quick one for me!" [002]

OPPOSITE: The Bowies arrive at the Odeon Leicester Square for the premiere of *Live And Let Die*.

SATURDAY 7 JULY

✪ PRESS

Charles Shaar Murray's interviews with Garson and Ronson, 'Say Hello to Weird and Gilly', published in *NME*.

SUNDAY 8 JULY

✪ PRESS

Charles Shaar Murray spoke to Bowie about the retirement announcement and asked if his new plans affected his relationship with Defries. "What's so great about Defries' management is it's so flexible that it can handle something like this," Bowie explained. "There's absolutely no question of any ructions between us. I couldn't ever work with anybody else."

MONDAY 9 JULY

► TRAVELLING

LONDON – PARIS

Bowie arrived at Victoria Station with Angie, who saw him onto the 10.30am boat train for the trip to Dover and Calais and on to the Château d'Hérouville studio complex, located north-east of Paris.

TUESDAY 10 JULY

■ CHART

'Life On Mars?'
UK Chart Peak No.3

OPPOSITE: Bowie on the boat train to Paris from Victoria Station.

TUESDAY 10 – TUESDAY 31 JULY

▲ RECORDING

Strawberry Studios
Château d'Hérouville
Hérouville, France

'PIN UPS' ALBUM

David Bowie/Ken Scott: Producers
Dennis MacKay: Engineer
David Bowie/Mick Ronson: Guitars
Trevor Bolder: Bass
Aynsley Dunbar: Drums
Mike Garson: Piano
Geoff MacCormack: Percussion/Backing Vocals

A residential studio, The Château had become popular with bands looking for more relaxed and isolated locations where they could record whenever inspiration struck them. Both Ken Scott, who engineered Elton John's *Honky Château*, and Marc Bolan, who recorded *The Slider* there in 1972, recommended it to Bowie. There was also a financial advantage.

Ken Scott (2006)
For a period of time in England there was a tax benefit to artists writing their songs and recording them out of England. They wouldn't get taxed as much if the money was kept outside of England and the money would be paid to wherever they wrote and recorded the songs. So that was the reason for recording in France. But of course Gus and I had done so much at Trident, we wanted to mix there so that's where we'd go for mixing. [417]

Rather than learning the songs from the records, Bowie decided to leave the pile of singles at home and brought along rough hand-scored notes for each song, to encourage improvisation and spontaneity.

Bowie told Martin Hayman: "I've got all these records back at home, but we don't have them here or anything. We just took down the basic chord structures and worked from there. Some of them don't even need any working on – like 'Rosalyn' for example. But most of the arranging I have done by myself and Mick… and Aynsley too.

Mike Garson (1995)
They were fun sessions. I didn't know any of those songs, so they could have been written by anybody. I had never heard the originals. I was just enjoying Mick's playing; he was just doing his thing. [010]

Trevor Bolder (1995)
It was really bad – the band thing had gone then. Once you pull any member out of a band, it changes. It was sad not having Woody there. [010]

In marathon sessions lasting up to 12 hours Bowie and the musicians worked quickly, completing the backing tracks in the first week, after which Bolder went home to England.

WEDNESDAY 11 JULY

✪ RADIO

Kid Jensen interviewed Bowie for his Radio Luxembourg show, asking him about his plans for the immediate future.

"I've still not thought it out too well," Bowie told Jensen. "I knew I had to stop performing for a little while. There's a lot of things that I've always wanted to do on stage and I found I wasn't fulfilling those particular needs at the moment. So I have to step back a little bit and have a look at what I was doing and see what adjustments can be made before I think of coming back on stage again.

"I'm retracing my own past really, my own likes and preferences for music in the early to mid-Sixties. Very much the London sound, because we were at the height of the Liverpool sound, which was sweeping England and America. And there was a lot of material that really went unnoticed in those days and that's the kind of stuff I wanted to put down. Things like the early Yardbirds things, even things that had some kind of nominal success like 'See Emily Play'. We're doing a lot of very interesting tracks, all my favourites."

▮Broadcast: July 14 (Radio Luxembourg).

MONDAY 16 JULY

▲ RECORDING

Strawberry Studios
Château d'Hérouville
Hérouville, France

LULU SINGLE

'The Man Who Sold The World'
'Watch That Man'

David Bowie/Mick Ronson: Producers
Andy Scott: Engineer

As Ken Scott was only contracted to work on *Pin Ups*, he set the levels for the house engineer Andy Scott and left him to it. Mick Rock took photos as Bowie conducted the session, playing the originals on a record player to refresh their memories. They recorded one take of 'The Man Who Sold The World' with Bowie providing a guide vocal for Lulu – she recorded her vocals later at Morgan Studios.

The 2006 reissue of the track (on *Oh! You Pretty Things: The Songs Of David Bowie*) includes a snippet of Bowie directing the session: "Play it with just a little bit more guts, Trev. We're starting a bit too relaxed. Let's hit it as a single, not as an album track, alright?" 'Watch That Man' was recorded in two takes.

Lulu (1973)
We had Aynsley Dunbar on drums and oh, he's sensational. It was amazing we got it together so quickly, because I was working, and he was working. I had two days, and flew over to Paris, did it and came back. It's a kind of mutual admiration thing. But we're from the same era and that's what it's all about. [313]

Geoff MacCormack (2007)
She's very easy to get on with. A really lovely lady. I remember wandering around the place with her one night singing soul songs. We sang harmonies together on a version of Aretha Franklin's 'Do Right Woman, Do Right Man' that got us a burst of spontaneous applause from the studio technicians. [054]

Lulu (2008)
In the studio Bowie kept telling me to smoke more cigarettes, to give my voice a certain quality. [298]

WEDNESDAY 18 JULY

✪ PHOTO SESSION

***Vogue* Studio**
Paris, France

'BRITISH VOGUE' COVER
'PIN UPS' ALBUM COVER

Justin de Villeneuve: Photographer
Pierre Laroche: Make-up

Two days later Bowie was working with another Sixties icon, Twiggy and her manager/partner/fashion photographer Justin de Villeneuve.

Twiggy (2012)
He'd done a song called 'Drive-In Saturday' and there was a line where he said, "She sighed like Twig the Wonder Kid." I heard it on the radio and went, "Oh my God, David Bowie just mentioned me in a song!" I rushed out to buy it because I thought maybe I'd misheard it. [287]

De Villeneuve, who had already shot several *Vogue* covers, suggested the idea of putting Bowie and Twiggy together on the cover. Editor Bea Miller loved the idea and they flew to France to meet Bowie at the Château.

At the small Paris studio, Pierre Laroche devised and applied make-up masks to reverse the contrast of Bowie's pallor against Twiggy's suntan.

Justin de Villeneuve (2012)
This worked out even better. When I showed Bowie the test Polaroids, he asked if he could use it for the **Pin Ups** ***record sleeve. I said: "I don't think so, since this is for*** **Vogue.** ***How many albums do you think you will sell?" "A million," he replied. "This is your next album cover!" I said. When I got back to London and told*** **Vogue,** ***they never spoke to me again.*** [243]

MONDAY 23 JULY

Bowie became the first solo artist to have all five of his RCA albums in the UK Top 40, three of them in the Top 15.

✪ PRESS

Angie made her debut as model/actress Jipp Jones in a fashion spread published in the *Daily Mirror*.

Terry O'Neill had visited earlier in the week to photograph Bowie and Angie modelling a variety of new outfits and posing in and around the Château.

Bowie (1973)

I thought it was funny because I didn't wear any Paris fashions. All my stuff was made by Fred. They tried to put me in their clothes, and I thought they were awful. There was only one thing I liked, and that was a dress that Angie wore. No, I just wanted Angie to get the centre pages because she looks nice. [141]

"It's a good place for nostalgia," Bowie told Martin Hayman. "These are all songs which really meant a lot to me then – they're all very dear to me. These are all bands which I used to go and hear play down The Marquee between 1964 and 1967. It's my London of the time." [141]

At that stage Bowie was toying with the idea of linking the songs with newly recorded couplets from his 1966 song 'The London Boys' to evoke his own experiences: "A young boy who comes up to London, gets pilled out of his head, all those things. I used to do that – get dressed up, go up to town on Friday night, see what was going on, stay for the night." [141]

The idea was dropped, along with other songs considered for a possible America-oriented *Pin Ups 2*, such as 'God Only Knows' and 'Summer In The City'. 'White Light White Heat' was recorded but left unfinished.

OPPOSITE: Justin de Villeneuve's photograph of his partner Twiggy and Bowie was intended for *Vogue*. Fortunately, de Villeneuve agreed to let Bowie have it for his *Pin Ups* cover. ABOVE: Recording *Pin Ups* at the Château outside Paris.

Bowie (1976)

I was intending to do an album of songs by New York people that I liked, but I never finished it. [085]

Mick Ronson used the 'White Light White Heat' backing track for his 1975 solo album *Play Don't Worry*.

Mick Ronson (1975)

Dave was thinking of doing it for **Pin Ups*****, and in a spare moment the band did a one-off. He didn't want to use it so I kept the 16-track and just overdubbed some guitars. After the first verse I made up the lyrics myself because I could never hear what Lou sung, couldn't make head nor tail of it, and there would be this little line here and this line here and I just filled the rest around.*** [158]

Bowie played Hayman a rough working mix of another new project (thought by some to be the *Aladdin Sane* outtake 'Zion'). "There are no vocals on it yet, just my la-la-la-ing," Bowie explained. "It's going to be a musical in one act called *Tragic Moments*, probably running straight through two sides. This is something I've always wanted to do." [141]

"We listen to perhaps seven minutes of music," Hayman reported. "I am confused. The contrast between *Tragic Moments* and *Pin Ups* could not be greater. The former is a highly arranged, subtly shifting music with just a touch of vaudeville: Mike Garson's piano flashes through like quicksilver. Perhaps the closest approximation to what has gone before would be the title track of *Aladdin Sane*." [141]

During the last week at the Château, Charles Shaar Murray looked in on the sessions. Ken Scott was back and Bowie and Ronson were working on vocals and various overdubs. Ronson spent any spare time crouched over his manuscript paper writing string arrangements.

"The session finally breaks up at around three in the morning," Murray reported. "Ronson goes up to bed, still declaring his intention to write some more string parts. Bowie commandeers the piano in the dining room to work on a new song, and by eight o'clock he's still working."

Bowie and Ronson also began remixing the tapes of the retirement concert for a planned live album, provisionally titled *Bowie-ing Out*. Meanwhile Defries was with Pennebaker at RCA Studios in New York viewing rushes of the film, which he hoped to release in 1974.

"It really is live," Ronson told Murray. "There's been no going back and redoing it in the studio. A lot of groups take the tapes into the studio and then strip it and start correcting the mistakes. They might put a fresh guitar solo on or something." [222]

Following her disappointment of the cancelled US tour, Ava Cherry had moved to Europe and was in Paris with a ballet production when she heard Bowie on the radio.

"I was supposed to work with this man," she told a friend, who replied, "His friend is staying at my house." The friend – Geoff MacCormack – took Cherry out to the Château where she resumed her affair with Bowie. He renewed his promise to help her career and they began working together on demos with a view to having her signed as a MainMan artist.

On the last day of July, as *Pin Ups* sessions finished, the BBC told MainMan that they would not be showing Mick Rock's 'Life On Mars?' promo film on *Top Of The Pops*.

AUGUST

■ **SINGLE RELEASED**
'Let's Spend The Night Together' (Jagger/Richards) (3:01)/
'Lady Grinning Soul' (3:42)
US (RCA APBO 0028)

■ **SINGLE RELEASED**
'Time' (3:38)/
'Panic In Detroit' (4:27)
Japan (RCA SS-2299)

WEDNESDAY 1

► **TRAVELLING**
PARIS – ROME
In the evening Bowie, MacCormack, Angie and Stuart George left Paris on a sleeper train for the overnight journey to Rome, where Bowie had originally planned to mix *Pin Ups* in the RCA studios.

THURSDAY 2 AUGUST

▼ **SOCIALISING**
The party holidayed just outside Rome in Tenuta San Nicola where they were joined by Zowie (in the care of Daniella Parmar) and Bowie's personal assistant Gloria Harris.

TUESDAY 7 AUGUST

► **TRAVELLING**
TENUTA SAN NICOLA – LONDON
Bowie, Angie and Stuart George returned by train and boat to London, where Ken Scott was mixing *Pin Ups* at Trident Studios. Mick Ronson and Sue Fussey stayed behind at the villa.

Sue Fussey/Ronson (2010)
We actually fell in love in Italy, right after he'd done the Bowie* Pin Ups *album. We had a villa outside Rome and everything just came together. It was a wonderful romance. [206]

A fire broke out in the surrounding countryside, burning the telephone wires and cutting them off from contact for three days. During that time Ronson came up with the concept for his debut album *Slaughter On 10th Avenue*.

ABOVE: *Best Deluxe*, a compilation double album released only in Japan. OPPOSITE: When the Stones tour reached Newcastle, Jagger invited Bowie to watch from the wings, with unexpected results.

WEDNESDAY 22 AUGUST

▼ **SOCIALISING**
Bowie went to Hampstead Theatre for the opening night of *Mad Dog*, starring Marianne Faithfull, whom Bowie had asked to be in his planned stage show based on *Nineteen Eighty-Four*.

SEPTEMBER

▲ **RECORDING**
Bowie travelled to the Château where Mick Ronson was recording *Slaughter On 10th Avenue*. Bowie contributed 'Growing Up And I'm Fine' and lyrics for Ronson's 'Hey Ma Get Papa', as well as an English lyric for 'Music Is Lethal'. Ronson had heard the song on Italian television and found out the music was available but the lyrics were untranslatable.

FRIDAY 7

▼ **SOCIALISING**
Bowie watched The Rolling Stones play the Empire Pool, Wembley and visited them backstage.

THURSDAY 13 SEPTEMBER

▼ **SOCIALISING**
Bowie and Scott Richardson hired a chauffeured Bentley for the trip to Newcastle to see the Stones playing at the City Hall. According to Zanetta, the sight of Bowie standing in the wings during the show was distracting the audience. After Jagger glared at him, Bowie withdrew further into the wings. After the show the Jaggers took Bowie and Richardson to a casino where Bowie and Jagger competed to lose the most money at the tables.

TUESDAY 18 SEPTEMBER

▼ **SOCIALISING**
The Bowies, the Jaggers and Richardson watched Diana Ross play the Royal Albert Hall.

SATURDAY 29 SEPTEMBER

◆ **AWARDS**
'MELODY MAKER' READERS' POP POLL

British Singer #1
International Singer #1
Single 'The Jean Genie' #1
Single 'Drive-In Saturday' #2
Album *Aladdin Sane* #2
International Album *Aladdin Sane* #2
International Producer #1
International Composer #1
Arranger (with Mick Ronson) #2
Live Act #2
Group (David Bowie And The Spiders From Mars) #6

OCTOBER

■ **ALBUM RELEASED**
'BEST DELUXE'
Compilation album released in Japan (RCA SRA 9412/13).

▌Reissued as *Special* (RCA 1976) with a new cover featuring a still from *The Man Who Fell To Earth*.

THURSDAY 4

Angie began the search for a new house following complaints about noise from their flat in Maida Vale, which they were renting from Diana Rigg.

FRIDAY 12 OCTOBER

■ **SINGLE RELEASED**
'Sorrow' (Feldman/Goldstein/Gottehrer) (2:53)/
'Amsterdam' (Brel/Shuman) (3:20)
UK (RCA 2424)
US (RCA APBO-0160)
UK Chart Peak No.3

The first release of 'Amsterdam', recorded during the November 1971 *Ziggy Stardust* sessions.

▌Reissued on *Rare* (RCA 1982) and with slightly different mixes on *Pin Ups* (Ryko 1990) and *Ziggy Stardust* 30th Anniversary 2 CD Edition (EMI 2002).

WEDNESDAY 17 OCTOBER

The Bowies moved into 89 Oakley Street, Chelsea accompanied by nanny Marion Skene, personal chef Anton Jones, Freddie Burretti and Daniella Parmar, who took the basement with Bowie's secretary Ava Clarke.

Bowie's new address suited Defries, who lived nearby in Gunter Grove, as he would be able to keep an eye on his employee. The monthly rent of £600 was paid as usual by MainMan and deducted from Bowie's profit-and-loss account.

Chelsea was a chic district appropriate to Bowie's new rock-star status. At one end was the fashionable King's Road, at the other the Chelsea Embankment. Here, overlooking the Thames was the exclusive Cheyne Walk, where Mick and Bianca Jagger lived at No.48. Keith Richards had lived a little further along at No.3 before moving to France in 1971. (Jagger and Richards bought the houses in 1968 and sold them in 1978.)

Cheyne Walk had a history of rich cultural life, which in the Sixties centred on the apartment of designer and Stones insider Christopher Gibbs at No.100. Here Gibbs held a salon for the cultural aristocracy and provided the setting for the party scene in Antonioni's 1966 film *Blowup*.

▲ REHEARSING
Manticore Studios
Fulham
London, England

THE 1980 FLOOR SHOW

Ava Cherry arrived in London for her appearance on *The 1980 Floor Show*. She checked into the Portobello Hotel before Angie suggested she move into Oakley Street.

Ava Cherry (1986)
David said, "Yeah, that's a great idea," so I said okay. I was new to this whole thing – you know, wife's there – but I thought, maybe this is the way things are done in England. [013]

The 1980 Floor Show was devised as an expedient way of giving Bowie nationwide exposure on American television. This would compensate for the cancelled tour and promote *Pin Ups* in full-page *Billboard* advertisements for the show. NBC agreed to stage the show for their *Midnight Special*.

Bowie initially wanted to do the performance live at the Hammersmith Odeon, which was rejected by NBC as too expensive. He opted for The Marquee Club, which was appropriate as *Pin Ups* paid tribute to the bands Bowie had watched there. During that period he also played at The Marquee with The Lower Third.

Bowie (2002)
At that time no one would book us. We were considered a freaky band, and got booed at every gig we did. The only place that would let us play regularly was The Marquee, and then only on Saturday afternoons for a free audience. [037]

Ziggy would be brought back for a one-off special that was both a *Pin Ups* showcase and a preview of his next, funkier direction in the shape of new song '1984/Dodo' and a hastily assembled trio of backing singers featuring Ava Cherry, Jason Guess (discovered in a 'soul food' restaurant) and honorary soul brother Geoff MacCormack, who adopted a joke stage name, Warren Peace.

They were dubbed The Astronettes (after Kemp's dance troupe from the Rainbow shows), and Defries added them to his MainMan roster, happy to have another act to promote in America. This would be their debut performance ahead of an album Bowie would produce in November.

Marianne Faithfull agreed to perform on the show and introduced Bowie to Amanda Lear, an exotic model of indeterminate age and gender who compered the show as the faux Russian 'Dooshenka'.

Amanda Lear (1978)
Marianne Faithfull rang me up one night and said David was at her house and wanted to meet me. He sent his car for me and we soon became good friends. [194]

They had almost met in August 1972. Bryan Ferry had Lear introduce Roxy Music on stage when they supported Bowie at the Rainbow. She had been Ferry's fiancée when she featured on the cover of Roxy Music's *For Your Pleasure*.

THURSDAY 18 – SATURDAY 20 OCTOBER

✪ TELEVISION
The Marquee Club
90 Wardour Street, Soho
London, England

'THE MIDNIGHT SPECIAL – THE 1980 FLOOR SHOW'

With Carmen, Marianne Faithfull and The Troggs.

Stan Harris: Producer/Director
David Bowie: Concept/Design
Matt Mattox: Choreography
David Bowie/Freddie Burretti: Bowie Costumes
Barbara Daly: Make-up
Natasha Korniloff: Costumes for dancers, Marianne Faithfull/Amanda Lear
Billy The Kid: Hair
George Underwood: Graphics
Ken Scott/Ground Control (Robin Mayhew): Sound Mix
'Dooshenka' (Amanda Lear): Compere
David Bowie: Vocals/Guitar/Tambourine/Harmonica
Mick Ronson: Guitar/Backing Vocals
Trevor Bolder: Bass
Aynsley Dunbar: Drums
Mike Garson: Piano
Mark Pritchett: Guitar
The Astronettes: Ava Cherry, Geoff MacCormack, Jason Guess: Backing Vocals/Percussion

OPPOSITE: Day one of *The 1980 Floor Show*: Bowie sings 'Sorrow' to Amanda Lear.

"At that time no one would book us. We were considered a freaky band, and got booed at every gig we did."

David Bowie on the early days with The Lower Third

THURSDAY 18 OCTOBER

✪ TELEVISION

The Marquee Club
90 Wardour Street, Soho
London, England

'THE MIDNIGHT SPECIAL – THE 1980 FLOOR SHOW'

Choreography
'20th Century Blues'
(Marianne Faithfull)
'Sorrow'

On the first day the club was a closed set as they filmed choreography for the opening titles, with dancers arranging themselves to spell out the letters – an idea inspired by the drawings of Erté – on a chequerboard painted stage. Behind them, white panels swung into view on pivots to form black and white stripes – evoking the old Marquee backdrop.

The dancers' crocheted elastic spider web costumes, designed by Natasha Korniloff, were originally used in the August 1972 Rainbow concerts and the 'John I'm Only Dancing' video.

Bowie emerged wearing a new Freddie Burretti suit, and serenaded Amanda Lear with 'Sorrow', singing live to a backing track, followed by a surrealistic conversation based on the Caterpillar episode in *Alice in Wonderland*.

FRIDAY 19 OCTOBER

■ ALBUM RELEASED

'PIN UPS'

UK (RCA RS 1003)
US (APL1-0291)
UK Chart Peak No.1
US Chart Peak No.23

SIDE ONE

1. **'Rosalyn'** (Duncan/Farley) (2:27)
2. **'Here Comes The Night'** (Berns) (3:09)
3. **'I Wish You Would'** (Arnold) (2:40)
4. **'See Emily Play'** (Barrett) (4:03)
5. **'Everything's Alright'** (Crouch/Konrad/Stavely/James/Karlson) (2:26)
6. **'I Can't Explain'** (Townshend) (2:07)

SIDE TWO

1. **'Friday On My Mind'** (Vanda/Young) (3:18)
2. **'Sorrow'** (Feldman/Goldstein/Gottehrer) (2:48)
3. **'Don't Bring Me Down'** (Dee) (2:01)
4. **'Shapes Of Things'** (Samwell/Smith/McCarty/Relf) (2:47)
5. **'Anyway, Anyhow, Anywhere'** (Townshend/Daltrey) (3:04)
6. **'Where Have All The Good Times Gone'** (Davies) (2:35)

David Bowie/Ken Scott: Producers
David Bowie/Mick Ronson: Arrangers
Dennis MacKay (credited as Denis Blackeye): Engineer
David Bowie: Vocals/Guitar/Moog/Harmonica/Tenor Saxophone/Alto Saxophone
Mick Ronson: Guitar/Piano/Backing Vocals
Trevor Bolder: Bass
Aynsley Dunbar: Drums
Mike Garson: Piano/Organ/Harpsichord/Electric Piano
Ken Fordham: Baritone Saxophone
Geoff MacCormack: Backing Vocals
Mick Rock/David Bowie: Design
Justin de Villeneuve: Photographer (front cover)
Mick Rock: Photographer (back cover)
Pierre Laroche: Make-up
Ray Campbell: Lettering
Recorded at Strawberry Studios Château d'Hérouville, France

TOP: Justin de Villeneuve's partner Twiggy was a perfect fit for Bowie's homage to Sixties London.
ABOVE: Back cover and insert with Bowie's notes and Mick Rock's photos, featuring the saxophone series specially shot for the album.
OPPOSITE: 'Time' (top) and Bowie between takes of 'Everything's Alright' (below) with Mick Ronson (left) and Mark Pritchett (middle).

Mick Rock (2002)
He has occasionally played sax on records over the years, including tenor and alto saxes on Pin Ups. It's like a transitional picture: he still has the Ziggy hairdo but without all the glitzy make-up and clothes. [037]

SELECTED REISSUES

▮ CD (RCA 1984).

▮ CD (remastered) (Ryko 1990).

BONUS TRACKS
1. 'Growin' Up' (Springsteen) (3:26)
2. 'Amsterdam' (Brel/Shuman) (3:19)

▮ CD (remastered) (EMI 1999).

▮ CD (mini LP replica) (Toshiba EMI 2007).

✪ TELEVISION

The Marquee Club
90 Wardour Street, Soho
London, England

'THE MIDNIGHT SPECIAL – THE 1980 FLOOR SHOW'

'As Tears Go By'
(Marianne Faithfull)
'Time'

For the second and third days of shooting, groups of 200 drawn from the Bowie fan club were brought in to inject some live energy into the show. However, with the club too small for multi-camera shooting, the audience endured five to six retakes and interrupted performances as two cameras were re-positioned between takes to cover the different angles.

Marianne Faithfull reprised her 1968 *Rock'n'Roll Circus* performance of 'As Tears Go By', her angelic appearance masking her serious heroin addiction.

Five or six takes were filmed of 'Time' to allow for shots of Bowie doing his 'gimme your hands' routine with the front row of the audience.

Above: Leee Black Childers, Cherry Vanilla, Tony Zanetta, Freddie Burretti and Suzi Fussey backstage at the Marquee. OPPOSITE: 'I Got You Babe' with Marianne Faithfull and '1984/Dodo' with the Astronettes, including Geoff MacCormark on congas.

SATURDAY 20 OCTOBER

✪ TELEVISION

The Marquee Club
90 Wardour Street, Soho
London, England

'THE MIDNIGHT SPECIAL – THE 1980 FLOOR SHOW'

■ SESSION 1

'Bulerias' (Carmen)
'Everything's Alright'
'Space Oddity'
'I Can't Explain'

The third day of shooting was devoted to the majority of the live performances. The music press was invited to report on a show that UK fans were unlikely to see. Showtime was advertised as 11.30am, but the shoot was already behind schedule as Carmen filmed takes of their song 'Bulerias', delayed when the wrong backing track was played over the PA.

Carmen was a Latino 'flamenco rock' band from Los Angeles recommended by Tony Visconti, who had recently produced their album *Fandangos In Space*.

Tony Visconti (1974)
Carmen brought David and me back together. David heard Carmen's first album and wanted to use them in his TV special. [271]

As Bowie dressed in the adjoining back room where Ken Scott and Robin Mayhew had set up the soundboard, Ronson directed the band through a couple of instrumental run-throughs of 'Everything's Alright'.

Bowie finally appeared at 3.15pm and launched into the song, only to be signalled to an abrupt halt when one of the lights went off.

"Frustrating ain't it?" Bowie remarked to the crowd as techs fixed the problem. "Well these are The Astronettes, and you all know the Spiders. And what 'ave you lot been up to?"

The next take got as far as the opening riff. By the fourth take Bowie and the technicians were satisfied and they reshot it from the audience and side stage, playing to the audio of the fourth take.

The kids at the front besieged Bowie and the band for autographs – as they did in every break in the filming. There was a flurry of interest with the arrival of MainMan artiste Wayne County, whom Charles Shaar Murray described as "a gay dude's nightmare of a woman". Mild hysteria greeted Angie's arrival with Zowie.

'Space Oddity' followed, with Ronson and Dunbar playing harder and heavier than usual. Ronson broke a string playing his guitar solo, but the take was deemed good enough and they reshot from another angle.

Bowie vanished again to change, re-emerging in thigh-length black PVC boots, a scarlet PVC corset, a big feather starting at his navel and extending up past his ears, and matching feather wristlets. He announced the next number as 'The Laughing Gnome' (the reissued 1967 Deram single had reached No.6 the previous week) before launching into 'I Can't Explain'.

■ SESSION 2
'The Jean Genie'
'1984/Dodo'
'I Got You Babe'
(with Marianne Faithfull)

The 200 fans were ushered out to make way for the next batch.

Ronson broke another guitar string during the solo in 'The Jean Genie'. He persevered before deciding the solo would suffer unless the string was replaced.

Bowie performed in a netted costume with a pair of glittery hands reaching across his chest. The hand over his crotch had been deemed too risqué for American television and was removed. After a playback of the first take showed his jockstrap was visible, Bowie went backstage to remove that as well.

For the second take, they mimed to the previous take with Bowie revealing more now his underwear was gone. Then Bowie reached for his harmonica to mime to his already-recorded solo, realised it was missing from its place on top of Trevor Bolder's amp, shrugged and mimed the part without it. Despite this the television crew was happy with the take, confident that "it won't show". On the broadcast, however, Bowie appeared clearly perplexed.

Following another costume change, Bowie announced the next song. "We've written a musical, and this is the title song called '1984'. We'll be doing the show in March next year." After a number of false starts and yet another broken guitar string, they managed a complete take, after which Bowie gave Ronson a pat on the back. After a fourth take (miming to playback for the other angles) Bowie vanished backstage, reappearing in his 'Angel Of Death' red PVC and black feathers outfit.

"Marianne Faithfull on stage now, please" came the announcement and she appeared in a backless nun's cowl to join Bowie on the Sonny and Cher duet 'I Got You Babe'. As she reached to adjust the microphone between takes, the cowl gaped open, revealing she wore nothing underneath but a body stocking.

'Rock'n'Roll Suicide' was also filmed but not included in the broadcast.

As roadies packed up Bowie's gear, most of the audience left and The Troggs recorded their three numbers – 'Wild Thing', 'I Can't Control Myself' and 'Strange Movie'.

LATE OCTOBER

▲ RECORDING
Trident Studios
17 St Anne's Court, Soho
London, England

'DIAMOND DOGS' ALBUM
'1984/Dodo'

Ken Scott: Producer

Bowie's first session for his next project was also his last with the two most significant collaborators of the past three years, Mick Ronson and Ken Scott – the producer he called "my George Martin".

Bowie (1997)
I had particular ideas that I wanted to expand upon, and it wasn't stuff that Mick would be terribly happy to follow in. It was getting harder all the time to get Mick to move along into the possibility of where we could go. His two role models were Jeff Beck and Free. If Mick had been more open to widening that which he already knew, we may have lasted as a partnership. [123]

Ken Scott (2006)
When we recorded '1984/Dodo' it became obvious that he was starting to change direction, so it was probably for the best. [394]

Mark Pritchett (2009)
Within the first couple of takes, it became fundamentally clear that all of us – but Mick was the lead musician – weren't black funky. This was not it. [045]

ABOVE: Bowie arriving at Olympic studios.

Mick Ronson (1975)
After the British tour it was decided that David wasn't going to play any more. The only plan we had was to record the Pin Ups album. Then we all went on a bit of a holiday. Then I thought I'd do a bit of recording as well. It was just for fun really. So then I started this album **Slaughter.** ***We just sort of drifted apart.***

When David decided he was going on the road again, I was going to be doing some concerts and finishing off in the studios. So I never went to America with him. We didn't fall out or become enemies or anything. When he asked me if I would go to America with him and I said no, it was only because I had one or two things to do myself. It was hard for me to say no. But he understood why. [275]

▌Released: *Diamond Dogs* (Ryko 1990)/ *Diamond Dogs* 30th Anniversary 2 CD Edition (EMI 2004).

▲ RECORDING
Studio 2
Olympic Studios
117 Church Road
Barnes
South West London, England

'DIAMOND DOGS' ALBUM

David Bowie: Producer

Keith Harwood: Engineer

Bowie moved the *Diamond Dogs* sessions from Trident (and all its Ziggy associations) to Olympic, the south London studios favoured by The Rolling Stones. Engineer Keith Harwood had recently mixed Led Zeppelin's *Houses Of The Holy* and later worked on *It's Only Rock'n'Roll*.

Retaining only Mike Garson on piano, Bowie decided (initially) to play most of the guitar and saxophone parts himself. "Angie bought me a baritone sax," Bowie later told Martin Kirkup, "so I've got the whole set now and I can do a brass section." [178]

Bowie (1997)
I knew how it had to sound, but I was a bit too embarrassed to work with other musicians. I always felt slightly awkward telling musicians who played so much better than I did what to play. Rather than have to tell those people who knew how to play really well what to play, I did it myself. [131]

I knew that the guitar playing had to be more than okay. That couple of months I spent putting that album together before I went into the studio was probably the only time in my life where I really buckled down to learn the stuff I needed to have on the album. I'd actually practise two hours a day. I knew the sound in my head, and at that time I didn't know musicians who could carry it off. [133]

"I always felt slightly awkward telling musicians who played so much better than I did what to play."

David Bowie

Bowie (1991)
I don't think I really got into messing about with recording technique until then, where it was virtually just myself doing everything. I played a great percentage of everything on Diamond Dogs, apart from the odd lead guitar, and the bass and drums. But most of the other lead guitars and the rhythm guitars and the keyboards, and saxophones, were just me. [153]

Herbie Flowers replaced Trevor Bolder on bass and the drumming was shared between Aynsley Dunbar and Tony Newman, who, like Dunbar, had played in The Jeff Beck Group. Bowie needed a more proficient guitarist for a new version of '1984' without the 'Dodo' section. He called in Alan Parker, who played a wah-wah guitar part à la 'Theme From Shaft', and Tony Visconti, whom he asked to write "some sort of Barry White strings" for it. Also working at Olympic in the neighbouring studio was Brian Eno, who was mixing *Here Come The Warm Jets*.

Bowie (1997)
We never actually had any contact at that time, except when passing each other in the hallway. I think we both caught a snatch of what the other one was doing. I know I heard his, and I know he heard mine because he would come in and lean on the doorpost.

That is the first time that I was aware that Brian and I were going off into different worlds from what we had done before. I was more into the William S Burroughs cut-up thing and that more American approach, and Brian was much more European than me at that time. [131]

SATURDAY 27 OCTOBER

By the end of the week, *Disc* reported that Bowie had already completed six songs including '1984'. Tony Ingrassia said he was working with Bowie on a script for a stage musical based on George Orwell's *Nineteen Eighty-Four*.

Bowie had announced the show the previous Saturday at The Marquee, where Ingrassia explained, "We have not fully acquired the rights to the book yet and it is still possible we will have to call it *Nineteen Eighty-Three*, or something like that!"

Later in the week, Cherry Vanilla intimated as much: "I don't know how closely David will follow the script. It might be quite unrecognisable from the original but Bowie will definitely be playing the lead role of Winston."

In fact MainMan had failed – like others before – to win the approval of Orwell's widow Sonia Brownell for the project.

Bowie (1976)
She put the clappers on it by saying no. So I, at the last minute, quickly changed it into a new concept album called Diamond Dogs. [117]

Bowie (1987)
My office, MainMan, didn't bother to do anything about it… But, I mean… well, it wasn't a real office in those days. Nobody did anything. [184]

WEDNESDAY 31 OCTOBER

✪ TELEVISION

APPEARANCE CANCELLED

Top Of The Pops producer Robin Nash had to cancel Bowie's planned performance of 'Sorrow' at the last minute due to misunderstandings. Bowie had intended to perform with live vocals and strings accompanied by a backing tape prepared at Trident. The Musicians' Union ruled that the tape could not be used. Either they record a new tape at the television studio or perform it entirely live, which Bowie deemed unfeasible.

▲ RECORDING
Morgan Studios
Willesden
North West London, England

With Herbie Flowers (and Olympic Studios) unavailable for the moment, Bowie called up Bolder out of the blue into Morgan Studios to play on a song. Bowie, Garson and Newman had been working on a slow acoustic number, which they ran through with Bolder, before recording a take (which never saw the light of day).

His job done, Bolder packed up and left saying, "I'm off now Dave, I'll see you later on," as Bowie sat with his back to him saying nothing. Bolder left the studio in silence, for the last time.

ABOVE: Bowie at the launch of 'flamenco rock' band Carmen's debut album, *Fandangos In Space*, which Tony Visconti produced.

NOVEMBER

SATURDAY 3

■ **CHART**

'Sorrow'

UK Chart Peak No.3

SATURDAY 10 NOVEMBER

◆ **UK ALBUM CHART**

Pin Ups #1

Aladdin Sane #10

Hunky Dory #17

Ziggy Stardust #25

FRIDAY 16 NOVEMBER

✪ **TELEVISION**

The 1980 Floor Show broadcast on *The Midnight Special* in US (NBC). Two months later *NME* reported that ITV had secured the British screening rights for *The Midnight Special 1980 Floor Show*, but hadn't fixed on a transmission date. The show was never broadcast in the UK.

Ava Cherry was moved, on Angie's insistence, to Daska House in nearby King's Road where Defries paid the rent, which was deducted from The Astronettes' account.

SATURDAY 17 NOVEMBER

✪ **PRESS**

Rolling Stone writer Craig Copetas moderated a two-way interview with Bowie and William Burroughs, conducted over lunch at Oakley Street.

"Bowie's house is decorated in a science fiction mode: a gigantic painting, by an artist whose style fell midway between Salvador Dali and Norman Rockwell, hung over a plastic sofa.

"Soon Bowie entered, wearing three-tone NASA jodhpurs. He jumped right into a detailed description of the painting and its surrealistic qualities. Burroughs nodded, and the interview/ conversation began. The three of us sat in the room for two hours, talking and taking lunch: a Jamaican fish dish, prepared by a Jamaican in the Bowie entourage, with avocados stuffed with shrimp and a Beaujolais nouveau, served by two interstellar Bowieites." [093]

They had expressed an interest in meeting each other and in the weeks leading up to the interview Bowie found time to read only one of Burroughs novels (*Nova Express*) that Copetas sent him. But he was already familiar with Burroughs' cut-up writing methodology.

ABOVE: William Burroughs showed Bowie the cut-up technique of writing, which Bowie employed from *Diamond Dogs* onwards.
OPPOSITE: Lulu and Bowie, promoting her career-reviving single 'The Man Who Sold The World'/'Watch That Man', which they made together during Bowie's *Pin Ups* sessions.

Bowie (1977)
Burroughs was very instrumental, as soon as I met him. He convinced me about the marvellous things you can do with the cut-up technique and I incorporated that in some of the stuff like* Diamond Dogs *and I've never dropped it. In fact it reveals itself to its fullest extent I guess, on "Heroes", more than anything else. [338]

Bowie (1980)
It was taking three different points of view of any given subject. You have one subject and you look at it from three different perspectives. And then you intercut the different perspectives. Logistically you just take sentences and cut the sentences up. [332]

Bowie (1974)
It seemed that it would predict things about the future or tell me a lot about the past. It's really quite an astonishing thing. I suppose it's a very Western tarot. [353]

'Beat Godfather Meets Glitter MainMan' was published in *Rolling Stone*, February 28, 1974.

LATE NOVEMBER

▲ **RECORDING**

Studio 2
Olympic Studios
117 Church Road
Barnes
South West London, England

'Growin' Up'

During a hiatus in the *Diamond Dogs* sessions, Ronnie Wood dropped in and played guitar on this, the first of three Springsteen covers recorded during the Olympic sessions. 'It's Hard To Be A Saint In The City' was begun (left unfinished until 1975) and Bowie produced 'Spirit In The Night' for The Astronettes.

▮Released on *Pin Ups* (Ryko 1990).

DECEMBER

MONDAY 3

▲ **RECORDING**

Studio 2
Olympic Studios
117 Church Road
Barnes
South West London, England

ASTRONETTES ALBUM

David Bowie: Producer

Keith Harwood: Engineer

Bowie turned his attention to The Astronettes' album that he had promised to produce for Ava Cherry. As with Arnold Corns, he used the Astronettes project as a dry run for his next project – a fusion of Afro-American soul music with Latin rhythms and Springsteen street-cool.

Ava Cherry, Geoff MacCormack and Jason Guess took turns on vocal, with Mark Pritchett, Herbie Flowers, Mike Garson and Aynsley Dunbar providing the backing.

Mark Pritchett (2009)
You'd get a call, turn up, it might be just you and a drummer, it might just be you laying down something on your own. David would say, "These are the chords, can you give it a funky feel?" He may use your part, he may decide he doesn't like it, or he might use the idea as part of something else. [045]

Songs recorded over the next few weeks included Bowie compositions 'I Am Divine', 'I Am A Laser', 'People From Bad Homes' and 'Things To Do'.

Tony Visconti (1982)
One of the songs David recorded with them was 'God Only Knows', which they did about four times slower than The Beach Boys, a very funky, laid-back version, and I did strings for a few of those tracks. [015]

Tony Visconti (2006)
The arrangement features mandolins playing what would normally be for violins. I thought I would have to persuade David to accept it, but he did so without hesitation. [047]

▲ **RECORDING**

LULU

David Bowie: Producer

Engineer: Keith Harwood

Bowie also started work on a backing track for a Lulu project at Olympic. At some stage a version of 'Dodo' (detached from '1984') was recorded as a possible Lulu single. A version with Bowie's guide vocal was released on the Ryko reissue and the EMI 30th Anniversary 2CD Edition of *Diamond Dogs*.

TUESDAY 4 DECEMBER

Bowie and Amanda Lear arrived in a white limousine to see Marianne Faithfull starring in John Osborne's play *A Patriot For Me* at the Palace Theatre, Watford. After the show they visited Faithfull backstage and joined the party afterwards. Bowie was interviewed at the theatre for local radio.

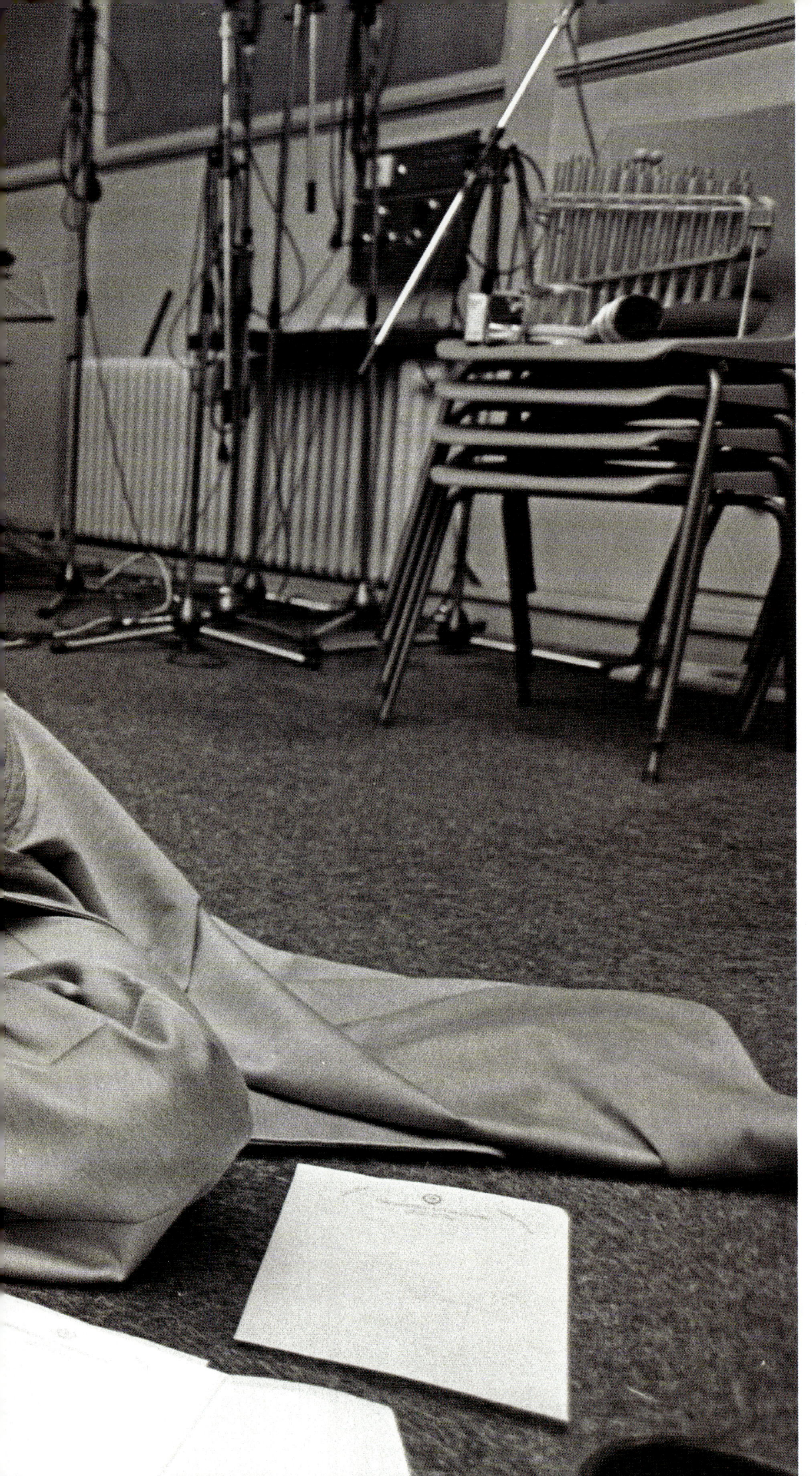

LEFT: Bowie writing songs for *Diamond Dogs* using the cut-up technique of assembling lyric phrases.

ABOVE: Ronnie Wood at 'The Wick', his home in Richmond, Middlesex, which British rock royalty frequented to jam and record in the home studio he had built there.

WEDNESDAY 5 THURSDAY 6 DECEMBER

▲ RECORDING

The Wick
Richmond
Surrey, England

THE ROLLING STONES
'It's Only Rock'n'Roll'

Mick Jagger was back in England during a break from recording the new Stones album in Munich. He was hanging out at Ronnie Wood's house – The Wick in Richmond – where Wood was recording *I've Got My Own Album To Do* in his home studio. Also at the sessions were top session bass player Willie Weeks and drummer Andy Newmark.

Wood had seen Newmark playing in Sly And The Family Stone and when he was preparing his own album, Wood called him. "We thought that I was going to play bass until he mentioned that he knew this bass player in New York that wouldn't mind the gig." When Newmark told him it was Weeks, Wood eagerly agreed. "I never thought I'd meet Willie, let alone play with him." [198]

Bowie dropped in and jammed with Jagger, Wood and Faces drummer Kenney Jones on a new song that became 'It's Only Rock'n'Roll'. Bowie joined in on backing vocals and handclaps.

Keith Richards knew the song had potential when he later heard the recording: "It's Mick's song and he'd cut it with Bowie as a dub. Mick had gotten this idea and they started to rock on it. It was damn good." [036]

Richards reclaimed the song for the new Stones album and its first single. Several overdubs later rendered Bowie's vocal contribution on the finished version inaudible.

FRIDAY 14 DECEMBER

▼ SOCIALISING

Kris Needs later described Mott The Hoople's show at the Hammersmith Odeon as "one of the greatest rock'n'roll moments this correspondent has experienced in over 40 years". Bowie and Jagger watched from behind Morgan Fisher's grand piano as Hunter led the group back on for the encore and announced: "Three things made tonight so enjoyable: David Bowie, Mick Jagger and you."

TUESDAY 25 DECEMBER

▼ SOCIALISING

The Bowies hosted Christmas for Mick and Bianca Jagger at home in Chelsea. Bowie gave Jagger a video recorder, an expensive luxury at the time (around £500), which had become one of Bowie's new obsessions.

THURSDAY 27 DECEMBER

▲ RECORDING

Trident Studios
17 St Anne's Court, Soho
London, England

'Rebel Rebel' (early demo)

Alan Parker (2004)

On 'Rebel Rebel', he had the riff about 75% sorted out. He wanted it a bit like a Stones riff, and he played it to me as such, and I then tinkered around with it. I said, "Well, what if we did this and that and made it sound more clangy and put some bends in it?" and he said, "Yeah, I love that, that's fine." I used an old Les Paul standard, a black one, and it was an old Fender reverb amp with a single Wharfedale speaker in them. [326]

FRIDAY 28 DECEMBER

✪ PRESS

'The Odd Couple: Lulu teams up with Bowie' by Deborah Thomas published in the *Daily Mirror* with photos by Gavin Kent.

This surely is the year's strangest showbiz combination. Lulu, the family favourite joining forces with David Bowie, the bizarre pop phenomenon. Lulu, 25, agreed because she wants to get away from her cosy television image claiming, "rock is where my roots are." She says, "My relationship with David is a kind of mutual admiration thing." [291]

SATURDAY 29
SUNDAY 30 DECEMBER

▲ RECORDING

Studio 2
Olympic Studios
117 Church Road
Barnes
South West London, England

ASTRONETTES ALBUM

ABOVE AND BELOW: Bowie with the RCA award for his outstanding performance in the 1973 UK album charts.

MONDAY 31 DECEMBER

✪ PRESS

Rules Restaurant
Covent Garden
London, England

RCA Records held a press lunch at the prestigious Covent Garden restaurant in Bowie's honour, for having six different albums in the charts for five weeks in 1973 and five in the Top 50 for 19 consecutive weeks.

Bowie rose from the head of a long table in an upstairs room to thank everyone: "I don't know what to say, I feel like a rock'n'roll star. At least it keeps the kids on the streets. Thanks to everyone who bought or were given the albums."

He was given a framed album presentation with a plaque inscribed "Awarded to David Bowie for outstanding musical achievements. From your friends at RCA."

JANUARY

TUESDAY 1

▲ RECORDING

Studio 2
Olympic Studios
117 Church Road
Barnes
South West London, England

'Take It In Right' (demo)
'Candidate' (demo)

Keith Harwood/Andy Morris: Engineers

This early version of 'Take It In Right' (later retitled 'Can You Hear Me') was a basic acoustic recording with lyrics still in progress. Bowie wrote it as a potential follow-up single for Lulu. 'Candidate' was written for the projected musical based on *Nineteen Eighty-Four*.

Released on *Diamond Dogs* reissue (Ryko 1990) and (as 'Alternative Candidate') on 30th Anniversary 2 CD Edition (EMI 2004).

TUESDAY 1 – SATURDAY 5 JANUARY

▲ RECORDING

Studio 2
Olympic Studios
117 Church Road
Barnes
South West London, England

ASTRONETTES ALBUM

MONDAY 7 JANUARY

⊙ BUSINESS

After two years of overspending, MainMan was running out of money. The London office had no cash flow and Corinne Schwab was fending off the creditors. Olympic Studios threatened to ban Bowie from further sessions until they were paid £4,935 in outstanding fees. Cherry Vanilla contacted Defries in New York asking him to pay Olympic so Bowie could complete the album.

TUESDAY 8 JANUARY

▼ SOCIALISING

To celebrate Bowie's 27th birthday, Amanda Lear took him and George Underwood out to an afternoon screening of *Metropolis* at the Everyman Cinema in Hampstead.

Amanda Lear (1978)

It was a real big thing for him. He was so paranoid about going out in daylight and being recognised. We saw Fritz Lang's **Metropolis** ***and David was in awe of it. He rented the film and ran it over and over again in his house. And that's where*** **Diamond Dogs** ***came from, the whole staging and album and everything Bowie got from*** **Metropolis.**
[194]

Bowie used the German expressionist film as a key reference point in the stage design of the new *Diamond Dogs* show.

TOP: Bowie recorded most of *Diamond Dogs* at Olympic Studios in Barnes, despite the owners' threats to ban further sessions due to unpaid bills.
ABOVE: Amanda Lear – model, muse, aspiring actress and later a queen of Euro disco.
LEFT: Ava Cherry and Geoff MacCormack, two-thirds of the Astronettes project that Bowie eventually shelved.

WEDNESDAY 9 – FRIDAY 11 JANUARY

▲ RECORDING

Olympic Studios
117 Church Road
Barnes
South West London, England

ASTRONETTES ALBUM

FRIDAY 11 JANUARY

■ SINGLE RELEASED

LULU
'The Man Who Sold The World' (3:58)/
'Watch That Man' (5:11)
UK (Polydor 2001 490)
Chart Peak No.3

David Bowie/Mick Ronson: Producers

Bowie supplied the backing track and supervised the sound for Lulu's appearance on BBC's *Top Of The Pops*, performing 'The Man Who Sold The World' wearing a suit and fedora.

▮ Reissued on *Oh! You Pretty Things: The Songs Of David Bowie* (Castle 2006).

Lulu (2009)
It was very Berlin cabaret. 'The Man Who Sold The World' saved me from a certain niche in my career. [298]

Bowie (1976)
It was hard for Lulu to do anything after that with the particular thing that I gave her, and she started dressing up in these funny suits and looking like a boy. She was trying to get lost in my identity of her, so when I'd done Lulu I thought, "I'd better stop doing this" because I felt somewhat like a Svengali and it was very easy for me to do that, fall into that role. I was again giving vent to my cinematic pretensions and creating little pastiche filmlet things for people and casting them in roles and sort of directing the whole thing. [332]

ABOVE: Lulu on *Top Of The Pops* performing 'The Man Who Sold The World' which Bowie wrote, produced and played on. OVERLEAF: Terry O'Neill's photograph of Bowie with the Great Dane (circled on the contact sheet) was the basis of a MainMan promotional poster for *Diamond Dogs*, painted by Guy Peellaert.

MONDAY 14 JANUARY

▲ RECORDING

Studio 2
Olympic Studios
117 Church Road
Barnes
South West London, England

'DIAMOND DOGS' ALBUM
'Rock'n'Roll With Me'
'Candidate'
'Big Brother'
'Diamond Dogs'

Andy Morris: Engineer

Photographer Kate Simon was at Olympic on assignment for *Disc*, taking pictures of Stomu Yamashta, who was recording in a room adjacent to Studio 2. After the session she ventured next door.

Kate Simon (2011)
I can see David clearly now, sitting behind the huge desk in the main room, in a long green synthetic fur coat and a green felt hat, singing and playing acoustic guitar.

I was overwhelmed at how good he was, just accompanying himself. And he was lovely, gave me absolute freedom that day. He kept calling me 'Bette' – he believed I looked like Bette Midler – and once I was done, said: "Bette, do you need a lift back into town?"

He was heading to Oakley Street and so I got a ride in this huge limousine to my flat in Fulham. He was very, very nice, but all the way – on what was quite a long journey – he didn't say a word, until I got out. Then he said: "I'll see you again."Maybe he was kind of wistful that day. [410]

ASTRONETTES ALBUM

With his days at Olympic numbered, Bowie shelved the Astronettes project to concentrate on finishing his album. He promised Ava Cherry that they would make her solo album later in the States.

The tapes of The Astronettes' sessions were retained by Tony Defries and eventually released as *People From Bad Homes* (Golden Years 1995).

Geoff MacCormack (2008)
They were just demos that we abandoned to come back to at another time. He had the tapes and without asking anybody just put them out. To my ears, the music wasn't good. They were just demos, just ideas being thrown around. [280]

WEDNESDAY 16 JANUARY

▲ RECORDING

Studio 2
Olympic Studios
117 Church Road
Barnes
South West London, England

'DIAMOND DOGS' ALBUM
'We Are The Dead'

THURSDAY 24 JANUARY

▲ RECORDING

Studio 2
Olympic Studios
117 Church Road
Barnes
South West London, England

'DIAMOND DOGS' ALBUM

Visitors to the *Diamond Dogs* sessions included Mick Jagger, Pete Townshend, Ronnie Wood and Rod Stewart, who donated an uncredited sample from the opening track of *Coast To Coast: Overtures And Beginners* – The Faces' live album released two weeks before. Bowie sampled the roar of the crowd and Rod Stewart's "Hey!" greeting for the opening of 'Diamond Dogs'.

SATURDAY 26 JANUARY

✪ PRESS

NME reported that Bowie was working on tracks 'Big Brother' and 'Are You Coming? Are You Coming?' for the *Nineteen Eighty-Four* stage show, now renamed *The 1980 Floor Show*, "to avoid any copyright problems which might otherwise arise".

WEDNESDAY 30 JANUARY

✪ PHOTO SESSION

'DIAMOND DOGS' ALBUM

Terry O'Neill: Photographer

Terry O'Neill (2013)

I had shot the dog first and then a few frames of Bowie posing in his inimitable way – which was at ease but totally in control. Then I said, "What about trying one with you and the dog?" Just as I started shooting, the bloody dog leapt up into the air towards the camera. It was quite aggressive and I was a bit taken aback, but I kept thinking: "Thank God I'm using a wide-angle lens." David just sat there throughout. He was totally unfazed. [236]

FEBRUARY

■ **MIXING**
Good Earth Studios
9 Melrose Terrace
Shepherd's Bush
London, England

Tony Visconti: Engineer

With Olympic Studios no longer an option, Bowie had to look elsewhere to finish the album and called up Tony Visconti for advice.

Tony Visconti (1982)
He said, "I'm having trouble mixing and finishing this album, so why don't we get together again?" and he asked if I could recommend a good studio. I said I was building my own, so he wanted to come and see it, and when he did, it obviously felt right, and he decided he must finish the album there.

We didn't even have chairs at that time, but he said it didn't matter, and the next day he went to Habitat or some place like that, and this big van showed up in front of my house, and out came tables, chairs, lounges and all that, and he completely furnished my studio so that he could finish his album there.

We actually did our first day's work, before all the stuff arrived, sitting on a carpenter's horse – we were sitting on this horse mixing, and it was the following day, when everything arrived, that he said, "Well, we couldn't spend another day sitting on this wooden horse." [015]

TUESDAY 12

⊙ **BUSINESS**
Since Bowie had to leave England for tax reasons, RCA organised a short promotional tour of Holland for Bowie to promote 'Rebel Rebel', receive an award and put the final touches on the album.

LEFT AND ABOVE: With Angie and Zowie at the Amstel Hotel, Amsterdam.
RIGHT: Downstairs at the press conference, Bowie has a glass of Schelvispekel.
OVERLEAF: Angie, Zowie and Bowie, holding his Edison Award for the Most Popular Male Vocalist.

WEDNESDAY 13 FEBRUARY

✪ **PRESS**
Amstel Hotel
Amsterdam, Netherlands

Accompanied by Angie and Zowie, Bowie attended a press reception where Ad Visser, host of Dutch music show *Top Pop*, presented Bowie with the Edison Award for the Most Popular Male Vocalist.

Visser then poured them glasses of Schelvispekel, recalling they had drunk it a few years before at Bowie's house in London. Visser toasted the Bowies' health, explaining it was an old fishermen's drink. Bowie quipped, "It's made out of old fishermen."

Bowie's Burretti-designed outfit was inspired by Carmen, the flamenco rock group who had appeared on *The 1980 Floor Show* in October.

Bowie (1993)
I had conjunctivitis so I made the most of it and dressed like a pirate. Just stopped short of the parrot. I had this most incredible jacket that I was wearing that night. It was a bottle-green bolero jacket that Freddie made for me, and he got an artist to paint, using the appliqué technique, this supergirl from a Russian comic [Octobriana] ***on the back. But I took the jacket off during the press conference and somebody stole it.*** [111]

✪ **TELEVISION**
AVRO Studio
Hilversum, Netherlands

'TOP POP'
'Rebel Rebel'

▮ Broadcast: February 18 (AVRO).

▮ Released on *Best Of Bowie* (EMI 2002).

◆ **AWARDS**
That evening Bowie and Angie attended the Edison Awards ceremony in Amsterdam. The Edisons – the Dutch equivalent of the Grammys – included a performance by Tony Orlando and Dawn singing their hit 'Tie A Yellow Ribbon'. Orlando broke off singing the last verse when he spotted Bowie and Angie in the audience: "Is that you? Is that really you? Is that David? A fantastic star, David Bowie."

▮ Broadcast: *Grand Gala du Disque* (AVRO).

THURSDAY 14 FEBRUARY

■ **MIXING**

Studio L Ludolf
Machineweg 8–12
Hilversum, Netherlands

Bowie and Tony Visconti completed work on the *Diamond Dogs* album at Ludolf.

FRIDAY 15 FEBRUARY

■ **SINGLE RELEASED**

'Rebel Rebel' (4:22)/
'Queen Bitch' (3:14)
UK (RCA LPBO 5009)
Chart Peak No.5

FRIDAY 22 FEBRUARY

▼ **SOCIALISING**

Bowie was at The Rainbow Theatre to see the first of Mick Ronson's two concerts at the venue, backed by Trevor Bolder, Mike Garson, Ritchie Dharma, Mark Pritchett and a horn section.

Mick Ronson (1975)
When I did the Rainbow, I don't know if it was good or bad. I think I wanted to do it. Maybe I should have hung on for a while. [162]

SATURDAY 23 FEBRUARY

■ **CHART**

'Rebel Rebel'
UK Top 30 Chart Entry No.6
Charting 7 weeks

THURSDAY 28 FEBRUARY

✪ **PRESS**

'Beat Godfather Meets Glitter MainMan' by Craig Copetas published in *Rolling Stone*.

Craig Copetas had introduced William Burroughs to Bowie and moderated the three-way interview at Bowie's Oakley Street home the previous November.

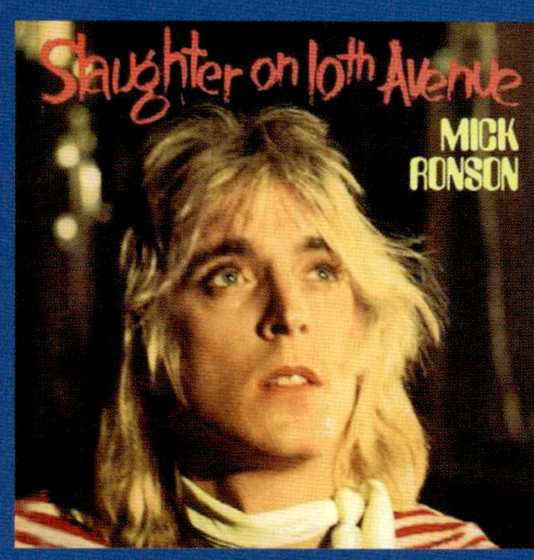

MARCH

FRIDAY 1

■ ALBUM RELEASED

MICK RONSON
'SLAUGHTER ON 10TH AVENUE'
UK (RCA APL1-0353)

Included Bowie's 'Growing Up And I'm Fine', the Bowie–Ronson composition 'Hey Ma Get Papa' and 'Music Is Lethal', for which Bowie contributed English lyrics.

MainMan promoted Ronson's first album with all the fanfare expected of an established star. A coinciding UK tour helped *Slaughter On 10th Avenue* make its chart debut at No.9. MainMan then rented one of New York's most expensive billboards in Times Square to advertise the album with a half-nude 'sex god' image of Ronson.

Ronson told *Circus*, "It was pretty weird. I thought it would be an actual photograph, like the album cover, but it was a painting. I looked like a doll or something."

One British writer commented later, "He's just a figure in a publicity campaign, a guy who wants a crack at the big pot. He wasn't ready for this big hype and he couldn't sustain it." [273]

SATURDAY 2 MARCH

■ CHART

'Rebel Rebel'
UK Chart Peak No.5

FRIDAY 8 MARCH

▼ SOCIALISING

Bowie attended the exhibition and book launch of Belgian artist Guy Peellaert's *Rock Dreams* at The Rainbow Room in London. The book was concerned with the iconography and mythology of rock history and included a double portrait of Bowie and Lou Reed.

Guy Peellaert (1974)
Those two are as provocative as they can be on stage; there are thousands of good pictures of them. I wanted a more inside point of view. David Bowie is always anxious about what is going to happen. He is clever and somewhat cold. [075]

Bowie also featured on the cover, sitting in a diner with the artists who Peellaert said "started the big movements during the last 20 years": Elvis, Dylan, Jagger and Lennon, who bought the painting.

Jagger had seen the *Rock Dreams* paintings while the book was still in production and commissioned Peellaert to illustrate the cover of the next Stones album, *It's Only Rock'n'Roll*. Jagger then told Bowie about the commission and showed him some examples of the Belgian artist's work to Bowie, who immediately contacted Peellaert.

Bowie had already sketched out his *Rock Dreams*-style visual concept for the *Diamond Dogs* front and back gatefold cover, based on a photo of Josephine Baker, with a mutant twist that referenced the title song's lyric, *"Tod Browning's Freak he was"*.

Following a breakfast meeting on 30 January at Peellaert's hotel, Bowie invited him to come to a hired studio where Terry O'Neill would be shooting the cover photographs of Bowie morphing into a dog – a Great Dane that O'Neill had borrowed from a friend.

ABOVE: The Terry O'Neill session produced reference images for Guy Peellaert's *Diamond Dogs* cover paintings.
ABOVE LEFT: Ronson's solo debut album, recorded straight after *Pin Ups* in the same studio with the same personnel. Cover by Leee Black Childers.
LEFT: Guy Peellaert's cover for the Rolling Stones LP *It's Only Rock 'n' Roll*.
OPPOSITE: AVRO Studios, Hilversum. Bowie mimes to 'Rebel Rebel' on *Top Pop*.

Guy Peellaert (2000)
It was only when we were at the session that he finally asked me if I would do a painting for him. The idea was so interesting I couldn't refuse. [007]

The night before the *Rock Dreams* book launch, Bowie took delivery of the artwork, and *Diamond Dogs* was in the record shops six months before the Stones album.

Bowie (1976)
Mick was silly. I mean, he should never have shown me anything new. I went over to his house and he had all these Guy Peellaert pictures around and said, "What do you think of this guy?" I told him I thought he was incredible. So I immediately phoned him up. Mick's learned now, as I've said. He will never do that again. [101]

MID-MARCH

Plans for the West End stage show of *Nineteen Eighty-Four* were ditched in favour of an extensive American tour with a strong theatrical element.

Defries planned to 'unretire' Bowie by relaunching him in America as an entertainer. In the tradition of Frank, Elvis, Judy and Liza, he would be known from then on as 'Bowie'.

Broadway designer Jules Fisher flew to London to meet Bowie, who briefed him on the concept for the *Diamond Dogs* stage show. Fisher then brought in Mark Ravitz to design the Hunger City set.

Jules Fisher (1985)

He had an attitude, a perspective of what he wanted, a very clear vision of what it should feel like. When an artist can communicate what he really feels, he can leave it up to other artists to execute. For* Diamond Dogs*, he had an understanding of German expressionist art and film – he wanted that image. He said, "I see a town, like the one in* The Cabinet Of Dr Caligari.*" [016]

Mark Ravitz (1985)

***David gave me three clues – power, Nuremberg and Fritz Lang's* Metropolis.** [016]

Jules Fisher (1995)

There were four towers that were the basis of the design, and they were made of newsprint that could be torn apart, so Bowie could actually climb one of these towers and destroy the building during the concert. There was also a bridge across here, and during the concert the bridge lowered down to the stage so that he could step off of it and sing downstage. And at the end it raised up again. And there was a door that opened up and a cherry picker arm came forward and extended out over the first six rows of the audience. [354]

Angie told Bowie about Toni Basil, a choreographer working with The Lockers, an urban dance troupe with a 'street' sense that fitted Bowie's *Diamond Dogs* concept. Bowie asked Defries to secure her services.

TOP: Fritz Lang's *Metropolis* was one of the key sources of inspiration for the Hunger City set.
ABOVE: The Hunger City set design model, showing Bowie on the bridge. This, the designers' copy, toured with the *David Bowie Is* exhibition. Jules Fisher and Mark Ravitz gave their other copy to Bowie, who in turn gifted it to Nicolas Roeg at end of filming *The Man Who Fell To Earth* in 1975. Roeg later gave it to Candy Clark.

Toni Basil (2002)
When I was taken to dinner, David wasn't there but there were several people with us. The money that was being thrown around was a lot of money. He was just willing to do theatre, rock'n'roll, dance, story – everything. [370]

As Bowie made plans for his move to America, Corinne Schwab was planning to move on from the London MainMan office, where she'd been keeping creditors at bay.

LEFT: Tour choreographer Toni Basil.
ABOVE: Bowie with Corinne 'Coco' Schwab at the Live Aid concert in London, July 1985.
RIGHT: Dana Gillespie's debut album with cover photography by Gered Mankowitz. 'Andy Warhol' and 'Mother Don't Be Frightened' were produced by Bowie and Ronson in 1971 with the *Hunky Dory* line-up, including Rick Wakeman.

Tony Visconti (2000)
Toni Basil taught him things like "Don't ever waste a movement. If you have to put your microphone down, do it with a flourish. If you have to walk from one side of the stage to the other, do it with great dramatic gestures. Throw your head back before you put your first step out." [030]

Toni Basil (1985)
We talked about the Living Theatre, we talked about mime. David had this idea about having ropes tied around the necks of some dancers. When I told him he could do it if he was careful he yelled at Corinne, "The Diamond Dogs number is back in!" [016]

Corinne Schwab (2001)
I got started working with David by answering an ad in the Evening Standard *in London asking for "Girl Friday needed for busy office". I had run my finger down the page and stopped there in totally arbitrary fashion. I needed a job to earn expense money for a trip my photographer friend and I were planning to take. We had a magazine interested in us to do a story of two girls on a Greyhound bus tour of America, kind of Jack Kerouac* On The Road *style, but two girls as opposed to two guys. They were only willing to pay a certain amount upfront and we thought to save a bit more we'd get short-term jobs.*

When I was ready to leave MainMan six months later, David called and asked me why I was leaving. I explained about this Greyhound bus tour of America thing. He paused for a minute and said, "How about a limousine tour of America?" I paused for about a nanosecond and said something like, "Uh, okay." Needless to say, I don't think my photographer friend ever truly forgave me. [389]

Since Gloria Harris had moved on, Bowie appointed Corinne Schwab (whom Geoff MacCormack nicknamed Coco) as his personal assistant. She later became his manager, a position she still held in 2016.

FRIDAY 22 MARCH
■ ALBUM RELEASED
DANA GILLESPIE
'WEREN'T BORN A MAN'
UK (RCA APL1 0354)

Included Bowie/Ronson productions 'Andy Warhol' and 'Mother Don't Be Frightened'. 'Backed A Loser' was credited as a Bowie composition.

MONDAY 25 MARCH
▲ RECORDING
Studio 2
Olympic Studios
117 Church Road
Barnes
South West London, England

LULU SINGLE
'Can You Hear Me'

David Bowie: Producer/Guitar
Tony Newman: Drums

FRIDAY 29 MARCH
► TRAVELLING
LONDON – PARIS
Bowie and Geoff MacCormack travelled by ferry across the Channel to France, where they stayed for a few days at the Hotel Raphael in Paris.

APRIL

WEDNESDAY 3

▶ TRAVELLING

PARIS – CANNES – NEW YORK

People magazine reported:

"Noted for his metallic jumpsuits, Martian spaceman costumes and gobs of eye make-up, Bowie appeared rather conservatively dressed in Cannes recently, sporting nothing louder than a satin-quilted suit and a borsalino hat."

After stopping off for a couple of hours at the Carlton Hotel in Cannes, Bowie and Geoff MacCormack boarded SS *France* for New York.

Geoff MacCormack (2007)

We nearly missed the boat from Paris. David fell in love with a girl on a revue show and I had a girlfriend there at the time. We had a suite in the Carlton Hotel for three nights but all we managed was to get back just in time to grab a banana, have a quick wash and get in a limo taking us back to get our boat, which we nearly missed. [021]

After Bowie heard the crew were disappointed that he was not scheduled to play on the voyage, he turned up in the canteen with an acoustic guitar.

Bruno Rabreau

(*Le France* Receptionist) (2006)

We enjoyed more than ten songs and especially 'Space Oddity' which was the first one, and a few crew members took instruments too and played with him. It was a really, really good time. He was a very ordinary person and very friendly to us. [161]

THURSDAY 11 APRIL

▶ TRAVELLING

Bowie and MacCormack sailed into New York on the SS *France*. After signing autographs for a small group of fans waiting on the dock, they checked into the Sherry Netherlands hotel on Fifth Avenue.

■ SINGLE RELEASED

'Rock'n'Roll Suicide' (2:58)/
'Quicksand' (5:03)
UK (RCA LPBO 5021)
Chart Peak No.22

The first record credited to 'Bowie' and his first RCA single to miss the British Top 20 since 'Changes' in January 1972.

▲ RECORDING

RCA Studios
Studio 4D
155 East 24th Street
New York City
New York, USA

'Rebel Rebel' (US version)

One of Bowie's first jobs in New York was to rework the new single for the American market, with tape effects, more percussion and a new arrangement, which he retained for the 1974 tour.

Geoff MacCormack (2008)

David and I got very heavily into Latin music. He decided we should put down a new backing vocal and have some congas all the way through 'Rebel Rebel'. So when we got to New York, they ordered some congas for me and I put a heavy conga thing all the way through and we sang those backing vocals. [280]

■ TELEVISION

RCA Studios
Studio 4D
155 East 24th Street
New York City
New York, USA

✪ COMMERCIAL FLMING

'DIAMOND DOGS' ALBUM

Defries had appointed MainMan publicist Cherry Vanilla head of the film division of MainMan, part of the strategy to sell Bowie to America on television. He assigned her to produce a television commercial for the new album. Photographer Macs McCarey filmed Bowie sitting at the recording console at work on the new version of 'Rebel Rebel'. Cherry Vanilla provided the voiceover: "*Diamond Dogs* by Bowie, available on RCA Records and Tapes worldwide. *Diamond Dogs* by Bowie – a MainMan production."

▲ RECORDING

RCA Studios
Studio 4D
155 East 24th Street
New York City
New York, USA

LULU SINGLE

'Can You Hear Me'

"Have you heard Ann Peebles?" Bowie asked Martin Kirkup a few days later. "Yeah, well Lennon's right, ain't he, best record in years. I mean, that's what I'd like to do producing Lulu – take her to Memphis and get a really good band like Willie Mitchell's and do a whole album with her, which I will do. Lulu's got this terrific voice, and it's been misdirected all this time, all these years. People laugh now, but they won't in two years' time, you see! I produced a single with her, 'Can You Hear Me', and that's more the way she's going. She's got a real soul voice, she can get the feel of Aretha, but it's been so misdirected." [178]

Carlos Alomar played guitar on the session – the beginning of a long working relationship with Bowie.

Alomar had got his start at The Apollo Theatre in Harlem in the vocal group Listen My Brother (Luther Vandross, Robin Clark and Fonzi Thornton), who opened for bigger acts such as Sly And The Family Stone in 1969. While in the house band, Alomar substituted for James Brown's guitarist and soon afterwards toured with Brown for eight months. He also backed Chuck Berry and The O'Jays.

By 1971 he was working in the RCA studio house band, where he joined The Main Ingredient. Their singer, Tony Silvester, suggested Alomar when Bowie said he was looking for a guitarist for the session.

Carlos Alomar (2004)

He was so thin, about 100 pounds, and one of the first things I said to him was, "Man, you look like shit. You've gotta come to my house and eat some decent food." And he did. [062]

That night Bowie asked Alomar to join the *Diamond Dogs* tour band. Alomar was equally keen to join, pending fee negotiations with Bowie's management.

▼ SOCIALISING

In the meantime Alomar spent the evenings showing Bowie and Ava Cherry around The Apollo Theatre, one night featuring The Temptations and The Spinners on the same bill.

Carlos Alomar (1997)

Here we are… in the centre of Harlem, at the front entrance of the theatre. There is a line. A long line! And a stretch limousine pulls up. Out comes the whitest white man imaginable with stark red flaming hair, who proceeds to walk right up to the front entrance and pass right through, ignoring the obvious gawks, stares, gaping mouths and probable profanities. [196]

Bowie (2002)

It rekindled the affection for soul and R&B which I had in the Sixties… seeing it for real in the States. It was unlike anything I'd seen or witnessed before. [116]

WEDNESDAY 17 APRIL

▼ SOCIALISING

Bowie, MacCormack and Cherry Vanilla attended the New York premiere of *Rodin, Mis en Vie*, a ballet based on the life of sculptor Auguste Rodin. Bowie was impressed with the performance and staging concepts, particularly in the final scene, 'The Gates of Hell', in which the entire company climbed up and descended from an ominous 50-foot scaffolding.

Afterwards Bowie met Michael Kamen, who scored the production, and invited him to join the tour as musical director.

OPPOSITE: Bowie working on the 'Rebel Rebel' US remix in RCA's New York studios.

FRIDAY 19 APRIL

▼SOCIALISING

Following Todd Rundgren's three-hour concert at Carnegie Hall, Bowie and Ava Cherry attended the 3am party thrown by Rundgren's record label Bearsville at the midtown Shun Lee restaurant.

"Looking casual in blue denims," *Melody Maker*'s New York editor Chris Charlesworth reported, "he drank champagne with his companion Ava Cherry and fled when the snapping flashbulbs began to irritate." [080] Before he left, Bowie raved to *Sounds* magazine about his first week in New York.

"I've got to spend the next two months here getting the tour ready for a June 14 start in Montreal. The new album will be out as soon as the cover art's okayed by RCA. It's a painting of me changing into a dog and they're a bit worried that its cock shows. But apart from the cock, everything's alright.

"Also, I'm putting a very good new band together. There'll be three people from the *Diamond Dogs* album, Mike Garson on piano again, Herbie Flowers on bass – yeah, I managed to persuade Herbie to tour with me, and you know he's got to be the best bassist in the country – and there's Tony Newman, who used to drum in the old Jeff Beck Group.

"And I've found a really incredible black guy called Carlos, just Carlos! And there's another black guy I want to get to play guitar in the band. I want a really funky sound. I've been going down to the Apollo in Harlem. Most New Yorkers seem scared to go there if they're white, but the music's incredible. I saw The Temptations and The Spinners together on the same bill there, and next week it's Marvin Gaye, incredible! I mean I love that kind of thing!" [178]

⊙ BUSINESS

Carlos Alomar was set to join the tour until Defries refused to match the $800 a week Alomar was making playing with The Main Ingredient. Bowie would have to do without Alomar – for the moment.

Michael Kamen then recommended Frank Madeloni, aka Earl Slick, a young guitarist from Staten Island who had played in Kamen's New York Rock Ensemble. Initially Slick had worked as a roadie for the band, jamming with them on soundchecks.

Earl Slick (2000)

David was looking for a new guitarist. And I tell you, if you were looking for this type of gig, you'd never find it. Something like this has to fall on your head. But one day Michael comes to me and says, "You'll never guess who's interested in your playing." [418]

Slick turned up with his guitar at the RCA studios to audition, and found there was no band – just Bowie and an engineer behind the console in the darkened control room.

Earl Slick (1999)

I came in, went in the main studio (they had already set up an amp that I had requested) and I put the headphones on. They played me a couple of tracks from **Diamond Dogs*****, took the guitars out of the mix, told me what key it was in and told me to play…! He then came into the studio with a guitar, we started talking, he plugged the guitar into an amp and we jammed around for a little while and that was it. Corinne said that they would call me in a week, because they had other people to listen to. I got a phone call the next morning. Then I shot up to the hotel, we talked and that was it.*** [004]

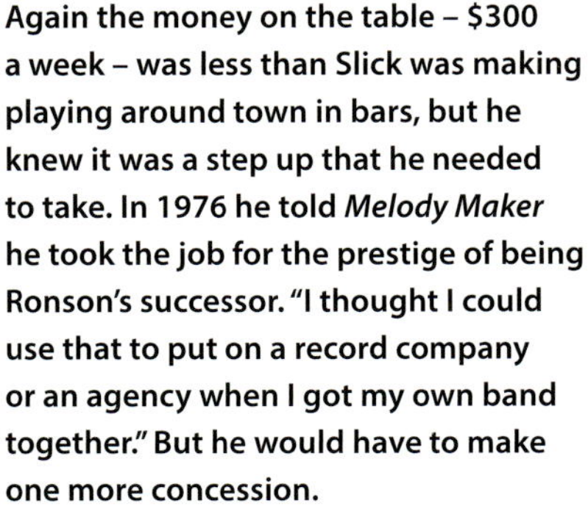

Again the money on the table – $300 a week – was less than Slick was making playing around town in bars, but he knew it was a step up that he needed to take. In 1976 he told *Melody Maker* he took the job for the prestige of being Ronson's successor. "I thought I could use that to put on a record company or an agency when I got my own band together." But he would have to make one more concession.

Earl Slick (1999)

I had really, really long hair when I met David and he had it all cut off for the tour because it was part of the show. [004]

Once Slick was hired, Kamen also suggested New York Rock Ensemble saxophonist David Sanborn, who had played with Stevie Wonder.

SATURDAY 20 APRIL

■ CHART

'Rock'n'Roll Suicide'
UK Top 30 Chart Entry
Charting 7 weeks

✪ PRESS

NME reported the completion of Jules Fisher's elaborate Hunger City set.

TUESDAY 23 APRIL

In Venice California, performance artist Chris Burden was crucified on the roof of a Volkswagen, which was then wheeled out, revved for two minutes and wheeled back in. In 1977 Bowie referenced the performance in 'Joe The Lion' – "Tell you who you are if you nail me to my car."

ABOVE: Guitarist Frank Madeloni, better known as Earl Slick.
LEFT: With Ava Cherry at Todd Rundgren's after-show party at Shun Lee restaurant, New York.
OPPOSITE TOP: Bowie and Geoff MacCormack (back, left) arriving at the party.
OPPOSITE BOTTOM: Sharing a table with journalist Chris Charlesworth, as the snapping flashbulbs begin to irritate.

> "If you were looking for this type of gig, you'd never find it…"
>
> Earl Slick

MAY

■ SINGLE RELEASED

'Rebel Rebel' (2:58) (US remix)/
'Lady Grinning Soul' (3:19)
US & Canada (RCA APBO-0287)
Mexico (RCA SP-4049)
US Chart Peak No.64

This new version, remixed in April for the American market, was later withdrawn and replaced by the original UK single mix.

▮Reissued on
Sound + Vision (Ryko 1989)/
The Best Of David Bowie 1969/1974 (EMI 1997)/*Diamond Dogs* 30th Anniversary 2 CD Edition (EMI 2004).

SATURDAY 11 MAY

Record Mirror reported Bowie's plan to produce *Octobriana*, a feature film based on the Russian strip cartoon character with Amanda Lear in the title role.

FRIDAY 31 MAY

■ ALBUM RELEASED

'DIAMOND DOGS'
UK (RCA APL1-0576)
US (CPL1-0576)
UK Chart Peak No.1
US Chart Peak No.5

SIDE ONE
1. **'Future Legend'** (1:00)
2. **'Diamond Dogs'** (5:50)
3. **'Sweet Thing'** (3:29)
4. **'Candidate'** (2:39)
5. **'Sweet Thing (Reprise)'** (2:32)
6. **'Rebel Rebel'** (4:21)

SIDE TWO
1. **'Rock'n'Roll With Me'** (3:54)
2. **'We Are The Dead'** (4:58)
3. **'1984'** (3:27)
4. **'Big Brother'** (3:25)
5. **'Chant Of The Ever Circling Skeletal Family'** (1:48)

David Bowie: Writer/Arranger/Producer, except 'Rock'n'Roll With Me' (Bowie: Words. Bowie/Peace: Music)
Keith Harwood: Engineer
David Bowie/Tony Visconti: Mixers Tracks 1–5 Side One/Tracks 3–5 Side Two
David Bowie/Keith Harwood: Mixers Track 6 Side One/Tracks 1–2 Side Two
Tony Visconti: '1984' Strings Arranger
David Bowie: Vocals/Guitar/Saxophones/Moog/Mellotron
Mike Garson: Keyboards
Herbie Flowers: Bass
Tony Newman/Aynsley Dunbar: Drums
Alan Parker: Guitar
AGI: Design
Guy Peellaert: Cover Artist
Leee Black Childers: Photographer (inside)
Recorded at Olympic Studios South West London, England/Island Studios, London, England/Studio L Ludolf, Hilversum, Netherlands

ABOVE: The original UK gatefold cover of *Diamond Dogs* featuring Guy Peellaert's artwork with the canine genitalia airbrushed out. The offending parts were restored for the Ryko 1990 reissue and subsequent editions.

The inside gatefold was originally to be a second painting Peellaert had made based on Terry O'Neill's leaping Great Dane photo. When it was repurposed as a promotional poster, Leee Black Childers was asked to make a photomontage of Hunger City – the album's dystopian setting.

Leee Black Childers (1985)
I don't think David ever thought of me as a photographer. I don't think it was even his idea to use me on Diamond Dogs*; it was Tony Defries trying to save money.* [043]

SELECTED REISSUES

▮ CD (RCA 1984).

▮ CD (remastered with bonus tracks) (Ryko 1990).
1. 'Dodo' (2:53)
2. 'Candidate' (5:09)

▮ CD (remastered) (EMI 1999).

▮ CD 30th Anniversary 2 CD Edition (remastered with bonus tracks) (EMI 2004).
1. '1984/Dodo' (5:27)
2. 'Rebel Rebel' (US single version) (2.58)
3. 'Dodo' (2:53)
4. 'Growin' Up' (Springsteen) (3:23)
5. 'Alternative Candidate' (demo) (5:09)
6. 'Diamond Dogs' (K-Tel *Best Of Bowie* edit) (4:41)
7. 'Candidate' (intimacy mix) (2:58)
8. 'Rebel Rebel' (2003 version) (3:09)

▮ CD (mini LP replica) (Toshiba EMI 2007).

ABOVE: Bryan Ferry holds court at the Roxy Music party in New York, with Amanda Lear, Bowie and Shaun Cassidy.

JUNE

SATURDAY 1 JUNE

■ CHART

'Rebel Rebel' (reworked)
US Chart Entry No.85

SUNDAY 2 JUNE

▼ SOCIALISING

Roxy Music received a standing ovation for their New York debut at the Academy of Music, part of their East Coast mini-tour headlining in smaller venues.

Artist Larry Rivers threw an after-show party for them at his East Village loft studio, which Bowie attended with Roxy Music cover star Amanda Lear.

Chris Charlesworth (1974)
Roxy's image has attracted a clique following of film stars, artists and general Warhol-type personalities and they turned up in droves for the after-show party. [081]

Lisa Robinson (1976)
The crowd was like an issue of Interview *come to life. For Bryan, who had initially been an artist and probably semi-worshipped Andy Warhol in his younger days, it must have been satisfying.* [254]

FRIDAY 7 JUNE

★ LIVE

SHOW CANCELLED

Bowie was forced to cancel a surprise warm-up gig in a small club upstate in Connecticut. He had planned to perform under an assumed name, only revealing his identity as he came on stage. Not even the club owner was told who was performing and had to be persuaded to take the booking. With the pressures of rehearsal, Bowie reluctantly called it off.

SATURDAY 8 JUNE

■ CHART

'DIAMOND DOGS'
Album Top 20 Chart Entry
Charting 14 weeks

SATURDAY 8 – MONDAY 10 JUNE

▲ **REHEARSING**

Capitol Theatre
Port Chester
New York, USA

Although the Hunger City set was complete, many technical issues had to be resolved before the tour could begin. The cherry picker used in 'Space Oddity' was playing up, the sound was distorted and the wiring was overloaded to the point of melting.

Tony Visconti (2000)

I was there the night when the cherry picker got stuck during 'Space Oddity', and David had to crawl back down the pole. The fans were trying to grab his bottom and his clothes, and he made it look like it was part of the act! [030]

On the first day of rehearsals with the set, the hydraulics controlling the bridge failed and it crashed to the ground with Bowie on it.

Toni Basil (1985)

I've never met anyone who could think so fast on his feet. As the bridge was falling, he calculated precisely when it would hit, jumping into the air just before the crash to avoid the shock. [016]

After this, Porsche brakes were installed in the bridge to control its descent.

"A Porsche brake?" Bowie asked the engineer. "Isn't that how James Dean died?"

Nick Russyian (1985)

The technical problems were never resolved before we left Port Chester. David was in great danger physically, and could have gotten electrocuted or killed. [016]

WEDNESDAY 12 JUNE

► **TRAVELLING**

NEW YORK – MONTREAL

Three trailer trucks, specially extended in length to contain the enormous set and stage equipment, left the Capitol Theatre for Montreal.

Bowie, Coco Schwab, Stuart George and driver Jim James left the Sherry Netherlands Hotel to begin the 'limousine tour of America' Bowie had suggested to Coco (shown in the *Cracked Actor* documentary), starting with a nine-hour drive to Montreal for the opening concert.

'DIAMOND DOGS' TOUR

Tony Defries: Executive Producer
Tony Zanetta: Producer
David Bowie: Vocals
Mike Garson: Piano/Mellotron
Earl Slick: Lead Guitar
Herbie Flowers: Bass Guitar
Tony Newman: Drums
Pablo Rosario: Percussion
David Sanborn: Alto Saxophone/Flute
Richard Grando: Baritone Saxophone/Flute
Michael Kamen: Musical Director/ Electric Piano/Moog/Oboe
Warren Peace/Gui Andrisano: Dog
David Bowie: Direction/ Mime Improvisation
Toni Basil: Co-direction
Jules Fisher: Production Supervisor
Mark Ravitz: Set Designer
Jules Fisher: Lighting Designer
Showco: Sound
Freddie Burretti: Costumes
Design Associates: Set Construction
Tom Fields Associates: Lighting
Fran Pillersdorf: Production Co-ordinator
Patrick Gibbons: Tour Co-ordinator
Eric Barrett: Tour Manager
Nick Russyian: Production Stage Manager
Stuart George: Security
Jac Colello: Hairstylist/Wardrobe
Corinne Schwab: David Bowie's Personal Assistant
Creative Management Associates: David Bowie's Agents

THE SUIT

Bowie wore a Freddie Burretti-designed pale blue suit, red braces, knitted blue and gold jumper, gold key chain with red Mary Jane shoes.

Bowie (1976)

I had been living in New York for some time and I was wearing a lot of Puerto Rican clothing. [356]

Ava Cherry (2010)

My dad was a musician in the Forties [in Chicago] – black guys used to wear baggy pants and they called them Gousters. I told David once, "My dad has got a couple of pairs of ties and suits." He was, "Really? Where? Can you bring some over?" So I ended up bringing over a couple of my dad's silk ties and a pair of Gouster pants that had suspenders [braces] on them. [045]

FRIDAY 14 JUNE

★ **LIVE**

Montreal Forum
Montreal, Quebec, Canada

Jules Fisher attended the first few dates to ensure that stage equipment worked properly. After 36 hours the Hunger City stage preparation was complete, although the bridge remained stationary as the hydraulics failed again.

Colin Davies (*Disc*)

The Forum is a huge stadium normally used for ice-hockey games and its acoustics are worse than the Albert Hall's. Even so, Bowie received a 20-minute standing ovation. His new act is far more than a collection of songs – it's an elaborate and brilliantly staged show. [109]

The Montreal Star

The whole set-up was an immaculately contrived display of staging. And it was all for nothing, because Bowie is one of the most undynamic performers on stage today. He strikes poses, and opens his mouth and emits bland sounds.

■ **SINGLE RELEASED**

'Diamond Dogs' (6:03)/
'Holy Holy' (2:16)
UK & Europe (RCA APBO 0293)
Chart Peak No.21

The first release of the re-recorded 'Holy Holy' from the November 1971 *Ziggy Stardust* sessions.

OPPOSITE: Bowie performing 'Time'.

"Bowie received a 20-minute standing ovation..."

Colin Davies

SATURDAY 15 JUNE
★ LIVE
Civic Centre
Ottawa
Ontario, Canada

Bowie received a standing ovation but refused to return for an encore. Following the announcement "David Bowie has left the building", a chair-throwing spree broke out on the arena floor.

SUNDAY 16 JUNE
★ LIVE
O'Keefe Centre
Toronto, Ontario, Canada

2 SHOWS

Angie was at the first few shows with Dana Gillespie and Zowie, who took his seat at the front of the stage, telling everyone, "I'm going to see Daddy earn dinner."

Despite suffering from laryngitis, Bowie impressed the rock writers Defries had flown in.

Lisa Robinson (*NME*)
Diamond Dogs *is a great show. It would be better if some of the unnecessary theatrical bits were eliminated. Bowie alone is theatre enough sometimes. The sets are fine, the sound and the lights are superb, the band is first rate.* [253]

Lenny Kaye (*Disc*)
The audience has become a spectator, watching with near-stunned attention. At an ordinary concert they would be asked to participate, to clap their hands, to rise and boogie in place. There is none of that here; this is theatre in the traditional sense. [171]

Gordon Fletcher (*Rolling Stone*)
The stage show Bowie has put together for this tour is intelligent, creative and entertaining. 'TheaTour' is what he calls it and it carries visual effects several steps beyond their heretofore supportive role at a rock concert. In his wake Bowie left 3,500 people marvelling at the professionalism of a show that transcended rock'n'roll. [124]

The success of the first dates of the tour helped to put *Diamond Dogs* at the top of the Canadian album charts for two weeks in July.

MONDAY 17 JUNE
★ LIVE
War Memorial Auditorium
Rochester
New York, USA

TUESDAY 18 JUNE
★ LIVE
Public Auditorium
Cleveland
Ohio, USA

Bowie's return to Cleveland left a big impression on Jerry Casale from nearby Akron.

Jerry Casale (2007)
At the start, an eight-foot diamond descended to the floor of the stage. The front opened forward and Bowie jumped out wearing a Kabuki outfit, pulling dance moves reminiscent of Broadway. I'd never seen anything as spectacular before. It was hypnotic, weird and fantastic. I lost count of the number of set changes and dance routines. It was seamless – an incredible fusion of rock music energy, theatrics and disturbing asexual innuendos. The show solidified right then and there what I wanted to do with Devo. We'd spent way too much time smoking pot talking about ideas and doing nothing about it. Here was someone who'd taken the time to do it for real. [078]

WEDNESDAY 19 JUNE
★ LIVE
Public Auditorium
Cleveland
Ohio, USA

THURSDAY 20 JUNE
★ LIVE
Sports Arena
Toledo
Ohio, USA

With temperatures reaching 130°F degrees in the arena, Bowie was given oxygen after collapsing from heat exhaustion.

FRIDAY 21 JUNE
▼ SOCIALISING
Bowie spent the evening at a small nightclub operated by Sixties activist John Sinclair in a downtown Detroit hotel.

SATURDAY 22 JUNE
★ LIVE
Ford Auditorium
Detroit
Michigan, USA

SHOW CANCELLED

Leee Black Childers (1974)
Someone had unwisely booked Bowie into the Ford Auditorium, a small, beautifully equipped theatre with only one drawback. That same afternoon they were having a high school commencement.

After the commencement the Bowie crew would have about three hours to set up a set that takes twelve hours to build. Impossible. [089]

■ CHART
'Diamond Dogs'
UK Top 30 Chart Entry
Charting 6 weeks

SUNDAY 23 JUNE
★ LIVE
Cobo Hall
Detroit
Michigan, USA

Leee Black Childers (1974)
The set-up had gone beautifully and everything would be in perfect working order. The lights were wonderful. Bowie's voice was in fine form. I have rarely seen a rock show so effective as that night. Everything went exactly as planned and the fans showed their appreciation wildly. [089]

Ray Bennett (*Windsor Star*)
English glitter-rock star David Bowie's Sunday night show at Cobo Hall was his most theatrically ambitious Detroit concert so far but the least satisfying musically. Backed by a raucous and unimaginative new band, Bowie churned out many songs from his most popular albums and a couple from his new one, Diamond Dogs, *but his mind appeared to be more on showmanship than singing and his vocal performance lacked the depth and clarity he's displayed in the past.*

MONDAY 24 JUNE
★ LIVE
Hara Arena
Dayton
Ohio, USA

TUESDAY 25 JUNE
★ LIVE
Civic Theatre
Akron
Ohio, USA

Replaced cancelled show at Cincinnati Gardens, Ohio.

WEDNESDAY 26 THURSDAY 27 JUNE
★ LIVE
Syria Mosque
Pittsburgh
Pennsylvania, USA

FRIDAY 28 JUNE
★ LIVE
Civic Center
Charleston
South Carolina, USA

SATURDAY 29 JUNE
★ LIVE
Municipal Auditorium
Nashville
Tennessee, USA

Paul and Linda McCartney were in town and came to the concert. Linda McCartney photographed Bowie in his dressing room.

Record Mirror reported that Bowie hoped to return to Britain in December for five consecutive concerts at Wembley.

SUNDAY 30 JUNE
★ LIVE
Mid-South Coliseum
Memphis
Tennessee, USA

OPPOSITE: Live at the Municipal Auditorium, Nashville.

JULY

MONDAY 1

★ LIVE

Fox Theatre
Atlanta
Georgia, USA

TUESDAY 2 JULY

★ LIVE

Curtis Hixon Hall
Tampa
Florida, USA

"Good evening, ladies and gentlemen. The concert you're going to see tonight is not the show we had planned for you. Due to an unfortunate road accident, half of our stage scenery, costumes, lighting equipment is in a local swamp 15 miles north of here. There was talk of cancelling tonight's performance but David Bowie would not hear of it and insisted we go on in the remaining half condition. So, in a few minutes, we'll go on with the concert – thank you."

A bee had flown into the cabin of the truck carrying the massive set and stung the driver.

Leee Black Childers (1974)

He drove the truck into a swamp somewhere near Tampa, Florida. Bowie went on that night on a bare stage. He says it's the best audience reception he's had to date. [089]

Bowie received a 20-minute ovation before returning for an encore.

WEDNESDAY 3 JULY

★ LIVE

Seminole Jai-Alai Fronton
Casselberry
Florida, USA

THURSDAY 4 JULY

★ LIVE

Exhibition Hall
Jacksonville
Florida, USA

SHOW CANCELLED

► TRAVELLING

ORLANDO – HAMLET – NORTH CAROLINA – CHARLOTTE

Bowie, Coco and Stuart George took the 12-hour journey by rail from Orlando to Hamlet, North Carolina and on to Charlotte.

FRIDAY 5 JULY

★ LIVE

Park Center
Charlotte
North Carolina, USA

SATURDAY 6 JULY

★ LIVE

Coliseum
Greensboro
North Carolina, USA

SUNDAY 7 JULY

★ LIVE

Scope Convention Center
Norfolk
Virginia, USA

MONDAY 8 – SATURDAY 13 JULY

★ LIVE

Tower Theatre
Philadelphia
Pennsylvania, USA

Tony Defries decided that a live album would serve as a contract filler and help to offset the huge cost of the tour (as well as publicise it) and organised to record the Tower dates. With Tony Visconti unable to supervise the recordings, the job fell to engineer Keith Harwood, who had the road crew rig the stage with recording equipment.

Tony Visconti (1976)

Recording it live, David had to have eight microphones all around the set because he'd be singing 'Ground Control to Major Tom' on top of this cherry picker seat. He'd be about six rows out over the audience and he'd be singing into a telephone handpiece. That was the microphone that recorded his vocal on that. [332]

Defries had neglected to tell the musicians, but Herbie Flowers soon realised what was going on when he noticed the extra microphones. He assembled them to decide how much they should be paid on top of their usual fee. Based on probable album sales figures, they calculated they were entitled to $50,000 ($5,000 each).

Flowers went to Bowie's dressing room to ask Defries what the band would be paid. Defries told him, "You'll get the $70 union rate for a live album." Flowers demanded they receive $5,000 each. Defries retorted, "You'll bankrupt us! We'll have to cancel the tour!" Flowers stood firm. "We want the money now or we won't go on the stage tonight."

Bowie shouted at him, "I've bloody well got to go on in ten minutes. I don't need this shit!"

Stuart George (1986)

He kicked the chair and it flew backwards. It wasn't directed at any person. David wouldn't actually get physical with anybody. Verbally he could be very cutting but bodily, no. [013]

Flowers told them, "That'll cost you a bonus for the stage crew." Defries wrote out the cheques (which later bounced) and the show went on, 30 minutes late.

Herbie Flowers (1985)

I can claim to be a genius for setting up the tension before we did the show, because when we went on stage, the feeling of liberation in the band was glorious. [016]

OPPOSITE: Tower Theatre, Philadelphia. Dagmar was invited to photograph the concerts, two of which – the 12th and 13th July – were being recorded for the *David Live* double album. Bowie later went through her shots and selected the images for the cover.

"Bowie went on that night on a bare stage. He says it's the best audience reception he's had to date."

Leee Black Childers

TUESDAY 9 JULY

▲ RECORDING

Sigma Sound Studios
Philadelphia
Pennsylvania, USA

AVA CHERRY
'Everything That Touches You'
'Give It Away'
'Sweet Thing'

Ava Cherry had been waiting for Bowie to record her promised solo album since January when he had shelved the Astronettes project. Eventually Defries had Michael Kamen arrange and produce a session for her at Sigma Sound Studios, where they recorded three tracks: 'Everything That Touches You', 'Give It Away' and 'Sweet Thing'. Sigma was home to the R&B empire run by Thom Bell, Kenny Gamble and Leon Huff, Philadelphia International Records. PIR was red hot since the house rhythm section MFSB (Mother Father Sister Brother) had scored a No.1 in May with 'TSOP (The Sound of Philadelphia)', featuring vocals by The Three Degrees.

When Bowie dropped in to the session, he was greatly impressed by the sound of the studio and was convinced that this would be the sound of his next album.

Michael Kamen (1986)
He met the guys, these fantastic black guys. Something really fundamental shifted in him. [013]

Despite having said in 1972, "I'm never gonna try and play black music 'cos I'm white. Singularly white!" [212], Bowie was now convinced that this would be the sound of his next album. Tony Visconti told *Circus Raves*, "He's been working to put together an R&B sound for years. Every British musician has a hidden desire to be black." [272]

SUNDAY 14 JULY

★ LIVE

Veterans Memorial Coliseum
New Haven
Connecticut, USA

MONDAY 15 JULY

★ LIVE

Palace Theater
Waterbury
Connecticut, USA

TUESDAY 16 JULY

★ LIVE

Music Hall
Boston
Massachusetts, USA

WEDNESDAY 17 JULY

★ LIVE

Bushnell Auditorium
Hartford
Connecticut, USA
(Memorial Coliseum,
Cape Cod concert cancelled)

Tony Defries and his wife divorced. According to his niece, "He was very nice until all this Bowie thing began."

▲ MIXING

Electric Lady Studios
Greenwich Village
New York City
New York, USA

'DAVID LIVE'
Working title:
Wham-Bam-Thank-You-Ma'm

Tony Visconti: Producer
Eddie Kramer: Engineer

Hoping to have the album ready for release in September to coincide with the West Coast tour, Tony Defries had Tony Visconti flown over from England to mix the recordings for an album as quickly as possible.

When they played back the tapes from the Tower Theatre shows, Visconti realised that the microphones had been set up incorrectly for recording. The instruments were not isolated properly, making it more difficult to mix.

Tony Visconti (1974)
I missed the recording of the Philadelphia concerts by a day because of transportation problems. I wasn't as happy with the basic tracks that I had to work with as I might have been. The most important thing in recording a live album is to keep the instruments as acoustically separate as possible. A rule of thumb is to maintain the level of instruments like the bass drum throughout the set. Although Keith Harwood is a good engineer, the levels he set for recording Bowie live were a bit inconsistent, and it took ages to clean up the master. We had that trouble on 'Diamond Dogs' where the bass drum and the bass guitar weren't distinguishable enough from each other. [271]

Tony Visconti (1982)
It was a mess, and like a lot of live albums. If we'd had the time, we could have salvaged it, but at least it was an honest live album, and David didn't replace a single note of his vocal. The only thing we did replace was the backing vocals, because the backing vocalists were also dancing, and they were better dancers than singers, added to which they were usually out of breath by the time they got to the microphone. [015]

Tony Visconti (2004)
Geoffrey and Gui sang their original parts in a few hours, but we used as much of the original vocals as possible. Some of the horn parts were also re-recorded because of technical difficulties. [328]

Eddie Kramer engineered the mixes the following day.

Tony Visconti (1982)
On the night we listened back to it, David invited about 60 people to the playback. And we mixed that album in quadraphonic, because RCA demanded it, although they never released it in quad. So we sat with about 60 people between four enormous speakers in a studio, and everyone was saying how fantastic it was, except David and I, who were the only people present with big frowns on our faces. We looked at each other, and we were just cringing. [015]

FRIDAY 19 JULY

★ LIVE

Madison Square Garden
New York City
New York, USA

Mick Jagger (1974)
He was very nervous, but everyone gets nervous in New York. [314]

Lisa Robinson and Chris Charlesworth noted that nothing about the show had changed since Toronto, except that Bowie included 'Knock On Wood' instead of 'Drive-In Saturday' and spoke to the audience.

Chris Charlesworth (*Melody Maker*)
The show was, as before, more visual than musical and the Garden is really too large a venue to attempt a concert of this kind. It belongs in a small theatre. [082]

▼ SOCIALISING

Promoter Ron Delsener threw a lavish after-show party at the Plaza for an exclusive guest list of 40, including Mick Jagger. Bette Midler arrived with two of her Harlettes, Charlotte Crossley and Sharon Redd. "Where's Bowie?" Midler demanded.

Charlotte Crossley (1977)
After a while I noticed Bette was missing, so I went to look for her. I heard some commotion in a walk-in closet. I walked in and saw her smoking a joint with David and Mick. I freaked out. They asked me to join them but I said no, thank you. It was too heavy in there. [288]

OPPOSITE: 'Cracked Actor' and 'Panic In Detroit', Madison Square Garden, New York.

SATURDAY 20 JULY

★ LIVE

Madison Square Garden
New York City
New York, USA

The New York concerts were videoed for MainMan by John Dove for Bowie to review later. Bowie had become obsessed with video, so Dove taught him how to shoot, edit and apply effects and arranged for Bowie to take lessons in film theory and history.

Soon his hotel rooms became mini-studios, crammed with video recorders, lights, video cameras and television monitors as he constructed and filmed miniature sets for his planned theatrical projects.

With the first half of the tour over, Bowie prepared to record his next album at Sigma Sound in Philadelphia.

He booked 120 hours of recording time in mid-August and gave Coco his wish list of Philly musicians to recruit. Bowie had wanted Sigma's house rhythm section MFSB (Mother Father Sister Brother). At one stage Bowie announced he had secured the services of MFSB founder Norman Harris, a guitarist/arranger/producer. In the event, only conga player Larry Washington was available for the sessions.

Drummer Tony Newman went back to session work, as did bassist Herbie Flowers, who later said, "If I'd done the second half of the tour, I'd have died." [016]

In their place Bowie was able to recruit bass guitarist Willie Weeks and drummer Andy Newmark, whom he'd met at Ronnie Wood's home studio.

Determined to get Carlos Alomar for the sessions, Bowie called him and assured him that this time he would make Defries match his asking price.

The rest of the musicians came from the *Diamond Dogs* tour band.

SATURDAY 27 JULY

▼ SOCIALISING

Madison Square Garden
New York City
New York, USA

JACKSON 5
OHIO PLAYERS

Bowie watched from the wings as the support act Ohio Players took the stage. Ava Cherry had turned him onto the group – then riding high on recent hits 'Funky Worm' and 'Jive Turkey' – and Bowie had added their 1968 song 'Here Today And Gone Tomorrow' to his set.

Circus Raves writer Joe Bivona noted the show's effect on Bowie: "At the climax of the performance the syncopated strutters accomplished an orgasm of audience participation the like of which their guest in the wings had seldom known to unite a rock audience. Twenty thousand voices began to shout in unison 'Part-tee!! Par-tee!!' while thousands of shrieking whistles punctuated their chant." [061]

LATE JULY

One night Bowie and Zanetta were bemoaning MainMan's excesses and financial woes. Bowie was finding it increasingly difficult to pay for anything or for anyone to buy things for him, yet thousands of dollars were being spent on MainMan staffers, indulgences and loss-making projects. As they spoke, Zanetta realised that Bowie assumed he was a partner in MainMan. When he explained how it really worked, Bowie vowed to terminate his relationship with Defries and MainMan.

AUGUST

MONDAY 5

■ SINGLE RELEASED

'1984' (3:21) /
'Queen Bitch' (3:14)
US (RCA PB-10026)

WEDNESDAY 7 AUGUST

✪ PRESS

Disc reported that the *Diamond Dogs* show "seems virtually certain to come to Britain in the New Year". Mike Garson told the paper that week, "There are only a certain number of places where it could be presented because the set requires 40 feet in height above the stage. At present they are talking of not doing a tour as such, but putting on the show in a London venue for a whole week." [115]

SUNDAY 11 – THURSDAY 22 AUGUST

▲ RECORDING

Studio A North
Sigma Sound Studios
Philadelphia
Pennsylvania, USA

'YOUNG AMERICANS' ALBUM
'The Young American'
'Shilling The Rubes'
'Lazer'
'After Today' (fast tempo)
'I'm Only Dancing' (later retitled 'John, I'm Only Dancing (Again)')
'Never No Turnin' Back' (later re-recorded as 'Right')
'Somebody Up There Likes Me'
'Who Can I Be Now?'
'Come Back My Baby' (later retitled 'It's Gonna Be Me')
'Take It In, Right' (later re-recorded as 'Can You Hear Me')
'It's Hard To Be A Saint In The City'
'Funky Music (Is A Part Of Me)' (later rewritten as 'Fascination')

Tony Visconti: Producer
Carl Paruolo: Engineer
Mike Hutchinson: Tape Operator
David Bowie: Vocals
Mike Garson: Piano
David Sanborn: Saxophone
Willie Weeks: Bass
Andy Newmark: Drums
Pablo Rosario/Larry Washington: Percussion
Warren Peace/Ava Cherry/Diane Sumler/Antony Hinton/'Luther' Luther Vandross/Robin Clark: Backing Vocals

"When Andy and Willie came to see me in the studio, they were very wary," Bowie later said. "They didn't know what to expect. They came in looking for silver capes and all, I imagine. But once we started playing the songs it worked itself out. It ended in a very, very solid friendship and a group that is going to work with me." [143]

'The Young American', as it was originally called, was one of the first songs that evolved, starting off as a jam.

OPPOSITE: Madison Square Garden, New York.

Carlos Alomar (2004)

It started off just as little fragments, ideas and riffs that he'd bang out on the piano or on his acoustic guitar, and then I would work with those ideas, supplying him with signature guitar lines, so he could choose, like one from column A, one from column B and so on. It was only about four hours into the first session. We got to the guitar breakdown and we knew we'd got something. [062]

Alomar's wife Robin Clark and Luther Vandross – who tagged along initially just to keep him company – came on the second day to help out with backing vocals. Bowie overhead them working out parts based around the phrase "Young Americans".

Luther Vandross (1987)

I said to Robin, "What if there was a phrase that went, 'Young American, Young American, he was the Young American – all right!' Now, when 'all right' comes up, jump over me and go into harmony." [302]

Bowie realised it was the hook the chorus needed and invited them both to join the sessions. He seized on Vandross' skill as a vocal arranger, consulting him on every song.

Carlos Alomar (1976)

That album was conceived and written in the studio. We'd be there at four in the morning, falling asleep virtually, and David would still be dashing off ideas for crazy vocal arrangements, ridiculous things for 'Right', you know? Crazy. [163]

Tony Visconti arrived on the third day at 8pm, jetlagged from London, to find the group had already recorded rehearsals of several tracks, including 'The Young American', 'Shilling The Rubes', The Astronettes' 'Lazer' and 'After Today'.

Bowie had originally asked Carl Paruolo to engineer the sessions as he'd worked on most of the Philly hits at Sigma, but now he told him he wasn't happy with the sound and Visconti would handle the recording once he arrived.

Tony Visconti (2002)

I could hear the problem he had with the sound. In those days, in America, engineers recorded 'dry' and 'flat', waiting for the mix to add the equalization, reverbs and special effects. But the British often recorded with the special effects right on the session! I was British-trained and David was used to this sound! So I rolled up my sleeves and got right into it. By 2am we'd recorded our first official backing track – 'Young Americans'. [420]

The sessions continued in this way with Bowie working up song fragments on guitar or piano, and the musicians picking up on it. Immediacy was the order of the day and Visconti set up the studio with the baffles positioned to allow eye contact between everyone and provide separation for microphone placement. On top of this, Bowie announced he wanted to sing live with the band.

Tony Visconti (2002)

Because the instruments were much louder than his voice, I had to rig up a special microphone technique, which cancelled the band but recorded his voice. This required two identical microphones placed electronically out of phase. In other words, the diaphragm of one mike is pushing when the other is pulling. The band's sound is picked up by the two mikes, but is out of phase and consequently cancelled. David was told to sing only into the top mike so that his voice was not cancelled. [420]

One of the backing tracks recorded at Sigma in August was a Vandross composition, 'Funky Music (Is A Part Of Me)', which Bowie revisited during the November sessions, rewriting some of the lyrics and retitling the song 'Fascination'.

In eight days, they had recorded nine basic backing tracks for most of the album, but only some of these made it onto the finished album. The rest came together in November, December and the following January.

Bowie (1997)

The original title for the* Young Americans *album at one point was* Shilling The Rubes, *which is circus slang for taking money off people. I was advised that my stunning wit would not go down well. [377]

The project had several other working titles during its production: *Dancin'*, *The Young American*, *Somebody Up There Likes Me*, *The Gouster* and *One Damn Song*.

▮ 'Who Can I Be Now?' and 'It's Gonna Be Me' released on *Young Americans* reissues (Ryko 1990, EMI 2007)

▮ 'After Today' released on *Sound + Vision* (Ryko 1989)

FRIDAY 16 AUGUST

■ SINGLE RELEASED

DANA GILLESPIE

'Andy Warhol' (2:58)/
'Dizzy Heights' (Gillespie) (3:34)
UK (RCA 2446)

To promote her 'new' single (A-side recorded with Bowie and Mick Ronson in 1971), Dana Gillespie made a whistle-stop tour of Britain's regional radio stations with Angie.

▮ Reissued on *Andy Warhol – The Best Of The MainMan Years* (Golden Years 1995).

SATURDAY 17 AUGUST

Melody Maker reported that Eddie Jobson had been approached to play on Bowie's autumn American tour but had declined, saying "I'm a member of Roxy Music."

THURSDAY 22 AUGUST

Throughout the sessions a group of devoted Philadelphian fans, dubbed the Sigma Kids, kept a nightly vigil outside Sigma Studios.

They waited outside the Barclay Hotel on Rittenhouse Square, where Bowie and his entourage would emerge each evening. They took pictures of him walking to the limo, and then quickly drove across town to Sigma in time to see him arrive.

Patti Brett (2005)

If he was already out of his limo when we were pulling up, we would stop our cars in the middle of the street, get out and halt traffic just to say hi to him again. In that time we got to be fairly friendly with everyone. We sent Carlos into the studio with a Polaroid, and we got the engineer, Carl, whose window was behind the soundboard, to open it so we could hear it. [004]

After Bowie put in a long last night of finishing touches to vocals and keyboard overdubs, he invited the Sigma Kids into the studio.

Bowie (1974)

We let them in and played them some things from the album and they loved it, which was amazing. Fabulous, because I really didn't know what they'd think about the change in direction. [143]

Matt Damsker (*Rolling Stone*)

Bowie played the album for the ten blissed-out, formerly camped-out, devotees, who'd been ushered into the studio, finally, at 5am by Stuart George. Bowie was an affable host as he signed more autographs, apologised for the unfinished mix of the album and agreed to play it a second time, at which point the party erupted into dance. Bowie took centre floor with a foxy stomp. [107]

SATURDAY 24 AUGUST

▶ TRAVELLING

PHILADELPHIA – LOS ANGELES

Euphoric from the Philadelphia sessions, Bowie began his three-day train journey to Los Angeles to prepare for the seven (already sold out) Amphitheatre shows.

FRIDAY 30 AUGUST

✪ PHOTO SESSION

'YOUNG AMERICANS' ALBUM COVER

Eric Stephen Jacobs: Photographer

With the album considered to be finished, Bowie worked on ideas for the sleeve design. Eric Stephen Jacobs had recently shot a portrait of Bowie's tour choreographer Toni Basil, which appeared on the cover of the September issue of *After Dark* magazine. For the *Young Americans* sleeve Jacobs replicated the portrait, including the hand-colouring and airbrushed cigarette smoke trail.

OPPOSITE: Sigma, Philadelphia, August 22. Dagmar recalls: "I went to Sigma Sound Studios, where Bowie was recording the latest songs. Found the fans waiting outside and joined them. To pass the time, I made them write BOWIE with their bodies on the pavement outside... and took pictures, of course. We just talked and had fun, until the doors were opened – sometime late at night, or early in the morning and everybody was invited inside. David played the songs for us all, we listened and I just kept taking pictures..." (Bottom right) Mike Garson, Bowie and Tony Visconti (on the floor).

Bowie

Bowie

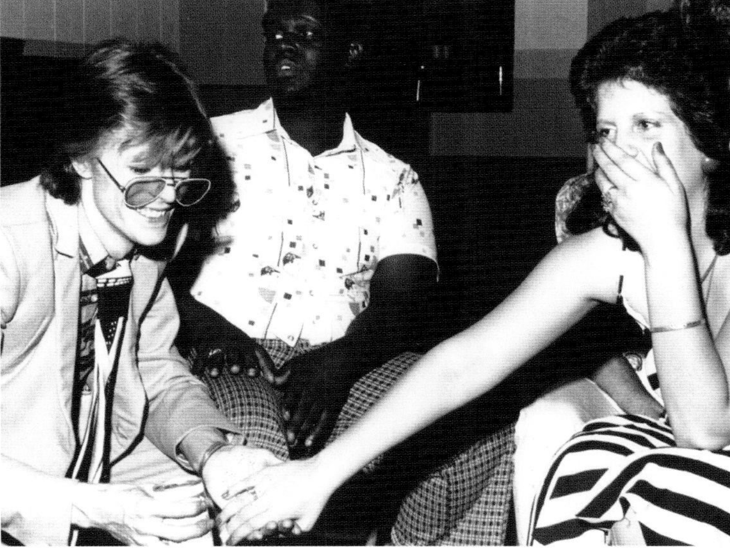

Bowie told Defries that he wanted to ditch the elaborate and expensive Hunger City set. Defries accepted this stoically, but requested that it be retained for the Universal Amphitheatre shows so that Los Angeles – a major media marketplace – could see the extravagant show.

The band members stayed at the Sunset Marquis, nicknamed 'The Plantation'. Bowie and his small entourage were at the Beverly Wilshire –'The Castle' where 'the Prince' lived. $5,000 worth of security was brought in to keep the hordes of fans and freaks at bay.

✪ **TELEVISION**

'CRACKED ACTOR'

Alan Yentob: Producer
Michael Murphy/David Myers: Cameramen
Pat Darrin: Sound

British filmmaker Alan Yentob arrived to document Bowie's experiences in America for BBC's *Omnibus* programme. Earlier that year, Bowie had seen one of his recent documentaries and he had asked Defries to arrange a meeting.

Alan Yentob (1985)

When I started, I wanted to make a film about him called 'The Collector' – about this man who seemed to adopt other people's gestures, presences or personalities… there were lots of allusions in his records, references to movies and all sorts of things. [016]

The idea had occurred to Yentob the year before, when Bowie had described himself on *Russell Harty* as "a collector – I collect things".

Bowie (1997)

I'm not an original thinker. Probably what I'm best at doing is synthesising those things in society or culture that I find rivetingly exciting and what I end up doing is refracting those things. [348]

Alan Yentob (1985)

He was a very eclectic singer… He was a bit arty. The dressing up stuff. The costumes… He was rather pretentious but always adventurous. He was always trying to get engaged with ideas. [016]

Bowie liked both Yentob and the idea and gave him unrestricted access as well as full control over editorial decisions. Yentob hired a local camera crew and spent two weeks following Bowie – backstage before a show, cocooned in the limo, riding through the streets of Hollywood and the desert highways – and gained a rare insight into his ambitions and fears, while the bemused American media tried to make sense of him.

In his suite at the Wilshire at three in the morning, Bowie literally opened up, pulling out a trunk full of Kansai costumes – Bowie has always kept everything – to illustrate the evolution of his image and demonstrating the cut-up writing method.

WEST COAST TOUR

Earl Slick: Lead Guitar
Carlos Alomar: Guitar
Michael Kamen: Musical Director/Electric Piano/Moog/Oboe
Mike Garson: Piano/Mellotron
David Sanborn: Alto Saxophone/Flute
Richard Grando: Baritone Saxophone/Flute
Doug Rauch: Bass Guitar (ex-Santana)
Greg Errico: Drums (ex-Sly And The Family Stone)
Pablo Rosario: Percussion
Ava Cherry/Warren Peace/Gui Andrisano/Luther Vandross/Diane Sumler/Anthony Hinton: Backing Vocals

Andy Newmark and Willie Weeks left to play on George Harrison's American tour.

When Bowie secured Carlos Alomar for the *Young Americans* sessions the previous month, tour co-ordinator Pat Gibbons had called Earl Slick to say he probably wouldn't be needed for the rest of the tour either.

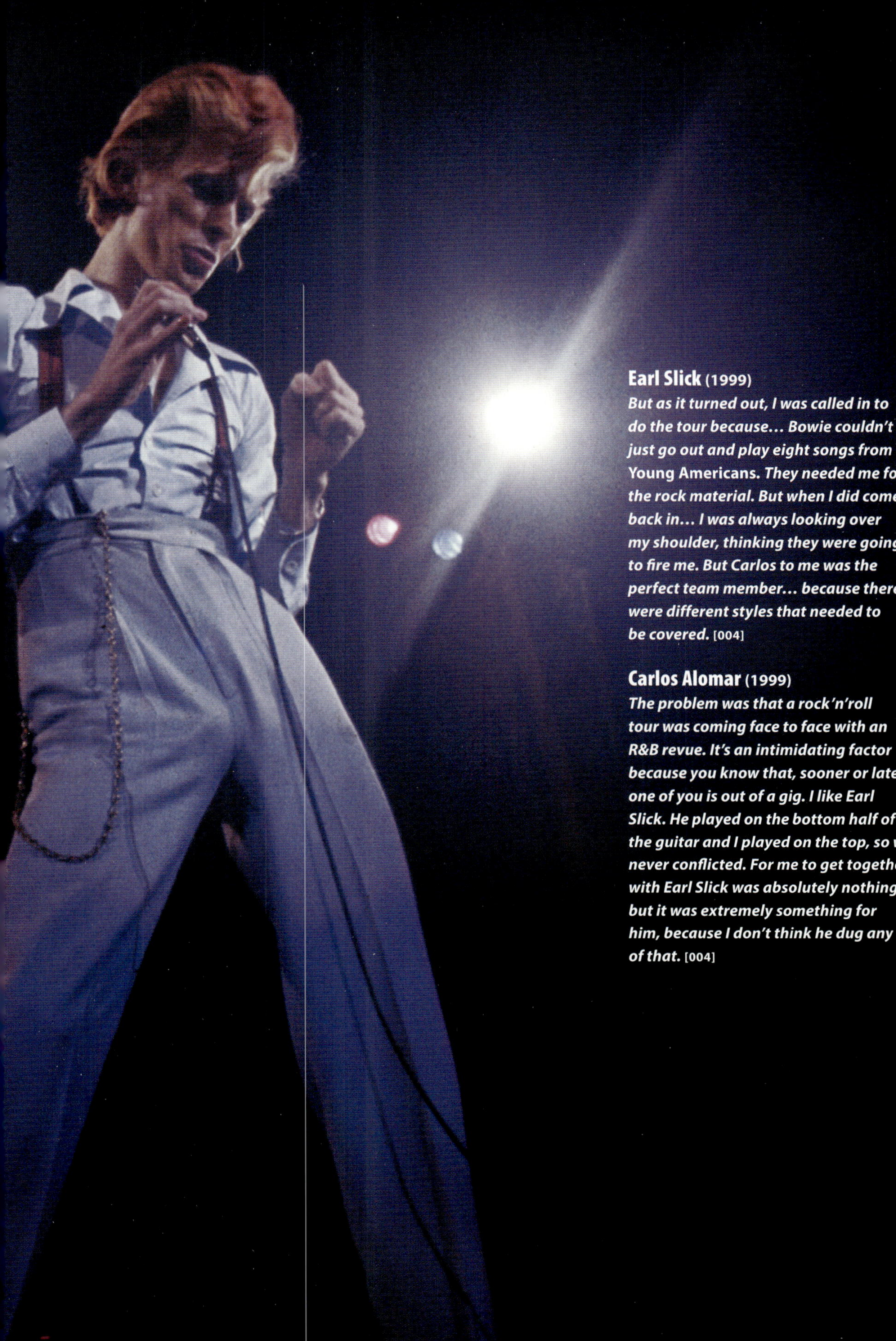

Earl Slick (1999)
But as it turned out, I was called in to do the tour because… Bowie couldn't just go out and play eight songs from Young Americans. *They needed me for the rock material. But when I did come back in… I was always looking over my shoulder, thinking they were going to fire me. But Carlos to me was the perfect team member… because there were different styles that needed to be covered.* [004]

Carlos Alomar (1999)
The problem was that a rock'n'roll tour was coming face to face with an R&B revue. It's an intimidating factor because you know that, sooner or later, one of you is out of a gig. I like Earl Slick. He played on the bottom half of the guitar and I played on the top, so we never conflicted. For me to get together with Earl Slick was absolutely nothing, but it was extremely something for him, because I don't think he dug any of that. [004]

Earl Slick (2004)
It was a bit strange because the musical direction changed. It went Philly. At the time I'm a 22-year-old testosterone-run fuckin' rocker and I'm going, "Hmm, this is kinda strange." [387]

Bowie agreed to keep the Hunger City set for the Los Angeles audiences, but he stuck to his decision to shift the focus from the theatrics to the new R&B feel. The set list was revamped with songs from the Sigma sessions: 'Young Americans', 'It's Gonna Be Me' and 'John, I'm Only Dancing (Again)' as the encore. Vandross was retained to handle vocal arrangements.

Luther Vandross (1982)
I had a little group at that time and I brought two of the singers [Diane Sumler and Anthony Hinton] with me. It was the group that ended up being 'Luther' on Atlantic Records. I told Bowie I wouldn't leave my group at home to go on the road, so he said, "Well, bring them because I really want you." [276]

Luther Vandross (1987)
Bowie would always come in the room while we were singing backgrounds and I'd say, "David, listen. If I'm ruining your song, let me know, but check this out. We have these new vocal parts for 'All The Young Dudes'" and he'd say, "Put it in tonight." [302]

Defries had wanted Ava Cherry to stay in New York to work on her solo album, but Bowie insisted she join the tour.

Rehearsals for the second leg of the *Diamond Dogs* Tour in Los Angeles: Geoff MacCormack and Gui Andrisano (far left), Doug Rauch (behind Bowie), Earl Slick (third from right), Greg Errico (at the drum kit, right) and Carlos Alomar (back).

MONDAY 2 – SUNDAY 8 SEPTEMBER

★ LIVE

Universal Amphitheatre
Los Angeles
California, USA

Robert Hilburn reviewed the first night's show and afterwards came to the Wilshire to talk about the new live album, but Bowie had other ideas.

"This isn't the new album," Bowie told him, "but the one after it, and the record company doesn't like me to do that. We cut it in a week in Philadelphia and it can tell you more about where I am now than anything I could say."

He played Hilburn some tracks from the new album, tentatively named *One Damn Song*. "I think it is the closest thing I've ever done on record to being very, very me. I always said that on most albums I was acting. It was a role generally. And this one is the nearest to actually meeting me since that very first *Space Oddity* album, which was quite personal. I'm really excited about it." [143]

Many celebrities attended the Los Angeles shows, including John Denver, Neil Diamond and the Jackson 5, who came with Diana Ross. Michael Jackson was especially intrigued with the choreography and afterwards invited Bowie for dinner at the Jackson house.

Bowie (2003)

Michael spent much of the evening asking me about the production and how we built the city and where the ideas came from for all the different visuals.

I was taught a 'backwards walk' by Toni Basil who choreographed The Lockers, one of the first black street-dance troupes. It was basically the Marcel Marceau walk but propelled backwards. It didn't have a name at that time, of course. She'd devised it with them and taught it to me for the Diamond Dogs show.

It's entirely possible that he copped the walk fourth hand, so to speak. I believe the nature of the show made a big impression on him. [390]

Each night the rock aristocracy converged on Bowie's suite at the Wilshire. At one after-show party he met Cameron Crowe, a journalist still in his teens when he began writing freelance for *Rolling Stone*.

Cameron Crowe (2006)

One of the artists I'd profiled was guitarist Ronnie Wood, then with The Faces, and one of the most gregarious fellows on the scene. Without knowing he had stepped over a line, Wood invited me to a private party with David Bowie. [102]

Crowe arrived with Wood, who ushered him past Stuart George and into the suite.

Cameron Crowe (2006)

Inside was Bowie himself, buzzing between guests, full of chaotic energy, still wearing the stage clothes, complete with red suspenders and a red newsboy's cap. He was always returning to the tape deck, discussing and fussing over favourite records, blasting Philadelphia soul music. [102]

Crowe was a fellow enthusiast and as they talked about The Spinners and the recent *Young Americans* sessions, Bowie played him an early version of 'Somebody Up There Likes Me'.

Cameron Crowe (2006)

I had met Bowie, and now it was on to the next step. An interview. It was Ronnie Wood, along with another musician I'd interviewed, Glenn Hughes, who pitched the idea to Bowie. [102]

Bowie also socialised with Marc Bolan and his new girlfriend, soul singer Gloria Jones, who dropped in after one of the Amphitheatre concerts. Bolan was in America looking for a new deal since Warner Brothers had dropped him. His album *Zinc Alloy And The Hidden Riders Of Tomorrow* had flopped, he had gained weight and the English press were calling him 'The Porky Pixie'.

The BBC filmed the September 5 concert in its entirety but only snippets were included in the final finished documentary: 'Cracked Actor', 'Time', 'Sweet Thing', 'Moonage Daydream', 'Diamond Dogs', 'Rock'n'Roll Suicide', 'Aladdin Sane', 'John, I'm Only Dancing (Again)'.

WEDNESDAY 11 SEPTEMBER

★ LIVE

Sports Arena
San Diego
California, USA

FRIDAY 13 SEPTEMBER

★ LIVE

Community Center Arena
Tucson
Arizona, USA

■ SINGLE RELEASED

'Knock On Wood'
(Floyd/Cropper) (3:08)/
'Panic In Detroit' (5:51)
UK (RCA 2466)
Chart Peak No.10

■ SINGLE RELEASED

'Rock'n'Roll With Me'
(Bowie/Peace) (4:17)/
'Panic In Detroit' (5:43)
US (RCA PB 10105)

SATURDAY 14 SEPTEMBER

★ LIVE

Arizona Coliseum
Phoenix
Arizona, USA

MONDAY 16 SEPTEMBER

★ LIVE

Anaheim Convention Center
Anaheim
California, USA

The BBC film crew captured Elizabeth Taylor arriving at Anaheim with her companion Henry Wynberg. Also in the audience for the last *Diamond Dogs* show were Elton John, Desi Arnaz, Sally Kellerman and John Carpenter.

After the show, Taylor went backstage and swept into the dressing room. Witnesses remarked that the two hit it off – an instant mutual admiration that quickly became an intense but brief friendship.

TUESDAY 17 – MONDAY 30 SEPTEMBER

▲ REHEARSING

A promoter had cancelled seven dates after exorbitant demands from Defries, creating a 17-day break between the concerts in Anaheim and St Paul on October 5. Bowie used the time to reshape and rehearse the new show – a stripped-down soul revue with a plain backdrop.

Bowie (1976)

Once I got to Los Angeles and did the shows in the Amphitheatre there, I'd already done 30 of them and it was terrible. There's nothing more boring than a stylised show, because there was no spontaneity and no freedom of movement. Everything was totally choreographed and it was very stiff. It didn't look it if you went and saw the show once. The first time it was probably a gas, but there's nothing much in it if you are doing it every night. It just becomes repetition. I can't speak as an audience but certainly, as a performer, it was hard to keep it up, trekking all over the country doing the same thing night after night. [085]

Yentob's crew filmed Bowie going through vocal arrangements with Vandross, Cherry and Robin Clark, who was joining them for the Soul Tour. They practised the *Young Americans* track 'Right' as photographer Terry O'Neill snapped away in the corner.

Elizabeth Taylor was a frequent visitor at the rehearsal studio and Bowie spent much of his downtime with her.

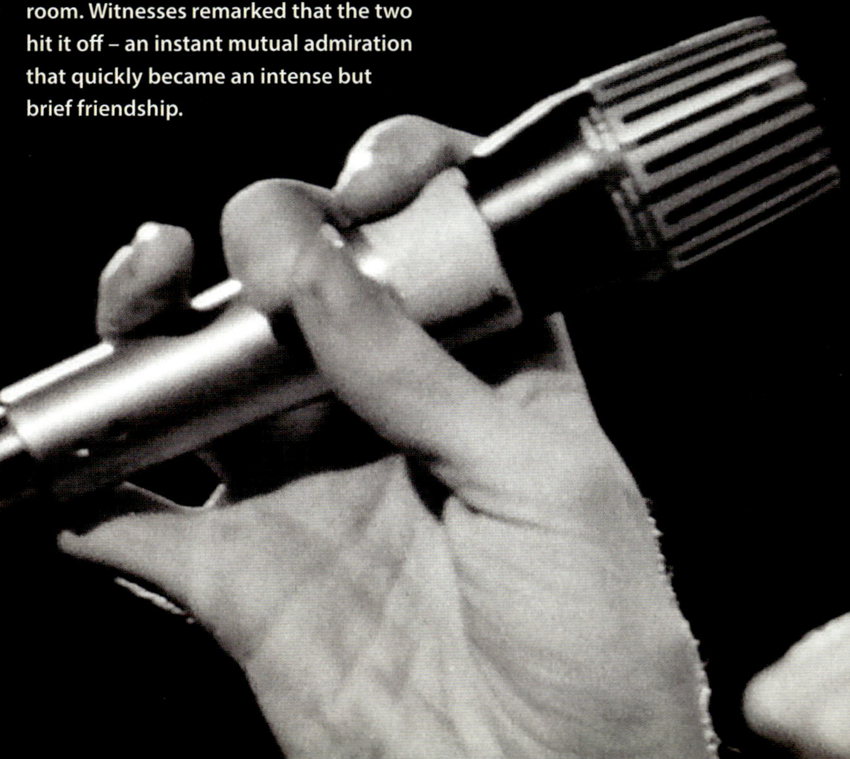

Universal Amphitheatre, Los Angeles. Alan Yentob's film crew shot footage of the September 5 concert for his BBC Omnibus documentary *Cracked Actor*.

✪ PHOTO SESSION

'YOUNG AMERICANS' PROMOTION

Terry O'Neill: Photographer

At a studio in the Playboy building in Hollywood, Terry O'Neill shot a series of publicity photographs to accompany the new *Young Americans* album.

The Eric Stephen Jacobs cover image presented Bowie in the 'old Hollywood' star tradition. Terry O'Neill's shots showed off Bowie's 'new Hollywood' look.

FRIDAY 20 SEPTEMBER

▼SOCIALISING

Taylor invited Bowie to join her at Dean Martin's house on Mountain Drive, Beverly Hills (pointed out by a tour bus guide in *Cracked Actor*) for the 21st birthday party of Martin's son Ricci.

When Bowie arrived at the party, he went looking for Taylor, and found her talking with Elton John, John Lennon and May Pang. They had come with Ringo in the hope of meeting Taylor, whom Ringo knew.

May Pang (2005)

And at that same party we met David Bowie. We were actually introduced to Bowie by Elizabeth Taylor. [396]

Bowie (1999)

John was sort of: Oh, here comes another new one. And I was sort of: It's John Lennon! I don't know what to say. Don't mention The Beatles; you'll look really stupid. And he said, "Hello, Dave." And I said, "I've got everything you've made – except The Beatles." [380]

RIGHT AND OPPOSITE: Terry O'Neill became Bowie's photographer of choice during his time in Los Angeles. When Elizabeth Taylor fixated on Bowie as a James Dean-like figure, O'Neill documented their fleeting affair (above) and Bowie's new 'old Hollywood' image (right and opposite). Bowie later told Cameron Crowe, "Dean was probably very much like me. Elizabeth Taylor told me that once. Dean was calculating. He wasn't careless. He was not the rebel he portrayed so successfully. He didn't want to die. But he did believe in the premise of taking yourself to extremes, just to add a deeper cut to one's personality." O'Neill also photographed the Universal Amphitheater shows (previous page) and tour rehearsals (seen in *Cracked Actor*, when Ava Cherry waves at him).

TUESDAY 24 SEPTEMBER

■ CHART

'Knock On Wood'

UK Top 30 Chart Entry

Charting 6 weeks

WEDNESDAY 25 SEPTEMBER

◆ AWARDS

Amanda Lear accepted Bowie's award for Top Male Singer at the *Melody Maker* Pop Poll Awards 1974 at the Global Village, a club located beneath Charing Cross station in London.

SATURDAY 28 SEPTEMBER

✪ PHOTO SESSION

'PEOPLE MAGAZINE' WITH ELIZABETH TAYLOR

Terry O'Neill: Photographer

O'Neill arranged the shoot at George Cukor's Bel Air home, where Elizabeth Taylor was staying at the time.

Cukor would be directing her the following year in *The Blue Bird*, the first joint Soviet–American production to be shot in Russia. Taylor had asked Bowie to co-star with her and a photo session was arranged to accompany the announcement in the press.

Terry O'Neill (2003)

David was two and a half hours late for his first meeting with Liz. He arrived dishevelled and out of it. Liz was pretty annoyed and on the verge of leaving, but we managed to persuade her to stay. She was thinking of asking him to appear in* The Blue Bird*, but she went off the idea after that. [026]

Bowie (1975)

That was a rotten film she wanted me to do, and a rotten part. She's finding out about it now. She's in Russia stuck out there. The thing she's in is a very dry, high French fairytale with nothing to say. It is being directed by a wonderful director. But the whole film stinks and I turned it down. [233]

In the New York studios of WNEW-FM, John Lennon sat in on the afternoon show and announced some of the commercials: "Tonight, at the Joint in the Woods, guess who's there! It's Ladies' Night! All females admitted at half-price. Oh, good! Well, Bowie can get in!"

OCTOBER

THE SOUL TOUR

The $400,000 Hunger City set was finally junked, donated to a public school in Philadelphia.

The new show added 'Can You Hear Me' and 'Somebody Up There Likes Me' and dispensed with Toni Basil and the choreography.

The other key player of the *Diamond Dogs* show, Michael Kamen, had been replaced as musical director by Mike Garson, who promptly asked for a pay rise. Defries responded by firing him, but Bowie demanded his reinstatement.

Bassist Doug Rauch was replaced by Emir Ksasan, who had played in The Main Ingredient with Carlos Alomar. Greg Errico was replaced by Dennis Davis.

Carlos Alomar (1997)

I met Dennis when we were playing with Roy Ayers. When you're a working musician in a big city like New York, you always should try to find the people you sound best with. So I found Dennis, Emir, and the three of us were a massive rhythm section… The first opportunity I got, I told David, "You've got to get these guys. These guys will wipe out anyone else."

When he heard Dennis, he was like, "That's it, it's over, the door's closed." Emir did the same thing, but he has a different personality so he only lasted a certain amount of time. That's when George Murray came in… his style and approach is more laid back. And that rhythm section lasted up until Scary Monsters. [196]

The shows were billed as David Bowie and The Garson Band.

David Bowie: Vocals/Guitar
Mike Garson: Musical Director/Keyboards
Carlos Alomar: Rhythm Guitar
Earl Slick: Lead Guitar
Emir Ksasan: Bass
Dennis Davis: Drums
Pablo Rosario: Percussion
David Sanborn: Alto Saxophone
Warren Peace/Ava Cherry/Robin Clark/Luther Vandross/Anthony Hinton/Diane Sumler: Backing Vocals

Luther Vandross (1982)
Bowie made me go out and do an opening 45-minute act for him every night with my own material. I remember the first night I went on stage and did my thing. Some people were shouting "Bowie, Bowie". That was very disconcerting to me that night. Bowie said, "Please. Later for these people. Later for them. You go out there and get your art together." [276]

SATURDAY 5 OCTOBER

★ **LIVE**
Civic Center
St Paul
Minnesota, USA

TUESDAY 8 OCTOBER

★ **LIVE**
Indiana Convention Center
Indianapolis
Indiana, USA

Backing singers Luther Vandross, Anthony Hinton and Geoff MacCormack with Bowie on the Philly Dogs tour.

FRIDAY 11 OCTOBER

★ LIVE

Dane County Coliseum
Madison
Wisconsin, USA

Michael Bauman

(*Wisconsin State Journal*):
Take away the gimmicks and the glitter, drop the overt decadence, and what have you got left? Boredom. Bowie appeared before a crowd of 5,000 that glittered a lot more than he did, he having ditched the old bisexual haircut and make-up. If you like your concerts bereft of any musical benefits, there was a lot going on. For most of the crowd however the reaction is summed up best by comments heard while heading toward the exit. To wit: "The next time that (bleep) plays here it'll be to an empty house."

SATURDAY 12 – TUESDAY 15 OCTOBER

▲ RECORDING

Star Studio
37th and National Avenue
Milwaukee
Wisconsin, USA

ZIGGY STARDUST AND THE SPIDERS FROM MARS SOUNDTRACK

MainMan had arranged for D A Pennebaker's film of the Ziggy retirement show – then known as *Bowie '73 With The Spiders From Mars* – to be screened on American television with a stereo simulcast on FM radio. Bowie went into the studio with Mike Garson and Earl Slick to overdub some piano and guitar parts for the soundtrack, with help from Dean and Sam Halonen and Robert Sage.

Michigan Palace, Detroit with Earl Slick. The musicians had been hidden away behind the set for most of the tour. Bowie brought them more to the fore after the LA shows.

SUNDAY 13 OCTOBER
★ LIVE
Mecca Arena
Milwaukee
Wisconsin, USA

TUESDAY 15 – SUNDAY 20 OCTOBER
★ LIVE
Michigan Palace
Detroit
Michigan, USA

WEDNESDAY 16 OCTOBER
✪ TELEVISION
Windsor
Ontario, Canada

✪ COMMERCIAL FILMING
'DAVID LIVE'
CHANNEL 9 (CKLW-TV)

The television station derived much of its income by making commercials at a fraction of what production houses in New York would charge. As a result the *David Live* commercial cost MainMan $5,000 instead of $30,000.

Bowie arrived for the shoot accompanied by a security squad, but there were only a dozen fans on the lawn outside the studio. News photographers were dispersed before they could get a shot. Management was concerned that the sudden flash of a camera – unnecessary on the bright day that it was – would be enough to make Bowie pack the whole thing in and leave.

Local record store workers were invited to watch the taping and, during a break in the studio work, joined Bowie for a snack of Kentucky Fried Chicken and Coca-Cola.

TUESDAY 22 WEDNESDAY 23 OCTOBER
★ LIVE
Arie Crown Theatre
Chicago
Illinois, USA

FRIDAY 25 OCTOBER
✪ TELEVISION
'BOWIE '73 WITH THE SPIDERS FROM MARS' WIDE WORLD: IN CONCERT (ABC)

The broadcast version was heavily censored as ABC objected to the references to death and suicide in the lyrics.

DA Pennebaker (2003)
They demanded that we beep them. The guy came in from ABC and went through and told me where to beep them and there were maybe 20 places. But we did it on the mono version, which was going out on regular network programming. Meanwhile we had the stereo version that I'd made where there are no beeps. [373]

This uncensored stereo version was used for the simultaneous FM radio broadcast. This cut included Jeff Beck's appearance, which was removed for the film's 1983 release as *Ziggy Stardust And The Spiders From Mars*.

Tony Visconti (2003)
David phoned up and said, "Beck doesn't want to be in the film. He doesn't like his guitar solo. I can book this studio tonight, let him record his solo to his satisfaction. I'm sure if it works out it'll be in the film." I went to the studio and he set up a guitar amp and we could view and play to the film. It was CTS Studios in north London and they could lock up film and tape. Jeff played his solo and it sounded great. He played it in two parts, we edited one part into the other, he was really happy with it. The next day David phoned me, "Beck still doesn't want to be in the film." Jeff kind of felt out of place in the show. All the guys in the band were dressed in glam outfits and he came onstage with flared trousers and an ordinary jacket. [373]

TUESDAY 29 OCTOBER

■ **ALBUM RELEASED**

'DAVID LIVE'
UK (RCA APL2-0771)
US (CPL2-0771)
UK Chart Peak No.2
US Chart Peak No.8

SIDE ONE
1. **'1984'** (3:21)
2. **'Rebel Rebel'** (2:42)
3. **'Moonage Daydream'** (5:10)
4. **'Sweet Thing'** (8:48)

SIDE TWO
1. **'Changes'** (3:36)
2. **'Suffragette City'** (3:46)
3. **'Aladdin Sane'** (4:58)
4. **'All The Young Dudes'** (4:19)
5. **'Cracked Actor'** (3:29)

SIDE THREE
1. **'Rock'n'Roll With Me'** (4:19)
2. **'Watch That Man'** (4:23)
3. **'Knock On Wood'** (3:08)
4. **'Diamond Dogs'** (6:34)

SIDE FOUR
1. **'Big Brother'** (4:11)
2. **'The Width Of A Circle'** (8:14)
3. **'The Jean Genie'** (5:19)
4. **'Rock'n'Roll Suicide'** (4:49)

"It was my ecstatic pleasure and great honour to be accompanied by some of the finest musicians I have ever worked with. Also eternal thanx to my friends and fans at the Tower for your wonderfulness. love on ya! Bowie 74."

All songs by David Bowie except 'Rock'n'Roll With Me' (Bowie/Peace)/ 'Knock On Wood' (Floyd/Cropper)

Tony Visconti: Producer
Tony Visconti/Edwin H Kramer: Mixers/Electric Lady Studios, New York City, New York, USA
Earl Slick: Guitar
Herbie Flowers: Bass
Gui Andrisano/Warren Peace: Backing Vocals
Michael Kamen: Electric Piano/Moog/ Oboe
Tony Newman: Drums
Pablo Rosario: Percussion
David Sanborn: Alto Saxophone/Flute
Richard Grando: Flute/Baritone Saxophone
Mike Garson: Piano/Mellotron
Keith Harwood: Live Recording Supervisor
Showco: Live Sound
Dagmar (uncredited): Photographer

Recorded live at the Tower Theatre, Philadelphia with the assistance of Record Plant.

In a bid to get the album to the top of the UK charts in its first week, *David Live* was priced at £3.78 for two months before reverting to the usual two LP price of £4.88.

Tom Nolan (*Rolling Stone*)
Rather than serving as a welcome introduction to or summation of David Bowie's oeuvre, this two-record live album lumps together the several facets of his music into a thin, samey oneness. Any power these 16 originals had can only be guessed at from hearing these cursory versions. The backing is one-dimensional, mixed into a flat canvas to highlight Bowie's presence, and despite extended solos, the band does not establish an engaging identity. Bowie is centre-stage all the way and the thinness and flaccidity of this outing are, in large part, due to his often perfunctory, slurred, and hurried vocals. Instead of providing for a more intimate performance, the live setting has only brought out Bowie's more unfortunate theatrical mannerisms; any magic these may have worked in person is, on platter, only so much heavy breathing. Bowie also indulges the greater weakness of taking himself too seriously. When 'Changes' is framed like a Watergate prophecy, you figure you're hearing Bowie on the wrong night.

ABOVE: Bowie selected the cover image from Dagmar's photos of the Philadelphia concerts. He famously remarked to Allan Jones in 1977 that "it looks as if I've just stepped out of the grave. That's actually how I felt." OPPOSITE: Radio City Music Hall. The tour was back in New York after only three months, revamped as a soul revue.

SELECTED REISSUES

■ LP *Rock Concert* (abridged to one disc) (RCA 1979).

■ LP *At The Tower Philadelphia* (reissue of *Rock Concert*) (RCA 1982).

■ 2 CD (remastered with bonus tracks) (Ryko 1990).
1. Band intro (0:09)
2. 'Here Today, Gone Tomorrow' (Satchell/Robinson/Webster/Harris/ Bonner/Middlebrooks/Jones) (3:32)
3. 'Time' (5:19)

■ 2 CD (remastered with bonus tracks and original running order restored) (EMI 2005).
1. 'Here Today, Gone Tomorrow' (Satchell/Robinson/Webster/Harris/ Bonner/Middlebrooks/Jones) (3:40)
2. 'Space Oddity' (6:27)
3. 'Panic In Detroit' (5:41)
4. 'Time' (5:21)

WEDNESDAY 30 OCTOBER

★ **LIVE**

Radio City Music Hall
New York City
New York, USA

John Rockwell (*New York Times*)
He has now dropped most of the overt theatrics, written a clutch of new songs and retooled his whole show. The result, on Wednesday, was disappointing. Mr Bowie's theatrics last summer may have had their problems – shapelessness, erratic pacing, pretension. But, at least there were some striking moments, and everything snapped along crisply, both dramatically and musically.

On Wednesday, the proceedings led off with a lame half-hour by Mr Bowie's band and mostly black back-up singers. When the star finally appeared, he seemed to be attempting to humanize his previous space-mutant image. But he looked self-consciously uncomfortable without routines to act out, and he was in hoarse voice indeed. The old songs were mostly unsuccessful, mannered and erratically distorted in phrasing. The four new songs appeared to be attempts at something a bit more conventional and direct, although the sound system and Mr Bowie's vocal state made a real judgment of them impossible.

THURSDAY 31 OCTOBER

★ **LIVE**

Radio City Music Hall
New York City
New York, USA

NOVEMBER

FRIDAY 1

★ **LIVE**

Radio City Music Hall
New York City
New York, USA

SATURDAY 2 NOVEMBER

★ **LIVE**

✪ **TELEVISION**

Radio City Music Hall
New York City
New York, USA

'THE DICK CAVETT SHOW'
'1984'/'Young Americans'/interview/'Footstomping' (Collins) – 'I Wish I Could Shimmy Like My Sister Kate' (Piron) medley/'Can You Hear Me'

Following Dick Cavett's preamble ("I'm explaining this for the square johns at home"), Bowie swept on to the stage to perform '1984' and 'Young Americans' live with the band.

ABOVE: Dick Cavett wonders what Bowie is drawing with his cane. BELOW: 'Young Americans' with David Sanborn, Earl Slick, Pablo Rosario and Carlos Alomar.

The interview was somewhat stilted, with Bowie being more nervous and evasive than ever. Dick Cavett attempted to keep the tone upbeat and casual, but Bowie's obsessive fiddling with the cane betrayed his agitation and inability to converse on a normal level.

Bowie (1994)
It was horrendous. I had no idea where I was, I couldn't hear the questions. To this day, I don't know if I bothered answering them, I was so out of my gourd. [388]

After the interview Bowie played a medley of early Sixties R&B covers: 'Footstomping' (The Flares) and 'I Wish I Could Shimmy Like My Sister Kate' (The Olympics), where Ava Cherry took the spotlight.

Before it went to air, the end of the broadcast tape was wiped, so the medley was never shown, nor was 'Can You Hear Me', which Bowie also performed. The band's introduction music and Cavett's preamble have also since been erased. Although the 'Footstomping' medley was never officially released, it circulates via bootlegs and online.

▮ Broadcast: December 5 (ABC).

▮ 'Footstomping' (audio) released on *Rarest One Bowie* (Golden Years 1995).

▮ 'Young Americans' released on *Best Of Bowie* DVD (EMI 2002).

▮ '1984'/'Young Americans'/interview released on *Dick Cavett's Rock Icons* DVD (Shout Factory 2005).

▮ '1984'/'Young Americans'/interview released on *Young Americans* CD/DVD (EMI 2007).

SUNDAY 3 NOVEMBER

★ **LIVE**

Radio City Music Hall
New York City
New York, USA

After a series of scathing reviews of Wednesday's opening night, Bowie rallied to deliver a show that Mick Farren had nothing but praise for.

Mick Farren (*NME*)
All reports seemed to agree that the first early stagings in the five-night stint were on the abject side of rotten. On the Sunday night, however, Bowie finally pulled it together and staged one of the finest live rock spectaculars that New York has been treated to in years. The phenomenon of David Bowie fronting what amounts to an avant-garde soul show is a strange thing to watch. It's also a joy. [122]

▼SOCIALISING

At the after-show party at the Gramercy Park Hotel, Bowie entertained David Johansen, Tony Visconti, Wayne County and others with sturgeon and Dom Perignon, telling them about his plans for the New Year. In January the new album would be released, and he planned to tour Brazil for three weeks with Geoff MacCormack, taking a boat to Caracas then going overland by Land Rover to Brazil, visiting Amazon villages along the way.

At that point he was still intending to do *The Blue Bird* with Liz Taylor, followed by a tour of Europe, beginning in April, and a tour of England in May.

ABOVE: The after-show party at the Gramercy Park Hotel with Ava Cherry (left) and Tony Visconti (right).
LEFT: Deep in conversation with David Johansen.

WEDNESDAY 6 NOVEMBER

★ LIVE

Public Hall
Cleveland
Ohio, USA

FRIDAY 8 NOVEMBER

★ LIVE

War Memorial Auditorium
Buffalo
New York, USA

MONDAY 11 NOVEMBER

■ SINGLE RELEASED

'Changes' (2:32)/
'Andy Warhol' (3:03)
US (RCA 74-0605)
Chart Peak No.41

★ LIVE

Capital Center
Landover
Maryland, USA

TUESDAY 12 NOVEMBER

■ CHART

'DAVID LIVE'
UK Chart Entry No.17
US Chart Entry No.30

THURSDAY 14 – SATURDAY 16 NOVEMBER

★ LIVE

Music Hall
Boston
Massachusetts, USA

Peter Gelzinis (*The Boston Herald*)
His impression of a nightclub singer was tailored to an audience of 4,500. His white made-up face and luminous eyes made you think of Joel Grey's caricature in Cabaret, *there was still that glamorized decadence to his swagger. He also kept everyone off guard musically for a while. 'Changes' and 'Sorrow' took on the new flavour of soulish show tunes, while a new song 'Young Americans', sung with a big acoustic guitar slung at his waist, was a chaotic blend of Elvis and Watergate all rolled up in a cha-cha close.*

Michael Nicholson (*The Boston Globe*)
'1984' was the first echo of the outrageously staged productions of the past, but it was only an echo with merely harsh lights played on the audience and a stage light casting an immense shadow of Bowie on the simple white backdrop to suggest a totalitarian presence. Then back to the mundane with 'Footstomping' and the new 'When You Rock'n'Roll With Me'.

It took the exuberant 'Jean Genie' to get the unusually sedate audience moving, albeit rather nonchalantly, toward the stage, and some monumental crashing guitar to keep things going, but 'Suffragette' and 'Rock'n'Roll Suicide' finished things off nicely for the encore of 'Diamond Dogs' featuring a wardrobe change to an army fatigue outfit with a red belt and a polo mallet accessory.

ABOVE: Sigma Sound Studios with Philadelphia DJ Ed Sciaky and Bruce Springsteen.

MONDAY 18 NOVEMBER

★ **LIVE**

Spectrum Theater
Philadelphia
Pennsylvania, USA

After the immediate sell-out of the 16,000-seat Spectrum, a second night was booked for the 25th. The concert was plagued by sound problems, which only increased the audience's hostility to The Garson Band who opened the show with an eight-song set.

Meanwhile in New York, Tony Ingrassia's play *Fame* (a comedy based on Marilyn Monroe's life) opened at The Golden Theatre on Broadway – and closed after one night, a resounding critical failure. It reportedly left MainMan $250,000 in the hole, adding to Defries' financial woes and Bowie's anger towards him.

TUESDAY 19 NOVEMBER

★ **LIVE**

Civic Arena
Pittsburgh
Pennsylvania, USA

WEDNESDAY 20 – SUNDAY 24 NOVEMBER

▲ **RECORDING**

Sigma Sound Studios
Philadelphia
Pennsylvania, USA

'YOUNG AMERICANS' ALBUM
'John, I'm Only Dancing (Again)'
'Can You Hear Me' (version 2)
'After Today' (version 1/slow tempo)
'Fascination'
'Win'
'It's Hard To Be A Saint In The City'

Tony Visconti/Harry Maslin: Producers

Bowie booked more time at Sigma to rework some of the songs with the Soul Tour line-up. Luther Vandross had been performing his song 'Funky Music (Is A Part Of Me)' as part of The Garson Band's opening set. Bowie took the song and reworked it with new lyrics as 'Fascination'. When Bowie asked his permission, Vandross replied, "You're David Bowie. I live with my mother. Of course you can change the lyrics!"

THURSDAY 21 NOVEMBER

A *Rock Dreams* exhibition opened at Star Gallery, 465 West Broadway, New York. Seventy-two of the 116 paintings featured in Guy Peellaert's book were offered for sale with prices from $1,500 to $2,500. Sales of the book had already reached 200,000 even before publication.

SUNDAY 24 NOVEMBER

▲ **RECORDING**

Sigma Sound Studios
Philadelphia
Pennsylvania, USA

Bowie was working on a cover of Bruce Springsteen's 'It's Hard To Be A Saint In The City' which he had started in late 1973, and hoped to get Springsteen involved. Earlier in the week, Tony Visconti called Philadelphia DJ Ed Sciaky at WMMR and asked him if he could get Springsteen into the studio.

Sciaky got in contact with Springsteen, who caught a bus from New Jersey to Philadelphia, where Ed and Judy Sciaky found him "hanging with the bums in the station". At midnight he arrived at Sigma.

Bowie (1997)
Springsteen came down to hear what we were doing with his stuff. He was very shy. I remember sitting in the corridor with him, talking about his lifestyle, which was very Dylanesque – you know, moving from town to town with a guitar on his back, all that kind of thing. Anyway, he didn't like what we were doing, I remember that. At least, he didn't express much enthusiasm. I guess he must have thought it was all kind of odd. I was in another universe at the time. I've got this extraordinarily strange photograph of us all – I look like I'm made out of wax. [324]

As Visconti worked, Bowie told Springsteen how he and MacCormack saw his set at Max's in February 1973, and since then Springsteen had been the only American artist he had wanted to cover.

Bowie *(1987)*
I didn't want to play ['It's Hard To Be A Saint In The City'] to him because I wasn't happy with it anyway. And I was out of my wig. I just couldn't relate to him at all. It was a bad time for us to have met. I could see that he was thinking, "Who is this weird guy?" And I was thinking, "What do I say to normal people?" [159]

As the night wore on, Ed Sciaky watched Bowie recording his vocal for 'Win'.

Ed Sciaky (2002)
He'd sing three lines, then have the engineer play them back, keeping the first line every time. It was spectacular, watching him work like a painter, hitting every line the way he wanted. [301]

Around 7am Bowie asked Carl Paruolo to play the whole track from start to finish, twice. After the second listen, he nodded and said, "That's it. It's done." As if on cue, the Sigma Kids outside started applauding and calling up at the studio windows.

▮ 'John, I'm Only Dancing (Again)' released as a single in 1979.

▮ 'After Today' released on *Sound + Vision* (Ryko 1989).

▮ 'It's Hard To Be A Saint In The City' released on *Sound + Vision* (Ryko 1989)/ *The Best Of David Bowie 1975/1979* (EMI 1997).

Mick Rock (2007)

I recall asking Bowie why he never released this great cut. He told me that Springsteen didn't respond when he'd sent a copy to him; presuming this meant he wasn't keen, Bowie decided to can the whole thing. [260]

ABOVE: Leaving Artemis nightclub, assisted by Philadelphia's finest.

MONDAY 25 NOVEMBER

★ LIVE

Spectrum Theater
Philadelphia
Pennsylvania, USA

After the scathing reviews of the previous Monday's concert were attributed to poor sound, Visconti was asked to conduct a more thorough soundcheck to ensure a better show.

Matt Damsker (*Philadelphia Bulletin*)

In general, it works, and last night's audience seemed won over by the fast-paced opening segment, which features the five vocalists (in various combinations) warming up with an affecting program of some new Bowie songs – thoroughly funky vehicles – as well as a powerful version of The Supremes' 'You Keep Me Hangin' On' and Geoffrey MacCormack's fine solo handling of Bruce Springsteen's 'Growin' Up'. Unfortunately, Bowie's voice has not been able to withstand so much recent touring, and his edge was considerably blunted by raw, uneven and generally strained singing. [108]

In a backstage interview with *Disc* magazine, Mike Garson revealed the album, titled *Fascination,* was complete, consisting of seven tracks.

'John, I'm Only Dancing (Again)'/ 'Young Americans'/ 'Fascination'/ 'Right'/ 'Win'/ 'It's Gonna Be Me'/ 'Can You Hear Me'

▼ SOCIALISING

Sciaky and Springsteen watched the concert and afterwards Bowie celebrated the completion of *Young Americans* with a private party at Le Club Artemis, during which Philadelphia police entered the bar looking for under-age drinkers.

Patti Brett (1999)

The bars close at 2am, and it was a quarter after three and we were still in the bar. It was a private party, but the police raided it and started taking David away! There's actually a photograph of all the cops in leather jackets leading him down the steps. He had this big green mohair fur coat and this little red beret and sunglasses, he looked like a little Christmas tree! He was very calm. Everyone else in the bar was freaking out.

They were arresting everyone in the bar and the bar staff were sneaking people out the back door. Nothing ever came of it though. He wasn't charged and I think they were doing it more for show. It was just so funny to see these tons of police coming in as if we were these horrible people who needed controlling, and then them escorting him down the steps. [004]

When Bowie and his entourage attempted to leave, Ava Cherry led the way. The captain blocked her path saying, "If you ain't got no proof of your age, sit down, miss!" She turned away and Bowie stepped forward. "You don't actually believe that I'm not at least 21 years of age? Incredible! That's quite flattering, actually. Why, everyone knows that I'm at least 52."

Throughout it all, Bowie signed autographs and chatted cheerfully with the kids. One young girl who was detained offered Bowie her body "when I get out of jail". [245]

WEDNESDAY 27 NOVEMBER

▼SOCIALISING

Mid South Auditorium
Memphis
Tennessee, USA

GEORGE HARRISON

The night before he played the same venue, Bowie went to see Willie Weeks and Andy Newmark playing in George Harrison's tour band and visited backstage. Bowie and Harrison reportedly "didn't hit it off that well".

George Harrison (1974)
All I really meant was what I said. I pulled his hat up from over his eyes and said, "Hi man, how are you, nice to meet you" – pulled his hat up and said, you know – "do you mind if I have a look at you, to see what you are because I've only ever seen those dopey pictures of you." [339]

THURSDAY 28 NOVEMBER

★LIVE

Mid South Auditorium
Memphis
Tennessee, USA

Bowie called up Harry Maslin, an engineer at Record Plant in New York, to arrange another *Young Americans* session. Bowie was hoping to finish the album in time to spend Christmas in London.

SATURDAY 30 NOVEMBER

★LIVE

Municipal Auditorium
Nashville
Tennessee, USA

Marc Bolan, on the road in Detroit, told Chris Welch, "Next year I'm hoping to make a film with David Bowie. I'll be directing and he'll be writing the script. The film will be a science fiction story, and we'll probably write it between us. We really want to work together.

"I've been hanging out a lot with him lately, and we'd like to do a concert together, just the two of us with acoustic guitars, to recreate the atmosphere of the old days. We did a tour of England together, years ago. Yeah, David's fine. He's pretty 'up' at the moment – like me, working on the road." [315]

LEFT: George Harrison, 1974. Bowie and the ex-Beatle got off on the wrong foot in Memphis.

DECEMBER

SUNDAY 1

★ **LIVE**

The Omni
Atlanta
Georgia, USA

The last show and the only performance of 'Win' on the tour.

TUESDAY 3 DECEMBER

▲ **RECORDING**

Record Plant
New York City
New York, USA

'YOUNG AMERICANS'
'Win'
'Fascination'
'Right'
'Somebody Up There Likes Me'

Tony Visconti: Producer
Harry Maslin: Engineer
Kevin Herron/David Thoener: Tape Operators

Tony Visconti began mixing the album and adding overdubs. During this time Bowie ran into John Lennon who was also at Record Plant, finishing the mixes on his covers album *Rock'n'Roll*. Bowie invited him over and later called Visconti at the studio. "John Lennon's coming to my suite at the hotel tonight and it would be great if you could be there to buffer the meeting between us." Visconti was happy to help out – he was keen to meet John Lennon – and he turned up at Sherry Netherlands and knocked.

After a while, an unfamiliar voice asked, "Who is it?" Visconti identified himself and the door was opened by Beatles aide-de-camp Neil Aspinall. He saw Lennon emerging from the bathroom with May Pang – they had been worried it was the police, as a drug bust would destroy his chances of getting a green card.

As requested, Visconti chatted with Lennon while Bowie sat on the floor drawing on a sketchpad. After a while, Lennon asked Bowie, "Do you have another one of those sketchpads?" and they began drawing caricatures of each other. The ice broken, Bowie and Lennon began to see each other socially and Lennon offered him advice on the pitfalls of management – he was in litigation with Allen Klein at the time. Bowie wanted to leave Defries but he didn't know how. He had assumed that he needed someone to deal with the business and the contracts.

Bowie (1976)
John sorted me out all the way down the line. He took me to one side, sat me down and told me what it was all about. I realised that I was very naïve. [085]

▼ **SOCIALISING**

Dana Gillespie began a week of shows at Reno Sweeney in New York. One night Bowie dropped in with Bette Midler and bumped into Bob Dylan, who was in town looking at artwork for *Blood On The Tracks*.

Bowie (1976)
We don't have a lot to talk about. We're not great friends. Actually, I think he hates me. We went back to somebody's house after some gig at a club. We had all gone to see someone, I can't remember who, and Dylan was there. I was in a very, sort of… verbose frame of mind. And I just talked at him for hours and hours, and whether I amused him or scared him or repulsed him, I really don't know. I didn't wait for any answers. I just went on and on about everything. And then I said good night. He never phoned me. [101]

ABOVE: May Pang and John Lennon, who offered Bowie advice concerning his impecunious state and how to break free from Defries's management.

Bowie (1978)
The funniest part about it was that I'd been talking about his music and what he should do and what he shouldn't and what his music did and what it didn't, and at the end of the conversation he turned to me and – I hope it was in jest, but I have a feeling it wasn't – he said, "You wait till you hear my next album."

I thought, "Oh no, not from you, please! Not that, anything but that!" I don't know whether I was in the correct state to appreciate him, but it was the first and last time I ever met him. [308]

THURSDAY 5 DECEMBER

✪ **TELEVISION**

The Dick Cavett Show broadcast (ABC)

MID-DECEMBER

▲ MIXING

'YOUNG AMERICANS' ALBUM

With the album sessions now considered complete, Visconti took the master tapes and left for London. Passing through Kennedy Airport, Visconti stopped to buy chewing gum. At the departure gate he realised he had left the tapes by the shop counter and ran back to find them still there.

Back in London, Visconti added string arrangements to 'Can You Hear Me' and 'Who Can I Be Now?' at George Martin's Air Studios. He mixed the album at Good Earth Sound House with the aid of an 18-page telex of mixing ideas Bowie sent from New York.

The album's track list at this stage:

SIDE ONE

1. **'John, I'm Only Dancing (Again)'**
2. **'Somebody Up There Likes Me'**
3. **'It's Gonna Be Me'**

SIDE TWO

1. **'Who Can I Be Now?'**
2. **'Can You Hear Me'**
3. **'Young Americans'**
4. **'Right'**

LATE DECEMBER

▲ RECORDING

▲ MIXING

Record Plant
New York City
New York, USA

'YOUNG AMERICANS' ALBUM

David Bowie/Harry Maslin: Producers

Harry Maslin: Engineer

Kevin Herron/David Thoener: Tape Operators

Bowie called Harry Maslin back into the studio to add more overdubs and to remix all the tracks (except 'Young Americans', which Visconti had already mixed and delivered to RCA to release as the new single).

MONDAY 23 DECEMBER

▼ SOCIALISING

Over dinner at the Sherry Netherlands Bowie told Mike Garson, "I want you to be my pianist for the next 20 years."

Garson visited Bowie the next day to exchange Christmas presents – the last he saw of Bowie for many years. Ten years on, Garson recalled the revolving door of musicians in Bowie's career: "The joke had been, 'When it's my time, David, just let me know.'" [013]

ABOVE AND OPPOSITE: Another cover concept for *Young Americans*, devised by Bowie and photographer Steve Schapiro.

Bowie was moved from the Sherry Netherlands to the slightly less expensive Pierre Hotel, where he kept two suites (at $700 a week) – one for living in, the other made into a studio, where he immersed himself in making films of the scale models of Hunger City.

Bowie (1980)

I recreated the set for* Diamond Dogs *– this was in the Pierre Hotel in New York – and I built three or four-foot high buildings out of clay on tables. Some were standing up, others were crumbling and I took the camera and put a micro-lens on it, zooming down the streets in between the tables.

I tried animation out and had all these characters; the whole thing is so bizarre I'm going to put it together and put it out as a cassette. And as it's silent – there's a few bits of strange music on it but nothing much else; mainly I used the* Diamond Dogs *album as a backing track…

You know, I wanted to make a film of* Diamond Dogs *so passionately, so badly; I really wanted to do that, I had the whole roller-skating thing in there. We had no more cars because of the fuel problems – which was super stuff to look back on and say yes, I thought that then – and these characters with enormous, rusty, sort of organic-looking roller-skates with squeaking wheels that they couldn't handle very well. Also I had groups of these cyborg people wandering around looking so punky it's going to be a lovely tape to put out. I want to write some new music for it though: a piece of music accompanied by a sort of strange black-and-white vision. [189]

TUESDAY 31 DECEMBER

Bowie spent New Year's Eve at home with Zowie. He intended to take Zowie to see the fireworks in Central Park but the weather kept them indoors, where they continued to play with the video equipment instead.

JANUARY

WEDNESDAY 8

▼SOCIALISING

Bowie spent his birthday night with Ava Cherry and Coco at the opening of the Lajeski Gallery at 801 Madison Avenue in New York. Guests including Andy Warhol, Larry Rivers, Yoko Ono, Roman Polanski, Karl Lagerfeld, Lance Loud and Richard Bernstein crammed in for the gallery's first show, 'The Tie'. Sixty artists exhibited their interpretation of the theme 'The condition of the tie today'. Bowie was among the invitees who were shuttled back and forth to the Plaza Hotel by carriage.

FRIDAY 10 JANUARY

▼SOCIALISING

After The Beatles' partnership was finally dissolved in London's High Court, Paul and Linda McCartney flew to New York. McCartney wanted to meet Lennon to discuss the dissolution before leaving for New Orleans to record *Venus And Mars*.

Lennon and May Pang took the McCartneys out to dinner at Nartells and Bowie came up in the conversation. At McCartney's suggestion they called him at the Pierre and Bowie invited them up.

May Pang (1983)

John and I had seen him a couple of times before our Christmas holiday and he had always insisted upon playing us the tracks of his new album. That night he played the album for Paul and Linda, even though John and I had heard it many times before. When it was over he played it again. I could see Paul getting restless. "Can we hear a different album?" he asked. David ignored him and when he began to play it a third time John said, "It's great. Do you have any other albums that might be of interest?" For a moment Bowie seemed startled by John's request and then he smiled and told me to pick another record. I selected an Aretha Franklin album and put it on the turntable and then David said, "Excuse me for a second." He marched out of the room. "I think you hurt Bowie's feelings," I told John. [029]

ABOVE: Cherry Vanilla photographed by Matthew Rolston for her 1978 RCA LP *Bad Girl*.

Lennon and Pang returned to her apartment on 52nd Street, and the phone was ringing as they walked in the door – it was Bowie. Lennon assured him he hadn't meant to offend and everything was fine.

EARLY JANUARY

⊙BUSINESS

In December, MainMan's accountant Alice Gartman drew up a list of creditors and found MainMan's debts totalled $350,000 and were increasing every week.

The list was much like the one that the London office had telexed to Defries at the beginning of 1974. The musicians had been paid their modest fees to ensure the shows went on and the albums recorded, but anything that could be invoiced – recording studios, hotels, equipment hire, contractors, even their own lawyers – remained unpaid.

Bowie had run up around $20,000 of room service in a month in his two-bedroom suite at the Pierre so Defries asked Jaime Andrews to find a cheaper option. Bowie was moved into a rented brownstone opposite St Peter's Episcopal Church on West 20th Street, a quiet tree-lined area in Chelsea.

Cherry Vanilla lived on the same street a couple of blocks away. She had served as Bowie's publicist for MainMan, working alongside Leee Black Childers and Tony Zanetta since Defries had enlisted them in 1972. He had indulged them for the past three years but eventually the axe fell on the New Yorkers.

Cherry Vanilla (1977)

He suddenly decided we were all getting carried away. He realised we'd spent about £200,000 on film stock… we filmed everything! Hours of stuff remains unedited. He suddenly freaked out at us. We were carrying the whole thing away, and he just said, "Stop! You're all fired!" [228]

Bowie too was about to split with Defries, following his realisation that all his money had paid for MainMan's excesses. Since settling in New York he had sought solace from Vanilla.

Cherry Vanilla (2011)

David liked my apartment on 20th Street, and he also liked Norman Fisher's coke, something for which he'd recently acquired an insatiable appetite and for which I had, of course, hooked him up. And since my days were winding down at MainMan, I guess David felt comfortable getting high with me and opening up about anything and everything that was on his mind. [046]

▼SOCIALISING

Vanilla had assembled a proto-punk band and was doing the rounds of the clubs. Bowie had promised to produce her album and watched her headline at Trude Heller's club, supported by Lance Loud's band Mumps.

Another night Bowie and Jagger watched her and Holly Woodlawn perform at Reno Sweeney's. Afterwards they moved on to the Café Carlyle to see Manhattan Transfer. The gossip columns reported that they "misbehaved" over the bill and were bounced by the maître d'.

MID-JANUARY

▲ RECORDING

Studio A
Electric Lady Studios
52 West 8th Street
New York City
New York, USA

'YOUNG AMERICANS' ALBUM
'Fame'
'Across The Universe'

David Bowie/Harry Maslin: Producers
David Bowie: Lead Guitar/Vocals
John Lennon: Guitar/Vocals
Carlos Alomar: Rhythm Guitar
Dennis Davis: Drums
Emir Ksasan: Bass
Eddie Kramer: Engineer
David Whitman: Tape Operator

John Lennon (1975)
David told me he was going to do a version of 'Across The Universe' and I thought 'great', because I'd never done a good version of that song myself. It's one of my favourite songs, but I didn't like my version of it. So I went down and played rhythm on the track. [083]

Having finished the song, Lennon suggested they do something else. Bowie suggested they try 'Foot Stomping', a 1961 Flares song they'd played during November shows and on *The Dick Cavett Show*. As Bowie, Lennon and Alomar began adding riffs to it, the song evolved into 'Fame'.

Bowie (1983)
We'd spent quite a few nights talking and getting to know each other before we'd even gotten into the studio… we spent endless hours talking about fame, and what it's like not having a life of your own any more. I guess it was inevitable that the subject matter of the song would be about the subject matter of those conversations. God that session was fast. While John and Carlos Alomar were sketching out the guitar stuff in the studio, I was starting to work out the lyric in the control room. [318]

ABOVE: John Lennon on the roof of the Dakota in New York, February 24.

John Lennon (1980)
He goes in with about four words and a few guys, and starts laying down all this stuff and he has virtually nothing – he's making it up in the studio. So I just contributed whatever – you know like backwards piano and oooohhh [hits a high note] and the repeat of 'fame'. Then we needed a middle eight so we took some Stevie Wonder middle eight and did it backwards, you know. And we made a record out of it, right? So he got his first No.1, so I felt that was like a karmic thing, you know. With me and Elton, I got my first No.1, so I passed it on to Bowie and he got his, and I like that track. [031]

Bowie (1976)
There's always a lot of adrenalin flowing when John is around, but his chief addition to it all was the high-pitched singing of 'Fame'. The riff came from Carlos and the melody and most of the lyrics came from me. But it wouldn't have happened if John hadn't been there. He was the energy, and that's why he got a credit for writing it. He was the inspiration. [085]

Tony Visconti (1985)
About two weeks after I'd mixed the album, David phoned me to tell me about 'Fame'. He was very apologetic and nice about it. He said he hoped I wouldn't mind if we took a few tracks off and included these. The first I heard of 'Fame' and 'Across The Universe' was when the record was released! [043]

The two new tracks replaced 'Who Can I Be Now?' and 'It's Gonna Be Me'.

Tony Visconti (1985)
Beautiful songs, and it made me sick when he decided not to use them. I think it was the personal content of the songs that he was a bit reluctant to release. [043]

SUNDAY 26 JANUARY

✪ TELEVISION

Cracked Actor broadcast on *Omnibus* in the UK (BBC 1).

WEDNESDAY 29 JANUARY

⊙ BUSINESS

To free himself from Tony Defries, Bowie had engaged Los Angeles entertainment lawyer Michael Lippman as his new manager. Formerly a CMA booking agent, Lippman had pitched film work to Bowie and Angie in the past so he was a logical choice given Bowie's film aspirations.

Lippman began legal proceedings against Defries, declaring a motion to end all agreements between Bowie and MainMan, including publishing, management and recording controls.

Lippman flew in from California and accompanied Bowie to RCA, where they met with Ken Glancey, Mel Ilberman and Geoff Hannington. When Bowie announced his intention to leave Defries, RCA reassured Bowie of their loyalty to him and granted Bowie's requests: financial support, office space and a car, as he had been relying on the MainMan limo.

The next issue was the new album. Bowie had the masters in a bank vault but the new recordings with Lennon were still at Electric Lady. Only MainMan was legally entitled to pick up the tapes, but Hannington retrieved them from the studio in the dead of night.

Defries later asked Ilberman why RCA had sided with Bowie when they were legally bound to MainMan. Ilberman explained that in any such dispute, RCA would always side with the artist. After all, he pointed out to Defries, "You can't sing."

FEBRUARY

⊙ BUSINESS

English film director Nicolas Roeg was casting the lead role for *The Man Who Fell To Earth*. As the character Thomas Jerome Newton in Walter Tevis' book was unusually tall, Roeg's first choice was the six foot nine inches tall Michael Crichton, despite the fact he had no acting experience, but he was unavailable. Roeg and executive producer Si Litvinoff met with CMA casting agent Maggie Abbott.

Si Litvinoff (2002)
She was David's agent at the time. She represented all their 'boutique' people, who were not necessarily known as actors or movie stars. [365]

She suggested Mick Jagger, whom Roeg had directed in *Performance*.

Maggie Abbott (2005)
I tried to talk him into Mick but Nic knew him so well and said he wasn't what he had in mind. He wanted someone who looked frail – as if he had no bones in his body – and I immediately cried out, 'David Bowie!' [054]

Abbott had seen *Cracked Actor* and realised "he had just the charisma the character required. It had nothing to do with acting experience." [154]

Following their meeting she managed to smuggle out a copy of *Cracked Actor* to show to Litvinoff and Roeg.

Bowie (1976)
Nic watched it and I guess it was my attachment to Ziggy, the alter ego that captured his interest and imagination. And my looks helped, too. Roeg wanted a definite, pointedly stark face – which I had been endowed with. [101]

They immediately recognised that, like Newton, Bowie was a 'foreign body', uncomfortable in a new climate.

ABOVE: Nic Roeg on the set of *The Man Who Fell To Earth* in the room where Bowie's character Newton was incarcerated by the government, located in the dilapidated section of the Hotel Artesia.

Bowie (1993)
I think one of the things that Nic identified with me is that I was definitely living in two separate worlds at the same time. My state of mind was quite fractured and fragmented but I didn't really have much emotive force going for me so it was quite easy for me not to relate too well with those around me. [364]

Roeg and Litvinoff were convinced – now they had to convince Bowie. Maggie Abbott took Paul Mayersberg's script round to him and was shocked at his 'ghastly' appearance. Bowie's initial response to the script was cautious, but he agreed to meet them at his house on West 20th Street.

Ava Cherry (2010)
He'd spoken of doing movies, but I don't think anyone offered him a serious script before Nic Roeg. He wanted to be a movie star because he admired musicians who had acted, the Frank Sinatras. It was a natural progression for him. Mick [Jagger] had done some films. They were friends – he wanted to do films, too. [252]

Paul Mayersberg (2012)
Bowie took some persuading. As a joke, I put in a scene showing Newton unable to sing. [146]

Bowie would be in a recording studio till 10pm, so Roeg arrived at 9.30, followed later by Litvinoff.

Si Litvinoff (2002)
After midnight, I got the call to go downtown, in the snow, to David's house. The door was opened by a lovely looking black girl with orange-coloured short hair wearing a Clockwork Orange *sweater.* [409]

Litvinoff had produced Kubrick's film and took this as a good omen. As Roeg chatted to the "strangers coming and going" they waited. And waited.

Bowie (1993)
I was out and when I remembered the appointment I was already an hour late, so I thought, "Oh, no, I missed him, he won't be there now," and just forgot about it. When I finally got home, there was Nic waiting for me, sitting in my kitchen very patiently. Eight hours late and the man waited for me! That's persistence, you know, isn't it? [364]

Nicolas Roeg (1993)
At about five o'clock he arrived. We spoke for about five minutes. He said, "I'm tired." I said, "I can understand that – so am I," and he said, "Don't worry, I'm going to do it." And he showed me to the door. I was obviously looking a bit stunned – having been from 9.30 'til 5.30 in the morning there! [He said] "I tell you, don't worry. Let me know when you want me. I'll be there." [364]

Bowie (1993)
What I didn't tell him that day when he turned up was that I hadn't actually read The Man Who Fell To Earth. *And it was a combination of having seen* Walkabout *and actually meeting Nic in person that convinced me that this was something I should definitely get involved with… I tried to kill the conversation as quickly as possible because I didn't want him to suss that I hadn't read it. So he was throwing bits of the film at me and I was, "Yes, quite, quite… oh absolutely… oh yes, I can see that." But it was probably the best decision based on absolutely nothing – other than a man's previous work – that I've probably ever made.* [364]

WEDNESDAY 12 FEBRUARY

▼SOCIALISING

Madison Square Garden
New York City
New York, USA

LED ZEPPELIN

Watching the concert with Ava Cherry, Mick and Bianca Jagger, Bowie was particularly interested in the lighting design, which featured 'Led Zeppelin' spelt out in lights and 'krypton' laser effects illuminating Jimmy Page's violin bow interlude.

During the first two weeks of February, Bowie and Cherry visited Zeppelin at the Plaza Hotel where they were based for their fortnight of East Coast dates.

THURSDAY 13 FEBRUARY

▼SOCIALISING

Ronnie Wood joined Led Zeppelin on stage at Nassau Coliseum in Long Island for their encore number 'Communication Breakdown'.

Wood and Jimmy Page later visited Bowie and Ava Cherry at West 20th Street. Bowie was intrigued by Page, whom he knew from the old days in London. They had first met in 1965 when Page, a top session guitarist at the time, was called in to add a guitar solo to 'I Pity The Fool', a single Bowie was recording with The Manish Boys. For the past six years, Page had maintained a well-documented interest in the work of Aleister Crowley, going so far as to purchase and restore his famed magical headquarters Boleskine House in 1971.

ABOVE: Bowie was interested in Led Zeppelin's lighting effects and shared Jimmy Page's fascination with Aleister Crowley and the occult.

Ava Cherry (1986)

David had heard that Jimmy Page was mentally very powerful and able to influence people and there was a battle of wits to prove who was the stronger. I watched their eye contact and it was very weird. [013]

Ronnie Wood gamely suggested that Bowie leave the seclusion of his house and socialise with them, which backfired when Page spilled his glass of red wine on the satin cushions. When he let Ava take the blame, Bowie turned on him demanding, "How could you let her take the blame for something you did?"

Page got up to leave and Bowie suggested, "Why don't you leave by the window?" Page stared at him and walked out the door without a word. [013]

For Bowie the confrontation confirmed what he suspected about Page's psychic aura. He began to read obsessively about Aleister Crowley and mysticism.

MONDAY 17 FEBRUARY

■ **SINGLE RELEASED**

'Young Americans' (3:11)/
'Knock On Wood'
(Floyd/Cropper) (2:59)
US (RCA PB-10152)
Chart Peak No.28

■ **SINGLE RELEASED**

PROMO

'Young Americans' (3:11)/
'Young Americans' (5:10)
UK (RCA 2523 DJ)
US (RCA JB 10152)

FRIDAY 21 FEBRUARY

■ **SINGLE RELEASED**

'Young Americans' (5:01)/
'Suffragette City' (3:45)
UK (RCA2523)
Chart Peak No.15

▼ **SOCIALISING**

Bowie attended Roxy Music's concert at The Academy of Music, followed by a get-together at the new restaurant Lady Astor's.

MONDAY 24 FEBRUARY

✪ **PRESS**

Diane Kelly, from English magazine *Hi*, visited Bowie at home and found him pottering about, showing her his junk shop finds and hanging pictures in his attic bedroom. Asked what he had been doing lately, he replied, "Well, I've written some films. If nothing else happens, at least I'll have all these portfolios of artwork to show."

The folio was full of storyboards for several films he planned to direct. "I don't think I want to be a film star," Bowie said and added that he wanted to shoot his film in England. "I'd really love that, to come home and do the film there. But I mustn't talk about it, I get really homesick if I do."

Pat Gibbons arrived with an advance copy of *Young Americans* for Bowie's approval and Coco reminded him he had a fitting that afternoon with a tailor for his Grammy Awards suit.

"Tickets arrived for a Rod Stewart concert that night and David asked Coco to remind him to ring John Lennon to see if he would like to go along too. Then it was back to the serious business of picture hanging, stopping only to light a cigarette, autograph some photographs for me to take back to England or to show me some more finds – like the old Christmas snow scene inside a glass dome and the dozens of plastic circles moulded to look like bronze plaques. "I can do so many things with those," David said." [172]

▼ **SOCIALISING**

That night Bowie, Ava Cherry and Geoff MacCormack went to Madison Square Garden to see Rod Stewart and The Faces, watching from the side of the stage.

ABOVE: Ava Cherry, Bowie and Geoff MacCormack watch from the side of the stage as Rod Stewart and The Faces play Madison Square Garden.
RIGHT: Rod Stewart offers Bowie a glass of Blue Nun backstage.

OPPOSITE TOP: Grammy Awards presenters photo call: Bowie, Art Garfunkel, Paul Simon, Yoko Ono, John Lennon and Roberta Flack.

OPPOSITE: Bowie and Ann-Margret at the post-awards party.

MARCH

SATURDAY 1

■ **CHART**

'Young Americans'
UK Top 30 Chart Entry No.18
Charting 7 weeks

★ **LIVE TELEVISION**

Uris Theater
New York City
New York, USA

17TH ANNUAL GRAMMY AWARDS (CBS)

Presenter: Andy Williams

Introduced as "the consummate rock performer", Bowie greeted the audience: "Ladies and gentlemen, and others… My personal award is to salute *ces premières femmes noires.*" He then gave the Black Power salute and continued, "Those of us that benefit from the sweet things found, within their intimate world, a message and a language of love." He announced the nominations for the 'Best Rhythm & Blues Performance by a Female Artist' award which he then presented to Aretha Franklin. [343]

Bowie (1999)
Before the show I'd been telling John [Lennon] that I didn't think America really got what I did, that I was misunderstood. Remember that I was in my twenties and out of my head. So the big moment came and I ripped open the envelope and announced, "The winner is Aretha Franklin." Aretha steps forward, and with not so much as a glance in my direction, snatches the trophy out of my hands and says, "Thank you everybody. I'm so happy I could even kiss David Bowie." Which she didn't! And she promptly spun around, swanned off stage right. So I slunk off stage left. And John bounds over and gives me a theatrical kiss and a hug and says, "See, Dave? America loves ya." [380]

Also at the ceremony to present awards were Simon & Garfunkel, John and Yoko and Roberta Flack, as well as Bette Midler, Stevie Wonder, Sarah Vaughan, Tony Orlando and Dawn, The Righteous Brothers, Ann-Margret and David Essex.

Bowie (1975)
The Grammys were very significant for me. It was like walking a tightrope. There were mostly aging middle-class show business people in that audience. It was a question of entertaining them or coming off like just another rock singer. I really did feel I was David Bowie and not a rock singer. [100]

Backstage in the crowded conference room, Bowie talked with Chris Charlesworth about the ManMan situation. "Yes, the reports are true, I am leaving. I am not saying any more than that because the matter is in the hands of my lawyers." [084]

After the televised awards ceremony a dinner was held at the Americana Hotel, where more presentations were made.

▼ **SOCIALISING**

Bowie, Lennon and Ono went on to a Motown party at Le Jardin, a discotheque upstairs in the Diplomat Hotel in West 43rd Street, where they hung out with Stevie Wonder and The Temptations' Eddie Kendricks. Originally a gay discotheque, Le Jardin had become a trendy mainstream scene that Lou Reed name-checked in 'Sally Can't Dance'.

Bob Gruen (2005)
David Bowie and John became engaged in a deep conversation, then disappeared. Tony King… who was an old friend of John and Yoko said to me, "Yoko's looking for John. Do you know where he is?" I didn't, but later I happened to be standing in the hallway when someone opened the door to the women's bathroom. I noticed three pairs of cowboy boots – suspiciously under one stall. The boots were David Bowie's, John's and a limo driver's. I can't help but think of that night when I hear 'Fame' – "What you like is in the limo…" [014]

THURSDAY 6 MARCH

Bowie's performance of 'Young Americans' from *The Dick Cavett Show* broadcast on *Top Of The Pops*.

Record Mirror
His physical deterioration was sad to behold. His corpse-like appearance only made more grotesque by a severe Fifties-style haircut and ill-fitting suit. His voice too was in appalling shape and it was almost pitiful to watch him aiming hoarsely at notes he could once reach with ease.

FRIDAY 7 MARCH

■ ALBUM RELEASED

'YOUNG AMERICANS'

UK (RCA RS 1006)
US (APL1-0998)
UK Chart Peak No.2
US Chart Peak No.9

SIDE ONE
1. **'Young Americans'** (5:10)
2. **'Win'** (4:44)
3. **'Fascination'** (Bowie/Vandross) (5:43)
4. **'Right'** (4:13)

SIDE TWO
1. **'Somebody Up There Likes Me'** (6:30)
2. **'Across The Universe'** (Lennon/McCartney) (4:30)
3. **'Can You Hear Me'** (5:04)
4. **'Fame'** (Bowie/Alomar/Lennon) (4:12)

Tony Visconti (Track 1 Side One)/ Tony Visconti/Harry Maslin (Tracks 2-4 Side One)/Track 1 Side Two)/ David Bowie/Harry Maslin (Tracks 2-4 Side Two): Producers/Mixers

David Bowie: Vocals/Guitar

Andy Newmark/Dennis Davis: Drums

Willie Weeks/Emir Ksasan: Bass

Mike Garson: Musical Director/Keyboards

Carlos Alomar: Rhythm Guitar

John Lennon: Guitar on 'Across The Universe'/'Fame'

Earl Slick: Lead Guitar

David Sanborn: Alto Saxophone

Ralph McDonald/Pablo Rosario/ Larry Washington: Percussion

Warren Peace/Ava Cherry/ Robin Clark/Luther Vandross/ Anthony Hinton/Diane Sumler/ Jean Fineberg: Backing Vocals

Jean Millington: Backing Vocals on 'Fame'

Eric Stephen Jacobs: Cover Photographer

Recorded at Sigma Sound, Philadelphia (Tracks 1-4 Side One/ Track 1 Side Two)/ Electric Lady, New York City (Tracks 2 & 4 Side Two)

Mixed at Sound House, London (Track 1 Side One)/ Record Plant, New York, USA (Tracks 1-3 Side One/ Tracks 1-4 Side Two)

Controversy surrounded the album's release. About 200,000 copies of *Young Americans* had been shipped when Defries filed an injunction to prevent RCA from distributing the album. Michael Lippman successfully fought the injunction and the restraining order was removed.

Bowie (1976)

I really wanted Norman Rockwell to do the cover of* Young Americans. *I got his phone number and called him up. Very quaint. His wife answered and I said, "Hello, this is David Bowie," and so on. I asked if he could paint the cover. His wife said in this quavering, elderly voice, "I'm sorry, but Norman needs at least six months for his portraits." [101]

SELECTED REISSUES

▮CD (RCA 1984).

▮CD (remastered with bonus tracks) (Ryko 1991).
1. 'Who Can I Be Now?' (4:35)
2. 'It's Gonna Be Me' (6:29)
3. 'John, I'm Only Dancing (Again)' (6:58)

▮CD (remastered) (EMI 1999).

ABOVE: Hand-coloured cover photograph by Eric Stephen Jacobs, based on a similar portrait he had made of Bowie's 1974 tour choreographer Toni Basil for *After Dark* magazine. RIGHT: Bowie at the Roxy in LA for Manhattan Transfer's debut, March 18.

▮CD/DVD (remastered with bonus tracks and 5.1 surround mix DVD) (EMI 2007).
1. 'John, I'm Only Dancing (Again)' (7:03)
2. 'Who Can I Be Now?' (4:39)
3. 'It's Gonna Be Me' (strings version) (6:28)

The Dick Cavett Show
1. Dick Cavett interviews David Bowie (16:01)
2. '1984' (3:07)
3. 'Young Americans' (5:11)

ISSUES OF OTHER YOUNG AMERICANS RECORDINGS

▮'After Today' (3:50) released on *Sound + Vision* (Ryko 1989).

▮'It's Hard To Be A Saint In The City' (Springsteen) (3:49) released on *Sound + Vision* (Ryko 1989)/

SATURDAY 8 MARCH

✪ PRESS

Speaking to Ray Fox-Cumming in *Record Mirror*, Angie dismissed reports of Bowie playing dates in Britain in May as "bunkum". Bowie would be starting work on *The Man Who Fell To Earth* in April and she didn't expect him back in Britain until the end of July.

She confirmed that Bowie was in litigation with Defries. "But David told me not to worry about it so I'm not getting involved at all. It should have happened a while back, but you can't start litigating while you're in the middle of an important tour." [127]

Bowie later told *Rolling Stone*, "Defries never really understood what I wanted to do. The Colonel Tom Parker trip wasn't what I had in mind." [264]

Bowie packed up his books and a few possessions and called Glenn Hughes in Los Angeles. Six months earlier Bowie had befriended the Deep Purple bassist and had kept in touch since September with vague plans to work together. During that time both Hughes and Ronnie Wood had pitched to Bowie the idea of an extended interview feature with rookie *Rolling Stone* writer Cameron Crowe.

Cameron Crowe (2006)

Bowie told Hughes to give me this message from New York. Some big changes were coming, he said, and he would soon be travelling from New York to Los Angeles by train. He would call when he arrived in Los Angeles. At this point, I knew I'd probably never hear from Bowie again. [102]

Between various legal complications caused by the split with Defries and relationship problems with Ava Cherry, New York was beginning to close in on him.

Since litigation with Defries had begun, Bowie had no money coming in, so Hughes invited him to stay at his house while he was on tour with Deep Purple. Bowie would spend the next few months couch-surfing as he waited for the call to start shooting his first film.

SUNDAY 16 MARCH

Glenn Hughes sent his driver to collect Bowie from the train at Union Station in Los Angeles. Bowie called Crowe at his parents' home. "I've left my manager, I'm here in LA staying at Glenn Hughes' home. Nobody knows I'm here. I'm not sure what's coming next. But if you want to talk… we'll talk." [102]

Geoff MacCormack joined Bowie a few days later and Lippman's wife Nancy lent them her yellow convertible VW bug to get around.

✪ TELEVISION
✪ COMMERCIAL FLMING
'YOUNG AMERICANS' ALBUM

Chuck Braverman: Director

The ad was filmed in a Los Angeles studio where Bowie, dressed in a white shirt and trousers with red suspenders, danced and mimed to a playback of the new single.

The commercial ended with a voiceover: "David Bowie, happening now on his new album *Young Americans* on RCA Records and Tapes."

During a practice run Bowie noticed photographer Ellen Graham taking pictures, so called a halt to filming and disappeared into the dressing room. He sent a message out stating she could not take photos as his make-up wasn't complete and he had clips in his hair. Distraught, she apologised and promised to destroy the photos. She then asked for permission to photograph him when he was ready. "I am a fair person," Bowie told her. "All you needed to do was ask… Yes." [265]

TUESDAY 18 MARCH

▼SOCIALISING

Bowie and Claudia Lennear (both "real, real skinny-looking," said *Rolling Stone*) were spotted watching Manhattan Transfer's first show at the Roxy Theatre on Sunset Boulevard. [264]

WEDNESDAY 26 MARCH

Mick Ronson was on tour with Ian Hunter, promoting their collaboration, the *Ian Hunter* album. Allan Jones caught up with Ronson for an extensive interview following the concert at Newcastle City Hall.

"I wish that Dave would get himself sorted out," Ronson reflected. "He's so very confused – I know he is. What he really needs is to have some good friends around him. I'll tell you he hasn't got one good friend now. He needs somebody around him to say, 'David fuck off, you're fucking stupid.' He needs one person who won't bow to him." [162]

When Crowe mentioned this, Bowie responded, "I've got God. Who's Mick got?" [100]

SATURDAY 29 MARCH

✪ PRESS
'MELODY MAKER' REPORT

Bowie's legal battle with Tony Defries is surging towards a final settlement in a matter of weeks. Incidentally, Bowie's proposed British tour in March, delayed through the courtroom tussle, will still happen.

APRIL

Production of *The Man Who Fell To Earth* was delayed as Roeg and Litvinoff looked for financial backers and so Bowie would be at a loose end for a couple of months. He heard that Iggy Pop was a voluntary patient at UCLA's Neuropsychiatric Institute. He had been running amok until the LAPD gave him a choice – jail or rehab. Danny Sugerman told *Rolling Stone* at the time, "He lives every day to play in front of people, but he can't and it kills him emotionally." [266]

Iggy Pop (1979)
By 1975, I was totally into drugs and my willpower had been vastly depleted. But I still had the brains to commit myself to a hospital, and I survived with willpower and a lot of help from David Bowie. I survived because I wanted to. [185]

Bowie had been visiting the nearby UCLA Department of Parapsychology where Dr Thelma Moss was researching Kirlian photography. She had a camera – a Kirlian Photographic Device – that was supposed to translate energy in pulses from living organisms onto film.

Bowie (1997)
Highly dangerous camera it was, too. It would regularly explode. Nic Roeg wanted to use some examples of it in **The Man Who Fell To Earth*, but it wouldn't film well enough.*** [079]

On one of his visits to the facility he dropped in to see Iggy, accompanied by Dean Stockwell.

Iggy Pop (1996)
He came up one day, stoned out of his brain in his little space-suit. They were like, "We want to see Jimmy. Let us in." There was a strict rule – you never let outsiders in: it was an insane asylum. You don't let people in the ward. But the doctors were star-struck, so they let them in. And the first thing they did say was, "Hey, want some blow?" They tried to give me drugs. I think I took a little, which is really unpleasant in there. I basically was just staying in touch. [346]

WEDNESDAY 9 APRIL

▼SOCIALISING

Bowie was spotted with George Harrison, Rod Stewart and Britt Ekland watching Leo Sayer's set at The Troubadour.

▲RECORDING

Oz Studios
Hollywood
Los Angeles
California, USA

IGGY POP DEMOS

Bowie was driving around with Cameron Crowe when they saw Iggy Pop, who had checked himself out of the Institute, on the street. Bowie coaxed him into the recently opened Oz Studios to record some demos with him.

The studio was a modest recording set-up consisting of two small TEAC decks. Artists could rehearse and record demos for a mere $15 per hour – an economical alternative to the big prestige studios charging upwards of $100 an hour. This suited Bowie as the MainMan days of limitless spending were over.

Bowie and MacCormack spent nine hours recording backing tracks with Iggy and ended up with three songs: 'Sell Your Love', 'Drink To Me' and an early version of 'Turn Blue', co-written with MacCormack.

Geoff MacCormack (2006)
I was playing this series of chords, which had a gospel feel. The next thing I know Iggy's standing beside me giving it large with the vocals. Then Bowie comes over, all excited, telling us to keep going and runs into the control room to get it recorded. [054]

Bowie and Iggy revisited the song in 1977 for *Lust For Life* and Iggy also recorded 'Sell Your Love' with James Williamson (released on *Kill City*).

Crowe described 'Drink To Me' as "an ominous, dirge-like instrumental track" with an improvised rant that he transcribed for his article. "They just don't appreciate Iggy," Bowie exclaimed as he watched. "He's Lenny fucking Bruce and James Dean. When that adlib flow starts, there's nobody like him. It's verbal jazz, man!" [100]

Iggy Pop (2010)
Bowie liked what I was doing, and had an interesting dialogue with a sort of a representative composite American of the kind he could relate to. A little bit sullen teen, a little bit Neal Cassady, a little bit Jack Kerouac. [252]

Ever since his brother Terry had introduced him to bebop jazz and Jack Kerouac, Bowie was in awe of fearless exponents of improvisational writing and performance. Iggy Pop was their modern counterpart and in him Bowie saw his own future. The sessions at Oz pointed the way to a new spontaneous working method. For now, he just had to keep Iggy upright long enough to get something down on tape.

"We have a lot more work to do tomorrow – please keep healthy," Bowie called out, as Iggy staggered out into the night with a girlfriend after the session. In the predawn Bowie lingered in the studio, writing and recording a new song, 'Movin' On', which was never heard of again.

"Another song," he observed, locking up the studio at 7am. "That's the last thing I need. I write an album a month as it is. I've already got two new albums in the can. Give me a break."

Bowie and Crowe drove up to Glenn Hughes' house in Benedict Canyon, behind the Beverly Hills Hotel. After a quick breakfast, they headed back down to the Beverly Wilshire. Bowie intended to check in to catch up on sleep, but when they found out Ronnie Wood was staying, they dropped in for a chat.

The conversation turned to the MainMan lawsuits. "The split had been building up for some time," Bowie said. "For the last year and a half, I've had no empathy with them whatsoever. It took me that long to stop touring and come back to finding out where the office was really at."

Iggy Pop overslept and failed to show up at the studio that day. He called up drunk several nights later and Bowie told him to "go away". Iggy took it literally and disappeared. "I hope he's not dead," Bowie said to Crowe. "He's got a good act." [100]

SATURDAY 19 APRIL

■ CHART

'Young Americans'
US Top 30 Chart Entry
Charting 4 weeks

ABOVE AND OPPOSITE: Bowie and Angie at Greystone Mansion in Beverly Hills for the party in honour of *The Passenger* director Michelangelo Antonioni.

SUNDAY 27 APRIL

▼SOCIALISING

Bowie, Angie and Litvinoff attended the American Film Institute cocktail party in honour of film director Michelangelo Antonioni at Greystone Mansion in Beverly Hills.

His film *The Passenger* had its US premiere on April 9 and was the official Italian entry at the Cannes Film Festival in May. Other guests included the film's lead Jack Nicholson, Donald Sutherland, Diane Ladd, Richard Chamberlain and Sally Kellerman.

MAY

✪ PHOTO SESSION
Tom Kelley Studio
Santa Monica Boulevard
West Hollywood
Los Angeles
California, USA

Tom Kelley: Photographer

While Angie was in town, Hollywood PR firm Rogers & Cowan organised a portrait session for her and Bowie with Tom Kelley. He had made his name in 1953 when he sold his 1949 calendar shot of Marilyn Monroe (posed nude on red velvet) to Hugh Hefner for the centrefold of *Playboy*'s first issue. As such he was ideal for the assignment – photography for the promotion of 'Fame', soon to be released as a single.

Tom Kelley

Bowie took me back to the golden age of movie stars. He's a visionary who looks into the camera as though he can see the finished pictures. [017]

The results of the sessions were so striking that RCA used them for several record sleeves, notably *Changes One Bowie* in 1976.

Bowie and MacCormack stayed for a few weeks with Michael and Nancy Lippman in their house on Sunset Strip in Hollywood.

Michael Lippman (1978)

He lived in my house during the period of The Man Who Fell To Earth *and* Station To Station, *and did a lot of paintings then. Their subjects were clear to him but not anybody else. My wife and he were good friends and they used to talk about his manifestations and his dreams – or nightmares – all the time. I kept out of that. At one point we gave him a gold cross as a gift. He also asked to have a mezuzah up in his room because of his revival and belief in religion, and felt that it would create more security for himself.* [317]

ABOVE: The portrait by Hollywood golden age photographer Tom Kelley used to promote the 'Fame' single.

✪ PRESS

Sunday Times writer Tina Brown visited him there for a feature. "It blows me out, having DB to stay," Lippman told her. "I've never met a guy so hyped on energy."

"Me and rock'n'roll have parted company," Bowie declared. "I'll still make albums with love and with fun, but my effect is finished. I'm very pleased. I think I've caused quite enough rumpus for someone who's not even convinced he's a good musician. Now I'm going to be a film director. I've always been a screenwriter. My songs have just been practice for scripts."

According to Lippman, Bowie had written nine scripts. Bowie had told Crowe about *Dogs*, which would star Terence Stamp and Iggy Pop. "Terence is going to be Iggy's father," Bowie laughed. "Isn't that lovely? I can't wait to direct it." [070]

Bowie was holed up in Lippman's spare room with a suitcase overflowing with books, including *The Manson Murder Trials*. He had become fixated on the subject when he discovered that Glenn Hughes lived four homes away from the site of the LaBianca murders in August 1969, which occurred just the day after the Tate murders.

After Bowie wore out his welcome with the Lippmans, Angie found him his own place at 637 North Doheny Drive in Beverly Hills, where his paranoia reached new heights.

Bowie (1983)

It was one of those rent-a-house places but it appealed to me because I had this more-than-passing interest in Egyptology, mysticism, the Cabala, all this stuff that is inherently misleading in life, a hodgepodge whose crux I've forgotten. But at the time it seemed transparently obvious what the answer to life was. So the house occupied a ritualistic position in my life. [318]

Angie Bowie (1993)
Built in the late Fifties or early Sixties, it was a white cube surrounding an indoor swimming pool. David liked the place, but I thought it was too small to meet our needs for very long, and I wasn't crazy about the pool. In my experience, indoor pools are always a problem. This one was no exception, albeit not in any of the usual ways. Its drawback was one I hadn't encountered before and haven't seen or heard of since: Satan lived in it. With his own eyes, David said, he'd seen HIM rising up out of the water one night. [003]

Bowie (1997)
It was pure straightforward, old-fashioned magic… there was a guy called Edward Waite who was terribly important to me at the time. And another called Dion Fortune who wrote a book called Psychic Self-Defence. *You had to run around the room getting bits of string and old crayons and draw funny things on the wall, and I took it all most seriously, ha ha ha! I drew gateways into different dimensions, and I'm quite sure that, for myself, I really walked into other worlds. I drew things on walls and just walked through them, and saw what was on the other side.* [013]

Ola Hudson was an African-American costume designer who in 1965 had a son, Saul, during a sojourn in England. She returned alone to Los Angeles to resume her career, which was given a boost by a Dewar's Scotch ad. Her husband and son later joined her in Laurel Canyon, where he designed covers for Asylum records. By 1974 she was single again with two sons. Saul, who later became Guns N' Roses guitarist Slash, remembers when his mother met Bowie.

ABOVE: ***The Man Who Fell To Earth*** **wardrobe mistress Ola Hudson's son Saul, later known as Slash (third row, second from left), in his sixth grade class photo from Third Street School in 1977 in Los Angeles, California. RIGHT: One of several magazine covers that featured Schapiro's photo session with Bowie.**

Slash (2007)
She and Bowie embarked on a semi-intense affair. Looking back on it now, it might not have been that big a deal, but at the time, it was like watching an alien land in your backyard. Bowie came by often, with his wife, Angie, and their son, Zowie, in tow. The Seventies were unique: it seemed entirely natural for Bowie to bring his wife and son to the home of his lover so that we might all hang out. [039]

Bowie (2002)
*I sometimes used to put him to bed at nights, little Slash. Who'd have guessed. Anyway, I got Ola involved as the wardrobe mistress of the film (*The Man Who Fell To Earth*); she designed all the clothes for it, and she continued designing clothes for* Station To Station *as well.* [116]

✪ PHOTO SESSION
Steve Schapiro: Photographer

In a Los Angeles studio Schapiro made a series of photographs with Bowie in a marathon session that began at 4pm with Bowie drawing diagrams of the Kabbalah on the wall and paper taped to the floor. They experimented with various outfits and backgrounds before finishing up at 4am with Bowie on a motorbike, lit by car headlights.

MONDAY 2

■ **SINGLE RELEASED**

'Fame' (3:30)/
'Right' (4:13)
US (RCA PB-10320)
Chart Peak No.1 (2 weeks)

MONDAY 2 JUNE – MONDAY 25 AUGUST

✪ **FILMING**

New Mexico, USA

'THE MAN WHO FELL TO EARTH'

Nicolas Roeg: Director
Si Litvinoff: Executive Producer
Michael Deeley/Barry Spikings: Producers
Paul Mayersberg: Screenwriter
Anthony Richmond: Cinematographer
Brian Eatwell: Production Designer
May Routh: Costume Designer
Principal cast: David Bowie: Thomas Jerome Newton
Rip Torn: Nathan Bryce
Candy Clark: Mary-Lou/Newton's wife on Anthea
Buck Henry: Oliver Farnsworth

Bowie and MacCormack rode the Amtrak Santa Fe *Super Chief* train from Los Angeles to Albuquerque, arriving on the set in a limo similar to the one seen in *Cracked Actor*. Roeg cast both the car and Bowie's driver Tony Mascia as Newton's chauffeur Arthur.

For the first two weeks of production Bowie was based at the Albuquerque Hilton Inn. Bowie's presence in the town was kept under wraps. Reporters were warned, "Mr Bowie does not wish to be interviewed or photographed."

Visiting the set in Los Lunas, *The Belen News Bulletin* was told that its cameras would be smashed by "a real big guy" if any pictures were taken of Bowie. A spokesman later explained that the threat had been made jokingly and that "David Bowie probably will be made available for interviews and photographs later. This is the first movie he has ever made, and he wants to be left alone for a while." [071]

During the first two weeks Bowie, MacCormack and Coco moved to a ranch in the hills above Albuquerque.

Principal photography began in Los Lunas, which Roeg was pleased to discover was Spanish for 'The Moons'. The first day of shooting covered Newton's arrival in Haneyville (a fictitious name from the original book), the pawn shop where Newton sells the first of his rings and the river where he toasts his first sale with a cup of murky water.

Bowie (1976)

I couldn't have worked with a director unless it was somebody I knew instinctively would become a mentor. I couldn't have worked with someone I considered to be less than myself – and I have a very, very high opinion of my own abilities. Within the first hour on the set, I knew that I'd picked the right one. [100]

Newton's first appearance was shot at an abandoned mine in Madrid, a small town 20 miles east of Santa Fe. Albuquerque locations included the First National Bank, the First Plaza and its water fountain. David Cammell (brother of *Performance* director Donald) told *The Albuquerque Tribune*, "There have been no problems, and everything is going fine. We have found everybody to be most cooperative." [071] Some 25 Albuquerque residents were given speaking roles and used as extras in the movie.

Bowie (1993)

My one snapshot memory of that film is not having to act. Just me being as I was was perfectly adequate for the role. I wasn't of this Earth at that particular time. [111]

Rip Torn (2005)

Here's a guy that gets out on the stage in front of 100,000 people and commands with a flick of his finger. If that's not an actor, I don't know what the hell it is. [364]

ABOVE: The oversized clapperboard, designed to be visible by airborne camera units shooting from above, was gifted to Candy Clark at the end of filming.
LEFT: Bowie looks at the framing at White Sands Missile Range, the location for Newton's home planet Anthea.

ABOVE: Candy Clark, Nic Roeg and Bowie discuss Newton's first scene with Mary-Lou in the hotel. OVERLEAF: Bowie in his dressing room trailer on the set of *The Man Who Fell To Earth* in New Mexico.

Tony Richmond (2012)
I can't think of anyone else who could have played Newton. Bowie was so strange, so ethereal, so androgynous. I never saw him using any drugs on set. He was great to work with – a bit weird, but great. He always turned up on time. He went a bit funny for a few days, because he thought someone had put something in his orange juice. He was a very sensitive guy. In one scene, surgery is performed on him. I didn't like the colour of the make-up blood, so I said to the props boy: "Nip down to the butcher and get some pig's blood." Bowie heard that and wouldn't entertain it. But he would entertain human blood. [146]

Candy Clark (2005)
There were some long speeches and monologues and interaction between me and David and, luckily for me, David likes to rehearse and run lines and I think that's because he's a musician and they're used to rehearsal. A lot of actors hate to run dialogue – they say it takes away the spontaneity. [364]

After two weeks, production moved north to Artesia for the scenes in the eight-storey Hotel Artesia, which was abandoned except for the bar on the ground floor.

Brian Eatwell (2005)
Because it was empty, the owner didn't care too much what we did, so I had a local contractor come in and knock down several walls to make filming easier. [364]

Scenes set on Newton's planet Anthea were shot at White Sands Missile Range near Alamogordo. Bryce's house was a converted park ranger's house beside Fenton Lake. On the far side of the lake was Newton's house, but the interiors were shot in a brand-new unoccupied adobe house in Santa Fe.

Paul Mayersberg (2012)
As a location, New Mexico was heaven sent: there are more sightings of UFOs over its deserts than in the rest of the world. It gave Nic a wonderful palette: you really got the feeling you were on a planet floating in space. We shot near Alamogordo and White Sands, near where they tested the atomic bomb. They still had 'no entry' signs up. [146]

Tony Richmond (2012)
We were on a short schedule for this – movies were different then. We were a lean, light crew, mostly British, and we found going on the road through New Mexico a wonderful experience: Albuquerque, Santa Fe, Fenton Lake, all over. [146]

Candy Clark (1979)
We were filming in New Mexico, but they had to do some exterior shots in New York. Bowie wouldn't fly, and I wanted a trip to New York so I did the scene for him. [342]

The scene called for Clark (playing Newton) to walk from World Enterprises to the waiting limo. Her resemblance to Bowie was convincing enough for onlookers to ask for an autograph. Clark obliged, signing as David Bowie.

Bowie spent his downtime writing new songs and stories, including his autobiography, *The Return Of The Thin White Duke*, to be published by Bewlay Bros in December. He also continued his compulsive reading.

Bowie (1999)
I took 400 books down to that film shoot. I was dead scared of leaving them in New York because I was knocking around with some pretty dodgy people and I didn't want any of them nicking my books. Too many dealers, running in and out of my place… [244]

Bowie (1975)
I take everything with me I would normally have at home. That's one of the benefits of travelling by train: you can fill up all the compartments as there are usually so few other people travelling. [200]

Bowie (2000)
All my reading at that particular time was people like Israel Regardie, Waite and Mathers and Manly Hall. It was an intense period of trying to relate myself to this search for some true spirit. And I thought I was gonna find it through reading all this material. [030]

JULY

Brian Duffy arrived on the set with *Sunday Times* writer George Perry, assigned to do a feature on the filming ("The Space Oddity", published 14 March the following year). During a break in Bowie's shooting schedule, Duffy organised a separate shoot with Bowie at White Sands National Monument, a heritage-protected white desert composed of soft gypsum crystals.

Geoff MacCormack (2014)
We were in New Mexico, close to White Sands desert, to film scenes with David and his alien family walking across the desert to replicate their planet terrain. For that shoot with Duffy, which was probably the evening before, I remember we were all waiting for David in the hotel lobby. Duffy was getting concerned as the afternoon wore on that we would lose the light, as David was taking his time faffing around getting ready. Sure enough, by the time we got to White Sands the sun was going down fast so they did what they could with reduced light. [008]

Chris Duffy (Duffy's son) (2014)
Being a photographer myself I know how easily that session could have failed. They were late to get to the location and the sun was dropping rapidly, Duffy had no assistant, very little time to get it together and would not have had another chance to get David down there if it had all gone wrong. No Polaroid, no autofocus in dim light, a one second, triple flash exposure with movement in the arms while David kept his body dead still – risky, really risky, but that's the way Duffy played the game, all or nothing. [008]

Duffy's triple exposure of Bowie at White Sands National Monument.
OVERLEAF: Bowie and Nic Roeg prepare for a scene at Lake Fenton.

U-HAUL

JULY

FRIDAY 18

■ **SINGLE RELEASED**
'Fame' (3:30)/
'Right' (4:13)
UK (RCA 2579)
Chart Peak No.17

SATURDAY 19 JULY

✪ **PRESS**
Melody Maker reported that Bowie was offered a role in *I Never Promised You A Rose Garden*, a movie being planned by Palomar Films. Singles reviewer Colin Irwin proclaimed the new single 'Fame' a hit.

SUNDAY 20 JULY

✪ **PRESS**
'The Bowie Odyssey' by Tina Brown published in *Sunday Times Magazine*.

AUGUST

■ **SINGLE RELEASED**
'Fame' (4:12)/
'Space Oddity' (5:15)
Italy (RCA TPBO 7013)

SATURDAY 9

✪ **PRESS**
Melody Maker announced Bowie's plans to play British dates for 1976. "The World Tour pencilled in for February and January next year will come after Bowie's legal dispute with his former manager Tony Defries has been settled." [199]

Steve Shroyer and John Lifflander from *Creem* interviewed Bowie at the Hilton Inn Albuquerque.

"It's lovely here," Bowie told them. "I like New Mexico, it's so clean and pure – and puritanical, too – not just the people but the land, too. There's something about the land that's very… This is the way I'd like America to be; the rest of America, I mean. It's so open and the people are very friendly. I wouldn't do a film in LA – I wouldn't even attempt it. But I'm enjoying it here. And I love the cowboys – they're fascinating. They can look at a leaf and tell you what kind of tree it's from and where it grows. It's a different breed."

Shroyer asked him if he was doing any music for the film. "Yeah, all of it," Bowie told him. "That'll be the next album, the soundtrack. I'm working on it now, doing some writing. But we won't record until all the shooting's finished. I expect the film should be released around March, and we want the album out ahead of that, so I should say maybe January or February." [282]

Si Litvinoff (2002)

David worked like a professional. Despite staying up late at night composing music for the soundtrack, he was always on time with his lines ready.

When Rip Torn arrived to do his first scene with David in the spacecraft, it became clear to me that Rip was wound up like a caged animal. David was not only tense, but exhausted from staying up all night. I quickly got tequila for Rip and I ground up No-Doz for David to snort. He had kept his promise to do no cocaine on the shoot but snorting worked better for him than pills. [409]

ABOVE : Bowie on set for the last scene of the film.
LEFT: French sleeve for 'Fame'.
BELOW LEFT: Bowie on the cover of *The Sunday Times Magazine*.
OPPOSITE: Steve Schapiro's photo of Bowie practising shooting a pellet gun on set was used for the cover of *Rolling Stone* the following February.

SUNDAY 24 AUGUST

While Bowie was filming his last scenes for *The Man Who Fell To Earth*, the papers were seeking confirmation of a rumour that Bowie had requested approval from Frank Sinatra to make and star in a Sinatra biopic.

Three weeks earlier *Record Mirror* had reported that Bowie had been asked to do the film and was "over the moon" about the idea. Michael Lippman had said, "The combination of these two talents and the subject matter of the proposed film could make it the biggest box office draw of the century." [249]

Bowie, contacted on set in New Mexico, told an RCA representative that he considered Sinatra one of his favourite singers but had no such plans. RCA said the rumour probably came from Sinatra's over-zealous publicists, who in turn pointed the finger at Bowie's people.

Other rumours had Nancy Sinatra suggesting the idea. One report said Bowie had tried to get backstage to meet Sinatra, who sent him a message that he didn't have time. Another rumour had Sinatra describing Bowie as "a limey faggot full of gimmicks to disguise his limited talent".

Bowie, asked about it years later, quipped that he "wasn't very good with horses' heads" – a reference to the gruesome scene in *The Godfather*, supposedly based on the story of Sinatra turning to the Mob for help in reviving his acting career.

With principal photography completed, Bowie returned to Los Angeles where Coco found him a house at 1349 Stone Canyon Road in Bel Air. Here he resumed his self-destructive lifestyle on a steady diet of milk, finely chopped red peppers and pure Merck pharmaceutical cocaine from LA's supplier to the stars, Freddy Sessler.

Bowie (1978)

I was totally out of hand and spouting for hours at two people who were either terrified or bored with what I was saying. I never moved out of this big room and everything came in to me: food and milk and people. I'd say, "Tonight I want to make sculptures." I'd order all kinds of materials, have them brought in and I'd build vast, incredible things in the living room next to the television set. This was in Bel Air, good ol' Bel Air.

Definitely a fractured person, by confounding myself with images and characters that I found I was living with – and actually seeing them in my apartment. A combination of that and a year and a half of fairly hard drugs. I was being threatened by my own characters, feeling them coming in on me and grinning at me, saying "We're gonna take you over completely!" I thought, "This is it. Terry, I'm just about to join you." [317]

SEPTEMBER

EARLY SEPTEMBER

▲ **RECORDING**
★ **GUEST APPEARANCE**
Clover Studios
Santa Monica Boulevard
Hollywood
Los Angeles
California, USA

'Real Emotion'

Steve Cropper: Producer
Barry Rudolph: Engineer
Keith Moon: Vocals
Steve Cropper: Guitar
Klaus Voorman: Bass
Ringo Starr: Drums
David Bowie: Backing Vocals

Returning to Los Angeles meant doing the rounds of parties, hotels and studios, where sessions became 'super-jams' with whoever was in town at the time. Keith Moon was recording the planned follow-up to his first solo album, *Two Sides Of The Moon*, at Clover Studios on Santa Monica Boulevard.

Barry Rudolph
David Bowie came in to do backing vocals. Bowie's entourage looked like a casting call for a circus movie – a pretty freaky-looking crowd that filled up the entire control room. David was very fast at composing and singing and I don't remember Cropper adding anything to Bowie's ideas – Crop sat back and enjoyed.

At one point Bowie asked "to ADT his voice"... ADT or Artificial Double Tracking (also called Automatic Double Tracking) was a tape-recording trick developed in England for The Beatles and used subsequently by others. Apparently it was du jour *for Bowie recording sessions at that time.* [379]

▮ Released as bonus track on *Two Sides Of The Moon* (reissue) (Mausoleum Classix 1997)/ (iTunes 2006).

ABOVE AND BELOW: Bowie jamming at Peter Sellers' birthday party with (above) Bill Wyman, Ronnie Wood and (below) Keith Moon. Wyman later recalled, "It was hopeless. We couldn't get one song together between us."

SATURDAY 6 SEPTEMBER

Melody Maker reported:

Ziggy Stardust will be returning next year – as a movie. Stardust, David Bowie's mythical pop persona, will be the subject of the first film to be made by Bowie's new production company, Bewlay Bros. The Ziggy Stardust movie has been written by Bowie, who will also take the lead role. Further Bewlay Bros film projects include Young Americans, *a story Bowie has written about astronauts.*

This film idea was possibly inspired by meeting Apollo 13 commander Jim Lovell, who played himself in *The Man Who Fell To Earth*. Bowie got as far as posing in a NASA jumpsuit in front of an American flag.

MONDAY 8 SEPTEMBER

▼ **SOCIALISING**

As 'Fame' climbed steadily up the US chart, Bowie and MacCormack attended Peter Sellers' 50th birthday party and entertained the guests as part of an impromptu supergroup.

David Bowie: Saxophone
Bill Wyman: Bass
Joe Cocker: Vocals
Ronnie Wood/Jesse Ed Davis/
Danny Kortchmar: Guitar
Bobby Keys: Saxophone
Nigel Olsson: Drums
Keith Moon: Organ/Vocal/Drums
Steve Madaio: Trumpet

Bowie (2002)
Bill Wyman was already discontent with being a Stone and coaxed Ronnie Wood and me into forming the band Trading Faces. The idea was to cover the big hits of the time, with each of us impersonating a popular singer while the others played in the style of a bad discordant to the chosen singer. This would lead to hybrids like Wayne Newton with The Troggs or, my personal favourite, The Singing Postman with Tower Of Power. [116]

Terry O'Neill (2003)
I was invited to what I thought was just a small private party by Peter, who was a close friend and didn't realise he'd invited so many stars. I'm glad I took my camera – it was a one-off moment in rock'n'roll history. I never knew Bowie could play the sax. [415]

Geoff MacCormack (2006)
Neither David nor any of the other musicians seemed to be playing the same songs and they made such a racket it disturbed the neighbours. The police were called and Keith Moon, of all people, tried to politely reason with them whilst they threatened to arrest Sellers. Sellers didn't say a word: he just looked bemused by it all.
He looked exactly like Chauncey, the character he later played in Being There. [021]

SATURDAY 13 SEPTEMBER

◆ AWARDS

'MELODY MAKER' READERS' POP POLL

UK Male Singer #7

International Male Singer #5

THURSDAY 18 SEPTEMBER

✪ TELEVISION

CBS Television City
7800 Beverly Boulevard
Los Angeles
California, USA

'CHER' (CBS)
'Fame'/
'Can You Hear Me' (with Cher)/
'Young Americans' medley
(with Cher)

Cher: Presenter

Cher's show was suffering a slump in ratings when she invited Bowie to perform three songs.

He opened with his first US No.1, 'Fame', followed by a duet – at Cher's request – of 'Can You Hear Me', both songs performed live to a backing track. They finished with a medley of oldies beginning and ending with 'Young Americans', accompanied by the studio orchestra.

Bowie (1999)

I'd got this thing in my mind that I was through with theatrical clothes and I would only wear Sears & Roebuck, which on me looked more outlandish than anything I had made by Japanese designers. They were just like this middle America dogged provincialism. They were loud check jackets and check trousers. I looked very bad. And very ill. [244]

Bowie

I was probably this crazed anorexic figure walking in and I'm sure she didn't know what to make of me. But she warmed up when we sang together. [032]

▮ Broadcast: November 23 (CBS).

ABOVE RIGHT: Bowie on *Cher*, between takes of 'Can You Hear Me'.
RIGHT: Bowie and Cher perform their medley of oldies.

SATURDAY 20 SEPTEMBER

■ CHART

'Fame' reached No.1 on the US chart while *Young Americans* reached 15.

Cameron Crowe reported:

Corinne has watched Bowie shrewdly work up to his most difficult move yet: the switch from cultish deco rocker to a wide-appeal film and recording star/ entertainer. "I want to be a Frank Sinatra figure," Bowie declares. "And I will succeed."

Wheeling a cart in a Hollywood supermarket just three blocks from where David is working on his new LP Station To Station, *Corinne says she has no doubts about something so obvious as Bowie's success in achieving his stated goal. The way she sees it, David has only one problem.*

"I've got to put more weight on that boy," she sighs. And with that she carefully places eight quarts of extra rich milk in the basket.

Down the street at Cherokee Studios, David Bowie is just back from three vice-free months in New Mexico where he starred in Nic Roeg's film, The Man Who Fell To Earth. *He is still glowing from the experience and, says Corinne, the healthiest he's been in years. He is so relaxed and almost humble as he scoots around the studio and directs his musicians through the songs.* [100]

▮ Published: 'Ground Control To Davy Jones', *Rolling Stone*.

SUNDAY 21 SEPTEMBER – EARLY DECEMBER

▲ **RECORDING**

Studio Instrument Rentals
6465 Sunset Boulevard
Hollywood
Los Angeles
California, USA

Cherokee Studios
751 North Fairfax Avenue
West Hollywood
Los Angeles
California, USA

Record Plant West
8456 West Third Street
Los Angeles
California, USA

'STATION TO STATION' ALBUM

David Bowie/Harry Maslin: Producers
David Bowie: Guitar/Vocals
Carlos Alomar: Guitar
Roy Bittan: Piano
Dennis Davis: Drums
George Murray: Bass
Earl Slick: Guitar
Warren Peace: Vocals

Bowie began work on the new album with Harry Maslin – an obvious choice since he had worked on much of *Young Americans*, including 'Fame', which was now topping the American charts. For a few days at Sound Instrumental Rentals Studios, Bowie and the band worked on songs from fragments he'd written – 'Word On A Wing', 'TVC 15', written in New Mexico, and 'Golden Years', which he had written for Angie and offered to Elvis to cover.

Earl Slick (1976)
He had one or two songs written but they were changed so drastically that you wouldn't know them from the first time anyway, so he basically wrote everything in the studio. [097]

Harry Maslin (1976)
There was no specific sound in mind. I don't think he had any specific direction as far as whether it should be R&B, or more English-sounding, or more commercial or less commercial. I think he went out more to make a record this time than to worry about what it was going to turn out to be. [097]

Moving recording to Cherokee on North Fairfax Avenue, one of the first tracks they tackled was 'TVC 15'. Bowie had let go of Mike Garson – the last musician of the Ziggy era – and called up British pianist Roy Young, whom he'd first met on the 1972 UK tour, to invite him to play on the sessions, but Young was held up by visa problems. Earl Slick mentioned that Springsteen's band had just checked into his hotel and suggested their pianist, Roy Bittan, with whom he had played on an obscure album, *Even A Broken Clock Is Right Twice A Day* by Tracks (1972).

As Cherokee boasted a 24-track desk, Bowie and Maslin had the luxury of experimentation, which led to long open-ended sessions.

Bowie (1993)
I would work at songs for hours and hours and days and days and then realise after a few days that I had done absolutely nothing . I hadn't got past four bars. [240]

Harry Maslin (1976)
It was rigorous. We tried to keep it on a private basis. Not too many people in there – usually no one. We started at 10 or 11 at night and went to anywhere from eight in the morning to whatever, 36 hours later. David knows exactly what he wants, it's just a matter of sitting there and doing it until it's done. [097]

Earl Slick (2010)
Everything else around you pretty much disappeared – your personal life, everything. David's good at creating that. You're in there [the studio], and that's what you're doing, period. We went into the void. [252]

Harry Maslin (2010)
Once after doing an all-nighter at Cherokee, they essentially threw us out in the morning as they had another session booked. I called Record Plant and we went over to continue to record. That was the session when David and I both played saxophone on 'TVC 15'. [327]

Carlos Alomar (2010)
Bowie threw us into the deep end. He was telling us that we could do whatever we wanted. "Make the sound of a train? We've got all the time you need…" [252]

Bowie (1997)
The 'Station To Station' track itself is very much concerned with the Stations of the Cross. All the references within the piece are to do with the Cabala. It's the nearest album to a magick treatise that I've written. I've never read a review that really sussed it. It's an extremely dark album. Miserable time to live through, I must say. [079]

Earl Slick (2010)
It started out with David and me in the studio. We had a couple of Marshall stacks and we were just feeding back. [252]

Carlos Alomar (2010)
We had six amps chained one to another, each with a different effect, with one microphone in front of them to see what it would sound like. [252]

Earl Slick (1976)
We both played all the way through the song, and then Harry took part of David's and part of mine and stuck them all together. [097]

Earl Slick (2010)
On 'Golden Years' there was no riff. I came up with something I stole from a 1960s song called 'Funky Broadway' [by Dyke and The Blazers in 1967, later a hit for Wilson Pickett]. I think it might have come from there. [252]

Geoff MacCormack (2007)
Unfortunately David lost his voice halfway through doing the backing vocals. He's an incredible singer – his pitch and timing are exceptional – so the parts, which were difficult for him, were murder for me. [021]

Bowie (1976)
'Word On A Wing' I wrote when I felt very much at peace with the world. I had established my own environment with my own people for the first time. I wrote the whole thing as a hymn. What better way can a man give thanks for achieving something that he had dreamed of achieving, than doing it with a hymn? [144]

Harry Maslin (1976)
'TVC 15' is about a television that ate his girlfriend. David is very interested in electronics, he's very interested in video, and that's supposed to be the epitome of where it could go. A hologramic television set with anything you could fit into a television. [097]

Earl Slick (2006)
'Stay' was originally going to be a remake of 'John, I'm Only Dancing', if my memory is any good. The session was very quick as the band was tight! I'd, however, put some time into the guitar solo. I guess it paid off. [190]

Earl Slick (1976)
It wasn't worked out in advance. I was very spaced out that night. It was done about five in the morning. I'd been waiting around for hours, drinking a lot of beer. [097]

Ronnie Wood and Bobby Womack dropped in on the sessions for a jam with Murray, Davis, Bittan and Bowie on sax, which Harry Maslin recorded and MacCormack photographed.

THURSDAY 25 SEPTEMBER

▲ **RECORDING**

Cherokee Studios
751 North Fairfax Avenue
West Hollywood
Los Angeles
California, USA

Bowie recorded seven vocal takes of 'Wild Is The Wind', but it was the first that ended up on the record.

FRIDAY 26 SEPTEMBER

■ **SINGLE RELEASED**

'Space Oddity' (5:15)/
'Changes' (3:33)/
'Velvet Goldmine' (3:09)
UK (RCA 2593)
Chart Peak No.1

RCA reissued 'Space Oddity' again, this time as part of its Maximillion EP series. The inclusion (against Bowie's wishes) of the previously unreleased *Ziggy Stardust* session 'Velvet Goldmine' helped 'Space Oddity' become Bowie's first UK No.1.

Bowie (1980)
That whole thing came out without my having the chance to listen to the mix; somebody else had mixed it – an extraordinary move. [189]

OPPOSITE: Recording at Cherokee Studios.

SATURDAY 27 SEPTEMBER

▲ RECORDING
Cherokee Studios
751 North Fairfax Avenue
West Hollywood
Los Angeles
California, USA

Bowie recorded his vocal for 'Golden Years' – the first song of the album to be completed.

Harry Maslin (2010)
Knowing that it might be a challenging vocal, David sat next to me and said: "Remember, I'm not really a vocalist, I'm more of a songwriter… be patient with me." The reason why this sticks out in my mind is because he proceeded to go into the studio and nail the vocal in one take… blowing my mind as to how proficient he truly was. [278]

OCTOBER

▲ RECORDING
Cherokee Studios
751 North Fairfax Avenue
West Hollywood
Los Angeles
California, USA

'STATION TO STATION' ALBUM

David Bowie/Harry Maslin: Producers

SATURDAY 11

■ CHART
'Space Oddity' EP
UK Top 30 Chart Entry
Charting 10 weeks

NOVEMBER

MONDAY 3

✪ TELEVISION

KTTV Studios
Metromedia Square
5746 Sunset Boulevard
Hollywood
Los Angeles
California, USA

'SOUL TRAIN'

Interview/'Golden Years'/'Fame'

Don Cornelius: Presenter

Bowie was accorded the honour of being the third white act (after Elton John and Average White Band) to be invited to perform on the popular syndicated African-American music show *Soul Train*.

Host Don Cornelius introduced Bowie and asked him some questions about his immediate plans before inviting questions from the audience. Somewhat awed by the occasion, Bowie had been drinking to calm his nerves before the programme.

He proceeded to stumble awkwardly through the segment with disjointed answers – how he first got into soul music, his plan to play in Russia, and working on the soundtrack for *The Man Who Fell To Earth* with Paul Buckmaster. When asked, "Is it true that you're gonna be teamin' up with Elizabeth Taylor to do a film?" Bowie flatly replied, "No."

At that point Cornelius wrapped it up and asked Bowie to introduce his performance of the new single 'Golden Years'.

Bowie (2000)

I hadn't bothered to learn it and the MC, who was a really charming guy, took me to one side after the third or fourth take, and he said, "Do you know there were kids lined up to do this show, who have fought their whole lives to try and get a record and come on here?" [004]

▮Broadcast: January 3, 1976 (ABC).

Cameron Crowe came to the taping, accompanied by his friend Andy Kent, who took photographs. Bowie admired Kent's work and his unobtrusive nature and invited him to join his 1976 tour as official photographer.

ABOVE: 'Golden Years' Japanese single release, with Steve Schapiro's photo of Bowie on Cher's show. After the *Cher* taping *Melody Maker's* Harvey Kubernik had asked Bowie whether he might consider appearing on *Soul Train*, since Elton John's recent performance on the show had helped 'Philadelphia Freedom' up the R&B charts. Bowie replied, "Don't you think that would be pushing it a bit?", but six weeks later he was there, performing 'Fame' and 'Golden Years'.
OPPOSITE: Bowie arrives at Cherokee Recording Studios for another midnight to morning session, recording music for the soundtrack of *The Man Who Fell To Earth*.

MONDAY 17 NOVEMBER

■ SINGLE RELEASED

'Golden Years' (3:22)/
'Can You Hear Me' (5:04)
UK (RCA 2640)
US (RCA PB-10441)
UK Chart Peak No.8
US Chart Peak No.10

SUNDAY 23 NOVEMBER

Bowie's appearance on *Cher* broadcast in US (CBS).

THURSDAY 27 NOVEMBER

✪ TELEVISION

NBC Studios
Burbank
California, USA

'RUSSELL HARTY' (LWT)

Interviewed via satellite from Burbank, Bowie appeared on Russell Harty's show to announce he would be returning to play shows in Britain for the first time in three years.

The British public had seen nothing of Bowie since *Cracked Actor*, where he was skittish verging on paranoid and far from well. Nevertheless he still seemed articulate and enthusiastic about his work, and as relaxed as he had been with Harty when they last spoke in early 1973.

This time round he seemed bemused by Harty's questions and responded to them guardedly. Harty persevered, mindful that he had a scoop as well as an exclusive satellite link. At the same time Juan Carlos was being anointed King of Spain at a Holy Spirit Mass in Madrid. The Spanish government wanted the satellite line to broadcast the ceremony but Bowie refused to surrender it.

Eventually Bowie relaxed sufficiently to discuss the tour and *The Man Who Fell To Earth*. "It's finished in visual," he explained "but it's not finished in sound. I've got to record the sound, we've written a lot of it." An excerpt of the film was shown, along with 'Golden Years' from *Soul Train*.

▮Broadcast: Live via satellite (LWT)

SATURDAY 29 NOVEMBER

■ CHART

'Golden Years'
UK Top 30 Chart Entry
Charting 10 weeks

Six months before, Bowie had said "touring… kills my art. I will never, ever tour again." Cameron Crowe asked Bowie about his change of mind: "Because it's going to make an obscenely large amount of money, which I desperately need to set up my media-production company, Bewlay Bros… I'm actually anxious to try something I've never done in the past – work with a small band, perform with no set whatsoever and use no production gimmickry.

No sets. I'm just going to go out and sing. It's exciting to me. I want to see if I can cut it. My main consideration at this point is just to present an upbeat musical show. That will keep me amused. None of the depressive starkness of the *Ziggy* and *Diamond Dogs* tours.

"I'm sorry I lied. Really, what can I say? Every time I've said I wouldn't tour again, I've meant it. Nothing matters except whatever it is I'm doing at the moment. That's what keeps me excited." [099]

DECEMBER

▲ RECORDING
Cherokee Studios
751 North Fairfax Avenue
West Hollywood
Los Angeles
California, USA

'THE MAN WHO FELL TO EARTH' SOUNDTRACK

Harry Maslin: Producer
David Hines: Engineer
David Bowie: Guitar/Synthesisers/Drum Machines
Carlos Alomar: Guitar
Paul Buckmaster: Cello
Herbie Flowers: Bass
J Peter Robinson: Electric Piano

Since September, Bowie had been working on both *Station To Station* and writing the soundtrack for *The Man Who Fell To Earth*. Once the album was complete he turned his attention to the soundtrack, working with Paul Buckmaster, who had arranged strings and played cello on 'Space Oddity'.

Bowie (1993)
I presumed – I don't know why but probably because I was arrogant enough to think it so therefore I acted upon it – that I had been asked to write the music for this film. And I spent two or three months putting bits and pieces of material together. I had no idea that nobody had asked me to write the music for this film; that, in fact, it had been an idea that was bandied about. [364]

Bowie and Buckmaster began work using a TEAC four-track tape recorder at Bowie's Bel Air home before moving to Cherokee Studios. By the end of December they had produced only five or six working tracks.

Paul Buckmaster (2007)
There were a couple of medium tempo rock instrumental pieces, with simple motifs and riffy kind of grooves, with a line-up of David's rhythm section (Carlos Alomar et al.) plus J Peter Robinson on Rhodes-Fender piano and me on cello and some synth overdubs, using ARP Odyssey and Solina. There were some more slow and spacey cues with synth, Rhodes and cello, and a couple of weirder, atonal cues using synths and percussion.

There was a ballad instrumental by David that appears on **Low** ***('Subterraneans'). It was performed by David, me and J Peter Robinson on various keyboards.***

There was also a piece I wrote and performed using some beautifully made mbiras (African thumb pianos) I had purchased earlier that year, plus cello, all done by multiple overdubbing. And a song David wrote, played and sang, called 'Wheels', which had a gentle sort of melancholy mood to it. The title referred to the alien train from his character Newton's home world. [072]

Nic Roeg was cutting the film at Shepperton Studios in Surrey, where Mike Flood Page interviewed him for UK music paper *Street Life*.

"[Roeg] has before him a miniature Sony cassette machine and offers an exclusive preview of the Bowie soundtrack just in from LA. It's a simple melodic instrumental based around organ, bass and drums, with atmosphere courtesy of studio wizardry all put together and performed by Bowie himself." [238]

Roeg and executive producer Si Litvinoff thought the recordings were "brilliant", but well short of being a usable soundtrack.

Harry Maslin (1985)
David was so burned out by the end of Station To Station, *he had a hard time doing movie cues. The movie was complete and we had all the videotapes and that was what we were working with.*

We had about about nine cues down – of the 60 that we needed – and David had a big blow-up with Michael Lippman. [016]

Paul Buckmaster (2001)
I considered the music to be demo-ish and not final, although we were supposed to be making it final. We also didn't have a producer at the time and we were just trying to hammer it out together. All we produced was something substandard and Nic Roeg turned it down on those grounds. [004]

Si Litvinoff (2002)
To make matters worse, [British Lion producer] Deeley tried to outsmart David on the music rights. David turned him down. Thus, the great music Bowie wrote for the picture couldn't be used. The soundtrack is a meaningless last-minute replacement for what was superb. [409]

Bowie (2002)
I got angry about it, with no real rational reason. I thought I should be contracted by the film company to do the soundtrack, not just make a presentation of ideas. A stupid juvenile reason but I kind of walked away from it. [116]

Although the sessions stalled in December, it was still assumed that Bowie's soundtrack would be released along with the film in March 1976. Pan Books was preparing a movie tie-in edition of Walter Tevis' novel with a cover illustration by George Underwood. The blurb on the first edition read "Music by David Bowie. Album available on RCA."

When it was apparent this would not be the case, the second printing read "Musical Director John Phillips".

With Bowie now focussed on tour rehearsals, Roeg had turned to The Mamas & The Papas' founder – then based in London – to put a soundtrack together. Phillips thought Bowie's recordings were "haunting and beautiful, with chimes, Japanese bells, and what sounded like electronic winds and waves" and asked Roeg why he wasn't using them.

John Phillips (1986)
Roeg wanted banjos and folk music and Americana for the film. Roeg said, "David really can't do that kind of thing. We asked him who he thought he would like to do it and you were the first name that popped out of his mouth." [033]

Bowie (1993)
I constructed a thing, which never became the soundtrack to the movie, but became the album Low. *Some of it went onto* Station To Station, *but another chunk of it went onto* Low. [364]

Ricky Gardiner
He spent quite some time writing a score, and he wasn't pleased it wasn't used in the film. He let us hear it and it was excellent, quite unlike anything else he's done. [049]

Brian Eno (1976)
*Two of the [*Low*] pieces are from the soundtrack he made for* The Man Who Fell To Earth *and he added things and remixed them.* [207]

Nic Roeg (1993)
Some time later, David sent me the album – he said, "This was the music I would have done for The Man Who Fell To Earth.*"* [364]

'THE VISITOR'

In the film, Thomas Jerome Newton records and releases an album called *The Visitor* in the hope that it will be broadcast on the radio and heard by his wife on his home planet, Anthea. In a local record store (which surreally has a display of *Young Americans*), Bryce finds a (heavily discounted) copy of *The Visitor*. Using the cover as a clue, he tracks down Newton.

NEWTON: Did you like it?

BRYCE: Not much.

NEWTON: Oh, I didn't make it for you anyway.

A bootleg purporting to be Bowie's soundtrack music called (appropriately) *The Visitor* turned out to be a hoax perpetrated by Roy Carr and Charles Shaar Murray in their book, *Bowie: An Illustrated Record*.

Charles Shaar Murray (2011)
Yes, Roy and I made that one up. It was an old trick of Roy's, designed to let him know whether anybody else was nicking his research rather than doing their own. [384]

In September 1992 *Vox* magazine reported that Netherlands-based Farnsworth label was to release a limited edition CD soundtrack of *The Man Who Fell To Earth*. Housed in a steel box, the set would include a copy of the script, a set of 12 production stills, a cinema lobby card and a replica of Newton's gold wedding band. The CD would include all of the music from the original soundtrack (this too had never been released), intercut with dialogue from the movie. The main attraction was the inclusion of a "10-minute segment of instrumental ambient music, composed by Bowie, but never used in the final cut". This too was a hoax.

OPPOSITE: Bowie leaves Cherokee with notes and tape boxes for the soundtrack of *The Man Who Fell To Earth*, following an all-night recording session with Paul Buckmaster (right).

"The soundtrack is a meaningless last-minute replacement for what was superb."

Si Litvinoff on the John Phillips soundtrack that was used instead of Bowie's

MID-DECEMBER

As *Station To Station* was being prepared for release, Earl Slick spoke to *Circus* magazine about the upcoming world tour: "It's the smallest band of David's that I've ever been in. The first was with two saxes, two keyboards, guitar, bass, drums, and percussion. It's interesting. David's writing is going back in a rock direction, which suits me better than the R&B does, 'cause I like to play a lot. And the tour's perfect for that because there's lots of nice things that the band gets to do.

"Another reason I'm happy I'm doing this tour is that this time I have much more freedom, obviously because there's less people, plus the rock and roll. I just can't help feeling good about this tour." [149]

ABOVE: Dr Feelgood's album cover influenced Bowie's minimalist design on *Station To Station*.
OPPOSITE: Bowie chose Steve Schapiro's still from *The Man Who Fell To Earth* for the cover of *Station To Station*. According to production designer Brian Eatwell, the pictured interior of Newton's spacecraft was lined with plastic coffee cups which he procured from catering, glued to a backing and sprayed black. The entire structure was then backlit through a white sheet thrown over it.

Bowie, meanwhile, had changed his mind about the *Station To Station* cover design after Roy Young sent him a copy of Dr Feelgood's album *Down By The Jetty*. Impressed by the no-nonsense design, Bowie cropped Steve Schapiro's production still from *The Man Who Fell To Earth* from a colour full bleed to a monochrome 35mm frame, emphasising the red modernist typography in the process.

SATURDAY 20 DECEMBER

► TRAVELLING

Record Mirror reported "David Bowie will be spending Christmas on a train with his wife and son. He is travelling from Los Angeles to Jamaica for a 10-day holiday."

When the Bowies – accompanied by Pat Gibbons and a nanny – reached New Orleans, there were no arrangements for their accommodation and no representative to meet them. For Bowie it was the last straw after a month of strained relations and miscommunication. He called Lippman to terminate his role as manager.

Michael Lippman (1978)

I spent most of my time working with him during the middle of the night. Most of these exchanges went well. But the week before Christmas I was totally unable to communicate with him. I do recall dramatically erratic behaviour, when I was cut off from seeing him. He would not come out of his house – a house he rented in Bel Air. From my personal observations he was overworked and under a lot of pressure… and unable to accept the realities of certain facts. It would manifest itself by him remaining incommunicable. Our falling out came as a complete surprise. David can be very charming and friendly, and at the same time he can be very cold and self-centred. [317]

The Bowie party travelled on to Florida, where they took a boat to Jamaica. They saw in the New Year at Point Of View, Keith Richards' gated estate on a hill overlooking Ocho Rios.

"David can be very charming and friendly, and at the same time he can be very cold and self-centred."

Michael Lippman

JANUARY

▲ REHEARSING

In early January, Bowie assembled his band in Jamaica, to rehearse for the Isolar 1976 World Tour.

Earl Slick had been confirmed as playing on the tour and was establishing a solo career, with an album coming in March. However, Lippman's dismissal found Slick edged out since Lippman managed him as well.

Earl Slick (1999)

Somehow David and I ended up having a falling-out. I left the band early in '76 and that was based on a conversation I had with Pat Gibbons. David had gone to Jamaica and we were supposed to rehearse there but I couldn't get in touch with David at all. The last time I'd seen him he wasn't in the best of shape, and I was trying to get details about finances; you know, what we were going to get paid. Pat was very vague with me, and I said, "Look, I need to talk to David." "Well, David's busy. I can't get through to him. He's not taking calls." Obviously I'm not going to accuse anybody of anything, but it seems awfully suspicious how ready he was to take over at the time. [004]

Slick explained to *Rolling Stone* why he left the tour. "Between all the drug trips going down and the assholes he has surrounded himself with, I just wanted to get myself out. As an artist, David is very talented. I just started losing contact with him as a person." [267]

He also expressed doubts that Bowie had the physical stamina needed for a four-month tour. Bowie's publicist Barbara DeWitt responded that Bowie had put on ten pounds in Jamaica, had begun karate lessons with bodyguard (former US Grand Champion and Rolling Stones bodyguard) Dwain Vaughns and that he was now referring to his 'Playgirl physique'.

Following the split with Defries and now Lippman, Bowie decided to share management with Pat Gibbons, determined to avoid the pitfalls of previous tours.

Bowie (1976)

Things were handled so badly that it was painful to go out to receptions and be with everybody and have false gaiety, because there wasn't any gaiety. There was often bitterness and terrible arguments happening. So I preferred to stay on my own, get the tour over and end up saying, "I'll never tour again." I wasn't trying to be particularly mysterious or clever about it. I just couldn't imagine ever touring again by the time I'd get through with a tour. [144]

Bowie (1976)

I always got so I hated a tour. The management was never around when I needed them and everyone came to me with their problems. It took me all these years to understand what I want out of working. I want a lot of control over events. [076]

Bowie (1976)

My office is a suitcase that stays in my room. It's far better than before when I never knew what was going on, and this is how I used to do it back in England before. [085]

SATURDAY 3 JANUARY

✪ TELEVISION

Bowie's appearance on *Soul Train* broadcast in US (ABC).

SATURDAY 10 JANUARY

✪ PRESS

Nic Roeg interview published in *Street Life*.

■ CHART

'Golden Years'
US Top 30 Chart Entry
Charting 16 weeks

SUNDAY 11 JANUARY

▲ REHEARSING

Roy Bittan had returned to the E Street Band, so Bowie's tour manager, Eric Barrett, tracked down ex-Yes keyboard player Tony Kaye, who was celebrating his birthday at The Rainbow in Los Angeles. Kaye accepted Barrett's invitation to join the tour band and flew out to Jamaica.

With Earl Slick off the tour, the search began for his substitute. Jobbing jingle writer/guitarist Stacy Heydon was at home in Toronto when he got the call to audition as lead guitarist and naturally assumed it was a prank until he was assured, "If you don't believe me, call Air Canada. Your tickets are at the desk. We need you down here for a rehearsal tomorrow at 2pm."

Heydon was collected at the airport and chauffeured up to Point Of View, where he found the other musicians already set up. Bowie stepped forward as he came in: "You must be Stacy." [252]

Stacy Heydon (2010)

When I was offered the job I was told that if there was one fuck-up, I was gone. They came in my room with a tape and a cassette player and they wanted me to learn the show for the next day's rehearsal. And I did. [252]

Carlos Alomar (2010)

Bowie's concept was simple – take the musicians away from the phone, away from their loved ones, away from any kind of distractions, and put them on an island where all they can do is eat, sleep and play music. [252]

With the entire band assembled, rehearsals moved to Dynamic Sound Studios in Kingston, where The Rolling Stones had recorded *Goats Head Soup*. As well as working through the set list for the tour, the band's jams resulted in at least two new songs, 'Calling Sister Midnight' and 'Jamaica', both of which were eventually recorded as 'Sister Midnight' and 'Fashion'.

SUNDAY 18 JANUARY

▼ SOCIALISING

Geoff MacCormack, on holiday in Jamaica with Gui Andrisano, visited the Kingston rehearsals and was struck by the visible improvement in Bowie's health.

WEDNESDAY 21 JANUARY

► TRAVELLING

Bowie boarded a boat to Florida to begin his train journey to Vancouver for the start of the tour. The band flew home and joined him there at the end of the month.

ABOVE: Earl Slick whilst touring with Ian Hunter on June 12 1977. After leaving Bowie in 1976, Slick concentrated on his own band (Slick), recorded and toured with Ian Hunter and played on the John Lennon/Yoko Ono albums *Double Fantasy* and *Milk And Honey*. Slick returned to Bowie in 1983 to work on the *Serious Moonlight* tour, the albums *Heathen* (2002) and *Reality* (2003), their supporting tours and *The Next Day* (2013).

FRIDAY 23 JANUARY
■ ALBUM RELEASED
'STATION TO STATION'
UK & US (RCA APL1 1327)
UK Chart Peak No.5
US Chart Peak No.3

SIDE ONE
1. **'Station To Station'** (10:14)
2. **'Golden Years'** (4:00)
3. **'Word On A Wing'** (6:03)

SIDE TWO
1. **'TVC 15'** (5:33)
2. **'Stay'** (6:15)
3. **'Wild Is The Wind'** (6:02)

All songs by David Bowie except 'Wild Is The Wind' (Washington/ Tiomkin)

David Bowie/Harry Maslin: Producers
David Bowie: Vocals/Guitars/ Tenor Saxophone/Alto Saxophone/ Moog/Mellotron
Carlos Alomar: Guitar
Roy Bittan: Piano
Dennis Davis: Drums
Earl Slick: Guitar
George Murray: Bass
Warren Peace: Backing Vocals
Recorded at Cherokee Studios, Hollywood, California, USA
Mixed at the Hit Factory, New York, USA November 1975
Mastered at Allen Zentz Mastering, Hollywood, California, USA

REISSUES
▮ CD (RCA 1985).

▮ CD (remastered) (Ryko 1991).

BONUS TRACKS
1. 'Word On A Wing' (live) (6:10)
2. 'Stay' (live) (7:24)

▮ CD (remastered) (EMI 1999).

▮ CD (mini LP replica) (Toshiba EMI 2007).

▮ Super Deluxe Edition (remastered with bonus discs) (EMI 2010).
DVD *Station To Station*
5.1 surround sound
CD of singles versions
CD *Station To Station* (RCA 1985 CD master)
LP *Station To Station*
2 LP *Live Nassau Coliseum '76*
2 CD *Live Nassau Coliseum '76*

▮ Deluxe Edition (remastered with bonus discs) (EMI 2010).

ABOVE: Bowie's cover design, a monochrome Steve Schapiro still from *The Man Who Fell To Earth*, established the stark minimalist aesthetic of the tour – right down to the Ola Hudson-tailored suit he kept from the film to wear onstage. The original design (using a colour version of the still) was initially proofed – a small number of sleeves were made up – before the change to monochrome. The colour version was later restored for the 1991 Ryko and 1999 EMI reissues.

MONDAY 26 JANUARY
▶ TRAVELLING
Bowie broke his train journey in Chicago, stopping in at the Drake Hotel for a brief rest before boarding the train for Vancouver in the afternoon.

FEBRUARY

Bowie's tour band, now named Raw Moon, regrouped with Bowie in Vancouver for a final dress rehearsal, which was filmed by a local film crew hired for the day.

The concerts of the Isolar 1976 Tour began with piped music from Kraftwerk's recent album *Radio-Activity*, followed by a screening of the 1929 surrealist short film *Un Chien Andalou* by Salvador Dali and Luis Buñuel.

The lighting was devised by Bowie and Eric Barrett and represented a dramatic shift from the 1974 presentation. No longer consigned to the wings, the musicians were out front, drenched in dramatic white light.

Later in the tour Bowie explained to Chris Charlesworth, "I wanted to use a new kind of staging, and I think this staging will become one of the most important ever. It will affect every kind of rock and roll act from now on, because it's the most stabilised move that I've ever seen in rock and roll. I've reverted to pure Brechtian theatre and I've never seen Brechtian theatre used like this since Morrison and The Doors, and even then Morrison never used white light like I do.

"I think it looks like a corrupted version of the Thirties German theatre, what with the waistcoat, which has always been a favourite with me. I should have had a watch chain to make it perfect. I'm trying to put over the idea of the European movement with the Dali film and playing Kraftwerk over the speakers. I'd like to get my hands on the new Eno album to play, actually. I think side one is absolutely fabulous." [085]

'ISOLAR: BOWIE 1976'
'Station To Station'/ 'Suffragette City'/ 'Fame'/'Word On A Wing'/ 'Stay'/'Sister Midnight'/'TVC 15'/ 'Waiting For The Man'/ 'Life On Mars?'–'Five Years' medley/ 'Panic In Detroit'/'Changes'/ 'The Jean Genie'/'Rebel Rebel'/ 'Diamond Dogs'/'Queen Bitch'/ 'Golden Years' (occasionally)

Carlos Alomar: Rhythm Guitar
Dennis Davis: Drums
Stacy Heydon: Lead Guitar
Tony Kaye: Piano
George Murray: Bass
Eric Barrett: Tour Manager
Pat Gibbons: Tour Co-ordinator
Dwain Vaughns: Security
Eric Barrett/Showco: Sound/Lighting
David Bowie/Steve Schapiro: Programme Designers
Heather Harris: Graphic Co-ordination
Corinne Schwab: David Bowie's Personal Assistant
Tony Mascia: David Bowie's Driver
Barbara DeWitt: Worldwide Press/ Publicity
Andy Kent: Tour Photographer
Ola Hudson: Costume Designer

Bowie based the Isolar programme design on New York's *Picture* newspaper, using photographs by Geoff MacCormack and publicity shots by Tom Kelley and Steve Schapiro.

Steve Schapiro (2010)
We'd start to shoot, then he'd disappear, and come out with another incredible outfit. Then, just as I was about to shoot it, he'd say, "No, no wait a minute." He'd go in the dressing room and come out in something totally different. [252]

Bowie (1976)
A newspaper with no words. I want to bring that out again. Absolutely identical to* Picture *newspaper, but with different pictures. Mostly of me, at first, until it starts selling. And a lot of whoever's popular at the time. And slip in a few things... William Burroughs, Kirlian photography... [255]

MONDAY 2 FEBRUARY

★ LIVE

Pacific Coliseum
Vancouver
British Columbia
Canada

The 17,000-plus Coliseum quickly sold out for the opening date of the Isolar Tour.

At end of 'The Jean Genie' Bowie announced, "Ladies and gentlemen, my name is David Bowie. This is the first night of the tour, and you've been fucking great." After a rousing encore of 'Queen Bitch' and 'Rebel Rebel' they left, with the crowd stomping and applauding for five minutes. Then the announcement, which had become customary for Bowie concerts, came over the PA: "David Bowie has left the building."

After the concert, reps from RCA Canada were waiting backstage to present Bowie with gold records for sales in Canada. Someone mentioned that 'Golden Years' was enjoying a big chart breakthrough. "Oh, my god!" Bowie laughed, "We forgot to do it!"

Bowie then picked up the 12-string acoustic guitar – a gift from Pacific Presentations, promoters of the concert – and played 'Wild Is The Wind' to the group in the dressing room.

TUESDAY 3 FEBRUARY

✪ TELEVISION

'GOOD MORNING AMERICA' (ABC)

Bowie and Angie interviewed by Rona Barrett.

★ LIVE

Seattle Center Coliseum
Seattle
Washington, USA

WEDNESDAY 4 FEBRUARY

★ LIVE

Memorial Coliseum
Portland
Oregon, USA

FRIDAY 6 FEBRUARY

★ LIVE

Cow Palace
Daly City
California, USA

Bowie was so disappointed by the turnout of 1,100 at the Winterland in 1972 he skipped San Francisco on the 1974 tour. This time round he had a US No.1 single behind him and was playing to a packed 14,000-seat Cow Palace.

Robert Hilburn (*Los Angeles Times*)
The response was phenomenal. Though his 90-minute set started slowly as Bowie concentrated on new material, he worked up such an enthusiasm in the arena with his versions of songs like 'Changes', 'Rebel Rebel' and 'Jean Genie' that a rare thing happened after the first, rather obligatory encore. The audience continued yelling for Bowie long after the house lights – normally the sign that a concert is irrevocably over – were turned on. An excited, but apparently unprepared Bowie finally came back on stage to do a hastily assembled version of 'Diamond Dogs'. Though he messed up some of the song's lyrics, the audience continued to roar its approval and kept doing so for a full five minutes after the house lights were again turned on. Bowie clearly has arrived as a rock superstar in America.

Afterwards, Bowie explained the numerological implications for the concert to Robert Hilburn. "It was a lovely night. And it should be even better in Los Angeles. The numbers were a bit tough for us tonight. We were a four and the audience was a four. That can sometimes mean resistance. In LA we'll be a five – in the realm of the magician, and the audience will be a six – meaning comfortable, agreeable. That should really be something."

Promoter Bill Graham presented Bowie with a silver cape and a radio station rep turned up with a plaque to commemorate 'Fame' reaching the top of the charts.

"Record sales can only do so much for your confidence," Bowie told Robert Hilburn. "Real confidence comes from things much closer. It comes from being able to put together a tour like this one almost single-handedly and see it come off so well, see people around me enjoying themselves. Over the last year I've become a businessman. I used to think an artist had to separate himself from business matters, but now I realise you have more artistic freedom if you also keep an eye on business." [144]

SUNDAY 8 FEBRUARY

★ LIVE

The Forum
Inglewood
California, USA

▼ SOCIALISING

Following the first of three concerts at the 18,000-seat Forum, Bowie threw a post-concert party for 350 at the Forum lounge. Four-year-old Zowie was allowed to stay up late to join in.

Guests included Rod Stewart and Britt Ekland, Alice Cooper, Ringo Starr, Neil Sedaka, Lou Adler, Ray Bradbury, Linda Ronstadt, Carly Simon, Flo & Eddie, Henry 'Fonzie' Winkler, Jimmie Walker and Valerie Perrine.

President Ford's 19-year-old son Steven was there with five conspicuously inconspicuous Secret Service men.

Bowie (1976)
I told him I could ride horses English style. He said that he rode Western style and knew that riding English style was a lot harder. I agreed with him and said, "Yes, it has a lot more to do with etiquette and discipline than to do with horsemanship." He agreed. That was it, really. I liked him very much. I asked him what he thought of using rock'n'roll as a political vehicle. [101]

Bowie later held a private party for some of the guests in his room, where Ford chatted until 2.30am with fellow horse enthusiast Ringo.

ABOVE: Bowie, Angie and Dwain Vaughns (behind) arriving at the *Good Morning America* studio for the interview with Rona Barrett.
OPPOSITE: Live at the Forum.

"Bowie clearly has arrived as a rock superstar in America."

Robert Hilburn

TONIC
WATER

MONDAY 9 FEBRUARY

✪ TELEVISION

CBS Television City
7800 Beverly Boulevard
Fairfax
Los Angeles
California, USA

'DINAH!'

'Stay'/ David Bowie interview/ Bowie interviewed together with Nancy Walker, Henry Winkler, Natalie Cole and Candy Clark/ 'Five Years'

Dinah Shore: Presenter

During the run of shows at the Forum, Bowie featured on Dinah Shore's afternoon talk show. After Bowie had performed 'Stay' live with the tour band, he joined host Dinah Shore for an interview, which continued after the break with the other guests, Nancy Walker and Henry Winkler.

In the next segment Shore introduced Bowie's bodyguard Dwain Vaughns to demonstrate karate with Bowie, who explained, "A number of my friends in rock, before going on tour, have taken up karate as a form of exercise and I thought I might as well join in with what everybody else is doing and learn some. I'd been studying mime when I was younger, so… the two kinds of movement are very similar."

Also on the show was Natalie Cole, who was in California for concerts and the Grammy Awards on February 28. Bowie presented her with a gold record for her album *Inseparable*.

Candy Clark, Bowie's co-star in *The Man Who Fell To Earth*, joined them to talk about the film. The film was due to open on March 18 in England. Meanwhile, US distributors Cinema 5 had drastically cut the film down by 20 minutes to two hours for its US premiere in May.

ABOVE: Inglewood Forum in Los Angeles with (from left) Carlos Alomar, George Murray and Stacy Heydon.
OPPOSITE: Bowie and Candy Clark in *The Man Who Fell To Earth*.

Si Litvinoff (2002)

Editing is my favourite stage after development. But in this movie, [British Lion producers] Deeley and Spikings replaced me in London. They had promised Nic that nobody would recut his cut. As my lawyer described it politely, Deeley tried to outsmart Paramount, which pulled out of the deal. The rights to the picture were then sold to an exhibitor, not a studio. And the exhibitor had the picture recut. [409]

Candy Clark (2005)

You really couldn't make head or tail of the cut version. They hired some people who edited commercials to do it. And this after Nic Roeg and editor Graeme Clifford had spent nine months cutting it. I was due to go on the road for Cinema 5 to promote it, but I bailed out after a day. It was making me sick. [154]

After the interview Bowie and band returned to the stage to perform 'Five Years'. Afterwards, Bowie told Robinson, "I think with this stage show, I've put myself in a position of being more like the real David Bowie the audience has wanted. This show is more bisexual, more theatrical than anything I've ever done, I think. Ostensibly because it's the most real show I've done. Now I can start work." [255]

Lisa Robinson was on set, covering the tour for *Hit Parader*. "Angela wanted to be here," Barbara DeWitt told her, "but she's home cooking for a dinner party they're having later with Alice Cooper and Ray Bradbury."

Broadcast: March 3 in US (CBS)

★ LIVE

The Forum
Inglewood
California, USA

Rolling Stone
The civilised panache of it all was absent the next night when an obviously awed Patti Smith stopped backstage to say hello and managed to spill beer over Angela Bowie's mink.

WEDNESDAY 11 FEBRUARY

★ LIVE

The Forum
Inglewood
California, USA

In the audience were Linda Blair, David Hockney, Christopher Isherwood, Henry Winkler, Carole King and Cameron Crowe, who tracked down the lyrics to 'Diamond Dogs' for Bowie, who had forgotten the words the week before.

Backstage after the show, Christopher Isherwood introduced Bowie to David Hockney. Isherwood was the original Berlin-exiled Brit whose writings inspired the film *Cabaret*. Bowie was intrigued by Isherwood's recollections of Berlin and began to give it serious consideration as his next move.

THURSDAY 12 FEBRUARY

✪ PRESS

'Ground Control To Davy Jones' by Cameron Crowe published in *Rolling Stone*.

FRIDAY 13 FEBRUARY

★ LIVE

Sports Arena
San Diego
California, USA

Iggy was in San Diego when Freddy Sessler called him: "Listen, you should do yourself a favour. David's down there, and I'm gonna see him." Iggy declined the invitation but the following day Sessler pressed the point: "I saw David. He's interested in working with you. You should call him."

Iggy Pop (1997)

Finally I called him up and basically he had a song, a single he'd written, and he said, "Look, you're not doing anything else. Come on, come on, do you want to do this single?" I said, "Sure, I'll do it." [023]

The song 'Sister Midnight' was already in the set list, and Bowie had recorded a demo in Kingston, Jamaica during the January tour rehearsals.

Bowie's accountants had told him he could not return to Britain or take residency in America without facing crippling tax bills. Angie suggested Switzerland and, through connections with her old Swiss school, arranged permits to live there.

As Angie looked at houses to buy, Bowie returned to the Bel Air house to pack up his belongings into crates to be freighted to Switzerland.

Bowie (1978)

I was cocooned in America, getting involved in the trappings of rock'n'roll and dealing with all these precious people… And I found I was being manipulated subconsciously, through my own choice. So I went back to Europe and lived in Berlin for a bit, then went to Thailand and Hong Kong and finally Japan. [338]

SATURDAY 14 FEBRUARY

◆ AWARDS

'RECORD MIRROR & DISC' READERS' POLL

- UK Male Singer #4
- UK Songwriter #6
- World Male Singer #2
- World Songwriter #3
- World Musician #9
- World Album *Young Americans* #10
- World Single 'Space Oddity' #4

SUNDAY 15 FEBRUARY

★ LIVE

Veterans Memorial Coliseum
Phoenix
Arizona, USA

Lisa Robinson arrived at the Double Tree Inn to interview Bowie, and was greeted by Iggy Pop, who had joined the tour.

Iggy Pop (2004)

I had never seen anybody work that hard! He was getting up at eight in the morning to travel by car to the gig. Gets to the town, does a couple of interviews, catches a half hour of sleep and he's onstage doing a show. Then after the show, the guy won't stop! He's out checking out whatever band is in town. I was exhausted just watching him. He really knows what it is to work hard. No wonder he was doing so well and I was not. [001]

Discussing the tour, Bowie confessed to Robinson, "I'm a little bored now – I guess I'll have to change the show around, maybe just the order of songs. I definitely left some numbers out like 'Time', 'Space Oddity', precisely for the reason that I'd rather the energy level come from the eye line, rather than an association with any particular piece of theatre.

"I'm doing it for the money. I'm only really playing to about 3,000 people. I wouldn't know if the rest of the place was empty. I mean it sounds loud, but I can only see about 3,000 people. It would have been nice to do it at the Tower (in Philadelphia) and places like that, but then I wouldn't have made any money." [255]

MONDAY 16 FEBRUARY

★ LIVE

Tingley Coliseum
Albuquerque
New Mexico, USA

TUESDAY 17 FEBRUARY

★ LIVE

McNichols Sports Arena
Denver
Colorado, USA

FRIDAY 20 FEBRUARY

★ LIVE

Mecca Arena
Milwaukee
Wisconsin, USA

SATURDAY 21 FEBRUARY

★ LIVE

Wings Stadium
Kalamazoo
Michigan, USA

SUNDAY 22 FEBRUARY

★ LIVE

Roberts Municipal Stadium
Evansville
Indiana, USA

MONDAY 23 FEBRUARY

★ LIVE

Riverfront Coliseum
Cincinnati
Ohio, USA

WEDNESDAY 25 FEBRUARY

★ LIVE

Forum
Montreal
Quebec, Canada

THURSDAY 26 FEBRUARY

★ LIVE

Maple Leaf Gardens
Toronto
Ontario, Canada

FRIDAY 27 FEBRUARY

★ LIVE

Cleveland Public Hall
Cleveland
Ohio, USA

After a mix-up at the airport the trunks containing Bowie's regular stage clothing were left behind and he performed the first night in Cleveland wearing a pair of light blue slacks and a plain white shirt.

SATURDAY 28 FEBRUARY

★ LIVE

Cleveland Public Hall
Cleveland
Ohio, USA

2 SHOWS

The clothing trunks arrived for the second night and Bowie was back in Thin White Duke mode.

SUNDAY 29 FEBRUARY

★ LIVE

Cobo Arena
Detroit
Michigan, USA

OPPOSITE: Bowie on stage at the Cobo Arena in Detroit.

"He really knows what it is to work hard. No wonder he was doing so well and I was not."

Iggy Pop

MARCH

MONDAY 1

★ LIVE

Cobo Arena
Detroit
Michigan, USA

As 17-year-old Madonna Louise Ciccone made her way into the Cobo Arena, Chris Charlesworth interviewed Bowie in suite 1604 at the Pontchartrain Hotel.

David Bowie is balanced delicately in an armchair, his legs bent and hunched up, gazing absently at his bare feet which, like the rest of him, look remarkably clean. In his blue tracksuit he looks healthy and, although he could add a few pounds in weight, his brain is as trim as his figure.

ABOVE: Madonna in 1976. Twenty years later at Bowie's induction into the Rock Hall Of Fame, she recalled the Detroit show: "It was the first rock concert that I ever saw and it was a major event in my life. I was wearing my highest platform shoes and a long black silk cape. We arrived at Cobo Hall and the place was packed and the show began. And I don't think that I breathed for two hours. I came home a changed woman." [412]
OPPOSITE: LIve in Nashville.

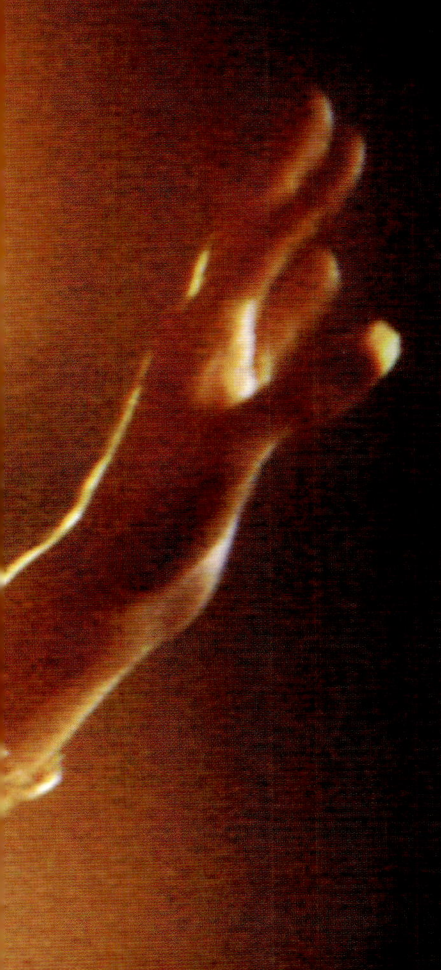

"It's the most efficient tour I've been on, and I can truthfully say it's the most efficient tour I've seen. Everybody on this tour is in a wonderful mood, and we're well through half the tour. This time no one comes to me with problems, so we get together as people instead, and I actually find I'm spending time with the band, which is rare. I've actually written on the road this time. The band and I have written three things and I've never been able to do that before.

"I think people look on the show as an honest appearance, and that's why they develop such a strong empathy for it. For the first few minutes they are absolutely alarmed at what they are seeing, they don't understand it, but there's one point when it breaks out and people realise what it is all about. It's not honest, really, but then I've never been a let-it-all-hang-out entertainer."

Bowie elaborated on his recently announced casting in The Eagle Has Landed*, playing Max Radl, a German officer who organises a plot to kidnap Winston Churchill during WWII.*

"I'm getting into my Nazi bit for this one. I have an inert left hand and a patch over my left eye for the part. Michael Caine and Donald Sutherland are in it, too, so it'll be one hell of a film. Sutherland is the reason that I chose to do it.

"If it wasn't for Sutherland and the money I wouldn't be interested. I'm more interested in a Bergman film called The Serpent's Egg *which is coming up, and I'd do that for nothing, just to work with Bergman."* [085]

WEDNESDAY 3 MARCH

★ LIVE

International Amphitheatre
Chicago
Illinois, USA

✪ TELEVISION

Bowie's appearance on *Dinah!* broadcast (CBS).

FRIDAY 5 MARCH

★ LIVE

Kiel Auditorium
St Louis
Missouri, USA

SATURDAY 6 MARCH

★ LIVE

Mid-South Coliseum
Memphis
Tennessee, USA

SUNDAY 7 MARCH

★ LIVE

Municipal Auditorium
Nashville
Tennessee, USA

MONDAY 8 MARCH

★ LIVE

Omni Coliseum
Atlanta
Georgia, USA

THURSDAY 11 MARCH

★ LIVE

Civic Arena
Pittsburgh
Pennsylvania, USA

FRIDAY 12 MARCH

★ LIVE

Norfolk Scope
Norfolk
Virginia, USA

SATURDAY 13
SUNDAY 14 MARCH

★ LIVE

Capital Center
Landover
Maryland, USA

MONDAY 15
TUESDAY 16 MARCH

★ LIVE

The Spectrum
Philadelphia
Pennsylvania, USA

WEDNESDAY 17 MARCH

★ LIVE

Boston Garden
Boston
Massachusetts, USA

Photographer Steve Schapiro sued Bowie for $85,000 in Los Angeles Superior Court for using promotional photos without paying for them, in violation of an agreement.

THURSDAY 18 MARCH

✪ PREMIERE

Leicester Square Theatre
London, England

'THE MAN WHO FELL TO EARTH'

Nicolas Roeg: Director
Si Litvinoff: Executive Producer
Michael Deeley/Barry Spikings: Producers
Paul Mayersberg: Screenplay from the novel by Walter Tevis
Anthony Richmond: Cinematography
John Phillips: Music Director
Graeme Clifford: Editor
David Bowie: Thomas Jerome Newton
Rip Torn: Nathan Bryce
Candy Clark: Mary-Lou/Anthean wife
Buck Henry: Oliver Farnsworth
Bernie Casey: Peters
Jackson D Kane: Professor Canutti
Rick Riccardo: Trevor
Tony Mascia: Arthur
Captain James Lovell: Himself

Among the guests were Angie Bowie, Paul and Linda McCartney, James Coburn, Lee Remick, Rick Wakeman, John Peel and Amanda Lear. Candy Clark and Rip Torn attended, as did Stomu Yamashta, who contributed to the soundtrack.

FRIDAY 19 MARCH

★ LIVE

Memorial Auditorium
Buffalo
New York, USA

Bowie struggled through the show, suffering from influenza.

SATURDAY 20 MARCH

★ LIVE

Rochester
Community War Memorial
Rochester
New York, USA

Before the show, Bowie told Al Rudis about his plans following the tour. "I'm going to finish off some silk screens and lithographs that I've worked on. I did some earlier this year, which I thought were very successful." [006]

▼ SOCIALISING

After the concert, Bowie threw a party in his three-room suite at the Flagship Americana hotel in State Street and invited a couple of ladies he met in the hotel bar. In the early hours of Sunday morning, the two women revealed themselves as narcotics officers and at 2.25am four vice squad detectives and a state police investigator charged Bowie, Iggy Pop, Dwain Vaughns and a 20-year-old Rochester woman, Chiwah Soo, on suspicion of possession of eight ounces of marijuana. This was a Class C felony, carrying a maximum sentence of 15 years in prison.

The four were held in the Monroe County jail for a few hours before being released on bond – at Bowie's expense. Bowie later said he bore the police no grudge: "They were just doing their job."

Bowie (1976)

Rest assured the stuff was not mine. I can't say much more, but it did belong to the others in the room that we were busted in. Bloody potheads. What a dreadful irony – me popped for grass. The stuff sickens me. I haven't touched it in a decade. [101]

ABOVE: The UK poster for *The Man Who Fell To Earth*.
LEFT: Angie Bowie, Lionel Bart and Candy Clark at the UK premiere in London.

SUNDAY 21 MARCH

★ LIVE

Springfield Civic Center
Springfield
Indiana, USA

MONDAY 22 MARCH

★ LIVE

New Haven Coliseum
New Haven
Connecticut, USA

TUESDAY 23 MARCH

★ LIVE

Nassau Coliseum
Uniondale
New York, USA

'Station To Station'/'Suffragette City'/'Fame'/'Word On A Wing'/'Stay'/'Waiting For The Man'/'Queen Bitch'/'Life On Mars?'/'Five Years'/'Panic In Detroit'/'Changes'/'TVC 15'/'Diamond Dogs'/'Rebel Rebel'/'The Jean Genie'

The concert was broadcast live to air by DIR on the *King Biscuit Flower Hour* FM radio show. As a result it was soon bootlegged as *Resurrection On 84th Street* and *The Thin White Duke*. Harry Maslin recorded the concert using the Record Plant mobile studio truck.

▮'Stay' and 'Word On A Wing' released on *Station To Station* (Ryko 1990).

▮Entire concert released on *Station To Station* deluxe editions (EMI 2010).

► TRAVELLING

Following the show Tony Mascia drove Bowie, Iggy and Dwain Vaughns to Rochester in upstate New York, arriving at four in the morning.

Iggy Pop (2003)

Bowie played the Ramones for me in the car. He always had whatever was new. I remember thinking 'Blitzkrieg Bop' sounded vaguely dangerous. [208]

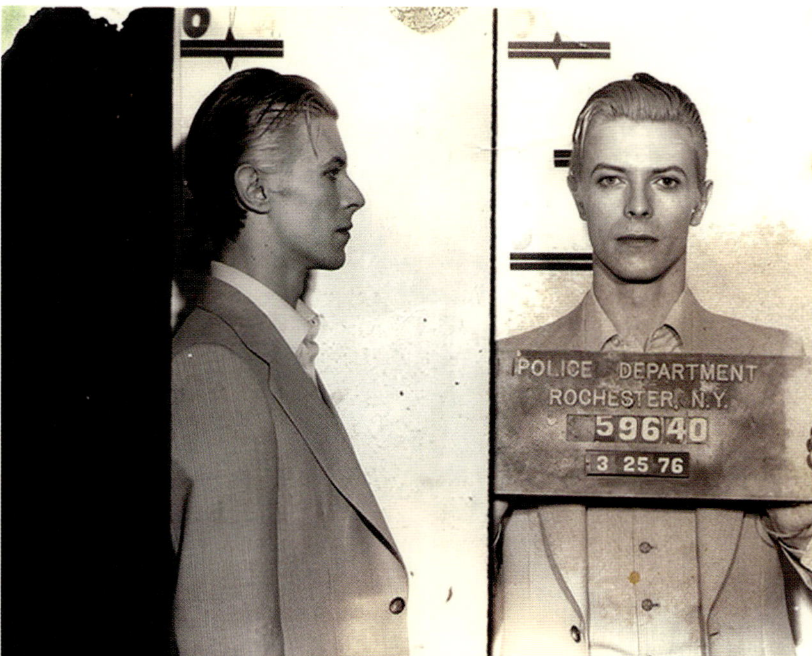

THURSDAY 25 MARCH

Fans mobbed Bowie as he arrived at Rochester City Court, pleading not guilty to charges of fifth-degree criminal possession of marijuana, as did Iggy Pop, Dwain Vaughns and Chiwah Soo. The case was adjourned until April 20 and Judge Cassetti allowed Bowie to remain free on $2,000 bail, as well as continuing the $2,000 bond on the other three. Bowie's LA attorney, Stan Diamond, told the press, "He's not a user of marijuana and it is my opinion that he is not guilty of any illegal possession."

Leaving the court, Bowie was besieged by reporters. He appeared on Channel Five News later in the day, saying he had been treated well by the police. One reporter asked him if he thought the marijuana could have been planted by a former business associate. Bowie looked shocked but declined to comment.

A five-by-four inch mugshot was taken when Bowie appeared at the city court for arraignment. In 2007 the photo was rescued from the rubbish during an estate sale of a retired Rochester police officer by Gary Hess, who was working for the auction house handling the sale. Hess didn't realise its value until he became ill and his brother Tom put the photo up for sale.

ABOVE: The right profile – Bowie's police mugshot.
LEFT: Bowie visits his attorney, Stan Diamond, before his city court appearance in Rochester.

FRIDAY 26 MARCH

★ LIVE

Madison Square Garden
New York City
New York, USA

▼ SOCIALISING

After the last concert of the US leg of the tour, a small party was held at the Penn Plaza Club for Bowie and the crew. Guests included Cyrinda Foxe, Flo & Eddie, Danny Fields, John Cale and Ronnie Spector.

Ronnie Spector (2006)

I didn't know him. I was like, David who? A man in make-up? But he went straight for me. We became friends later. [056]

At the party Bowie described that evening's show as getting the best reaction he had ever received: "I was so nervous, I nearly threw up!" He spent much of the evening in a corner booth with Iggy. He told Lisa Robinson that he and Iggy would finish the album they had begun on the tour in either Munich or Switzerland. "It'll be a Bewlay Bros production and then we'll give it to whoever offers the best deal."

Jagger arrived in New York the following day, missing the concert. Bowie had hoped to hold a private viewing of *The Man Who Fell To Earth* for Jagger and Bolan (whom he'd offered to fly over), but Bowie was unable to obtain a print of the film.

SATURDAY 27 MARCH

► TRAVELLING

Bowie and Coco sailed to Cannes, Iggy stayed behind in New York to catch up with friends, and Andy Kent flew back home to LA, for a break before the European leg of the tour.

Record Mirror reported that Bowie was unlikely to play a role in *The Eagle Has Landed* as its production schedule overlapped with his European tour dates. The part was given instead to Robert Duvall.

■ **LEFT: Madison Square Garden.**

APRIL

WEDNESDAY 7

★ **LIVE**

Olympiahalle
Munich, West Germany

THURSDAY 8 APRIL

★ **LIVE**

Philipshalle
Düsseldorf, West Germany

FRIDAY 9 APRIL

★ **LIVE**

East Berlin

By this time Angie had found the family a house near Montreux – Clos des Mèsanges in Blonay – and moved the rest of their possessions from London. But Bowie was having too much fun in Berlin with Iggy to contemplate a quiet life in a Swiss chalet.

Andy Kent (2011)
We went through Checkpoint Charlie and drove around East Berlin in David's big limousine. It was the President of Sierra Leone's old Mercedes 600 and it had one of those windows where you could stand up and wave to the crowd. He had a great driver, Tony Mascia, and we went out a couple of times at night and drove round Berlin real fast. David and Iggy loved it. They were out all the time. [105]

SATURDAY 10 APRIL

★ **LIVE**

Deutschlandhalle
West Berlin, West Germany

In the audience that evening was flamboyant transgender cabaret star Romy Haag and her entourage, who danced and disrobed in the front rows to attract Bowie's attention. Also at the concert was 13-year-old Christiane Felscherinow, who later described the concert in the autobiographical *Christiane F*.

PRESS
Stuart Grundy interviewed Bowie for a six-part BBC Radio 1 documentary, *The David Bowie Story*. "I'm supposed to be living in Switzerland," Bowie told him, "but I don't know how long that will last. I've got to come back to Berlin." [322]

SUNDAY 11 MONDAY 12 APRIL

★ **LIVE**

Congress Centrum
Hamburg, West Germany

TUESDAY 13 APRIL

★ **LIVE**

Festhalle
Frankfurt, West Germany

Following technical issues with the Dali–Buñuel film, the band took the stage 40 minutes late and launched into 'Station To Station'. As the song reached its climax, a fan was stretchered out after a drug overdose. The 1981 film of *Christiane F* alluded to the incident in the Berlin concert scene.

WEDNESDAY 14 APRIL

★ **LIVE**

Friedrich-Ebert-Halle
Ludwigshafen, West Germany

ABOVE: Hotel Bayerischer Hof, Munich with Pat Gibbons (right). OPPOSITE: Bowie relaxes in his Munich hotel suite.

SATURDAY 17 APRIL

★ **LIVE**

Hallenstadion
Zurich, Switzerland

SUNDAY 18 APRIL

▶ **TRAVELLING**

With a week off before the next date in Helsinki, Bowie found himself at a loose end. Recalling his 1973 Trans-Siberian Express journey, Bowie asked Andy Kent and Iggy if they fancied a side trip to Moscow. Kent organised the tickets and transit visas and they set off with fellow travellers Pat Gibbons and Coco Schwab for Moscow via Warsaw.

WEDNESDAY 21 APRIL

▶ **TRAVELLING**

Iggy celebrated his 29th birthday at Basel railway station where Bowie gave him a Polaroid camera to document their travels.

Arriving in Brest, on the Polish–Russian border, they were detained by the KGB after embassy contacts had failed to put their names on a transit list.

Andy Kent (2001)
The train stops and an albino KGB man comes in! He takes us off the train, we go into this huge Russian inspection place and an interpreter comes up and says, "We weren't expecting you." We were all separated. Iggy and David got strip-searched. I think they took some books away, that was all. I don't know what they took from David, but they took a* Playboy *away from me. [105]

The KGB found books on Josef Goebbels and Albert Speer, which Bowie explained were 'research' materials for a film he was planning to make about Hitler's minister for propaganda.

THURSDAY 22 APRIL

▶ **TRAVELLING**

Moscow
When they finally reached Moscow, there was more drama when their assigned contact in Moscow failed to appear.

Andy Kent (2011)
We got into two separate taxis, they had all the passports in one taxi and I was in another with the baggage. It was the most alone I ever felt in my life. But eventually we got to our hotel, and then spent the rest of the day seeing Moscow. [413]

After a quick stop at the Aeroflot head office for assistance, the group arrived at the Hotel Metropol. Bowie had been through this before in 1973 and remained calm.

Andy Kent (2011)
He was a confident, experienced traveller. We were on our own but David knew how to make his way around. When he gave me the thumbs up, I knew that everything was going to be fine. [413]

Andy Kent (2001)
We went to Red Square and the GUM department store, then back to the Metropol for caviar, then we met the next train in a different train station and left. We were in Moscow for seven hours, that's where all those pictures came from. [105]

SATURDAY 24 APRIL

★ LIVE

Nya Masshallen
Helsinki, Finland

Bowie and party arrived in Helsinki in time for the concert, but a day later than expected.

Andy Kent (2011)

Barbara DeWitt had invited all the members of the Scandinavian press to meet David at the train station when we arrived from Moscow. She thought the trip took two days – actually, it took three. So all the press was there but not David. People started to worry. [413]

The newspaper headline the next day was 'Bowie Lost in Russia!'.

Marc Bolan and Gloria Jones joined the tour in Helsinki and stayed until the 28th. Bowie had secured a print of *The Man Who Fell To Earth* and was keen to show it to Bolan.

Gloria Jones (2012)

David had been calling Marc, telling him that he'd been doing the film and it's going to be released. So we flew to Stockholm and then we got on the boat to go to Helsinki, Finland. He was doing a concert there, so when we arrived David rented the cinema, so there it was, just the three of us.

David was very humble because it was the first time seeing the actual film and Marc was, "Yeah well, that scene's OK there but I would've shot it like this and I would've had you coming in here and…" so it was slowly building up. Suddenly, I see Marc's arms flying and you could tell David was just like, "Man, just let me look at the film!" They were such good friends and when we left the cinema Marc told me that he was really proud of him.
[427]

ABOVE: More gold records from RCA, Stockholm.
OPPOSITE AND OVERLEAF: Despite arriving in Helsinki a day later than expected, there was still time for a press conference and a large brandy.

MONDAY 26 APRIL

★ LIVE

Kungliga Tennishallen
Stockholm, Sweden

✪ PRESS

Following the concert, a rep from the company that licensed RCA Records in Sweden presented Bowie with gold records for *Pin Ups*, *Diamond Dogs* and *Young Americans*. At the press conference Bowie was asked about the incident on the train in Russia.

BOWIE: *I'm working on a film based on the life of young Goebbels – when he was a young man – and they found all my references, [laughs] which didn't go down very well at all. They found books on the young SA uniforms, Goebbels' history and Albert Speer's Spandau diary and a lot of basic histories of German Romantics – that was the pre-National Socialists, the whole of the 18th, 19th century German history.*

Q: *Why do you travel around with that?*

BOWIE: *Well, I travel – generally – with about four or five hundred books and I cut down to a hundred books for Russia but I didn't – and I've been to Russia before; I should have known better – I didn't realise I had quite so many reactionary books on me.*

Inevitably Bowie was asked about the political ambitions he expressed in February's *Rolling Stone*. ("Maybe I should be prime minister of England. I wouldn't mind being the first English president of the United States either. I'm certainly right wing enough.")

BOWIE: *I think that maybe by the time I'm willing to throw myself into that kind of position, which would be a good 10, 15 years from now, I think I might be able to cope with it as well as everybody else.*

Q: *You said England needed a fascist leader, do you still think that?*

BOWIE: *Oh yes, not a Nazi leader, a fascist leader. Fascism is an extension of nationalism; a radical conception of what Lenin was going for. It's an intense form of Communism. And for a few years – until I get killed, [laughs] – as prime minister, one would need that kind of leadership just to tighten up reins and to pull people into perspective, into definition, so that they can really see what their country's made of and what they really want. But they won't know what they really want until they are ruled. When they are ruled then they decide what they really want.*

Q: *You want to be Prime Minister of England. Why not King of Sweden?*

BOWIE: *Because I have great respect for Swedes themselves and they have every right to have their own king! Have I met him? No. I saw somebody who looked like him in the third row, but I don't think it was him.*

TUESDAY 27 APRIL

★ **LIVE**

Kungliga Tennishallen
Stockholm, Sweden

Replaced cancelled show at Ekeberghallen, Oslo, Norway.

WEDNESDAY 28 APRIL

★ **LIVE**

Scandinavium
Gothenburg, Sweden

THURSDAY 29 APRIL

★ **LIVE**

Falkoner Teatret
Copenhagen, Denmark

FRIDAY 30 APRIL

★ **LIVE**

Falkoner Teatret
Copenhagen, Denmark

■ **SINGLE RELEASED**

'TVC 15' (3:29)/
'We Are The Dead' (4:53)
UK (RCA 2682)
US (RCA PB-10664)
UK Chart Peak No.33

Skivspegeln Radio broadcast Bowie's controversial interview conducted in Sweden four days earlier. The comments went unremarked in the Swedish media, but were quickly picked up by the British papers.

LEFT: Falkoner Teatret, Copenhagen.

ABOVE: Station to station: from Copenhagen (left) to Victoria Station (right), where Bowie waves to the fans. *NME* ran this Chalkie Davies photograph with the headline 'Heil and Farewell', implying he gave a Nazi salute. OPPOSITE: Bowie and a phalanx of security survey the commotion behind the crush barriers, as London's constabulary holds the line.

MAY

SUNDAY 2

▶ TRAVELLING

In the afternoon Bowie took the Boulogne hovercraft to Dover where he boarded a specially chartered train to Victoria Station. During the trip he fielded questions from Maggie Norden (Capital Radio) and, cognisant of the media furore surely awaiting him, his replies were guarded. Asked if he liked Russia, Bowie replied, "Yes, it's er… no Penge but it's quite good, quite fun. I didn't stay there for long – eight hours."

For Bowie's homecoming after a three-year absence RCA had set up a PA system on a podium supplied by British Rail so Bowie could address the adoring crowd of 2,000 that included teenage fans 'Boy George' O'Dowd and Gary Webb (later Numan).

Ignoring the podium, Bowie chose instead to stand in the back of the open-top Mercedes to wave to the fans. A photographer snapped him mid-wave and got a shot of what appeared to be a Nazi salute. The tabloids, looking to capitalise on his recent comments, seized on the symbolism of the gesture.

Gary Numan (2000)

I didn't see anyone walking around saying, "What a wanker, he did a Nazi salute." No one. People just thought he was waving at them, and I'm sure he was. [030]

Bowie (1993)

I didn't give a Nazi salute. I don't think I'd have done anything as daft as that. It's a bit like the shot of me 'kissing' Lou Reed. They were waiting for me to do something like a Nazi salute and a wave did it for them. [111]

Bowie (1978)

I hadn't seen England for a few years and when I got back there [for the European leg of the tour] I found that I'd taken back to England with me a character who was the epitome of everything that it looked like could be happening to England. I saw the National Front and it was obvious to me: there was a Nazi Party in England. Whether or not it was a good thing that I did, I don't know. I believe it was good – the best way to fight an evil force is to caricature it. [317]

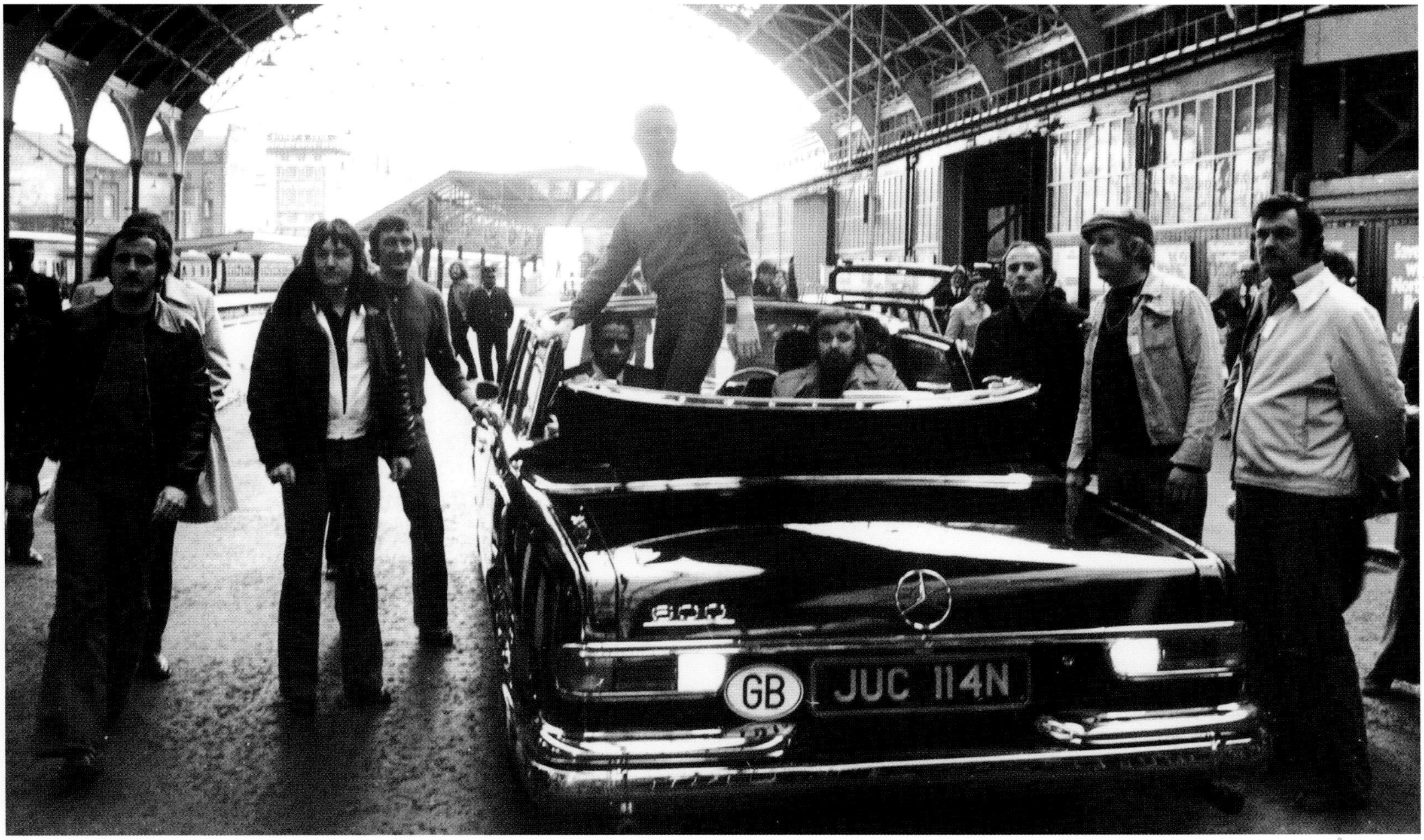
GB
JUC 114N

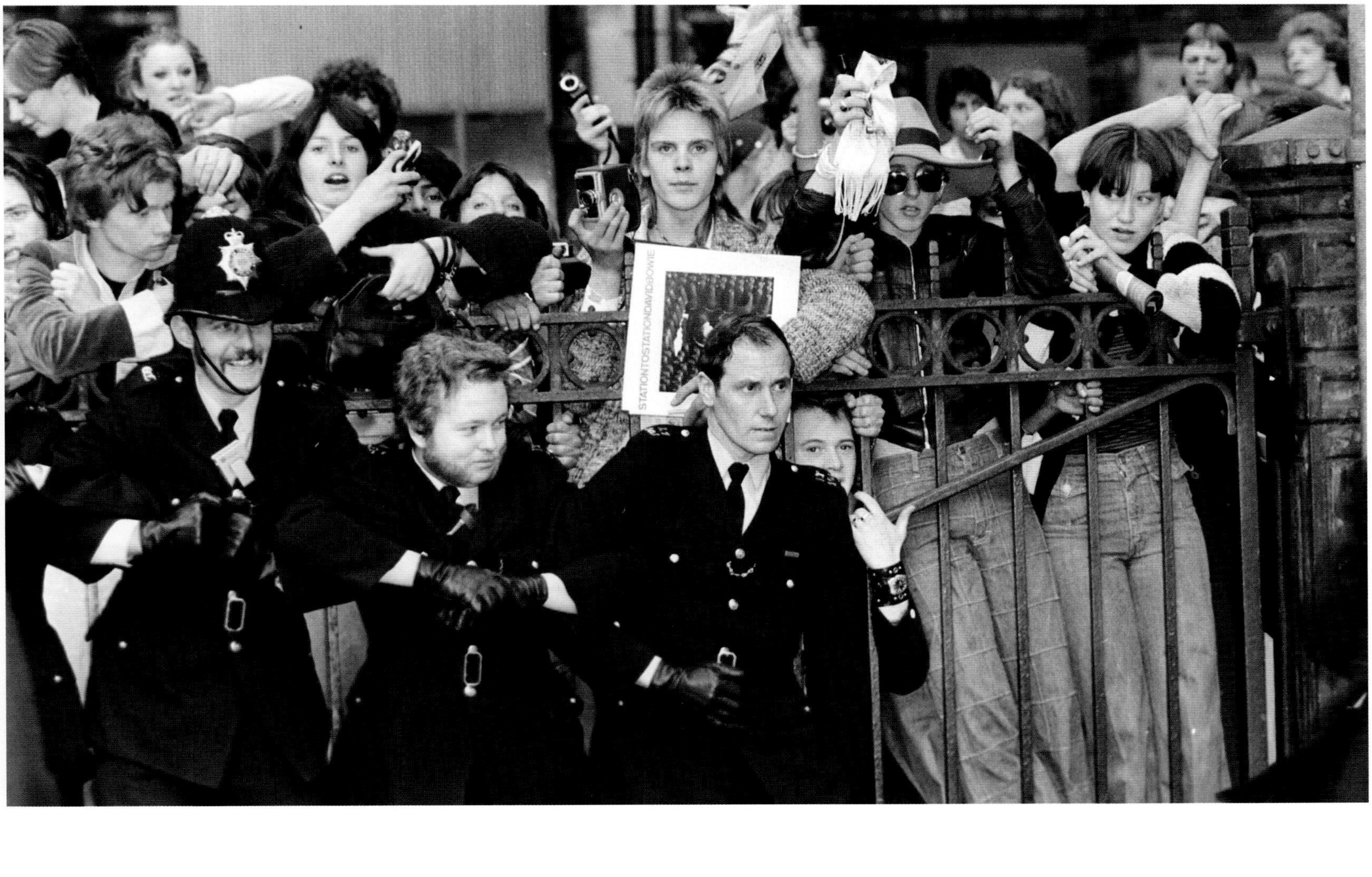
STATIONTOSTATIONDAVIDBOWIE

MONDAY 3 MAY

★ **LIVE**

Empire Pool
Wembley
London, England

TUESDAY 4 MAY

★ **LIVE**

Empire Pool
Wembley
London, England

PRESS

In an effort to pour oil on the troubled waters, Barbara DeWitt granted Jean Rook an exclusive interview for the *Daily Express*.

Yesterday, they were together at his secret London hideout – Angie glamorous, thinner even than he is, with ginger eye make-up to match his hair, and looking incestuously like his twin sister.

Physically, Bowie is not disappointing. He looks terribly ill. Thin as a stick insect. And corpse pale as if his lifeblood had all run up into his flaming hair. Did Bowie say that Britain needs a fascist Prime Minister and that, at 28, he is the man to fit the goose-stepping boots? Bowie would blush if he could spare the blood.

"If I said it – and I've a terrible feeling I did say something like it to a Stockholm journalist who kept asking me political questions – I'm astounded anyone could believe it. I have to keep reading it to believe it myself. I'm not sinister. I'm not a great force. Well, not that sort of force. I don't stand up in cars waving to people because I think I'm Hitler. I stand up in my car waving to fans – I don't write the captions under the picture.

"I'm Pierrot. I'm Everyman. What I'm doing is theatre, and only theatre. All this business about me being able to raise 7,000 of my troops at the Empire Pool by raising one hand is a load of rubbish. In the first place the audience is British, and since when will the Brits stand for that? What you see on stage isn't sinister. It's pure clown. I'm using myself as a canvas and trying to paint the truth of our time on it. The white face, the baggy pants – they're Pierrot, the eternal clown putting over the great sadness of 1976."
[268]

RIGHT AND OPPOSITE: Live at the Empire Pool.

WEDNESDAY 5 MAY

★ LIVE

Empire Pool
Wembley
London, England

THURSDAY 6 MAY

★ LIVE

Empire Pool
Wembley
London, England

▮ *Cracked Actor (Omnibus in Hollywood)* repeated in UK (BBC 1).

FRIDAY 7 MAY

★ LIVE

Empire Pool
Wembley
London, England

▼ SOCIALISING

After the concert Brian Eno met up with Bowie backstage. They had been in contact since Bowie was quoted in the American press expressing his admiration for Eno and Robert Fripp's albums. Eno sent him a copy of *Another Green World* and they agreed to meet.

Brian Eno (1999)
So I went backstage and we then drove back to where he was living in Maida Vale. He said that he'd been listening to **Discreet Music** ***which was very interesting because at the time that was a very out-there record, which was universally despised by the English pop press. He said he'd been playing it non-stop on his American tour, and naturally flattery always endears you to someone. I thought, 'God, he must be smart!'*** [104]

Bowie (1977)
I picked on Brian because he got out of a band that in the beginning had been one of the most inspirational bands in England and as far as New Wave went because it was a juxtaposition of fine arts against rock'n'roll, which is what I'd been trying to do, when I started mime back in the early Seventies. [335]

Eno returned with Bowie to his rented hideout in Maida Vale, where they made plans to collaborate with Fripp on an Iggy Pop album to be recorded in Canada, followed by a separate Eno, Bowie and Fripp project.

■ **Live at the Empire Pool.**

SATURDAY 8 MAY

★ LIVE

Empire Pool
Wembley
London, England

Max Bell (*NME*)

Bowie ambles upfront like Sinatra in his Songs For Swinging Lovers *days. He smiles a lot but the nerve ends show up as taut as wires. He chews the inside of his mouth, though when he swings into action, his voice is excellent, immediately negating rumours that he'd lost it after the season.*

They do 'Diamond Dogs' superbly. Elegant he is on all the SF monster kinks, trailing his fingers over the stage and bolstering the last lines with some fine improvised singing. He takes his bows and waves to Mick Jagger and Ron Wood at the side. They wave back. Jagger is flanked by two lusty spades, spinning round his Bowielite and generally drawing attention to himself.

Bowie is moved at the response. "Thank you. I'll see you all very soon." It is very soon. They return for the encores, 'Rebel Rebel' and 'Jean Genie', both of which are entirely relaxed, timeless interpretations and not the rather effete little numbers they once were. He turns on a sharp heel to every side of the auditorium, combining the peace sign with the Nazi salute, then leaps for joy and splits.

Allan Jones asked Bowie's band leader Carlos Alomar about their post-tour plans. "It seems that we're going to be doing some more gigs in the States and David wants to cut a new album fairly soon. David has the album planned and all the songs are together. It's just down to him, when he wants to record. And then, after that, he wants to come back to Europe later this year."

ABOVE: Bowie at Vorst Nationaal in Brussels. OPPOSITE: At the Sportpaleis van Ahoy in Rotterdam.

"I'm working for this band to stay together for as long as possible. As far as David is concerned, I know he loves this band and wants to keep it. He knows it's a good band. After this tour we have to consider what he wants to do. We'll be there if he wants us. We'll be keeping ourselves together in New York. And we're also working on the possibility of recording together." [163]

The Rochester drug charge was reduced from a felony to a misdemeanour, meaning the maximum punishment could be no more than a year in jail.

MONDAY 10 MAY

► TRAVELLING

London – Brussels

TUESDAY 11 MAY

★ LIVE

Vorst Nationaal
Brussels, Belgium

THURSDAY 13
FRIDAY 14 MAY

★ LIVE

Sportpaleis van Ahoy
Rotterdam, Netherlands

MONDAY 17 MAY

★ **LIVE**

Pavillon de Paris
Paris, France

▼ **SOCIALISING**

Bowie hired L'Ange Bleu nightclub on the Champs-Élysées for his after-show party and invited members of Kraftwerk.

Maxime Schmitt (1993)

When Ralf and Florian walked in they received a five-minute standing ovation. Iggy Pop was gazing devotedly at them, he completely adored them. Both he and Bowie were transfixed, Bowie was saying to Iggy Pop, "Look how they are, they are fantastic!" [005]

Iggy Pop (2003)

David Bowie turned me on to **Radio-Activity** ***when I was hanging out with him on his*** **Station To Station** ***tour, trying to get him to produce*** **The Idiot.** ***I heard this and thought, "Aha – the world has changed."*** [208]

TUESDAY 18 MAY

★ **LIVE**

Pavillon de Paris
Paris, France

▼ **SOCIALISING**

The second Paris show was the last of the world tour (as the third show was cancelled). Bowie celebrated at L'Alcazar club with Romy Haag, whom he'd met in Berlin.

✪ **TELEVISION**

'SPÉCIAL DAVID BOWIE' (TF1)

Yves Mourousi: Presenter

The 11-minute news segment included a short interview with Bowie, live footage of 'Life On Mars?', 'Suffragette City' and 'TVC 15' from the Paris concert and a profile of French Bowie fan club founder Natacha Smolianoff.

WEDNESDAY 19 MAY

► **TRAVELLING**

★ **LIVE**

Pavillon de Paris
Paris, France

SHOW CANCELLED

Bowie, Iggy and Coco had intended to stay on at the Plaza Athénée in Paris but were constantly besieged by fans outside the hotel. Pierre Calamel, the enterprising studio manager of the Château d'Hérouville, called to invite them out to the Château for a couple of days of peace and quiet. They checked out of the Plaza and arrived at the Château that evening.

RIGHT: Bowie and Romy Haag celebrate the end of the tour with friends and crew at L'Alcazar club in Paris. OVERLEAF: Bowie interviewed by *Paris Match*.

THURSDAY 20 MAY

Bowie rose late after a restless night – he'd been found sleepwalking in the grounds, wearing nothing but a Burberry mac – and met with chief engineer Laurent Thibault. Bowie dragged out a pile of records to play and as they talked about the music, Bowie decided to book Thibault and the studio for June and July to work on Iggy's album.

The plan had been to record in Munich but the Château was a residential studio, meaning they wouldn't have to worry about living expenses – RCA would pick up the tab. Money was still tight as the split with MainMan had choked Bowie's royalties.

After a couple of days Bowie left with Zowie and his nanny Marion Skene to join Angie in Switzerland to look at Clos des Mésanges in Corsier-sur-Vevey.

Bowie spent the next week planning his next album, recording rough ideas on a small cassette machine. Iggy arrived and they began some rough sketches of songs for *The Idiot* on keyboard and guitar.

Bowie (1995)
I spent a lot of time writing for him as well as producing. For me, Iggy's strength was as a lyricist – I thought he was the funniest, darkest lyricist of the time. I really wanted to give him some musical support that would get him a wider audience. It just seemed so unfair that he was virtually neglected. I was going through a very experimental stage when I first started working with Iggy on* The Idiot. *I had some ideas on that which reached their fruition when I started working with Brian on* Low. The Idiot, *for me, was a kind of format for devising a new kind of musical scenario. [242]

Bowie (1977)
Towards the end of my stay in America, I realised that what I had to do was to experiment, to discover new forms of writing, to evolve, in fact, a new musical language. That's what I set out to do. That's why I returned to Europe. [164]

Iggy Pop (1996)
He has a work pattern that recurs again and again – if he has an idea about an area of work he wants to enter, he'll use side projects or work for other people to gain experience and get a little taste of the water before he goes in and does his, and I think he used working with me that way. [346]

ABOVE: The cover featured one of the portraits from the 1975 Tom Kelley session. OPPOSITE: The US teaser poster.

FRIDAY 21 MAY

■ ALBUM RELEASED

'CHANGES ONE BOWIE' COMPILATION
(RCA RS 1005)
UK Chart Peak No.2
US Chart Peak No.10

SIDE ONE
1. **'Space Oddity'** (5:14)
2. **'John, I'm Only Dancing'** (2:43)
3. **'Changes'** (3:34)
4. **'Ziggy Stardust'** (3:13)
5. **'Suffragette City'** (3:25)
6. **'The Jean Genie'** (4:07)

SIDE TWO
1. **'Diamond Dogs'** (6:03)
2. **'Rebel Rebel'** (4:28)
3. **'Young Americans'** (5:10)
4. **'Fame'** (4:12)
5. **'Golden Years'** (4:03)

Tom Kelley: Cover Photographer

Bowie selected the tracks for the first compilation (outside Japan) of his work since leaving Decca.

'John, I'm Only Dancing' made its first appearance on LP, though due to an error in the mastering, the first 1,000 copies of the UK pressing used the 'sax version' cut during the *Aladdin Sane* sessions in 1973.

Subsequent pressings of *Changes One Bowie* featured the original version of the single that had been recorded and released in 1972. Though mainly a singles collection, 'Ziggy Stardust' had been a B-side (of 'The Jean Genie') and 'Suffragette City' was only released as a single in July 1976 to promote the compilation.

▌Reissued on CD (RCA 1984).

SATURDAY 22 MAY

■ CHART

'TVC 15'
UK Top 30 Chart Entry
Charting 4 weeks

WEDNESDAY 26 MAY

The Man Who Fell To Earth finished its run at Leicester Square Cinema.

FRIDAY 28 MAY

✪ PREMIERE

The Man Who Fell To Earth premiered in New York.

SUNDAY 30 MAY

▼ SOCIALISING

The Bowies hired a room at the Montreux Casino (recently rebuilt since the 1971 fire) to celebrate Zowie's fifth birthday with his friends.

Angie Bowie (1985)
We went and got all these instruments and put them there for the kids. David was fabulous. He's so good at that. He loves that street theatre and improvisation with kids. We have a wonderful video of them doing a 'thematic' representation of* Jack And The Beanstalk *with David narrating and the kids acting all the parts.

It wasn't long after this that David decided the last person he could talk to or have anything to do with was me and it was at this point that he went into hiding. [019]

Angie had hoped for a new beginning with Bowie in Switzerland following the 1976 tour, but soon after the party, Bowie left for the Château d'Hérouville with Iggy and Corinne Schwab to begin work on Iggy's new album.

David Bowie

The man who fell to Earth

JUNE

▲ RECORDING
Château d'Hérouville
Hérouville, France

IGGY POP
'THE IDIOT' ALBUM

Sessions began with a few days of Bowie recording rough backing tracks on his Baldwin electric piano, while Iggy scribbled out lyrics.

Iggy Pop (1977)
It was done very much in the manner that I've always worked. We sat in the basement, me on the drums and him on piano. [307]

Iggy Pop (1984)
The basic idea was to do it without anybody. Just the two of us – although we started fudging, bringing in a bass player here, a drummer there. [183]

When Bowie asked for a "very solid, very rough" drummer, Laurent Thibault called Michel Santangeli. When he arrived the next day from Brittany he was shocked to find it actually was Bowie in the studio, not one of Thibault's jokes, and was coaxed in from the foyer, where he stood paralysed with fear.

Bowie played through the songs on keyboard with Santangeli learning the drum parts as they went, quickly moving onto the next. Later Santangeli realised the tape was on the whole time – they were the finished takes, and Bowie moved onto his guitar overdubs.

Iggy Pop (1986)
David plays better Angry Young Guitar than any Angry Young Guitar player I've ever heard, including James Williamson. When David plays guitar he gets nuts. You know that little part on 'Dum Dum Boys', that 'bowwwwaaah'? That's his part, that's David doing that. He struggles with that thing when he plays. His fingers start cramping and we have to stop halfway through and he's yelling "I don't know why the fuck I'm doing this for you, you jerk!" We have a very abrasive relationship, it's a clash. [043]

Bowie left Thibault to write and record bass parts, all of which were retained except 'Borderline', for which Bowie hummed a new bass line to him.

Bowie continued to experiment in the studio while Iggy roamed the grounds with sheaves of lyrics. One source of inspiration arrived one afternoon in the form of Kuelan Nguyen, the Vietnamese girlfriend of musician Jacques Higelin.

They were staying at the Château as guests of owner Michel Magne. Despite the language barrier, a brief affair soon developed, inspiring Iggy to rewrite 'Borderline' as 'China Girl', acknowledging the hopelessness of the affair with the warning "you shouldn't mess with me – I'll ruin everything you are."

Bowie (1993)
An extraordinary lyric, and it was really sort of thrown out as he was writing it. It was literally thrown out on the recording session, almost verbatim. He changed maybe three or four lines. But it is an extraordinary talent that he has for spontaneous free thought. [049]

Kuelan Nguyen (2011)
I only said to Iggy "Shhh..." because I worried he was too 'speed' and could hurt himself. It's Iggy who created the words 'shut your mouth' to make it rock'n'rolling in the song. I would never say 'shut up' to one of the most beautiful voices in rock'n'roll! [401]

THURSDAY 17 JUNE

✪ PRESS

Circus magazine reported on troubles Bowie had been having that year. There were ongoing complications arising from his split with manager Michael Lippman in January. Cherokee Studios was planning a court action to recover $30,000 in studio fees from Bowie's soundtrack sessions in December.

Steve Schapiro had sued him for $85,000 for using his promotional photos without permission and New York's *Picture* newspaper claimed Bowie had defaulted on a payment of a $4,000 consultant's fee for his Isolar Tour programme.

An exhibition of Bowie's paintings, silk screens and videotapes, which had been cancelled in February due to the tour, was now being scheduled for later in the year, in galleries across America, starting in New York.

JULY

FRIDAY 9

■ SINGLE RELEASED
'Suffragette City' (3:25)/
'Stay' (3:21)
UK (RCA 2726)

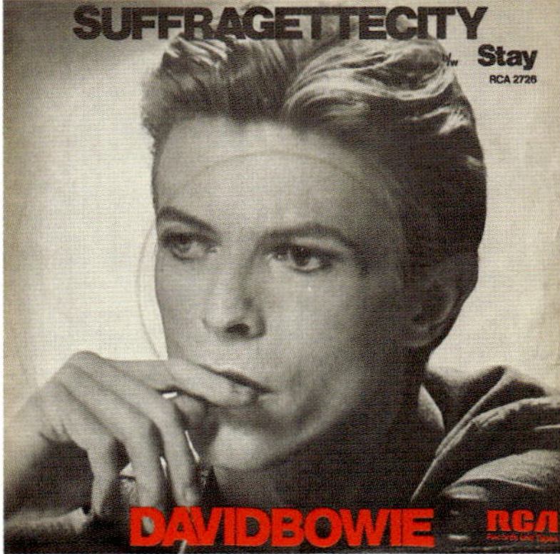

WEDNESDAY 21 JULY

The Man Who Fell To Earth opened in Chicago.

▲ RECORDING

The Idiot recording sessions continued at the Château until the end of July, when George Murray and Dennis Davis arrived to overdub bass and drums.

⊙ BUSINESS

Bowie's financial difficulties worsened as his royalties were frozen, pending resolution with Lippman.

Laurent Thibault (2010)
He told us he had to sell his Mercedes. He came with a big Mercedes and a chauffeur. In fact he asked us to find a garage to sell it. It was a big class Mercedes and the value of the car was terrible because he'd had a car crash. So they offered only a very low price. David was very angry because he said that the Mercedes was paid for by RCA as an advance in royalties and it was very, very expensive and they wanted him to sell it for nothing. [425]

Bad Company had booked the Château for August, so Bowie and Iggy borrowed engineer Thibault and moved the sessions to Munich. As they left, Bowie asked Calamel to book them into the Château for September.

AUGUST

▲ RECORDING
Musicland
Munich, West Germany

IGGY POP
'THE IDIOT' ALBUM

Sessions resumed at Musicland, a basement studio beneath the Sheraton where they stayed on the 22nd floor. Bowie, Iggy and Thibault recorded vocals and overdubs, working through the night as Thin Lizzy had the studio by day.

Iggy Pop (1996)
To work with as a producer, Bowie was a pain in the ass. Megalomaniacal loco... but who had good ideas. I was working on a lyric for 'Funtime' and I had a good idea for the song and he's the kind of guy who would stop you and say, "Okay, the words are good but don't sing it like a rock guy, sing it like Mae West," which is informed of another genre, informed of cinema, it's also a little bit gay, that suggestion. And that suggestion worked and the vocal got more menacing 'cos of that. And that was very good. [346]

Bowie wanted some of his guitar parts redone and called Visconti.

Tony Visconti (1986)

He was always changing guitarists like we change socks and I got this guy called Ricky Gardiner who I'd been making some demos with and he was one of the best guitarists I've ever worked with. [019]

Gardiner was called and invited to join, but uninvited shortly afterwards.

Ricky Gardiner (1986)

I had this last-minute telephone call saying it was no longer necessary for me to go and that Mr Bowie sent his apologies. [043]

Mr Bowie had found his man, another name from Visconti – British guitarist Phil Palmer, so green he still lived with his parents.

Phil Palmer (2005)

At two o'clock in the morning the phone rang, and my mum answered it and came upstairs and said, "There's a Mr Bowie on the phone for you," and I thought it was someone messing around, as you do. Yeah, "Get over here as soon as you can and it will all be taken care of," and it was. I just threw a few things in a bag, and a guitar, and off I went. [045]

Palmer arrived with his Telecaster to join them on the sessions, which he described as 'vampiric' – working through the nights on bizarre soundscapes, playing guitar parts to their cryptic instructions. On 'Nightclubbing' he was told: "You're walking down Wardour Street. Now play the music you hear coming out of each club."

FRIDAY 20 AUGUST

▲ MIXING

Hansa Tonstudio
West Berlin, West Germany

IGGY POP
'THE IDIOT' ALBUM

After Thibault returned to Paris, Iggy and Bowie moved to Berlin to finish the mix with Tony Visconti at Hansa Tonstudio on the Kurfürstendamm, which Edgar Fröese recommended at the Château.

Corinne Schwab soon found them a seven-room flat above a car spares shop at Hauptstrasse 155, Schöneberg, within walking distance of Hansa, while Visconti stayed at the Schlosshotel Gerhus in Grunewald. Initially Visconti was brought in to work on *The Man Who Fell To Earth* soundtrack tapes that were still at Cherokee, pending payment of studio fees.

The tapes hadn't arrived so they completed the mix on Iggy's album instead, working in the afternoons and nightclubbing afterwards, often at Romy Haag's cabaret.

In the relative anonymity of Schöneberg Bowie and Iggy sought a simple life, away from the pressures of fame. They had a vague plan to clean up, partly driven by Zowie living there, having started school in Berlin.

Bowie (1989)

The whole reason for going there was because it was so low key. Jim and I – we were both having the same problems – knew it was the kind of place where you walk around and really are left alone and not stopped by people. They're very blasé, there. Cynical, irony-based people and it's a great place if you really want to try and do some soul-searching and find out what it is that you really want. [110]

Corinne Schwab (2001)

I loved how Jim would pick new neighbourhoods in Berlin and then just go out and walk them. Then he'd come back and say, "Wanna go for a walk?" He'd show us from time to time what he found. It was always fun. I remember one elevated subway ride where you rode into East Berlin with no checkpoints and then back out again into the West. Trust Jim to find that one... [389]

With a potentially expensive lawsuit with Lippman coming up, Coco put them both on a strict budget of 10 Deutschmarks a day, which they spent at cafés and galleries. They fixated on Neo-Expressionist painters hanging in the Brücke Museum. Eventually Bowie went out and bought art materials so they could paint their own.

He also bought the reproduction rights for Heckel's *Roquairol* for the cover of *The Idiot*. In the event it was decided instead to have Andy Kent shoot Iggy in the same pose, wearing his girlfriend Esther's jacket.

Bowie (2001)

Since my teenage years I had obsessed on the angst-ridden, emotional work of the Expressionists, both artists and filmmakers, and Berlin had been their spiritual home. This was the nub of Die Brücke movement, Max Reinhardt, Brecht and where **Metropolis** ***and*** **Caligari** ***had originated. It was an art form that mirrored life not by event but by mood. This was where I felt my work was going. My attention had been swung back to Europe with the release of Kraftwerk's*** **Autobahn** ***in 1974. The preponderance of electronic instruments convinced me that this was an area that I had to investigate a little further.*** [105]

■ SINGLE RELEASED

'Stay' (3:21)/
'Word On A Wing' (3:10)
US (RCA PB-10736)

TOP: Iggy at the entrance of Hauptstrasse 155, the West Berlin home he shared with Schöneberg and Bowie. ABOVE: The US 'Stay' single sleeve with another portrait from the 1975 Tom Kelley session.

SEPTEMBER

▲ RECORDING
Château d'Hérouville
Hérouville, France

'LOW' ALBUM

David Bowie/Tony Visconti: Producers

Bowie and Iggy returned to the Château, joined by Tony Visconti who had brought his secret weapon. When Bowie and Eno were planning the album they had conference called him and asked, "What are you going to bring to the table?" He thought quickly. "An Eventide Harmonizer. It fucks with the fabric of time."

In fact, Harry Maslin had used the same device on *Station To Station*, but Visconti's experiments had resulted in an innovative effect that was widely copied afterwards.

Tony Visconti (2001)
It was a radical sound, especially on the drums. I had the second Harmonizer in Europe and I guessed it would be a matter of time before other producers figured out what I was doing. But when the album came out the Harmonizer still wasn't widely available. [105]

Carlos Alomar, George Murray and Dennis Davis arrived from America and began to develop Bowie's song ideas and record some backing tracks. Alomar had known back in May that an album was being planned but was not privy to its exact nature.

Carlos Alomar (2012)
The situation with me, George and Dennis is that we get a call, telling us to show up. Then we have to start from scratch; we have to pluck it from the air. [296]

Ricky Gardiner had missed out on *The Idiot*, but soon afterwards got the call "asking could I go off and perform miracles on his new album?" He arrived a few days later with Roy Young, whom Bowie had tracked down at The Speakeasy. The renowned boogie-woogie pianist had guested with Bowie one night in 1972 and was invited to play on *Station To Station*, but was unable to make the sessions. On the flight over from Britain to Paris, Young and Gardiner agreed they had no idea how they would fit in with Bowie's plans.

ABOVE: Château d'Hérouville, outside Paris. Three years after recording *Pin Ups* there, Bowie was drawn back to the residential-style studio by its unhurried atmosphere and tax advantages to record *The Idiot* and *Low*.

As it happened, he had no definite plan other than to record two sides of sharply contrasting styles under the Eno-esque title *New Music: Night And Day*. Since May he had been in discussions with Eno about the nature of their collaboration.

Tony Visconti (1977)
David described the album to me as far back as July, because he asked me if I could produce Iggy's album first and then his own, which he said was going to be very revolutionary. [306]

Bowie had determined a prudent course of action – six or seven songs that were conventional enough to keep RCA happy and a side of experimental instrumental pieces to keep him and the public "interested and excited", as he had put it in 1974.

Bowie (2002)
I had brought the idea of having fundamentally an R&B rhythm section working against this new zeitgeist of electronic ambience that was happening in Germany. It was terribly exciting to know that one had stumbled across something that was truly innovative. At that time I was vacillating badly between euphoria and incredible depression. Berlin was at that time not the most beautiful city of the world, and my mental condition certainly matched it. I was abusing myself so badly. My subtext to the whole thing is that I'm so desperately unhappy, but I've got to pull through because I can't keep living like this. There's actually a real optimism about the music. In its poignancy there is, shining through under there somewhere, that it will be all right. [239]

For the first side of "raw rock'n'roll" they recorded more than enough for Bowie to consider abandoning the first concept – until it came to writing lyrics.

Tony Visconti (1977)

Ever since* The Man Who Sold The World *he has written the lyrics after the music, but in this case he couldn't come up with more than one verse for some things, which is why a lot of the tracks fade out. [306]

Eventually Bowie adopted Iggy's 'write what you know' approach and drew vignettes of his isolation and disenchantment in California, meltdowns in Berlin and, in at least one case, immediate problems. One night Angie turned up with her boyfriend, Roy Martin, resulting in a spectacular fight, and a new lyric – 'Breaking Glass' – was born.

Bowie's dented Mercedes provided another. Months before, Bowie was convinced that a coke dealer had ripped him off and set off in hot pursuit, repeatedly ramming the car from behind. Bowie eventually gave up the chase and returned to the hotel where he reached, in his words, "some kind of spiritual impasse" and proceeded to race round and round the hotel garage. As he contemplated letting go of the wheel, the Merc sputtered to a standstill.

Tony Visconti (2001)

I remember David wrote a third verse to 'Always Crashing In The Same Car' and sang it in the style of Bob Dylan. It was done half in jest, but we were a little freaked because Dylan had just been in that motorcycle accident and this seemed like bad taste, I guess. David asked me to erase it and I did. I can't recall there being any alternative lyrics to any other songs. [105]

Two and a half weeks later, the basic backing tracks were complete, Murray and Davis had gone home, leaving Gardiner and Young to work on solos and overdubs.

Around this time Eno arrived and the next recording phase began with a reviewing of the soundtrack tapes, which Bowie played to the remaining musicians as a possible starting point, although little of the film music made it onto *Low* in the end. They would basically start from scratch. He explained, "We don't know if this will ever be released, but I have to do this."

ABOVE: Incidents occurring – Angie's visit to the studio with her boyfriend led to a fight that inspired Bowie to write 'Breaking Glass' and the plaintive 'Be My Wife'.

Tony Visconti (2009)

We had defined it as an experiment. Before we went in, we said this might be a waste of a month of our lives. And it was three weeks before we knew it was working. [045]

Bowie (1978)

We didn't expect anything. We were really excited when we had some very good material and we sort of, just lumped it together and I called it* Low. *I'd been interested in how remote you can get with traditional methods of writing, but it hadn't occurred to me to take the plunge and try to evolve myself. I was very cautious about getting into deep water in areas that I didn't feel that I was competent, but I was given a shoulder to lean on with Brian. [338]

Brian Eno (1980)

The way he worked impressed me a lot. Because it reminds me of me. He'd go out into the studio to do something, and he'd just come back hopping up and down with joy. And whenever I see someone doing that, I just trust that reaction. It means that they really are surprising themselves. [006]

Bowie had to leave the sessions for four days to negotiate a settlement with Michael Lippman's legal representatives at the Hotel Raphael in Paris, although in 1999 Eno remembered it as a dispute with Angie over custody of Zowie.

Eno was only at the Château for a week, so he used the downtime to start work on an instrumental on the understanding that if they didn't develop it for the album, Eno would use it for himself and pay for the studio time. Inspired by a three-note figure he heard Visconti's son Morgan picking out on the living room piano, Eno laid the groundwork for 'Warszawa', as it became when Bowie returned and commented that it reminded him of a Polish choir he had once heard. Accordingly, he added some phonetic speech, which they slowed down and pitch-shifted. The result sounded to Bowie like "a 12-year-old Polish boy glorifying the Socialist state".

Bowie (1977)

It was a phonetic language, it doesn't exist – just sounds. But it seemed to capture the feeling between East and West, West Germany and Poland. The different kinds of tension. [186]

Disconsolate and stressed from the legal meetings, Bowie relied on Visconti and Eno for motivation. Iggy buoyed him up with humour, telling outrageous stories that they eventually decided to record for posterity.

Tony Visconti (1977)

His mood was far from optimistic. It was absolutely the worst. A lot of things were happening to him, and we had a lot of setbacks. [306]

Apart from the dire state of Bowie's finances (his first cheque to the Château bounced), his management and his marriage, there were reports of ghosts and food poisoning.

Tony Visconti (2001)

We would get ravenous at night so we'd eat this cheese that they left out uncovered since dinner. David and I got food poisoning as a result. Even the French doctor couldn't be bothered to look at me because I got out of bed to request that he see me after David. He said, "He's okay, he can walk!" David shared his medicine with me.

There was certainly some strange energy in that Château. On the first day David took one look at the master bedroom and said, "I'm not sleeping in there!" He took the room next door. [105]

Bowie (2001)

It was a spooky place. I did refuse one bedroom, as it felt impossibly cold in certain areas of it. To my knowledge though, the place itself had no bearing on the form or tonality of the work. The studio itself was a joy, ramshackle and comfy feeling. I liked the room a lot. [105]

On top of this, Visconti had issues with Thibault, as did Bowie who accused him of leaking session information to *Rock et Folk* magazine. Bowie decided to complete the album in Berlin.

SATURDAY 25 SEPTEMBER

◆ **AWARDS**

'MELODY MAKER' READERS' POP POLL

UK Male Singer #3

International Male Singer #4

OCTOBER

▲ RECORDING
Hansa Tonstudio 1
Kurfürstendamm/
Hansa Tonstudio 2
Köthenerstrasse 38
West Berlin, West Germany

'LOW' ALBUM

With house engineer Edu Meyer, Bowie and Visconti continued recording for a week and a half, completing 'Weeping Wall', 'Subterraneans' and 'Art Decade', for which Bowie coaxed a cello part from classically trained Meyer.

Bowie (1977)
On Low, the subject I was dealing with was so intangible to actually talk about, it was preferable to try and put it into music rather than words. I'm not well-equipped enough or articulate enough to put the experience into lyrics really. It's really about that whole area of Poland/Germany/Austria where the album was recorded. It was a very new feeling and experience being there... because I hadn't been there very much before. Really it was a first experience with that part of the world and that is what came out. [234]

ABOVE AND OPPOSITE: Hansa Tonstudio 2 – the Meistersaal – on the Köthenerstrasse, now restored to its former grandeur. Situated by the Berlin Wall, the building was derelict for most of the Second World War and still largely decrepit in 1976 and 1977 when Bowie worked there on *Low*, *Lust For Life* and *"Heroes"*.

Bowie (1977)
'Warszawa' is about Warsaw and the very bleak atmosphere I got from the city. 'Art Decade' is West Berlin – a city cut off from its world, art and culture, dying with no hope of retribution. 'Weeping Wall' is about the Berlin Wall – the misery of it. And 'Subterraneans' is about the people who got caught in East Berlin after the separation – hence the faint jazz saxophones representing the memory of what it was. [186]

Tony Visconti (2002)
We loved Berlin. David was living there now. He was pleased that he could go out in public unmolested. During Low *I gave David and Iggy very close-cropped haircuts, and the moustache David sported during this period made him hardly recognisable. There were great clubs to go to, fabulous restaurants, and plenty of German friends to share these days of stability and upbeat moods.* [421]

NOVEMBER

SATURDAY 20

PRESS

'Melody Maker' reported:

A new David Bowie album New Music: Night And Day *is scheduled by RCA in January. The album – the first Bowie studio record since the highly-acclaimed* Station To Station *came out at the start of this year – has been recorded at the Château d'Hérouville, France and also features Eno, Ricky Gardiner, Carlos Alomar, Roy Young and Dennis Davis.*

It is currently being mixed in Berlin, and Bowie is designing the cover himself. A spokesman for RCA told Melody Maker *that one half of the record represents "a new departure" for Bowie. It is understood there are several instrumental tracks.*

"Bowie usually does his final mix," quipped an RCA operative, "after the first 10,000 albums are shipped. He's never satisfied." [289]

DECEMBER

BUSINESS

When Bowie sent the masters of the new album to RCA in time for its January release, RCA was likely anticipating something that would capitalise on the successes of 1976. Executives were dumbfounded to discover the record contained nothing resembling a hit.

Initially RCA set up a meeting with Bowie to discuss the album. They told him the album was not marketable in its present state and asked how it might be fixed. One executive famously promised him a house in Philadelphia if he'd record another *Young Americans*.

Bowie was adamant that there was nothing to fix – he saw no problems with it and the fact that it had no commercial potential did not concern him. RCA told him in that case they would not invest any money in it, not even to press the record. Bowie could keep his masters as they had no use for them – they would not be releasing the album.

Following the stand-off, Bowie was both furious and perplexed since the company had been supportive in the past. He believed strongly in the album and, since he'd spent much of the year in litigation, he decided to fight for this too. After receiving legal advice, he was able to point out that, under the terms of the contract, RCA was obliged to release the album.

JANUARY

SATURDAY 8

▼SOCIALISING

Bowie celebrated his 30th birthday with Iggy, Romy Haag, Coco, Pat Gibbons and friends at L'Ange Bleu in Paris.

FRIDAY 14 JANUARY

■ ALBUM RELEASED

'LOW'

UK (RCA PL 12030)
UK Chart Peak No.2
US Chart Peak No.11

SIDE ONE

1. **'Speed Of Life'** (2:46)
2. **'Breaking Glass'** (1:52)
3. **'What In The World'** (2:23)
4. **'Sound And Vision'** (3:05)
5. **'Always Crashing In The Same Car'** (3:33)
6. **'Be My Wife'** (2:58)
7. **'A New Career In A New Town'** (2:53)

SIDE TWO

1. **'Warszawa'** (6:17)
2. **'Art Decade'** (3:43)
3. **'Weeping Wall'** (3:25)
4. **'Subterraneans'** (5:37)

All songs by David Bowie except 'Breaking Glass'(Bowie/Davis/Murray)/ 'Warszawa' (Bowie/Eno)

David Bowie/Tony Visconti: Producers

David Bowie: Vocals/ARP/ Tape Horn/Brass/Synthetic Strings/ Saxophones/Tape Cellos/Guitar/ Pump Bass/Harmonica/Piano/ Pre-arranged Percussion/Chamberlin

Brian Eno: Vocals/Report ARP/ Splinter Mini-Moog/Piano/Keyboards/ Guitar Treatments/Synthetics/ Chamberlin/Other Synthesisers

Carlos Alomar: Rhythm Guitar

Dennis Davis: Percussion

George Murray: Bass

Ricky Gardiner: Guitar

Roy Young: Piano/Farfisa Organ

J Peter Robinson/Paul Buckmaster (Peter/Paul): Piano/ARP Synthesiser on 'Subterraneans'

ABOVE: Bowie sent a copy of *Low* to Nic Roeg with a note - "This was the music I would have done for *The Man Who Fell To Earth*," and illustrated the point with a treated still from the film on the cover.

Eduard Meyer: Cellos

Mary Visconti 'Sound And Vision'/ Iggy Pop 'What In The World': Backing Vocals

David Bowie: Cover Designer

Steve Schapiro: Photographer

Recorded at the Château & Hansa By The Wall, West Berlin, West Germany

Mixed at Hansa By The Wall

REISSUES

▮CD (RCA 1984).

▮CD (remastered) (Ryko 1991).

BONUS TRACKS

1. 'Some Are' (3:24)
2. 'All Saints' (3:25)
3. 'Sound And Vision' (1991 remix) (4:43)

▮CD (remastered) (EMI 1999).

▮CD (mini LP replica) (Toshiba EMI 2007).

At the last minute Bowie decided to change the title from *New Music: Night And Day* to *Low*.

Bowie (1977)

Really the reason was very corny. You see the album cover has a profile of me on it, and on the album itself I keep a very 'low profile'. I was very disappointed no one picked up on that. I thought it would have been obvious. [234]

Following his dispute with RCA over *Low*'s release, Bowie refused all interview requests, saying: "It doesn't need to be discussed. It speaks for itself."

Although several critics found it incomprehensible, just as many were intrigued by Bowie's attempt to make a new kind of music. *Record Mirror*'s Tim Lott concluded his review: "So. This album might be Bowie's best ever. Eno's best ever. A mechanical classic."

Bowie (1978)

It was received with caution when it came out. I didn't expect otherwise. I certainly didn't expect people to embrace it with open arms as the long lost 'new language of music'. And I realise I might be alienating a lot of people that had maybe only recently got into the idea that I change from record to record. I'd gathered a whole lot of new people listening to me at the* Young Americans *stage which I was worried about because I hoped that they didn't expect that, that was it – that I was going to continue from there and that's what I was, so I knew I'd lose a few of them on the way. [338]

Bowie (1989)

I was a very different guy by then. I mean, I'd gone through my major drug period and Berlin was my way of escaping from that and trying to work out how you live without drugs. It's very hard. You're up and down all the time, vacillating constantly. It's a very tough period to get through. So my concern with* Low *was not about the music. The music was literally expressing my physical and emotional state… and that was my worry.

So the music was almost therapeutic. It was like, "Oh yeah, we've made an album and it sounds like this." But it was a by-product of my life. It just sort of came out. I never spoke to the record company about it. I never talked to anybody about it. I just made this album… in a rehab state. A dreadful state really. [110]

Circus magazine discussed the album with an RCA rep and Bowie's PR, Barbara DeWitt – usually an unseen presence in interviews. She described side one as "Fantastic. Strange, but very commercial. Very Bowie. He's very anxious to hear what everybody's going to have to say about it."

"It's avant-garde," the RCA rep remarked. "It's ambitious. Frankly, I think it needs more work."

"When you say avant-garde," DeWitt protested, "you fall into a category of no melodies, very bizarre-sounding stuff, and it's not like that at all. Some of it is very pretty, some of it is very up…" [289]

SATURDAY 15 JANUARY

■ CHART

RCA's initial response to *Low* had been "What are we going to do with this?", but when *Circus* asked the RCA rep the same question he replied, "Bowie albums sell themselves." In the event the latter was true and there was no need to do anything. Bowie's conviction (or obstinacy) was vindicated when *Low* entered the UK Top 30 at No.25, charting for 18 weeks and peaking at No.2. Having refused to promote *Low*, Bowie then persuaded RCA to sign Iggy to a three-album recording contract, the first release being *The Idiot*. Bowie would tour that instead.

◆ AWARDS

For his performance in *The Man Who Fell To Earth*, Bowie was named Best Actor of 1976 (shared with Gregory Peck for *The Omen*) at the annual Golden Scroll Awards, presented by The Academy of Science Fiction, Fantasy and Horror Films at the Directors Guild Theater in Hollywood.

SATURDAY 29 JANUARY

✪ PRESS

Melody Maker reported "plans are afoot for both David Bowie and Iggy Pop, whom he now manages, to appear in Britain this year. Bowie wants to do a tour in the autumn with Brian Eno on keyboards, Tony Visconti on bass and Ricky Gardiner on guitar."

On March 5 'Bowie Writes' appeared on the letters page in *Melody Maker*. "I would like to correct the misconception that Iggy Pop is managed by myself. Iggy looks after his own business affairs. I would appreciate a printed correction. – David Bowie, Berlin." [201]

In April, Bowie told *RAM* magazine, "That's amazingly false. I wouldn't wish that on *anyone*… no, I haven't got a manager and Jimmy hasn't a manager. We're the only ones I think who've broken away… no, John Lennon has too… he's broken away from all that too. Who needs them? We look after ourselves." [234]

With Bowie refusing interview requests, Michael Watts turned to Tony Visconti and Brian Eno to shed light on *Low*'s creation. Visconti described how he became involved in the sessions.

"He was trying to produce Jimmy's album [*The Idiot*] at the Château but he said the engineers were proving hopeless." Visconti was referring to Thibault, with whom he'd clashed while making *Low*.

"We found the studio totally useless. The people who own it don't seem to care. We all came down with dysentery. David and I were in bed for two days." [306]

On March 12, *Melody Maker* published a rebuttal from the Château's studio manager Pierre Calamel.

"Yes, Mr Visconti, 'The Château's hopeless engineer' went to record and to mix in Munich on David Bowie's special request. Yes, Mr Visconti, this is now the fourth time that David Bowie has come to what you called a 'useless studio'. No, Mr Visconti, neither you nor anyone came down with dysentery as the doctor told you here." [202]

FEBRUARY

FRIDAY 11

■ SINGLE RELEASED

'Sound And Vision' (3:00)/
'A New Career In A New Town' (2:50)
UK (RCA PB 0905)
Chart Peak No.3

SATURDAY 12 FEBRUARY

■ CHART

'LOW'
UK Album Chart Peak No.2

▲ REHEARSING

UFA Studios
West Berlin, West Germany

Ricky Gardiner arrived in Berlin to join rehearsals for the Iggy tour as UK dates were announced. For the rhythm section Bowie called in two of Iggy's LA friends, Hunt and Tony Sales, who had been sending him demo tapes periodically since he met them in New York. Sons of comedian Soupy Sales, the Sales brothers had grown up around the Sinatra scene and played for the mob-connected Roulette label run by Morris Levy.

Hunt Sales (1991)

Me and my brother Tony first met David in the back room of Max's Kansas City when we were working with Todd Rundgren in the ill-fated Utopia. David had come over to our table to say hello, possibly because Tony had pink hair and I had black hair with a white stripe down the middle, like a skunk. David gave us some passes to see his Ziggy show at Radio City, and I thought it was amazing. I didn't see or speak to him again until '75 or '76. I was laying around in LA when I got a phone call from Iggy Pop, whom David had scraped off the street. Iggy and I once hung together in LA, and he thought of me and my brother when he got a shot to make the record with David. [090]

Tangerine Dream's Peter Baumann lent them The Vic, their rehearsal studio on Viktoriastrasse, which was soon to be demolished. The converted screening room was part of one of the UFA studios, which had produced such films as Fritz Lang's *Metropolis*. The studio was later co-opted by Goebbels to produce Nazi propaganda pictures. The band members found some old filing cabinets full of dusty film reels and Weimar era paperwork, which they rummaged through.

Iggy Pop (1982)

Many, many great films were made at UFA. They still had all these wonderful German Expressionist films just sitting in cans rotting, because they still can't figure out the politics of who should get them. You could smell the film slowly going bad. [035]

SATURDAY 19 FEBRUARY

■ CHART

'Sound And Vision'
UK Top 30 Chart Entry No.29
Charting 11 weeks

MARCH

IGGY POP
'THE IDIOT' TOUR

Iggy Pop: Vocals
Ricky Gardiner: Guitar
Tony Sales: Bass
Hunt Sales: Drums
David Bowie: Keyboards/Backing Vocals
The Vibrators: Support Act (UK)
Blondie: Support Act (Canada/USA)

The initial press announcement omitted the fact that Bowie would be playing keyboards on the tour – though rumours spread of his involvement – as Bowie wanted the focus squarely on Iggy.

Bowie (1978)
He encouraged me to play piano with him and I thought the idea was thoroughly enticing and very tempting and I did it for the nerve of it, really. I never enjoyed a tour so much, because I had no responsibilities on my shoulders at all. I mean I just had to sit there, drink a bit, have a cigarette, wink at the band, I mean y'know, and watch him. [293]

Tony Sales (2010)
It was a very loving relationship in a sense. David was at a place where he needed to recharge and got behind Iggy – and in return that helped him [Bowie], taking the pressure off being David Bowie. [045]

Bowie (1993)
It was the first time I'd ever really put myself into a band since the Spiders. It was great not having the pressure of being the singer up front. But there were too many drugs around at the time. I was trying to get away from those drugs and I was going through these really ambivalent things because I kept wanting to leave the tour to get off drugs. The drug use was unbelievable and I knew it was killing me, so that was a difficult side of it. But the playing was fun. Iggy would be preening himself before he went on and I'd be sitting there reading a book. [111]

THIS SPREAD: Iggy and Bowie at the Hippodrome in Birmingham. OVERLEAF: Bowie exits the Rainbow Theatre stagedoor with Tony Mascia and Stuart George.

TUESDAY 1 MARCH

★ LIVE
Friars
Vale Hall
Civic Centre
Aylesbury
Buckinghamshire, England

In the Gun Bar of the Bell Hotel, nearby in Market Square, Bowie spent the afternoon waiting for the band. After delays getting the equipment through customs they arrived late. Bowie saw the queue at the hall getting longer and told promoter David Stopps, "Just let them in. We'll forget the soundcheck."

David Stopps (1999)
He said it was more important that they come in out of the rain, rather than keep the audience out while they did a soundcheck. When people realised David was the keyboard player, the entire audience shifted to one side of the venue. [004]

Jim Evans (*Daily Mirror*)
His performance was interesting if not totally enjoyable. It was difficult to hear exactly what he was trying to sing at times although he managed to express himself perfectly in other ways – with his body. Without Bowie's presence, the concert would have become boring. His musicianship managed to lift it above tedium.

WEDNESDAY 2 MARCH

★ LIVE
Newcastle City Hall
Newcastle upon Tyne
Tyne and Wear, England

THURSDAY 3 MARCH

★ LIVE
Apollo
Manchester
Lancashire, England

FRIDAY 4 MARCH

★ LIVE
Hippodrome
Birmingham
West Midlands, England

SATURDAY 5 MARCH

★ LIVE

Rainbow Theatre
Finsbury Park
North London, England

'Raw Power'/'TV Eye'/'Dirt'/'1969'/'Turn Blue'/'Funtime'/'Gimme Danger'/'No Fun'/'Sister Midnight'/'I Need Somebody'/'Search And Destroy'/'I Wanna Be Your Dog'/'Tonight'/'Some Weird Sin'/'China Girl'

Iggy's first London show was marred by scuffles between the crowd and security as Bowie and the group came on stage and the audience rushed to the front. Fans were ejected and seats were damaged.

For the London dates, Iggy checked into the Montcalm Hotel, while Bowie stayed with Marc Bolan at his house at 142 Upper Richmond Road West, hanging around nearby King's Road and dining at Toscanini's. Bolan was still telling reporters that he and Bowie were working together on a film, with Bowie writing the script and Bolan the soundtrack.

"I hope it's going to be out in the year," he told *Record Mirror* in April. "All I can tell you is that it's about a future society and reflects our own feelings. We're also bringing out an album, doing a side each. What a combination it's going to be, the two greatest musical influences of the Seventies joined together."

By some accounts Bowie and Bolan recorded a rough demo during this time – 'Madman' – which was released on a Bolan fan club cassette. In 1980 Cuddly Toys released their cover of the song on Fresh Records.

NKLER
VALVE

MONDAY 7 MARCH

★ LIVE

Rainbow Theatre
Finsbury Park
North London, England

Howard Devoto of Buzzcocks handed Iggy a copy of their record, *Spiral Scratch*, saying, "I've got all your records, now you've got all mine."

Bowie (1987)

Johnny [Rotten] and Sid [Vicious] – they individually turned up to different shows, you know? 'Cause, I mean, they just worshipped the ground that Iggy... spat on. [184]

THURSDAY 10 MARCH

▶ TRAVELLING

Bowie, Iggy and Andy Kent flew from Heathrow to New York to begin the US leg of the tour. For the first time since 1972, Bowie conquered his fear of flying, having realised that a boat to America would take seven days.

Bowie (1984)

The first gig was in four days... I thought, well, I've got to take a plane. It's the only way I can get over there in time. So I thought, sod it. So I took a plane, and it was all right. [012]

▼ SOCIALISING

That night Bowie and Iggy dropped in to Mickey Ruskin's Lower Manhattan Ocean Club in Chambers Street, where The Patti Smith Group were performing (without Patti Smith, who was recuperating after falling off the stage in Tampa). Bowie told Lisa Robinson, "I flew for the first time in five or six years. I think the airplane really is a wonderful invention." Taking in the atmosphere of the club packed with local musicians, Bowie observed, "This is like the early London scene." [256]

TOP RIGHT: Iggy (in a Rainbow Theatre T-shirt) and Bowie ride the TWA buggy for their flight from Heathrow to New York. BOTTOM RIGHT: At the Lower Manhattan Ocean Club: Iggy, Cyrinda Foxe, Bowie and Lisa Robinson, with Nancy Spungen behind.

"It's strange to be playing without Patti," guitarist Lenny Kaye announced, "but she sends her love and she'll be back real soon." They launched into a set of rock'n'roll nuggets with special guest vocalists including David Johansen. Then Iggy ripped off his jacket, shoes and sunglasses and took the stage to belt out '96 Tears'. Robinson noted that Bowie smiled "like a proud father" as the audience erupted.

Afterwards Bowie talked to the band in the basement dressing room and took Polaroids of Cyrinda Foxe and Johansen. When someone observed that The Eagles would be performing in New York the same night as Iggy (the 18th), Bowie joked, "I thought Blondie was opening for us."

Clem Burke (Blondie) (1978)

We got word that we were going to do the Iggy tour and we were totally floored. This was just coming from playing clubs twice a month in New York. David Bowie had heard our album while he was in Berlin and wanted us to do the tour. We got to know Iggy really well... we learned a lot from him, and David would help us too. Like we'd be doing a soundcheck and he would prop his head on his elbows right in front of Debbie and take in the whole thing. He'd give us suggestions, too. [001]

Clem Burke (1980)

We used to tell Bowie to comb his hair down in little bangs, like Debbie, and this was at a time when his hair was swept back in that pompadour look. Then one night he came to the side of the stage waiting to go on, and his hair was in these little bangs. He said, "This is my Tom Verlaine look. How do you like it?" [128]

FRIDAY 11 MARCH

Iggy flew to Toronto to appear on Peter Gzowski's CBC television talk show. He had planned to perform but the American Federation of Musicians ruled it out. Iggy settled instead for a show of attitude, which Gzowski said afterwards was just an act, because backstage Iggy Pop was "quite a pleasant young guy". Meanwhile, Blondie finished their New York dates with a 2am show at Max's, before travelling up to Canada in their Winnebago tour bus to join Iggy.

SATURDAY 12 MARCH

■ **CHART**

'Sound And Vision'
UK Chart Peak No.3

▶ **TRAVELLING**

NEW YORK – MONTREAL

Bowie travelled by limo to Montreal for the first date of the Iggy Pop US/Canada tour.

SUNDAY 13 MARCH

★ **LIVE**

Le Plateau Theatre
Montreal
Quebec, Canada

MONDAY 14 MARCH

★ **LIVE**

Seneca College
Toronto
Ontario, Canada

WEDNESDAY 16 MARCH

★ **LIVE**

Harvard Square Theatre
Boston
Massachusetts, USA

FRIDAY 18 MARCH

★ **LIVE**

New York Palladium
New York City
New York, USA

Bob Gruen (2004)

Bowie was kind of dark in the background, not spotlighted, not highlighted. He was the piano player. It was kind of funny. People were going, "Who is this guy Iggy Pop, who has Bowie as his piano player?" It suddenly gave him a lot of respect, a lot of attention. [001]

The Rolling Stones were in New York for a band meeting in the wake of the Toronto drug bust. Mick Jagger, Ron Wood, Bill Wyman and their wives came to the Palladium show.

✪ **PHOTO SESSION**

During the day Wood joined Bowie and Iggy for a photo session with Milton H Greene, another legendary Hollywood photographer who, like Tom Kelley, made his name shooting Marilyn Monroe.

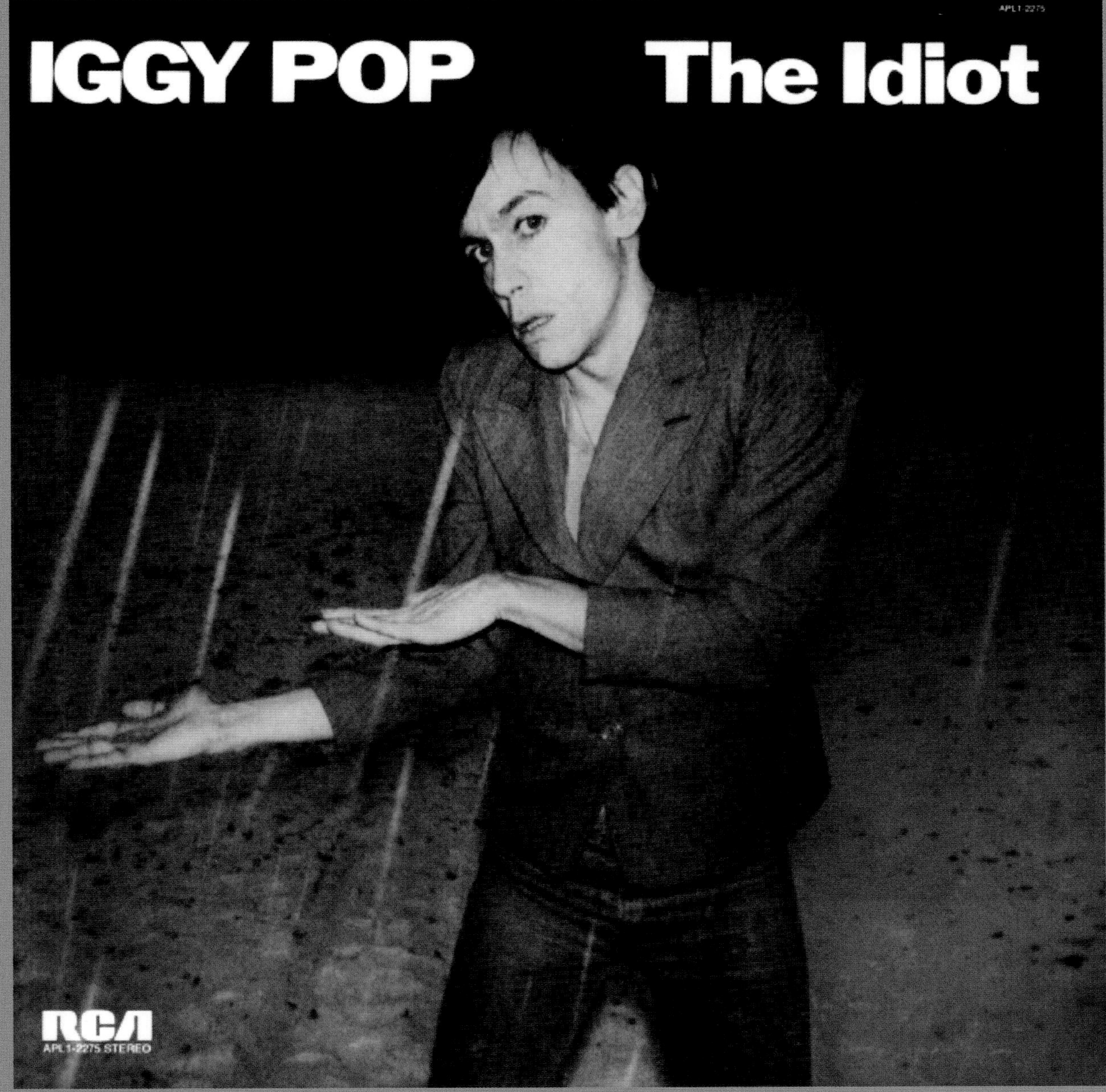

ABOVE: Bowie and Iggy had planned to use – and even acquired the reproduction rights to – Erich Heckel's *Roquairol* painting for the cover. They decided instead to have Andy Kent photograph Iggy in the same pose, wearing a jacket he borrowed from girlfriend Esther Friedman.

■ **ALBUM RELEASED**

IGGY POP
'THE IDIOT'
(RCA PL 12275)
UK Chart Peak No.30
US Chart Peak No.72

SIDE ONE
1. **'Sister Midnight'** (4:23)
2. **'Nightclubbing'** (4:18)
3. **'Funtime'** (2:53)
4. **'Baby'** (3:20)
5. **'China Girl'** (5:12)

SIDE TWO
1. **'Dum Dum Boys'** (7:12)
2. **'Tiny Girls'** (3:03)
3. **'Mass Production'** (8:28)

All songs written by Iggy Pop and David Bowie except 'Sister Midnight' (Pop/Bowie/Alomar)

David Bowie: Producer
Iggy Pop: Vocals
David Bowie: Keyboards/Synthesiser/Guitar/Piano/Saxophone/Xylophone/Backing Vocals
Carlos Alomar: Guitar
Dennis Davis: Drums
George Murray: Bass
Phil Palmer: Guitar
Michel Santangeli: Drums
Laurent Thibault: Bass
Andrew Kent: Photographer
Recorded at Château d'Hérouville, Hérouville, France/
Musicland Studios, Munich, West Germany/
Hansa by the Wall, West Berlin, West Germany

ABOVE: Iggy, Ricky Gardiner and Bowie at Berkeley Community Theatre, San Francisco. OPPOSITE: Tower Theatre, Philadelphia.

SATURDAY 19 MARCH

★ LIVE

Tower Theatre
Philadelphia
Pennsylvania, USA

MONDAY 21 – WEDNESDAY 23 MARCH

★ LIVE

Agora Ballroom
Cleveland
Ohio, USA

Members of Akron band Devo were in the audience. Around this time Bowie was given their demo tape by the wife of Michael Aylward, guitarist from Akron band Tin Huey. Bowie initially put it aside until Iggy recommended he listen to it.

▮'TV Eye', 'Dirt' and 'Funtime' released on *TV Eye: 1977 Live.*

FRIDAY 25 MARCH

★ LIVE

Masonic Temple
Detroit
Michigan, USA

Iggy's parents brought his nine- year-old son Eric to see his sold-out hometown show.

SATURDAY 26 MARCH

★ LIVE

Masonic Temple
Detroit
Michigan, USA

SUNDAY 27 MARCH

★ LIVE

Riviera Theatre
Chicago
Illinois, USA

MONDAY 28 MARCH

★ LIVE

Riviera Theatre
Chicago
Illinois, USA

▮'I Wanna Be Your Dog' released on *TV Eye: 1977 Live.*

TUESDAY 29 MARCH

★ LIVE

Leona Theatre
Pittsburgh
Pennsylvania, USA

WEDNESDAY 30 MARCH

★ LIVE

Agora Ballroom
Columbus
Ohio, USA

THURSDAY 31 MARCH

★ LIVE

Taft Auditorium
Cincinnati
Ohio, USA

APRIL

FRIDAY 1

★ LIVE

Oriental Theatre
Milwaukee
Wisconsin, USA

MONDAY 4 TUESDAY 5 APRIL

★ LIVE

Paramount Theatre
Portland
Oregon, USA

THURSDAY 7 APRIL

★ LIVE

Vancouver Gardens
Vancouver
British Columbia, Canada

SATURDAY 9 APRIL

★ LIVE

Paramount Theatre
Seattle
Washington, USA

WEDNESDAY 13 APRIL

★ LIVE

Berkeley Community Theatre
San Francisco
California, USA

FRIDAY 15 APRIL

✪ TELEVISION

CBS Television City
7800 Beverly Boulevard
Fairfax, Los Angeles
California, USA

'DINAH!' (CBS)
David Bowie and Iggy Pop interview/ 'Sister Midnight'/'Funtime'

SHORE: *Where did you meet?*

POP: *In a bar in New York. We were both unrecognised at the time. So we had a lot in common.*

BOWIE: *What Jimmy was doing… I'd never seen Jimmy really but I'd heard some of his albums. It sounded like, uh… nihilistic rock. It was nihilism, which fascinates me. I love nihilism!*

POP: *My music is just basically, I look for things to tear apart.*

BOWIE: *In the studio, Jimmy would make up the lyrics on the spot and keep everything that he did and occasionally change a line after we recorded. I'd never seen anybody be able to make lyrics up so fast, just out of his head for a track. And it's more like – he'll hate me – the beatnik era. Jimmy and I collaborated because I was intoxicated with what I thought he stood for and I never want it to be thought that I'm some kind of hand manipulator or Svengali behind what Jimmy's doing now because he's getting popular now. It's only because he was six years too early with what he was doing with The Stooges.* [357]

▮ Broadcast: May 6 (CBS).

★ LIVE

Civic Auditorium
Santa Monica
California, USA

▼ SOCIALISING

After the show, Bowie spent the rest of the evening carousing with Mick Jagger at a cabaret, where they heckled one of the acts.

SATURDAY 16 APRIL

★ LIVE

Civic Auditorium
San Diego
California, USA

In the audience for the last show of the tour was Gary Heffern, who was inspired that night to start punk band The Penetrators.

Gary Heffern (2010)

I was in the audience, in the second row, and Iggy came out and gave the microphone to the guy next to me, Tom Griswold. Tom wouldn't sing, so I grabbed it and started singing ['96 Tears'] and wouldn't give Iggy the microphone back! I was looking directly at Bowie, who was singing back-up vocals. I knew then that I had to sing. [385]

ABOVE: Bowie faces the press at the Hotel New Otani, April 25.
OVERLEAF: Bowie at Victor Vasarely's workshop at Annet-sur-Marne, near Paris.

MID-APRIL

Hotel New Otani
Chiyoda-Ku
Tokyo, Japan

Bowie and Iggy arrived in Tokyo with Coco for a two-week holiday and some interviews to promote *The Idiot*.

Some 5,000 Japanese fans mobbed them at the airport and Bowie had to be rescued by a large security guard, who picked him up and carried him over the heads of the crowd.

They stayed at the Hotel New Otani, famous for the 400-year-old Japanese garden on its premises.

THURSDAY 21 APRIL

▼SOCIALISING

Iggy celebrated his 30th birthday with Bowie and Coco in their hotel room in Tokyo

SATURDAY 23 APRIL

✪ PRESS

Hotel New Otani
Chiyoda-Ku
Tokyo, Japan

Hideaki Okada from *Music Life* magazine interviewed Iggy and Bowie at Hotel New Otani. Although Iggy was largely unknown in Japan, Okada was familiar with his music and history and noted how confident and positive Iggy now looked.

Asked about the years since *Raw Power*, Iggy went quiet. "I lived like Dorian Gray. Now I'm into German Expressionism."

They discussed the aggression in his music and whether it figured in *The Idiot*. Iggy explained that the violence was explicit on the earlier records but implicit on *The Idiot*.

"The theme of the album is the story of man torn apart in his heart between his need for what you call egotism and animalism and desire to be human. But when he indulges in human things he's consistently disappointed. I got that from reading the lyrics on the back of the album."

Bowie had been refusing interviews. To Okada's surprise, he agreed to be interviewed for the next half hour. Okada hadn't recognised Bowie at first, as he was so "cheerful, clean and elegant". Bowie ordered drinks from room service and they talked about *Low*. When Okada remarked on the departure from American music, Bowie explained that America had gone from a dreamland to a nightmare-land for him, that he was expected to be an entertainer and he was losing his sense of self. Okada pointed out,"But didn't you say that you wanted to be like Frank Sinatra?" Bowie laughed, "In this business you have to say stupid things sometimes."

MONDAY 25 APRIL

✪ PRESS

Hotel New Otani
Chiyoda-Ku
Tokyo, Japan

Bowie told the assembled media, "The album *Low* was the effect of Europe upon me having lived in Europe for nine months. Everything I write has a lot to do with the environment that I live in because that's all I can write about. It's much easier to live here. That's why I don't live in America or England."

Asked about the difference between Western and Eastern markets, Bowie said, "I only know about teenagers, I don't know about markets. Remember we are here on holiday so we've not… the only thing I've noticed is that we get mobbed here more than we do in America or England."

LATE APRIL

✪ PHOTO SESSION
Masayoshi Sukita
Harajuku Studio
Tokyo, Japan

"HEROES" ALBUM COVER

Masayoshi Sukita brought Bowie and Iggy to Harajuku Studio where stylist Yasuko 'Yacco' Takahashi assisted with the photo shoot.

Masayoshi Sukita (2011)
The photos were meant to have a 'punk' feel. David-san had asked Yacco to get as many leather jackets as possible and instead of shooting on a straight white background, I included the door edge to break the image up and give a rougher feel.

Elegantly wearing several layers of leather jackets, it reminded me of Kenneth Anger's movie* Scorpio Rising. *The whole session was over in an hour. Afterwards, I selected about 20 photos to give to David-san, including the shot on the "Heroes" LP sleeve. When he contacted me to say he wanted to use it, I was delighted. [042]

The session also produced several images that were used on singles and promotional material. One of the Iggy Pop portraits was used on the front cover of his *Party* album (1981).

MAY

✪ PRESS
Hotel New Otani
Chiyoda-Ku
Tokyo, Japan

While in Tokyo, Bowie was interviewed over the phone by Anthony O'Grady for *RAM* magazine.

BOWIE: *I'm coming over to Australia next year… in the spring. Been going to festivals… I'm very tired actually. I need a holiday after my holiday. Japan's a very energetic country, lots of traffic jams… takes all your energy to get through them.*

O'GRADY: *You've lost your fear of flying?*

BOWIE: *Fear of flying… fear of elevators… fear is not a word in my vocabulary any more. I am a man of great inner strength and courage these days. The flying bit ended, actually, when I had to get to America and there were no ships, so I had to, excuse the expression, take the plunge.* [234]

FRIDAY 6

■ SINGLE RELEASED
IGGY POP
'China Girl' (3:26)/
'Baby' (3:20)
UK (RCA PB 9093)

■ SINGLE RELEASED
IGGY POP
'Sister Midnight' (2:54)/
'Baby' (3:20)
US (RCA 10989)
Australia (RCA 102923)

▮ Bowie and Iggy's appearance on *Dinah!* broadcast in USA (CBS).

LATE MAY

▼ SOCIALISING
During a Hong Kong stopover, Bowie, Iggy and Coco ran into John and Sean Lennon in the foyer of the Mandarin Hotel.

Iggy Pop (2005)
We learned en route to Hong Kong that he would be there in our hotel for the same few days that we were. He was travelling with Sean, who was about two years old, and was on his way to meet Yoko in Japan. I was with David Bowie and Coco Schwab on our way back to Europe from Japan. A pair of elevator doors opened, and he stood in the hotel foyer, wearing a basketball jersey that was way too big, and he gave David a very big hug and a kind of laughing, greeting smile. I was surprised to see an English industry giant exhibit such warmth. [027]

Each night, after Lennon put Sean to bed, the trio headed out to paint the town red. They went to restaurants, dined on Peking duck and had tea at a posh country club. When service was not forthcoming, Lennon rose from his place and called out, "Have you ever heard of The Beatles?" They took in a show at a topless bar, The Sea Palace, and went swimming in the South China Sea.

JUNE

WEDNESDAY 8 – SUNDAY 12 TUESDAY 14

▲ RECORDING
Hansa Tonstudio 2
Köthenerstrasse 38
West Berlin, West Germany

IGGY POP
'LUST FOR LIFE'

Eduard Meyer: Engineer

With a new contract and a $2,500 advance from RCA, Iggy decided to move into his own apartment, a smaller one at the rear of Hauptstrasse 155.

Iggy Pop (2010)
I was living on coke, hash, red wine, beer and German sausages, had my own little place and I was sleeping on a cot with cold-water showers. [045]

Bowie (2003)
When I settled there I found the claustrophobia of the Wall almost comforting. I agree that at times it was like living in a timeless zone. No English TV to speak of, except AFN, the American Forces Network. One night, Iggy and I were sitting around when the news came on. I got hooked by the little blippy intro music and picked up a ukulele and started playing along with it. This became 'Lust For Life'. [065]

The tour band was retained for the album and were encouraged to contribute ideas. Ricky Gardiner played them a chord sequence he had thought of on a spring walk. Iggy seized on it and came back the next day with the Jim Morrison-inspired 'The Passenger'.

Iggy recalled later that he took a more assertive role than he did on *The Idiot*.

Iggy Pop (1977)
We did it quick, this record. The entire thing was done in just two weeks, including the mixing. The best of the stuff was written in about two and a half days. The music is hard, and fast, and stiff, the direct opposite of* The Idiot. *I am singing with my full range instead of just deep down low, like I did on that album.

We worked so fast that almost everything was done in one take, with only a couple of overdubs necessary because of my unusual microphone technique, and one lead guitar thing, or whatever you call it when the guitar players start doodling around with their instruments.

During the preparation and recording of the album it would appear that I was having a stronger effect on David than him on me – I think that is valid. He wanted nothing more than to be involved in one of my 'brash albums', as he called them, and I think that is a good description. But I don't want to underplay his effect. He co-wrote most of the songs and had a great deal to do with the record.

We worked very quickly together, but I don't want you to think it was all togetherness and walking hand-in-hand or anything like that. We had a lot of friction between us, and I think that's why we have done some pretty good work. [237]

✪ PRESS
Plaza Athénée Hotel
Avenue Montaigne
Paris, France

With *Lust For Life* completed, Bowie and Iggy flew to Paris to do some promotion for *Low*. Bowie stayed at the five-star Plaza Athénée Hotel on Avenue Montaigne with his PR Barbara DeWitt, whose husband Michael was Iggy's PR at the same time. Iggy stayed nearby at the Trémoille Hotel.

While in Paris, Bowie did several photo sessions with Sygma photographers Christian Simonpietri and Philippe Auliac.

▼ SOCIALISING
Bowie visited the workshop of Hungarian-French artist Victor Vasarely at Annet-sur-Marne near Paris. One of the paintings from his 'Planetary Folklore' series had featured on the cover of the 1969 *David Bowie* album.

FRIDAY 17 JUNE

■ **SINGLE RELEASED**
'Be My Wife' (2:55)/
'Speed Of Life' (2:45)
UK (RCA PB-11017)

TUESDAY 21 JUNE

✪ **PHOTO SESSION**
Plaza Athénée Hotel
Avenue Montaigne
Paris, France

Philippe Auliac: Photographer
Serge Behnamou: Assistant

SATURDAY 25 JUNE

✪ **PHOTO SESSION**
Plaza Athénée Hotel
Avenue Montaigne
Paris, France

Christian Simonpietri: Photographer

SUNDAY 26 JUNE

✪ **PHOTO SESSION**
Plaza Athénée Hotel
Avenue Montaigne
Paris, France

Jean-Claude Deutsch: Photographer

MONDAY 27 JUNE

✪ **TELEVISION**
ACTUALITÉS (TF1)
Interview with Yves Mourousi.

✪ **TELEVISION**
MIDI PREMIÈRE (TF1)
Interview with Danièle Gilbert.

TUESDAY 28 JUNE

✪ **PROMO FILM**
'Be My Wife'

Stanley Dorfman: Director

▮ Released on *The Video Collection* (PMI 1993)/*Best Of Bowie* (EMI 2002).

ABOVE AND RIGHT: Photo sessions at the Plaza Athénée Hotel with (clockwise from top left) Jean-Claude Deutsche (for *Paris Match*), Phillippe Auliac and Christian Simonpietri. OPPOSITE: Shooting the clip for 'Be My Wife' directed by Stanley Dorfman.

JULY

MONDAY 4

✪ TELEVISION

ACTUALITÉS RÉGIONALES ILE DE FRANCE (FR3)

Interview with Marie Claire Gautier.

WEDNESDAY 6 JULY

✪ PROMOTION

Gaumont Champs-Elysées Paris, France

'THE MAN WHO FELL TO EARTH' FRENCH PREMIERE

As Bowie and his companion Sydne Rome entered the theatre, a fan grabbed Bowie's scarf and wouldn't let go. Bowie surrendered it to avoid being choked. Moments later Bowie grabbed his wallet back from a pickpocket and ran inside.

Bowie later commented on the film to *International Herald Tribune*, "It's very slow. It's one of the slowest movies I've ever seen in my life. One of the saving graces is the speed it moves at."

Sydne Rome, an American actress based in Europe, was in Paris to discuss working with Bowie on the film *Wally*. Director Clive Donner was planning to make the film about Expressionist artist Egon Schiele (to be played by Bowie) and his mistress Valerie 'Wally' Neuzil in Vienna in September.

Donner never made the fim, but in 1978 Bowie and Sydne Rome worked together on *Just A Gigolo*.

RIGHT: Leaving a Paris party with Bianca Jagger. OPPOSITE: With Sydne Rome at the Gaumont Theatre in Paris for the French premiere of *L'homme qui venait d'ailleurs* (*The Man Who Fell To Earth*).

WEDNESDAY 20 JULY

✪ PRESS

Mary Blume interview:

The man in tweeds drinks beer, smokes Gitanes and has a six-year-old son who, he says, is going to be very nice. "He's into the process of living, not the result."

"[Turning 30] is the best thing that ever happened to me. Until 30 I was a dedicated artist. Now I've discovered privacy, I've lost contact. My writing's much better, my music's better, I've played more music in the last year and a half than in all my life."

His next album, not yet written, will be put together in a Berlin studio with a three-week time limit.

"I want to go with disposable music. That's a good catch phrase, music you can disregard completely. I've always been interested in muzak beyond the use it's put to in elevators so you won't be frightened when they fall down, or in airports. I like the idea of plain narrative music with a sudden gem. It's like Ayers Rock in Australia – a huge, huge rock jutting out of miles of sand. If I could write a piece of music like that rock… But I'm talking out of line because I'm not a musician as such, I haven't accomplished anything in music." [063]

▌Published: *Los Angeles Times*.

▼SOCIALISING

Bowie spent late July socialising with Bianca Jagger, who was in Paris working on the François Weyergans film *Couleur Chair* (*Flesh Colour*). They had a short holiday together at Costa del Sol in Spain where they were seen at The Marbella Club.

Speaking to the *Los Angeles Times*in September, she dismissed the inevitable rumours of an affair between them. "It's so ridiculous. I know they say ours is an open marriage, but it isn't. Mick's much too old-fashioned for that. Of course, when we're apart, the stories start. We take no notice. He trusts me. He knows I see other men, but he knows they're only friends – people I can trust and can talk to, like David Bowie." [192]

AUGUST

▲ RECORDING
Hansa Tonstudio 2
Köthenerstrasse 38
West Berlin, West Germany

"HEROES" ALBUM

Tony Visconti/Colin Thurston: Engineers

When Bowie returned to Hansa By The Wall with Tony Visconti, Brian Eno and the band, he had only one song prepared – 'Sons Of The Silent Age'. The rest of the songs – as with *Low* – evolved in the studio.

Brian Eno (1977)
David would say "Okay, it's that, that, twice as long on that, and then that – and we do this a couple of times and then back to that again." And after that very brief instruction, we'd start playing – and, in that tiny space of time, Carlos would have worked out this lovely line. He's quite remarkable. He gives those pieces a lot of character.

The whole thing was evolved on the spot in the studio. Not only that, everything on the album is a first take! I mean, we did second takes but they weren't nearly as good. [187]

Bowie (1999)
A couple were very definitely first and only takes. I think the rest were probably run at two or more times until the feel was right. With such great musicians the notes were never in doubt so we looked at 'feel' as being the priority. [106]

Brian Eno (1977)
It was all done in a very casual kind of way. We'd sort of say "Let's do this then" – and we'd do it, and then someone would say "Stop" and that would be it, the length of the piece. It seemed completely arbitrary to me. [187]

Tony Visconti (1999)
We always started these albums as making demos. That went right on until Scary Monsters. *Then we'd realise that the 'demos' needed just a little editing without re-recording. Sometimes I would take a great section and copy it and edit it into the song later on, cutting right across the 24-track tape. I wouldn't say they were first takes, we worked hard and long on each track. We didn't go into say 25 takes, but I'd say that most tracks were done in about five takes.* [105]

Eventually they decided to call on Robert Fripp, Eno's collaborator on *No Pussyfooting*, to deploy the layered guitar technique he called Frippertronics on the backing tracks.

Robert Fripp (1979)
[David] said, "We tried playing guitars ourselves; it's not working. Do you think you can come in and play some burning rock-and-roll guitar?" I said, "Well, I haven't really played guitar for three years... but I'll have a go!" [166]

Brian Eno (1977)
Fripp did everything he did in about six hours – and that was straight off the plane from New York too! He arrived at the studio at about 11pm and we said "Do you fancy doing anything?" and he said "Might as well hear what you've been doing." And while we were setting up the tapes, he got out his guitar and said "Might as well try a few things."

So I plugged him into the synthesiser for treatments and we just played virtually everything we'd done at him – and he'd just start up without even knowing the chord sequences. [187]

Robert Fripp (1979)
And the very first thing they did was put up 'Beauty And The Beast'. And I played straight over it. This is the way I did the rest of the album. They'd put up a track and I'd play. I wouldn't bother rehearsing it. I'd just play. [166]

Brian Eno (1977)
It was a very extraordinary performance. By the next day, he'd finished, packed up, and gone home. All first takes again. Incredible. [187]

Bowie (1999)
Most of my vocals were first takes, some written as I sang. Most famously 'Joe The Lion' I suppose. I would put the headphones on, stand at the mike, listen to a verse, jot down some key words that came into mind then take. Then I would repeat the same process for the next section, etc. It was something that I learnt from working with Iggy and I thought a very effective way of breaking normality in the lyric. [105]

Bowie (1977)
I had no melody, so I only sang the lines I'd written for four or five bars at a time. Having sung one line, I'd take a breath and do the same thing again, and so on to the end. I never knew the complete melody until I'd finished the song and played the whole thing back.

We spent a lot of time laughing, actually. Laughing at ourselves, laughing at our pretentiousness and at some of the stuff that came out and never got on to the album. It was rich with self-parody as well as a lot of inventive ideas. There's a sense of foreboding that one wouldn't have expected to come out of that environment, but it did. [Berlin] is not a relaxed place, certainly, and it produces a kind of nervous mirth – whistling in the dark. [129]

Bowie (1977)
Berlin is a city made up of bars for sad disillusioned people to get drunk in. One never knows how long it is going to remain there. One fancies that it is going very fast.

That's one of the reasons why I was attracted to the city. It's a feeling that I really tried to capture in the paintings while I was there, of the Turks that live in the city. There's a track on the album called 'Neukölln', and that's the area of Berlin where the Turks are shackled in bad conditions. [164]

LATE AUGUST

▲ MIXING
Mountain Studios
Montreux, Switzerland

"HEROES" ALBUM

Dave Richards/Eugene Chaplin: Assistant Engineers

OPPOSITE: 'Heroes' recording sessions at Hansa by the Wall: Robert Fripp, Colin Thurston, Bowie and Brian Eno in the control room (top) and with Fripp and Eno in the studio (bottom).

"Berlin is a city made up of bars for sad disillusioned people to get drunk in."

David Bowie

SEPTEMBER

WEDNESDAY 7

✪ TELEVISION
Granada Studios
Quay Street
Manchester
Lancashire, England

'MARC'
'Heroes'/untitled jam
(known as 'Sleeping Next To You')

Muriel Young: Producer
Nicholas Ferguson: Director
David Bowie: Vocals/Guitar
Herbie Flowers: Bass
Tony Newman: Drums
Dino Dines: Keyboards
Marc Bolan: Guitar on untitled jam ('Sleeping Next To You')

In early 1977, Marc Bolan was making a comeback of sorts. With a new band and a new album he toured the UK, with The Damned supporting to attract the audience too young to remember his heyday.

On the strength of this, Muriel Young, a friend and producer at Granada Television, commissioned Bolan to front a series of six shows (with an option to renew) for its afternoon slot. Bolan would be playing his own songs, introducing new bands and jamming with them.

OPPOSITE AND OVERLEAF: **Bowie's performance on Bolan's TV show was the first and last time they shared a stage. Bolan fell off it mid-song, bringing 'Sleeping Next To You', their hastily prepared collaboration, to a premature end. For the occasion Bolan wore a Raleigh Grifter bike t-shirt and red Mary Jane shoes, much like the pair Bowie wore on the 1974 tour.**

Chris Welch (1977)
The show was born out of Marc's dream to be a media man, dating back to when he once did some interviews for London television. Here he could invite his favourite guest artists, do a bit of chat and generally camp it up in time-honoured Bolan fashion. [316]

Bolan and Jeff Dexter (co-manager with Tony Howard) persuaded Bowie to fly over from Switzerland to Manchester to perform on the final show. Bowie would be playing with the current T. Rex line-up, which included Flowers and Newman from the *Diamond Dogs/David Live* band.

Rehearsals got under way in the morning at Granada Studios in Quay Street. After Eddie And The Hot Rods, Generation X did six run-throughs of 'Your Generation' with Bolan repeating the same introduction: "This is Generation X. They have a new singer Billy Idol, who is supposed to be as pretty as me. I ain't so sure. Check it out."

Herbie Flowers (1985)
David's appearance on the show proved Marc was a mentor to him, but David arrived with his entourage – the limo, the secretaries, his publicist, the media. So if he was acknowledging his debt to Marc, at the same time he was demonstrating his greater success. Marc was the star of the show, but he didn't have an entourage and he didn't have any hit records and David did. [016]

Cliff Wright (2012)
When David arrived Marc said to him, "This is Cliff." To me it was, "Look after David for the day, whatever he wants." Marc gave David a Fender Strat: a Sunburst with a maple neck. We set up an amp and cabinet in the studio for him, and they recorded 'Heroes' for the show. [018]

Cliff Wright (2012)
David just sat on a chair, and somehow got that feedback, it was really cool. [045]

Cliff Wright (2012)
David also wanted a bottle of red and a bottle of white. By the end of the day, Marc had got so pissed off that he wound up drinking both of them himself. [018]

Bowie and Bolan then ran through some musical ideas for the show. They recorded several takes of an untitled jam based on a Bolanesque riff that Bowie played on the borrowed guitar. Bolan practised his introduction to their first and only appearance on stage together: "Thank you very much, David Bowie… an amazing song… it's going to be a stunning smash!"

Bowie performed a live vocal 'Heroes' for the cameras, then it was time for their duet. At this point they were running behind due to delays. This was mainly due to Bowie's security barring everybody from the set, including Bolan's team and the production crew.

Jeff Dexter protested to Corinne Schwab and all hell broke loose.

Jeff Dexter (2012)
"How dare you?" I say, "Do you realise what you're doing? This is their show, not yours. It's not yours, David," I said to him when I saw him. I lost it. And then Marc lost it. [018]

After a hastily convened meeting Bolan announced, "We've got to do this." Bowie offered, "Well I didn't even know I *had* a crew throwing people out. What's going on?"

Rehearsals resumed and after a short introduction from Bolan they launched into the jam, which soon broke down when Bolan fell off the lip of the stage, much to everyone's amusement. But there was no time for a retake – it was 7pm. The floor manager, who had been barred from the studio earlier, was also the head of the union, and the regulations banned overruns on the programme. The technicians downed tools and the ending went to air as it was.

Chris Welch (1977)
I thought it funny, but I'm sure producer Muriel Young didn't, nor did the manager of Generation X, who turned up three hours late without any equipment, nor Barrie Masters and his famous Rods who never got to appear on the show after waiting around for two days. [316]

▮Broadcast: September 28 (ITV).

Afterwards Bowie took the train back from Manchester to Euston, sharing a carriage with Eddie And The Hot Rods. Tim Lott, covering the Rods tour for *Record Mirror*, lucked into an exclusive interview with Bowie.

Tim Lott (2008)
I took the train back to London with them and Bowie invited us all to join him in first class for the journey back. He thought I was a member of the band, and I didn't disabuse him of that notion. In the meantime, I noted down everything he said on a paper plate hidden under the table. Bingo – my first ever world exclusive.

I remember thinking that Bowie had a few of his pages stuck together. He talked of meeting the astronaut John Glenn, who had told him that he had seen something on the moon that he wouldn't ever tell anyone about. And Bowie seemed convinced that NASA kept a cosmic black hole confined in a small metal box in the Midwest, which, if it escaped, would swallow the whole universe. But other than that, he was extremely engaging. [186]

Back in London, Bowie and Bolan went to dinner at a Soho restaurant with Colin Thurston. Afterwards they dropped in to see Visconti at his studio, where Thurston was chief engineer.

Visconti had taken over the lease of Zodiac Studios, which had been a film studio in the Fifties. He rebuilt the original 16-track studio located in the basement of the building and re-equipped it as a 24-track, renamed Good Earth Studios.

FRIDAY 9 SEPTEMBER

■ ALBUM RELEASED

IGGY POP
'LUST FOR LIFE'
UK (RCA PL 12488)
US (AFL1-2488)
UK Chart Peak No.28
US Chart Peak No.120

SIDE ONE
1. **'Lust For Life'**(Pop/Bowie) (5:13)
2. **'Sixteen'** (Pop) (2:26)
3. **'Some Weird Sin'** (Pop/Bowie) (3:42)
4. **'The Passenger'** (Pop/Gardiner) (4:44)
5. **'Tonight'** (Pop/Bowie) (3:39)

SIDE TWO
1. **'Success'** (Pop/Bowie/Gardiner) (4:25)
2. **'Turn Blue'** (Pop/Lacey/Bowie/Peace) (6:56)
3. **'Neighbourhood Threat'** (Pop/Bowie/Gardiner) (3:25)
4. **'Fall In Love With Me'** (Pop/Sales/Sales) (6:30)

David Bowie/Iggy Pop/Colin Thurston: Producers
Iggy Pop: Vocals
David Bowie: Keyboards/Piano/Backing Vocals
Carlos Alomar/Ricky Gardiner: Guitar/Backing Vocals
Tony Sales: Bass/Backing Vocals
Hunt Sales: Drums/Backing Vocals
Andrew Kent: Photographer
Recorded at Hansa Tonstudio 2
West Berlin, West Germany

The timing of the album's release couldn't have been worse. When Elvis Presley died on August 16, RCA record presses went into overdrive to meet renewed demand for his records, most of which were out of print.

The first UK pressings of *Lust For Life* sold well but retailers could not restock as 95 per cent of the machines at RCA's UK plant in Hayes had been turned over to Elvis. As a result, *Lust For Life* stalled at No.28 in UK and barely made an impression in America.

ABOVE: Andy Kent took the cover photo for *Lust For Life* in London following a BBC radio interview in March.
BELOW AND OVERLEAF: Recording the 'Peace On Earth'/'Little Drummer Boy' duet with Bing Crosby at Elstree Studios in England.
OPPOSITE: Bowie performs 'Heroes' on Bing Crosby's Christmas special.

SUNDAY 11 SEPTEMBER

✪ TELEVISION

Elstree Studios
Hertfordshire, England

'BING CROSBY'S MERRIE OLDE CHRISTMAS'
'Heroes'/'Peace On Earth'–'Little Drummer Boy'
Duet with Bing Crosby

Gary Smith/Dwight Hemion: Producers

Bing Crosby, aged 74, was still suffering from spinal injuries following his fall into an orchestra pit in March. He arrived in London to play two weeks of concerts at the Palladium and film his annual Christmas special, this time with an English setting.

The producers booked various British guest stars, including Bowie's pin-up Twiggy. Bowie was induced to appear with the promise to include a performance of 'Heroes', which he taped at the studios, incorporating a mime sequence.

Given that the two titans of pop barely knew each other, the scriptwriter, Buz Kohan, prepared a 'getting to know you' segment set in an English country manor. Bowie and Crosby would meet and talk about their Christmas customs, such as singing carols. Bowie would choose 'Little Drummer Boy' ("my son's favourite") which they would sing as a duet.

However, when the time came, as the show's musical arranger Ian Fraser recalls, "David came in and said, 'I hate this song. Is there something else I could sing?' We didn't know quite what to do." [120]

Fraser, Kohan and songwriter Larry Grossman hastily left the set and, working on a piano in the basement, wrote 'Peace On Earth' as a counterpoint to 'Little Drummer Boy'. After less than an hour of rehearsal Crosby and Bowie performed the new arrangement, after which Crosby mused, "It's a pretty theme, isn't it?"

Bowie (1999)
I was wondering if he was still alive. He was just… not there. He was not there at all. He had the words in front of him. "Hi, Dave, nice to see ya here…" And he looked like a little old orange sitting on a stool. 'Cos he'd been made up very heavily and his skin was a bit pitted, and there was just nobody home at all, you know? It was the most bizarre experience. I didn't know anything about him. I just knew my mother liked him. [244]

Crosby later remarked, "He sings a lovely counterpoint."

Like Bolan, Crosby never saw his Bowie duet go to air. He died in Spain on October 14 directly after a round of golf (he won).

▮ Broadcast: November 30 in USA (CBS)/December 24 in UK (ITV).

FRIDAY 16 SEPTEMBER

Marc Bolan and Gloria Jones were heading home just after 5am following a night out at The Speakeasy and Morton's. After going over a humpback bridge on Queens Ride in Barnes, Jones lost control of the Mini and ran off the road into a steel-reinforced concrete post. Bolan was killed instantly – two weeks short of his 30th birthday – and Jones was hospitalised with serious injuries.

Despite singing frequently about cars, Bolan had never learnt to drive, fearing a premature death.

TUESDAY 20 SEPTEMBER

Bowie flew from Switzerland to attend Marc Bolan's funeral at Golders Green Crematorium, London, where his ashes were buried.

Bolan's manager, Tony Howard, arranged for a four-foot-high white swan sculpted in chrysanthemums to be displayed as a symbol of his biggest hit, 'Ride A White Swan'. At its base was the word Marc, traced in flowers.

Among the mourners were Rod Stewart, Elton John, Alvin Stardust, Tony Visconti, his wife Mary Hopkin, Linda Lewis, Dana Gillespie, members of The Damned (who supported him on his recent tour) and various musicians who had played with Bolan over the years, including Steve Harley.

Steve Harley (2012)

I'd travelled there in a limo with Rod. Bowie was sat right in front of me – the only time I ever met him. Rod was staying at the Intercontinental on Park Lane. We were going back there to have our own little wake. We asked David to join us. He didn't come. [018]

Bowie was visibly upset and wept openly during the service. Visconti and Cliff Wright noticed Bolan's estranged wife June had come despite being *persona non grata*.

RIGHT: Arriving at Golders Green Crematorium for Bolan's funeral. .

Cliff Wright (2012)

Outside, she was just standing there afterwards, helpless and alone among the crowd. Then David Bowie came past in his limo. June spotted him, and called out to him, "David, David!" Bowie opened the door and let her in. [018]

Bowie asked Tony Mascia to take him past his childhood home at 40 Stansfield Road, Brixton. He got out and stared up at the window of his old bedroom, then got back in the Mercedes. They continued on to Haddon Hall in Southend Road, Beckenham. As Bowie stood outside the rambling Gothic façade, his old landlord Ralph Hoy emerged with a bill for unpaid rent.

FRIDAY 23 SEPTEMBER

■ **SINGLE RELEASED**
'Heroes' (3:32)/
'V-2 Schneider' (3:10)
UK (RCA PB 1121)
Chart Peak No.24

■ **SINGLE RELEASED**
'Héros' (French version) (3:35)/
'V-2 Schneider' (3:10)
France (RCA PB 9167)
Canada (RCA PB-50398)

■ **SINGLE RELEASED**
'Helden' (German version) (3:32)/
'V-2 Schneider' (3:10)
Germany (RCA PB 9168)

Bowie described the song as "a combination of Brian's piano technique and my piano technique, which are both dastardly and end up sounding like The Velvet Underground".

The BBC's Nicky Horne asked Bowie why the German version had more power than the English version:

BOWIE (1979): *Well, a number of reasons I think. Atmospherically, I was in Berlin, I was looking at the Wall [from the Hansa studio window]… that's where the incident was written which is the main central theme of the song. Plus the fact that I was singing in the native, in a foreign language and so I was fighting the language and I think I probably gave it more impetus. And I did that version before I did the English version. So when I eventually got to the English version, I think I might have tempered it down a bit and started getting a bit too sophisto about how I was going to deal with the interpretation.* [315]

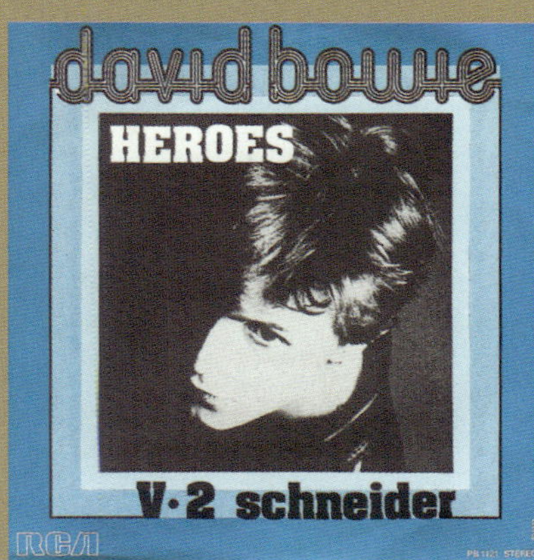

REISSUES

▮'Héros' English/French version (6:07) on French *"Heroes"* album (RCA 1977).

▮'Helden' English/German version (6:07) on German *"Heroes"* album (RCA 1977).

▮'Heroes', 'Helden' and 'Héros' single versions on Australian EP (RCA 1978).

▮'Héros' English/French and 'Helden' English/German versions on German 12-inch EP (RCA 1982).
▮'Helden' English/German version on *Rare* (RCA 1982)

▮'Helden' 1989 remix on *Sound+Vision* (Ryko 1989).

▮'Helden' 2002 remaster on German/Swiss/Austrian *Best Of Bowie* (EMI 2002).

▮'Héros' on *The Record Producers: Tony Visconti* (EMI 2007).

▮'Helden' 2002 remaster and 'Héros' 2007 remaster on 'Heroes'/'Helden'/'Héros' EP (iTunes 2009).

ABOVE: Single sleeves for 'Heroes' (Germany), 'Helden' (Germany), 'Heroes' (Belgium) - all with Sukita photos.

SUNDAY 25 SEPTEMBER

Iggy Pop opened his UK *Lust For Life* tour at the Apollo in Manchester, supported by The Adverts. Scott Thurston took Bowie's place on piano and Stacy Heydon replaced Ricky Gardiner on guitar. 'The Passenger' was filmed by Granada for *So It Goes*, which also included Tony Wilson's interview with Iggy.

TUESDAY 27 SEPTEMBER

✪ **PROMO FILMS**
'HEROES'
'BLACKOUT'
'SENSE OF DOUBT'

Nicholas Ferguson/Stanley Dorfman: Directors

▮'Heroes' released on *The Video Collection* (PMI 1993)/ *Best Of Bowie* (EMI 2002).

✪ **TELEVISION COMMERCIAL**
"HEROES"

Nicholas Ferguson: Director

"Tomorrow belongs to those that can hear it coming," intoned a Cockney voice (possibly Bowie's) over excerpts from the three promotional films.

WEDNESDAY 28 SEPTEMBER

▮Bowie's appearance on *Marc* – the last show of the series – broadcast on UK afternoon television (ITV).

THURSDAY 29 SEPTEMBER

Bowie set up a trust fund for Rolan Bolan after he found out that, since Bolan never married Gloria Jones, neither she nor their son had any claim on the estate.

Gloria Jones (2012)

He did it so that we could live; and he did it without being asked. It was simply that he loved Marc. He wanted to look after us. He didn't say anything and he didn't have to. It was from the heart. [427]

FRIDAY 30 SEPTEMBER

■ **SINGLE RELEASED**
IGGY POP
'Success' (4:23)/
'The Passenger' (4:40)
(RCA PB 9160)
'Iggy rules' is etched in the run-out groove.

OCTOBER

SATURDAY 1

ITALY

✪ TELEVISION
'L'ALTRA DOMENICA'
'The Other Sunday'
Interview with Fiorella Gentile.

✪ TELEVISION
'ODEON' (RAI UNO)
Interview / 'Heroes' / 'Sense Of Doubt'

THURSDAY 13 OCTOBER

AMSTERDAM

✪ TELEVISION
'POP SHOP'
Interview with Vic Dennis.

▮Broadcast: November 6.

✪ TELEVISION
'TOP POP' (AVRO)
'Heroes'

Gold record presentation
Ad Visser: Presenter

Bowie returned to the popular Dutch music show where he had performed 'Rebel Rebel' in February 1974 to sing 'Heroes' live to a backing track. The show's host, Ad Visser, then presented Bowie with a gold record for *Low*, then another for *"Heroes"*, which had achieved gold in the Netherlands in two weeks.

Afterwards Bowie did a photo call for the press, posing on a stool. Two young boys presented him with a book on Egon Schiele, saying "This is a book for your movie on Schiele."

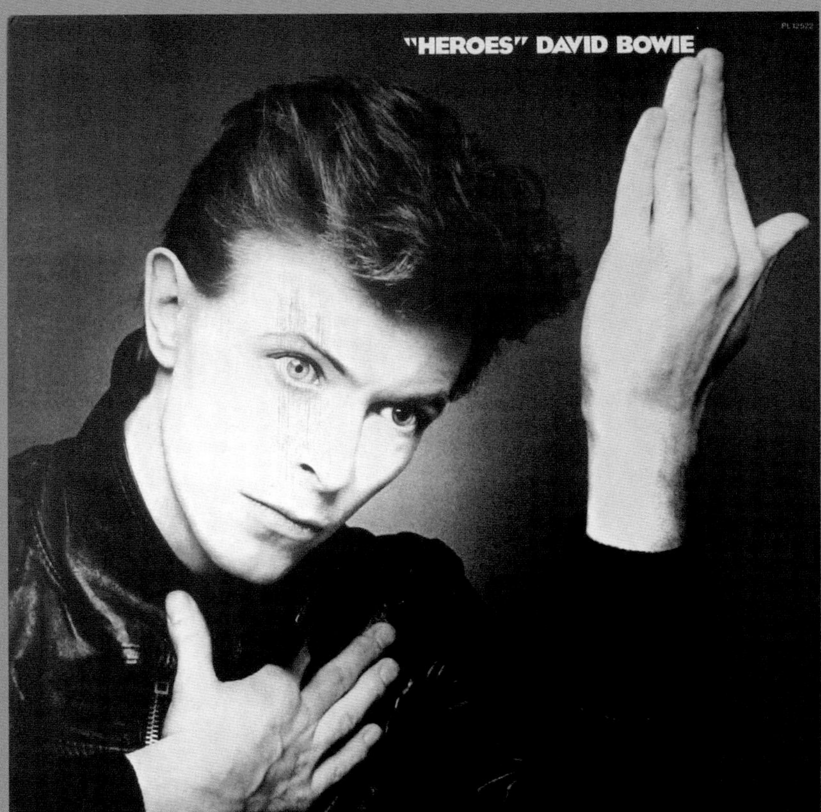

ABOVE: The cover photograph is one of a series Masayoshi Sukita took during Bowie's Japan trip in April.
RIGHT: *Top Pop* host Ad Visser presents Bowie with his gold records for *Low* and *"Heroes"*.

FRIDAY 14 OCTOBER

■ ALBUM RELEASED
"HEROES"
UK (RCA PL 12522)
US (AFL1-2522)
UK Chart Peak No.3
US Chart Peak No.35

SIDE ONE
1. **'Beauty And The Beast'** (3:32)
2. **'Joe The Lion'** (3:05)
3. **'Heroes'** (Bowie/Eno) (6:07)
4. **'Sons Of The Silent Age'** (3:15)
5. **'Blackout'** (3:50)

SIDE TWO
1. **'V-2 Schneider'** (3:10)
2. **'Sense Of Doubt'** (3:57)
3. **'Moss Garden'** (Bowie/Eno) (5:03)
4. **'Neuköln'** (Bowie/Eno) (4:34)
5. **'The Secret Life Of Arabia'** (Bowie/Eno/Alomar) (3:46)

David Bowie/Tony Visconti: Producers
David Bowie: Vocals/Keyboards/Guitar/Saxophone/Koto
Carlos Alomar: Rhythm Guitar
Dennis Davis: Percussion
George Murray: Bass
Brian Eno: Synthesiser/Keyboards/Guitar Treatments
Robert Fripp: Lead Guitar
David Bowie/Antonia Maass/Tony Visconti: Background Vocals
Tony Visconti/Colin Thurston: Engineers
Dave Richards/Eugene Chaplin: Assistant Engineers
Sukita: Cover Photographer
Recorded at Hansa By The Wall West Berlin, West Germany/Mountain Studios, Montreux, Switzerland
Mixed at Mountain Studios Montreux, Switzerland

SELECTED REISSUES

▮CD (RCA 1984).

▮CD (remastered with bonus tracks) (Ryko 1991).
1. 'Abdulmajid' (3:40)
2. 'Joe The Lion' (1991 remix) (3:08)

▮CD (remastered) (EMI 1999).

▮CD (mini LP replica) (Toshiba EMI 2007).

SATURDAY 15 OCTOBER

■ **CHART**

'Heroes'

UK Top 30 Chart Entry No.7

Charting 8 weeks

Bowie called the *San Francisco Chronicle* columnist Herb Caen from Amsterdam after learning that a Bowie imposter was at large in the city. "I have not been in San Francisco since April of 1977 and I am highly irritated by this imposter," he told Caen, who wrote, "Last Monday night he bought bottles of wine for every diner at Chez Michel and handed out $100 tips to waiters at Enrico's." [087]

Bowie (1984)

Then he ran off with some film producer's wife and $500,000 of the film producer's money – as me – and flew to Hawaii. Where he promptly was greeted with banner newspaper headlines: 'Bowie Arrives With Producer's Wife.' Newspapers were doing a whole number on it. And I was in Scotland. This guy was flashing around a credit card in the name of David Bowie, and people were of course accepting it.

ABOVE: Michel Drucker interviews Bowie on *Les Rendez-vous du Dimanche*.

So all this money was being spent in my name. The newspapers wouldn't believe it wasn't me. They insisted it was me. And they said, well, if it's really not you, you contact us from wherever you are, because we know this is you. So I had to go through this great farce of phoning all these columnists and gossip writers and say, listen, check the lines, this is a call from David Bowie, and I have an international operator to prove it. It was quite absurd.

He got the idea to do it when he was in reform school. His cellmate was a Jimi Hendrix clone! [012]

SUNDAY 16 OCTOBER

PARIS

✪ **TELEVISION**

'LES RENDEZ-VOUS DU DIMANCHE' (TF1)

'Heroes'

Interview with Michel Drucker.

✪ **RADIO**

'POSTE RESTANTE'

RADIO LUXEMBOURG (RTL)

An hour-long show with Bowie interviewed by Jean-Bernard Hebey live in the studio, answering questions phoned in by French fans. The special included selections from the album, including the English/French version of 'Heroes'.

WEDNESDAY 19 OCTOBER

✪ **TELEVISION**

BBC Television Centre

London, England

'TOP OF THE POPS'

'Heroes'

Tony Visconti: Bass

Ricky Gardiner: Guitar

Sean Mayes: Piano

On his arrival in London, Bowie asked Visconti to prepare a backing track for his return to *Top Of The Pops*. Sean Mayes hadn't heard from Bowie since 1973 when his band Fumble had supported Bowie on the UK and US tour.

Ricky Gardiner (2001)

We recorded 'Heroes' for* Top Of The Pops *at Good Earth Studios, Tony's studio in London. There was a full band and it was recorded minus vocals. I was asked to reproduce Robert Fripp's line. I did not realise at the time that he had used an EBow. I did my best using feedback alone. **[According to Visconti, Fripp had also used feedback, not an EBow.]** ***As we went through the song, my amplifier started dying. As the song finished, so did the amp.*** [105]

Bowie performed the song live to the backing track. After the taping, Bowie and Visconti went to a pub in Soho.

Bowie surveys Park Lane from the balcony of the Dorchester Hotel during a two day stopover in London to promote "Heroes".

SAFETY
FILM
ILFORD
HP5

THURSDAY 20 OCTOBER

✪ PRESS
Dorchester Hotel
Mayfair
London, England

Allan Jones interview:

"The only reason I've decided to do these interviews is to prove my belief in the album. Both Low *and "Heroes" have been met with confused reactions. That was to be expected, of course. But I didn't promote* Low *at all, and some people thought my heart wasn't in it.*

"This time I wanted to put everything into pushing my new album. I believe in the last two albums, you see, more than anything I have done before. I mean I look back on a lot of my earlier work, and although there's much that I appreciate about it, there is not a great deal that I actually like. I don't think they are very likeable albums at all.

"There is a lot more heart and emotion in Low*, and especially the new album. And, if I can convince people of that, I'm prepared to be stuck in this room on the end of a conveyor belt of questions that I'll do my best to answer."* [164]

▮Published: *Melody Maker*.

Having finished the rounds of interviews at the Dorchester, Bowie attended a private viewing of a film that he had been invited to score. Afterwards he headed over to Capital Radio for an appearance on Nicky Horne's show.

✪ RADIO
Capital Radio
Euston Tower
Camden
London, England

'YOUR MOTHER WOULDN'T LIKE IT'

Interview with Nicky Horne.
Phone-in Q&A with listeners.

ABOVE: Bowie backstage at Max's Kansas City with Devo – Mark Mothersbaugh, Gerald Casale and Bob Mothersbaugh. RIGHT: At the bar in Max's with Monique van Vooren and Tony Mascia (behind). OPPOSITE: Photographed by Barry Plummer for *Melody Maker*, Dorchester Hotel.

FRIDAY 21 OCTOBER

► TRAVELLING

Bowie took some time off from promoting *"Heroes"*, flying from Heathrow to Kenya for a safari visit with Zowie. They stayed overnight at Treetops, before travelling onto Masai Mara to visit the Masai and other tribes, accompanied by a local who translated for him. Bowie later described the trip to Flo and Eddie, reporting for Canadian show *90 Minutes Live*.

David Bowie (1977)

I went there to show my son how animals really live, that they're not always behind bars, because he's seen the Berlin Zoo and things like that and that's about it. I mean, he's only six and he's only seen them in zoos. So we got there and he started looking at all the animals and found it was a real country, with real people, it wasn't just one great big safari. [344]

SATURDAY 29 OCTOBER

▮*Rock On* interview with Stuart Grundy broadcast (BBC Radio 1).

NOVEMBER

MONDAY 14

★ LIVE
★ GUEST APPEARANCE
Max's Kansas City
213 Park Avenue South
New York City
New York, USA

DEVO

Bowie came to the show with actress Monique van Vooren, who had starred in Andy Warhol's *Flesh For Frankenstein* in 1973.

Bowie had been raving about Devo ever since Iggy Pop made him listen to their demo tape. He told *ZigZag*, "I like them very much indeed. I've been listening to them for a long time since they sent me their tapes, and I hope if I have the time at the end of this year to record them."

Mark Mothersbaugh (2009)

David Bowie showed up and on the second set before we came out, he introduced us, "This is the band of the future! I am producing them in Tokyo this winter!" And we're like, "Okay, we're sleeping in a car tonight – that sounds good to us!"

Then afterwards, he said, "Yeah, I really want to produce you guys. The only thing is, I'm up for this movie called Just A Gigolo*. If I get it, I have to go to Berlin for a couple months. So that would push it off." And we go, "Well, we don't even have anywhere to go when we leave here." We're homeless, you know – we don't know what we're gonna be doing for those two months.*

The next week, we played again, and Robert Fripp and Brian Eno came. And they invited us over to Robert Fripp's house. And he fed us. And they both said, "We would want to produce you guys if you were up for it." And we said, "Well, Brian, David Bowie last week said he was producing us in Tokyo!" And Brian Eno starts going, "He's full of shit."

At the time I didn't know that Brian Eno was kinda pissed at Bowie because he felt he didn't get credited

properly on "Heroes". And Low*. Brian Eno said, "Let's just go right now. Don't even worry about a record company. I'll loan you the money. We'll go over to Germany, at this studio I work at all the time – Conny Plank Studio." It's the place where bands like Birth Control and Guru Guru and Kraftwerk and you know – Can, Moebius, Roedelius, they all recorded at that studio. "Sure, that's great – you're gonna pay for us to go to this?" So he flew us over to Germany.* [092]

TUESDAY 15 NOVEMBER

PRESS

Mayfair House
New York City
New York, USA

Bowie spent the day doing interviews in his uptown hotel suite, discussing *Low*, *"Heroes"* and his peripatetic lifestyle. One of the interviews was recorded with Sonny Fox for the Superstars Radio Network. Bowie described his recent trip to Kenya:

BOWIE: *I took a straightforward corny safari. I spent a few hours – with the Masai tribe in Masai Mara, which is western Kenya, just on the border of Tanzania. I went to look at the lifestyle of the people – especially the Masai tribe. They've been living their particular way, untouched for at least 800 years.*

And it took a long time to get permission to get to the village. I had to find a Masai who spoke English who worked in that area, who would get me into the village. It's very hard to get to see them, and they were very, very wary and cautious of me in the beginning. I intend going back – I haven't finished there. I had to come here, break up my stay there.

FOX: *Did you do any recording – on cassette or something?*

BOWIE: *Not this time. I wanted to understand what I was seeing before I was presumptuous enough to start recording anything. So I wanted to make more stringent investigations. There's a lot of other tribes there that I didn't know much about. The Giriama are one of the most musical tribes and I saw them playing which was spectacular.* [338]

▮ Released in US as promo LP *An Evening With David Bowie* (RCA DJL1-3016).

SOCIALISING

Monique van Vooren was again Bowie's date for the celebrity premiere of *Close Encounters Of The Third Kind* at The Ziegfeld Theater, New York. Bowie joked a few days later in a radio interview with Dave Herman: "I think it's marvellous. I think it's incredible fun, a really good movie to go and see because the price is so reasonable."

ABOVE: With Tony Mascia in 1978.
OPPOSITE: Arriving at The Ziegfeld Theatre with Monique van Vooren.

MID-NOVEMBER

RECORDING

RCA Studios
New York City
New York, USA

DAVID BOWIE NARRATES PROKOFIEV'S 'PETER AND THE WOLF' ALBUM

Bowie narrated the traditional children's story accompanied by the Philadelphia Symphony Orchestra conducted by Eugene Ormandy.

Charles M Young interview:

Bowie is sitting in an RCA recording studio between takes of a recitation of Peter And The Wolf*, Prokofiev's chestnut being made into yet another children's album. Dressed in a grey shirt, black corduroys and green clogs, his hair its natural shade of light brown, he looks as normal and healthy as anyone with Martian features can.*

Bowie has mellowed enough in his pursuit of platinum that the lack of huge sales doesn't bother him that much. "I'm incredibly happy," he says. "I don't care if I'm understood or not. I have less formulated ideas about this time than ever. It's probably why I'm enjoying it so much."

▮ Published: *Rolling Stone*. [321]

SUNDAY 20 NOVEMBER

SOCIALISING

New York City
New York, USA

TONY MASCIA'S WEDDING

Bowie was best man for driver Tony Mascia (who also played Arthur, Bowie's driver in *The Man Who Fell To Earth*).

Tony Mascia (1983)
David's a cool kid to work for, I got offered twice the money to work for Rod Stewart, but I turned it down. David's a brilliant guy, the painting, the writing. He's a very generous kid, very shy, but with me he can be himself. I'm like his father. [006]

Guests include Iggy Pop and photographer (and Barbara DeWitt's brother) Bruce Weber.

Bruce Weber (1993)
David was there – tanned, for a change – and was asked to sing by the bride and bridegroom. He, of course, obliged like the gentleman that he is and this Mafia-style wedding became a royal one with the sound of his voice. [240]

FRIDAY 25 NOVEMBER

TELEVISION

"90 MINUTES LIVE"

Flo and Eddie's interview with Bowie, recorded at the Plaza Hotel, New York.

TUESDAY 29 NOVEMBER

TELEVISION

'GOOD MORNING AMERICA' (ABC)

Interview with David Hartman.

WEDNESDAY 30 NOVEMBER

TELEVISION

▮ *Bing Crosby's Merrie Olde Christmas* broadcast in US (CBS).

Reviewers praised Bowie's duet with Crosby as the highlight of the special, but criticised his performance of 'Heroes' as "a jarring note" and "inappropriate".

DECEMBER

AWARDS

'NEW MUSICAL EXPRESS' READERS' POP POLL

Singer and Songwriter #1
Best Album *"Heroes"* #2

SATURDAY 17

Melody Maker declared *"Heroes"* Rock Album Of The Year.

LATE DECEMBER

BUSINESS

David Hemmings visited Bowie at Clos des Mésanges in Switzerland to persuade him to take a leading role in his new film *Just A Gigolo*, to be filmed in Berlin. Whether or not Bowie accepted as a favour to Hemmings, the project was certainly geographically convenient, giving him a legitimate excuse to remain in Berlin.

Asked later why he took the part, Bowie flippantly explained, "Marlene Dietrich was dangled in front of me."

Dietrich returned the compliment, saying, "The reason I did this film was that David is the only young person today who has anything to say."

THURSDAY 22 DECEMBER

The Bowie family had planned to spend Christmas in Switzerland until David told Angie he would be staying in Berlin to prepare for the film. Enraged, Angie left Zowie with Marion Skene and flew to New York to spend the holiday with friends. The nanny called Bowie, who asked her to come to Berlin with Zowie.

SATURDAY 24 DECEMBER

TELEVISION

▮ *Bing Crosby's Merrie Olde Christmas* broadcast in UK (ITV).

SUNDAY 25 DECEMBER

SOCIALISING

Bowie spent Christmas with Zowie at Hauptstrasse 155, where Coco cooked goose for their guests, including Edu Meyer.

1978

JANUARY

■ **ALBUM RELEASED**
'BOWIE NOW' PROMO
US (RCA DJL1-2696)

SIDE ONE
1. **'V-2 Schneider'** (3:10)
2. **'Always Crashing In The Same Car'** (3:26)
3. **'Sons Of The Silent Age'** (3:15)
4. **'Breaking Glass'** (Bowie/Davis/Murray) (1:42)
5. **'Neuköln'** (Bowie/Eno) (4:34)

SIDE TWO
1. **'Speed Of Life'** (2:45)
2. **'Joe The Lion'** (3:05)
3. **'What In The World'** (2:20)
4. **'Blackout'** (3:50)
5. **'Weeping Wall'** (3:25)
6. **'The Secret Life Of Arabia'** (Bowie/Eno/Alomar) (3:46)

MONDAY 2

Angie returned to Switzerland with her friend, Heartbreakers soundman Keeth Paul, with whom she had stayed in New York. They arrived at Clos des Mésanges to find that Zowie and Marion Skene had gone.

Despondent and in need of cash, she called David Lewin, a journalist friend who contacted the *Sunday Mirror*. The editor called Angie and agreed to send some cash over with a reporter and a photographer.

FRIDAY 6 JANUARY

■ **SINGLE RELEASED**
'Beauty And The Beast' (3:29)/
'Sense Of Doubt' (3:57)
UK/Germany/France/Belgium/Netherlands (RCA PB-1190)
US (RCA PB-11190)
UK Chart Peak No.39

■ **SINGLE RELEASED**
12-INCH PROMO
'Beauty And The Beast' (extended mix) (5:18)/
'Fame' (Bowie/Alomar/Lennon) (4:12)
US (RCA JD-11204)

SATURDAY 7 JANUARY

Sunday Mirror reporter Tony Robinson arrived at the chalet to find Angie groggy from sedatives, but ready to air her grievances, which were published the following day.

SUNDAY 8 JANUARY

✪ **PRESS**

In the early hours of the morning Angie got up, realising what she'd done. She took an overdose of sleeping pills and went on a rampage, smashing up the house and attacking Keeth Paul with a rolling pin when he tried to calm her. She tried to stab herself with a carving knife, and finally passed out on the bed.

Later in the day, as Keeth Paul and Tony Robinson decided what to do, she roused herself and threw herself down the stairs, breaking her nose. They called the ambulance and accompanied her to the Samaritan's Hospital.

The *Sunday Mirror* reported:

Angie Bowie, wife of superstar David Bowie, is furious with her husband. She said angrily last night, "Without my knowledge he has taken our son to Berlin."

Weeping in the lounge of their home in Switzerland, she told The Sunday Mirror *of the latest conflict in her tempestuous marriage. She claimed that while she was staying with friends in New York, David telephoned the nanny of their six-year-old son Zowie and said: "Come to Berlin." Angie said: "I found out when I got back. They went either by air or in the train." How did she think Zowie would cope with being looked after by his father?*

"I'm sure he's perfectly all right," she said. "David's a perfect father."

Would she like to have Zowie back?

"You're absolutely right," she told me. "That's why I want a divorce, to get custody of him. I have to seek a divorce… I really want David to suffer." [257]

▌Published: 'Bowie Rapped By His Missus', *Sunday Mirror.*

MONDAY 9 JANUARY

✪ **PRESS**

Bowie issued a statement from Berlin in response to Angie's allegations:

"My wife was not aware that my son was with me. A few days before Christmas she decided she would leave Switzerland and spend the holidays with friends elsewhere. From that day to her arrival back on 2 January, she didn't phone me or the boy to say where she was."

Angie was discharged from Samaritan's Hospital after making so much commotion that a woman in the next bed suffered a cardiac arrest relapse.

THURSDAY 12 JANUARY

Marion Skene and Daniella Parmar, accompanied by Stuart George, returned Zowie to Angie in Switzerland.

ABOVE: ***Bowie Now*****, a promotional sampler LP of *Low* and "*Heroes*" songs, some of which would feature in the upcoming world tour.**
RIGHT: The German sleeve featured a Sukita photo from the "*Heroes*" session.
OPPOSITE: Angie Bowie and boyfriend Keeth Paul at Clos des Mésanges in the aftermath of her meltdown and discharge from hospital.

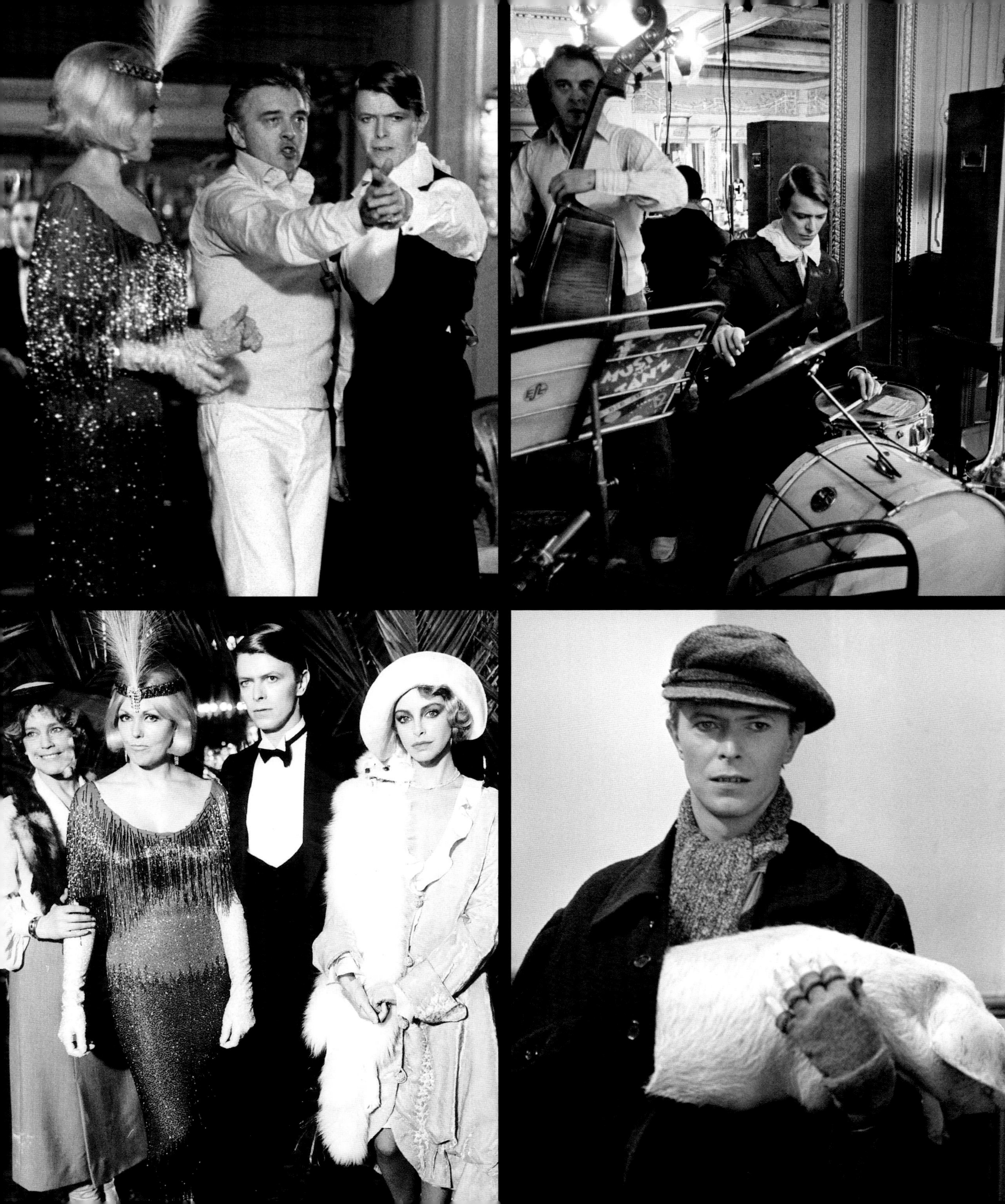

BOWIE: *I'm finding it enthralling to be really getting into a person's flesh this time around. I really feel very much at home – with this character, being led and shown how to do it.*

WATTS: *Tell me how you got involved in the movie about Egon Schiele.*

BOWIE: *It was originally suggested to me that I should play the part by Clive Donner, the guy who did* The Caretaker *and* Mulberry Bush. *He sent me the original script and I jumped at the idea of it, 'cause Schiele was somebody I was aware of. Wally is just a working title. It will go through the time from as he was leaving Klimt as a pupil and setting himself up as a painter, through his prison sentence and to the end of his relationship with his girlfriend, Wally. Charlotte Rampling is on board to play her at the moment.* [308]

Despite his world tour coming up, Bowie told Watts he was also planning to meet Rainer Werner Fassbinder to discuss the possibility of working on a remake of Brecht's *The Threepenny Opera*.

On the weekends, he headed over to Cologne, where Brian Eno was producing Devo's debut album at Konrad Plank's studio. [092]

Mark Mothersbaugh (2009)

David Bowie still wanted to be involved and showed up every day on the weekends and hung out with us, and then bickered with Eno.

Ian Birch (*Melody Maker*) phoned the band at the studio to talk about the album and spoke to Jerry Casale.

"We always had a desire to be produced by either Brian or David, or possibly both, and they both were, like, equal choices, and as it's turned out we're going to eventually have both of them. Out of anyone in the business they were obviously the closest to the devolved end of the scale. The sounds they achieved, the way they approached the art and, in the case of David, of course, his understanding of media and total image. There weren't too many choices." [057]

MID-JANUARY

✪ FILMING

'JUST A GIGOLO'

David Hemmings: Director

Rolf Thiele: Producer

Shooting of Bowie's second feature film began, continuing until mid- February at various locations, including the Café Wien on the Kurfürstendamm in Berlin. Bowie spent the evenings working on his art, taking Polaroids of them to mount in a photo album.

Chris Hodenfield reported:

Outside an old-time transvestite bar, the Lützow Lampe, in a dressing room trailer, David Bowie sat and looked at pictures. His bicycle was in the trailer, too. A cassette played Vivaldi's Four Seasons. *In his photo album there were snapshots of his recent paintings and woodcuts. Most were stark, howling messages, reminiscent of Twenties Expressionism. A room with a table. There was a startling woodcut of an Argentine dancer.*

"Have I shown them?" he said, recoiling. "Never have, but I think I might be getting the confidence up again. That's a self-portrait," he said, turning over a snake-faced headshot. "That's Iggy, without his professor's glasses. That's his 'I just want to be taken seriously' look." Iggy, with parted hair, had a sad, up-from-under stare.

ABOVE: Bowie in 1990 with his 1976 painting of Iggy, *Portrait of J.O.*
OPPOSITE: The *Just A Gigolo* set, West Berlin. Director David Hemmings shows Bowie how to tango with Kim Novak and takes to the upright bass with Bowie on drums; Bowie with the pig he had to carry through the production as it grew steadily larger and heavier; with Maria Schell, Kim Novak and Sydne Rome.
OVERLEAF: Bowie and Kim Novak dance the tango.

Another self-portrait, this one with ravenous eyes and a stricken face. A portrait of a man with child, gnarled limbs like old, dry cornstalks, hands like shovels, expressions of severity. Even more severe was a painting of Yukio Mishima, the Japanese author, with huge, almond eyes. A sketch of a man looking into the distance. "That's a bartender. He built his bar right alongside the Wall. His parents live on the East side and that's just how he sits, looking out the window at the East." [147]

▮Published: 'Bad Boys In Berlin', *Rolling Stone*.

⊙ BUSINESS

Australian promoter Paul Dainty announced that he had to move Bowie's Australia/New Zealand tour dates from February to November. The *Just A Gigolo* contract required Bowie to be available for two weeks after the end of filming in January to cover the possibility of extra shooting in February. "Unfortunately, I couldn't just set the tour dates back two weeks," Dainty explained. "The venues just weren't available."

FEBRUARY

✪ PRESS

In between shooting *Just A Gigolo* scenes in the Café Wien, press interviews were conducted with Chris Hodenfield (*Rolling Stone*) and Michael Watts (*Melody Maker*).

WATTS: *How do you feel about this film compared with* The Man Who Fell To Earth?

BOWIE: *This has so far been a far more enjoyable experience. For one reason or another, I'm a lot closer to David than I was with Nic. Nic is less approachable. David is a far more generous personality.*

WATTS: *Roeg's an intellectual.*

BOWIE: *Yes, he has those leanings. David not so much; though, of course, he is of a sophisticated nature. Creatively, quite as extraordinary as Roeg in his way.*

WATTS: *You appear to be enjoying acting, anyway.*

WEDNESDAY 15 FEBRUARY

Eno called up Bowie in the morning from Cologne. He had been to Frank Zappa's concert the night before and was impressed by Zappa's guitarist Adrian Belew. Remembering that Bowie was looking for a lead guitarist for the upcoming tour, he told Bowie to check out the concert that night at the Deutschlandhalle in Berlin.

Adrian Belew (2007)

The following night David comes to the show, ostensibly to see me play. There is a break in the show where I normally leave the stage while Frank plays an extended guitar solo. As I'm leaving, I glance over to the monitor board. I'm shocked to see David Bowie and Iggy Pop! I walk over, shaking David's hand. I say, "I've always loved your music."

"Great," he says, "how'd you like to join my band?"

"Well, I'm playing with this guy right now..." I stammer, pointing to Frank.

"Yes, I know, but your tour ends in two weeks and mine begins two weeks later."

We agree to meet back at the hotel after the show. David and Coco tried to rendezvous with me without letting Frank know I was being wooed away from his band. We stepped into the hotel elevator when no one was around. Coco said, "We have a car out front. We'll meet you there in ten minutes."

David wanted to take me to one of his favourite restaurants to discuss my future. So his driver set off with the three of us in the back. We pulled up to a nice looking restaurant and walked in. At the table right in front of us sat Frank and some of the band! David said, "Really enjoyed the show." Frank shot back, "Fuck you, Captain Tom." No matter what David tried, Frank kept saying, "Fuck you, Captain Tom." So we left the restaurant.

Outside David said, "That went down rather well, didn't it?" [398]

ABOVE: Bowie poached Nashville guitarist Adrian Belew from Frank Zappa after Robert Fripp declined the invitation to join the tour.

Bowie continued planning the world tour and contacted Natasha Korniloff, who had designed several of his outfits over the years, to prepare some ideas. She flew to Berlin where Coco took her to see Bowie on location. After filming finished for the day, they returned to Bowie's hotel, and spent an hour scribbling costume design ideas on the backs of envelopes, which she took to London to work on.

Natasha Korniloff (1984)

We had torn bits out of magazines and we did small drawings and we had lots of ideas and wanted trousers that were kind of big and we also wanted to combine them with Hawaiian shirts that they used to wear in the Forties with strange prints on them. We had also seen a funny mess jacket in another photograph and I went off and combined the large trousers with the mess jacket. I made him a series of tracksuits in velour. I made a snakeskin jacket to go over the tracksuits. I made loads of things – corduroy suits, sailor suits and hats. [009]

✪ PHOTO SESSION

Lord Snowdon photographed Bowie for a feature in British *Vogue* (published in September).

MONDAY 20 FEBRUARY

✪ PRESS

Dorchester Hotel
Mayfair
London, England

After *Just A Gigolo* wrapped, Bowie returned to Britain to announce the 1978 World Tour. During the stopover, Natasha Korniloff sent him some designs for his stage costumes.

Natasha Korniloff (1986)
I didn't see him but he tried it on and sent it back with messages like "more of this – one in red as well." So I just got on with it until eventually I was to fly to Dallas where they were rehearsing. [019]

TUESDAY 21 FEBRUARY

Tour plans were announced in the press, with Stacy Heydon still slated as lead guitarist, pending commitment from Adrian Belew, who would play his last Zappa show on March 1.

MARCH

MONDAY 13 – SATURDAY 25 MARCH

▲ REHEARSING

Dallas
Texas, USA

Bowie was still en route from another Kenya trip when his new tour band assembled in a rehearsal studio, located in a large windowless warehouse on a freeway 15 miles out of town.

Carlos Alomar, who resumed his role as bandleader, took the band through the set list, handing out chord charts to the musicians, four of whom were new to the material.

Adrian Belew, fresh from his tour with Frank Zappa, had signed up as Stacy Heydon's replacement. Bowie's first choice for lead guitarist had been Robert Fripp, but he had baulked at the prospect of a five-month tour. He told Bowie, "I don't think you have the room to give me."

Eno declined to join for the same reason, telling *ZigZag*, "I gave it some serious consideration. I don't like doing gigs very much, but I think there are a few people I'd like to do them with, and he's one of them. But the trouble was he was talking about a long tour… it would

ABOVE: Sean Mayes, pianist with Fumble, a Fifties retro band Bowie first saw on *Old Grey Whistle Test* in 1972, who subsequently supported Bowie and the Spiders on the UK/US Ziggy Stardust tour. In 1978 Fumble was providing the music for the West End musical *Elvis!* when Sean Mayes got the call to join the Bowie tour.

Bowie later added, "He'd love to have done this tour but he's not strong enough. Both his lungs collapsed on tour once – he just couldn't have taken this."

Eno recommended Roger Powell, whom Bowie knew from his work with Todd Rundgren's Utopia. Powell was technically and musically adept, having recently developed one of the first polyphonic synthesisers.

Bowie had known violinist Simon House since the early days in London, when he played in High Tide with Tony Hill, who had briefly played with Bowie (and Hermione Farthingale) in Turquoise, aka Feathers, in 1968. House played with Hawkwind until Bowie called him to join the tour.

Sean Mayes (1999)
David had chosen us for our individual abilities and didn't really interfere with us much. So the music found its own level and became very much the band's music played in our own way. [022]

Adrian Belew (1999)
He gave me full rein to be his guitarist and to add a lot of colours and sounds; to play solos and to be involved in the shape and form of the music itself. [004]

Sean Mayes (1985)
He told me later on the tour, "I'm very suspicious of virtuosity. I like people who play with an original style and I choose people who I think can contribute something." [009]

Carlos Alomar (1999)
That was a wonderful band. You wouldn't normally find a band that would have a violin player, a lead guitar player, a synth player and a piano player – these are all soloist instruments. [004]

"Bowie is uncanny in his ability to pick musicians," *Variety* later commented.

First Class

WEDNESDAY 15 MARCH

▶ TRAVELLING

Following his return from Kenya, Bowie spent the day in London, then flew from Heathrow to join the band in Dallas.

Bowie arrived at Dallas airport in the afternoon and called in at the rehearsal studio to say hello.

Although tired from the 11,000-mile flight from Kenya (via London), he was healthy and showing off an uncharacteristic suntan. Excited by the prospect of playing live again with a new band, Bowie jumped on stage to run through some songs. Eventually Coco took him away to preserve his voice.

THURSDAY 16 MARCH

▲ REHEARSING

Rehearsals with Bowie got properly underway in sessions from 10am to 8 or 9pm. With only two weeks to prepare, there was much work to be done, with four musicians learning 30 to 40 songs. Early on, Bowie announced, "Let's do the whole *Ziggy Stardust* album – that'll surprise them!" After learning all of the songs, they ended up doing only six.

Natasha Korniloff arrived with two suitcases of stage outfits for Bowie to try. That night they all went out to a French restaurant, where everyone (except Korniloff) ordered snails and fell ill.

FRIDAY 17 MARCH

Korniloff and Bowie decided on the final selections, including a snakeskin jacket and a double-breasted mess jacket they had seen in a magazine cutting combined with large trousers. On the night, Bowie would select one or two different combinations from a large wardrobe.

Natasha Korniloff (1985)

His favourite combination was the white trousers with the snakeskin jacket. The cut of the trousers was based on Jacobean breeches but I made them in white drill and down to the ankles. [009]

Towards the end of the rehearsals Bowie's voice was fatigued, so the last few days were spent going through the set so the crew could devise the lighting for the show.

ABOVE AND OPPOSITE: Bowie at Heathrow airport with Eric Barrett, before his Concorde flight to New York, and a connecting flight to Dallas for tour rehearsals with the band.

SATURDAY 25 MARCH

Melody Maker announced that Devo were confirmed to sign a contract with Warner Brothers and would tour the UK in June, and were "likely to support Bowie on several British dates".

▼ SOCIALISING

After the Showco trucks left for San Diego to set up for the first concert, Bowie and the band spent the evening at a bowling alley. Bowie, who was playing pool and chalking his cue, asked a local about the rules. Looking as ordinary as he did, Bowie spent the evening untroubled by the unsuspecting Texans – a far cry from the Houston local who pulled a gun on him

MONDAY 27 MARCH

Bowie and the band flew to San Diego, where they had two days for rest and last-minute preparations for the opening show of the tour.

Natasha Korniloff spent the time finishing off the sewing of the outfits on a machine delivered to Tony Mascia's room at the hotel. The company rep began to explain the workings of the machine until Mascia became impatient, picking up the man by the shoulders and placing him outside the door.

Bowie told the *Chicago Tribune* that the shows would be "low profile, nothing very dramatic visually. No characters. I've finished with characters. Now it's just me." He was asked whether the rampant egomania that characterised his time in Los Angeles was still a problem:

"Good Lord, I hope not. But I think you'd have to ask the people around me. The fact that they're still with me would, I hope, mean that I've lost a lot of that. But it built up to quite a pitch when I was living in Los Angeles, it's true.

"It was completely my own fault, though it would have been hard to avoid it, given the conditions of that kind of cocooning. Breaking out, breaking off – it was hard. But getting out was the best thing I did.

"Getting out and trying to realise another kind of existence in another environment. I have no fixed address. I never intend to. I think it would be ruinous to the kind of songwriting I do, which is intrinsically change." [300]

ISOLAR 2 – WORLD TOUR

'Warszawa'/'Heroes'/ 'What In The World'/ 'Be My Wife'/'The Jean Genie'/ 'Blackout'/'Sense Of Doubt'/ 'Speed Of Life'/'Breaking Glass'/ 'Beauty And The Beast'/ 'Fame'/'Five Years'/'Soul Love'/ 'Star'/'Hang On To Yourself'/ 'Ziggy Stardust'/'Suffragette City'/ 'Rock'n'Roll Suicide'/'Art Decade'/ 'Station To Station'/'Stay'/'TVC 15'/ 'Rebel Rebel'/'Alabama Song'/ 'Sound And Vision'

David Bowie: Vocals/Keyboards

Carlos Alomar: Rhythm Guitar/ Musical Director

Adrian Belew: Lead Guitar

Dennis Davis: Drums/Percussion

Simon House: Electric Violin

Sean Mayes: Piano/String Ensemble

George Murray: Bass

Roger Powell: Keyboards/Synthesisers

Dennis Garcia: Keyboards/Synthesisers on November 11/14

Eric Barrett: Tour Manager

David Bowie/Eric Barrett: Lighting Designers

Showco: Sound/Lighting

David Bowie: Programme Designer

Natasha Korniloff: Costume Designer

Rob Joyce: Stage Manager

Jan Michael Alejandro/ Vern 'Moose' Constan/Leroy Kerr/ Edd Kolakowski: Road Crew

Produced in association with Winterland Productions

WEDNESDAY 29 MARCH
★ LIVE
Sports Arena
San Diego
California, USA

Sean Mayes (1999)
You open a tour generally at a place not too big and famous, so we had about three or four gigs before the first biggie, which was Los Angeles, but nonetheless it was big – it was 15,000 people in a big stadium. We were all very keyed up for it. [022]

Despite pre-show nerves all round, the first show of the tour went without a hitch and the ecstatic capacity crowd brought them back for two encores. Fans followed them back to the hotel where the band joined the hotel band on stage in the bar.

THURSDAY 30 MARCH
★ LIVE
Veterans Memorial Coliseum
Phoenix
Arizona, USA

FRIDAY 31 MARCH
▼ SOCIALISING
Still in Phoenix, the band spent their day off lingering around the hotel pool and had dinner at a traditional Japanese restaurant.

ABOVE: Oakland-Alameda County Coliseum, Oakland.
BELOW : Convention Centre, Fresno.
OVERLEAF: Sports Arena, San Diego.

APRIL

SATURDAY 1

In a statement published in *Melody Maker*, Richard Branson said that Devo had signed with Virgin, not Warner Brothers as reported. He told *Melody Maker* that Brian Eno had produced the album and had agreed to pay the recording costs. Prior to this, it was thought that Bowie's production company had signed the band and paid for the recording.

SUNDAY 2 APRIL
★ LIVE
Convention Center
Fresno
California, USA

ABOVE: The cover featured a portrait from the 1975 session with Tom Kelley.

MONDAY 3 APRIL

★ LIVE

The Forum
Inglewood
California, USA

▼ SOCIALISING

After the show, two limos ferried the entourage to The Rainbow Club on Sunset, where Bowie held court at a large corner table.

✪ TELEVISION

'EYEWITNESS NEWS'

The report from the Inglewood Forum featured an interview with Bowie backstage and showed him with the band preparing to perform, as well as a clip of 'The Jean Genie' from the show.

TUESDAY 4 APRIL

★ LIVE

The Forum
Inglewood
California, USA

WEDNESDAY 5 APRIL

★ LIVE

Oakland-Alameda County Coliseum
Oakland
California, USA

THURSDAY 6 APRIL

★ LIVE

The Forum
Inglewood
California, USA

▼ SOCIALISING

After the show, Bowie held a party at Ma Maison restaurant on Melrose Avenue. Bowie provided limos for all the guests, including Nic Roeg, Si Litvinoff, Alan Bates, Jacqueline Bisset, Tom Waits, Bette Midler and Mark Rydell, who was directing Midler in *The Rose*.

FRIDAY 7 APRIL

▼ SOCIALISING

In the afternoon Bowie and the band attended a party at tour manager Eric Barrett's house in the canyon. Barrett was an expatriate Scot who had settled in Los Angeles and worked with a succession of high-profile West Coast artists such as James Taylor and Linda Ronstadt. Later in the evening they all crowded around a television to watch the *Eyewitness News* coverage of the Forum show.

■ ALBUM RELEASED

PROKOFIEV'S
'PETER AND THE WOLF'

US (RCA Red Seal ARL1-2743)

SIDE ONE

'Peter And The Wolf, Op.67' (27:08)

SIDE TWO

'Young Person's Guide To The Orchestra, Op.34' (Britten) (17:10)

David Bowie: Narrator
Jay David Saks: Producer
Paul Goodman: Engineer
J J Stelmach: Art Director
Jeffrey Schrier: Art
Tom Kelley: Cover Photographer
Recorded with Eugene Ormandy/ The Philadelphia Orchestra at RCA Studios, New York City, New York, USA, December 1977

A limited number were pressed on translucent green vinyl and stickered 'The Green Record'.

▮ Reissued on CD
(RCA Red Seal 1984)
(RCA Gold Seal 1992)
(RCA Victor 2004).

SATURDAY 8 APRIL

► TRAVELLING

After a five-hour flight the entourage arrived in Houston, unaware that Lou Reed was also staying at the Hyatt and playing that night.

SUNDAY 9 APRIL

★ LIVE

The Summit
Houston
Texas, USA

MONDAY 10 APRIL

★ LIVE

✪ TELEVISION

Convention Center
Dallas
Texas, USA

In the morning Bowie and the entourage flew back to Dallas, this time staying at the upmarket Fairmont (as opposed to last month's functional hotel on the edge of town). Before the show they celebrated Pat Gibbons' birthday backstage.

The concert was filmed by RCA. Performances of 'What In The World', 'Blackout', 'Sense Of Doubt', 'Speed Of Life', 'Hang On To Yourself' and 'Ziggy Stardust' were later broadcast as *David Bowie On Stage* on US TV. Four were broadcast on *The Old Grey Whistle Test* in the UK.

TUESDAY 11 APRIL

★ **LIVE**

Louisiana State University Assembly Center
Baton Rouge
Louisiana, USA

WEDNESDAY 12 APRIL

▶ **TRAVELLING**

Travelling via Atlanta to Adrian Belew's hometown, Nashville. With a night off before the next concert, Belew suggested they go out to Fanny's, the club where Frank Zappa first discovered him.

THURSDAY 13 APRIL

★ **LIVE**

Municipal Auditorium
Nashville
Tennessee, USA

▼ **SOCIALISING**

After a subdued show, Bowie and the band returned to the bar at the Hilton, then headed out to a Thirties-style restaurant.

FRIDAY 14 APRIL

★ **LIVE**

Mid-South Coliseum
Memphis
Tennessee, USA

SATURDAY 15 APRIL

★ **LIVE**

Municipal Auditorium
Kansas City
Missouri, USA

The entourage flew to Chicago in the afternoon and checked into the Whitehall Hotel.

Arie Crown Theatre, Chicago, one of the smaller venues on the tour.

The Arie Crown held only 4,000, significantly fewer than the arenas and halls they had been playing. It would have made for an intimate setting with better audience interaction, but with the equipment set up downstage, and an orchestra pit at the front, the band found they were unable to see the audience.

TUESDAY 18 APRIL

★ **LIVE**

Arie Crown Theatre
Chicago
Illinois, USA

On the second night, the orchestra pit was taken out and Bowie was able to work the crowd. As the house lights went down, he called for them to be turned back up a little "so I can see you all out there!"

John Milward (*Rolling Stone*)

David Bowie's career has been predicated on abrupt stylistic changes, and the most surprising aspect of his new live show is the ease with which he melds the disparate strands into a tightly woven whole. During the two-hour show, Bowie places equal emphasis on the adventuresome new music he's made with Brian Eno and the souped-up and blown dry hard rock that made him a star.

The new Ziggy is a dramatic crooner – Bowie turns everything into a prop, from his Gitanes to his mike-over-the-shoulder delivery of 'Suffragette City' – with a different story. Marching in time with the manic "I want to touch you" phrase that concludes 'Breaking Glass', Bowie leaped from the stage, touched somebody in the first row, and was back on stage before most of the audience knew what had happened. The time lapse was just a second but if you caught Bowie's face, you saw his features screaming with insecurity.

Then during a stunning interpretation of 'Moon Of Alabama', Bowie's face again became the focal point, changing with each verse and making Bowie appear to be a man of a thousand visages. That we can't tell which face is real is what makes Bowie's show so intriguing. [209]

FRIDAY 21 APRIL

★ LIVE
Cobo Arena
Detroit
Michigan, USA

SATURDAY 22 APRIL

★ LIVE
Richfield Coliseum
Cleveland
Ohio, USA

The entourage arrived in Cleveland and checked into Swingo's Inn, a hotel favoured by musicians. As they arrived, Count Basie, who was there for a show, stopped to greet Dennis Davis and Tony Mascia, who used to chauffeur him in New York.

In the evening Bowie called a meeting with the band, Eric Barrett and Pat Gibbons to discuss recording the live album the following week in Philadelphia.

MONDAY 24 APRIL

★ LIVE
Mecca Arena
Milwaukee
Wisconsin, USA

WEDNESDAY 26 APRIL

★ LIVE
Civic Arena
Pittsburgh
Pennsylvania, USA

Pete Bishop (*Pittsburgh Press*)
He proved what he has hidden under excessive theatrics all these years: that he's one of the very best rock'n'rollers around. "If I play music, it's going to be straight and I'll take the consequences," Bowie told an interviewer recently. And play it straight, backed by a fine band, is just what he did. And the shockingly small but enthusiastic crowd (5,671) loved it. [060]

THURSDAY 27 APRIL

★ LIVE
Capital Center
Landover
Maryland, USA

Tom Zito (*The Washington Post*)
One must admire Bowie for attempting to broaden the musical parameters of rock concerts, although in the process he may have managed to cut his audience in half.

ABOVE: Bowie's favourite of Natasha Korniloff's designs for the tour – white trousers with snakeskin jacket.
OPPOSITE: Maple Leaf Gardens, Toronto, with Simon House (obscured) and Carlos Alomar behind.

FRIDAY 28 APRIL

★ LIVE
Spectrum Arena
Philadelphia
Pennsylvania, USA

Tony Visconti flew Concorde from London to New York, arriving in Philadelphia in time to set up the equipment to record both of the Spectrum dates for the live album, *Stage*.

Tony Visconti (2002)
RCA loaned us their excellent mobile studio, which we parked outside each venue. I was the engineer, assisted by two senior RCA engineers. Each show was miked exactly the same way and no one was permitted to change the settings on the console from show to show. So consistent was the sound (and the tempo of each song) that we were able to use the intro and outro of 'Station To Station' from Boston and the bulk from Rhode Island. [422]

Tony Visconti (2006)
I had to make sure that the band was close miked for maximum separation between their sounds to ensure more control during mixing. I wanted the audience to sound big and real and I wanted the natural reverb in the concert halls to enhance the sound of the record. I used four microphones for the audience, not the more common two that are usually placed left and right in the house. Quadraphonic recording was still viable in the late 1970s and I wanted to cover the possibility; years later my surround sound mix recreated the spatial feeling of being in the audience. [047]

SATURDAY 29 APRIL

★ LIVE
Spectrum Arena
Philadelphia
Pennsylvania, USA

Ahead of the second night's live recording the band had a complete rehearsal in the afternoon. The tapes from the previous night's performance had showed they had been playing too fast, so Alomar re-established the studio tempos.

MAY

MONDAY 1

★ LIVE
Maple Leaf Gardens
Toronto
Ontario, Canada

▼ SOCIALISING
At the hotel bar after the show Bowie caught up with Lindsay Kemp, who was playing a season of *Salome* and *Flowers* in Toronto and had been to the concert that night with Jack Birkett, aka The Incredible Orlando.

TUESDAY 2 MAY

★ LIVE
Civic Center
Ottawa
Ontario, Canada

WEDNESDAY 3 MAY

★ LIVE
Forum
Montreal
Quebec, Canada

In Canada, 'Heroes' had been released in both languages but Bowie declined to sing the French version, explaining, "I can't remember the words now."

THURSDAY 4 MAY

After arriving in Boston and checking in to the Sheraton, the tour party had a day off before the show in Providence.

FRIDAY 5 MAY

★ LIVE
Civic Center
Providence
Rhode Island, USA

Recorded for *Stage* album.

SATURDAY 6 MAY

★ LIVE
New Boston Garden Arena
Boston
Massachusetts, USA

'The Boston Rock Thrower' regularly attended concerts armed with rocks from the venue's car park. At some point during a performance he would get up, say "Excuse me" and hurl them at the stage. Tonight, one narrowly missed Dennis Davis, whilst another smashed Roger Powell's keyboard. Oblivious, Tony Visconti was outside, recording the show for *Stage*.

SUNDAY 7 MAY

Arriving in New York, the party settled in at the Westbury Hotel, uptown on Madison Avenue, for a night off before the two sold-out Madison Square Garden concerts.

While in New York, David was interviewed on WPLJ-FM.

▼SOCIALISING

Carlos Alomar celebrated his 27th birthday at Hurrah disco at 32 West 62nd Street. Bowie turned up at the party with Bianca Jagger, but disappeared soon afterwards. Coco explained later, "He was rather shy about coming here tonight as several of his ex-girlfriends were here. But you should have seen their faces when he walked in."

MONDAY 8 MAY

★LIVE

Madison Square Garden
New York City
New York, USA

The atmosphere backstage at the Garden was thick with the pungent smells of animals – the circus was in town. Barnum and Bailey were at the venue for a month, but Pat Gibbons had bought two nights from them for Bowie's engagement. Naturally, the animals remained there, just down the passage from Bowie's dressing rooms.

Adrian Belew (2010)

We had a banquet room where there was lots of food laid out, and some of the wives, children and band associates were there. The door burst open and suddenly a chimpanzee in a houndstooth suit and roller skates came whirling around the table, chasing the kids all over the place, followed by his handler in an identical suit, holding a little placard that read "Here's my chimp. He's done a thousand commercials and movies." [040]

RIGHT: With Carlos Alomar, Dennis Davis and George Murray at Madison Square Garden, New York.
OPPOSITE: Maple Leaf Gardens, Toronto.

Belew was nervous at the prospect of playing to the rarefied New York crowd of 20,000, specifically those whose music he was playing: "Bob Fripp will be out there," he worried, "Earl Slick might be coming."

Sean Mayes was more unnerved by the presence of Bianca Jagger watching from the wings with Coco, Andy Warhol and Yoko Ono. During a break in the show, Bianca visited Bowie backstage and arranged to go to lunch with Warhol the following day at Quo Vadis – which was later cancelled when Bowie was too busy.

Adrian Belew (2007)

I remember scanning the front row and seeing Dustin Hoffman looking back at me. Off to one side of the stage sat Andy Warhol with his ever faithful entourage trying their best to look nonchalant. Somewhere in the audience were the Talking Heads, Mick Jagger, Bianca, etc. It was a rubberneck fest. [397]

Tony Visconti also attended as there had been a plan to record the New York dates, but it was scrapped as it involved a costly recording fee.

Paul Rambali (*NME*)

The first hour was the province of Low *and "Heroes", his avowedly conscious and uncaring rejection of the commercial avenues he opened up for himself with* Young Americans *and* Station To Station. *The actual song 'Heroes' seemed to find a space in the audience's collective attention span but the rest of the songs left them plainly restless. The applause seemed to be directed at the thin, fashionably attired presence on stage for being there and being who he is rather than for his music.* [246]

The New York Times critic John Rockwell described the concert as "one of the highlights of the year".

TUESDAY 9 MAY

★ **LIVE**

Madison Square Garden
New York City
New York, USA

Brian Eno visited backstage and showed Roger Powell how he had created the synthesiser sounds on *Low* and *"Heroes"*.

▼ **SOCIALISING**

After the show – the last of the US leg of the tour – Eno and Bianca Jagger joined the party to celebrate at CBGB.

Leaving the club, they found their limo's hubcaps had been removed (by *Punk* magazine's Legs McNeil, who later donated them to a punk Hall of Fame exhibit). They moved on to Studio 54 where they met up with members of Blondie.

ABOVE: Iggy's contractual obligation album, compiled from tapes of his two 1977 tours. Bowie appears on four of the tracks.
OPPOSITE: Festhalle, Frankfurt.

WEDNESDAY 10 MAY

► **TRAVELLING**

While the tour party spent their day off relaxing in New York, Bowie flew to Paris to post-sync some dialogue on *Just A Gigolo*, in preparation for its screening at the Cannes Film Festival.

Tony Visconti returned to Good Earth Studios in London to mix the live tapes for the live album that became *Stage*. RCA wanted the album out as soon as possible both to promote the tour and to thwart bootleggers, who had cashed in on Bowie's 1976 tour with albums such as *The Wembley Wizard Touches The Dial* and *The Thin White Duke*.

■ **ALBUM RELEASED**
IGGY POP
'TV EYE: 1977 LIVE'
(RCA AFL1-2796)

Iggy Pop's live album, which fulfilled his RCA contract and gained him a full album advance, was culled from soundboard tapes from *The Idiot* and *Lust For Life* tours and cleaned up by Edu Meyer at Hansa Tonstudio.

Bowie played piano and sang backing vocal on four of the tracks: 'TV Eye', 'Funtime', 'Dirt' (recorded March 21 and 22 in Cleveland) and 'I Wanna Be Your Dog' (recorded March 28 in Chicago).

THURSDAY 11 MAY

In the afternoon the touring party (minus Bowie) flew to Frankfurt.

FRIDAY 12 MAY

■ **ALBUM RELEASED**
PROKOFIEV'S
'PETER AND THE WOLF'
UK (RCA Red Seal RL-12743)

SATURDAY 13 MAY

▲ **REHEARSING**

Festhalle
Frankfurt, West Germany

Bowie arrived from Paris and joined the band at 7pm to rehearse and check that the equipment had survived the flight from New York.

SUNDAY 14 MAY

★ **LIVE**

Festhalle
Frankfurt, West Germany

MONDAY 15 MAY

★ **LIVE**

Congress Centrum
Hamburg, West Germany

The entourage arrived in Hamburg and checked in at the Plaza Hotel by the lake. That night they played to an audience of 3,000, who were appreciative but remained seated throughout the concert. A solitary fan ventured to the front at the end of 'Ziggy Stardust' and returned to his seat after Bowie leaned down to shake his hand.

TUESDAY 16 MAY

★ **LIVE**

Deutschlandhalle
West Berlin, West Germany

As in Hamburg, the audience remained seated throughout the show and again a solitary fan from the front row got up to dance during 'Station To Station'. A person of military appearance, also in the front row, motioned to the bouncers to subdue him. Bowie ordered them to stop but he was ignored, so he stopped the band and repeated "No! Nein! Stop!" They released the boy and the show resumed.

THURSDAY 18 MAY

★ **LIVE**

Grugahalle
Essen, West Germany

FRIDAY 19 MAY

★ LIVE

Kölner Sporthalle
Cologne, West Germany

✪ TELEVISION

'ARENA ROCK'

"Absolute ruhe bitte!" Bowie barked in mock German officialese when someone in the room called out off-camera. *Cracked Actor* producer Alan Yentob was interviewing Bowie in his hotel room against the Cologne skyline.

YENTOB: *Well, it's been a long time…*

BOWIE: *The last time you were with me was in Los Angeles – one of the worst periods in my life, I think. I got into a lot of emotional and spiritual trouble there and so I decided to split and discover new ways of relating to the music business per se. I wasn't sure exactly what I was in it for any more.*

YENTOB: *Was there a clash between the materialism, the need to be a rock star, successful?*

BOWIE: *Yes, very much so. And as I really didn't want to be one myself, I was living more and more in the style of one of my characters who wanted terrific success – because they're all messiah figures… I really felt the material aspect was something that had to be done in Los Angeles because it's driven into you, it's the food of Los Angeles – Hollywood, rather, not Los Angeles. And so I just packed up everything one day and I moved back to Europe… It was finding out what used to interest me when I was at art school and mime companies and mixed media productions when I was young. That's the first thing I did when I got back to Europe, was to stop thinking about music and performing for a bit and think about something that I hadn't done for a long time, which was paint. And that helped me get back into music again. And also from a different perspective about music and what I wanted to write. And it was a form of expressionistic realism [laughs] – if there's such a thing! I'm not quite sure where to go now. The East beckons me. I'm a bit scared of moving over there really, because I fall in love so much with the life style that I get very Zen about it and won't write anything any more. And I want to keep contributing.* [347]

▮ Broadcast: May 29 (BBC 2).

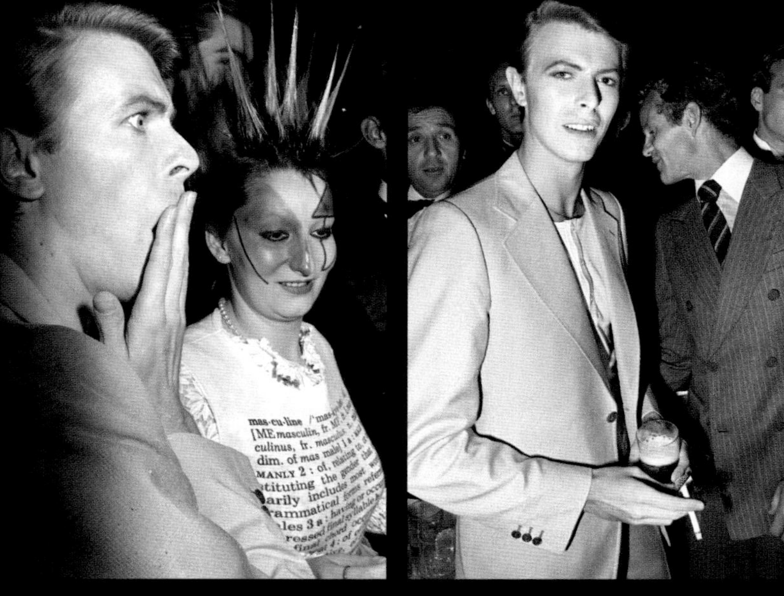

SATURDAY 20 MAY

★ LIVE

Olympiahalle
Munich, West Germany

Tony Visconti arrived with the finished mixes of *Stage*, which he played to Bowie and some of the band in a studio hired for the evening.

Tony Visconti (2002)

They loved it and jumped out of their seats when they heard the descending notes on 'Fame' (we were playing it back very, very loud). David loved it just as I'd mixed it and didn't want to change a single thing. I suggested that maybe the ambient instrumentals could be edited shorter, but he insisted they remain on the album in their entirety. [422]

ABOVE: Cannes International Film Festival. The *Just A Gigolo* party with the waiters dressed as gigolos (top) and Sex Pistols stylist Jordan (above left) who was attending the screening of Derek Jarman's 1977 punk film *Jubilee*, in which she played Amyl Nitrate.
OPPOSITE: Onstage in France.
OVERLEAF: Bowie speaks to the press at the Cannes International Film Festival.

MONDAY 22 MAY

★ LIVE

Stadthalle
Vienna, Austria

TUESDAY 23 MAY

✪ PROMOTION

Cannes, France

CANNES INTERNATIONAL FILM FESTIVAL

The rest of the band and crew flew to Paris, staying at the Hotel de la Trémoille, for a day off before the first of the two shows there.

Meanwhile Bowie attended the Cannes International Film Festival to promote *Just A Gigolo*. David Hemmings had organised a preview screening of a French dubbed version for potential film distributors. With the editing still incomplete, Hemmings and the film's backers felt that Bowie's presence at the screening might help its chances.

Hemmings had also organised a 'Gigolo' party, complete with a group of men dressed in appropriate Twenties tuxedos. With crowds milling everywhere, Bowie ducked through the kitchen and made his entrance. Bowie was also there to push his own film projects: Clive Donner's *Wally* and Rainer Werner Fassbinder's film of *The Threepenny Opera*.

Bianca Jagger was also at the festival promoting the François Weyergans film *Couleur Chair (Flesh Colour)*, in which she appeared with Dennis Hopper. The film ran in the *section parallèle* of the festival but was never released.

WEDNESDAY 24 MAY

★ LIVE

Pavillon de Paris
Paris, France

After partying all night with film industry people who might help him bring his film ideas to fruition, Bowie had Tony Mascia rush him back to Paris. He joined the band for a 4pm soundcheck, returning to the Plaza Athénée Hotel to rest up before the first Paris concert. After the show, he broke his cocaine abstinence and stayed up for the next 24 hours.

THURSDAY 25 MAY

★ LIVE

Pavillon de Paris
Paris, France

▼ SOCIALISING

After the show Bowie and the band partied at The Palace, the local equivalent of Studio 54.

FRIDAY 26 MAY

★ **LIVE**

Palais des Sports de Gerland
Lyon, France

The touring party boarded the plane at Orly Airport for the short flight to Lyon. There was a lengthy delay on the tarmac – it was announced that they were changing an engine. Bowie groaned, "Oh God, that means the pilot's drunk and they're feeding him black coffee."

Recalling the flight from Cyprus in 1972 that put him off air travel for five years, he gripped the armrest tightly as they finally took off.

In the evening Bowie arrived at the venue, which was surrounded by fans. His French driver tried to drop him off out the front next to the crowd, explaining, "I must go back to the hotel to collect some more people."

SATURDAY 27 MAY

★ **LIVE**

Palais des Sports
Marseilles, France

Replaced cancelled Parc Chaneau show.

The concert went well with the band in high spirits and an enthusiastic crowd, until they finished playing 'Blackout'. As if on cue, the speakers sputtered and died, along with the lights.

Sean Mayes (1986)
Carlos was very quick-witted and shouted for us all to get off the stage **très vite.** ***There was no real division between the audience and the backstage area and it was felt that we should leave the building.*** [009]

Marseilles had a reputation for rough crowds. Keith Richards had told Bowie they'd had chairs thrown at them.

Eric Barrett hustled them quickly backstage into the limos and back to their rooms at the hotel. An hour later the roadies had located the loose connection and restored power. Barrett then called them all back and they finished the concert.

Sean Mayes (1986)
It was like giving a show to the troops just behind the front line. It was a hell of a show because everyone had so much nervous energy. [009]

MONDAY 29 MAY

✪ **TELEVISION**

Arena Rock broadcast in UK (BBC 2).

TUESDAY 30 MAY

✪ **TELEVISION**

'MUSIKLADEN EXTRA'
'Sense Of Doubt'/
'Beauty And The Beast'/
'Heroes'/'Stay'/'The Jean Genie'/
'TVC 15'/'Alabama Song'/
'Rebel Rebel' (encore)/
'What In The World' (encore)

Radio Bremen Production
Michael Leckebusch: Director

Bowie put together a 45-minute version of the set for the concert, filmed live in the studio, which was done up like a music club with an audience of 150 sitting at tables amidst pot plants.

▮ Broadcast: August 4 (ZDF).

WEDNESDAY 31 MAY

★ **LIVE**

Falkoner Teatret
Copenhagen, Denmark

GITANES FILTRE SEITA FRANCE
1664
Kronenbourg

JUNE

THURSDAY 1

★ LIVE
Falkoner Teatret
Copenhagen, Denmark

FRIDAY 2 JUNE

★ LIVE
Kungliga Tennishallen
Stockholm, Sweden

SUNDAY 4 JUNE

★ LIVE
Scandinavium
Gothenburg, Sweden

MONDAY 5 JUNE

★ LIVE
Ekeberghallen
Oslo, Norway

WEDNESDAY 7 – FRIDAY 9 JUNE

★ LIVE
Sportpaleis Ahoy
Rotterdam, Netherlands

After the Friday show, Bowie, Coco and Sean Mayes headed out to the Amsterdam nightlife. Some clubs they would visit were the sort where the presence of a superstar went unremarked, apart from a discreet glance or a "Hi, David!" The first club they tried in Amsterdam turned out to be the other sort – full of younger people who quickly noticed Bowie in their midst. In the end they headed for Bonaparte's, a mixed gay club where they socialised and danced without fans milling around him.

SUNDAY 11 JUNE

★ LIVE
Vorst Nationaal
Brussels, Belgium

✪ TELEVISION
Cracked Actor rebroadcast in UK (BBC 2).

MONDAY 12 JUNE

★ LIVE
Vorst Nationaal
Brussels, Belgium

TUESDAY 13 JUNE

▼ SOCIALISING

Iggy Pop's TV Eye Tour (with a new band that included Stooges drummer Scott Asheton and Fred 'Sonic' Smith on guitar) crossed paths with Bowie's tour when it finished with two nights at The Music Machine in Camden Town.

Eno was at the Monday show, playing pool throughout the set, which a reviewer said "didn't rise above the ordinary".

Bowie and Sean Mayes came to the second night, which was better, according to reports. Johnny Rotten was standing at the bar with his back to the stage wearing a huge overcoat with the collar up, despite the tropical heat in the venue.

Later when Bowie and Mayes were backstage with Iggy, security knocked at the door, calling out, "I have a Mr Rotten here." Bowie opened it for Rotten who, Mayes said, "was soon complaining about the place being too hot, the beer shitty." He then told Iggy the show was "a load of rubbish". Bowie later recalled, "Being a Capricorn, I just stayed in the background and listened," but others in the room remember otherwise.

ABOVE: Iggy Pop at The Music Machine, Camden Town. OPPOSITE: Newcastle City Hall.

Scott Asheton (1997)
They're all sitting around a big table, and Bowie and Iggy just kept telling Johnny flat out what he should do. You know, "You should do this, get rid of these guys, straighten up your act, go talk to this person..." And he's just sitting there not saying a thing. Finally Johnny just stood up and said, "Fuck you guys. You're full of shit." [023]

John Lydon (1993)
I went backstage to say hello because I had met Iggy a year before. Mr Bowie wanted me removed – thrown out in fact. He wasn't touring with Iggy – he was just backstage. I thought it was odd. It was Iggy's gig, and Mr Bowie got his personal bouncers to have me removed. [020]

After a while Coco arrived and they left to go clubbing with Iggy at Monkberry's (a cabaret/disco in Mayfair) and Tramps.

WEDNESDAY 14 JUNE

★ LIVE
Newcastle City Hall
Newcastle upon Tyne
Tyne and Wear, England

The entourage arrived in Newcastle, basing themselves at the Gosforth Park Hotel for the three dates at the modest 2,000-seat City Hall. It was Bowie's first UK show in two years and rabid fans were laying siege to the hotel and venue alike. The limos circled the venue nine times before the stage door was cleared for Bowie and the band to get inside. Inside, the enthusiasm of the audience in the comparatively small hall made for a show Sean Mayes described as "amazing", with two "glorious encores".

THURSDAY 15 JUNE

★ LIVE
Newcastle City Hall
Newcastle upon Tyne
Tyne and Wear, England

Backstage visitors included Trevor Bolder and Iggy Pop, who joined the tour for a week. Pat Gibbons told the press that the Egon Schiele film had been postponed for at least a year, and that the live album would be released mid-July.

FRIDAY 16 JUNE

★ LIVE
Newcastle City Hall
Newcastle upon Tyne
Tyne and Wear, England

✪ TELEVISION
'NORTHERN LIGHTS'
(TYNE TEES)

Some sections of the media questioned the absence of artifice in Bowie's act as much as they had questioned its presence in the past.

Q: *Are you afraid perhaps that the fans might sort of go off you a little bit without all the characters that you play and the theatrical performances?*

BOWIE: *I've never really wanted to think about that. That would have stifled my work. I'm very pleased that they still come – it's very nice!*

Q: *You're not living in England at the moment. Why is that? Why do you choose to live abroad?*

BOWIE: *I don't live anywhere really; I travel 100 per cent of the time.* [367]

SATURDAY 17 JUNE

▶ **TRAVELLING**

Bowie, Iggy and the entourage (including girlfriends, wives and children) boarded the coach for the trip to Glasgow. They made tourist stops along the way – a country pub (where the barmaid had a chat with Bowie and stole a kiss) near the Scottish border, and Edinburgh Castle.

MONDAY 19 JUNE

★ **LIVE**

The Apollo
Glasgow, Scotland

The Apollo was an old theatre with two balconies, which had previously been deemed structurally unsound and closed off. Since then they had been fortified and reopened. As the Glasgow fans were whipped into a frenzy by the opening bars of 'Suffragette City', the balconies were bouncing up and down to the beat. They left the stage to tumultuous applause following the 'Station To Station' finale, then returned for an encore of 'TVC 15', and again for a second encore – 'Stay' and 'Rebel Rebel'.

✪ **TELEVISION**
'REPORTING SCOTLAND' (BBC SCOTLAND)

The report included an interview and live tour footage of 'Hang On To Yourself'.

TUESDAY 20 JUNE

★ **LIVE**

The Apollo
Glasgow, Scotland

✪ **PRESS**

Interviewed by Jonathan Mantle for *Vogue*.

MANTLE: *With Ziggy, you appealed to the devotion of a generation. Your music isn't directed at one age group any more, is it?*

BOWIE: *I'm getting older, so I don't think in terms of generation as much as I used to. Before, I was trapped into the archetype of writing for a generation, which is what I think most young rock and rollers do. I'm bored with narration. It died out of all the other arts years ago. Rock and roll follows the rest of the arts about ten years later.*

MANTLE: *Whether you're protected, or you protect yourself deliberately now, you keep yourself cut off. Is there a danger of cutting yourself off from things you might not want to miss?*

BOWIE: *I keep myself cut off from hotels and things, out of deference to the English countryside. At the moment I'm staying way outside of Glasgow, so most of my time has been spent walking on the hills and fishing in the lakes, and running every day. I've been with a friend, Jimmy Osterberg – Iggy Pop. We're from very different backgrounds – that's why we get on really well. I've spent this tour in a very civilised fashion. I've been able to live as I do when I'm not on the road. I get up at seven or eight in the morning, and walk.*

MANTLE: *How long will you stay in Berlin?*

BOWIE: *I think I've finished there now. I've been in Japan and Thailand recently and I may go back to Japan, somewhere round Tokyo.* [193]

THURSDAY 22 JUNE

★ **LIVE**

The Apollo
Glasgow, Scotland

FRIDAY 23 JUNE

▶ **TRAVELLING**

Bowie travelled to Birmingham by rail with Coco, Sean Mayes, Rob Joyce and Leroy Kerr. Travelling first class, Bowie was occasionally accosted by fans who were following the tour. He indulged them with autographs, but Coco had to fend off one persistent waiter from the dining car.

SATURDAY 24 – MONDAY 26 JUNE

★ **LIVE**

Bingley Hall
Stafford
Staffordshire, England

After the Sunday concert, a party was held for the road crew at a club in Birmingham, featuring a disco and a strip show. Taking the stage with a microphone, Dennis Davis livened up the occasion with a mock fashion commentary.

TUESDAY 27 JUNE

▶ **TRAVELLING**

The touring party boarded the coach in the morning for the long ride down the M1 to London for the last three dates of the UK tour.

THURSDAY 29 JUNE

★ **LIVE**

Earls Court Arena
London, England

For his triumphant homecoming, Bowie chose Earls Court rather than Wembley where he had finished the 1976 UK tour.

Bowie's mother Peggy sat with Clive Donner and Michael Watts in the royal box, where Bowie visited her before the concert.

Despite the rapturous receptions the shows had received, Bowie suffered from hometown nerves, as did fellow Londoners Simon House and Sean Mayes.

FRIDAY 30 JUNE

★ **LIVE**

✪ **FILMING**

Earls Court Arena
London, England

David Hemmings and a film crew arrived early to set up for shooting concert footage at Earls Court for a feature-length documentary film of the tour – one of the first Bewlay Bros productions.

In the afternoon the band played a technical rehearsal for Hemmings' crew to set the recording levels and camera angles. A giant crane arm was used to lift one of the camera operators above the stage and audience. Tony Visconti was on hand to supervise recording.

✪ **TELEVISION**
'LONDON WEEKEND SHOW' (ITV)

Janet Street-Porter came with a film crew to make a special focusing on Bowie's relationship with his fans, some of whom she interviewed outside the venue, as well as Michael Watts and David Hemmings.

WATTS: *I think he attracts the punks because they like the idea of somebody who's in a constant state of change and also doesn't represent the hippy period. When Bowie first came out in the Seventies, he was such a relief from all the earnest, rather boring music that was happening and the kind of po-faced attitude that existed in the pop music scene.*

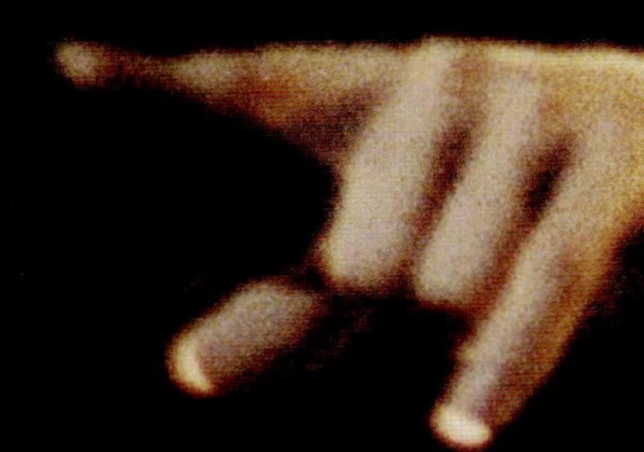

HEMMINGS: *I think it's much more exciting for an audience to have that kind of association with somebody that they really can't touch or understand completely than it is with somebody who's a lot more open and immediately communicative.* [362]

Shortly before show time, Bowie emerged from his trailer in the cavernous backstage area to give a short interview with Street-Porter. "I think that this is not so much of an act really," Bowie said. "It's more… sort of… a performance of songs. This tour has been somewhat of an eye opener because I've really enjoyed just performing songs and not having the commitment of having to be a character, which has made it less of a strain than it normally is."

With Hemmings inside about to shoot the concert, Bowie evaded her question about *Just A Gigolo*.

"I don't know, I haven't seen it. I don't usually see rushes when I'm filming so I really don't have any real idea of what the film's like."

Of his future plans he ventured, "Possibly a little tour next year, very simple one. But definitely a big tour in two years' time – 1980." [362]

▌Broadcast July 9 (ITV).

OPPOSITE: Earls Court Arena, London. David Hemmings' film of the Friday concert, *Stage*, remains unreleased.

ABOVE: On stage with Simon House, Sean Mayes and Carlos Alomar at Earls Court.

JULY

SATURDAY 1

★ LIVE
✪ FILMING
Earls Court Arena
London, England

The show marked the end of the European leg of the tour. In the audience: Brian May, Roger Taylor, Ian Dury, Dustin Hoffman, Bob Geldof and Iggy Pop.

David Hemmings and his film crew were back, getting more footage for the documentary. Backstage one of the cameras turned to film Bowie's arrival with Bianca Jagger, until Pat Gibbons instructed them to stop.

Sean Mayes (1999)
The gig was sensational, the final high of the tour. The surge to the front started almost immediately so we played to a seething crowd of excitement. The first half was magnificent, the second just wild. [022]

Midway through the first set, Bowie turned to ask the band if they remembered how to play 'Sound And Vision'.

"Here's something we haven't done before," he told the 20,000-strong audience as the band kicked into the song. "This is all last night stuff, folks!"

▮ 'Be My Wife'/'Sound And Vision' released on *Rarest One Bowie* (Golden Years 1995).

▼ SOCIALISING
Bianca Jagger and David Hemmings joined Bowie's party at Tramps nightclub to celebrate the end of the European tour.

✪ 'STAGE' FILM
Bowie and Hemmings envisaged the film as a 90-minute feature incorporating Bowie's life on and off the stage, which they hoped would be in cinemas late autumn, pending a distribution deal.

In February 1979, when Nicky Horne interviewed Bowie on Capital Radio, the film was still a going concern, intended as a companion to *Stage*.

Bowie (1979)
We had great ambitions in the beginning to do some kind of surreal thing but what we've ended up with is a very straightforward film of the concert as it stands and I hope that it sort of matches the album. There's a little bit more to do with the editing, then it's ready. I don't know when it's going to come out, exactly. [341]

David Hemmings (2000)
We shot it with about 10 cameras over two nights. We put it all together in Majorca, where I had a house, and David came out and stayed with us. But at the end of it he didn't like the cut, or he didn't like the fact that we had to cut in between numbers in order to get all the coverage. So he never released it. [105]

Bowie (2000)
I simply didn't like the way it had been shot. Now, of course, it looks pretty good and I would suspect that it would make it out some time in the future. [105]

SUNDAY 2 JULY

▲ RECORDING
Good Earth Studios
Dean Street, Soho
London, England

'Alabama Song' (Brecht/Weill)

Tony Visconti: Producer

During his Berlin period, Bowie had become a fan of Brecht and Weill (though nothing came of *The Threepenny Opera* film with Fassbinder) and their 'Alabama Song', popularised by Kurt Weill's wife Lotte Lenya and later by The Doors.

The song had become a highlight of his set, so Bowie decided to take the match-fit tour band into Visconti's studio in Dean Street to record it.

Sean Mayes (1999)
David wanted Dennis [Davis] to play very freely against the rhythm to give an unstable, insane atmosphere to the track. When we tried to do this, it proved hilariously difficult so we finally laid the backing down without drums, then Dennis overdubbed his demolishing attack when his efforts wouldn't disturb the beat. [022]

Bowie presented the recording to RCA as his next single, a move so perverse it was interpreted as a provocation to RCA to release him from his contract. RCA refrained from issuing it until 1980.

SUNDAY 9 JULY

✪ TELEVISION
London Weekend Show broadcast in UK (ITV), featuring interviews and excerpts of 'Star', 'Heroes' and 'Hang On To Yourself' from Earls Court.

AUGUST

FRIDAY 4

✪ **TELEVISION**

Musikladen Extra broadcast in Germany (ZDF) without the second encore, 'What In The World'.

Bowie returned to the relative anonymity of Berlin, where he had a crew cut and grew a short beard. He packed up his belongings at Hauptstrasse 155 to move to Switzerland.

SEPTEMBER

✪ **PRESS**

Vogue published in UK, including Jonathan Mantle's June interview with Bowie and portraits by Lord Snowdon.

▲ **RECORDING**

Mountain Studios
Montreux, Switzerland

'LODGER' ALBUM

After a two-month break the tour band reconvened in Switzerland, where Bowie was now living, to record what became *Lodger*, the third album of the 'Berlin triptych'. Mountain Studios was located on the shore of Lake Geneva, part of the casino complex that had been rebuilt since the 1971 fire Deep Purple immortalised in 'Smoke On The Water'. The band was staying nearby at the Hotel Excelsior.

They set up in the smaller of the two studios with in-house engineers Dave Richards and Bowie's neighbour in Vevey, Eugene Chaplin.

Tony Visconti (2006)
It wasn't really a studio for recording a band at all, but was used to record live concerts in the huge auditorium that was below us. It was small and really an overdub studio, but the main auditorium was booked out for the summer. [047]

Adrian Belew (2007)
The control room of the studio was on the first floor, while the actual recording room was above it on the second floor. There was a camera in the recording room, which allowed David, Eno and Tony to see the players. [399]

The album's working title was *Planned Accidents*, continuing the experimental, spontaneous approach of its predecessors. With little in the way of specific song ideas, Bowie and Eno instead directed the musicians using the Oblique Strategies methodology that Eno developed with Peter Schmidt.

Sean Mayes (1985)
He and Brian were determining the direction everything should take. Basically we were getting down backing tracks. We'd be given a chord sequence and a rhythm and, in one case, Brian would point to different chords with a baton. It seemed deliberately to make things difficult for us. If anyone was getting too comfortable with what they were playing, he'd then change it and give them something else, so you were making mistakes all the time. [019]

Tony Visconti (2006)
Eno asked for a blackboard and wrote his eight favourite chords [B flat, F, C, E, G, E flat, A minor and C minor] in big block letters. He then said to Carlos, Dennis and George, "Okay, I'd like you to play a funky groove. I will point to a chord and you will change over to that chord after four beats." I could see the rhythm section exchanging irritable looks as if to say "what an asshole". [047]

Bowie (2001)
Brian and I did play a number of 'art pranks' on the band. They really didn't go down too well though. [105]

Tony Visconti (2003)
He was telling these three black guys who came from the roughest part of New York, "Just play something funky." [176]

Another strategy they devised for Boys Keep Swinging' (originally called 'Lewis Reed') was to have the musicians swap instruments – Alomar on drums, Davis on bass and Murray on guitar, though only Alomar's drum part was kept.

Bowie (1979)
What was extraordinary was the enthusiasm that came from musicians who weren't playing their usual instrument. They became kids discovering rock 'n' roll for the first time again. [310]

Tony Visconti (2002)
'Boys Keep Swinging' and 'Fantastic Voyage' are the same exact chord changes and structure, even in the same key; just the tempo and instrumentation are different. We even recorded a third song with the same structure, but it never got finished. [423]

At one point they considered recording the entire album with these chord changes. In the two weeks at Mountain they tried various strategies – oblique and standard – to generate new song ideas. 'African Nightlife' came from jamming on Dale Hawkins' 'Susie Q'. Others were the result of recycling. Bowie borrowed back 'Sister Midnight', which he had originally written with Alomar and given to Iggy. They slowed down the original backing track, removed some instruments and added others as well as new lyrics, which became 'Red Money'.

Tony Visconti (2006)
'Move On' was inspired by playing the recording of 'All The Young Dudes' backwards and then everyone learning to play it that way. [047]

Bowie (1979)
I had put one of my reel to reel tapes on backwards by mistake and really quite liked the melody it created. So I played quite a few more in this fashion and chose five or six that were really quite compelling. 'Dudes' was the only one to make the album, as I didn't want to abandon the 'normal' writing I was doing completely. But it was a worthwhile exercise in my mind. [106]

At the end of each recording day Bowie and Visconti would run off a quarter-inch tape of the recordings and review the takes. Then they looped the section with the 'mistakes' to form song structures.

Sean Mayes (1985)
Because the mistakes come up again each time, they cease to be mistakes – they become part of the music. You'd end up with the structure of a song in multi-track made from the loops that you could continue adding to and it ceased to be obvious that it came from loops in the first place. [019]

With the backing tracks complete, Alomar, Davis and Murray flew home to New York. Mayes, House and Belew then alternated in the studio recording overdubs alone upstairs with Bowie running back and forth with suggestions.

Tony Visconti (2001)
Adrian Belew was a champion because he'd do whatever strange thing that was requested of him. [015]

Adrian Belew (2010)
The idea, in keeping with the theme 'planned accidents', was to capture my accidental responses to the backing tracks they had already recorded. So they insisted I never hear the tracks beforehand, nor was I allowed to know the key of the songs. I simply heard a count-off and was instructed to play something along with the tracks as best I could. After no more than three tries, we would move on to the next song. (Just about the time I knew when to expect the chorus.) Later, David, Eno, and Tony chose their favourite bits from what I had played and made them into a single composite guitar part, a guitar part I never actually could or would have played. [399]

After two weeks the musicians were sent home, to regroup in a month for the last leg of the tour. Bowie and Visconti made plans to finish the album – still untitled and without lyrics – in the new year.

MONDAY 25 SEPTEMBER

✪ PHOTO SESSION

Paris, France

'L'UOMO VOGUE'

(December issue)

FRIDAY 29 SEPTEMBER

■ ALBUM RELEASED

'STAGE'

UK (RCA PL 02913)
US (CPL2 2913)
UK Chart Peak No.5
Charting 10 weeks
US Chart Peak No.44
Charting 13 weeks

SIDE ONE

1. **'Hang On To Yourself'** (3:26)
2. **'Ziggy Stardust'** (3:32)
3. **'Five Years'** (3:58)
4. **'Soul Love'** (2:55)
5. **'Star'** (2:31)

SIDE TWO

1. **'Station To Station'** (8:55)
2. **'Fame'** (Bowie/Alomar/Lennon) (4:06)
3. **'TVC 15'** (4:37)

SIDE THREE

1. **'Warszawa'** (Bowie/Eno) (6:56)
2. **'Speed Of Life'** (2:46)
3. **'Art Decade'** (3:10)
4. **'Sense Of Doubt'** (3:11)
5. **'Breaking Glass'** (Bowie/Davis/Murray) (3:28)

SIDE FOUR

1. **'Heroes'** (Bowie/Eno) (6:20)
2. **'What In The World'** (4:22)
3. **'Blackout'** (4:02)
4. **'Beauty And The Beast'** (5:08)

David Bowie/Tony Visconti: Producers
David Bowie: Vocals/Keyboards
Carlos Alomar: Rhythm Guitar
George Murray: Bass
Dennis Davis: Drums/Percussion
Adrian Belew: Lead Guitar
Simon House: Violin
Sean Mayes: Piano/String Ensemble
Roger Powell: Synthesiser/Keyboards
Recorded April/May in Boston/Philadelphia/Providence

ABOVE: Delayed by a change of cover photo and legal issues, *Stage* was still released in time to promote the tour it documented.

RCA had asked Tony Visconti to hurry with the mix (as with *David Live*) to ensure the album was out in time to promote the tour. By the end of May it was ready and advertisements for pre-orders appeared in late July with Bowie's self-portrait in lieu of a cover.

Then RCA put back the release date, citing problems with the artwork – the problem being that Bowie had changed his mind about the cover after seeing a live photograph in French rock magazine *Best*. It had been shot unauthorised by reporter Gilles Riberolles, but Bowie halted the release in order to make it the cover image.

The release was delayed further by a contractual dispute between RCA and Bowie, who wanted to fulfil his contract and move to WEA (and its movie affiliations). He argued the album counted as two LPs and RCA countered it was worth one, as it was taken from a single performance, despite the fact it was collated from three different dates.

Stage received the same lukewarm response as *David Live*, although the criticism focused more on the format rather than the performances. Bowie and Visconti had decided to sequence the songs chronologically rather than follow the order of the set list, and put fades between the tracks. This rendered the audience almost inaudible and diminished the energy and atmosphere of the concert.

Bowie corrected this in 2005 when he asked Tony Visconti to restore the original set list sequencing for the 5.1 surround sound edition.

REISSUES

▮ CD (UK/Germany only) (RCA 1985).

▮ CD (remastered) (Ryko 1991).

BONUS TRACK

'Alabama Song' (4:00)

▮ 2005 EMI CD (remastered, 5.1 surround sound). Resequenced with bonus tracks 'Be My Wife'/'Stay'.

SIDE ONE

1. **'Warszawa'** (Bowie/Eno) (6:50)
2. **'Heroes'** (Bowie/Eno) (6:19)
3. **'What In The World'** (4:24)
4. **'Be My Wife'** (2:35)
5. **'Blackout'** (4:01)
6. **'Sense Of Doubt'** (3:13)
7. **'Speed Of Life'** (3:44)
8. **'Breaking Glass'** (Bowie/Davis/Murray) (3:28)
9. **'Beauty And The Beast'** (5:08)
10. **'Fame'** (Bowie/Alomar/Lennon) (4:06)

SIDE TWO

1. **'Five Years'** (3:58)
2. **'Soul Love'** (2:55)
3. **'Star'** (2:31)
4. **'Hang On To Yourself'** (3:26)
5. **'Ziggy Stardust'** (3:32)
6. **'Art Decade'** (Bowie/Eno) (3:10)
7. **'Alabama Song'** (Brecht/Weill) (4:00)
8. **'Station To Station'** (8:55)
9. **'Stay'** (7:17)
10. **'TVC 15'** (4:37)

▮ 'Station To Station' also released on *Christiane F* soundtrack (RCA 1981, EMI 2001) and *Sound + Vision* (Ryko 1989).

■ ALBUM RELEASED
'AN EVENING WITH DAVID BOWIE' PROMO
US (RCA DJL1-3016)

SIDE ONE
1. **Open** (0:33)
2. **Segment 1** (7:29)
3. **'Ziggy Stardust'** (3:32)
4. **Segment 2** (2:26)
5. **'Station To Station'** (8:47)

SIDE TWO
1. **Segment 3** (2:53)
2. **'Beauty And The Beast'** (5:02)
3. **Segment 3** (continued) (6:22)
4. **'Fame'** (Bowie/Alomar/Lennon) (4:05)
5. **Segment 4** (5:18)

Released to promote *Stage*, the exclusive Superstars Radio Network interview was recorded the previous November in New York, where he spoke about his life, career and influences. Intercut with live music tracks taken from *Stage*.

Sonny Fox: Producer/Editor

■ SINGLE RELEASED
12-INCH PROMO
'Star' (2:31)/
'What In The World' (4:22)/
'Breaking Glass' (Bowie/Davis/Murray) (3:28)
US (RCA DJL1-3255)

Live versions from *Stage*, pressed on white vinyl.

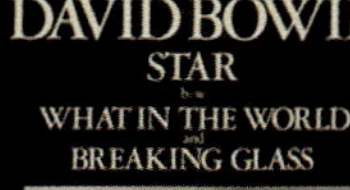

OCTOBER

Bowie's office issued a press release to quash rumours that he was considering leaving RCA for another label:

"In answer to the numerous rumours concerning my recording activities, I wish to clear the air and set the record straight. At present and for the foreseeable future I am under contract to RCA Records and at no time have I engaged in any negotiations to alter that status. My relationship with RCA has been a long and rewarding one and any rumours that I am signing with another label are completely false and erroneous."

The world premiere of *Just A Gigolo* in Germany was postponed for a month due to problems translating from English to German. Hemmings' original cut of the film was longer and dramatically different to the version eventually released in 1979.

SATURDAY 14

■ CHART
'STAGE'
UK Chart Peak No.4

ABOVE: The interview promotional album featured a David James still from *The Man Who Fell To Earth*.
BELOW LEFT: The promo 12-inch live single 'Star' featured another shot from the 1975 Tom Kelley session.

NOVEMBER

THURSDAY 2

AUSTRALASIAN TOUR

"I'm looking forward to it," Bowie told Australian journalist John Hanrahan. "It's a long way to go and there have been times in the past when I considered it. But now we're about to start, I'm very happy." [135]

SATURDAY 4 NOVEMBER

▶ TRAVELLING

Bowie arrived in Sydney for his first tour of Australia after an almost incident-free flight from Hong Kong. He woke at 3am to the announcement that one of the four engines had cut out and was spilling oil into the ozone.

"Nothing to worry about," the captain assured the passengers, "We'll bypass Melbourne and limp up to Sydney. Go back to sleep, everyone."

"Awfully decent of him to tell us," he recalled later. "I think that flying should be treated like being in shock," he added. "You should be wrapped up and drink cups of tea while it is happening." [148]

Despite having no prior notice of Bowie's arrival, the media were waiting at the airport, but he eluded them with a ruse and quietly slipped outside into the waiting Rolls-Royce.

Bowie (1978)
The first thing that happened was that there were three or four press people behind me in the line saying, "Have you seen David Bowie yet?" I said, "You can't miss him, he's just over there, he's got a green raincoat on and bright red hair" and they went off and hassled the poor guy for a few minutes. [350]

The band arrived at 4pm on a separate flight from Los Angeles and joined Bowie at the Sebel Townhouse, a small European-styled hotel in Elizabeth Bay, near Kings Cross. At the time, the Sebel was recognised as Australia's premier celebrity hotel.

MONDAY 6 NOVEMBER

▲ REHEARSING

Hordern Pavilion
Sydney, Australia

The band assembled for a week of rehearsals, working from late afternoon until early morning. The stage was fully constructed to ensure all technical aspects ran smoothly, with the lighting crew practising synchronising the spots for each song.

✪ PRESS

Over the next two days Bowie gave interviews to the press in his room at the Sebel. Tour promoter Paul Dainty's publicist, Margaret St George, allocated 30 minutes to each group of five.

Anthony O'Grady (*RAM*)

He absolutely refused to do an all-in general press conference. Apparently he'd heard some of the classic stories – like the time Fleetwood Mac were asked five times within the hour just why they had a penguin as a logo.

We ascend to the ninth floor or thereabouts… Barbara DeWitt invites us into the actual interview room, seats everyone around the sofa where Bowie will actually sit and explains the rules. Half an hour of questions, and a five-minute warning before end of play. Barbara disappears to fetch The Man. [235]

The Australian press focused mainly on Bowie's apparent normality – one writer described his hair as "unfashionably short and conservatively groomed."

John Hanrahan (*The Sun*)

I was expecting a washed-out little man with a midnight sun tan who would nod shyly and retire to the furthest seat in the room. He's slender, wiry, but Bowie's colouring is closer to midday at Bondi. He bounces on to the lounge and sinks, one leg tucked under the other, pulls out a packet of cigarettes and lights up, tossing the packet onto the lounge. "How are ya, then?" The question sounds like it's come from an old mate.

Bowie explained his tanned healthy appearance came from his recent trip to Eastern Africa, where he had spent three days with a Masai tribe. "I get my musical influences from societies like Masai, rather than from the past in this society," he said. "I'm a born traveller. I'm obsessed by it, can't stop. When I travel I take a Jeep and do it alone. When I go to Kenya, for instance, I'm on the road all the time and I make the most of any environment that I'm in.

"While I'm here I'll take one flight out to Ayers Rock because I promised Brian Eno I would – that's his famous symbol in life, Ayers Rock. To him that's music – long barren passages with one jewel dropped in the middle. That's how he writes. [136]

"Ziggy has gone, so has the Thin White Duke and all the other characters. Now I'm just David Jones, the real me. I don't write character songs any more… so I suppose I am about as natural as I can be on stage in front of 20,000 people, which is a pretty unnatural thing to do. I do regret that Australian audiences never had a chance to see the characters. [134]

"They have missed out on all the build-up to what I'm doing now. It's a shame because they were important as pre-stages of what's happening now." [235]

WEDNESDAY 8 NOVEMBER

Bowie's old schoolmate Peter Frampton arrived in Sydney for the premiere of *Sgt Pepper's Lonely Hearts Club Band* film and his concert at the Sydney Sports Ground on the 18th. A reporter asked him, "Bette Midler showed us her cleavage. David Bowie was incoherent. What are you going to do for us, Peter?"

✪ TELEVISION
'COUNTDOWN'

Ian Meldrum interviewed Bowie on the tennis court at the Hordern Pavilion, where they talked about his arrival in Australia, how Bowie had used theatre in his music, the origins of 'Golden Years' and 'Fame', *Just A Gigolo*, *Ziggy Stardust* and 'Heroes'.

▮Broadcast: November 12 (ABC).

THURSDAY 9 NOVEMBER

▼ SOCIALISING

In the evening Bowie and a small group went out to some clubs, ending up at the Manzil Room in Kings Cross. The Walker Street Cinema screened *The Man Who Fell To Earth* and again the following night.

FRIDAY 10 NOVEMBER

In the evening Bowie and entourage flew to Adelaide for his first concert in Australia.

Synthesiser player Roger Powell missed the Adelaide and Perth shows as he was still playing Todd Rundgren dates. Melbourne musician Dennis Garcia took his place.

Garcia's 1977 album, *Jive To Stay Alive*, was the result of his experimenting with the creation of music using biomechanical feedback devices. Electrodes were attached to his head and wired up with cables to trigger both drums and synthesisers. Bowie had liked the album and recruited Garcia for the tour. "He was a gentleman," Garcia later said. "He gave me a lot of good raps in the Australian press."

OPPOSITE: Bowie fields questions in his suite at the Sebel Townhouse in Kings Cross, Sydney. He was so taken with the area – and Australia – that in 1983 he bought an apartment in the nearby Kincoppal block in Elizabeth Bay. He kept the waterfront apartment as a base for his regular month-long visits until 1992.

"Ziggy has gone, so has the Thin White Duke and all the other characters. Now I'm just David Jones, the real me."

David Bowie

SATURDAY 11 NOVEMBER

★ **LIVE**

Adelaide Oval
Adelaide, Australia

The Australian tour was the first time since 1973 that Bowie had a support act. The Angels formed in Adelaide, originally as a 'jug band', and had reinvented themselves as a hard rock group. In 1978 their chart-topping album *Face To Face* and the exposure from the Bowie tour made them one of Australia's most popular bands.

John Brewster (2012)
We had done the Meatloaf tour earlier in the year... then the Bowie tour took our album to triple platinum. I was told that he chose us on the strength of our music – he liked the sound of the band, and the songs.

Bowie and the band arrived at the Adelaide Oval a couple of hours before the show.

Sean Mayes (1999)
This was our first open-air gig, the huge rig looking magnificent with a canopy covering the stage in case of rain. We all strolled out front on the grass while support group The Angels did a soundcheck. [022]

John Brewster (2012)
We did our soundcheck in the late afternoon and there was a lone figure sitting out on the grass about 60 metres away in a pair of slacks and a v-neck jumper and fairly short hair. I looked at him and I thought, "I wonder if that's David Bowie" and then I thought, "Nah, don't be silly, that can't be David Bowie." But in fact it was, and when we finished the soundcheck he was just on his own and as we started walking off the stage this guy got up and walked around the back of the stage and we were walking down the steps and he was at the bottom of the steps and he introduced himself to each and every one of us. And that's when he said, "I really like your music" and "Would you like to have dinner with me and the band tonight?" It was really good to be made to feel so much a part of their tour.

Doc Neeson (2007)
Bowie insisted we be called 'special guests' rather than the support act. He said we could have his lights and did we want to borrow his guitars? He showed how to treat a support band. [319]

OPPOSITE AND ABOVE: Adelaide Oval, the opening concert of Bowie's first Australian tour.

Later, as the crowds were filing through the gates, Bowie was in his caravan in the backstage compound behind the stage, watching Peter Frampton co-host the *Countdown* music show.

At the end of the first set, Bowie announced, "We're just going off for 10 minutes and when we come back, we won't be wearing any slippers." When they returned the excited crowd became even more worked up, despite the unseasonably cold conditions.

Sean Mayes (1999)
People were throwing streamers onstage, also a sparkler, a camera sling and a blue puppet wearing a Devo badge. Towards the end, Carlos was losing his voice and David forgot some of the words in 'Station To Station'. But we stormed through the encores... [022]

Bowie placed the puppet (a Sesame Street Grover doll) on Mayes' piano, where it sat for most of the concert.

The piano Mayes played on the tour was a Bechstein. It had gone through several colour changes in its history, from wood grain to black (studio work) to blue (television show) to black (private use) to white (Rod Stewart's 1977 Australian tour) and back to black for the Bowie tour.

SUNDAY 12 NOVEMBER

▶ **TRAVELLING**

Bowie and the band flew to Perth and checked in to the Sheraton Hotel overlooking the Swan River.

✪ **TELEVISION**

Countdown broadcast in Australia (ABC)

The eight-minute report included the Ian Meldrum interview, footage of the band rehearsing 'Alabama Song' and clips from 'Fame' (*Soul Train*), the 'Heroes' video and 'Ziggy Stardust' live in Dallas.

TUESDAY 14 NOVEMBER

★ **LIVE**

Entertainment Centre
Perth, Australia

Perth was not originally on the tour itinerary but Bowie ended up playing two concerts at the Entertainment Centre, a relatively new circular indoor venue with a capacity of 8,200.

After the show, Sean Mayes, Carlos Alomar and some of the crew went to the club Hernando's Hideaway. Alomar refused to pay his admission, saying, "You don't charge Bowie's band!" Mayes noted the house band was "very un-together" and was told that it was all they could get, with nearly all of Perth's musicians at the Bowie show that night.

WEDNESDAY 15 NOVEMBER

★ **LIVE**

Entertainment Centre
Perth, Australia

The second Perth concert was only scheduled and announced that morning. It was only half full as a result, but those who had returned for the second night said it was the pick of the two concerts and had Bowie joking with the crowd.

▼ **SOCIALISING**

After the gig Bowie and Coco went to Connections nightclub. Australian bodyguards Bob Jones and Richard Norton stood by their table, keeping over-interested fans away as Stuart George muttered, "I wish those two weren't so obvious." Bowie later stopped outside the club on his way out and autographed a fan's car.

Richard Norton was part of Paul Dainty's security unit and doubled as a martial arts instructor to his charges.

Richard Norton (1979)
David's in great shape. The first time we met in Australia, he says, "Well, give me a look at your push-ups." This is in a restaurant. So I'm down doing ten push-ups, and he says, "Oh, I can do 'em better than that." He jumps down and does arms-stretched ones. They're very hard to do. [181]

THURSDAY 16 NOVEMBER

Bowie and the band spent their day off in Perth cruising along the Swan River in a boat hired for them by Australian tour promoter Paul Dainty.

Sean Mayes (1986)

On that tour, David was very relaxed and looking very healthy. We were all out on this boat in the sun, all in our swim suits and things, and David was pulling at his middle and just about managing to pinch a bit of flesh between his fingers saying, "Dear me, they'll be calling me plump next." [019]

Most of the cast (except Bowie) attended the world premiere of *Just A Gigolo* (*Schöner Gigolo, Armer Gigolo*) in West Berlin at the Gloria Palast on Kurfürstendamm, where Dietrich's film *The Blue Angel* had opened to rave reviews in 1930.

This film, however, was so poorly received that David Hemmings cancelled further screenings before the German public could see it.

Bowie (1979)

During the filming we'd had a lot of aggravation from the German production company – we wanted to do things in a particular manner and they wanted to do them in quicker time and a bit cheaper than everything that David [Hemmings] had in mind. David went on holiday after the film. By the time he got back from holiday they'd taken the thing away and they'd cut it themselves and had already started to try and sell it and David freaked at that and that's why the thing only came out in Germany because he was able to stop it. [337]

Hemmings returned to London to work on a new edit, cutting it from 147 minutes to 105 minutes for its UK opening the following year.

FRIDAY 17 NOVEMBER

Bowie and entourage arrived in Melbourne, checking in to the Hilton Hotel, opposite the venue, Melbourne Cricket Ground.

ABOVE: Bowie arriving in Melbourne.
OPPOSITE: Melbourne. Bowie keeps his promise – "We play rain or shine."

■ **SINGLE RELEASED**
7-INCH LIVE EP
'Breaking Glass' (Bowie/Davis/Murray) (3:28)/
'Art Decade' (3:10)/
'Ziggy Stardust' (3:32)
UK (RCA BOW 1)
Europe (PB 9337)
UK Chart Peak No.59

SATURDAY 18 NOVEMBER

★ **LIVE**
Melbourne Cricket Ground
Melbourne, Australia

The MCG, with its capacity of 40,000, was the largest venue Bowie had played to date.

Determined Melbourne fans had been camping outside the venue for three weeks before the concert to get in first for the good vantage points.

The tickets promised, "We play rain or shine." Melbourne, notorious for its inclement weather, obliged with a downpour that never let up throughout the entire concert. The stage was so slick with water that Bowie slipped and almost fell into the front row. The energy of the crowd kept him in a jovial mood and he substituted the word 'rain' when they played 'Fame'.

Sean Mayes (1999)

It was pouring and the bedraggled fans had a punk look with their ruined hair and streaky make-up. But the mood was fantastic – when you're soaked you don't give a damn. [022]

Adrian Belew (1999)

That was an incredible show. There was a huge expectation and everyone's waiting for you to come out and finally you do come out and there's this concern whether everyone will be electrocuted! [004]

Debra Robertson (*The Sun*)

It was a truly miserable night in Melbourne. More than 25,000 fans gathered to stick by their hero through his three-hour show. It was well worth the drenching. At least that was the general feeling of fans who stayed. The crowds even had the patience to wait for Bowie while he took intermission – so he could show off the gear from his unique wardrobe. In a considerate gesture, he told them he wouldn't be long. During the second half of the show, the crowd went wild. Bowie almost caused a riot at the end when he threw his microphone into the crowd. [251]

SUNDAY 19 NOVEMBER

▶ TRAVELLING

It was still raining as they left Melbourne and flew to Brisbane.

The Courier Mail

If it had not been for the security entourage surrounding the 31-year-old singer and actor, no one would have realised he had arrived. He and the guards walked quickly across the tarmac to a fleet of waiting limousines. He smiled pleasantly and said hello to photographers. Inside the Ansett terminal an agitated American gave orders to Brisbane tour promoter Harvey Lister. He seemed to feel security was not tight enough.

Bowie and the band had a couple of spare days in Brisbane before the next concert. Fans were already camping outside the venue gates – some of them since Friday – with canvas awnings spread above their sleeping bags. [094]

MONDAY 20 NOVEMBER

▼ SOCIALISING

Bowie and the entourage went out to celebrate Tony Mascia's first wedding anniversary at the Brisbane nightclub Top Of The State. Peter Maslen (later of Australian group Boom Crash Opera), was drumming in the house band, Stax, when Bowie and his entourage arrived.

Peter Maslen (2010)

Being an early week night, there weren't many people out, so Bowie et al had a hassle-free venue in which to drink and party. The champagne was flowing that night. Stax played a variety of music, but when we saw who had arrived, we played our most 'funky' tracks.

In a break, Dennis Davis, who had heard us playing BT Express and Stevie Wonder songs, asked me if he could play my kit. People kept getting up and jamming on stage and Dennis Davis loved playing drums to BT Express and T-Connection songs.

ABOVE: Bowie crosses the tarmac with Stuart George and Tony Mascia on arrival in Brisbane. OPPOSITE: With Simon House, Sydney Showground.

The house band from the nightclub at Lennons Plaza arrived and joined in. I was back on the drums (Dennis wanted to sing by this stage) with Barry Sullivan on bass, most of the Bowie band playing guitars and keyboards to some funky tune and as I looked up out of my drunken haze, I see David Bowie on the centre mic singing something that resembled 'Fame'. I remember saying in my head… "I'm onstage, playing with David Bowie!!" [381]

TUESDAY 21 NOVEMBER

★ LIVE

Lang Park
Brisbane, Australia

Rory Gibson (***The Brisbane Telegraph***)

'Station To Station' was stunning. Roger Powell unleashed an awesome sound from his synthesisers, giving the impression of a giant train speeding between the speaker banks. Bowie, if you were close enough to see him, oozed a talent and stage presence that is rare. His movements were fluid and exact and the famous voice was as powerful and as versatile as expected. The sound system was huge and the music that poured out of it was crystal clear. [130]

For those who couldn't join the 16,000 at the concert, a cinema in Annerley held a late-night screening of the uncut version of *The Man Who Fell To Earth*.

WEDNESDAY 22 NOVEMBER

There were several reports in the press about noise from the concert, which spread across the still night air.

The Brisbane Telegraph

David Bowie today received some noisy feedback from Queensland's minister in charge of noise, Mr Russ Hinze, following the pop star's open-air concert last night. "These pop singers come out here to make a quick quid by disturbing our peace and tranquillity," Mr Hinze said. "The fact that he's a pommie as well wouldn't help." It was reported that the noise was loud enough to be heard 6km away. Residents of the suburbs of Paddington, Bardon and Milton described it as "intolerable". [069]

The Courier Mail

One Bardon man said the concert drowned out the television. A spokesman for the concert promoters, the Paul Dainty Corporation, Margaret St George, said there were only eight telephone complaints about noise. The concert ended at 10.30pm she said. [095]

Bowie and the band returned to Sydney and the Sebel Townhouse. On the night of their arrival, Dennis Davis and Roger Powell jammed with Bette Midler's band at the Manzil Room in nearby Kings Cross.

A few days before, Midler had said of Bowie, "He loves me and I love him. And we've been talking about doing a film for a long time. But who wants to make a movie with a guy who's prettier than you are?"

THURSDAY 23 NOVEMBER

Bowie visited Peter Frampton at his hotel. "He's very friendly," Bowie told Mayes. "Just as sweet as he used to be in school." Bowie had gone to the same school as Frampton, whose father was Bowie's art teacher.

In the evening Bowie, Coco and Mayes went to see Bette Midler's show at the State Theatre, standing at the back as all seats were sold out.

FRIDAY 24 NOVEMBER

★ LIVE

RAS Showground
Sydney, Australia

Demand was high after more than 40,000 tickets sold out quickly at $12.50. Despite this, the first show was "subdued, but went well", according to Mayes.

While in Sydney, the Australian office of RCA presented Bowie with a plaque for Outstanding Sales, which he later gave to charity.

SATURDAY 25 NOVEMBER

★ **LIVE**

RAS Showground
Sydney, Australia

The second Sydney show was said to be the best of the whole tour.

Les Murray (*The Sun*)
His stunningly diverse material… if anything outmatched the quality we recalled on record – in many cases his superb seven-piece band dabbling inventively with the new arrangements. Re-emerging in angelic white after his own intermission, from the rear of the arena, he looked like some divine prophet's post-resurrection apparition in front of his beguiled multitude. [224]

For the second encore, Bowie returned to the stage alone. Leaning on the mic stand, Bowie asked the roaring crowd, "What would you do if I sang out of tune?" and proceeded to sing the anthemic song from a popular Australian beer advertisement: "I feel like a Tooheys, I feel like a Tooheys, I feel like a Tooheys or two… We'll be back next year, I promise."

SUNDAY 26 NOVEMBER

▼ **SOCIALISING**

On their last day in Australia, Bowie and the band drove north to Gosford where Dennis Garcia had a bungalow near a small lake.

They returned in the evening to celebrate the end of the Australian tour with The Angels at the Sebel Townhouse.

John Brewster (2012)
I'm sure we were all probably imbibing things more than we should have – I remember the beginning of it, I don't remember the end too well!

MONDAY 27 NOVEMBER

Bowie remained in Sydney while the tour party took an early flight to Christchurch, New Zealand.

TUESDAY 28 NOVEMBER

✪ TELEVISION

Seven Studios
Epping, Australia

'WILLESEE AT SEVEN' (SEVEN)

Interviewed by Mike Willesee.

Bowie's other television appearance in Australia was a 13-minute segment, which included an interview with Mike Willesee and clips of 'Heroes', 'Space Oddity' and *Just A Gigolo*.

WEDNESDAY 29 NOVEMBER

★ LIVE

Queen Elizabeth II Park
Christchurch, New Zealand

As The Angels were unavailable for the New Zealand dates, the support spot was given to New Zealand-born Australian guitarist Kevin Borich. The QEII Park was an open-air athletic stadium built for the 10th Commonwealth Games, which opened at the venue in 1974.

J D McLellan (Bowie fan)

DB only faltered once: to interrupt the set to berate some members of the audience for giving the Nazi salute and 'seig heiling' him. He made some comments about how the National Front would soon be raising their heads in our country and that we shouldn't be seduced by them. "That's no way to be a rebel," he said, then performed 'Rebel Rebel'. [381]

DECEMBER

FRIDAY 1

► TRAVELLING

Bowie arrived at Auckland airport where heavy security had been laid on, but there were no crowds – only five photographers awaited his arrival. The tour party checked in at the Mon Desir, a single-storey hotel backing onto a beach at Takapuna.

SATURDAY 2 DECEMBER

★ LIVE

Western Springs
Auckland, New Zealand

Some 41,000 turned out to see the concert at Western Springs, an open-air natural amphitheatre stadium. Bowie set a national attendance record, beating previous record-holders The Rolling Stones and Neil Diamond. With fans milling everywhere, the limos had to clear a path through the cars and crowds to reach the backstage area.

After the interval, the band came on holding cameras. Bowie wanted them all to take pictures of the audience as a gesture of tribute.

SUNDAY 3 DECEMBER

► TRAVELLING

At 7.30pm the party began the four-hour flight from Auckland back to Sydney, where they boarded a small JAL jet bound for Tokyo.

Bowie drew the biggest concert crowd in Auckland's history.

MONDAY 4 DECEMBER

They landed at 6am at New Tokyo International Airport at Narita and were greeted by the tour promoter Seijiro Udo.

After exchanging a few words with the television crews filming their arrival, the party headed to the limos, which ground through the morning traffic. Three hours later they settled in at the Tokyo Prince Hotel in Shiba-koen, Minato-ku.

During the tour, Bowie did the promotional rounds of radio stations and TV shows.

TUESDAY 5 DECEMBER

► TRAVELLING

Osaka, Japan

Shinkansen Bullet Train

WEDNESDAY 6 DECEMBER

★ LIVE

Koseinenkin Kaikan

Osaka, Japan

The first show in Japan was small – the theatre held only 1,500 – and the audience subdued. At a recent concert there had been a fatality when the crowd had rushed the stage. Dennis Davis tried to liven up the concert by occasionally bashing two Chinese gongs until they were taken away from him.

▌Broadcast: Japanese radio.

✪ TELEVISION

'STAR SENICHIYA'

The ten-minute interview, recorded in Bowie's Tokyo hotel room, was intercut with a clip of 'Ziggy Stardust' from the Dallas concert.

▌Broadcast: December 6.

ABOVE: Bowie being interviewed in his Tokyo hotel room. OPPOSITE: NHK Hall in Tokyo, the last show of the tour.

THURSDAY 7 DECEMBER

★ LIVE

Koseinenkin Kaikan

Osaka, Japan

The concert was livelier than the previous night – the audience was less inhibited and threw streamers. Dennis Davis painted his face like a Native American and Bowie won a huge cheer when he addressed the crowd in Japanese.

After the show the head of RCA in Japan, Tokugen Yamamoto, took some of the entourage to a restaurant and introduced them to its specialty dish, Kobe beef.

SATURDAY 9 DECEMBER

★ LIVE

Banpaku Kaikan

Osaka, Japan

SUNDAY 10 DECEMBER

► TRAVELLING

The party left Osaka by train, seen off by a small group of crying girls. Arriving in Tokyo, they checked into the New Otani Hotel.

MONDAY 11 DECEMBER

★ LIVE

Budokan Arena

Tokyo, Japan

TUESDAY 12 DECEMBER

★ LIVE

NHK Hall

Tokyo, Japan

Before the last show in Japan the band was downbeat at the prospect of ending the tour, but after a few songs, they kicked into 'The Jean Genie' with renewed enthusiasm.

Sean Mayes (1999)

From that moment the show took off and became a stormer, one of the best of the whole tour, all the higher for starting low. [022]

✪ TELEVISION

'Warszawa'/'Heroes'/'Fame'/ 'Beauty And The Beast'/ 'Five Years'/'Soul Love'/'Star'/ 'Hang On To Yourself'/ 'Ziggy Stardust'/'Suffragette City'/ 'Station To Station'/'TVC 15'

NHK filmed the concert and edited it to one hour for broadcast on *The Young Music Show*.

▼ SOCIALISING

Bee Club

Roppongi, Japan

GIGOLO PARTY

Barbara DeWitt organised the end-of-tour party to be held after the show at 10.30. The theme for the night was *Just A Gigolo*, as the movie was due for release soon. The guests, mostly Europeans and Americans living in Tokyo, were invited to dress in Twenties style. Sean Mayes was drafted in to present a short cabaret piece with a violinist and a singer performing the theme tune.

MONDAY 25 DECEMBER

Bowie and Coco spent Christmas in Kyoto with make-up artist Antony Clavet, who had worked on *Just A Gigolo* and Bowie's Japan dates.

JANUARY

Bowie spent January with Zowie in Japan, mainly in Kyoto.

After *Just A Gigolo* received such a poor reception at the Berlin premiere, David Hemmings hastily recalled the various prints in circulation and returned to London to recut the film for the February UK release.

SATURDAY 13

Bowie told Michael Watts he was preparing to finish his next album, to be titled either *Despite Straight Lines* or *Planned Accidents*:

Bowie thinks it contains some of his most intimate lyrics ever and says that although he still uses cut-up techniques, he's also going back to narrative. "But more in a very emotionally driven way rather than from an objective point of view."

"I've not made any plans for the next couple of years at all, apart from keeping on with my painting. I'm still painting pictures of my favourite area in Berlin, the Turkish area. I started to say yes to an exhibition, but then I backed off. I'm still completely frustrated and scared by the idea of exhibiting that publicly. But it's certainly one of my more successful art forms over the last couple of years." [309]

▮Published: *Melody Maker*.

FEBRUARY

Bowie returned to London from Japan to promote Hemmings' new cut of *Just A Gigolo*.

Bowie (1979)

Fortunately David managed to get hold of all the bits and pieces and stole it in the night and came back to England and did his own cut in hiding and that's the one that's now going out in England, which is David's cut – the film that he wanted to make. It makes sense – there's a story there. It's not just bits of incidents, and all these sort of send-ups of the whole German period are back in again. [315]

MONDAY 12

✪ TELEVISION

'AFTERNOON PLUS' (ITV)

Interviewed by Mavis Nicholson.

BOWIE: *Thematically I've always dealt with isolation in everything I've written, I think.*

NICHOLSON: *Do you feel isolated though?*

BOWIE: *Not really, but I can quite imagine how it must feel to be isolated so I have often put myself in circumstances and positions where I am isolated just so that I can write about them… It's that peculiar part of the human mind that fascinates me – about the small universes that can be created inside the mind, some of them fairly schizophrenic and quite off the wall.* [345]

✪ TELEVISION

'THAMES AT SIX' (THAMES)

Interviewed by Rita Carter.

✪ TELEVISION

'TONIGHT' (BBC 1)

Interviewed by Valerie Singleton.

SINGLETON: *There is this tremendous tendency to think of rock stars or pop stars as being a bit thick and obviously there's a lot more to you than that. Did it worry you that people had that kind of image?*

BOWIE: *No, I'm very thick.*

SINGLETON: *Are you?*

BOWIE: *Yes – I became a rock star!* [371]

TUESDAY 13 FEBRUARY

✪ PRESS

Dorchester Hotel
Mayfair
London, England

Jean Rook interview:

I'm the only journalist who knows his hotel and even I don't know his room number. Our undercover meeting took place in a hired private suite, later cleared of any trace of us, down to the butts of the 60 cigarettes a day on which Mr Bowie is still hooked.

Today he looks 17. His undyed hair is pale brown and short back and sides. The unmade-up face is guileless and spotless. In grey flannel bags, grey shirt and tasteful tie, he looks like a public schoolboy. Or like Edward before he met Mrs Simpson. Has he really been reborn a brand-new Persil-washed man overnight?

"Not overnight – it's been a struggle," said the one-time glittering, diamante, lipsticked superstar. "I hated the pop lifestyle but it's hard to kick the habits of a lifetime. I'm learning to be happy. To go to bed at night instead of 5am and get up in the morning instead of halfway through the day. I'm painting pictures nobody wants to buy, but I love it. I've grown my hair back to mouse. I'm even practising walking down the street." [269]

▮Published: *Daily Express*.

✪ RADIO

'YOUR MOTHER WOULDN'T LIKE IT' (CAPITAL RADIO)

Interviewed by Nicky Horne.

Despite the cold, wet and windy conditions, a horde of fans had gathered at the front door of Capital Radio's studios in Euston Tower. Bowie arrived and ran the gauntlet, losing his three bodyguards and five police escorts in the melee.

"David, it's nice to see you back again," Nicky Horne said, "glad you got in without losing too much of your hair!" During the two-hour programme, Horne talked to Bowie about *Just A Gigolo*, the *Stage* film and the next album – and then opened the lines for listeners to phone through questions.

HORNE: *Now with the benefit of hindsight, do you think that being with Lindsay Kemp and around him at that time, you actually gained a lot of what you are today?*

BOWIE: *Oh God, an extraordinary amount. As you probably have gathered over the past few years, I'm pretty eclectic, and I borrow and steal everything that fascinates me. I'm sort of a jackdaw, or is it a magpie? I can never remember. And Lindsay introduced me to things like Cocteau and the Theatre of the Absurd and Antonin Artaud and the whole idea of restructuring and going against what people generally expect – sometimes for the shock value, sometimes as an educational force. He just gave me the idea that you could experiment with the arts and do things and take dangerous risks that you wouldn't do in real life. And so you can use it as a kind of experimental area for trying out new lifestyles without having to take the consequences.*

HORNE: *But you've always taken those chances in real life.*

BOWIE: *Yes, when I started with the characters, I would put myself through terrible experiences and terrible positions to write about what I thought they would feel. Until I really cottoned on to the idea, mainly through Brian Eno, who sort of put it more into focus for me, that you could do all the experimentation in the actual creating of the music and not actually have to put your body through the same kind of risks that you do when you put it through those things to write insights into how people go through terrible things.*

HORNE: *I heard that Eno's disappeared; he's gone away for a long holiday.*

BOWIE: *What happened was toward the end of the album, he said, "David, I'm going away for rather a long time. What I mean is, I'm going away for a year or two." I said, "You're not serious" and he said, "Yes, I am" and he left the next day and I didn't hear a word from him until last week, when he wrote me a letter… He's out on a desert island in the East and he said, "I'm going to stay here for another year and I think that my whole career will be left on the beach and swamped by new wave after new wave."*

HORNE: *How much of a bait was [Marlene Dietrich] for you to appear in [Just A Gigolo] and how much did it work the other way around?*

ABOVE: With Nicky Horne at the Capital Radio studio in Euston Tower, London.

BOWIE: *Well, it made an enormous impression on me that Miss D had said that she would do the film if I would do it. And likewise I said if it's a promise that she's doing the film, I'll do it and let's sort of leave it at that.*

HORNE: *You must have been terribly flattered that she even knew you.*

BOWIE: *Oh my God, it was incredible! She said very nice things about me and in fact she was playing the side two of the Low album to all her friends, which I thought was just terrific.*

HORNE: *You once said that one of your favourite writers was Christopher Isherwood. Do you have a fascination for that period [of German history] and was that one of the reasons why you [agreed to do the film]?*

BOWIE: *I think it was Christopher's idea of contradictions, that he always put himself in a position that was fairly dangerous – it was the same kind of thing. He went to Germany because he thought it was the political melting pot of Europe, that everything that was going to happen would show itself in Berlin. That applied then and I feel it has been applying over the last two or three years as well in Berlin, that all the unrest and the political unrest that's happening there – the breaking down of ethnic groups into different areas and the lack of liaison between them – is starting to show itself all over Europe. But I think it started in Berlin a few years ago and I wanted to be there. I would like to think I was some kind of Isherwood inasmuch that I'd like to say that I could have observed what was happening in Europe, being sort of on the outside looking in.*

CALLER: *Do you think you're going to live in London?*

BOWIE: *There's a stronger and stronger possibility because London is having the same kind of friction feel that I felt in other areas of the world. I'm feeling more and more disorientated every time I come to London so it's becoming more attractive to me.*

A caller talked about the atmospheric quality of tracks such as 'Subterraneans', 'Warszawa' and 'Sense Of Doubt' and how he would like to set them to films.

BOWIE: *Mine's not coming out, but when I was in Russia, when I took the Trans-Siberian Express, I took a lot of footage there and I started putting those particular pieces – 'Subterraneans' and 'Warszawa' – against what I'd taken – just 8mm. It is very effective, I advise you to go ahead!* [341]

The interview was interspersed with some songs that Bowie selected to talk about…

'Shapes Of Things' The Yardbirds/ **'The Batman Theme'** Link Wray/ **'Warning Sign'** Talking Heads/ **'La Düsseldorf'** La Düsseldorf/ **'White Light White Heat'** The Velvet Underground/ **'Baby's On Fire'** Brian Eno/ **'China Girl'** Iggy Pop

Broadcast: Live at 9pm.

Just a Gigolo
DAVID BOWIE • SYDNE ROME
JUST A GIGOLO
KIM NOVAK • DAVID HEMMINGS
MARIA SCHELL • CURT JURGENS
MARLENE DIETRICH
SCREENPLAY BY
PRODUCED BY
DIRECTED BY
JOSHUA SINCLAIR & ENNIO DE CONCINI • ROLF THIELE • DAVID HEMMINGS

WEDNESDAY 14 FEBRUARY

✪ PRESS
Café Royal
Regent Street
London, England

'JUST A GIGOLO'

Bowie arrived at midday for a 15-minute press conference with co-star Sydne Rome on his arm. Before going in, they obliged the reporters and photographers waiting in the foyer with a Valentine's Day kiss.

✪ PROMOTION
Prince Charles Cinema
Leicester Square
London, England

'JUST A GIGOLO' PREMIERE

Although the invitation stated that Twenties-style dress (or black tie) was compulsory, Bowie and Vivienne Lynn opted for a kimono and a Willie Brown dress.

FRIDAY 16 FEBRUARY

▼SOCIALISING
Nashville Room
171 North End Road
West Kensington
London, England

Formed in 1978 in Sheffield, The Human League was part of a new wave of UK bands influenced by Bowie and Bowie's own influences, such as Kraftwerk.

In 1981 Phil Oakey and Adrian Wright turned The Human League into a Top 40 act after Martyn Ware and Ian Craig Marsh left to form BEF and then Heaven 17. But when Bowie dropped in to The Nashville Room to watch them play to a capacity crowd (that included almost famous Gary Numan), they were still an experimental post-punk electronic band with an eclectic cultural literacy that appealed to Bowie.

He arrived dressed in a houndstooth jacket and cuffed jeans. Before the show he headed backstage to meet the band and their manager Bob Last.

Phil Oakey (1980)
Seems a very friendly bloke. Just not what everybody says about him. I thought he'd come in and be moody and hum selections from* Low *and try and depress you. And in fact he comes in, he's very nice, very friendly, very complimentary bloke. Really enjoyable bloke to talk to. [137]

Phil Oakey (1979)
He asked us before we went on how long we were working for. We thought, "Huh? Oh, about four years I suppose," and he said, "No, how long are you on for?"... "Oh, 43 minutes and 23 seconds." [210]

Bowie talked to them about his plans – to finish off *Lodger* in London and possibly move back to Britain permanently. "There are a lot of interesting things happening over here."

Director of Visuals Adrian Wright projected a series of 400 slides – derived from cult TV shows, such as *Doctor Who* and *Captain Scarlet*, as well as famous images from recent history – onto four screens at the back of the stage, creating a visual interest to balance the band's deadpan 'non-performance'. Bowie enjoyed their show, particularly when they finished with 'Nightclubbing'.

OPPOSITE TOP: At the press conference for *Just A Gigolo* with co-star Sydne Rome.
OPPOSITE BOTTOM LEFT: The UK premiere of *Just A Gigolo* with model Vivienne Lynn. A Blitz Club regular and friend of Steve Strange, she appeared on his Visage LP cover. She modelled for designers Zandra Rhodes and Willie Brown in Robyn Beeche photo sessions with make-up by Richard Sharah.
OPPOSITE BOTTOM RIGHT: *Just A Gigolo* film poster.

Phil Oakey (1980)
***For me, his best work is with Iggy Pop. The two LPs he did with Iggy Pop are fantastic, landmarks, especially* The Idiot.** [137]

Afterwards Bowie swapped phone numbers with the band, saying he'd be in touch. He told *NME*'s Adrian Thrills, "They were great. I was watching from behind the lighting desk so that I could see the audience as well as the group. It was like watching 1980!"

Adrian Wright (1999)
He was very complimentary and very nice. When he saw our visuals he said something like, "Oh bugger, I was going to do something like that on my next tour." [004]

SUNDAY 18 FEBRUARY

Richard Cromelin interviewed Iggy about *New Values*, which he recorded with James Williamson in Los Angeles, rather than with Bowie in Berlin.

"I basically went to Bowie's pop-star school, if you will, and he taught me a great deal. I sort of negated my own personality for two years, and now I've grafted my own personality to the skills I learned. We're still good pals, but we're not working together right now. I wanted to do an album myself. *The Idiot* is probably the best album I've ever made, but it was more of a James Osterberg album. The new one's more of an Iggy Pop album." [098]

WEDNESDAY 21 FEBRUARY

■ ALBUM RELEASED
'JUST A GIGOLO' SOUNDTRACK
UK (Jamco JAM 1)
Schöner Gigolo/Armer Gigolo
Germany (Ariola 200462)

Bowie appeared on one track:
'David Bowie's Revolutionary Song'
(Bowie/Fishman) (4:41)

Performed by The Rebels
Tim Hauser/Jacques Morali: Producers
John Altman/Frank Barber: Arrangers
David Bowie: Guitar/Vocal Refrain
Jack Fishman: Original Soundtrack Recording Supervisor

■ SINGLE RELEASED
'Revolutionary Song'
Japan (Overseas Records MA-185-A)

TUESDAY 27 FEBRUARY

✪ TELEVISION

The Old Grey Whistle Test screened four songs from *David Bowie On Stage*, the RCA film of the 1978 Dallas concert.

ABOVE: Ramones post-concert party at Mudd Club, March 9. Joey Ramone, co-manager Linda Stein, Bowie, Dee Dee Ramone, Vera Ramone and co-manager Danny Fields (behind, right).

MARCH

▲ RECORDING
▲ MIXING
Studio D
Record Plant
New York City
New York, USA

'LODGER' ALBUM

David Bowie/Tony Visconti: Producers

Tony Visconti (2002)

We went to New York to finish this album, and it suffered at the mixing stage because the studios simply were not as versatile or well-equipped as their European counterparts in those days! The heavy New York vibe added more darkness to this album. [423]

Bowie and Visconti resumed sessions for *Lodger*, begun in Montreux the previous September. Since then he had written lyrics and in the space of a week recorded vocals and further overdubs and completed the mixing.

Tony Visconti (2006)

We recorded some new jams with Belew on drums, myself on bass and David on guitar, but nothing came of it. Instead we settled for some Belew guitar overdubs and I replaced the bass on 'Boys Keep Swinging'.

Dennis Davis, who is left-handed, never played a satisfactory bass part on George Murray's right-handed bass. I played an over-the-top bass part on the song, in the spirit of **The Man Who Sold The World.** [047]

▼ SOCIALISING

Between *Lodger* sessions, Bowie was out with David Byrne at clubs like Mudd and Hurrah, an Upper West Side disco refashioned in May 1978 as a rock club. The new owners, Robert Boykin and Barbara Lackey, called it "the first rock disco". It was also the first rock club in New York to install a video system, operated by resident VJ Merrill Aldighieri, who played music videos on six 19-inch colour monitors suspended from the ceiling over the bar and near the banquettes at the back of the club.

The Mudd Club was named after Samuel Alexander Mudd, a doctor who treated John Wilkes Booth following his assassination of Abraham Lincoln. It was opened in October 1978 by Steve Mass, art curator Diego Cortez and Anya Phillips. Mass was a colleague of Eno, who lived in an apartment upstairs. Located downtown at 77 White Street TriBeCa, Mudd was designed as an underground alternative to Studio 54, though equally elitist. Entry was by exclusive laminated cards that were sent to those approved by Steve Mass.

ABOVE: Locked inside 'The Cage' at Mudd Club with Warhol superstar Jackie Curtis, March 29.

FRIDAY 9 MARCH

▼SOCIALISING

Bowie and Byrne were at CBGB to watch Nico perform, then at Mudd for the party following Ramones' Palladium show.

During this period Bowie was at Mudd to see The B-52s, which *Melody Maker's* New York correspondent described as "just about the most rated young band in town. 'Rock Lobster' has been one of the best – and best-received – independent 45s released over here. The group is to sign with Talking Heads' manager and a record deal is imminent." [283]

Lisa Robinson (*Rock Scene*)

He chatted about music backstage, saying, "Does any of it matter any more? There was a time, wasn't there, when the music seemed so much more important than it does today. In Europe the Ayatollah Khomeini is so much more important. Now I worry that by putting out more albums, I'm contributing to a useless medium. Eno has gone off to the South Seas. He doesn't want to do music any more. Of course, he has other alternatives." [256]

Bowie greeted Blondie's Debbie Harry and Chris Stein, danced behind the stage to The B-52s' second set, and, as he looked around, said, "I don't want to tour again. It got really boring the last time. But this kind of club would be fun to do, wouldn't it?" [256]

Keith Strickland (B-52s) (2008)

It was pretty amazing. I remember we had just finished our set at The Mudd Club, and someone came and told us, "David Bowie's here." And Cindy screamed, "DAVID BOWIEEE!!!" She had her back to the door and, as she screamed, he was walking in. She was like, "Oh no!" But he was great. He just laughed. [211]

SATURDAY 17 MARCH

✪ PRESS

'MELODY MAKER' REPORT

David Bowie recently approached Scott Walker with a view to producing his next album. Bowie was impressed by the European feeling of the last Walker Brothers' album Nite Flight, *which owed its critical acceptance to Scott's work. While Walker appreciated Bowie's interest, he turned down his help. He is working on his own solo album, and is anxious to avoid contact with other musicians at the moment, although it is thought he may team up with Bowie in the future.* [203]

THURSDAY 29 MARCH

▼SOCIALISING

Bowie and John Cale went to see Roxy Music's New York Palladium concert and hung out with Bryan Ferry and Lisa Robinson after the show. Later that night Bowie was back at Mudd Club.

APRIL

SUNDAY 1

★LIVE
★GUEST APPEARANCE
Carnegie Hall
New York City
New York, USA

THE FIRST CONCERT OF THE EIGHTIES (WKCR BENEFIT)
'Sabotage' (Cale)

John Cale: Vocals
David Bowie: Viola
Gregor Kitzis: 1st Violin

Taylor Storer, Mark Schuyler and Tim Page organised a benefit concert for WKCR designed to showcase new American music, featuring Steve Reich and Philip Glass. John Cale was scheduled to perform with Nico but she decided to stay home instead of performing. Bowie joined Cale on stage, wearing a black kimono and playing viola on Cale's song 'Sabotage'.

Bowie (1979)
I had never played viola in my life before but I learned four notes on it and it sounded great. I may learn another four and play it on my next album. [310]

John Cale (2008)
That was a lot of fun. That was when we were hanging out, so I asked David if he'd like to come and play 'Sabotage' with me. I ended up teaching him the viola part, which he had a whack at and then ended up playing on the stage for the first time. [298]

Philip Glass (1996)
I was very pleased to find people working in a contemporary way in the field of popular music but who were really interested in experimental music. And this is what made David interesting to me. [346]

ABOVE: Phil Oakey, The Human League. Bowie was impressed by the group's back projections (by Adrian Wright) when he saw them in London in February. "It was like watching 1980!" he told *NME*.
BELOW: Composer Philip Glass. In 1993 he released *Low Symphony*, three movements based on three instrumentals from *Low*: 'Subterraneans', 'Some Are' (attributed to the *Low* sessions and included on the Ryko reissue) and 'Warszawa'. In 1997 he followed it with *"Heroes" Symphony*.

Philip Glass (1996)
I was very pleased to find people working in a contemporary way in the field of popular music but who were really interested in experimental music. And this is what made David interesting to me. [346]

SATURDAY 7 APRIL

▼SOCIALISING

Back in London, Bowie watched The Human League supporting Siouxsie And The Banshees at The Rainbow Theatre – a charity gig in aid of mentally handicapped children.

TUESDAY 10 APRIL

▼SOCIALISING
Hammersmith Odeon
London, England

LOU REED

The Human League was scheduled to support until shortly before the show, when Reed decided he didn't want a support band after all. Bowie watched the concert from the wings, sitting on a flight case. Reed finished his set and greeted Bowie with open arms, overjoyed to see him again. They piled into the tour bus and headed off to the Chelsea Rendezvous in Sydney Street to have dinner.

They were up to dessert when writers Giovanni Dadomo (*Sounds*) and Allan Jones (*Melody Maker*) turned up. Arista press officer Howard Harding had brought them along at Reed's behest after Reed saw Dadomo's glowing preview of the concert in *Time Out*. After some friendly conversation the writers left Bowie, Reed and their companions to their Irish whiskeys. From their table they watched them laughing and talking about old times and toasting "to friends". Then Reed's guitarist Chuck Hammer heard Reed ask Bowie to produce his next album.

Bowie said, "Yes, if you clean up your act." Reed turned on Bowie, slapping him twice and shouting, "Don't you EVER say that to me!"

Everything settled down for a few minutes when suddenly Reed again exploded with rage. "I told you NEVER to say that!" he yelled as minders struggled to restrain him and eventually escort him blank-faced from the restaurant. [165]

Allan Jones then asked Bowie what had upset Reed. Bowie, enraged at the question, left the restaurant alone, trashing the pot plants as he went. The drama continued an hour later when Bowie turned up at the hotel, found Reed's room and hammered on the door, yelling, "Come on Lou – I know you're in there!" When no one answered, he gave up and left.

The next day Bowie sent 'a bodyguard' to the restaurant to pay for replacement of the demolished plants, a cost of about £60. Reed flew out early the next morning to Dublin, cancelling all engagements and offering no explanation to anyone.

Lou Reed (1979)
Yes, I hit [Bowie] – more than once. It was a private dispute… It had nothing to do with sex, politics or rock and roll. I have a New York code of ethics. Speak unto others as you would have them speak unto you. In other words, watch your mouth. [011]

SUNDAY 15 APRIL

✪ **RADIO**

'An Hour With David Bowie' broadcast in US (KLOS-FM).

WEDNESDAY 18 APRIL

✪ **RADIO**

Good Earth Studios
Dean Street, Soho
London, England

'YOUR MOTHER WOULDN'T LIKE IT: BOWIE THE TRAVELLER/ CONVERSATIONS WITH BOWIE'

Nicky Horne: Presenter

At Bowie's suggestion, RCA's Tony McGrogan organised a contest for Capital Radio. The listeners were asked to write about 'Bowie The Traveller' and the 12 best would join him in Tony Visconti's studio for an advance listen to the *Lodger* album.

Bowie greeted the 12 winners at the studio. "Hello, how lovely to meet you. Do please grab some food and something to drink," he said, pointing them to the smoked salmon, prawns, spare ribs and champagne laid on by RCA.

The show began with an hour of Bowie answering general questions, followed by a playback of *Lodger* with Bowie's track-by-track commentary.

"Every time I finish an album I think, 'Oh God, I can't stand this any more, I've got absolutely nothing to contribute, it's no good,' all hell has broken loose in my mind, you know, completely... illogical about the whole thing, I just curl up and die for a couple of weeks after making it. I don't know, it's always been like that with me, not one album that I've made that I've walked happily away from and gone about my business. None of it's pleasure any more; it started off not as pleasure and it's now still not pleasure."[330]

▮ Broadcast: May 14 (Capital Radio).

ABOVE: Kenny Everett's comedy show, performing 'Boys Keep Swinging', his first new single since 'Heroes'. The title provided music writers with a droll headline for the recent fracas with Lou Reed, and the slapstick with Angry of Mayfair at the end of the segment could even be construed as satirising the fight. Bowie's appearance on the show was the beginning of his collaboration with director David Mallet. He commissioned Mallet to direct the three music videos planned to promote *Lodger* and to co-direct 'Ashes To Ashes' in 1980.

MONDAY 23 APRIL

✪ **TELEVISION**

'THE KENNY EVERETT VIDEO SHOW' (ITV)

'Boys Keep Swinging'
(live vocal and backing track)

David Mallet: Director

Having performed recently with a viola, he decided to mime Adrian Belew's guitar solo by playing a violin theatrically on a rooftop set. Kenny Everett entered (as Angry of Mayfair), leering at Bowie and making snide remarks: "You know, I was in the war – but I didn't see you there. I fought for people like you – and I never got one!" The clip ended in farce as Bowie smashed the violin and chased Everett around the roof with the bow.

LATE APRIL

✪ PROMO VIDEO FILMING
Ewart Studios
Wandsworth and
Earls Court Road
London, England

'Boys Keep Swinging'/'D.J.'/
'Look Back In Anger'

David Mallet: Director
Michael Minas: Set Designer

Bowie was so impressed with the 'Boys Keep Swinging' segment on Everett's show, he asked Mallet to direct the promo video for the single as well as the two singles which would follow. Starting with a straight performance (based shot for shot on the Everett version), the 'Boys Keep Swinging' clip featured a catwalk of three drag acts paying wry homage to *Coronation Street* siren Bet Lynch, Lauren Bacall (both ending with Romy Haag's lipstick smear) and his *Gigolo* co-star Marlene Dietrich.

Bowie played out the melodrama of the DJ who has lost everything, trashing the mock radio studio and spraying his own initials on the wall (in case anyone missed the joke). Then he took to the street in Earls Court, unannounced, unstaged and seemingly without a security cordon.

Bowie was soon surrounded by fans hugging and kissing him as he walked on, lip-syncing the song to Mallet's camera.

David Mallet (2009)
That was real, as completely real as you can get. Wasn't even anybody notified that it was going to happen. [040]

▮Released on
The Video Collection (PMI 1993)/
Best Of Bowie (EMI 2002).

FRIDAY 27 APRIL

■ SINGLE RELEASED
'Boys Keep Swinging'
(Bowie/Eno) (3:17)/
'Fantastic Voyage' (Bowie/Eno) (2:55)
UK (RCA BOW2)
Chart Peak No.7
Deadwax inscriptions:
"Your Bicameral Mind"
"Mind Your Bicameral"

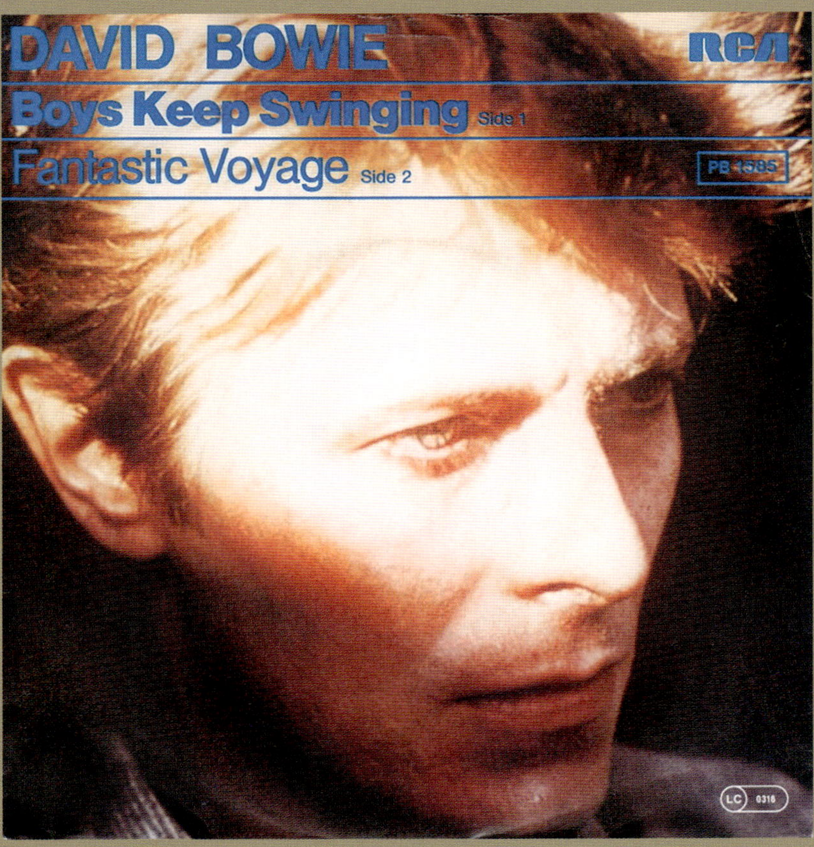

ABOVE AND BELOW: 'Boys Keep Swinging' German cover and Spanish promotional 7-inch picture disc.
OPPOSITE: I am what I play – Bowie playing and talking about records, as well as plugging *Lodger*. His playlist was a mixture of Sixties throwbacks, teenage obsessions, contemporaries and collaborators and recent acquisitions.

MAY

SATURDAY 5

✪ PRESS
'MELODY MAKER' REPORT
Bowie was recently seen buying up copies of Eno albums in a Virgin Records shop. The Dook expressed agitation when told that After The Heat, *the import LP his other musical accomplice made with Messrs Roedelius and Moebius, was out of stock but exited proudly showing the wax to his obviously impressed female companion.* [204]

SATURDAY 12 MAY

■ CHART
'Boys Keep Swinging'
UK Top 30 Chart Entry No.22
Charting 10 weeks

✪ RADIO
'STAR SPECIAL'
Bowie appeared on the two-hour show to play disc jockey again, talking about some of his favourite records.

"Hello, this is David Bowie. It's a bit grey out today and I've got some Perrier water and I've got a bunch of records. I think if I was walking outside at the moment, I would like to be walking on this street…" [337]

'Love Street' The Doors/
'TV Eye' Iggy Pop/
'Remember' John Lennon/
'96 Tears' ? And The Mysterians/
'A Wagon – The Nursery Suite' Edward Elgar/
'Inchworm' Danny Kaye/
'Trial Prison' Philip Glass/
'Sweet Jane' The Velvet Underground/
'Helen Fordsdale' Mars/
'He's A Star' Little Richard/
'21st-Century Schizoid Man' King Crimson/
'Warning Sign' Talking Heads/
'Beck's Bolero' Jeff Beck/
'Try Some, Buy Some' Ronnie Spector/
'20th Century Boy' Marc Bolan/
'Where Were You' The Mekons/
'Big City Cat' Steve Forbert/
'We Love You' The Rolling Stones/
'2 HB' Roxy Music/
'It's Hard To Be A Saint In The City' Bruce Springsteen/
'Fingertips' Stevie Wonder/
'Rip Her To Shreds' Blondie/
'Beautiful Loser' Bob Seger/
'Boys Keep Swinging'/
'Yassassin'/
'The Books I Read' Talking Heads/
'For Your Pleasure' Roxy Music/
'Something On Your Mind' King Curtis/
'Lies' The Staple Singers

▮Broadcast: May 20 (BBC Radio 1).

✪ RADIO
'ROCK ON'
BBC RADIO 1
Interviewed by Stuart Grundy, discussing 'Fantastic Voyage', 'Boys Keep Swinging' and 'Yassassin'.

FRIDAY 18 MAY

■ ALBUM RELEASED

'LODGER'

UK (RCA BOW LP1)
US (AQL1-3254)
UK Chart Peak No.4
US Chart Peak No.20

SIDE ONE

1. **'Fantastic Voyage'** (Bowie/Eno) (2:55)
2. **'African Night Flight'** (Bowie/Eno) (2:54)
3. **'Move On'** (3:16)
4. **'Yassassin'** (Turkish for 'Long Live') (4:10)
5. **'Red Sails'** (Bowie/Eno) (3:43)

SIDE TWO

1. **'D.J.'** (Bowie/Eno/Alomar) (3:59)
2. **'Look Back In Anger'** (Bowie/Eno) (3:08)
3. **'Boys Keep Swinging'** (Bowie/Eno) (3:17)
4. **'Repetition'** (2:59)
5. **'Red Money'** (Bowie/Alomar) (4:17)

ABOVE: Designed by Derek Boshier and Bowie, and photographed by Duffy at his London studio in February 1979. In the spirit of the album's working title, *Planned Accidents*, Bowie burnt his hand on the morning of the first day of the cover shoot, resulting in a bandage being added to his figure's already distressed state.

David Bowie/Tony Visconti: Producers
David Bowie: Vocals/Piano/Synthesiser/Chamberlin/Guitar
Adrian Belew: Guitar/Mandolin/Rhythm Guitar
Carlos Alomar: Guitar/Rhythm Guitar/Drums/Vocals
Brian Eno: Ambient Drone/Prepared Piano/Cricket Menace/Synthesisers/Guitar Treatments/Horse Trumpets/Eroica Horns/Piano
George Murray: Bass/Vocals
Dennis Davis: Drums/Percussion/Bass/Vocals
Sean Mayes: Piano
Roger Powell: Synthesisers
Simon House: Violin/Mandolins
Tony Visconti: Bass/Mandolins/Rhythm Guitar/Vocals
Stan: Saxophone
David Bowie/Derek Boshier/Brian Duffy (uncredited): Cover Designers
Recorded at Mountain Studios Montreux, Switzerland
Engineers: Tony Visconti/Dave Richards
Assistant Engineer: Eugene Chaplin
Mixed at Record Plant Studios New York City, New York, USA
Tony Visconti/Rod O'Brien: Engineers
Gregg Caruso: Assistant Engineer
Gregg Calbi: Mastering at Sterling Sound Studios New York City, New York, USA

Deadwax inscriptions:
"No sense is better…"/
"…than none at all"

REISSUES

▌CD (RCA 1984).

▌CD (remastered) (Ryko 1991).

BONUS TRACKS
1. 'I Pray Olé' (3:59)
2. 'Look Back In Anger' (recorded 1988) (6:59)

▌CD (remastered) (EMI 1999).

▌CD (mini LP replica)(Toshiba EMI 2007).

Derek Boshier (2003)
I loved the resolution to the problem of David being photographed falling. Shooting him from above, on a specially made table built to match the falling form. The table was designed to be completely obscured by David's body. (You can see the table in the photograph right centre on the inside of the book-style cover.) The wash hand basin was laid underneath the table on the floor. [395]

Jon Savage (*Melody Maker*)
So Bowie returns to RCA, rewarded by a personalised catalogue number, with what – playing the significance game – he likes to see as the final part of the Low / "Heroes" *trilogy. Mmmm. The new album appears as a piece of self-plagiarism unmatched since* The Seeds: *his last eight or so albums are cut up, played backwards and then reassembled. It's a credit to his craft that the end result is still fresh.* [277]

Bowie (1979)
Lodger *is really a hodgepodge of styles that create a lovely sort of mix. The areas we've been working in are so undefined at the moment that I find them hard to analyse, but I think probably a classification you can give the album is that it incorporates just about every style that I've ever got involved in, apart from rock. There are three or four narrative songs, though, which is something I haven't done in a long time, and two or three of what you might call Dada pop as opposed to rock. Now whether that's the kind of pop that people expect, I don't know. But it's definitely Bowie pop.* [311]

ABOVE: Designer Derek Boshier, who became involved when Duffy said to him, "I've got this friend who I think you will get on quite well with. I'd like you to meet."
OVERLEAF: Make-up artist Antony Clavet (left) and assistant applying prosthetics to Bowie's face. Lengths of nylon string, pulled from different directions, contorted his face, so he appeared to be falling.

Chris Charlesworth, who had left *Melody Maker* and was now RCA's press officer, invited journalists to RCA for a preview of *Lodger* and the new promotional videos.

Chris Charlesworth (2011)
For Lodger I helped organise a 'listening' session in the RCA boardroom and invited a bunch of writers to come along and hear it played very loud. The previous week David had introduced us to the album by coming into the offices for a buffet lunch in the boardroom attended by the senior staff.

Allan Jones (*Melody Maker*)
The playback of the record was virtually drowned out by a chorus of inebriated bickering, gossip and giggling. The tottering pen-pushers were only silenced when we were treated to a series of videos of the Thin White One. The first tapes, projected onto a massive screen in the far corner of RCA's plush fifth-floor banqueting suite, were from the Stage tour in Dallas. More striking were the recently completed promo flicks for the new album, certainly the most impressive video sales pitch since the original Devo epics.

"See those girls?" asked the chap from RCA. "Absolute goddess, the one in the middle," we replied, pointing out the Lauren Bacall-meets-Jerry Hall lookalike. "They're all Bowie," explained the chap from RCA. Mouths dropped open. [167]

SUNDAY 27 MAY

✪ RADIO
'RADIO RADIO' (WPIX-FM)
Interviewed in New York by John Ogle. Lou Reed was also on the show.

"It's a credit to his craft that the end result is still fresh."

Jon Savage

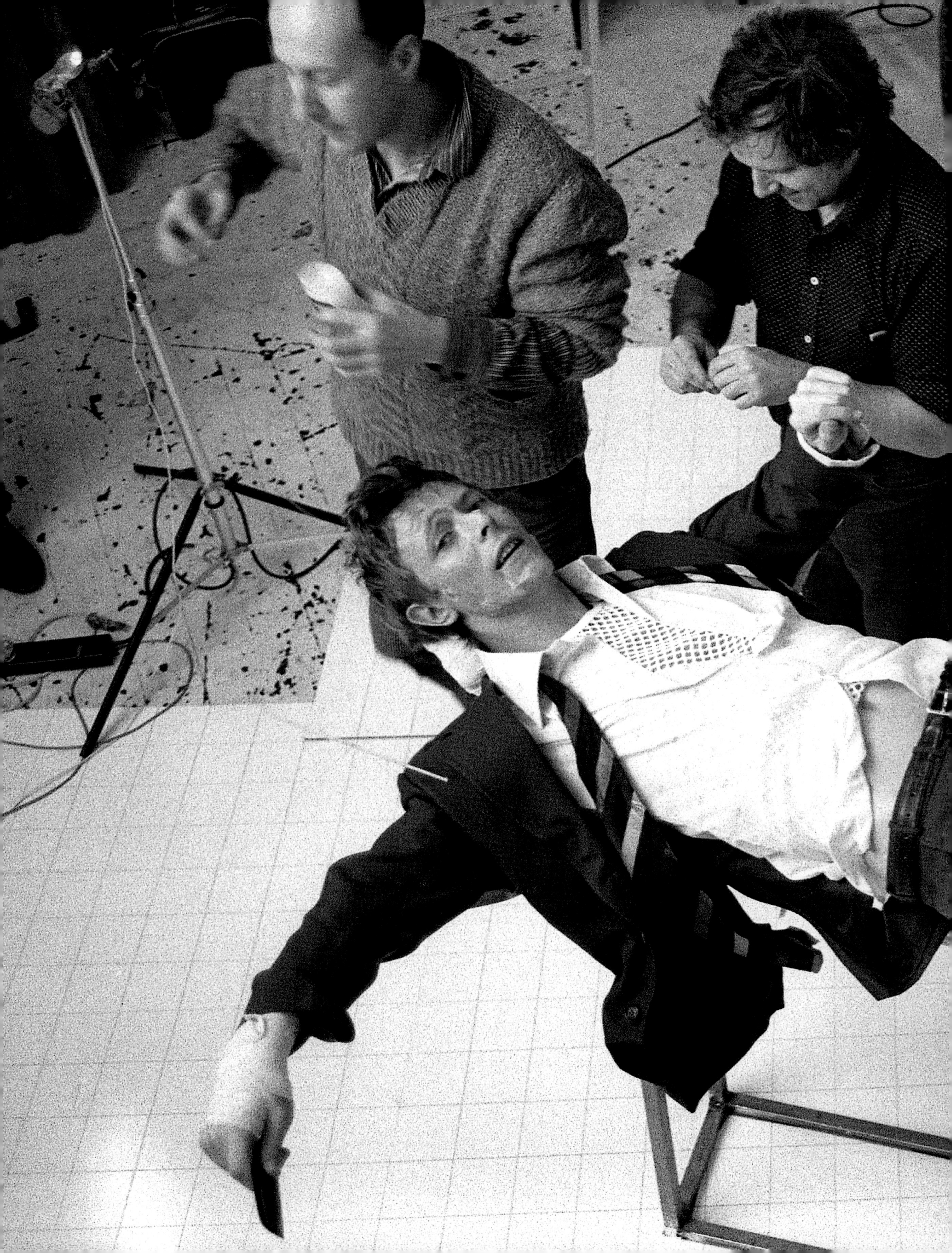

JUNE

SATURDAY 2

■ CHART

'Boys Keep Swinging'
UK Chart Peak No.7

The Friars' Club in Aylesbury celebrated its tenth anniversary. Rumours had spread that Bowie would be appearing since he had close links with Dave Stopps, the club's promoter. Stopps admitted he had approached Bowie, but he declined.

FRIDAY 8 JUNE

Lodger certified gold in UK.

SAVE THE CHILDREN CHARITY AUCTION

Sotheby's held an auction of 'Lipograms' contributed by celebrities, including Bette Davis, Jack Nicholson, Audrey Hepburn, Peter Ustinov and others. Bowie's contribution was the inspiration behind the auction – a card he had sent to Charles of the Ritz to thank him for a gift of make-up. The card had Bowie's lip-print and an inscription, "The lips part like silence set for alarm – Bo. '79."

FRIDAY 29 JUNE

■ SINGLE RELEASED

'D.J.' (Bowie/Eno/Alomar) (3:20)/
'Repetition' (2:58)
UK (RCA BOW3)
Chart Peak No.29

JULY

■ SINGLE RELEASED

'Yassassin' (3:06)/
'Repetition' (2:58)
Netherlands (RCA PB-9417)

■ SINGLE RELEASED

'Yassassin' (4:13)/
'Red Money' (Bowie/Alomar) (2:58)
Turkey (RCA 79.014)

MONDAY 2

■ SINGLE RELEASED

'D.J.' (Bowie/Eno/Alomar) (3:20)/
'Fantastic Voyage' (Bowie/Eno) (2:53)
US (RCA PB-11661)
Chart Peak No.106

THURSDAY 5 JULY

✪ RADIO

Interviewed in New York by Dave Herman (WNEW-FM).

SATURDAY 21 JULY

■ CHART

'D.J.'
UK Top 30 Chart Entry
Chart Peak No.29
Charting 5 weeks

AUGUST

MONDAY 20

■ SINGLE RELEASED

'Look Back In Anger' (Bowie/Eno) (3:08)/ **'Repetition'** (2:58)
US (RCA PB-11724)

FRIDAY 31 AUGUST

DA Pennebaker's 1973 concert film – then titled *Bowie* – was shown at the Edinburgh Film Festival. Allan Jones was highly critical of the film, describing it as an 'erratic mess' with poor photography, 'appalling sound' and absence of direction.

Allan Jones (*Melody Maker*)
The film's neutrality is overwhelmingly annoying. The most telling moments seem to have been captured accidentally. My favourite moment came toward the end. "This was written by a friend of mine," Bowie says announcing 'White Light/White Heat'. He pauses. "I think he's a friend of mine anyway," he concludes. [168]

DA Pennebaker (2003)
I made a 35mm Dolby print which I had to make by hand in my own studio and I got a mag-striped print and I put the tracks on and I took it to Edinburgh to show it and I thought, "This will just be a little film festival showing." Instead, this whole goddamn audience showed up. Everybody that was at the concert was in Edinburgh. You couldn't get in the theatre, and of course they went crazy in the film. It was one of the best screenings I've ever had of any film. And part of it even got out of sync because they didn't know how to handle Dolby very well in the theatre. But nobody seemed to mind. [373]

At that stage the film suffered from poor sound and still included Jeff Beck's two appearances – 'Round And Round' and 'Love Me Do'/'The Jean Genie" – which were edited out for the 1982 cinema release.

SEPTEMBER

▲ RECORDING
★ GUEST APPEARANCE

Rockfield Studios
Monmouth, Wales

IGGY POP
'SOLDIER' ALBUM

Iggy Pop was having problems recording his new album at Dave Edmunds' Rockfield Studios in Wales. Bowie and Corinne dropped in for a couple of days to lend moral support. Simple Minds were recording *Real To Real Cacophony* in the studio next door and wanted Bowie to play sax on their album. Bowie declined the request but asked if they could sing, gave them lyric sheets, and they ended up singing backing vocals with him on 'Play It Safe'. The song began life as an outrageous story Bowie recounted concerning bodyguard/hard man John Bindon, which Iggy turned into verse to Bowie's music.

▲ RECORDING

Good Earth Studios
Dean Street, Soho
London, England

'Space Oddity' (new version)
'Panic In Detroit' (new version)
'Rebel Rebel' (new version)

Bowie: Vocals/12-string Guitar
Zaine Griff: Bass
Hans Zimmer: Piano
Andy Duncan: Drums

Tony Visconti (2000)
The acoustic version of 'Space Oddity' was recorded for the Kenny Everett Show and was never meant to be a single. [383]

Bowie (1980)
That came about because Mallet wanted me to do something for his show and he wanted 'Space Oddity'. I agreed as long as I could do it again without all its trappings and do it strictly with three instruments. Having played it with just an acoustic guitar onstage early on, I was always surprised at how powerful it was just as a song, without all the strings and synthesisers. In fact the video side of it was secondary; I really wanted to do it as a three-piece song. [179]

With this in mind Bowie asked Tony Visconti to put together a band to re-record some of his songs. At the time Visconti was producing an album by New Zealand-born Zaine Griff (Glenn Mikkelsson). When Visconti arranged for them to meet at Good Earth Studios, Bowie was initially disconcerted by Griff's Bowie-like appearance.

▮ 'Panic In Detroit' released on *Scary Monsters* (Ryko 1992) and *Heathen* bonus CD (2002). 'Rebel Rebel' remains unreleased.

TUESDAY 18 SEPTEMBER

✪ TELEVISION
Ewart Studios
Wandsworth
London, England

'WILL KENNY EVERETT MAKE IT TO 1980?' (ITV)
'Space Oddity' (new version)

David Mallet: Director

The special, also known as *The Kenny Everett New Year's Eve Show*, was envisaged as a look back at the Seventies and forward to the Eighties. Gary Numan was originally going to be on the show and recorded his segment ('I Die You Die') the previous week.

▮ Broadcast: December 31 (ITV).

Gary Numan (1997)
It was an excellent and very important show to be on as the ratings were massive. After I'd recorded my bit for the show, Mallet told me that Bowie was going to be there the following Thursday and did I want to come along and watch?

I turned up a week later, very excited and a little nervous, to watch the great man in action. There was a little side room, which I stood at the back of, well out of the way, behind Bob Geldof and Paula Yates, and a reasonable group of other people whom I didn't recognise. I was very intimidated by the whole thing. I'd only been famous myself for a short time so I was still completely in awe of famous people.

TOP: Bowie with Daniella Parmar at Blitz Club, in the Willie Brown-designed jumpsuit he later wore on the Dick Clark Seventies special.
MIDDLE: With Daniella Parmar and Toni Basil.
BOTTOM: Bowie and Bob Geldof.

Bowie started performing his track and then suddenly everything stopped. A whispered discussion with Mallet followed and then Mallet came over, took me to one side, and said that Bowie had seen me, and it would be better if I left. So I was thrown out – which, apart from being extremely embarrassing, was really quite sad because I was a huge Bowie fan. Then, a few days after that, I was taken off the Christmas Special [sic] as well and I ended up on a normal Kenny Everett show a couple of months later. [024]

THURSDAY 27 SEPTEMBER

▼SOCIALISING
Bowie watched Talking Heads play at The Greek Theatre in Los Angeles.

OCTOBER

✪ PRESS
'Bad Boys in Berlin' by Chris Hodenfield published in *Rolling Stone*.

FRIDAY 5

▲RECORDING
Ciarbis Studios
New York City
New York, USA

'Piano-La'
'Velvet Couch'

David Bowie: Vocals
John Cale: Piano

John Cale (2008)
When we did that bootleg, it was like the good old bad old days. We were partying very hard. It was exciting working with him, as there were a lot of possibilities and everything, but we were our own worst enemies at that point. He could improvise songs very well, which was what that bootleg was all about. [298]

▮ Unreleased, but available on the *Two Gentlemen In New York* bootleg.

THURSDAY 25 OCTOBER

The uncut version of *The Man Who Fell To Earth* made its US debut at a nine-film Nicolas Roeg retrospective at Carnegie Hall Cinema in New York. The censored version originally released in the USA was 20 minutes shorter than the UK version.

NOVEMBER

SATURDAY 10

✪ **PRESS**

Melody Maker writers nominated the most significant and influential albums of the decade. *The Rise And Fall Of Ziggy Stardust And The Spiders From Mars* topped the list.

SATURDAY 24 NOVEMBER

✪ **PRESS**

Melody Maker published a number of pieces concerning the coming decade from various writers and musicians. Bowie's contribution:

All Clear 1980.
Personal – Eyes Only.
Tragedy Converted Into Comedy.
Indifference.
Complete Lack Of Task.
To Be 67 By 1990.
To win a revolution by ignoring everything else out of existence.
To own personal copy of *Eraserhead*.

DECEMBER

■ **ALBUM RELEASED**
PROMO
'1980 ALL CLEAR'
US (RCA DJL1-3545)

SIDE ONE
1. **'The Man Who Sold The World'** (3:58)
2. **'Space Oddity'** (5:15)
3. **'Ziggy Stardust'** (3:13)
4. **'Panic In Detroit'** (4:25)
5. **'Always Crashing In The Same Car'** (3:26)

SIDE TWO
1. **'1984'** (3:24)
2. **'Golden Years'** (4:03)
3. **'Fascination'** (Bowie/Vandross) (5:43)
4. **'Heroes'** (Bowie/Eno) (6:07)
5. **'Boys Keep Swinging'** (Bowie/Eno) (3:17)

ABOVE: The *1980 All Clear* promotional album sampled Bowie's Seventies on RCA with one track from 10 of his 12 studio albums (*Hunky Dory* and *Pin Ups* are not represented).

✪ **TELEVISION**
'SENSATIONAL SHOCKING WONDERFUL WACKY 70'S' (NBC)
'Space Oddity'

While in London, Bowie recorded a performance of 'Space Oddity' (1969 version) for Dick Clark's two-hour musical comedy tribute to the Seventies. Bowie wore a metallic grey jumpsuit designed by Willie Brown with a graphic pattern inspired by Le Corbusier.

▮ Broadcast: January 4 (NBC).

SATURDAY 1

✪ **TELEVISION**
'COUNTDOWN END OF THE DECADE SPECIAL' (ABC AUSTRALIA)
Interviewed by Ian Meldrum.

"We'll be talking about music in the Seventies, so I suppose I've got to be in it," Bowie said by way of an introduction. The special featured Bowie and other musicians discussing the last 10 years of popular music. Doing the interview in historic Kew Gardens was Bowie's idea.

Ian Meldrum (1979)
Getting in there is like trying to get an exclusive with the Queen on the lawns of Buckingham Palace. We managed it though, after telling the attendants that we were filming a special on beautiful English gardens. David posed as an expert on plants as we paid our penny to get in the gate. [006]

Meldrum asked him about the importance of punk, specifically The Sex Pistols…

BOWIE: *A very important enema. The only thing is that it was a shame that it all got manufactured so quickly, in a way. It would have been nice if they had come out on a hardy independent label. It's a shame that they jumped for those great giant idiots, because that's the perfect step not to take.*

MELDRUM: *Do you think that the audio vision is going play a lot of importance in the Eighties?*

BOWIE: *Undoubtedly, I thought it would have happened a bit sooner, really. But they didn't get their hardware out, everybody kept arguing about what sort of system they're going to have for video – video disc and whatever – and it took ages to get the stuff out. But now that it is out I think it will probably make a big cut into record sales generally as is probably being seen anyway.*

I think at the beginning of the Seventies when it was a bit dull, there was the idea of creating a flash of some kind and the flash was created but no one was seen holding the smoking pistol, so it went off at tangents after that. There was no real definite thing said at the beginning of the Seventies, but it did open everything up for investigation, and sub avenues of different kinds of music. People started working in all different areas of music. [351]

◆ **AWARDS**
'MELODY MAKER' READERS' POP POLL

Most Popular Male Singer #3

✪ **TELEVISION**
Brixton
London, England

'WILL KENNY EVERETT MAKE IT TO 1980?' (ITV)
'Panic In Detroit'

David Mallet: Director

Bowie spent a day with Mallet and a Thames TV crew shooting a video for the remade 'Panic In Detroit' to be included in Kenny Everett's New Year's Eve show. Bowie chatted between shots with the locals about squatters and German silent films.

Paul Tickell (*Melody Maker*)
Brixton is as good as any setting for a song which mentions urban guerrillas, but David said there were even more special personal reasons – like the fact he'd been born close by in Stansfield Road. "I love Brixton," he opined. [292]

The clip was left incomplete and the new version of 'Space Oddity' was used instead.

FRIDAY 7 DECEMBER

■ **SINGLE RELEASED**
7-INCH
'John, I'm Only Dancing (Again) (1975)' (3:25)/
'John, I'm Only Dancing (1972)' (2:47)
UK (RCA BOW 4)
Chart Peak No.12
A-side (7-inch version) reissued on *Rare* (RCA 1982).
B-side (1972 alternate mix) reissued on *Ziggy Stardust* (Ryko 1990).

■ **SINGLE RELEASED**
12-INCH
'John, I'm Only Dancing (Again) (1975)' (6:59)/
'John, I'm Only Dancing (1972)' (2:47)
UK (RCA BOW12 4)

Deadwax inscriptions:
"At last…"/"Shape of things…"

Both issued in limited edition of 50,000 in picture sleeves.

A-side (12-inch version) reissued on *Changes Two Bowie* (RCA 1981), *Young Americans* (Ryko 1991), *Best Of David Bowie 1974/1979* (EMI 1998) and *Young Americans* CD/DVD (EMI 2007).

■ **SINGLE RELEASED**
12-INCH
'John, I'm Only Dancing (Again) (1975)' (6:59)/
'Golden Years' (4:03)
US (RCA PD-11886)

■ **SINGLE RELEASED**
7-INCH
'John, I'm Only Dancing (1972)' (2:43)/
'Joe The Lion' (3:05)
US (RCA PD-11887)

Bowie (1980)
They're sort of out of the vault; it's an old new record. It came out first in the early Seventies with one particular mix and I dug it up again a few weeks ago and it was another mix. And it was a very loud, straight off the faders kind of mix and I thought that it would be nice to put it out. And then RCA found this disco version that I'd shelved, that I'd done at the time of Young Americans and so they decided to put the two out at the same time. The disco one I think is particularly interesting, outrageously funny, looking back at it now. It's an outtake – we thought it was too dancey! [333]

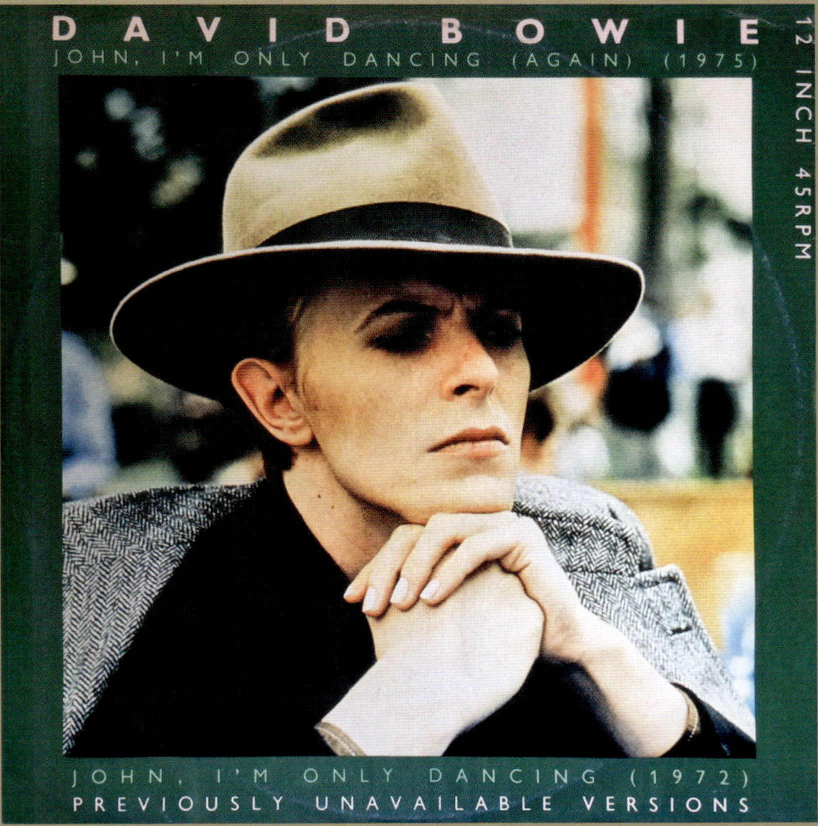

ABOVE: The first release of 'John I'm Only Dancing (Again)' from the *Young Americans* sessions. Sleeve photo by David James from *The Man Who Fell To Earth*. BELOW LEFT: Klaus Nomi.

Bowie (1980)
It seemed so right at the time and RCA wanted to put it out, and I agreed to it fully. It was just some more material that was held back there. I've still got lots of things canned like that, which I'd like to release, things like 'White Light/White Heat' with the Spiders. [189]

SUNDAY 9 DECEMBER

▼ **SOCIALISING**

Bowie was back in New York and caught Iggy Pop's set at Hurrah, the last stop on the *New Values* tour.

Another night Bowie was at Mudd with Blondie's Jimmy Destri when they spotted German singer/performer Klaus Nomi and Warhol scenester/Fiorucci store attendant Joey Arias.

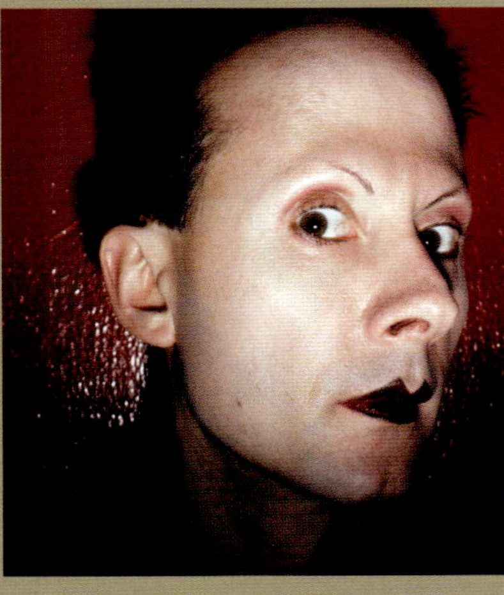

Madeline Bocchiaro (1997)
A strange, brilliant fellow from Germany had been living quietly in New York City for a few years, developing an act and a persona to complement his extraordinary singing talents. That persona became Klaus Nomi. [064]

Tony Frere (2004)
Klaus had created a lot of attention in the downtown scene and thankfully it got to Bowie. You know Bowie, always has his feelers out for what's next, for what's going on, for what's happening. [366]

Jimmy Destri (2009)
All the people who graduated from CBGBs would take over The Mudd Club. That was just the period when it was hopping. I was David's ambassador to these little bands. He was really, really interested in new wave. [040]

Joey Arias (2009)
The Nomi thing was happening really strongly at that moment that we first met Bowie. We were at The Mudd Club one night, and we were upstairs on the top floor. We were about to leave when someone said, "There's David Bowie, sitting there". We just froze. [040]

Bowie called them over to his table and introduced himself, though they had actually met before in 1973 at Berlin train station. Bowie was changing trains on his way back to England from Japan and Nomi (in those days a long-haired hippie named Klaus Sperber) carried Bowie's bags for him.

At Mudd they exchanged phone numbers, then met at Bowie's Chelsea loft a few days later to discuss ideas for an end-of-the-decade New Year's Eve concert, to be choreographed by Toni Basil. When that proved unfeasible, they adapted the ideas for Bowie's scheduled appearance on *Saturday Night Live*.

Bowie devised three set pieces based on Tristan Tzara's Cabaret Voltaire skits and John Heartfield's photomontages with help from *SNL* set designer Mark Ravitz, who had worked on the *Diamond Dogs* set in 1974.

Bowie's costume, a solid moulded plastic body painted in Thirties evening dress with a large bow tie, was made by *SNL*'s theatrical suppliers, Brooks Van Horn.

Page Wood (Art Director) (2004)
So we look at this thing and it's beautiful, and Pat Gibbons comes up and says, "Well, you're going to have to have something, you're going to need some costumes." And he whips out a big wad of cash and says, "How much do you need?" and starts peeling off bills, and Joey and Klaus look at him and their eyes widened and they look at each other and say, "We're going to need shoes, too." [366]

A few days later in a RCA rehearsal studio, Nomi and Arias watched as Bowie ran through the songs with the band: Carlos Alomar, George Murray and Dennis Davis, plus *SNL* guitarist George Wadenius and Jimmy Destri on keyboards.

SATURDAY 15 DECEMBER

✪ TELEVISION

NBC Studios
New York City
New York, USA

'SATURDAY NIGHT LIVE' (NBC)
'The Man Who Sold The World'/ 'Boys Keep Swinging'/'TVC 15'

Lorne Michaels: Producer
Dave Wilson: Director
Martin Sheen: Presenter

Studio 8H at 30 Rockefeller Plaza was buzzing with excitement as *SNL* regulars Jane Curtin and Laraine Newman ran around backstage squealing, "Bowie is in the building!"

After a brief introduction from Martin Sheen, Klaus Nomi and Joey Arias carried Bowie – encased in his solid body costume – to the front of the stage for 'The Man Who Sold The World'. Bowie then donned a blue Natasha Korniloff dress for 'TVC 15'. He described the idea as "a pipe-smoking Chinese airline stewardess, dragging a huge fake pink poodle on a leash. The dog had a TV monitor inside its mouth on which the real-time performance was playing." [065]

For 'Boys Keep Swinging' Bowie used a trick he had once seen at a German fair. He changed into a green costume and attached a small puppet's torso and limbs just beneath his head. With the aid of chroma key in front of a green screen, Bowie became a marionette with a huge human head.

▼SOCIALISING

After the show Bowie and the cast partied at One Fifth Avenue in Greenwich Village.

Page Wood (2004)

I said, "So, what are your plans? Are you going to be in New York, are you staying here?" and he said, "Yeah, I've got a loft, I'm going to be around for a while, I have a couple of things I have to tie up, and then I'm free." And I said, "Well, we've got some ideas." And he goes, "Well great, you'll be hearing from me." And Iggy Pop, who was smoking a big cigar, gave us the thumbs-up and we thought, "Great, we're in!" But we never really heard from him again. [366]

ABOVE LEFT: Backstage at NBC studios with presenter Martin Sheen.
ABOVE: With Klaus Nomi, Joey Arias and *Saturday Night Live* regulars Bill Murray, Laraine Newman, Jane Curtin, Gilda Radner and Martin Sheen (obscured).
OPPOSITE: 'The Man Who Sold The World' on *Saturday Night Live* with Carlos Alomar, Joey Arias, Klaus Nomi and house band guitarist Georg Wadenius; 'TVC 15' in Natasha Korniloff's 'Chinese airline stewardess' costume (bottom left and centre); using chroma key, Bowie becomes a little boy puppet singing 'Boys Keep Swinging' (bottom right).

■ CHART

'John, I'm Only Dancing (Again)'
UK Top 30 Chart Entry
Chart Peak No.12
Charting 8 weeks

SUNDAY 16 DECEMBER

✪ RADIO

'GOOD AFTERNOON' (WXRK-FM)

Bowie interviewed on air by Flo & Eddie.

▮ *Countdown End Of The Decade Special* broadcast in Australia (ABC).

LATE DECEMBER

▼SOCIALISING

Bowie went to see *The Elephant Man* at the Booth Theatre with friend and Hurrah co-owner Robert Boykin, who introduced him to director Jack Hofsiss afterwards.

TUESDAY 25 DECEMBER

Bowie spent Christmas in New York with Joey.

MONDAY 31 DECEMBER

✪ TELEVISION

The *Will Kenny Everett Make It To 1980?* show broadcast in UK, featuring David Mallet's video of Bowie's remade 'Space Oddity'. Bowie spent New Year's Eve at Rolling Stones manager Peter Rudge's apartment on Central Park with Mick Jagger and Jerry Hall.

JANUARY

TRAVELLING
Bowie flew back to Switzerland with Joey for a skiing holiday with George Underwood.

FRIDAY 4

TELEVISION
Dick Clark's 'Sensational Shocking Wonderful Wacky 70's' broadcast in US (NBC), including Bowie's lip-synched performance of 'Space Oddity'.

CHART
'John, I'm Only Dancing (Again)'
UK Chart Peak No.10

Melody Maker reported that Bowie was planning a series of British concerts in April/May and had designed the cover art for a compilation album of New York bands, which Blondie's Jimmy Destri was producing for ZE Records.

The record was eventually released as *2x5* on Marty Thau's Red Star label. The cover was designed by Peter Zaremba, the vocalist with The Fleshtones – one of the groups featured on the record.

OPPOSITE: Blondie at Hammersmith Odeon, where they performed 'Heroes' as an encore with guest guitarist Robert Fripp, who had mischievously hinted to reporters that Bowie might appear for a special duet with Debbie Harry.

FRIDAY 11 JANUARY

Bowie and RCA Records obtained a High Court injunction on behalf of the rest of the industry against record bootleggers M&C Pressings and associated companies.

In 1979, a British Phonographic Industry investigation of bootlegging activities in Britain had led to a raid in December on the operation in Northumbria. The BPI estimated that bootlegging had cost the industry £20 million in the last year alone.

SUNDAY 13 JANUARY

Blondie's last night at Hammersmith Odeon in London was buzzing with anticipation. On Friday guest guitarist Robert Fripp had let slip that Bowie would be making a special appearance to duet with Debbie Harry on 'Heroes'. Expectations built before the show as the PA played the *Stage* version of 'Beauty And The Beast' and peaked after it, when Blondie came back for the encore.

James Truman (*Melody Maker*)
'Heroes' began as a dark swell of sound, the band's nervous glances into the wings suggesting the arrival of a presence that the song dearly needed. It was Fripp who pulled the song back from the brink of disaster as it became painfully apparent that the legend was still in Switzerland building snowmen. [294]

SUNDAY 20 JANUARY

RADIO
During the hour-long special, recorded while Bowie was promoting 'John, I'm Only Dancing (Again)' in December 1979, Bowie reflected on the decade, and programmed some of its musical highlights, including his own.

'KING BISCUIT FLOWER HOUR' (KMET-FM)
DAVID BOWIE – A LOOK AT THE SEVENTIES
'Space Oddity'/
'Instant Karma' John Lennon/
'Saviour Machine'/
'Suffragette City'/
'Deborah' Tyrannosaurus Rex/
'Autobahn' Kraftwerk/
'I Feel Love' Donna Summer/
'DJ'/
'John, I'm Only Dancing (1972)'/
'John, I'm Only Dancing (Again)'/
'Virginia Plain' Roxy Music/
'I Wanna Be Your Dog' The Stooges/
'I'm Looking For A Love' Bobby Womack/
'I Can't Stand The Rain' Ann Peebles/
'Fame'/
'Trial-Prison' Philip Glass/
'Don't Worry About The Government' Talking Heads/
'Where Were You?' The Mekons

Released as a triple LP for syndicated radio station use (DIR Broadcasting).

FEBRUARY

SATURDAY 9

PRESS

Melody Maker reported that Bowie had scrapped plans for a spring tour and was looking at film scripts.

MID-FEBRUARY

Bowie's divorce from Angie was finalised. Angie was given a settlement of £500,000 to be paid over 10 years and Bowie was granted custody of Zowie.
Iggy Pop album *Soldier* was released, including 'Play It Safe', for which Bowie wrote music and sang backing vocals.

RECORDING

Power Station
441 West 53rd Street
New York City
New York, USA

'SCARY MONSTERS (AND SUPER CREEPS)'

David Bowie/Tony Visconti: Producers
Larry Alexander: Engineer

Bowie returned to New York to start work on the new album. Tony Visconti told *Melody Maker,* as he was packing for New York, "This album is going to be a departure from earlier experimentalism. David has written about 30 songs, and I can't reveal the concept, but I have something in mind which will give Bowie a new direction and dimension."

Visconti was keen to start on Bowie's new project, and excited by the sonic possibilities of Power Station, since owner Tony Bongiovi had built the studio to the same specifications as Motown's original studio. He rushed over at short notice to find Bowie actually had no finished songs, just some chord changes. Nevertheless, Bowie and his core band quickly worked up 'head arrangements' for nine or ten songs.

Tony Visconti (2002)

Although this studio was very businesslike and the staff hustled us out exactly when our time was up, there was a wonderful energy, which we tapped into. Carlos, George and Dennis were playing their best, now that they were in their own country and didn't have to deal with German and Swiss pubs for their only amusement. [424]

At various times the band was augmented by Jimmy Destri and Roy Bittan – on loan again from the E Street Band, at that time recording *The River* in the studio next door.

Tony Visconti (2002)

We often munched ribs and chicken sitting next to The Boss in the communal artists lounge. Dennis Davis actually turned to Bruce Springsteen, so casual was the ambience, and asked, "What band are you in?" [424]

Bowie came up with the piano figure for the 'Ashes To Ashes' intro, which he wanted Bittan to play on a stereo Wurlitzer he had delivered to the studio. It didn't work properly, but Visconti achieved the same effect putting a piano through an Instant Flanger.

Adrian Belew had been booked (and paid) in advance and he was disappointed to hear that Tom Verlaine was working on the album. As it turned out, Verlaine spent a whole day auditioning amplifiers and never recorded a note. His authorship of 'Kingdom Come' was his sole contribution.

Lou Reed's guitarist Chuck Hammer was invited to the sessions to demonstrate what he called Guitarchitecture, three examples of which he had sent to Bowie after they met in London. Hammer was using a guitar synthesiser to orchestrate parts for live performance as well as studio recordings. Visconti seized on this for the middle eight of 'Ashes To Ashes' (then known as 'People Are Turning To Gold'), and used the natural reverb of the four-level stairwell. Bowie and Visconti had a specific plan for where he would contribute.

Chuck Hammer (2012)

They appeared to be quite open to any idea I wanted to try. David understood quite clearly what 'textural zones' I was developing from the cassette demos I had forwarded. [274]

Hammer's Guitarchitecture was also deployed on 'It Happens Everyday' ('Teenage Wildlife') and 'Cameras In Brooklyn' ('Up The Hill Backwards'), though on the latter it wasn't used.

During a break in recording, Bowie was contacted by *The Elephant Man* director Jack Hofsiss, who told him that Philip Anglim, currently in the lead role of John Merrick, would be leaving the production in July.

Bowie (1980)

He asked if I would take over the role. I had never met him and I didn't know he knew anything about me, but he had apparently seen a few of my concerts and felt I'd be able to undertake the role successfully. I said, "If you want to take the risk, I'd love to take the plunge." [145]

Jack Hofsiss (1980)

I was familiar with his music, and I had seen him in concert. But the piece of work he did that was most helpful in making the decision was* The Man Who Fell To Earth*, in which I thought he was wonderful, and in which the character he played had an isolation similar to the Elephant Man's. His perceptions about the part and his interest were all so good that we decided to investigate the possibility of doing it. [182]

ABOVE: The UK picture sleeve folded out to a square colour poster featuring a still from Bowie's January appearance on Dick Clark's TV special.

FRIDAY 15 FEBRUARY

SINGLE RELEASED

'Alabama Song' (Brecht/Weill) (3:47)/
'Space Oddity' (4:49)
UK (RCA BOW 5)
Chart Peak No.23

Deadwax inscriptions:
"Ta Kurt"/"Sorry Gus" (Visconti's mock apology to Gus Dudgeon, who produced the original version).

'Alabama Song' recorded July 1978 at Good Earth Studios, London.

Reissued on *Rare* as 'Moon Of Alabama' (RCA 1982) and on *Scary Monsters* (Ryko 1992).

'Space Oddity' recorded September 1979 at Good Earth Studios, London.

Reissued on *Scary Monsters* (Ryko 1992)/*Space Oddity* 40th Anniversary EP (iTunes 2009).

MARCH

SATURDAY 1

CHART

'Alabama Song'
UK Chart Entry
Chart Peak No.23
Charting 5 weeks

WEDNESDAY 5 MARCH

SOCIALISING

Bowie, along with Tom Verlaine and most of the Patti Smith Group, watched Iggy Pop's show at Irving Plaza. Afterwards, Bowie and Iggy went to Hurrah to see Debbie Harry and Chris Stein make a guest appearance with James Chance & The Contortions at a benefit for their manager, Anya Phillips.

SUNDAY 9 MARCH

RADIO

'PROFILES IN ROCK MUSIC – DAVID BOWIE'

Broadcast: WPLJ-FM, New York.

SOCIALISING

Iggy was back in New York, playing at Great Gildersleeves on the Bowery. Bowie was in the audience, along with Mick Jagger and Chrissie Hynde.

MID-MARCH

After two and a half weeks of recording backing tracks and a further week of overdubs, Tony Visconti prepared a rough mix of the tracks in various stages of completion – covers of Tom Verlaine's 'Kingdom Come' (Alomar's suggestion) and Cream's 'I Feel Free', a staple of his 1972 set; 'Is There Life After Marriage', completed but later dropped; 'Lazer', recorded with The Astronettes and again for *Young Americans*, which was rewritten as 'Scream Like A Baby'. Of the new songs, only one was complete – 'It's No Game No.2', using the melody of 'Tired Of My Life' which Bowie had written as a 16-year-old and demoed in 1970.

Bowie opted to take a two-month break to compose melodies and lyrics for the remaining tracks – rather than improvise as he had done in the past – and finish the album in London.

TELEVISION COMMERCIAL

Kyoto, Japan

'CRYSTAL JUN ROCK'

With the bulk of the *Scary Monsters* backing tracks complete, Bowie accepted an invitation to promote Crystal Jun Rock, a brand of *shochu* (a Japanese distilled spirit similar to vodka) made by Takara Shuzo Co. Limited. He would appear in two television commercials, speak four words – 'Crystal Jun Rock Japan' – and provide the music. The shoot took place over two weeks at a temple in one of his favourite cities, Kyoto, staying at Osaka Teikoku Hotel. Between shooting, Bowie spent time with Masayoshi Sukita and Yacco Takahashi in Kyoto and Tokyo. Sukita photographed him in his hotel, riding the subway, at the markets and dining with Yacco at the Tofu Chinese restaurant in Roppongi.

Before he left Japan he was asked why he agreed to do the commercial...

BOWIE: *There are three reasons, the first one being that no one has ever asked me to do it before. And the money is a very useful thing. And the third, I think it's very effective that my music is on television 20 times a day. I think my music isn't for radio.* [006]

Q: *So did you write the music for the commercial?*

BOWIE: *Yes, this is the important point and the reason I agreed to do the commercial. It's a very slow one. I didn't use bass or drums, so it's very different from anything I have done before. It will be included in my next album. I don't drink while I work so I didn't drink while I wrote this one, of course.*

The music Bowie submitted, 'Fujimoto San', was originally intended to close *Scary Monsters* until it was used for the commercial and retitled 'Crystal Japan' for release as a single.

Takara Shuzo was initially disappointed that Bowie didn't actually sing on the track, but he submitted the elegant commercials and the print campaign had the desired effect, increasing demand for Crystal Jun Rock.

ABOVE: The 'Crystal Japan' single sleeve used a still from the Crystal Jun Rock commercial shoot.

SINGLE RELEASED

'Crystal Japan' (3:26)/
'Alabama Song' (Brecht/Weill) (3:50)
Japan (RCA SS-3270)

'Crystal Japan' was issued only in Japan, then later released in UK as the B-side of 'Up The Hill Backwards' (RCA 1981).

Reissued on *Rare* (RCA 1982)/ *Scary Monsters* (Ryko 1992)/ *All Saints – Collected Instrumentals 1977–1999* (EMI/Virgin 2001).

APRIL

SUNDAY 27

LIVE
GUEST APPEARANCE

The Metropol Theatre
Berlin, West Germany

IGGY POP

On his way back from Japan, Bowie dropped in to Berlin to see Iggy play a show in their old neighbourhood, Schöneberg. "Hi Dave, wherever you are," Iggy said from the stage as he introduced 'China Girl'. Bowie joined him for the encore to play keyboard on a couple of songs.

SOCIALISING

Afterwards Bowie, Iggy and the band headed to one of their favourite haunts, the Café Exil in Kreuzberg, finishing the night playing billiards.

MAY

RECORDING

Good Earth Studios
Dean Street, Soho
London, England

'SCARY MONSTERS (AND SUPER CREEPS)' ALBUM

Bowie returned to Visconti's studio in London, having written lyrics for all the songs as promised, and they began work on recording vocals, overdubs and mixing.

Bowie (1980)

Being settled into New York for longer than a month period, the influx of the general paranoia, high jet-set fashion and abject poverty all had a lot to do with the input that went into Scary Monsters. I had been living something that vacillates between a European to Far East existence for the last four and a half years. [342]

Bowie and Visconti decided, half in jest, that this album would be Bowie's *Sgt Pepper*. Accordingly, Bowie decided to open the album with 'It's No Game' and close with a reprise, and Visconti introduced the first part with the sound of spooling tape and Dennis Davis' count-in.

Bowie had his lyrics translated by a professor friend and had intended to sing it, even seeking coaching from Japanese actress (and Sparks' *Kimono My House* cover star) Michi Hirota, who was in the London production of *The King And I*. She found that the translation was literal rather than poetic, and was impossible to fit to the melody. Instead, Bowie asked her to recite the words, counterbalancing Bowie's histrionics.

Bowie (1980)

[She] says the lyric in such a way as to give the lie to the whole very sexist idea of how Japanese girls are so very prim. She's like a Samurai the way she hammers it out. It's no longer the little Geisha girl kind of thing, which really pisses me off because they're just not like that at all. [189]

Bowie almost discarded their recording of 'Jamaica', a relic from the 1976 tour rehearsals. Then a lyric idea occurred to him and 'Fashion' took shape with a berserk guitar part from Robert Fripp, who also recorded parts for 'It's No Game', 'Scary Monsters (And Super Creeps)', 'Kingdom Come', 'Up The Hill Backwards' and 'Teenage Wildlife'. At Bowie's request Pete Townshend turned up to play on 'Because You're Young'.

Tony Visconti (2006)

He seemed to be in a foul laconic mood... and asked what we wanted him to do. David looked at me and asked "Chords?" Townshend asked, "What kind of chords?" "Er, Pete Townshend chords." [047]

Townshend shrugged and played the part in his trademark windmill style, helped by a bottle of red. Thirty minutes later he was finished and out the door, but not before mentioning that the demo of 'Space Oddity' that Bowie gave him in 1969 was 'sure to be a hit'.

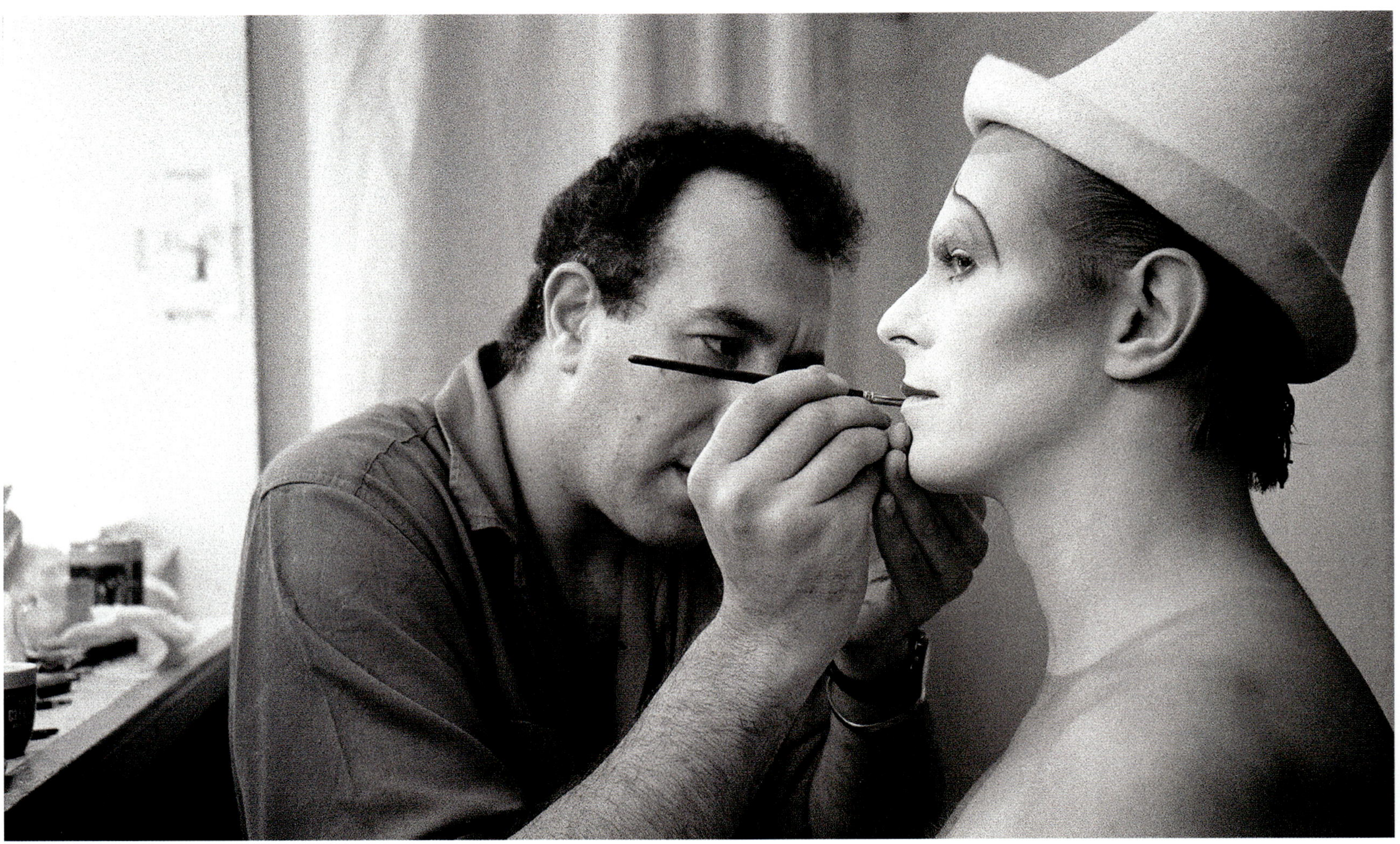

✪ PROMO VIDEO FILMING
Pett Level
East Sussex, England/
Ewart Studios
Wandsworth
London, England

'Ashes To Ashes'

David Mallet/David Bowie: Directors

Bowie (1980)

The other three [videos] that were done for Lodger were co-directions inasmuch as I gave David complete control over what I wanted put in there. But this one I storyboarded myself, actually drew it frame for frame. He edited it exactly as I wanted it and has allowed me to say [adopts Edward Heath voice] publicly that it is my first direction. I've always wanted to direct and this is a great chance to start – to get some money from a record company and then go away and sort of play with it.

ABOVE: Steve Strange's make-up artist Richard Sharah. "David came to me and said he wanted a Pierrot look, and he let me design from there. Most of the time I draw up some ideas and then work with the subject around those. The preparation for David's make-up took one-and-a-half hours." [119]
OPPOSITE: Natasha Korniloff's Blue Clown costume. "David rang me up and said, 'Tash, you know the beautiful clown in the circus? Well, I want to be the most beautiful.' I asked, 'Do you think blue?' He agreed." [019]

It was supposed to be the archetypal 1980s ideal of the futuristic colony that has been founded by the earthling, of what he looks like – and in that particular sequence the idea was for the earthling to be pumping out himself and to be having pumped into him something organic. So there was a very strong Giger influence there: the organic meets hi-tech. [189]

David Mallet (2002)

I think David Bowie's influence on early music videos was probably the greatest influence of all. He wasn't frightened to do something that was surreal, to go back to silent surrealist movies – he wasn't frightened to do anything. [370]

Two nights before the shoot, Bowie visited The Blitz Club to recruit extras for the video. On the door as usual was Steve Strange, who had told a journalist in March, "Mick Jagger turned up once. I had to explain he couldn't come in, just because he was Mick Jagger." Bowie was unlikely to be turned away – Strange regularly held 'Bowie Nights' at the club – but he chose a more discreet entrance.

Steve Strange (2002)

I clocked this limo that had been driving around two or three times. [Coco Schwab] came to me and said, "I have someone very important in the car and we need a table in an exclusive area upstairs." I was about to say, "He better be more important than the people about to go on stage" when the window wound down. And it was Bowie in there. I was a bit lost for words.

We managed to sneak them into the club the back way to avoid a fuss and usher him upstairs to a private area. David himself was charming and asked if I would join him upstairs for a drink when I had finished on the door. Word spread like wildfire. I had to have all the downstairs security on the stairs to stop everyone going up there. He said it was a great scene and asked me if I would like toappear in the video for his next single, 'Ashes To Ashes'.

He then said to me, "Look, I'd like you to pick the clothes you are going to wear, and to choose three other extras for the video. But there is only one snag. We have to meet tomorrow morning at 6am outside the Hilton to leave for the location shoot. I rushed around and found Judith Frankland, Darla Jane Gilroy and another girl for the video. [041]

Judith Frankland (2001)

Steve was resplendent in the wedding outfit that night and was chosen straight away. He was also asked to select people he felt could be right. I was invited, as was Darla Jane Gilroy, over to the table where David Bowie and his PA Coco were sitting and offered a glass of champagne. Darla and I were both dressed in a similar ecclesiastic style and were also asked to take part for what at that time was a decent sum of money for penniless, decadent students.

We were told Coco would call us the following day with the details. I awoke with a jolt, seriously wondering if this had all been a dream. I chose to believe not and sat at the door of the 'palatial' bedsit for hours waiting for the communal upstairs phone to ring so that I could sprint up in time to catch it. When the call finally came, I was instructed to be outside the Hilton the next day at some ungodly hour, fully dressed and made up the same way I had been at The Blitz, and to get the coach to a secret location. [419]

The Blitz kids were picked up from the Hilton Park Lane and taken by coach to Pett Level, a beach near Hastings that Mallet had closed off to the public for the filming.

David Mallet (2009)

The beach was my idea. It was a location I'd known since I was a little boy. One of the very rare places you can get right down to the water and there's a cliff towering over you. [040]

Judith Frankland (2011)

When we arrived at the beach, the crew was set up and David Bowie greeted us dressed in the Lindsay Kemp outfit he would wear that day. He coached us for a few minutes on the words we were to mime and then the day was spent in sinking sand and mud. [419]

The beach at Pett Level has an unusual feature at the western end under the cliffs – the fossilised remains of an ancient forest dating from the time of the land bridge linking England to Europe, which was submerged by the melt at the end of the Ice Age. Since the 16th century, the sea levels have dropped, exposing the remains of the trees at low tide.

Amidst the strange landscape, Bowie noticed a bulldozer sitting idle. Rather than shoot around it, Bowie decided to incorporate it – as a "symbol of oncoming violence", as he later explained. They located the owners – the local river board, which used it to repair the sea defences – and hired someone to drive the machine behind Strange and the others as they followed Bowie in procession.

Steve Strange (2002)

The difficulty was getting us all to move along at the correct speed. If I was too fast, I caught David up; if I was too slow, the bulldozer kept catching the robe I was wearing. There's a famous moment in it where it looks as if I am bending forward to bow. What I was actually doing was moving the hem of my robe to avoid getting pulled over by the bulldozer, but they decided to keep it in. [041]

Judith Frankland (2011)

We had done well, we were told at the end of the day, and asked to come to the studios in Wandsworth to shoot another scene. [419]

As the song was a sequel of sorts to 'Space Oddity', they returned to the padded cell and kitchen sets and approximated Bowie's outfits from the video of the 1979 version.

Judith Frankland (2011)

At the studios, David Bowie had lunch with us mere mortals in the canteen. The scene we were to do at the studio involved an explosion and I was at the back. In fact if you look at the video you can see my crucifix swing in. We were told to duck out and run after we had mimed our piece or we could be hurt. This was difficult in a hobble dress, so I hoisted it up as high as I could and got ready to run. Quite a sight for the superstar sat behind me. It took about three takes and we were done and told we could stay to watch the rest of the filming and that we should tell no one about the details of the video. It was all very hush-hush. [419]

The Blitz kids were handed £50 each and returned to London, clubbing all night at Hell.

The clip was later enhanced with solarising and other special effects using the new Quantel Paintbox, becoming the most expensive music video ever made at that time. It was voted best music video at MIDEM later in the year.

Released on
Sound + Vision (Ryko 1989)/
The Video Collection (PMI 1993)/
Best Of Bowie (EMI 2002).

PHOTO SESSION
'SCARY MONSTERS' ALBUM

Duffy: Photographer
Edward Bell: Photographer

Bowie turned again to *Aladdin Sane* and *Lodger* photographer Brian Duffy to shoot the *Scary Monsters* cover. Artist Edward Bell then developed the sleeve design using the photographs and cut-outs of old Bowie album sleeves, whitewashing them – as Bowie said at the time – to symbolise the discarding of his old personae.

Bowie was sufficiently pleased with the result that he commissioned Bell for another painting based on the Duffy photos. The artwork, entitled *Glamour*, appeared on the 1982 Bowie calendar and a poster.

SATURDAY 31 MAY

SOCIALISING

At Camden Music Machine Bowie watched Iggy Pop, supported by Hazel O'Connor.

Since the February sessions at Power Station, Visconti had been producing Hazel O'Connor's music for the film *Breaking Glass*, which was shooting at the same time. When he told Bowie about the film and O'Connor's Ziggyesque character, Bowie suggested they meet. Bowie had mentioned he needed a haircut, so Visconti asked O'Connor to come over with a pair of scissors – she had been cutting Visconti's hair as he had a small part in the film. Awestruck, O'Connor cut Bowie's hair and then invited him to the set, where she was filmed performing 'Give Me An Inch', acutely aware of Bowie watching her from the side of the stage.

JUNE

WEDNESDAY 4

SOCIALISING

Robert Fripp took Bowie to The Venue in London to see New Jersey group The Roches, whose debut album he had produced.

While in London, Bowie was spotted in the Virgin Megastore buying records by The Human League, Q-Tips, The Go-Go's, Throbbing Gristle and Elvis Costello.

ABOVE LEFT: Nightclub impresario, pop star and founding father of New Romanticism, Steve Strange. OPPOSITE: After Duffy had shot the Pierrot series, Edward Bell told Bowie, "I don't understand the clown make-up, shall we just mess it up and look like you've just had a fun night out" [008], then both Bell and Duffy shot Bowie in his dishevelled state. The *Scary Monsters* album cover was a composite of both.

THE
ELEP ANT MAN

JULY

WEDNESDAY 9

The New York Times announced that Bowie would be making his American stage debut in the touring company of *The Elephant Man*, playing a week in Denver followed by a month in Chicago. "He wanted to do the play," producer Nelle Nugent told Carol Lawson, "but it had to fit into his schedule. It happened that he could do it conveniently in Denver. David loves the role and has been talking about New York. If it can be fit into his schedule, he might do it."

Bowie (1980)
I wasn't given a chance to get cold feet because the whole thing was forgotten about. I didn't hear anything more until two weeks before rehearsal. Hofsiss said, "You're in – be over here in two weeks." [145]

Bowie (1980)
I had to say yes or no within 24 hours. I think they knew that as well. I think that Hofsiss knew that if I'd had time to think about it I would have dropped out. He was very clever psychologically in forcing me to face an issue like that. [189]

OPPOSITE: Promotional photo for the stage production of *The Elephant Man*.
RIGHT: John Merrick, the subject of Bernard Pomerance's play.

Bowie (1980)
So I couldn't do very much. So I went to the London Hospital and went to the museum there. Found the plaster casts of the bits of Merrick's body that were interesting to the medical profession and the little church that he'd made, and his cap and his cloak. Nothing much that you can get from that, just the general atmosphere. [336]

PG Nunn (London Hospital) (2009)
David asked pertinent questions… he wanted to know how Merrick walked, how he spoke. [040]

MID-JULY

► TRAVELLING

Bowie flew to San Francisco to watch Philip Anglim's last performance as John Merrick. Hofsiss allowed Bowie to see it just once as he wanted him to put his mark on the part. Bowie watched, soundlessly reciting the lines along with Anglim.

▲ REHEARSING

He then joined the company for two weeks of rehearsals, applying himself to the physically challenging role and drawing on his training in mime to suggest Merrick's deformity.

Hofsiss gave Bowie a chance to ease into the part with a week-long run at Denver's 2,400-seat Center For The Performing Arts, before moving on to Chicago.

Bowie (1980)
We didn't know if I was going to get to New York, but for me it was the idea of doing a straight play that had the greater appeal. [336]

"David asked pertinent questions... he wanted to know how Merrick walked, how he spoke."

PG Nunn

TUESDAY 29 JULY – SUNDAY 3 AUGUST

✪ THEATRE

Center For The Performing Arts
Denver
Colorado, USA

'THE ELEPHANT MAN'

DENVER CAST
Jack Hofsiss: Director
Ken Ruta: Frederick Treves/Belgian Policeman
David Bowie: John Merrick
Richard Neilson: Carr Gomm/Conductor
Thomas Toner: Ross/Bishop Walsham How/ Snork
Dennis Lipscomb: Pinhead Manager/ London Policeman/ Will/Lord John
Jeannette Landis: Streetwalker/Pinhead/ Miss Sandwich/Princess Alexandra
Concetta Tomei: Mrs Kendal/Pinhead
Thomas Apple: Orderly
David Heiss: Cellist
David Jenkins: Setting
Julie Weiss: Costumes
Beverly Emmons: Lighting

The play was a sell-out from the start, grossing $186,466, making it the biggest box-office attraction in the 38-year history of the venue.

Bowie (1980)
The only time I got real cold feet was just before opening night. I thought, "What on earth am I doing?" [145]

Variety
The acting debut on the American stage of rock singer David Bowie was greeted by a standing ovation in Denver when the singer, noted for his flamboyant musical style, took on the role of physically misshapen John Merrick, the human monster with a liking for culture. Drawing on an early mime background and the resourceful staging of his rock shows, Bowie displays the ability to project a complex character.

Playing a man too ugly to draw a freak audience, and too human to survive within a distorted body, Bowie shows a mastery of movement and of vocal projection. Bowie takes the stage with authority to create a stirring performance. Vocally, he is both quick and sensitive. In scene after scene he builds poignantly, crying for the chance to become civilised, though he knows he will always be a freak; pleading for a home; though he knows his presence disturbs; and questioning the rules of society; though his well being depends on their acceptance. Judging from his sensitive projection of this part, Bowie has the chance to achieve legit stardom.

Despite the good reviews, Bowie had misgivings about his performance.

Bowie (1980)
I was furious with myself on the first night that the thing that was preoccupying me during the performance was how people were adjusting or relating to my body movements and that I hadn't been considering the character at all. It took a good week to shake that feeling off and become interested and involved onstage with Merrick. [189]

Publicity still of Bowie as John Merrick, The Elephant Man.

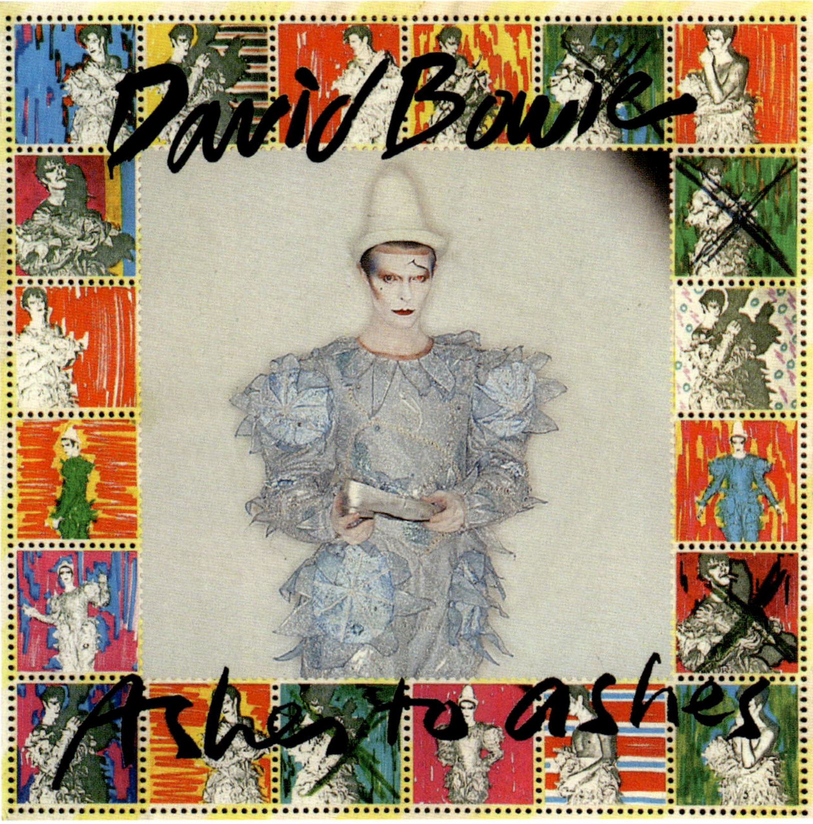

AUGUST

■ **ALBUM RELEASED**

PROMO INTERVIEW
'DAVID BOWIE:
RCA SPECIAL RADIO SERIES'
US (RCA DJL1-3829)

SIDE ONE
1. **Intro** (0:35)
2. **'Scary Monsters'** (5:25)
3. **Interview bridge** (0:20)
4. **'It's No Game (Part 1)'** (3:57)
5. **'Space Oddity'** (3:43)
6. **'Ashes To Ashes'** (4:21)
7. **'Fashion'** (4:48)

SIDE TWO
1. **'Up The Hill Backwards'** (3:24)
2. **Interview bridge** (0:30)
3. **'Kingdom Come'** (Bowie/Verlaine) (with interview bridge) (3:38)
4. **'Teenage Wildlife'** (5:35)
5. **'Scream Like A Baby'** (3:35)
6. **'It's No Game (Part 2)'** (4:30)

■ **SINGLE RELEASED**

12-INCH PROMO
The Continuing Story Of Major Tom
'Space Oddity' (5:15)/
'Ashes To Ashes' (3:35)/
'Ashes To Ashes' (4:21)
US (RCA DJL1-3840)

FRIDAY 1

■ **SINGLE RELEASED**

'Ashes To Ashes' (3:36)/
'Move On' (3:16)
UK (RCA BOW 6)
Chart Peak No.1

Released in three different covers using Duffy's photography. The first 100,000 copies containing one of a series of four sheets of nine stamps, designed by Bowie and inspired by Jerry Dreva's mail-art. The American conceptual artist was involved with Hollywood glam-art group the Bon Bons. Bowie acknowledged the inspiration by marking 'Bon Bon' on each one of the stamps on the covers.

SUNDAY 3 AUGUST

✪ **THEATRE**

The last night of a week of critically acclaimed performances in Denver. *The Elephant Man* closed and moved on to Chicago.

WEDNESDAY 6 – SATURDAY 30 AUGUST

✪ **THEATRE**

Blackstone Theatre
60 East Balbo Avenue
Chicago
Illinois, USA

'THE ELEPHANT MAN'

Starting with a Wednesday night preview, the Chicago run comprised 31 performances in 25 days. With only two days off in the season, Bowie was rarely seen out on the town, but was spotted one night with Iggy Pop at new wave club Neo's in Clark Street.

Opening night was attended by a large contingent of fans. At the cast party afterwards in Maxim's he told the *Chicago Tribune*, "I know that many of them haven't been to see serious theatre before, and that's why I'm so pleased that they were so attentive."

Bowie now had custody of Zowie and the pair spent their days sightseeing in Chicago, visiting aquariums and planetariums and the Museum of Science and Industry. "It is like a paean to General Motors," Bowie complained to *Rolling Stone*'s Kurt Loder, "quite ghastly in its corrupt values, including its splendiferous Muppet presentation, where you pay $1.50 to get in, see 15 stuffed Muppets in a glass case, and then that leads to a shop where you can buy merchandise! I mean... it was a fucking disgrace." [182]

✪ **PRESS**

Bowie was also interviewed by Angus McKinnon (*NME*) and Gordon Burn (*The Sunday Times*), both flown over and put up at the luxurious Whitehall Hotel for five days, courtesy of RCA.

Chris Charlesworth

(RCA Press Officer) (2007)

I was informed in no uncertain terms by 'Bowie's people' that each journalist would be allotted just one hour in which to talk with him. McKinnon wasn't happy and – unbeknownst to me – had brought along the Dutch photographer Anton Corbijn to take pictures exclusively for* NME*. This, said Bowie's people, was out of the question. I told McKinnon. "If you can engage David in an interesting, stimulating interview and along the way make it clear to him that you need to talk for more than an hour, he might just overrule his minders. But if you bore him you'll only get an hour. Oh – and mention Anton to him yourself."

So McKinnon did just that and David granted him not only extra time on the day of the interview but a further two hours the following day. And he agreed to pose for Corbijn, both in his Elephant Man costume backstage at the theatre and in a bar where McKinnon's interview took place.

Bowie's 'people' were furious with me but I couldn't care less. Next week's* NME *had a Corbijn picture of DB on the cover and five pages of McKinnon's interview inside, and a month or two later DB in his Elephant Man loincloth graced the front page of* The Sunday Times *colour magazine. The point of the story is that David knew better than his advisors how to achieve maximum coverage. [086]

During the Chicago run, Bowie went to see Roy Orbison play at the Park West and invited him to see *The Elephant Man* the following night.

Bowie also attended a party at Scampi's, a restaurant in the lobby of the Hyatt Regency, where he and Orbison sang 'Happy Birthday' for Orbison's promoter, Jam Productions' John Weitekamp.

SATURDAY 16 AUGUST

■ CHART

'Ashes To Ashes'
UK Top 30 Chart Entry No.4
Chart Peak No.1
Charting 10 weeks

SATURDAY 23 AUGUST

'Ashes To Ashes' reached No.1 in the UK. BBC's *Newsbeat* reporter Andrew Turner called Bowie in Chicago earlier in the week to tell him the news. "I'm very surprised," said Bowie. "God bless the English public is what I say!"

SATURDAY 30 AUGUST

✪ THEATRE

The Elephant Man closed in Chicago, having set a box-office record with receipts of $172,000.

SEPTEMBER

WEDNESDAY 3

✪ TELEVISION

**Times Square Studios
New York City
New York, USA**

'GOOD MORNING AMERICA' (ABC)

Q: *An awful lot of performers talk about how difficult it is to deal with what the public sees them as, and do you think you're alike? Do you have a problem with that because you've been so many different people?*

BOWIE: *Not really because I don't circulate in places where there's much public...*

Q: *You're a private person?*

BOWIE: *It's not that as much as that I prefer travelling than sticking in cities where you're sort of immersed in the rock'n'roll circus. So I end up in Africa or Germany or Japan… Mombasa, Berlin and Kyoto are my main ports of call.*

Q: *Opening night, do you get jitters, I mean, I'm wondering about the play, but even in your concerts, are you a little nervous before you go on?*

BOWIE: *Yes. I don't like riding in on a concert in too relaxed a state.*

Q: *You like to have the adrenalin flowing then?*

BOWIE: *Yes, very much so.*

Q: *How about* Elephant Man, *did you have many jitters opening night?*

BOWIE: *Yes, I was petrified. I didn't know what was going to happen, but once I got on stage, the supporting cast were just truly wonderful.* [361]

Broadcast: Live at 7am.

▲ REHEARSING

Bowie began three weeks of rehearsals for the Broadway run of *The Elephant Man* with the New York cast, taking over the role from Jeff Hayenga who joined the national touring company.

**LEFT: Bowie on *Good Morning America*.
OPPOSITE: *The Elephant Man* rehearsals in New York, September 13.**

FRIDAY 5 SEPTEMBER

TELEVISION

NBC Studios
Burbank
California, USA

'THE TONIGHT SHOW WITH JOHNNY CARSON' (NBC)
'Life On Mars?'/
'Ashes To Ashes'

Bowie took a break from rehearsals in New York to appear on America's most popular talk show. Earlier in the week, a crew from the *20/20* news programme filmed Bowie rehearsing for the appearance with the band that included GE Smith and Steve Goulding.

A large contingent of fans camped outside NBC on Thursday night for tickets to see Bowie's first US performance in nine months. By the morning the crowd had swelled to 200.

"I guess I'm sort of on top of the world at the moment," Bowie told Robert Hilburn in his dressing room before the show. Asked about the play, Bowie said, "There is discipline involved in both rock and straight theatre, but it's a different kind of discipline. The strange thing for me was to take one character and play him with an emotional chronology from beginning to end, knowing the emotional and psychological steps he was going to take in a two-hour period. In concert, I play with the characters and evoke different kinds of emotional drive anytime I wish.

ABOVE RIGHT AND RIGHT: Performing 'Ashes To Ashes' and 'Life On Mars' on *The Tonight Show With Johnny Carson*.

"I knew after the first night that I was credible. I felt, 'Yes, I was John Merrick tonight.'

That made me happy and I thought, it's a continual process. It may be imperceptible to some people, but I do find something new every night." [145]

Waiting for the Carson taping to begin, he chatted with friends and signed a few autographs for those lucky enough to get in.

Carson finally introduced Bowie, plugging *Scary Monsters* and his upcoming appearance in *The Elephant Man*. Over the loud cheering, Carson quipped, "He'd better be good after this."

MONDAY 8 SEPTEMBER

SINGLE RELEASED

'Ashes To Ashes' (3:35)/
'It's No Game (Part 1)' (4:16)
US (RCA PB-12078)
Chart Peak No.101

TUESDAY 9 SEPTEMBER

PRESS

'David Bowie: The View From The Top' by Robert Hilburn published in the *Los Angeles Times*.

FRIDAY 12 SEPTEMBER

■ ALBUM RELEASED

'SCARY MONSTERS (AND SUPER CREEPS)'

UK (RCA BOW LP2)
Chart Peak No.1

SIDE ONE
1. **'It's No Game (No.1)'** (4:17)
2. **'Up The Hill Backwards'** (3:13)
3. **'Scary Monsters (And Super Creeps)'** (5:10)
4. **'Ashes To Ashes'** (4:24)
5. **'Fashion'** (4:48)

SIDE TWO
1. **'Teenage Wildlife'** (6:55)
2. **'Scream Like A Baby'** (3:35)
3. **'Kingdom Come'** (Bowie/Verlaine) (3:42)
4. **'Because You're Young'** (4:51)
5. **'It's No Game (No.2)'** (4:20)

Japanese Translation
'It's No Game (No.1)': Hisahi Miura

Producers: David Bowie/Tony Visconti

Assistant Engineers:
Larry Alexander/Jeff Hendrickson

David Bowie: Vocals/Keyboards

Carlos Alomar: Guitars

George Murray: Bass

Robert Fripp: Guitar

Dennis Davis: Percussion

Chuck Hammer: Guitar

Roy Bittan: Piano

Andy Clark: Synthesiser

Pete Townshend: Guitar

Tony Visconti: Acoustic Guitar/Backing Vocals

Lynn Maitland/Chris Porter: Backing Vocals

Michi Hirota: Voice on 'It's No Game (No.1)'

Cover Designer: Edward Bell

Cover Concept: Brian Duffy/David Bowie

Natasha Korniloff: Clown Costume Designer

Make-up: Richard Sharah

Recorded at Power Station, New York, USA/ Good Earth Studios, London, England

ABOVE: Bowie had given artist Edward Bell free rein to incorporate the photographs from the earlier session into the sleeve design. "Bowie told me, 'I don't care what you do as long as I have red hair, because in America I'm known as the red-haired bisexual.' I actually reversed the transparency that I painted from for the cover, so that his eyes were the wrong way round on the album sleeve. The interesting thing was that when Bowie saw the finished painting with his face in reverse, he didn't notice anything wrong with the picture. I asked him to look closely, and in the end I had to point it out to him. Of course he was used to seeing his face that way round in the mirror." Duffy was dismayed to find his photography was obscured by Edward Bell's painting on the approved cover design.

REISSUES
- CD (RCA 1984).
- CD (remastered) (Ryko 1991).

BONUS TRACKS
1. 'Space Oddity' (recorded 1979) (4:57)
2. 'Panic In Detroit' (recorded 1979) (3:00)
3. 'Crystal Japan' (3:08)
4. 'Alabama Song' (3:51)

- CD (remastered) (EMI 1999).
- CD (mini LP replica)(Toshiba EMI 2007)

Angie Bowie's account of life with Bowie, *Free Spirit*, serialised in *The Sun* for a week. She told reporters in London the previous year, "This book will make me rich. Thank God this marriage is finally kaput."

SATURDAY 13 SEPTEMBER

✪ PRESS

Angus Mackinnon's interview feature, 'The Future Isn't What It Used To Be', published in *NME*.

MONDAY 15 SEPTEMBER

■ ALBUM RELEASED

'SCARY MONSTERS (AND SUPER CREEPS)'

US (RCA AQL1-3647)
Chart Peak No.12

WEDNESDAY 17 SEPTEMBER

PRESS

Booth Theatre
222 West 45th Street
New York City
New York, USA

After a dress rehearsal, Bowie told the press, "It's the most terrifying position I've ever put myself in. There isn't any room for spontaneity – very different from rock and roll."

SATURDAY 20 SEPTEMBER

RADIO INTERVIEW

(WHFS-FM)
New York City
New York, USA

TUESDAY 23 SEPTEMBER – SUNDAY 4 JANUARY 1981

THEATRE

Booth Theatre
222 West 45th Street
New York City
New York, USA

'THE ELEPHANT MAN'

NEW YORK CAST

Donal Donnelly: Frederick Treves/ Belgian Policeman
David Bowie: John Merrick
Richard Clarke: Carr Gomm/Conductor
LM Hobson: Ross/Bishop Walsham How/ Snork
Jeffrey Jones: Pinhead Manager/ London Policeman/Will/Lord John
Judith Barcroft: Streetwalker/Pinhead/ Miss Sandwich/Princess Alexandra
Patricia Elliot: Mrs Kendal/Pinhead
Dennis Creaghan: Orderly
Michael Goldschlager: Cellist
Benjamin Hendrickson: John Merrick Understudy

Evenings: Tuesday – Saturday 8pm
Matinees: Wednesday 2pm, Saturday 2pm, Sunday 3pm

Celebrities who turned out for the opening night included Andy Warhol, Christopher Isherwood, David Hockney, Lee Radziwill, John Belushi, Gilda Radner, May Pang, Tom Hoving, Diana Vreeland and Oona Chaplin, the 55-year-old widow of Charlie Chaplin, who flew in for the occasion from Switzerland.

ABOVE: Hurrah nightclub, the night Bowie watched The Psychedelic Furs play and met Richard Butler.
OPPOSITE: *The Elephant Man* opening night at the Booth Theatre on September 23, with co-star Patricia Elliott and Gilda Radner.

WEDNESDAY 24 SEPTEMBER

Nic Roeg's original cut of *The Man Who Fell To Earth* was given general release in USA. Advertising read: "*Before there was* Star Wars… *Before there was* Close Encounters… *There was* The Man Who Fell To Earth. *Now there is the complete uncut version never before seen in the United States. Experience a sci-fi original as it was originally intended."*

THURSDAY 25 SEPTEMBER

SOCIALISING

Following his evening performance at the Booth Theatre, Bowie went to Hurrah to check out a new group that Iggy had endorsed – The Psychedelic Furs. Their single 'Sister Europe', released in February, won them a support spot on Iggy Pop's UK tour. Their debut album, released in March, was a commercial success and word soon spread to America of this Bowie-influenced group. They came to New York in June.

Richard Butler (2001)
We played at The Mudd Club, and got to stay in New York for five days, which was incredible. After years of being a fan of The Velvet Underground and Bob Dylan and Andy Warhol, it was totally a different world, totally alien, incredibly exciting. And then we went back and planned to tour here. [405]

Hurrah's booker Ruth Polsky travelled to London to convince them to come to New York and play at the club.

Sara Salir (Hurrah DJ) (2011)
When The Psychedelic Furs came, everyone was really anxious to see them. And at Hurrah there was no VIP lounge and the DJ booth was the VIP lounge. The DJ booth was really, really small, so it was me and David Byrne, David Bowie, Mick Jagger and Jerry Hall. But of course I was so nervous and insecure. David Bowie was looking through the records and I practically slapped his hands – I might have slapped his hands – and said, "Nobody touches my records." [372]

After their set, Bowie went backstage to meet the Furs and chatted with Richard Butler.

Richard Butler (1982)
He just came round afterwards and said, "Hi, I'm David," and I thought, "Christ! I know who you are. I'm Richard Butler!" What was good was the simple fact that he took the trouble to come back and tell us how much he liked the show. [006]

Bowie (1987)
I've always had a penchant for The Psychedelic Furs. I think they're a great band. I've always wanted to produce them, and they've often asked me to, but I never had the time. I would never be forward enough with most bands to suggest producing them, because I always like what it is they have themselves. [184]

SATURDAY 27 SEPTEMBER

CHART

'Scary Monsters'
UK Chart Entry
Chart Peak No.1
Charting 32 weeks

Bowie poses beside George M Cohan's "Give My Regards to Broadway" statue in Times Square, New York City, September 29.

GEORGE
M
COHAN
1878-1942
Give my Regards to Broadway
Panasonic
just slightly ahead of o
reborn
MATERNI
3rd AVE... 81
THE HUNTER
MY BODYGUARD

OCTOBER

✪ FILMING
Hurrah
32 West 62nd Street
New York City
New York, USA

'CHRISTIANE F'

After an approach from German writer/director Herman Weigel, Bowie agreed to appear briefly in the feature *Christiane F* (under production in Berlin) on the condition they film his segment in New York. To simulate a 1976 Berlin concert, Bowie lip-synched to the *Stage* version of 'Station To Station' at Hurrah.

The footage, including cutaways of actress Natja Brunckhorst, was intercut with shots of AC/DC's November 27 Berlin concert.

✪ PROMO VIDEO FILMING
Hurrah
32 West 62nd Street
New York City
New York, USA

Various Manhattan locations.

'Fashion'
David Mallet: Director

The day after filming *Christiane F*, Bowie and David Mallet reused the set and the group to shoot the 'Fashion' video.

Merrill Aldighieri (Hurrah VJ) (2009)
David Bowie was a friend of the club owner, Robert Boykin, which was how he came to choose Hurrah for a location. The shoot was in the afternoon while the club was closed to the public. We see the club draped in a khaki grey canvas fabric, which must have been rented because normally the decor was black. There is some choreography on the dance floor where you can see the characteristic faceted mirror wall, which distinguished Hurrah's decor, creating a real-life effect that was somewhat like a magic lantern. [378]

Other characters in the scenes shot around the streets of Manhattan included May Pang saying "beep beep" and a self-referential street mime. Done up in white face and striped top and braces, struggling actor Alan Hunter got to see firsthand how this new video medium worked.

ABOVE: RCA Studios in New York, for a day of interviews with international press and television.
OPPOSITE: Bowie attends the premiere of David Lynch's film *The Elephant Man*, starring John Hurt, with whom Bowie formed a mutual admiration society. Although the film was not an adaptation of the play, Bernard Pomerance successfully sued the production company for the film's use of the play's title and much of its content.

Alan Hunter (2011)
Great gig – three days, three square meals and $50 per day and I got to meet the Thin White Duke. Only three months later, I got the MTV gig… how prophetic. [408]

Hunter became one of the first five presenters on the revolutionary music channel, where 'Fashion' and 'Ashes To Ashes' later went on to high rotation. UK *Record Mirror* readers later voted them best music videos of 1980.

▮ Released on *The Video Collection* (PMI 1993)/ *Best Of Bowie* (EMI 2002).

THURSDAY 2 OCTOBER

✪ TELEVISION
RCA Studios
6th Avenue
New York City
New York, USA

Bowie's publicist Barbara DeWitt organised a day packed with interviews to promote both *Scary Monsters* and *The Elephant Man*. The media blitz would counteract the publicity for the imminent release of David Lynch's film of the same name.

At a studio in the RCA building, television crews from Rai Uno, *Musik Szene*, *13 Heures* and *Apropos Music* were ushered in. Each was allotted 15 minutes of interview time and given a choice of different coloured seamless paper backdrops. The Italian Rai Uno crew chose mauve, followed by the French who chose black.

"That is so Left Bank. And theirs was so Milan," observed Bowie as the camera was reloaded for the next session. "What's Germany got?"

After lunch they moved uptown to a suite at the Carlyle Hotel for the rest of the interviews, including Tim Rice from the BBC's *Friday Night Saturday Morning*.

"I've just had the most coruscating interview with a woman from *Stern*. All she did was attack me about my 'decadent' audiences," Bowie told Gordon Burn from *The Sunday Times* magazine. "I keep telling myself every time I finish one of these forays into the public eye, never again. Because I feel fettered by cliché all the time, and become quite parrot-like. I don't help myself at all." [073]

Also interviewed by the Japanese show *De De Music Now Young Oh! Oh!*

FRIDAY 3 OCTOBER

Bowie attended the premiere of David Lynch's film *The Elephant Man* at New York's Coronet Theatre.

FRIDAY 10 OCTOBER

✪ TELEVISION
'FRIDAY NIGHT SATURDAY MORNING' (BBC 2)

TIM RICE: *Are you getting people saying, "I enjoyed your performance but I've never heard of you before"?*

BOWIE: *That element has crept into it, yes. There have been some regular theatregoers who've come… well, they had heard of me but in some sort of perverse fashion or some kind of really corrupted idea of what I was about and I suppose they've got a different impression of me now.*

RICE: *Would you like to go back on stage in due course?*

BOWIE: *Not particularly. I've learned an awful lot just in the few weeks that I've been doing this. I hope I can explore the part even further. If I don't then I'll be wasting a lot of time. I would like to be more adventurous with the part. I've been sticking very tightly to the way I first wanted to interpret the thing. Whilst all this palaver has gone on about press and opening nights and whatever, now things are relaxing more, I would like to stretch out into it more. There are certain avenues that I would like to follow that I haven't had the courage to do so, yet. But now I will probably take advantage.* [360]

WEDNESDAY 22 OCTOBER

TELEVISION

'13 HEURES – SPECIAL DAVID BOWIE' (TÉLÉVISION FRANÇAISE 1)

Yves Mourousi: Presenter

Patrice Drevet: Interviewer

The 15-minute special was based around the interview filmed at RCA Studios, and included clips from 'Boys Keep Swinging', 'DJ', 'Ashes To Ashes', the 1978 Dallas concert and *The Elephant Man*.

BOWIE: *It never occurred to me to even consider trying to work in the realm of straight dramatic theatre. I didn't think that I was qualified, nor that I had any particularly masterful technique which would put me anywhere near a stage in a credible fashion but [Jack Hofsiss] had the audacity, or courage… to put me in that position. And I met the challenge as I am of that nature to… leap into things without really thinking. And I accepted.*

DREVET: *Are you the last rock star?*

BOWIE: *In my family, definitely.* [342]

THURSDAY 23 OCTOBER

TELEVISION

'COUNTDOWN' (ABC AUSTRALIA)

Interviewed by Ian Meldrum in a Japanese restaurant near the Booth Theatre. Towards the end of the interview, Bowie mischievously grabbed Meldrum's interview notes and started tearing them up.

Meldrum presented Bowie with a platinum record for *Scary Monsters*, which had sold 250,000 copies in its first three weeks of release in Australia and topped the chart for five weeks.

FRIDAY 24 OCTOBER

SINGLE RELEASED

'Fashion' (3:23)/
'Scream Like A Baby' (3:33)
UK (RCA BOW 7)
UK (RCA BOW T7)
Chart Peak No.5

Brian Duffy: Photographer

Edward Bell: Sleeve Designer

Deadwax inscriptions:
"So There"/"So There"

ABOVE: Edward Bell's cover for 'Fashion' was composed of photos he had taken just before the *Scary Monsters* photo session at Duffy's studio. "We both arrived at the studio together and before he put any make-up on I said, 'Look, let's take some pictures now'". [008] OPPOSITE: Debbie Harry with Bowie in his dressing room at the Booth Theatre.

SINGLE RELEASED

'It's No Game (Part 1)' (4:16)/
'Fashion' (4:48)
Japan (RCA RPS-10)

Mushroom Publishing released Angie Bowie's *Free Spirit*. Bowie was reportedly unconcerned by the tell-all memoir: "The book doesn't worry me and won't worry the fans. They expect me to be outrageous anyway."

NOVEMBER

SATURDAY 8

CHART

'Fashion'
UK Chart Entry No.8
Chart Peak No.5
Charting 12 weeks

MONDAY 10 NOVEMBER

SINGLE RELEASED

'Fashion' (3:23)/
'Scream Like A Baby' (3:33)
US (RCA PB-12134)

THURSDAY 13 NOVEMBER

PRESS

'Scary Monster On Broadway' by Kurt Loder published in *Rolling Stone*.

TELEVISION

'20/20' (ABC)

Donovan Moore: Producer

Tom Hoving: Arts Correspondent

The US news programme showed Bowie rehearsing 'Ashes To Ashes' for his Carson appearance and painting in his Chelsea loft. Tom Hoving interviewed Bowie in a Soho art gallery, surrounded by some of Bowie's paintings he had shipped over from Germany.

The special also showed clips from the *Ziggy Stardust* film, *The Man Who Fell To Earth*, *The Elephant Man*, 'Ashes To Ashes' video, Bowie's *Peter And The Wolf* narration and 'Heroes' from *Bing Crosby's Merrie Olde Christmas*. Hoving also interviewed Allan Jones, Charles Shaar Murray and Cherry Vanilla.

SUNDAY 16 NOVEMBER

TELEVISION

Bowie's interview with Ian Meldrum broadcast on *Countdown* in Australia (ABC). The report included a clip from *The Elephant Man* and the promo clips of 'Ashes To Ashes' and the new single 'Fashion'.

THURSDAY 20 NOVEMBER

SOCIALISING

Bowie attended the launch party of The Peppermint Lounge at 128 West 45th Street. New wave act Buzz And The Flyers provided the live entertainment.

TUESDAY 25 NOVEMBER

PRESS

'Bowie's Achievement on the Legitimate Stage' by Patricia Barnes published in *The London Times*.

Barnes interviewed Bowie in the Japanese restaurant – the same as the *Countdown* interview – and he impressed her by addressing the waiters in fluent Japanese…

PATRICIA BARNES: *After several weeks in New York as an actor, is it now possible to walk down the street without being set upon by innumerable fans?*

BOWIE: *Oh yes, I have worked out a very coherent New York lifestyle and there are two ways of walking down the street – I really buy that one. You can walk down the street wanting to be recognised and you can walk down the street not wanting to be recognised. This is especially true of New York and, to a certain extent, most of America. The most you get is, "Hi Dave, how's it going?" It's very neighbourly. They don't get as excited at meeting you as they do in London, which is still a bit star conscious. Here you see Al Pacino walking around or Joel Grey jogging. It's quite easy to do that, it's great.* [053]

WEDNESDAY 26 NOVEMBER

Following Bowie's popularity surge in America, United Artists announced its intention to resurrect *Just A Gigolo*, despite its disastrous reception two years before in Europe and Great Britain. Since then, David Hemmings had re-edited and shortened the film, which would be tested in Atlanta on December 19, potentially to open in New York in January 1981.

SUNDAY 30 NOVEMBER

PRESS

'Bowie Holds Court' interview feature published in *The Sunday Times* magazine.

DECEMBER

FRIDAY 5 DECEMBER

BBC Radio 1 announcer Andy Peebles and his producer Paul Williams arrived in New York, having secured an interview with Bowie and tickets for *The Elephant Man*, which they attended on the Friday night. During the day they also met with Yoko Ono to arrange an interview with her and John Lennon for the following day at The Hit Factory, where they were recording the follow-up to *Double Fantasy*.

Paul Williams (Producer)
The original reason Andy Peebles and I planned to visit New York was to record an interview with David Bowie. Shortly before we set out I thought we should take the opportunity also to interview John Lennon and Yoko Ono. [031]

SATURDAY 6 DECEMBER

✪ PRESS

Andy Peebles' interview with Lennon and Ono touched on the subject of Bowie and the play…

PEEBLES: *We mentioned* Elephant Man *earlier – which we've been to see while we've been here in New York – I must say a stunning performance from Bowie, he's a very talented gentleman.*

LENNON: *Amazing guy, isn't he?*

PEEBLES: *I mean I was quite puzzled by that, because I thought, I wonder whether David starring in a stage play like that would encourage the wrong sort of people to turn up. The screamers may come to see Bowie and to say, to hell with the intellectual element of the play, we're just here to clock him, and it wasn't like that at all actually, it was a very sympathetic audience.*

ABOVE: BBC executive producer Doreen Davies and interviewer Andy Peebles with Yoko Ono and John Lennon at The Hit Factory, New York.

LENNON: *I must say I admire him for his vast repertoire of talent the guy has, you know. I was never around when the Ziggy Stardust thing came, because I'd already left England while all that was going on, so I never really knew what he was. And meeting him doesn't give you much more of a clue, you know, because you don't know which one you're talking to. But… and, you know, we all have our little personality traits, so between him and me I don't know what was going down but we seemed to have some kind of communication together, and I think he's great. The fact that he could just walk into that and do that. I could never do that.* [031]

SUNDAY 7 DECEMBER

✪ RADIO

BBC RADIO 1

Bowie interviewed by Andy Peebles.

The interview, which took place before his matinee performance at the Booth Theatre, covered the play, the recording of *Scary Monsters* and Bowie's work with John Lennon.

PEEBLES: *Could I get your views on [David Lynch's* Elephant Man*] film and how you felt John Hurt's performance was?*

BOWIE: *Unfortunately, I can't give them to you because I've not seen it and I probably won't see it until I finish my run at the moment on Broadway. I like John Hurt very much indeed; I think I would not want to see it, mainly because I wouldn't want to be influenced by anything he's doing. And I also like David Lynch's films very much indeed; I like his expressionist thing, very cult film.*

PEEBLES: *What about the diversification of interests? Have you found that easy to control? I mean, the fact that you were involved in a stage production here and yet you still have the inevitable pressure of keeping up the output of music. How do you manage to mix the two, or indeed how do you at all?*

BOWIE: *I think so, in terms of it, I don't have managers, I just have a couple of people who work with me. It's much more on a real basis. I don't feel like an organisation or something like that. Some of my contemporaries have got into that position. It's an unhappy one to be in. I'm not saying things are perfect, but it feels a lot more real. Yeah, I think there's not that much happening that I can't really look after. And the play's in the evenings, I do my writing in the day and I can paint when I come from the theatre. So it's all fairly logical.*

PEEBLES: *You're here on a regular basis now… you're not in Britain as much as you were.*

BOWIE: *Firstly, America isn't a place that I come to very often; I'm not that fond of this place either!*

PEEBLES: *Oh really? I hope they're not listening next door!*

BOWIE: *No, no, it's OK… it's OK… they know that as well. They have to live here. I don't mind working here, again, but it's a great stimuli as a place to work but again, as a living place, I don't know. I'm not at all sure about habitat and all that anyway. Never have been.*

PEEBLES: *Naturally nomadic?*

BOWIE: *Mmm.*

PEEBLES: *What do you see yourself doing stage-wise in the future – is there anything in the pipeline?*

BOWIE: *Probably… coming back to Europe at some point to do the minimal tour situation. I would do maybe one south of England thing, and one north of England thing. And do that from country to country over a two-week period, and do the same thing in America. As a commitment that I would still perform but under my own regulations about how I'm going to perform, in a restricted kind of area.* [336]

Broadcast: January 5, 1981 (BBC Radio 1).

✪ TELEVISION

Musik Szene broadcast in Germany (WDR/HR).

The programme included the interview filmed in October (dubbed German translation), clip from *The Elephant Man*, live clips from the Convention Centre in Dallas ('Ziggy Stardust'), promo video ('Ashes To Ashes'), Bowie's paintings and excerpts from promo videos ('Heroes' and 'Sense Of Doubt').

ABOVE: Mourners congregate outside Lennon's home, The Dakota, 1 West 72nd Street.

MONDAY 8 DECEMBER

After a morning photo shoot with Annie Leibovitz, John Lennon gave his last interview – for the RKO Radio. "I always consider my work one piece, whether it be with Beatles, David Bowie, Elton John, Yoko Ono, and I consider that my work won't be finished until I'm dead and buried and I hope that's a long, long time."

Lennon and Ono spent the evening recording 'Walking On Thin Ice' at The Hit Factory, before returning home just before 11pm. Outside the Dakota building Lennon was shot dead by Mark Chapman, six hours after Lennon had autographed his copy of *Double Fantasy*.

May Pang was having dinner at a girlfriend's house when she heard the news. She fled to her apartment where the phone kept ringing with everyone asking her for information. Thinking about the time she'd recently spent with Bowie talking about Lennon and his return to recording, she got back on the phone and called Bowie. Coco answered as Bowie was out on a date. "Are you alone?" she asked Pang, "Get here immediately!"

Shortly after she arrived to the loft, Bowie returned. Deeply distraught, numb and incredulous, Bowie kept screaming, "What the hell?! What the fuck is going on with this world?!" as they watched the news reports on television. They stayed up all night consoling each other as the crowds gathered outside the Dakota. [029]

TUESDAY 9 DECEMBER

Rumours abounded following Lennon's murder. It was said that Mark Chapman had been to one of Bowie's *Elephant Man* performances at the Booth Theatre and had photographed him at the stage door; he'd bragged that he could have killed either of them; and police searched Chapman's hotel room and supposedly found a Booth Theatre programme with Bowie's name ringed in black. Bowie later claimed the rumours were true.

Bowie (2010)

I was second on his list. Chapman had a front-row ticket to **The Elephant Man** ***the next night. John and Yoko were supposed to sit front-row for that show, too. So the night after John was killed there were three empty seats in the front row. I can't tell you how difficult that was to go on. I almost didn't make it through the performance.*** [407]

Jack Hofsiss (1985)

We asked David if he wanted to miss performances but he insisted not, because it was very important for all aspects of the experience to keep playing the role and to appear. It must have been very frightening for him. [019]

Both Lennon and Bowie had tried to assume normal lives and thought they had succeeded. Lennon had said as much to Andy Peebles the week before: "I can go out this door right now and go in a restaurant. Do you want to know how great that is?" [031]

Now the shutters would have to come down. Bowie scrapped plans for a *Scary Monsters* tour and told the producers of *The Elephant Man* that he would leave the play at the end of his contract on January 4.

MONDAY 15 DECEMBER

■ **ALBUM RELEASED**

'THE BEST OF BOWIE' COMPILATION

UK
(K-Tel NE 1111)
UK Chart Peak No.2

SIDE ONE

1. **'Space Oddity'** (5:07)
2. **'Life On Mars?'** (K-Tel edit) (3:34)
3. **'Starman'** (4:07)
4. **'Rock 'n' Roll Suicide'** (2:56)
5. **'John, I'm Only Dancing'** (saxophone version) (2:37)
6. **'The Jean Genie'** (4:03)
7. **'Breaking Glass'** (live version) (Bowie/Davis/Murray) (3:27)
8. **'Sorrow'** (Feldman/Goldstein/Gottehrer) (2:51)

SIDE TWO

1. **'Diamond Dogs'** (K-Tel edit) (4:36)
2. **'Young Americans'** (5:05)
3. **'Fame'** (edit) (Bowie/Alomar/Lennon) (3:25)
4. **'Golden Years'** (edit) (3:20)
5. **'TVC 15'** (edit) (3:28)
6. **'Sound And Vision'** (3:00)
7. **'Heroes'** (edit) (Bowie/Eno) (3:26)
8. **'Boys Keep Swinging'** (Bowie/Eno) (3:15)

K-Tel released *The Best Of Bowie* with saturation TV advertising and via mail order internationally, but passed on the North American rights.

ABOVE: 'Fashion' was still in the shops when K-Tel released the compilation *The Best of Bowie*, which adapted Edward Bell's cover design from the single.

George Lukan (K-Tel) (1985)

We didn't feel we would recoup our money in America. We're talking about $500,000 in advertising, which is what we needed to run a successful campaign in 1981. We would have had to sell 700,000 units to break even and we didn't feel we'd be able to do that in the US with Bowie. So we released it all over Europe and in Australia and Asia. There we did very nicely. [013]

EPILOGUE 1981–1982

Bowie had become increasingly disenchanted with RCA, particularly in America. Having delivered *Scary Monsters*, the last album he owed them, he decided to wait out both the RCA and Defries contracts, which would expire at the end of 1982.

He left New York and settled back in Switzerland, recording very little ('Under Pressure' with Queen and 'Cat People (Putting Out Fire)' with Giorgio Moroder), concentrating instead on his acting career. In August 1981 he played the lead in *Baal* for BBC TV and spent much of 1982 filming *Merry Christmas, Mr Lawrence* and *The Hunger*.

With nothing new by Bowie apart from the 1982 *Baal* EP, RCA resorted (with Defries' badgering) to exploiting Bowie's back catalogue (see Appendix 1). Bowie's influence and popularity grew in his absence and ensured that *Let's Dance*, the first album under his lucrative 1983 EMI contract, brought him worldwide mainstream success.

Bowie

I allowed myself to be pushed into the commercial arena because I'd never been there, and it was sort of "Ooh, what's it like?", but there it was and I jumped in with my future in my hands. [359]

POST-1980 ISSUES OF 1969-1980 RECORDINGS

1981 *Christiane F: Wir Kinder vom Bahnhof Zoo* (soundtrack)
1981 *ChangesTwoBowie*
1982 *Portrait Of A Star* (*Low*/*"Heroes"*/*Lodger* box set [France only])
1982 *Fashions* (10 picture disc singles)
1982 'Peace On Earth'/'Little Drummer Boy'/'Fantastic Voyage'
1982 *Rare*
1983 *Lifetimes* (20 picture sleeve singles)
1983 *Golden Years* (remastered)
1983 *Ziggy Stardust: The Motion Picture* (soundtrack)
1984 *Fame And Fashion*
1984 *BOPIC* (*Hunky Dory*/*Ziggy Stardust*/*Aladdin Sane*/*Pin Ups*/*Diamond Dogs* picture disc albums)
1984 RCA CD issues (13 studio albums/4 compilations/*Peter and the Wolf*/*Stage* [UK/Germany])
1985 *Early Years* (*The Man Who Sold The World*/*Hunky Dory*/*Aladdin Sane* box set [France])
1989 *Sound + Vision* (3CD + Video CD box set)
1990 *ChangesBowie*
1990-92 Ryko reissues (13 studio albums/*Ziggy Stardust: The Motion Picture*/*David Live* remastered with bonus tracks [all formats])
1993 *The Singles Collection*, *The Video Collection*
1994 *Santa Monica '72* (live [semi-official])
1995 *Rarest One Bowie* (live, rarities [semi-official])
1997 *The Best Of David Bowie 1969/1974*
1998 *The Best Of David Bowie 1974/1979*
1999 EMI reissues (13 studio albums, remastered)
2000 *Bowie At The Beeb: The Best Of The BBC Radio Sessions 68-72*
2001 *All Saints: Collected Instrumentals 1977-1999*
2001 *Christiane F: Wir Kinder vom Bahnhof Zoo* (remastered)
2002 *Best Of Bowie* (CD, DVD)
2002 *The Rise And Fall Of Ziggy Stardust And The Spiders From Mars* (30th anniversary edition, remastered with bonus tracks)
2003 *Aladdin Sane* (30th anniversary edition, remastered with bonus tracks)
2003 *Ziggy Stardust And The Spiders From Mars* (30th anniversary edition, remastered DVD, soundtrack CD with bonus tracks)
2003 *Sound + Vision* (reissued with added tracks)
2004 *Diamond Dogs* (30th anniversary edition, remastered with bonus tracks)
2005 *David Live* (remastered with bonus tracks)
2005 *Stage* (remastered with bonus tracks)
2005 *The Collection*
2005 *The Platinum Collection*
2007 *Young Americans* (CD/DVD, remastered with bonus tracks)
2007 *The Best Of David Bowie 1980/1987*
2007 Toshiba EMI vinyl replica CD reissues (13 studio albums [Japan])
2008 *Live Santa Monica '72*
2008 *iSelect* (tracks selected by Bowie)
2009 *David Bowie* (40th anniversary edition, remastered with bonus tracks)
2009 *'Heroes'/'Helden'/'Héros'* (iTunes EP)
2010 *Station To Station* (remastered with bonus tracks and 1976 live album)
2012 *The Rise And Fall Of Ziggy Stardust And The Spiders From Mars* (40th anniversary edition, remastered)
2013 *Aladdin Sane* (40th anniversary edition, remastered)
2013 *Zeit! 77-79* (*Low*/*"Heroes"*/*Stage*/*Lodger* box set)
2014 *Nothing Has Changed* (remastered)
2015 *Five Years 1969-1973* (6 studio albums/2 live albums/2 rarities compilations box set, remastered)
2012-15 40th anniversary singles (16 picture discs)
2015 'Amsterdam'/'My Death' (picture disc single [*David Bowie Is*, Netherlands only])

PHOTOGRAPHY

© Mick Rock, Photo Duffy © Duffy Archive, Bob Gruen, Terry O'Neill/Getty Images, Geoff MacCormack, Jack Kay/Express/Getty Images, Leee Black Childers/IPOL, Echoes/Redferns, Justin de Villeneuve/Hulton Archive/Getty Images, Mick Gold/Redferns, Gijsbert Hanekroot/Redferns, Duffy/Getty Images, NBC/NBCU Photo Bank, Keystone Press Agency/Rex/Shutterstock, ITV/Rex, Harry Myers/Rex/Shutterstock, Alan Messer/Rex, Michael Putland/Getty Images/Retna UK, Kevin Cummins/Getty Images, D Morrison/Daily Express/Hulton Archive/Getty Images, Steve Wood/Express/Getty Images, David Gahr/Getty Images, Denis O'Regan, Frazer Ashford/Arena Pal, The Sun/News Syndication, Lynn Goldsmith/Corbis/VCG via Getty Images, Richard Imre, John Rodgers/Redferns, Daily Express/Hulton Archive/Getty Images, Leonard Burt/Central Press/Hulton Archive/Getty Images, J. Stevens/Globe Photos INC, NBCU Photo Bank, Allstar Picture Library/British Lion/StudioCanal, Alpha Press, Neil Zlozower/Atlasicons.com, Dagmar/Michael Ochs Archives/Getty Images, Gems/Redferns, Joe Stevens, American Broadcasting Companies Inc, Tim Boxer/Getty Images, Art Zelin/Getty Images, Roger Bamber/Rex/Shutterstock, Steve Schapiro/Corbis, Nate Cutler/Globe Photos Inc, Phil Roach/IPOL/ Globe Photos Inc, CAP/PLF supplied by Capital Pictures, Mark Sullivan/Contour by Getty Images, Ron Galella/WireImage, Dick Barnatt/Redferns, GAB Archive/Redferns, Brad Elterman/Rex/Shutterstock, Stephen Morley/Rex, EMI/The Kobal Collection, Brian Hamill/Getty Images, Marc S Canter/Michael Ochs Archives/Getty Images, Estate Of Keith Morris/Redferns, Ian Dickson/Redferns, Matthew Rolston, Steve Schapiro/Scopefeatures.com, Esther Friedman, Jens Kalaene/DPA/Corbis, Gary Lewis, Chalkie Davies/Getty Images, Knps/Dalle/eyevine, Hollandse Hoogte/eyevine, Zuma/eyevine, Jan Persson/Redferns, Pictorial Parade/Getty Images, Central Press/Getty Images, Hulton Archive/Getty Images, Michael Ochs Archives/Getty Images, John Downing/Getty Images, Beth Gwinn/Redferns, Keystone/Hulton Archive/Getty Images, Jarnoux Patrick/Paris Match via Getty Images, Fin Costello/Redferns, V Anderson/Getty Images, Michael Marks/Donaldson Collection/Getty Images, Movie Poster Image Art/Getty Images, Allan Tannenbaum/Getty Images, Everett/Rex/Shutterstock, Rebel Images/Rex/Shutterstock, Jarmo Hietaranta/Rex/Shutterstock, Vesa Klemetti/Rex/Shutterstock, Christian Simonpietri/Sygma, Richard Imne, Christian Simonpietri/Sygma/Corbis, Scott Weiner/Retna Ltd/Corbis, Evening Standard/Getty Images, The Sun, Tolca/Sunshine, Barry Plummer, Jackie Giroux/Globe Photos/Zumapress.com, Jean-Claude Deutsch/Paris Match via Getty Images, Richard McCaffrey/Michael Ochs Archive/Getty Images, Bertrand Rindoff Petroff/Getty Images, Kypros/Getty Images, AP Photo, Sipa Press/Rex/Shutterstock, ITV/Rex/Shutterstock, Christian Simonpietri/Sygma/Corbis, Eyevine, Claude Gassian, Denis O'Regan/Getty Images, Brannan, George Rose/Getty Images, Gai Terrell/Redferns, GAB Archive/Redferns, Richard E. Aaron/Redferns, Jorgen Angel/Redferns, Peter Still/Redferns, Ralph Gatti/AFP/Getty Images, Ke.Mazur/WireImage, Purcell/The Sydney Morning Herald/Fairfax Media via Getty Images, Larry Hulst/Michael Ochs Archives/Getty Images, Ed Perlstein/Redferns/Getty Images, Paul Natkin/Getty Images, Kypros/Getty Images, Ullstein Bild via Getty Images, Koh Hasebe/Shinko Music/Getty Images, Ray Cash/Newspix, News Ltd/Newspix, Howard/Daily Mail/Rex, Dagmar, Graham Smith/PYMCA/Rex/Shutterstock, Tony Evans/Timelapse Library Ltd, Philippe Gras/Alamy Stock Photo, Robin Platzer/The LIFE Images Collection/Getty Images, Peter Noble/Redferns, Martin O'Neill/Redferns, Paul Trynka, George Chin/Iconicpix, Alan Singer/NBCU Photo Bank, Richard Young/Rex/Shutterstock, Andre Csillag/Rex/Shutterstock, Fremantle Media Ltd/Rex/Shutterstock, Everett/Rex/Shutterstock, Robert Rosen/Rex/Shutterstock, Alamy, WENN.com, AP Photo/Dave Pickoff, John Timbers/Arena Pal, Ron Scherl/Arena Pal, Keystone Features/Getty Images, AP Photo/Nancy Kaye, John Kalodner, Virginia Turbett/Redferns, AFP/Getty Images, Tom Gates/Pictorial Parade/Archive Photos/Getty Images, Ron Tom/NBC/NBCU Photo Bank, Mark and Colleen Hayward/Redferns, Gus Stewart/Redferns, Alamy Stock Photo, bpk/Digne Meller Marcovicz, Ulvis Alberts/mptvimages.com, Camera Press, Press Association, Tracks Ltd, BBC pictures, Gabi Nasemann, George Underwood, Julian Wasser/Online USA Inc, Michael Stroud/Express/Getty Images, Photo by Earl Leaf/Michael Ochs, Tony Russell/Redferns/Getty Images, Dick Barnatt/Redferns, Roberta Bayley/Redferns, David Gahr/Getty Images, Douglas Miller/Keystone Features/Hulton Archive/Getty Images, Jack Mitchell/Getty Images, Peter Hujar/Conde Nast via Getty Images, Jon Lyons/Rex, Ray Stevenson/Rex/Shutterstock, Ian Dickson/Rex/Shutterstock, P Felix/Getty Images, Charlie Gillett Collection/Redferns, CSU Archives/Everett Collection, GEMA Archive/IconicPix, David Gahr/Getty Images, Virginia Turbett/Redferns, Brian Cooke/Redferns, Thomas Monaster/NY Daily News Archive via Getty Images, Richard Creamer/Michael Ochs Archives/Getty Images, Barry Marsden/Retna Pictures, Leni Sinclair/Getty Images, Waring Abbott/Getty Images, Everett Collection/Rex, IconicPix Music Archive, Govert De Roos/GDR-LFI, Virginia Turbett/Redferns, Brian Cooke/Redferns, Pictorial Press Ltd/Alamy Stock Photo, Kent PhotoNews, Hans Wild/The LIFE Picture Collection/Getty Images, Associated Newspapers, Phillip Jackson/Associated Newspapers/REX

All photographs used with permission of the copyright holder.

REFERENCES

BOOKS

[001] Ambrose, Joe. *Gimme Danger* (Omnibus Press, 2004)

[002] Badman, Keith. *The Beatles Diary Volume 2: After The Break-Up 1970-2001* (Omnibus Press, 2001)

[003] Bowie, Angela. *Backstage Passes* (G P Putnam's Sons, 1993)

[004] Buckley, David. *Strange Fascination* (Virgin, 2005)

[005] Bussy, Pascal. *Kraftwerk: Man, Machine And Music* (SAF, 1993)

[006] Cann, Kevin. *David Bowie: A Chronology* (Vermilion, 1983)

[007] Cann, Kevin. *Any Day Now* (Adelita, 2010)

[008] Cann, Kevin and Duffy, Chris. *Duffy/Bowie – Five Sessions* (ACC Editions, 2014)

[009] Currie, David. *The Starzone Interviews* (Omnibus Press, 1985)

[010] Demattio, Eric and Laney, Karen. *The Spider With The Platinum Hair* (Independent Music Press, 2003)

[011] Doggett, Peter. *Lou Reed: Growing Up In Public* (Omnibus Press, 1991)

[012] Flippo, Chet. *Serious Moonlight* (Doubleday, 1984)

[013] Gillman, Peter and Leni. *Alias David Bowie* (Henry Holt & Co, 1987)

[014] Gruen, Bob. *John Lennon: The New York Years* (Stewart Tabori & Chang, 2005)

[015] Grundy, Stuart. *The Record Producers: Tony Visconti* (BBC Books, 1982)

[016] Hopkins, Jerry. *Bowie* (Elm Tree Books, 1985)

[017] Jones, Dylan. *When Ziggy Played Guitar* (Preface, 2012)

[018] Jones, Lesley-Ann. *Ride A White Swan* (Hodder & Stoughton, 2012)

[019] Juby, Kerry. *In Other Words: David Bowie* (Omnibus Press, 1986)

[020] Lydon, John. *No Irish, No Blacks, No Dogs* (Hodder & Stoughton, 1993)

[021] MacCormack, Geoff. *Station To Station: Travels With Bowie 1973-76* (Genesis Publications, 2007)

[022] Mayes, Sean. *Life On Tour With David Bowie: We Can Be Heroes* (Independent Music Press, 1999)

[023] McNeil, Legs and McCain, Gillian. *Please Kill Me* (Penguin, 1997)

[024] Numan, Gary and Malins, Steve. *Praying To The Aliens: An Autobiography* (André Deutsch Limited, 1997)

[025] O'Dowd, George. *Take It Like A Man* (HarperCollins, 1995)

[026] O'Neill, Terry. *Celebrity* (Little, Brown, 2003)

[027] Ono, Yoko. *Memories Of John Lennon* (It Books, 2005)

[028] Palin, Michael. *Diaries 1969-1979 – The Python Years* (Weidenfeld & Nicolson, 2006)

[029] Pang, May. *Loving John* (Warner Books, 1983)

[030] Paytress, Mark and Pafford, Steve. *Bowie Style* (Omnibus Press, 2000)

[031] Peebles, Andy. *The Lennon Tapes – John Lennon And Yoko Ono In Conversation With Andy Peebles, 6 December 1980* (BBC, 1981)

[032] Pegg, Nicholas. *The Complete David Bowie Sixth Edition* (Titan Books, 2011)

[033] Phillips, John. *Papa John* (Doubleday & Co, 1986)

[034] Pitt, Ken. *The Pitt Report* (Design Music, 1983)

[035] Pop, Iggy and Wehrer, Anne. *I Need More* (Karz-Cohl Publishing, 1982)

[036] Richards, Keith. *Life* (Little, Brown, 2010)

[037] Rock, Mick and Bowie, David. *Moonage Daydream* (Genesis Publications, 2002)

[038] Sheppard, David. *On Some Faraway Beach: The Life And Times Of Brian Eno* (Orion, 2008)

[039] Slash and Bozza, Anthony. *Slash* (HarperCollins, 2007)

[040] Spitz, Marc. *David Bowie* (Aurum, 2009)

[041] Strange, Steve. *Blitzed! The Autobiography Of Steve Strange* (Orion, 2002)

[042] Sukita, Masayoshi and Bowie, David. *Speed Of Life* (Genesis Publications, 2011)

[043] Thompson, Dave. *Moonage Daydream* (Plexus, 1987)

[044] Tremlett, George. *The David Bowie Story* (Futura Publications, 1974)

[045] Trynka, Paul. *Starman* (Sphere, 2010)

[046] Vanilla, Cherry. *Lick Me* (Chicago Review Press, 2010)

[047] Visconti, Tony. *Bowie, Bolan And The Brooklyn Boy* (Harper Collins, 2006)

[048] Warhol, Andy. *The Philosophy Of Andy Warhol* (Harcourt Brace Jovanovich, 1975)

[049] Wilcken, Hugo. *Low* (Bloomsbury Publishing, 2005)

PRESS

[050] Arthur, J. 'Hard Rockin' Mr Bowie' (*Record Mirror*, 9 September 1972)

[051] Baker, Danny and Needs, Kris. 'An Interview With Brian Eno' (*ZigZag*, January 1978)

[052] Bangs, Lester and Korinsky, Esther. 'Honey, Come And Be My Enemy, I Can Love You Too' (*Creem*, April 1974)

[053] Barnes, Patricia. 'Bowie's Achievement on the Legitimate Stage' (*The London Times*, 25 November 1980)

[054] Barr, Tim. 'Geoff MacCormack' (*A-Listed*, 1 March 2009)

[055] Beck, John and Cornford, Matthew. 'Home Counties Surrealism' (*Eye* 68)

[056] Bell, Max. 'Ronnie Spector: Be My Baby?' (*Uncut*, May 2006)

[057] Bell, Max. 'The Golden Years' (*Classic Rock*, November 2007)

[058] Benton, Michael. (*Melody Maker*, 14 July 1973)

[059] Birch, Ian. (*Melody Maker*, 25 February 1978)

[060] Bishop, Pete. 'Bowie Straight Just Plain Good' (*Pittsburgh Press*, 27 April 1978)

[061] Bivona, Joe. 'Why He Had To Go Disco-Soul' (*Circus Raves*, June 1975)

[062] Black, Johnny. 'The Story Of Young Americans' (*Blender*, January 2004)

[063] Blume, Mary. 'Bowie's Latest Profile: Low' (*Los Angeles Times*, 20 July 1977)

[064] Bocchiaro, Madeline. 'Klaus Nomi – Riding The New Wave' (*Roctober* 19, 1997)

[065] Bowie, David. 'Hedi Slimane interview' (*Vogue*, May 2003)

[066] Bowie, David. 'What I've Learned' (*Esquire*, 2004)

[067] Bowie, David. 'I Went To Buy Some Shoes, And I Came Back With Life On Mars' (*Mail On Sunday*, 28 June 2008)

[068] Briggs, Newt. 'Don't Leave Now: The Psychedelic Furs Survive Fame, Fortune And The '80s' (*Las Vegas Mercury*, 18 September 2003)

[069] *Brisbane Telegraph*, 22 November 1978

[070] Brown, Tina. 'The Bowie Odyssey' (*Sunday Times Magazine*, 20 July 1975)

[071] Bryan, Howard. 'Rock Star David Bowie Kept Under Wraps In Albq' (*The Albuquerque Tribune*, 14 June 1975)

[072] Buckley, David and Buckmaster, Paul. 'The Lost Bowie Album' (*Mojo Classic: 60 Years Of Bowie*, 2007)

[073] Burn, Gordon. 'Bowie Holds Court' (*Sunday Times Magazine*, 30 November 1980)

[074] Campbell, Mary. 'Mott The Hoople, Saved By Bowie, Hits Stardom' (*The Lowell Sun*, 2 January 1974)

[075] Campbell, Mary. 'Rock Stars Merit Painter's Attention' (Associated Press, December 1974)

[076] Campbell, Mary. 'Tightrope Keeps David Bowie On Toes' (Associated Press, 8 May 1976)

[077] Cann, Kevin. 'Play Don't Worry' (*Starzone*, Autumn 1984)

[078] Casale, Jerry. 'The Gig Of A Lifetime' (*The Telegraph*, 17 May 2007)

[079] Cavanagh, David. 'Changes Fifty Bowie' (*Q* 125, February 1997)

[080] Charlesworth, Chris. 'US News' (*Melody Maker*, April 1974)

[081] Charlesworth, Chris. 'Roxy Step Up The Ladder' (*Melody Maker*, 15 June 1974)

[082] Charlesworth, Chris. (*Melody Maker*, 19 July 1974)

[083] Charlesworth, Chris. 'Rock On!' (*Melody Maker*, 8 March 1975)

[084] Charlesworth, Chris. 'US News' (*Melody Maker*, 8 March 1975)

[085] Charlesworth, Chris. 'Ringing The Changes' (*Melody Maker*, 13 March 1976)

[086] Charlesworth, Chris. 'Watch That Man' (*Mojo: Bowie*, November 2003)

[087] *Chicago Tribune*, 20 October 1977. 'People'

[088] Chiccarelli, Joe. 'Shooting To Thrill' (*EQ*, 2005)

[089] Childers, Leee Black. 'On Tour With Bowie' (*Hit Parader*, December 1974)

[090] Cohen, Scott. 'From Ziggy Stardust To Tin Machine: David Bowie Comes Clean' (*Details*, September 1991)

[091] Coleman, Ray. 'A Star Is Born' (*Melody Maker*, 15 July 1972)

[092] Collins, Dan. 'Devo: Gonna Be A Man From The Moon' (*LA Record*, 4 November 2009)

[093] Copetas, Craig. 'Beat Godfather Meets Glitter Mainman' (*Rolling Stone* 155, 28 February 1974)

[094] *Courier Mail*, 20 November 1978. 'Four Guards – But No Fans'

[095] *Courier Mail*, 22 November 1978. 'Some Glum Over David's Strum'

[096] Cromelin, Richard. 'The Darling Of The Avant Garde' (*Phonograph Record*, January 1972)

[097] Cromelin, Richard. 'The Return Of The Thin White Duke' (*Circus*, 2 March 1976)

[098] Cromelin, Richard. 'Iggy: A Graduate Of Bowie's School' (*Los Angeles Times*, 18 February 1979)

[099] Crowe, Cameron. 'Bowie To Tour: No Gimmickry' (*Rolling Stone* 204, 15 January 1976)

[100] Crowe, Cameron. 'Ground Control To Davy Jones' (*Rolling Stone* 206, 12 February 1976)

[101] Crowe, Cameron. 'Candid Conversation' (*Playboy*, September 1976)

[102] Crowe, Cameron. 'All Access Bowie' (*Rolling Stone* 1000/1001, 18 May 2006)

[103] Dalton, Stephen. 'Drum 'n' Bass Oddity' (*NME*, February 1997)

[104] Dalton, Stephen. 'Brian Eno On A Series Of Inspired Collaborations' (*Uncut*, October 1999)

[105] Dalton, Stephen and Hughes, Rob. 'Trans-Europe Excess' (*Uncut*, April 2001)

[106] Dalton, Stephen. David Bowie and Tony Visconti interviews (for *Uncut*, April 2001)

[107] Damsker, Matt. 'Philly Stopover: Fans And Funk' (*Rolling Stone* 171, 10 October 1974)
[108] Damsker, Matt. 'Bowie's Soul Works But His Voice Is Off' (*Philadelphia Bulletin*, 26 November 1974)
[109] Davies, Colin (*Disc*, 6 July 1974)
[110] Deevoy, Adrian. 'Boys Keep Swinging' (*Q* 33, June 1989)
[111] Deevoy, Adrian. 'Golden Years' (*Q* 80, May 1993)
[112] DeMain, Bill. 'The Sound And Vision Of David Bowie' (*Performing Songwriter*, September 2003)
[113] DeMain, Bill. 'The Freakiest Show' (*Classic Rock*, April 2011)
[114] *Disc And Music Echo*, 20 March 1971. 'Rebirth Of A Hope'
[115] *Disc*, 7 August 1974. Mike Garson interview
[116] DuNoyer, Paul. 'Contact' (*Mojo*, July 2002)
[117] Edmonds, Ben. 'Bowie Meets The Press' (*Circus*, 27 April 1976)
[118] Edwards, Henry. 'David Bowie's Version Of Camp Rock' (*After Dark*, October 1972)
[119] *The Face*, 1981. Richard Sharah profile
[120] Farhi, Paul. 'Bing And Bowie: An Odd Story Of Holiday Harmony' (*Washington Post*, 20 December 2006)
[121] Farley, Chris. 'Hype Aside, Ava Cherry (And Her Name) Is For Real' (*Chicago Tribune*, 21 August 1987)
[122] Farren, Mick. 'Mr Bowie Has Left The Theatre' (*NME*, 16 November 1974)
[123] Fisher, Ben. 'But Boy Could He Play Guitar' (*Mojo*, October 1997)
[124] Fletcher, Gordon. 'Performance' (*Rolling Stone* 165, 18 July 1974)
[125] Fox-Cumming, Ray. 'Aladdin Scotland' (*Disc*, 2 June 1973)
[126] Fox-Cumming, Ray. 'Behind Bolan And Bowie' (*Disc*, 28 September 1974)
[127] Fox-Cumming, Ray. 'An Audience With Angie' (*Record Mirror*, 8 March 1975)
[128] Fricke, David. 'Debbie Harry: Female Vocalist Of The Year' (*Circus*, 19 February 1980)
[129] Gelly, Dave. 'Creating An Atmosphere Of Panic' (*The Observer*, 20 November 1977)
[130] Gibson, Rory. (*Brisbane Telegraph*, 22 November 1978)
[131] Gill, Chris. 'Mick Ronson – The Hero Of Glam' (*Guitar World*, April 1997)
[132] Girard, Jim. 'Not Just A Sideman' (*Scene*, 27 March 1975)
[133] Gore, Joe. 'New Digital Stimulation From David Bowie & Reeves Gabrels' (*Guitar Player*, June 1997)
[134] Green, Gavin. 'We'll See The Real Bowie' (*Sun Herald*, 12 November 1978)
[135] Hanrahan, John. 'The New Bowie – Without The Stardust' (*The Sun*, 2 November 1978)
[136] Hanrahan, John. 'Bowie… Seriously' (*The Sun*, 23 November 1978)
[137] Hart, Heather. 'The Plain Person's Guide To The Human League' (*The Face*, August 1980)
[138] Harvey, Peter. 'End Of The Road For The Spiders?' (*Record Mirror*, 14 July 1973)
[139] Harvey, Peter. 'Ziggy Played Guitar' (*Record Mirror*, 14 July 1973)
[140] Harvey, Peter. 'Bowie's Party Night Fiesta' (*Record Mirror*, 14 July 1973)
[141] Hayman, Martin. 'David Bowie In Search Of Lost Time' (*Sounds*, 5 August 1973) / 'Outside David Bowie...Is The Closest You're Gonna Get' (*Rock*, 8 October 1973)
[142] Hilburn, Robert. 'David Bowie Proves Himself With New Album Hunky Dory' (*Los Angeles Times*, 23 January 1972)
[143] Hilburn, Robert. 'I'm Just Searching: Brave New World For David Bowie' (*Los Angeles Times*, 8 September 1974); republished as 'Bowie Finds His Voice' (*Melody Maker*, 14 September 1974)
[144] Hilburn, Robert. 'Bowie: Now I'm A Businessman' (*Melody Maker*, 28 February 1976)
[145] Hilburn, Robert. 'David Bowie: The View From The Top' (*Los Angeles Times*, 9 September 1980)
[146] Hoad, Phil. 'How We Made: The Man Who Fell To Earth' (*The Guardian*, 25 June 2012)
[147] Hodenfield, Chris. 'Bad Boys In Berlin' (*Rolling Stone* 301, 4 October 1979)
[148] Hogan, Christine. 'The Man Who Fell To Earth Lands In A State Of Shock' (*Sydney Morning Herald*, 7 November 1978)
[149] Hogan, Tim. 'Bowie: City To City' (*Circus*, 2 March 1976)
[150] Hollingsworth, Roy. 'Cha-Cha-Cha-Changes: A Journey With Aladdin' (*Melody Maker*, 12 May 1973)
[151] Holloway, Danny. 'David Bowie' (*NME*, 29 January 1972)
[152] Holloway, Danny. 'Bowie At His Brilliant Best' (*NME*, 29 January 1972)
[153] Horkins, Tony. 'Tin Machine: Bowie & Gabrels' (*International Musician*, December 1991)
[154] Hughes, Rob. 'Loving The Alien' (*Uncut*, December 2005)
[155] Hughes, Rob. 'The Making Of Starman' (*Uncut*, June 2009)
[156] Hughes, Tim. 'Bowie For A Song' (*Jeremy*, March 1970)
[157] *Hull Daily Mail*, 13 February 1970. 'Ex-Rat Gets His Chance In Big Time'
[158] Ingham, Jonh. 'Rats To Riches' (*Creem*, August 1975)
[159] Isler, Scott. 'David Bowie Opens Up A Little' (*Musician*, August 1987)
[160] *Jackie*, 21 July 1973
[161] Jackson, Patrick. 'Surreal Times On The SS France' (*BBC News*, June 2006)
[162] Jones, Allan. 'Mick Ronson: I'd Like To Kick Some Sense Into Bowie' (*Melody Maker*, 5 April 1975)
[163] Jones, Allan. 'Bowie's Raw Power' (*Melody Maker*, 22 May 1976)
[164] Jones, Allan. 'Goodbye To Ziggy And All That' (*Melody Maker*, 29 October 1977)
[165] Jones, Allan. 'Fight Of The Week: Lou Bops Bowie' (*Melody Maker*, 21 April 1979)
[166] Jones, Allan. 'Riding On The Dynamic Of Disaster: An Interview With Robert Fripp' (*Melody Maker*, 28 April 1979)
[167] Jones, Allan. 'Absence Makes The Heart Grow Fonder?' (*Melody Maker*, 26 May 1979)
[168] Jones, Allan. 'Bowie At Edinburgh' (*Melody Maker*, 8 September 1979)
[169] Jones, Robert. 'Audience Mesmerised By Rick's Piano Playing' (*North West Evening Mail*, 16 June 2011)
[170] Kane, Peter. 'Cash For Questions' (*Q* 166, July 2000)
[171] Kaye, Lenny. (*Disc*, 29 June 1974)
[172] Kelly, Diane. 'The All New Adventures Of David Bowie' (*Hi!*, 7 June 1975)
[173] Kent, Nick. 'An Initiation Into Iggy Pop' (*NME*, 29 July 1972)
[174] Kent, Nick. 'Show Business In The Twilight Zone' (*NME*, 21 April 1973)
[175] Kent, Nick. 'A Walk On The Wild Side Of Lou Reed' (*NME*, 9 June 1973)
[176] Kent, Nick. 'Into The Abyss' (*Mojo: Bowie*, November 2003)
[177] King, Arthur. 'The Ziggy Stardust Years' (*Record Collector*, February 1987)
[178] Kirkup, Martin. 'Diamond Dogs' (*Sounds*, 4 May 1974) / 'Diamond David' (*Rock*, June 1974)
[179] Kubernik, Harvey. 'Fame At Last For Soulful Bowie' (*Melody Maker*, 25 October 1975)
[180] *Lancashire Evening Telegraph*, 1 June 1973
[181] Loder, Kurt. 'Karate Expert Puts The Muscle On Rock Stars' (*Chicago Tribune*, 11 November 1979)
[182] Loder, Kurt. 'Scary Monster On Broadway' (*Rolling Stone* 130, 13 November 1980)
[183] Loder, Kurt. 'Iggy Pop: Bowie's Main Man' (*Rolling Stone* 433, 25 October 1984)
[184] Loder, Kurt. 'Stardust Memories' (*Rolling Stone* 498, 23 April 1987)
[185] *Los Angeles Times*, 25 February 1979. '10 Survivors And Friends'
[186] Lott, Tim. 'The Thin White Duke Has Gone. Here's The New David Bowie' (*Record Mirror*, 24 September 1977); 'No Fun At The Ministry Of Drugs' (*The Guardian*, 25 July 2008)
[187] MacDonald, Ian. 'Eno Part 2: Another False World – How To Make A Modern Record' (*NME*, 3 December 1977)
[188] Machell, Ben. 'Hello Goodbye: Trevor Bolder' (*Mojo*, October 2005)
[189] MacKinnon, Angus. 'The Future Isn't What It Used To Be' (*NME*, 13 September 1980)
[190] Madman. Earl Slick interview (*Bowie Zone*, 1 September 2006)
[191] Madman. Mike Garson interview (*Bowie Zone*, 2 October 2006)
[192] Mann, Roderick. 'Bianca's Living Down Her Frivolous Image' (*Los Angeles Times*, 4 September 1977)
[193] Mantle, Jonathan. 'David Bowie' (*Vogue*, September 1978)
[194] Marlowe, Jon. 'A Walk On The Wild Side With Amanda Lear' (*Miami News*, 25 January 1978)
[195] Marszalek, Julian. 'Marc Bolan And David Bowie Nearly Formed Group' (*Spinner*, February 2010)
[196] McDonald, Colin. 'Carlos Alomar interview' (*Goldmine*, 24 April 1997)
[197] *Melody Maker*, 19 February 1972
[198] *Melody Maker*, 13 July 1974. 'The Faces – It's Like A Marriage!'
[199] *Melody Maker*, 9 August 1975
[200] *Melody Maker*, 23 August 1975. 'Hot Licks'
[201] *Melody Maker*, 5 March 1977. 'Letters'
[202] *Melody Maker*, 12 March 1977. 'Bowie at the Château'
[203] *Melody Maker*, 17 March 1979. 'Scott's No To Bowie'
[204] *Melody Maker*, 5 May 1979
[205] Mendelssohn, John. 'David Bowie: Pantomime Rock' (*Rolling Stone* 79, 1 April 1971)
[206] Midgely, Ian. 'Why Hull Should Honour My Mick' (*Hull Daily Mail*, 5 April 2010)
[207] Miles. 'Zing! Go The Strings Of My Art' (*NME*, 27 November 1976)
[208] Milner, Greg. 'My Life In Music: Iggy Pop' (*Spin*, November 2003)
[209] Milward, John. 'David Bowie: Man Of Many Phases' (*Rolling Stone* 267, 15 June 1978)
[210] Morley, Paul. 'A Career In Electronics Can Be Yours! Novices Welcome, All Letters Answered' (*NME*, March 1979)
[211] Mulholland, Garry. 'The Interview: B-52's' (*The Stool Pigeon*, 5 March 2008)

[212] Murray, Charles Shaar. 'David At The Dorchester' (*NME*, 22 July 1972)
[213] Murray, Charles Shaar. 'Bowie – Dry Ice, Nice Legs And Absolute Ascendancy' (*NME*, 26 August 1972)
[214] Murray, Charles Shaar. 'Bowie Is An Industry. Protected, Swaddled And Handled With Care' (*NME*, 2 December 1972)
[215] Murray, Charles Shaar. 'Ziggy Pulls The Squealers' (*NME*, 6 January 1973)
[216] Murray, Charles Shaar. 'Goodbye Ziggy And A Big Hello To Aladdin Sane' (*NME*, 27 January 1973)
[217] Murray, Charles Shaar. 'Brainful Of Bowie (*NME*, 14 April 1973)
[218] Murray, Charles Shaar. 'Aladdin Seine' (*NME*, 12 May 1973)
[219] Murray, Charles Shaar. 'The Bowie Experiment' (*NME*, 9 June 1973)
[220] Murray, Charles Shaar. 'Bowie-ing Out At The Chateau' (*NME*, 4 August 1973)
[221] Murray, Charles Shaar. 'Tight Rope Walker At The Circus' (*NME*, 11 August 1973)
[222] Murray, Charles Shaar. 'The Ronson Creative Flame (*NME*, 6 October 1973)
[223] Murray, Charles Shaar. 'The Man Who Fell To Earth' (*Arena*, May/June 1993)
[224] Murray, Les. 'The Divine Mister B' (*The Sun*, 27 November 1978)
[225] Musel, Bob. 'Rail Journey Through Siberia' (*UPI*, 1973)
[226] *Music Star*, 1973. 'How I Nearly Lost My Eye'
[227] *Music Star*, 1974. 'A Star Called David Bowie'
[228] Needs, Kris. 'NY Punk' (*ZigZag*, April 1977)
[229] Needs, Kris. 'Mott The Hoople: Teenage Riot!' (*Mojo*, May 2009)
[230] Nelson, Jim. 'Morrissey interview' (*GQ*, September 2012)
[231] *New York*, 9 November 1998
[232] *NME*, 2 September 1972. 'Bowie Opens Manchester Supergig'
[233] O'Grady, Anthony. 'Rock And Roll Is Just A Toothless Old Woman' (*RAM*, 26 July 1975)
[234] O'Grady, Anthony. 'David Bowie As The Laughing Gnome' (*RAM*, 3 June 1977)
[235] O'Grady, Anthony. 'On The Conveyor Belt With The Tall, Bronzed, Fragmented One' (*RAM*, 1 December 1978)
[236] O'Hagan, Sean. 'Who Is David Bowie?' (*The Observer*, 17 February 2013)
[237] Orme, John. 'Iggy's Lust Words' (*Melody Maker*, 13 August 1977)
[238] Page, Mike Flood. 'Nick Roeg On The Man Who Fell To Earth' (*Street Life*, 10 January 1976)
[239] Pareles, Jon. 'David Bowie, 21st Century Entrepreneur' (*New York Times*, 9 June 2002)
[240] Parsons, Tony. 'Bowie By Bowie' (*Arena*, May/June 1993)
[241] Petrie, Gavin. 'Bowie's Bow' (*Disc And Music Echo*, 12 March 1970)
[242] Petros, George and Blush, Steven. (*Seconds*, August/September 1995)
[243] Phillips, Sarah. 'Justin De Villeneuve's Best Photograph' (*The Guardian*, 16 May 2012)
[244] Quantick, David. 'My Work Here Is Done' (*Q* 157, October 1999)
[245] *RAM*, 8 March 1975. 'The Night They Raided Bowie'
[246] Rambali, Paul. 'David Bowie: Madison Square Garden NYC' (*NME*, 20 May 1978)
[247] Raven, Paul. 'Popping The Question: David Bowie' (*Mirabelle*, September 1972)
[248] *Record Mirror*, 26 August 1972. 'More Bowie, Fairies, Quicksilver'
[249] *Record Mirror*, 2 August 1975. 'Bowie Roles On'
[250] Roberts, Chris. 'Station To Station' (*Uncut*, 29 October 1999)
[251] Robertson, Debra. 'Bewitching Bowie' (*The Sun*, 21 November 1978)
[252] Robinson, John. 'Run For The Shadows' (*Uncut*, July 2010)
[253] Robinson, Lisa. 'Cracked Actor Zaps Canuck Thespians' (*NME*, 29 June 1974)
[254] Robinson, Lisa. 'Roxy Music: All Dressed Up With Nowhere To Go' (*Creem*, February 1976)
[255] Robinson, Lisa. 'The First Synthetic Rock Star. There Is No Other' (*NME*, 7 March 1976)
[256] Robinson, Lisa. 'Bowie' (*Spin*, August 1990)
[257] Robinson, Tony. 'Bowie Rapped By His Missus' (*Sunday Mirror*, 8 January 1978)
[258] Rock, Mick. 'David Is Just Not Serious' (*Rolling Stone* 110, 8 June 1972)
[259] Rock, Mick. 'Ronno' (*Music Scene*, September 1973)
[260] Rock, Mick. 'Going For A Song' (*Sunday Times*, 29 April 2007)
[261] Rockwell, John. 'David Bowie Keeps On Flirting With Extremes' (*New York Times*, 7 May 1978)
[262] Rohrer, Finlo. 'Why Would You Burn Your Life's Work?' (*BBC News Magazine*, 5 October 2009)
[263] *Rolling Stone* 152, 17 January 1974. 'Wakeman Sets Solo Concert'
[264] *Rolling Stone* 185, 24 April 1975. 'Random Notes'
[265] *Rolling Stone* 187, 22 May 1975. 'Random Notes'
[266] *Rolling Stone* 190, 3 July 1975. 'Random Notes'
[267] *Rolling Stone* 207, 26 February 1976. 'Random Notes'
[268] Rook, Jean. 'Waiting For Bowie' (*Daily Express*, 5 May 1976)
[269] Rook, Jean. 'Bowie Reborn' (*Daily Express*, 14 February 1979)
[270] Ross, Ron. 'Fleeting Moments In A Glamorous Career' (*Phonograph Record*, October 1972)
[271] Ross, Ron. 'Bowie Throws A Bone To His 'Dog' Fans' (*Circus*, December 1974)
[272] Ross, Ron. 'Who Will I Be Now?' (*Circus Raves*, February 1975)
[273] Ross, Ron. 'It's Strange Being On Your Own, Reveals Ronson' (*Circus*, April 1975)
[274] Russell, Rosalind. 'Mick Ronson Interview' (*Disc And Music Echo*, 15 July 1972)
[275] Russell, Rosalind. 'Hunter Ronson Walking On Gilded Odds' (*Disc*, 29 March 1975)
[276] Salaam, Kalamu ya. 'An Interview With Luther Ronzoni Vandross, Jr.' (*The Black Collegian*, February 1982)
[277] Savage, Jon. 'Avant-AOR' (*Melody Maker*, 26 May 1979)
[278] Seabrook, Thomas Jerome. 'White Shirt Black Noise' (*Record Collector*, February 2011)
[279] Seabrook, Thomas Jerome. 'An Axe To Break The Ice' (*Record Collector*, March 2012)
[280] Sharp, Ken. 'Travels With Bowie' (*Record Collector*, October 2008)
[281] Sharp, Ken. 'Hunky Dory' (*Record Collector*, June 2009)
[282] Shroyer, Steve and John Lifflander. 'Spaced Out In The Desert' (*Creem*, December 1975)
[283] Sigerson, Davitt. 'B-52's On Target At New Club' (*Melody Maker*, 24 March 1979)
[284] Simpson, Dave. 'Bet You Think This Song Is About You' (*The Guardian*, 13 December 2008)
[285] Sinclair, David. 'Station To Station' (*Rolling Stone* 658, 10 June 1993)
[286] Smith, Robin. 'Boastful Bolan' (*Record Mirror*, 16 April 1977)
[287] Sterdan, Darryl. 'Twiggy Struts Out With New Album' (*Toronto Sun*, 5 March 2012)
[288] Stone, Danny. 'Harlette Adds A Bright Layer Of Polish To Her Brassy Boss' (*Chicago Tribune*, 18 December 1977)
[289] Strick, Wesley. 'Bowie Now: New Music For Day And Night' (*Circus*, 28 February 1977)
[290] Telford, Raymond. 'Hype And David Bowie's Future' (*Melody Maker*, 28 March 1970)
[291] Thomas, Deborah. 'The Odd Couple: Lulu Teams Up With Bowie' (*Daily Mirror*, 28 December 1973)
[292] Tickell, Paul. 'Bowie: This Blessed Plot' (*Melody Maker*, 15 December 1979)
[293] Tobler, John. 'Secret Secret Never Seen: An Interview With David Bowie' (*ZigZag*, January 1978)
[294] Truman, James. 'Pop Goes Blondie' (*Melody Maker*, 19 January 1979)
[295] Trynka, Paul. 'Golden Year' (*Mojo*, August 2011)
[296] Trynka, Paul. 'Safe European Home' (*Mojo*, February 2012)
[297] Turner, Steve. 'The Rise And Rise Of David Bowie' (*Beat Instrumental*, August 1972)
[298] *Uncut*, June 2008. '30 Greatest David Bowie Songs'
[299] Valentine, Penny. 'A New Star Shoots Upwards' (*Disc And Music Echo*, 14 February 1970)
[300] Van Matre, Lynn. 'Bowie Alters Courses But Majors In Music' (*Chicago Tribune*, 9 April 1978)
[301] Volk, Steve. 'David Bowie's Young Americans' (*Philadelphia Weekly*, 24 July 2002)
[302] Walters, Barry. 'Soul God' (*Spin*, April 1987)
[303] Watts, Michael. 'Oh! You Pretty Thing' (*Melody Maker*, 22 January 1972)
[304] Watts, Michael. (*Melody Maker*, 1 July 1972)
[305] Watts, Michael. 'Stranger In A Strange Land' (*Melody Maker*, 24 February 1973)
[306] Watts, Michael. 'Funereal In Berlin' (*Melody Maker*, 29 January 1977)
[307] Watts, Michael. 'A New Career In A New Town' (*Melody Maker*, 5 March 1977)
[308] Watts, Michael. 'Confession Of An Elitist' (*Melody Maker*, 18 February 1978)
[309] Watts, Michael. 'Ethnic Bowie' (*Melody Maker*, 13 January 1979)
[310] Watts, Michael. 'Bowie's Lodger: Where New Muzik Meets Errol Flynn' (*Melody Maker*, 19 May 1979)
[311] Watts, Michael. 'David Bowie Introduces Lodger To An Awestruck World' (*RAM*, 15 June 1979)
[312] Webster, Charles. 'Live!' (*Record Mirror*, 13 July 1972)
[313] Welch, Chris. 'Honour Lulu' (*Melody Maker*, 24 November 1973)
[314] Welch, Chris. 'Jagger – It's Time For A Change' (*Melody Maker*, 10 August 1974)
[315] Welch, Chris. 'Marc Bolan' (*Melody Maker*, 30 November 1974)
[316] Welch, Chris. 'Bowie And Bolan Get It On' (*Melody Maker*, 17 September 1977)
[317] White, Timothy. 'Turn And Face The Strange' (*Crawdaddy*, February 1978)
[318] White, Timothy. 'The Interview' (*Musician*, May 1983)
[319] Wilmoth, Peter. 'Fallen Angel' (*The Age*, 3 June 2007)

[320] Yentob, Alan. 'What Bowie Means To Me' (*Mail On Sunday*, 17 February 2013)
[321] Young, Charles. 'Bowie Plays Himself' (*Rolling Stone* 256, 12 January 1978)
[322] Zell, Fran. 'Graffiti's Candy Clark: Serendipity Is Her Forte' (*Chicago Tribune*, 31 August 1979)

SLEEVE NOTES
[323] Bowie, David. *Sound + Vision* (Ryko, 1989)
[324] Bowie, David. *One Step Up/Two Steps Back: The Songs Of Bruce Springsteen* (The Right Stuff, 1997)
[325] Buckley, David. *Aladdin Sane 30th Anniversary Edition* (EMI, 2003)
[326] Buckley, David. *Diamond Dogs 30th Anniversary Edition* (EMI, 2004)
[327] Crowe, Cameron. *Station To Station Super Deluxe Edition* (EMI, 2010)
[328] Visconti, Tony. *David Live* (EMI, 2005)

SOUND
[329] An Appreciation Of David Bowie (Paul Gambaccini, BBC Radio 1, 12 November 1981)
[330] Bowie The Traveller / Conversations With Bowie (Capital Radio, 14 May 1979)
[331] Changes Now Bowie (Mary Anne Hobbs, BBC Radio 1, 8 January 1997)
[332] Changes: The David Bowie Story (Stuart Grundy, BBC Radio 1, May 1976)
[333] David Bowie: A Look At The Seventies (King Biscuit Flower Hour, KMET-FM, January 1980)
[334] David Bowie Interview (Kid Jensen, Radio Luxembourg, 14 July 1973)
[335] David Bowie Interview (US radio, November 1977)
[336] David Bowie Interview (Andy Peebles, BBC Radio 1, December 1980)
[337] David Bowie Star Special (BBC Radio 1, 12 May 1979 tx 20 May 1979)
[338] An Evening With David Bowie (Sonny Fox, December 1977, released RCA, 1978)
[339] George Harrison Interview (KHJ 930 AM, 21 December 1974)
[340] The Sunday Show (John Peel, BBC Radio 1, 5 February 1970)
[341] Your Mother Wouldn't Like It (Nicky Horne, Capital Radio, 13 February 1979)

VISION
[342] *13 Heures – Spécial David Bowie* (TF1, 22 October 1980)
[343] *17th Annual Grammy Awards* (CBS, 1 March 1975)
[344] *90 Minutes Live* (CBC, 25 November 1977)
[345] *Afternoon Plus* (ITV,12 February 1979)
[346] *A Part Ca* (Canal +, 1997)
[347] *Arena Rock* (BBC2, 29 May 1978)
[348] *Changes: Bowie At Fifty* (BBC2, 4 January 1997)
[349] *Classic Albums: Transformer* (Eagle Rock, 2001)
[350] *Countdown* (ABC Australia, 12 November 1978)
[351] *Countdown* (ABC Australia, 16 December 1979)
[352] *Countdown* (ABC Australia, October 1980 – broadcast 16 November 1980)
[353] *Cracked Actor* (BBC1, 26 January 1975)
[354] *Dancing In The Street* (BBC/WGBH-Boston, 1995)
[355] *David Bowie And The Story Of Ziggy Stardust* (BBC4, June 2012)
[356] *Dinah!* (CBS, 9 February, broadcast 3 March 1976)
[357] *Dinah!* (CBS, 15 April, broadcast 6 May 1977)
[358] *Duffy: The Man Who Shot The Sixties* (BBC, 2010)
[359] *Five Years In The Making Of An Icon* (BBC2, May 2013)
[360] *Friday Night Saturday Morning* (BBC2, 10 October 1980)
[361] *Good Morning America* (ABC, 3 September 1980)
[362] *London Weekend Show* (ITV, 30 June, broadcast 9 July 1978)
[363] *Lou Reed: Rock And Roll Heart* (American Masters, 1998)
[364] *The Man Who Fell To Earth* – Nic Roeg and David Bowie commentary (Criterion, 1993)
[365] *The Man Who Fell To Earth – Watching The Alien* (Studio Canal, 2002)
[366] *The Nomi Song* (Palm Pictures, 2005)
[367] *Northern Lights* (Tyne Tees, 16 June 1978)
[368] *Origins Of A Starman* (Chrome Dreams, 2004)
[369] *The Sacred Triangle: Bowie, Iggy And Lou 1971-1973* (Sexy Intellectual/MVD, 2011)
[370] *Sound And Vision* (Prometheus, 2002)
[371] *Tonight* (BBC1, 12 February 1979)
[372] *The V.J. Diaries* (Merrill Aldighieri, 2012)
[373] *Ziggy Stardust And The Spiders From Mars* – Visconti and Pennebaker commentary (EMI, 2003)

WEB
[374] 5years.com/rock.htm – Mick Rock: Ziggy Stardust Photographer (1999)
[375] 5years.com/mnnewcastle.htm – David Bowie (Mick Nixon, 1972)
[376] 5years.com/radint.htm – Ziggy On Radio (February 1972)
[377] aol.com – 50th Birthday Live Chat (8 January 1997)
[378] artclips.free.fr – David Bowie – Fashion
[379] barryrudolph.com – Keith Moon (Barry Rudolph, 2005)
[380] berklee.edu – David Bowie's commencement address at Berklee (8 May 1999)
[381] bowiedownunder.com – 1978 Low/Heroes Tour (AUS/NZ)
[382] bowiewonderworld.com – I Could Play The Wild Mutation (Paul Kinder, 29 January 2002)
[383] bowiewonderworld.com – Ground Control To Major Tom (Paul Kinder, 11 July 2001)
[384] bowiewonderworld.com/forum – The Visitor (Bowie Bootleg) (27 January 2011)
[385] cheunderground.com – You're Way On Top Now: Gary Heffern Meets Iggy Pop (Ray Brandes, 21 March 2010)
[386] chickfactor.com – Bridget St John (Sam Brumbaugh, December 1999)
[387] concertlivewire.com – Earl Slick (18 January 2004)
[388] davidbowie.com – News: Bowie and Dick Cavett (13 December 2000)
[389] davidbowie.com – Q&A with Coco Schwab (27 June–13 July 2001)
[390] davidbowie.com – message board (2 August 2003)
[391] davidbowie.com – News: Neil Tennant (15 December 2011)
[392] davidbowiefanclub.com – George Underwood (May 2006)
[393] davidbowiefanclub.com – Woody Woodmansey (2007)
[394] davidbowietribute.com – Ken Scott (David Brighton, January 2006)
[395] derekboshier.com – DB David Bowie
[396] earcandymag.com – May Pang (2005)
[397] elephant-blog.blogspot.com – Anecdote #373 (Adrian Belew, 30 April 2007)
[398] elephant-blog.blogspot.com – Anecdote #646 part 1 (Adrian Belew, 22 May 2007)
[399] elephant-blog.blogspot.com – Planned Accidents (Adrian Belew, 23 March 2010)
[400] facebook.com – David Bowie: Any Day Now
[401] facebook.com – Kuelan Nguyen (28 July 2011)
[402] flickr.com – Michael Oberman (2005)
[403] guerrillamonster.com – Bowie Visits MCA (2007)
[404] i94bar.com – James Williamson On Raw Power 30 Years On (Ken Shimamoto, 1 April 2001)
[405] ijamming.net – Richard Butler (Tony Fletcher, June 2002)
[406] indieethos.wordpress.com – Mike Garson (19 July 2011)
[407] inthestudio.net – In The Studio With Redbeard (30 August 2010)
[408] liketotally80s.com – Alan Hunter (8 June 2011)
[409] lukeford.net – Si Litvinoff (Luke Ford, 2002)
[410] paulgormanis.com – Photography: Kate Simon (Paul Gorman, February 2011)
[411] rockbandsandartists.com – Trevor Bolder (21 February 2012)
[412] rockhall.com – Madonna Accepts For David Bowie (17 January 1996)
[413] rockpaperphoto.com – Andrew Kent
[414] rockpopgallery.typepad.com – Terry Pastor (March 2007)
[415] sfae.com – Terry O'Neill
[416] shapersofthe80s.com – Wendy Kirby (21 December 2011)
[417] stevehoffman.tv – Ken Scott (Doug Hess, March 2006)
[418] teenagewildlife.com (2000)
[419] theswellelife.com – Frankly Frankland: The Blitz, David Bowie And Ashes To Ashes (Judith Frankland, 22 February 2011)
[420] tonyvisconti.com – Young Americans (2002)
[421] tonyvisconti.com – Heroes (2002)
[422] tonyvisconti.com – Stage (2002)
[423] tonyvisconti.com – Lodger (2002)
[424] tonyvisconti.com – Scary Monsters (2002)
[425] trynka.net – Tibo: Thunderstorms and Fire Day (Paul Trynka, 2010)
[426] tv.com – Morrissey Flaunts Brutal Honesty (Jim Welte, 16 March 2006)
[427] ultimateclassicrock.com – Late T. Rex Singer Marc Bolan's Girlfriend Gloria Jones Keeps His Memory Alive (Karen Laney, September 2012)
[428] warhol.org – Screen Test Activity
[429] youtube.com – Allen Midgette Warhol Film/Meeting David Bowie @ The Factory (3 July 2009)

ACKNOWLEDGMENTS

Many thanks to: David Barraclough, who commissioned this book in 2010, for his patience and support throughout its production; Michael Bell for his initial elegant design concept; a huge thank you to Paul Tippett for his brilliant design work, solving problems with grace and commensense; photo researchers Dave Brolan and Ian Whent who went to extraordinary lengths to track down rare pictures; Chris Charlesworth, John Hutchinson and Dagmar for stories; Edie for research and transcribing; Bon for editing and endless enthusiasm; Stu for constant encouragement and space to work; Claude for inspiration and source material; Gene, Tamara, family and friends for understanding my absence from social occasions for five years; all the supporters of bowiegoldenyears.com for contributions and feedback. Finally I am greatly indebted to the legions of writers, photographers and filmmakers whose work formed the core of my research. As the man would say, love on ya!